Magic Seasons

A Mystical Science Fiction Novel

L.D. LESLIE

Magic Seasons

Published by MysticSciFiPress

First Edition 2020 (Prepublication Copy)

ISBN-13: 978-0-578-53925-6

Library of Congress Card Catalog Number TXu 2-214-192

Printed in the United States of America

mysticscifi@gmail.com

mysticscifipress.com

Cover Artwork and Layout: L.D. Leslie

Cover / Interior Design and Self-Publishing Consultation:
Heidi Connolly, HarvardGirlEdits.com

For my parents, Joan Lola and Eugene Victor:
Thank you for your open minds and open hearts.

ACKNOWLEDGMENTS

Magic Seasons' philosophy is based on the *Unified Field Theory of Science and Spirituality* developed by Nassim Haramein at the Resonance Science Foundation. Dion Fortune's *Cosmic Doctrine* was my basis for the creation of the Universe according to the metaphysics of the Western Inner Traditions. Drunvalo Melchizedek's School of Remembering and Buckminster Fuller provided the groundwork for sacred geometry. Father Charlie Moore's descriptions of the correlation between spiritual evolution with the evolution of the galaxy as well as his vast religious scholarship wove together a vivid picture of humanity's origins. Decades long study of the Hermetic Principles presented by Builders of the Adytum continues to generate insights like the opening of a flower.

I owe the concept of planetary evolution to Dolores Cannon's *Convoluted Universe*. Although Delores explained that we are headed for a unique, one-time planetary schism and ascension, I adapted the notion to include cyclic planetary evolutionary events at ever-ascending frequencies throughout the ages.

As to the aliens or ETs, I couldn't include all species identified by die-hard UFOlogists. I relied on what I call Conspiracy Theory 101— which is to say, an amalgam of the most generally accepted paradigms regarding who's here, when they arrived, and their intentions. There are sure to be those that disagree. But until full disclosure, my fictionalized account serves the story.

Denise Coté, Ava Richey, Patricia Winslow, and the Bandon Writers Group provided wonderful editorial feedback. Thanks to Joyce Leslie, Colleen Dolan, Barry Slagle, Robin niCathain, and Rhonda Wiley for reading early drafts and sharing their reflections.

Other researchers work is implicit in *Magic Seasons*. Those who study alternate science, technology, and history often do so in unfunded obscurity; sacrificing support, respect from academia, and wider recognition in order to pursue valid theories that contradict those propagated by the conventional scientific theory. Your time is coming.

Here is a partial list of teachers and researchers whose ideas I've included and who informed my notion of the relationship between science and spirituality:

Alice Bailey, Ancient Aliens on the History Channel, Anne Davies, Art Bell, Barbara Hand Clow, Barbara Marciniak, Barbara Marx Hubbard, Brooks Agnew, Bruce Lipton, Buckminster Fuller, Carl Jung, Caroline Myss, Carolyn Casey, Charles Hapgood, Colin Wilson, Damanhur, David Icke,

David Wilcock, Debbie Ford, Deepak Chopra, Dolores Cannon, Dick Sutphin, Dion Fortune, Doreen Virtue, Drunvalo Melchizedek, Earlyne Chaney, Edith Hamilton, Edgar Cayce, Elisabeth Haich, Foster Gamble, Fr. Malachi Martin, Fritjof Capra, George Noory, George R. Stewart, Gordon-Michael Scallion, Graham Hancock, Gregg Braden, Helena Blavatsky, Hopi Prophecy and Petroglyphs, Ignatius Donnelly, Jamie Janover, Jane Roberts, John L. Lash, Jose Arguelles, Joseph Campbell, Josephine Brace, June Wakefield, Kimberly Carter Gamble, Laura Eisenhower, Laura Knight Jadczyk, Leonard Shlain, Lori Toye, Lynn Andrews, Machelle Small Wright, Marianne Williamson, Marshall Lefferts, Michael Cremo, Michael Talbot, Michael Tellinger, Nassim Haramein, Nikola Tesla, Osage Lore, Ovid, Paul Foster Case, Randall Carlson, Richard Thompson, Robert Schoch, Robert Sepehr, Ron Lampi, Rudolf Steiner, Rupert Sheldrake, Ruth Montgomery, Steven Greer, Terence McKenna, The Bible, The International Council of Thirteen Indigenous Grandmothers, The Ra Material, Trevor Ravenscroft, Vedic Scripture, Whitley Strieber, William Bramley, Zecharia Sitchin, and countless science fiction authors including DC and Marvel Comics.

PREFACE

A handful of nerdy girls loved science fiction from the time they could read. As I collected comic books and paperbacks, it bothered me that whenever a story took humans to alternate realities, we found ourselves in a hellish world where we had to battle demons or alien villains. If there are infinite alternate dimensions out there, surely one of them must have gotten it right. That's the story I want to tell and the reality I want to visit.

Welcome to Tellara, Earth's evolved sister planet vibrating at a higher frequency. Thirteen thousand years ago, we were one world. In an extraordinary schism, Gaia split into Earth and Tellara.

Tellaran science is in resonance with nature.

Tellaran technology is perpetual and implosive, meaning unlimited, free, healing, and clean.

Tellara has a resource-based economy centered on contributionism.

Tellarans revere the divine feminine and the divine masculine in all things.

Tellarans remember Atlantis and other previous cyclic civilizations including their spirituality, science, history, technology, glories, and follies.

Tellarans know how and why pyramids were built and continue to build them.

Tellaran humans socialize with species from all over the galaxy including evolved reptilians and grays.

On Tellara, unity consciousness has displaced Earth's divisive polarity. Tellarans are anticipating ascending en masse. They understand the vast cycles of galactic seasons and the ephemeral nature of planetary stability.

Tellara's final gift to Earth is the message that all sentient beings evolve spiritually, including biological species and celestial bodies. Throughout *Magic Seasons*, Tellarans share offhand references to self-evident knowledge of Inner-Earth civilizations, moon bases, the intelligence of water, ancient galactic history, and alternative science.

Magic Seasons is a heroine's journey. When a man takes the hero's journey, he saves or changes the world. Consider Hercules, Gilgamesh, Jesus, Neo in the Matrix, and even Harry Potter. When a female takes the hero's journey, she is invariably a pre-pubescent girl who returns to her home with such banal insights as, "There's no place like home," or "I've just had the most curious dream." It's time for an elder woman, a grandmother, a goddess to take the journey and change the world by revealing humanity's mythos for the next age.

Whatever you think is happening on Earth, take it up a fractal octave. The long seasons aren't just galactic, they're magic. If you think the bad guys are winning, expand your canvas. There's more to reality than is dreamed of in our philosophy. Humanity's collective consciousness is on the precipice of a perceptual leap.

~L.D.L. March 20, 2019

"*The world is like a ride in an amusement park, and when you choose to go on it you think it's real because that's how powerful our minds are. The ride goes up and down, around and around, it has thrills and chills, and it's very brightly colored, and it's very loud, and it's fun for a while. Many people have been on the ride a long time, and they begin to wonder, "Hey, is this real, or is this just a ride?" And other people have remembered, and they come back to us and say, "Hey, don't worry; don't be afraid, ever, because this is just a ride.*" ~ Bill Hicks

Part One

Summer in Tellara

CHAPTER 1

I live in my imagination. It is my way of staying sane in an insane world. It is another Monday morning in the mundane situation I inhabit for the sole purpose of survival. I have had jobs I loved, bosses I loved. This is neither. Still, it beats the hell out of unemployment. My name is Dana Mae Travers and I used to have all the answers. Then life happened. Attitude platitude shmattitude.

Loss of faith came slowly. I realized things that I can finally put into words. There is supposed to be more magic in the world, but dark forces have kept it suppressed. Are there forces inimical to the well-being of humanity? There might be. According to my best friend Louie, there are nasty aliens who probe our asses and suck our souls. There is a shadow government run by the one percent. Corporations intentionally create a throwaway stratum of humanity whose only way out of poverty is to fight wars that line the pockets of the colluding conspirators. Louie is a conspiracy theorist who has an answer for everything. Are aliens real? I don't know. But today is one of those soul-sucking, ass-probing days in corporate America.

But enough about that. Back to work; must refocus on the demographic spreadsheets. I work at the Midwest Regional Headquarters for Shelter Insurance & Trust, a huge, multinational corporation that does many things besides insurance. Shelter has big trust and investment branches on the right hand, of which, we on the left hand, are supposed to know nothing. But we see things and, of course, Louie interprets it all through his conspiracy theorist filter. Shelter Insurance & Trust is known by its employees and burned clients as its clichéd anagram, Sh.I.T. Is it a good place to work? Use your imagination. My boss is the chief claims adjuster. It is his job to deny claims. He loves his job. Louie thinks he's a reptilian in human disguise. He enjoys punishing people for being poor by making them poorer and, ideally, homeless, hungry and chronically ill. As a mid-level claims adjuster, my job is to inform policyholders that their claims have been denied.

1

Why do I stay at Shelter? From a misguided hope that I can bring some small measure of reform to the cesspool. Thinking globally, acting locally, sort of. There is more to it than that. I have internal debates about feeling trapped financially and wanting to remain in my home until I retire in order to be near family and friends. I have a deep sense of loyalty to my colleague Louie Robles-León, who feels significantly isolated in our corporate culture. In addition to being my best friend and conspiracy theorist, Louie is a senior claims adjuster, a handsome Hispanic wit. Without his wry irreverence at the office, I would wither. No job will ever be a comfortable fit for me, slipping, as I am wont to do, off the reality bus and into the sliding, gliding, winding train of daydreams. Yet I once was advised to 'grow where I was planted,' and I still believe I can make a difference and help the world.

Today Louie and I are off to lunch at our neighborhood Asian Noodle Factory. "Louie, you bring out the best and the worst in me. That is what I love about you." I declared over broccoli, nuts, and noodles.

"How so, Dana?"

"Well, you've trained me to work claims. I've learned to be more compassionate to strangers. I never knew the ongoing heartache of life's tragedies or the incredible resilience of the human spirit. But I find myself being snarky and catty about some people in the office who seem to intentionally cause suffering. I've started making a list of assholes."

"Share. Anybody I know?"

"Vincent R. Cretzky"

"The R stands for Reptile, sure, who else?"

"Bullies, most politicians, liars whose initials are FF, women who sleep their way to the top whose initials are SQ, and office gossips."

"I believe I have deciphered your sphinxlike code and identified several of our very own colleagues." Louie deserved my boss' job but was passed over five years ago. Louie processes insurance claims fairly, based on the spirit and the letter of the policy. This does not make him popular at corporate.

My boss is Vincent 'the Reptile' Cretzky. He's your stereotypical middle-aged, entitled white man. Once handsome, and still reasonably good-looking, his facade is spoiled by a perpetual scowl. His rare smile is a feral grimace. He's married to Gwen Cretzky, a brittle blonde wanna-be political wife who married the guy when he was young and promising. They had a son and life was good. But somewhere along the way, she discovered the appalling dirty tricks Vincent had used to climb the corporate ladder. Gwen Cretzky comes from serious money and uses it to keep him tied to the marriage. In her day Gwen was a brassy, sassy socialite. She has since retreated into genteel seclusion.

So, Vincent dallies with Suzy Quintana, the newly anointed, unqualified, slept-her-way-into-the job, Director of Human Resources for the Midwest Division of Sh.I.T. in Chicago.

Louie said, "Suzy was in rare form today. She burst into my office glaring daggers. She informed me that you and I are going to Sh.I.T.'s Underwriters, Agents, and Adjusters conference in San Francisco. She resents management including you."

"I resent it too. That's next week!" I cried.

"Yeah, the good news is we get a week away from the cesspool to spend in beautiful San Francisco. And we'll get to see Jay and Alice from Dallas. The bad news is that Suzy and the Reptile are going.

"That makes no sense. She's in HR. She's only going because she's Vincent's main squeeze."

"Right, his Squeezy. We'll be traveling with Squeezy and the Reptile. The other bad news is that Hal and I won't be hosting our summer solstice picnic this year. I'll be away."

I groaned, "But that's the best party of the year. No one from Shelter is invited! Except me!"

"And Carmela Benedetto in Accounts Receivable."

"She's nice. Suzy made her cry last week and I took her out to lunch to console her."

Louie sighed, "Do you think Squeezy actually likes the Reptile or is she using him as a stepping-stone in her career?"

"Either way, I don't take her seriously. She's an injection of toxic waste into the cesspool. I can't even figure out why she was hired. Vincent R. Cretzky, on the other hand, I do take seriously. He has the ear of Sheldon Walters, our CEO."

"So maybe Squeezy is sleeping with Vincent to get to Sheldon Walters, the T-REX. Do you think she's a natural blonde under all that teased peroxide? Do you think she has a nice complexion and pretty eyes under the layers of garish makeup?"

"I don't know. She might be physically fit beneath the voluptuous layers of flesh that are squeezed out below her hip-hugging mini-hemmed skirt."

"And above her plunging neckline."

"A perceptive observation for a man not taken with women."

"I can admire the female form as a work of art. Squeezy's certainly agile. She rocks 'n' rolls her hips while clickety-clacking atop lethal stiletto heels as she storms along corridors breathing fire." Louie did a little wobble in his chair in uncanny imitation of Squeezy's swing hips. "Only the Reptile seems to find Squeezy's overstated femme fatale attractive. What can I say? He's a cliché sniffing after a caricature."

I laughed mirthlessly. "This job is making me nasty."

"Forget about your guilt. Those two deserve to be snarked at. They are evil aliens whose real motives are to create misery. It is like a narcotic to them. Even though I call Vincent the Reptile, this is a disservice to actual reptiles who are not evil aliens."

"Louie, I'm being serious. I don't like office gossips and I've become one."

"One of the best! You say asshole, I say reptile."

"That's not comforting. OK, let's suppose, for the moment, there are evil alien reptiles on Earth."

"There are also good aliens."

"Fine Louie, I will stipulate to Extra-Terrestrial Aliens on Earth. I just don't believe any of them are working in our office."

"I'll make a true believer of you yet."

"It isn't just Squeezy and the Reptile. The whole corporate hierarchy at Sh.I.T. is causing me to lose faith in humanity. I have a front row seat to the unnecessary suffering of people at the bottom caused so that those on top can line their pockets with more wealth than they'll ever need. Maybe their callous indifference is rubbing off on me. When did I become a faceless number cruncher?"

"Corporations are, by definition, soulless entities. You, my fellow wage slave, are a soul in crisis. Keep fighting the good fight. Let's go back to the cesspool and do some good work for good people. Let's pay some valid claims."

All afternoon, these musings were running through my right brain while I was number crunching with my left. I was working on a spreadsheet for Shelter's annual insurance report when a rhythmic tapping distracted me. I glanced up. Five gold-lacquered two-inch nails were rapping an impatient tattoo on the corner of my desk. There stood Squeezy, all 5'8" of her, lording her height over my diminutive frame.

"What is it, Suzy?" I sighed. She had my attention. She was in gold today, a brassy, form-hugging power suit with lamé trim and matching gold, patent leather, spike heels. Coordinated vulgarity, her signature style.

"I want you and Carmela Benedetto to join me in Robles-Leon's office. Now."

So, Squeezy was calling a meeting. Not her prerogative, but there it was. Carmela is the manager in accounts receivable. She was just sitting down with Louie at his small conference table when Squeezy and I entered.

"Is this about next week's conference?" I asked.

"No," she gushed, "I've been promoted."

"To what?" Louie asked, his irreverence sailing right over Squeezy's head.

"Vice President of Corporate Human Resources. Therefore, I'm implementing a procedural change to be in compliance with corporate culture. From now on,

I am to be addressed as Ms. Quintana."

"Whatever you say, Suzy," Louie replied.

"You're announcing your own promotion?" I asked. "How does that work?"

"You don't have any actual authority over personnel outside the Human Resources Division, Suzy," said Carmela.

"I do now." Squeezy smirked.

"According to Shelter's organizational chart, Louie and I answer directly to our regional manager, Vincent Cretzky," Carmela refuted.

"Here is a copy of our new organizational chart," Squeezy declared, brandishing her trump card. "Take note that there is now a dotted line linking Ms. S. Quintana, the VP of HR, to Accounts Receivable, Claims, and Underwriting Divisions."

"Wow! A dotted line! Well, this changes everything, Suzy," Louie proclaimed. Her teased highlights shimmered when she creased her forehead.

"Ms. Quintana," she admonished. "You three need to set the example for others in the building. I am implementing higher professional standards in the Chicago Office."

"How?" Louie asked. "Has someone published a connect-the-dots primer to illustrate professionalism?" And this time his derision penetrated her narcissistic fog. Suzy was clearly aggrieved that her declaration of superior status was met with derision, indifference, and outright defiance. She had really expected us to be impressed.

"I'll get you written up, Robles-Leon, unless you conform to the new corporate culture and respect your superiors," she threatened, rocking back on her lethal heels.

"When I meet one, I'll make sure to introduce you, Suzy," Louie deadpanned. "And that's Mr. Robles-Leon, to you."

Squeezy stormed off and headed in the direction of Vincent Cretzky's office, probably to pout and demand our heads on a platter, followed by a stress-releasing shag.

"Bye, Suzy," this from me. I was more intimidated than Louie, but I had to get my licks in.

Carmela shook her head in bewilderment. "I didn't think this place could get any creepier."

Later that day, Vincent sauntered by my cube and into Louie's office. He left the door wide open, and berated Louie for all to hear. "Ms. Quintana deserved her promotion. Sheldon Walters himself signed off on it. Her new position will be an asset to Shelter. She's one of a kind."

"If by one of a kind you mean she's a parody of professionalism, we're in agreement."

At this point, Vincent shut Louie's door and continued his conversation privately. Louie had no fear for his job. He did half of Vincent's work, covering for our boss' long, late lunches with his sleazy squeeze.

No one in the Chicago Office called Squeezy, "Ms. Quintana." Fuming, she dropped the matter. As I was leaving on Friday evening, I overheard a custodian call her "Ms. Q." while emptying her wastebasket. She preened for all of five seconds before noticing that I was the only one there to overhear the subservient blandishment. She slammed her door in the poor guy's face, sending crumpled papers flying about for the abused employee to recover. Perhaps Squeezy was working late drawing dotted lines between herself and the custodial staff.

Squeezy, or anyone from Human Resources, has no actual professional justification for attending a conference for underwriters, adjusters, and agents. But she wants to go, the Reptile wants to show her off, and they prepare the conference paperwork. That's how shit works at Sh.I.T. Louie and I will connect with friends from the Dallas office. The Reptile and Squeezy will appear for nominal requisite presentations and then hit the sheets. So, it works out for everybody, minimum contact with assholes, maximum quality time with our favorite counterparts in our bizarre corporation.

I went back to my desk to call my son Jesse and ask if he could house sit and pet sit for me next week. "Whatcha doing, Jesse?"

"Landscape backgrounds for my alternate reality graphic novel." Jesse used cutting edge software to create visionary art of dreamscapes, spacescapes, and phantasmagoric panoramas; not to mention wizards, he-men, and scantily clad damsels with superpowers.

"What's this one like?"

"Mysterious woodlands populated with mythological creatures and ancient magic."

"Sounds like a place I'd like to visit."

"Me too. What's up?"

"I have to go to San Francisco next week. Can you dog sit Rip for me?" My son Jesse lives on the same property as I do. I live in an old Victorian mansion that was converted to separate condos. Mine is a spacious one-bedroom on the ground floor. There are several outbuildings on the property including a barn and a workshop that have been converted into condos and studios. Jesse lives upstairs in the former barn. It is an open great room that serves as his living quarters and art studio.

"Sure, San Francisco sounds great. There's an alternate reality you can enjoy."

"More so if it wasn't for work. It's an insurance conference." My job isn't my whole life. I have friends, neighbors, and grown kids who complete my circle.

Not to mention my dog Rip, a rescued mutt. I raised my son Jesse and daughter Ruth myself, working odd jobs that improved slightly every few years. I re-entered the workplace as a divorced single mom with a BA in liberal arts. Ruth lives a few miles away in a small condo in the city. She works for an IT company doing something with software programming. Jesse and Ruth are light-years ahead of me in computer technology. But if I might modestly say so, I have mastered the computer skills I need to do my job. I am the Spreadsheet Master of the Universe.

My kids have heard my political and spiritual diatribes for years. I used to be a political activist, but that changed with one disappointment after another. As the political landscape became more and more corrupt, my optimism faded in stages until I lost hope for humanity. I am not as far gone as Louie with his conspiracy theories, but I've lost faith in churchiosity and government. I lost my sense that the world was magical. I compensate for my pessimistic worldview by surrounding myself with beauty.

When I lost everything but my children in the divorce, my artistic dreams were derailed. As the planet was taken over by war-mongering psychopaths, magic went out of the world for me. It was a slow, downward spiral into that spiritual wasteland I refer to as my crisis in faith. My childhood was filled with enchantment, but magic moments have become rare since human civilization toppled into the abyss.

World events mirrored my inner apocalypse. When I was a young woman, I believed that humanity had a chance; we teetered on a precipice between destruction and enlightenment for centuries, counting down to decades, years, months, days, election days, vote counts, and lies. We had the collective choice to take ourselves to the next level of evolution, save our souls, and save Earth's habitat for all creatures, or let our heritage be stolen from us while we slept. So, we hit the snooze button and let the sociopaths win.

Today, I was just depressed about toxic office politics. I unearthed a claims conflict so I could call my friend Alice in Dallas to commiserate for the last half hour of the day. Alice is an assistant underwriter. Like me, she has all the responsibility, none of the rights. She's a Texas A&M educated African American woman. We're of a similar age, late fifties, have similar worldviews, and if we lived closer, we'd hang. I am glad it's Friday so I can spend the summer weekend with my dog, my art, my books, my hammock, and my music.

Monday morning came way too early. The four of us, Louie, the Reptile, Squeezy, and I departed Chicago for San Francisco at an ungodly hour. We'd be staying at the Regency Hotel off Union Square. Union Square is a favorite spot of mine because there are art galleries, restaurants, and boutiques on every block. The Reptile booked us into four separate rooms, the kind of economic extravagance in which Sh.I.T. wallows.

The Reptile didn't want to room with Louie (lucky Louie!). Squeezy did not want to room with me. The room arrangements were just a charade to maintain the appearance of separate rooms. The Reptile can afford it; our office is flush because he pulls reasons to deny claims out of his ass. Our crushed clients file repeated appeals to be considered for pennies on the dollar. It's a con. It should be illegal. Even the rest of the insurance industry looks askance at Shelter's practices. Corruption is company policy. The Reptile is a god among claim-denying managers. Squeezy is his trophy. The other Reptiles salivate over her. Do Reptiles salivate?

The Regency was filled to capacity with Shelter underwriters, adjusters, and agents from offices across the country. The conference rooms were brimming with California cuisine, salads, sushi, satay, and melon balls. We lunched before the afternoon sessions. So far, I'd attended breakout sessions on legal justifications for denying flood claims, traumatic injury claims, and auto accident claims. Shelter is an equal opportunity claim-denying operation. After the final session, the Reptile and Squeezy slipped off.

Dinner was on our own the first night. Louie and I met up with two kindred spirits, Alice Redding and Jay Andrews from the Dallas office.

"There is a lot of original art in this hotel," I commented. We viewed murals and sculptures throughout the lobby and dining rooms, paintings in alcoves and hallways.

"Even the reproductions in our rooms are beautiful abstracts," Alice commented. "I love the gray, turquoise, and burgundy mash up. Reminds me of Rothko."

"Reproductions are a gift for people who can only dream of viewing original masterpieces." I said. "Hey guys, it's early enough to visit an art gallery before dinner."

"Food first!" insisted Louie.

"I second that," said Jay. So, off we went in search of Italian food. Jay is a strapping, handsome, Ivy League-educated, likable, thirty-something, married yuppie with two young daughters and a stay-at-home wife, Val. She blogs about charter schools and organic food. "Say, did I tell you that the twins, Veronica and Vanessa, just won a piano competition playing a duet of Hungarian Rhapsody? They won statewide in their age group. They are going to the Nationals."

"I recall your mentioning it several times." Alice rolled her eyes.

"Jay, your bragging about your daughters would be obnoxious, if they weren't actual prodigies," I said.

"So, Jay," Louie asked, "Are you still the golden boy at Shelter?" Jay spent several years as an independent insurance agent writing up policies for folks, only to watch his most deserving clients have their claims denied. Altruistically, he switched sides to fix things from within.

Jay shook his head. "I've held my peace so far. The more I learn about Shelter, the more I recoil. How do you make sense of an exploitive, indifferent company policy?"

"By watching, learning, biding your time," said Alice. "There is a lot to observe if you know where to look."

"I thought I was on the inside track when I was promoted, but I don't know how much longer I can play the game."

"Be glad you don't have to work with Vincent Cretzky and his office squeeze Suzy Quintana."

"I'd take those two over Frank Fretz, Shelter's ubiquitous security sleaze," said Alice.

"Sleazy and Squeezy," Louie joked.

"Not to mention Sheldon Walters, our fearless CEO," said Jay.

"The T-Rex himself."

"Those two venomous snakes, Fretz and Walters, slither around the Dallas Office keeping morale abysmal."

"Disenchanted, are we Jay?"

"I'll probably leave Shelter within the year. I need to work for a company that has ethics. I'm too young to be this disillusioned."

"You're disillusioned. I'm burnt out." Alice said.

"Aren't we a pair?" Jay said to Alice. They smiled together.

She said, "If you and Louie were setting company policy, the world would be a better place. I've been at corporate headquarters in Dallas for ages and witnessed Sheldon Walter's shenanigans close up and personal."

"Our Alice has stories going back to the Big Bang," Jay confided.

"Do tell," said Louie. We were walking slowly because Alice walks with a cane.

"Why do you stay?"

"It's complicated. Shelter has been covering my disability insurance for years. If I try to switch, my costs would skyrocket."

"You could have found another job with benefits."

"The time for me to find a new career has long since passed." Alice didn't seem to want to talk about it anymore. I sensed there was more to her story. Corporate keeps her close, under their thumb. What does she have to lose?"

Given their age difference, Alice and Jay are unlikely best pals in the Dallas office. She's the old timer and he's the new kid on the block. But like Louie and me, they are kindred spirits.

Three blocks away from the Regency, we arrived at Tony's Casa Italia, one of the few West Coast Italian restaurants that prepare New York-style Italian cuisine. No frou-frou California Italian at Tony's. I ordered spaghetti Bolognese, a superb pasta delivery system. Alice got Eggplant Parmesan and the guys both ordered Ravioli Florentine. We drank Chianti first, and then switched to Port. Lips loosened. Stories poured forth.

Louie and I commiserated about the affair between Squeezy and the Reptile. "It's so blatant, it's gross. They're upper management."

"There's no accounting for our corporate culture." Louie shared stories about two families that the Reptile had indifferently destroyed by denying their claims. "It earned him a big bonus."

But our tales paled compared to offenses Jay and Alice described at Dallas Headquarters. Do you remember that business about my thinking that office gossips are assholes? This didn't count. We were discussing ethical and legal breaches by our management. We were essentially laying the groundwork to become corporate whistleblowers, although I didn't realize it that night. The anecdotes were increasingly hysterical, which is to say, hilarious and terrifying. We worked for criminals.

"How could he do that?" I gagged on my wine after hearing about Sheldon Walter's quid pro quo wrongdoings.

"That's not the half of it," Jay said. "He keeps spreadsheets of global power-players who owe him specific favors and those who have gotten perks from him."

"You've seen these spreadsheets? How?" Louie asked.

"It seemed like an accident. But Sheldon Walters doesn't make mistakes."

"I've seen them too, spreadsheets, memos, phone logs, you name it," declared Alice. "Sheldon Walters trusts me. Back in the day, and we're talking decades, I helped him develop the tables. I transferred his data from his handwritten journals to spreadsheet software for him. I don't know what all his codes stand for, but he tracks people on a global scale. Sometimes he seems to make entries prior to events occurring."

"Why does he trust you?" I asked.

"Like Jay said, Sheldon Walters and I go back to the Big Bang. He thinks of me as his loyal shadow."

Louie said, "A CEO only documents this kind of stuff if he's confident he has Congress in his back pocket, is above the law, and has offshore bank accounts."

"He has all that and more. He has sovereign governments and intelligence agencies at his beck and call. He's owned some presidents," said Alice. "He's cunning. He's untouchable." The way she said untouchable gave me goose bumps.

"I knew he was powerful, but you make him sound like one of the one percent," Louie said.

"More like the unnamed upper one percent of the one percent. Sheldon Walters is the public face of Shelter Insurance, however, the 'Trust' side of the house deals with clandestine transnational interests, not people," Alice answered. It was a good thing we were the only Shelter folks in Tony's that night, and better still that we had a booth in the back room.

It was past ten o'clock when we at last stumbled from our booth. "No galleries open this late," I sighed to no one in particular. We stepped out into the cool, foggy, San Francisco night to walk to the Regency. As I'd thought, the lights were out, and grates pulled down on the neighboring storefronts. All except one; a dimly lit, recessed door emerged through the mist. It was not a promising display from the outside. But peering within The Phoenix Gallery, I saw track lights illuminating 180° of walls covered with paintings and photographs. Stone plinths supported metal, ceramic, and glass sculptures. For me, entry was compulsory. Louie understood. Jay and Alice bid us good-night and set off for the hotel. Tomorrow was going to be a long, busy, corporate day.

We ste₋ ₋ed into The Phoenix Gallery. "Welcome sojourners. I am Phoenix. Make ₋ ₋selves comfortable and enjoy my artistic offerings." Phoenix was a handsome, well-made man with broad shoulders and strong, artist's hands. He had an unidentifiable accent, was of indefinable race, and indeterminate age. He smelled of sandalwood, wore a burgundy caftan, and pulled his long, wavy black hair back in a leather tie. Not all gallery owners share my taste. But when I find someone who loves the same styles I do; I step into heaven.

"You did all this art yourself?" I asked.

"It is my work." The walls were arrayed with landscapes, seascapes, cityscapes and abstracts. As I gazed painstakingly through the canvases, Phoenix's gaze traveled from the top of my head to my toes. A knowing smile creased his striking face. I looked at him, agog, until Louie poked me in the ribs with his elbow.

Phoenix had painted multiple viewpoints of a vaguely familiar landscape: not Tuscany, not the Amalfi Coast, not Provence, not California, but evocative of these favorite artists' destinations. Rolling hills covered with trees, meadows, flowers, and streams, gently sloping down to a picturesque harbor. The place looked real. I knew this place. Where had I seen it before? Phoenix stood at my elbow sharing my view. His brush strokes were tiny, yet thick. Multi-dimensional swirls that coalesced into fractal patterns. They merged into expanding coherent images until the entire canvas looked alive. I was going to have to own something by this artist.

I love scenes with people in them. The people have faces. The canvases have stories. How many tales can be discovered in Renoir's *Luncheon of the Boating Party*? Which two are paired up clandestinely? Who's in love? Who's bored? Who's along just to be near water? In street scenes, I see well-turned-out women with umbrellas rushing through the rain; a gentleman in a tall black hat escorting an elegantly dressed lady. Is she his mistresses or his wife? Are they on their way to the opera, a party, or perhaps the reading of a will? A flower vendor sells blossoms from a canopied stall. A young lady in a red dress waits and watches from the park across the street while a young man opens his purse. Are they together? Do they even know each other? Not yet, but as he crosses the street to the park, she asks him softly, "Are those for me?" They had not been. But in a moment, lives are changed. He hands the girl the flowers and promises to meet her here tomorrow. Then he departs to tell someone, not in the canvas, about his altered destiny.

Well-painted faces can carry the story in different directions. Not too photorealistic, yet not too impressionistic. Faces deep with lines, color, texture, and shadow speak to me. After a few years living with the still, silent companions in my art collection, I know these people. The stories in the paintings I live with always have happy endings. Paintings are magic.

One of Phoenix's canvasses leapt out at me. In the meadow at the top of a hill, young women in summer dresses lounged in the tall grass. She held an open book. I couldn't tell if she was reading, talking, laughing or sleeping. Her expression was whimsical, her eyes laugh-lined slits. A young man played fetch with a dog near a pond surrounded by fruit trees. Who is he to the women? Brother? Friend? Lover? A stone wall rose from a red rock terrace. Within the wall, a flower-covered archway revealed a vineyard sloping down to aquamarine water filled with sailboats. I was rapt by the view, drawn into the village beyond the arch, by the change of perspective, by the boats gently bobbing on the waves and the fluttering of their sails. Bobbing? Fluttering? The images in the canvas were actually moving. I shook my head to clear the vision. This picture had a story.

Phoenix leaned in and whispered to me, "It is called *Summer in Tellara* and it is part of a tableau of four paintings called *Magic Seasons*."

"Where is this panoramic landscape?"

"My homeland, Esselen Bluffs, along the west coast of this continent."

"I've never heard of it."

"Few have."

"Where are the other three paintings?"

Phoenix pointed to his forehead, "In here, waiting to be out pictured into your reality."

"My reality just got better."

CHAPTER 2

I won't say how much I paid for *Summer in Tellara*. It was more than I could afford, though it wouldn't break the bank. It was worth more than I paid because the painting promised to reawaken magic in my life. While I got lost in the paintings, Louie admired Phoenix's photos of San Francisco environs and his sculptures of human forms in postures of repose, lovemaking, and athletic exertion. It was past midnight when we resumed our walk to the Regency.

"Louie," I began tentatively, "I think that artist Phoenix was hitting on me."

"No Dana, he was selling to you. He was hitting on me."

"What did I miss? He was checking me out the whole time."

"He looked you over. He gave me 'the look.'"

"Oh, really? Mister Hot Stuff?"

"Trust me, Dana. He was interested."

"Yeah, in me."

"No, in me."

"Why not me? Cause I'm short and dumpy, and past my prime and you're a hot-blooded Latin stud?"

"Ease up, Dana. Phoenix is gay. And you're a petite, well-rounded woman of a certain age."

I sniffed prettily. "He must be bi."

"Maybe he's just a good salesman. You did buy a painting."

"Not because he flirted with me. Because..." I trailed off. I wasn't ready to share the moving images I'd seen on the canvas.

"Because?"

"We're kindred spirits. I can't wait to see the rest of *Magic Seasons*. Phoenix is special."

"Not to mention charming, charismatic, and good looking."

"That too."

"But who cares about that stuff?"

"Besides us?"

"And you were a little drunk."

"That too."

I unwrapped *Summer in Tellara* in my hotel room and drank in its vivid imagery for another hour before sleep enfolded me. I didn't see the boats or the sails move again. But the dog did seem to have jumped a smidgen further from the land and closer to the airborne stick. Was it my imagination? I fell asleep wondering about the stories of the young people in the painting.

Tuesday morning at the Regency arrived too soon. Today's conference sessions were pretty much the same as Monday's had been, same colleagues, different seminars: strategies for legally circumventing federal regulations, and keys to wooing new clients with a soft sell, warm and fuzzy media campaign. Vincent and Suzy schmoozed with CEO Sheldon Walters and his omnipresent appendage, Shelter Chief of Security, Frank Fretz.

Alice was late coming down to the first seminar and missed breakfast. I expected to be the last down since I was up 'til the wee hours. She looked beat. I gave her a hug and brought her a cup of strong coffee with cream and sugar. She perked up a little and we exchanged knowing looks. Perhaps we regretted the candor of last night's conversation. Nevertheless, we four knew the score and felt the sting as our company indifferently exacerbated the suffering of fellow human beings who had trusted us with their premiums.

Each of us was at a no-win crossroads of conscience: either walk away from Shelter at significant professional and personal loss, or dive into the deep end of the whistle blowing pool and face catastrophic loss. Then there was that third option: do nothing, keep our mouths closed, our heads down, and continue to collect our paychecks.

At the lunch break, Louie and I were grazing at the buffet table while a waiter was refilling a chafing dish with chalupas.

"*Estos son deliciosos, Oscar, pero no tan buenos como los de mi mama,*" said Louie, reading his nametag.

"*De mi mama's secret ingredient is chorizo,*" said Oscar.

"I'll have to try that."

Squeezy spun on Louie and hissed, "Don't speak to the help! It makes you look like."

"Like what Suzy? Mexican?"

She fumed for a moment and then condescendingly shook her blood red, two-inch fingernail in Louie's face,

"Unprofessional."

As she authoritatively clickety-clacked away on her deadly stilettos, Louie provided the play-by-play commentary.

"This reproach from a tarted-up sleaze in a crimson Frederick's of Hollywood ensemble featuring a hemline up to the Holy City and a neckline down to the Promised Land." We burst out laughing until I was gasping for air. Across the buffet table, Alice and Jay witnessed the exchange and were heartened to see us enjoying some comic relief from our office femme fatale. Oscar beat a hasty retreat to the kitchen. There was enough ambient noise in the room to mask our 'unprofessional' outburst. Squeezy rejoined the Reptile, Frank Fretz, and Sheldon Walters, the Lizard King, and gloated triumphantly at us from her strategic perch among Sh.I.T's great and famous.

14

"At least now we understand why she's attending this conference. She's raising our entire industry's standards," I said.

"Let's go find loopholes in federal insurance regulations," replied Louie.

That evening we endured a mandatory group bonding experience in a private dining room at a Chinatown restaurant. We danced the corporate dance, sitting with folks from other regional offices while playing icebreakers over moo goo gai pan, mu shu, and Kung pao. Shelter colleagues occupied dozens of tables. Each table held a foursome with one participant from the Eastern, Midwestern, and Western Regions, plus corporate headquarters in Dallas. I sat with Frank Fretz from corporate, Maggie Coutts from Eastern, and Phil Block from Western.

Maggie Coutts was a big woman; big bust, big butt, big curly orange hair, tall and loud, with a big voice, big laugh, big brain, and big opinions. I might have found her intimidating had I not found her buffoonish. But Maggie took herself seriously. She was ambitious and treated people like they were In. Her. Way. I liked Maggie Coutts in spite of myself, drawn as I am to colorful people, even if they are obnoxious.

Frank Fretz was debonair and handsome in a contrived way. Blond and blue eyed, he had a Kirk Douglas jaw and Jack Nicholson smile. Frank tried to be convivial, but his personality came across as invasive. I never met anyone with whom I cared to share less. Phil Block, on the other hand made the Ken Doll look soulful.

Alice was stuck at Squeezy's table. Jay was seated at the Reptile's table. Poor Louie was seated with T-Rex himself, Sheldon Walters. After dinner, we were given icebreaker fortune cookies and had to share something about ourselves with our colleagues. Mine read, "Describe a recent disappointment." I dissembled, kept my response out of the office.

"I'm disappointed that I could only buy one painting in San Francisco."

Frank Fretz read his fortune, "Share something about yourself that complements what your previous colleague just shared." So, Frank allowed that he liked art. Okay, promising.

Then Maggie read, "Share something that happened to you recently that was both disappointing and instructive." She related a story of a claimant who appealed a denied claim repeatedly, hired an attorney, and finally prevailed. Maggie got blamed. But she figured out a loophole that would prevent the next appeal from succeeding. "A major malpractice law firm with offices on the East Coast is kindly disposed to Shelter." She made air quotes around the words kindly disposed. "Appealing clients can be approached by ambulance chasers called Waldo Mannheim & Peters in a number of creative ways, all legal."

"How does that work?" I asked

"The Trust side of Shelter owns several subsidiaries." Maggie winked at me.

"That explains it," I mused, which everyone at the table took to mean that I was impressed.

Finally, Phil read his fortune, "Describe a recent disappointment that made you reconsider your priorities." Phil allowed he was keenly disappointed that the San Diego Chargers had moved to L.A. and he was seriously thinking of switching allegiance to the Oakland Raiders now that he lived in the San Francisco Bay area. A bit of a sports rant followed. I nodded in hearty agreement. Go Raiders.

"So, what kind of art do you like?" I asked Frank, because in the next round icebreaker, the question was to ask colleague Number Two something about his and my complementary interests. I asked him to name his favorite artist.

"Hieronymus Bosch," he replied. Hell and Damnation! Oh, there are magnificent faces and epic stories in Bosch's paintings. Not to mention the tortures of the damned. Bosch's canvases do not have happily ever afters.

Frank asked me to complement his last query by naming my favorite artist. Trying to stay neutral, I went mainstream: "Vincent Van Gogh."

"Ah, *The Potato Eaters* and *The Potato Harvest*," Frank concurred nodding. *The Potato Eaters*! Bleak, colorless scenes of impoverished farm families scratching out subsistence crops to sustain their drab, backbreaking existence. "Go Raiders!" I thought silently.

Now it was Maggie's turn to describe something about Frank's and my shared interest that complemented her first-round icebreaker story. "The family in *The Potato Eaters* look like the clients I worked so diligently to deny. They're equally, poor, stupid, unwashed, undeserving, and ugly." She slapped her thigh. Frank and Phil roared with glee. I choked on my water, which was taken to be a strangled cough of laughter. Our table was having a fabulously successful icebreaker. Corporate heads turned our way and beamed approval.

Phil's turn. He must now piggyback his first story on the now converged interests of his colleagues' second round icebreakers. There was no question in Phil's mind, if *The Potato Eaters* were alive in California today, they would be San Diego Chargers fans. Phil also opined that Maggie's clients, no doubt, supported losing teams everywhere. Even I had to laugh.

"Go Raiders." This time I said it out loud and was rewarded by a collegial slap on the back from snake oil salesman, Frank Fretz. The dinner ended on that high note.

Back at the Regency, Alice, Jay, Louie, and I gathered in Alice's room to recover from our corporate team building. I described my table mates and our icebreaker.

"Frank Fretz needs his bolts tightened," Louie quipped.

I asked, "What's Sheldon Walters like?"

"Like Dick Cheney without the warmth."

Alice said, "Suzy has tremendous confidence with nothing to back it up."

Jay was quiet while we bantered. But then said, "We're all in the same boat."

"And up the same creek," said Louie. We finished our wine, said good night, and adjourned to our rooms.

Back in my room, I contemplated *Summer in Tellara*. My eyes were drawn to the vine-covered stone archway, down across the rolling green hills to the coastal village and the boats in the harbor. Again, I was rapt by the sensation of bobbing hulls and fluttering sails. This time I didn't look away or shake my head to dislodge the moving image. I stared, transfixed, allowing my consciousness to flow with the wind and water. My peripheral vision caught movement of the dog as its image blurred across the meadow and jumped to catch the stick in its mouth! I continued to stare through the arch, while attending to the peripheral imagery. Tall trees, heavy with purple fruit, stirred gracefully. Leaves fluttered. A breeze brushed the side of my face. Whoa! I jerked back out of my trance. Was I hallucinating? Or was perceived motion within the canvas lulling me, luring me into a summer meadow? Did I want to go to *Summer in Tellara*? I had no way of knowing if the country in this picture was kinder and gentler than the reality I inhabited. But I knew magic was back in my life. It had reached out to me tangibly. And I needed magic to rekindle my hope.

My eyes returned to the canvas. I repeated the technique of focusing on the arch while attending to my peripheral vision. Images stirred. Wind rippled through the grass. Trees bowed and swayed. Heavy purple fruit fell to the ground. I heard it thunk. I felt the breeze. The girl's yellow dress fluttered. She stepped directly before me and smiled. Her eyes were a rich dark sable.

Our eyes locked. She made deliberate and lengthy eye contact until she was certain that we were actually seeing one another. She held out a hand to me. My own hand was extended into a blurry mist. When I switched my attention back to my peripheral vision, I felt a disorienting lurch. I was summersaulting through space. I didn't know up from down and seemed to have lost my gravitational center. My eyes sought my hand, the only tangible frame of reference I could identify. Through the mist, my fingertips became visible, entwined in a delicate brown hand that balanced me as I stumbled into the tall grass. The rest of my body tripped into the meadow. The young woman pulled me into a strong, steadying hug. "Welcome to Tellara."

Her companion rushed forward to greet me. More sounds and smells assailed my senses. The tree leaves whispered a lullaby. The low hanging purple fruit emanated a tangy aroma. The grass exuded the scent of new mown hay and the dog jumped and barked in excitement. My appearance seemed to be cause for rejoicing. The young people were tall and strong. Their eyes were shades of brown. Their skin was deep bronze and their hair dark and wavy.

"Welcome wayshower!" said the tall girl. I took a few steps further into the meadow and turned around to look behind me. Where I expected to see the interior of my hotel room, I saw terra cotta terraces, walls, arches, and benches.

"Welcome to Tellara," she repeated in that strangely accented English that reminded me of Phoenix.

"Thank you, I think. I'm Dana Travers," I said rather formally, "How do you do?"

"I am well. You are expected, wayshower."

"Why do you call me wayshower? What is this place?"

"Permit us to introduce ourselves. I'm Juniper, this is my brother Robin; and this hairy beast is Corky."

Corky was a medium-sized, black and tan mixed breed.

"This place is Heartplum Park, in the region of Tellara called Esselen Bluffs. Robin, Corky, and I come here often on summer afternoons. That is why the Circle of Thirteen appointed us to greet you. We knew you would arrive on the solstice. It was foretold."

"Foretold? Solstice? Wayshower? Circle of Thirteen? Heartplum Park? How did I get here?" I didn't know what to ask first.

"This is an alternate Earth if that is what you're wondering. This world is Tellara," Juniper answered. "We're on the west coast of Boreal Esselen, a region called Esselen Bluffs. The heartplum trees grow wild here in this park."

"How did I get here?" I repeated.

"You traveled through a quantum singularity in the painting, *Summer in Tellara*. The artist painted a fractal pattern that spiraled down to a singularity. You found the portal by staring at the fractal, geometrical brush strokes. When you saw the images moving, you slipped through the crack between our worlds."

"I don't understand anything you just said. What is a quantum singularity?"

"Well, you know what a singularity is, yes?"

"No."

"A blackwhole, where mass is drawn into the center of a spinning vortex and collapses under the weight of its own gravity. A singularity is a single point in spacetime with zero mass and infinite gravity. So, it is zero, one, and infinity all at once."

"I know of black holes from the Discovery Channel on TV."

"Well a blackwhole is a singularity. A quantum singularity is a singularity with magnitude and direction."

"Huh?"

"Like the difference between a scalar and a vector. A scalar is a line. It has magnitude. A vector is an arrow. It has magnitude and direction. Similarly, a quantum singularity is like a wormhole. It has a direction, a destination. When something enters a quantum singularity it emerges somewhere else."

I nodded, "So I came here through a wormhole. How do I get back?"

"The quantum singularity opens in both directions. You will emerge through the painting to wherever *Summer in Tellara* is displayed."

"That would be in my hotel room in San Francisco, the city where I bought this painting from an artist named Phoenix."

"Yes, Phoenix is the Tellaran artist who drew you to the portal. Phoenix opened the portal from Tellara to Earth. You opened it from Earth to Tellara. Wayshowers appear during the Magic Seasons to assist with the shift of the ages."

More riddles. "I'm in another Earthlike world. I got here through a wormhole in the painting. I'm expected. A shift is happening. You think I'm some kind of wayshower for you."

"Not for us. A wayshower to bring our message to your Earth."

"On my world, very few people listen to anything I have to say."

"They will, after you go through your training here in Tellara."

I looked around. The fruit trees looked like sugar maples with their graceful silhouettes and broad, variegated leaves. It appeared I was near San Francisco geographically. But the flora and terrain were unfamiliar, as were the people. "Is this a real world or am I inside a painting?"

"Tellara is a real world. Here, taste a heartplum. It should convince you," Robin offered, handing me the ripe purple fruit. I bit into it and was rewarded with a juicy orgasm of tangy sweetness. The heartplum was shaped like a small, elongated apple. Its skin was deep purple. Its pulp was reddish purple. This fruit was succulent like a mango, but crispy like a watermelon. It had a singular taste all its own. The heartplum spurted dark purple juice as soon as I bit into it. It was difficult to eat without getting messy. I felt like a kid with a melting popsicle, trying to capture every drop.

"Heartplums open up your heart chakra and your third eye. 'It is delicious, nutritious, and cyclopropitious,'" said Robin, laughing. "That is a rhyme for kids. It means the heartplum is all good things for body, mind, and spirit. You can live off the heartplum for days and even the pit has energizing nutrients."

"Is that hemp?" I pointed at a wild field of greenery that looked like marijuana only with larger stalks and buds of all sizes.

"Yes, hemp and heartplums grow wild all over Tellara. Come then, we'll escort you down to the Thirteen Elders of Esselen Bluffs," said Robin.

"How long will this take? I'm expected at a conference in the morning."

"You have been expected on Tellara for thirteen thousand years," Juniper teased gently.

"Oh, well in that case…." I trailed off.

"When in doubt, dance!" Juniper took my right arm while Robin took my left. Juniper skipped alongside Corky, who leapt across the meadow. I was more or less being hauled to the so-called Thirteen. Tellara didn't seem like a dangerous place and these young people didn't seem threatening. But how would I know? Sure, I visit alternate realities in my imagination. My son even illustrates them. But this was my first actual parallel world. We stepped through the arch and I got my first unobstructed view of the meadow overlooking Esselen Bluffs. "The entire region of the continent from the Boreal Pole to the equator is called Esselen Bluffs. The city is just called the Bluffs," Juniper informed me.

I was surprised to see that this was not some primitive fairytale realm but a highly organized, thriving, technologically advanced modern world. On yonder hills, winding roads were filled with pedestrians, cyclists, and floating vehicles. Travelers passed each other going up and down the knolls that wended to the coast. We came to a domed transport station where a passenger transport was waiting. Below the cars, several millimeters of air cushioned tongue-in-groove fittings aligned with what I guessed were magnetic tracks. We stepped on board and found seats. I was a short, pale, self-conscious blotch in a sea of tall, bronze gods and goddesses. People noticed me. They were curious but friendly. Smiling nods greeted me. I tried to look cool while gazing at the passing scenery.

From the moving vista I could see the Bluffs draw closer. The streets were laid out in a pattern of expanding, tree-lined, concentric circles with intersecting radial lanes. Only at the water's edge did the circles break into open arcs with breakwaters extending deep into the blue sea. Boats by the hundreds were docked and anchored. Others were slowly underway in the light breeze. "It's just like the painting," I mused.

Across the breadth of the city the coastline had several expanses of sandy beaches. Our coach glided downhill for about an hour in a smooth, nearly silent ride. I disembarked with my new companions, more uncertain than ever, first, if I belonged here; second, where here really was; and third, and most significantly, if I was having a psychotic break from reality.

The city streets bustled with tall, attractive, vigorous, bronze-skinned people of all ages heading in all directions. Laughing and talking, they carried all manner of food, drink, fabric, instruments, and parcels. The cityscape was filled with arches and domes of glass, wood, and stone containing elegant curves and nary a ninety-degree angle in sight. Domed and pyramidal structures were set in verdant flora and rock gardens. The streets were lined with sculptures on marble plinths. I saw metal and marble dancers, figures in flowing robes of stone.

"Let's turn this way," Juniper directed me through a winding labyrinth where turquoise tiles were laid amidst a lush carpet of moss. Our path led to a cathedral-sized, crystalline geodesic dome. Upon entering, I could see it was one great hall with alcoves at intervals. Juniper escorted me into an alcove. Robin waited outside with Corky.

Within the alcove sat thirteen ageless individuals. "Dana Travers, here is The Circle of Thirteen Elders of Esselen Bluffs." Juniper introduced me, nodded respectfully to the Elders, and departed silently.

A woman spoke, "My name is Violet. All of Tellara welcomes you. We Thirteen constitute the Council for Elders for Esselen Bluffs. I am the oldest person in Esselen Bluffs. There are several advantages to investing the oldest folks in society with the most oversight. One is that few hold power long enough to abuse it. Also, our tenure is naturally limited. In each region, the composition of the council has regular, albeit unpredictable, turnover. We each bring a lifetime of experience and consideration regarding the needs of society. So, Dana Travers, whose name means travelling mediator, you have certainly traveled far from home."

"I came here through a wormhole in Phoenix's painting."

"What do you think of Tellara so far?"

"It's surreal and beautiful. Thank you for your welcome, but why me?"

These gentle folk on the Council were seemingly centenarians, but for that, each was spry and bright. I would come to understand over the course of my visit that sacred vitalized water and the heartplum fruit were the keys to Tellaran longevity, mindfulness, and health. I surmised that Tellarans lived deep into twelve and thirteen decades of life. The Thirteen were dressed in comfortable caftan-like robes, all different colors. I was wearing my fancy fuchsia bathrobe and slippers, which seemed somehow suitable for the occasion. The circular room was rimmed with forest green, velvet-upholstered couches. The flocked wallpaper in shades of green, turquoise, and orange created the impression that the gardens outside interpenetrated the alcove. The crystal ceiling was an airy skylight. The Thirteen sat in a semi-circle, seven women and six men. I sat on a cushion indicated by a sweeping gesture of one woman. I had a zillion questions, but The Thirteen were running the show.

Violet spoke again. "The Bluffs is our capital city and a great trade center withinin the Pacific Ring." Violet wore lavender robes and had a purple flower in her hair. The others introduced themselves in order of descending age. I noticed a pattern to the names, many women had names that came from plants and many men had names that came from animals. Men and women both had names from the mineral kingdom. In addition to Violet, there was Jade, Saffron, Ginger, Ivy, Rain, and Hazel. The men were Wolf, Bear, River, Hawk, Stone, and Buffalo.

Violet continued, "Tellara is peaceful and prosperous. Our technology works in resonance with nature. We have a resource-based economy called contributionism. The heartdance is core to our essence as a global population. Ecstatic dance is a form of moving meditation. It brings about a higher state of consciousness. When done in synchronized groups, our collective consciousness reveals tableaus of possibilities."

I replied, "I learned about the collective consciousness in psychology classes. All members of a sentient species share the same instincts, archetypes, and symbols. We share a similar worldview. This is different from the personal unconscious which filters these archetypes through our individual experiences."

I wanted to hear more about the heartdance and the heartplum, but Violet took a deep breath and launched into an astounding revelation. "Earth and Tellara were once one planet. Planets evolve in vast cycles as they spiral through their galaxy, and galaxies spiral through galactic clusters, and galactic clusters dance through our Universe, and universes spiral through the Multiverse. Trillions, quadrillions of simultaneous, ascending vortices emerge from the Great Mother Sea and continue to advance in scale, coherence, and consciousness without end. Cycles of destruction and creation recur from the tiniest vortex to the expanding boundaries of the multiverse. These vortices organize the structure of all matter, energy, and life."

I whispered, "As above, so below; As within, so without."

"What was that?" asked Buffalo.

"A saying from Earth."

"Very good," affirmed Violet and continued. "From time to time, when the pressures on sentient bodies become unbearable, they outgrow the structures that can no longer contain their consciousness. Evolutionary transformation happens."

"Like a snake shedding its skin or a crab seeking a larger shell," I said.

"This outgrowing of structures happens in celestial bodies as well as biological creatures. Transformation can be gentle or brutal." Violet said.

"This breaking of boundaries happened to Earth and Tellara?" I asked.

"It happened in a series of cataclysms thirteen thousand years ago and foreseen thirteen thousand years hence. Thirteen thousand years ago, Earth was rent asunder. Historically, this shift coincided with the fall of Atlantis."

"Was Atlantis a city or an island?" I asked, remembering my Plato.

"Atlantis was a prosperous, global, maritime civilization that spanned tens of thousands of years. There was a main island the size of a small continent, but its cultural influence reached around the world," Buffalo answered.

Violet continued, "The destruction of Atlantis coincided with the rapid melting of the glaciers. In addition to unprecedented flooding, this redistributed weight of the planet's surface giving rise to tremendous siesmic acticity in a process called crustal displacement. Whole continents shifted around the globe. This redistribution of weight, in turn, altered the planet's axial balance and magnetic field. Geologic cataclysms flooded and submerged entire coastal regions of the globe. They remain submerged on both Earth and Tellara.

This upheaval coincided with monstrous power grabs in Atlantean governments. Insane, despotic, oligarchs seized totalitarian control of regimes. They used science, technology, and military might to control the masses. But all was not lost. A handful of priests and priestesses were able to preserve and protect our most precious schematics, blueprints, agriculture, medicine, science, technology, arts, seeds, sacred texts, and tools. These artifacts were transported all over the world to pockets of settlements that survived the global upheaval.

"This discontinuity in our collective psyches was a reflection of the schism within Gaia herself. Even as Earth and Tellara were separating, these initiates used the remnants of Atlantean knowledge to construct stone edifices that would endure for tens of thousands of years. Encoded in these edifices are mathematical, symbolic, and astronomical encryptions to inform and warn future civilizations of the stellar calendar that marks planetary cycles and galactic seasons." Violet paused and I needed a moment to gather my thoughts, but before I could, she continued.

"The difference between Earth and Tellara is that we remember it, all of it. We remember the planetary shift. We remember our Atlantean civilization from its peak to its destruction. We acknowledge the influences that brought it to ruin, both natural and man-made. We remember the meanings of the encoded messages in our megaliths. We remember that civilizations on this planet are cyclic; rising and falling over millions of years. We remember our history and science. We never stopped venerating the natural world."

I said, "On Earth, the antediluvian world is considered a legend. Some people believe in it from various religious scriptures. Those working in mainstream academic institutions consider it ridiculous. And yet, some independent researchers take ancient lost civilizations seriously."

Buffalo smiled at me and took over the narrative from Violet. "On Tellara, the priesthood shared all remnants of the Atlantean expertise with all survivors of the deluge. None were ever deceived about our true history, our resonant science and technology, the natural healing arts, and the wisdom of water. The entire repertoire of ancient sacred knowledge was openly shared.

"The survivors on Earth who retained the secret knowledge were an elite priesthood. For many generations, this knowledge was preserved as sacred and unsullied. After a time, the keepers of this secret knowledge recognized that they had access to power unattainable to the masses of humanity. They could use it to manipulate events to their advantage. Knowledge is power and power corrupts. Thus began a scheme to consolidate that power over generations with an eye toward global domination."

I said, "The elite are nothing if not patient. They play a long game. Some of us recognize the use of religion, education, and the media to manipulate the masses. My friend Louie calls these powerful people the Illuminati. So, you prevented this stranglehold of power on Tellara, how do you know what happened on Earth?"

"Because it was tried here. A small cabal of priests tried to conceal ancient knowledge within their secret circle. They were discovered and their plans overturned by means of the heartdance. As the planetary shift continued over seven generations, these duality-minded individuals reincarnated on Earth, finding themselves uncomfortable in Tellara's emergent harmony consciousness."

Duality-minded?" I asked.

"Look at it like this," Buffalo replied. "Polarity is essential to creation. The magnetic attraction between masculine and feminine, between yin and yang, positive and negative polarities draw together to create, to manifest. However, divisive polarity moves the poles so far apart so as to make them mutually exclusive to the point of destruction. Dualistic thinking sees only opposition. When polarities are balanced, unity thinking is possible. Heart and mind connect."

Buffalo stopped speaking and a woman wearing a goldenrod-colored caftan said, "My name is Saffron. Do you heartdance on your world?" Like the other elders, Saffron was tall with a bronze-toned complexion. Her ageless face featured prominent cheekbones, gentle, expressive eyes, and an Olympian nose that accentuated her powerful mien. Her hair was thick and white. She wore it in a braid to her waist over her right shoulder. All the elders remained seated in a semicircle facing me. My cushioned seat was at their height, but they seemed to tower over me owing to the fact that I was 5'2" and they all seemed to top 6'.

"Not that I am aware of. How can this moving meditation reveal possibilities and secrets?"

"Nature is balanced between radiative and contractive forces, projective and receptive. On Tellara we use this polarity dynamic to resonate with nature. This ecstatic dance is both an artistic expression and a living instrument connecting us to higher dimensions."

"I'm still not getting the picture." I fidgeted on my cushion.

"That is because your technology is based on the radiative aspect of science: explosions, projectiles, rockets," continued Saffron. "All your scientific processes end with entropy."

I quoted my high school chemistry teacher. "Any time there is a chemical reaction, it increases entropy. The Universe becomes less organized. Eventually, all will degenerate into chaos. But don't worry because we have billions of years before that happens."

Saffron nodded and continued, "This principle presupposes that at a prior moment, the Universe was more organized; that matter and energy existed in a coherent state. Where did this organization come from and why don't you study that? The contractive aspect of nature is its organizing principle. Gravity is metaphysical love. We call it syntropy."

"Syntropy," I liked that word. "But to be fair, on Earth, we use technology to organize as well. We have 3-D printers, and bio-medically engineered machines like heart pacemakers, and computers that solve problems. We don't just blow things up."

"Yes, but on Tellara, we have an endless supply of free energy. We have harnessed gravity. We use sound waves to heal, to levitate, to purify water, and to dampen seismic waves."

"How does this explain the heartdance?" I persisted.

"The heartdance utilizes sexual polarity, sound, movement, and geometry. Women form inner concentric circles. Men encircle them. Men sing, chant, and play instruments tuning in to the issue at hand. Women dance to synchronize with the heart of the concern. Vibratory attunement is attained. From a higher dimension, a sensory web externalizes our thoughts and feelings. Vibrating threads weave a tapestry. This shared vision gives rise to consensus."

"It must be difficult to argue about your decisions when you can all see the consequences together before they happen," I was getting a clearer picture.

"Indeed, it makes selfish choices impractical," Saffron agreed.

Husky and tall, Buffalo took over the narrative, "For example, a community wants to put in a vegetable garden in a meadow. We dance to determine if a parcel of land should remain a meadow or become a vegetable garden. The tapestry displays the meadow. It then phases and we see that a vegetable garden will disrupt a bird habitat. But if we use permaculture and the garden is woven through with indigenous flowering plants, it will offset the loss of habitat. The birds will thrive, so will the vegetables, and so will the community." Buffalo fit his name. He was a big, handsome man with a shaggy head of hair.

"Thank you, Buffalo, for helping me to visualize this consensus image. But I still don't understand how this protects Tellara globally."

Saffron replied, "Somewhere in the world, people are always heartdancing. The perpetual heartdance maintains a web of protective loving light over all Tellara. We collectively bring forth global harmony consciousness. Forces detrimental to the well-being of our world cannot tolerate or penetrate this vibratory shield."

"You dance a defensive shield?" I was skeptical, "using sexual polarity?"

Buffalo nodded. "Harnessed polarities are the creative life force. Destructive polarization traps people in an 'us versus them' mentality."

I spoke up, "Some people think I can't have mine unless you can't have any. This fear-based belief dominates much of my planet, my country, even my office."

"Wayshower, we brought you here to show you what is possible with a harmony collective consciousness. You, then, can share this vision with your Earthborn population. That is a wayshower's mission, a wayshower's dharma."

I laughed. "Yeah, because everybody on Earth listens to me. However, this does explain that those who amass the most wealth at the cost of others are the most fearful." I expressed another uncertainty, "On Earth, our sexual polarities are not absolutes. We have homosexuality, bisexuality, transgender individuals, and even hermaphrodites who don't fit into your scheme."

"We have that here too. People of all genders can be either masculine or feminine at different moments in their lives. Sometimes we're projective, sometimes we're receptive."

"You're overwhelming me with a lot of science and natural history. Why?"

Violet spoke, "Believe it or not, understanding our science is fundamental to our harmony consciousness and resonant technology."

Buffalo added, "Think of yin and yang."

"OK."

"It is She, the Primal Mother into which He, the primal Father is projected. Without both, creation has no form, no organizing structure to contain atoms, molecules, cells, even consciousness."

"Whereas a monotheistic Father God just projects an endless masturbatory ejaculation on and on to infinity." If the elders appreciated my irreverent humor, they didn't show it. Even if Earth religions gave lip service to God being both genders, masculine nouns and pronouns permeated our dominant languages. A not-so-subtle, persistent reminder to humanity's collective consciousness, to every human, every day, that the creator of the Universe was unequivocally male, ergo, the gender roles in all things great and small were so ordained. No wonder we like to light fires under phallic rockets and project them into space; and how easy to glorify the radiant masculine projection while debasing the dark, receptive feminine and equating it with sin.

I was pulled from my reverie by Buffalo, "Imagine gazillions of tiny ejaculations impregnating gazillions of cosmic wombs, endlessly. Continuous creation in the Universe at all scales, at all moments. Without beginning. Without end."

This was a completely different way of thinking about cosmology. "On Earth, we theorize one moment of creation called the big bang."

"Well, now you can consider gazillions of little bangs happening all the time."

I asked, "You figured this out by dancing?"

Violet answered, "We've known it since Atlantean times. The heartdance was revealed to us by Zola, our first Tellaran Elder and the last living Atlantean priestess. The heartdance balances our spiritual and biological evolution. It makes deception nearly impossible. We banished the hard-core, duality-minded individuals from Tellara after the shift. Duality-minded individuals had held positions of great power and put up a massive and bloody struggle to maintain control."

"The faction of priests who tried to keep Atlantean science secret?" I asked.

"You've been listening, wayshower," Violet affirmed. "As the heartdance web strengthened, polarized individuals either embraced harmony consciousness or reincarnated on Earth."

"So, my Earth became a dumping ground for selfish Atlanteans who never accepted this harmony consciousness?"

"Just so."

"And that would include, uh, me..." It wasn't a question, but a humbling realization.

"You are here now, Dana Travers, wayshower," said Violet, her lavender caftan shimmering in the afternoon sun's rays. Her hair was so black it looked almost purple.

I stood and addressed the Thirteen, wanting to view them at eye level. "Again, I ask you, why was I chosen to be this wayshower? I'm not so selfless. I'm kinda snarky and petty. You've created a paradise here. How can a flawed individual like me be a wayshower for anybody, anywhere, much less on my insanely corrupt world?"

"It's karmic. You volunteered thirteen thousand years ago," Violet answered.

"Oh? Did I?"

"Dana, you also found the painting. You opened the portal from your world to ours. All will be revealed once your lessons begin in earnest. In order to arrange your training regimen, we will do a heartdance now. Join us." Violet addressed the Circle.

All Thirteen rose from their seats. We moved from the small alcove into the crystal domed pavilion. Sunlight refracted through the translucent, faceted ceiling. Dozens of prisms cast intersecting rainbows on the white walls. The women formed an inner circle in the rotunda and drew me into the center with them. Men encircled the women and began a lilting chant accompanied by drums, flutes, and stringed instruments. The women swayed. The chanting grew stronger, took on rhythmic, melodic, and harmonic resonance. The women's swaying became synchronized and graceful. Men's voices combined to create a rich instrument. Patterns of light and geometry cohered in the space between dancers. Individual dance steps morphed into a multi-bodied, geometric pattern. It was a mysterious process that gently yoked me to the movements of the women around me.

Thrumming grew to a crescendo. Robes swirled together in eddies of color. Glittering monads of light materialized from nowhere. Movement fashioned strands of light that surrounded the dancers. Light coalesced around Saffron in her goldenrod-colored caftan. Then the strands surrounded me in my bright pink robe. She and I became woven together in a spinning infinity symbol. It grew into three dimensions, expanding and contracting enfolding us in swirling gold, pink, and orange currents. I saw, felt, and even smelled the fruit and flowers that emerged. Then all were dancing and singing. We moved in a brilliant frenzy until we were laughing, sweating, panting, and finally dropping to the floor.

Violet spoke again, "Consensus has been attained." Saffron rose and walked to me. She reached out her hands to help me to my feet as Violet declared, "Saffron will be your guide and mentor in Tellara." There was general murmuring of agreement. "Well met, wayshower."

CHAPTER 3

I went with Saffron to her charming domed house enclosed in lush, fragrant, flowering plants. It was a short walk through the moss-covered park lands. Juniper and Robin joined us. It turned out that they were Saffron's grandchildren. I spent the rest of the day and the night with them. Saffron told me more about Tellaran science and history and its significance to Earth's destiny. We meditated, talked, ate, napped, and laughed. I cried once as I became overwhelmed with the enormity of my situation. Saffron served a wonderful fruit salad and vegetable soup with bread.

"So, on your Earth, you are already considered a crone?" Robin asked between bites.

I was nonplussed and made no reply.

"On Tellara, the crone is venerated," Juniper explained. "Tellarans enjoy showing our age."

I said, "It also seems age does not diminish your vigor, health, or beauty. On Earth, our external aging process often mirrors the internal wear and tear our bodies undergo because we live in a rat race. That means we are running all the time to get nowhere. Age is not a cause for veneration in my culture. Some people aren't even lucky enough to live the rat race. They eek out life off the land in subsistence poverty."

"But the land is bountiful," cried Robin.

"Not always. Not on Earth. We have droughts and famine, floods, and shortage of clean water."

"We want to know more of your world of duality," Juniper said.

Saffron answered, "Phoenix is transporting Earth artifacts to Tellara to help us understand how our Earthborn counterparts have coped with duality for these long millennia."

The sun was coming up. "It was night in San Francisco, but it was noon when I arrived in Tellara. How much time has passed?"

"It won't always be noon now that you have opened the portal. The days, nights, and seasons will cycle."

"Have I been here a day and a night?" I was too enchanted with everything Tellaran to be concerned about returning to the Shelter Convention. But return I must.

"Will you return to Tellara soon?" Robin asked me.

"As soon as I can."

In a butter-colored kimono, Saffron escorted me to Heartplum Park. The damp grass soaked my slippers and the hem of my bright pink robe.

"Come Dana, take back some heartplums to Earth. They will sustain your spirits until you return to Tellara." Saffron picked handfuls of purple fruit and I stuffed my pockets until they became stained with juice. She showed me how to identify the portal on the Tellaran side. There was no painting here in Heartplum Park, but clearly, this was the spot where Phoenix had stood to paint *Summer in Tellara*. Beneath a copse of trees, ripples resembling rising thermal waves distorted a section of the red stone wall. I approached the wall and stumbled through the waves. I emerged clumsily into my hotel room and flopped onto my bed.

Had it all been a dream? My cold, wet feet belied that theory. So too did my juice-stained, bulging pockets. Unless I had been sleepwalking, sleep-dancing, and sleep-eating around the Regency, I had been in Tellara since the wee hours of Wednesday morning. Near as I could figure, I'd spent a day and a night there, about thirty-two hours. Had thirty-two hours passed in San Francisco? I turned on the television to view a news channel. Gemini Dallas, a bland blonde scandalmonger, assured viewers that it was Thursday morning and the world was in political and economic turmoil. I had missed a day of the conference. Alice, Jay, and Louie would be frantic. I hope they had covered for me. The Reptile would be nasty. Yikes! The Reptile. I hadn't thought about him in a lifetime. My stomach growled and I devoured two heartplums. I needed to put in an appearance at the Shelter conference ASAFP.

I showered, dressed in a conservative gray business suit, and took the elevator to the lobby to face the consequences of my Tellaran sojourn. Louie and Alice descended upon me in great agitation, "Where have you been?" asked Louie.

"Where's Jay?" asked Alice.

"What do you mean? Where's Jay?" I was bewildered.

"You both missed all of yesterday's sessions," said Alice.

"Sheldon Walters, FrankenFretz, and the Reptile are on a tear," added Louie. "Late yesterday when neither of you appeared for the conference, Frank Fretz pounded on your hotel doors. Neither of you answered. Finally, hotel security let him into your rooms. Both your rooms were empty, except all your belongings were still here. The general assumption was that you were together."

"No. I went out alone."

"For a day and a night?" Louie was mad at me.

Alice looked more worried than angry. "I called Val. She hasn't heard from Jay."

"Where have you been, Dana?" Louie pressed. "No one has heard from either of you."

"I'm going to need more privacy than this hotel lobby to tell you everything, Louie."

30

The Reptile and Squeezy approached. Righteous anger at my truancy stirred him to make a disrespectful joke. "So, you and young Jay, clandestine rendezvous, eh, Travers?"

I was speechless. Squeezy laughed. No one else did. Although still in my Zen state from Tellara, Jay's disappearance stunned me. My reticence didn't suit the Reptile, "Travers, we need to get a few things straight," he roared just in case anyone in Union Square couldn't overhear him

"As you wish." I conceded gracefully. After all, I had missed a day of the conference on Shelter's nickel. The Reptile had lost face. He bellowed. I demurred. He threatened. I acquiesced. Squeezy smirked. I met her gaze with bland serenity. "I'm sorry to have worried you. I'm fine. Yesterday, I met a revered mentor who persuaded me to join her in a vision quest." I wasn't lying, exactly. I had met Saffron yesterday. She is my mentor.

Not to be diverted, Vincent demanded, "Was Jay Andrews with you?"

"No. I only just learned of his absence."

Questions began flying at me from all sides. "When is the last time you saw him? Where do you think Jay is now? Have you been in contact with his wife? Why did you disappear without notifying anyone?"

Aware that curious colleagues were hanging on every word, I spoke directly to Vincent Cretzky, "I last spoke to Jay Tuesday night in Alice's room. We had a nightcap after the team-building dinner. My invitation came just after midnight. I went out alone."

"Nobody makes appointments in the middle of the night unless they're up to no good," said Suzy, sticking her nose in where it didn't belong.

"Are you interviewing with another company? Passing company secrets?" The Reptile was on a roll.

"Of course not. There was a message waiting for me in my room. I met up with Saffron later."

Vincent said, "Saffron! What kind of hippy-dippy name is that? You left without telling anyone, even your friends. You should have gotten my signed permission if you wanted time off."

"You should have turned in an absentee requisition to me! You can't play hooky during a conference," said Squeezy. There she stood, toe tapping, and squinting, the Mistress-of-All-Administrative-Paperwork. The idea of filling out a requisition with Squeezy and getting the Reptile's signature before dissolving across a quantum singularity into Tellara struck me as spectacularly absurd. Spontaneously I giggled. My inappropriate frivolity drew sharp looks from Sheldon Walters and Frank Fretz.

"Were there no phones where you went?" Vincent challenged.

"I was in a remote location," This public scolding was getting tedious. "Now,

I'm going to eat breakfast and attend the session regarding health claims based on contaminated water tables near landfills."

Vincent would have said more, but the FrankenFretz approached and laid a restraining hand on his sleeve. The Reptile had smoke coming out his ears. Squeezy looked constipated. But Frank Fretz and Sheldon Walters looked more vexed than a few missing hours by a middle-aged, middle-management claims adjuster should have signified. Alice was near tears and asked to leave the conference early, but Sheldon Walters wouldn't hear of it. "You're my Gal Friday, Alice. Stay put," his smile seemed threatening. Alice leaned heavily on her cane and walked over to the breakfast buffet. I followed.

"Apparently Dana didn't know Jay was missing," FrankenFretz said as he diverted the Reptile and Squeezy toward the buffet table. He hung back to speak to me. Frank purred in my ear. "Vincent is a fool. I'll minimize any reprimand that might appear in your file." Frank was being good cop to the Reptile's bad cop. But I didn't care. A reprimand in my file? Of all things to give a rip about at this point! Bring it on. I'll write the damn memo myself!

"*Instead of training on creative ways to deny claims, Ms. Travers was pickin' fruit and dancin' naked under the solstice moon in the Land of Milk and Honey.*" In his understated way, FrankenFretz was more menacing than the loud confrontational Reptile. "I saw the painting you bought in your hotel room," he whispered again, "charming, but a little saccharine for my taste."

"I'm sorry you felt the need to search my room."

"I alerted hotel security when neither you nor Jay Andrews could be contacted. I accompanied them into both your rooms." I could hardly blame my colleagues for calling out the militia. If I had been in trouble, I'd have been grateful for their intervention. I forced myself to thank him for his support.

Alice handed me a blueberry muffin. Louie handed me a cup of tea. Their faces were grim. Up until now, they had been doubly panicked on my behalf as well as Jay's. They must have worried that something threatening had befallen us if we had been overheard at Tony's Casa Italia. Speculation among the conference attendees was that Jay was either involved in corporate espionage or having a romantic rendezvous, maybe even with me since we were both missing. But those who knew Jay dismissed either possibility.

The conference dragged on all Thursday. As soon as I could escape, I retreated to my room and ordered a light meal from room service. As much as I wanted to reenter Tellara, I refrained. My first sojourn had caused an uproar. After a brief, longing look at Tellara, I climbed into bed and turned on cable news to watch Gemini Dallas dish the latest sensational celebrity scandal. I channel-surfed, looking for a good story. I was too restless to watch, read, or sleep. The arrival of Louie and Alice rescued me. They entered bearing California Pinot and hotel bar glasses. "We're here to make sure you stay in tonight," said Louie.

We fretted about Jay. Alice disclosed quietly that she suspected Jay was being spied on by Shelter Security, of which FrankenFretz was head. "It's his MO." Louie poured us each a glass of wine and I shared heartplums with my friends. The color, texture, and exotic taste momentarily distracted them.

"These are delicious," said Alice. "I don't recognize this fruit."

"Where were you really, Dana?" Louie pressed. I pointed to *Summer in Tellara* and started to share that I had traveled through a portal to an alternate world; but thought better of it after speculating about Jay being surveilled. FrankenFretz had probably done more than search my room. He had likely bugged it. I repeated my mentor-meditation story.

"People are calling you a cougar," Louie said.

"Yuck! That's insulting to both Jay and me. Let me guess, it was Squeezy."

"And her growing entourage," Louie confirmed. I groaned. Squeezy had an entourage.

"People are speculating regarding other, more untoward reasons for Jay and you to meet up in the wee hours," Alice half-laughed, half-sobbed. She lowered her voice to a whisper and turned up the TV volume. We leaned in close to each other.

"We crossed some dangerous lines at Tony's. I'm worried for Jay's safety. Ours too."

"It sounds like Jay had real evidence of criminal wrongdoing. We just have office gossip," Louie whispered.

"Who else knows that besides us?" I asked, sotto voce.

"Well," Alice murmured, "if your room has been bugged, we've done no more than speculate. We're probably safe for tonight."

"Not comforting, Alice," I sighed.

Louie stood, signaling the end of our conversation. "Time for bed kids. Don't go anywhere tonight Dana." I nodded compliantly. After they walked across the hall to their rooms, I sank sullenly into my cushy hotel mattress. Where in the world was Jay?

* * *

Jay Andrews' body was discovered early Friday morning. He washed up against the rocks of Alcatraz Island. The media reported that the boaters who found him said it looked like his skull had been bashed in. The official cause of death was unknown. The police declared the circumstances of his death suspicious. They would notify his next of kin.

Now, my own provocative disappearance became the object of sinister gossip. I was the focus of covert glances and hushed whispers that withered into embarrassed silences when I approached. FrankenFretz became my unwanted shadow. The Reptile and Squeezy brazenly watched my every move. I was the woman of the moment at Shelter, in a dark, ugly way. And to think I had compromised my integrity to stay with this miserable company in order to try to facilitate reform. So had Jay and look where it had gotten him. I held it together just enough to prop up Alice, who was slumped on a lobby couch in tears. Louie brought us coffee. We huddled in misery while colleagues ogled the train wreck of my life.

The police questioned everyone at the conference but concentrated on Frank Fretz and me. Frank, because he was head of Corporate Security who had notified hotel security to check our rooms; and me, because of my missing hours on the night in question. FrankenFretz wanted to remain at my side during police questioning. His unctuous hand rubbing was meant to convey support. Thankfully, the police would not allow him in the interrogation room with me.

At the police station, I was ushered into an ugly gray room with metal table and chairs. "Ms. Travers, I'm Inspector Javier Vazquez, San Francisco P.D. Have a seat." He gestured to the rigid metal chair. The detective was a darkly handsome, mature gentleman whose demeanor compelled my attention. He began by asking all the same questions my colleagues had shouted at me.

"Where were you Tuesday night after the company dinner in Chinatown?"

"Jay, Louie, Alice, and I met in Alice's' room for a nightcap. After I returned to my room, an old friend and spiritual mentor named Saffron contacted me. She invited me to join her for a healing meditation."

"How did she contact you? Phone? Email? We can check."

"I don't remember," I stammered.

"How did you connect with her?"

"I just walked outside the Regency and there she was."

"Why do you suppose you don't show up on any of the hotel's surveillance cameras?"

"I don't know."

"Did you use a back door?"

"I don't think so."

"You can't remember what door you used? Did you even leave the hotel?"

Ooh. Good one. I should have thought of that. Technically, I hadn't left the hotel. But now it was too late to change my story. "Yes, I went out."

"Did you depart the hotel with Jay Andrews?"

"No."

"Where did Saffron take you?"

"We went to her community outside San Francisco."

"How long was the drive?"

"About an hour." That was true. The ride from Heartplum Park to the Bluff took about one hour.

"Did you cross any bridges?"

"No."

"Did you enter any buildings?"

"Two. One was kind of a domed church. The other was a small hillside house where we ate and slept."

"You and Saffron?"

"Yes."

"I'd like to meet Saffron. Provide me with her contact information."

"I can't. She's not around." At the end of the day, and a very long day it was, I could not produce Saffron. I could not provide an address for any place in Tellara. I could not say how I got there, nor provide details about my so-called group meditation.

"Did anyone else see Saffron?"

"No," I was floundering in a morass of half-truths. Why didn't he ask me the difference between a singularity and a quantum singularity?

"Jay Andrews left the Regency at 1:50 A.M. Wednesday, the same time as you."

"No, I left earlier, just after midnight."

"The last time he was seen alive, around 3:00 A.M., Jay was strolling along Fisherman's Wharf with a petite brunette. Did you meet up with Jay later?"

"No. I wasn't anywhere near Fisherman's Wharf."

"Who was the petite brunette that was seen with Jay the night he was killed?"

"Not me." Was I really a suspect in Jay's murder? I was panicking when, mercifully, my interrogator changed the subject.

"Tell me about your dinner on Monday night."

"Well, Jay, Louie, Alice, and I went out for dinner at Tony's Casa Italia about three blocks from the Regency."

I started to tell him what we ate and drank, but he waved his hand in my face and said, "We'll get back to that. What did you talk about?"

"You know, work."

"Could you be more specific?"

"Jay said he knew Sheldon Walters trades favors with powerful people."

"What favors?"

"I don't know details."

"Can you name names?"

"Jay only named Sheldon Walters. He'd seen documents listing quid pro quos."

"Were there other diners in your vicinity?"

"We seemed to have the back room to ourselves."

"What else?"

I went blank. As whistleblowers go, I suck. Javier Vazquez crossed his arms over his chest and silently pinned me with his insistent gaze. I had to avert my eyes. He allowed the time to pass without pressing me. Something clicked: "Louie said that no one would keep such records unless they," I counted off on my fingers, "were above the law, had Congress in their back pocket, and had offshore bank accounts."

"Did the four of you return to the hotel together?"

"No, I stopped in an art gallery and bought a painting. Louie was with me."

After a dozen more detailed questions about our dinner conversation, the Inspector changed tacks, "Ms. Travers, do you like your job?"

"Nobody likes their job."

"I do."

"How could you? All that crime? With criminals and corruption?"

"I manage," said Inspector Vazquez dryly.

"This shabby office and ugly furniture and dubious goings-on?" I was babbling.

"Speaking of which, your alibi is a dubious muddle. You were not at the Regency from midnight Tuesday until 8:00 A.M. Thursday. That's thirty-two hours you can't account for."

I didn't know if I was more devastated by Jay's death or panic-stricken about being a murder suspect. Questions designed to entrap a guilty person might possibly help clear me since I was genuinely clueless. A dim inkling was tickling my brain. If the police considered me a suspect, did that make me less of a threat to Shelter? If Shelter guessed we'd discussed whistleblowing, I'd be in more danger from my employer than the criminal justice system. Was this police investigator thinking along similar lines? Was Shelter the big fish that Vazquez was angling for? Was I bait? That thought aside, I had the worst alibi in the history of alibis and my being uncooperative on that score seemed to be playing into everyone's agenda.

Vazquez unfolded his arms to reveal his hunky chest and let me fidget before he continued. "I don't know what to make of your crazy alibi, Ms. Travers. You might as well tell me aliens abducted you to Mars to dance the Fandango. I'm going to find out where you were and if you witnessed anything that can help solve Jay Andrews' murder."

"I want that too. Jay was a friend as well as a colleague. I think he was a potential whistleblower. But any evidence he possessed was never shared, unless it was to this other petite brunette."

Inspector Javier Vazquez rubbed his chin, never shifting his gaze from my wobbly composure. Finally, I looked down at the gray-green linoleum. At length, he signaled we were done. When I tried to stand, I slid back down with an unladylike thud. He was at my side helping me to my feet, holding my arm in a grip reminiscent of the FrankenFretz. But the Inspector's grasp conveyed support. He escorted me to the door and told me that he would be in touch. Stupidly, I said, "I look forward to it." He looked at me like I was an idiot.

We stood at the door a moment longer than seemed necessary for police protocol. I flushed with adolescent embarrassment. Now that the interrogation was over, I noticed that he had silver hair at his temples, combed into his wavy black hair. He was taller than me but didn't tower over me like the Tellarans. He had bulk from muscle rather than indulgence. "At some point, Dana Travers, I will get your entire alibi. I am not detaining you, but we are not through."

I nodded dumbly. How was I ever to explain my trans-dimensional travels to Mr.-No-Nonsense-Seen-It-All Police Inspector Javier Vazquez? Unless I ran with that Red Planet Fandango?

CHAPTER 4

I was the last to leave the police interrogations. FrankenFretz was waiting for me in the precinct vestibule. He placed his hand possessively on the small of my back and steered me out the door, onto the street, and back to the Regency. At the hotel, Louie, Alice, and I compared notes. We'd all pretty much corroborated each other's account of Monday's dinner. In fact, Alice had disclosed much more than I. She'd told the Inspector that she'd seen the memos, records, and spreadsheets herself.

Shelter personnel had all but cleared out of the hotel; no after-conference San Francisco excursions this year. The murder of a popular underwriter with a claims adjuster as the main suspect tends to cast a pall over an insurance gathering. Inspector Vazquez showed up at the hotel as we all were checking out. Within earshot of all, he said, "No one is presently being detained in this murder investigation. I will be back in touch with all conference attendees."

FrankenFretz, hovering nearby, declared, "Not to worry Inspector, as head of Shelter Corporate Security, Ms. Travers can be released into my custody." I was appalled that he had singled me out.

"You're getting ahead of yourself, Mr. Fretz. Dana Travers is being released on her own recognizance. Don't interfere with a police investigation. When I need to speak to her, she'll hear directly from me." I could have kissed Inspector Javier Vazquez.

"I am just looking out for the welfare of a valued employee," Frank casually assured Vazquez, inching closer to me as I inched away from him. Sheldon Walters was eyeing me speculatively. Did he suspect that I was the petite brunette on the wharf? Did everyone at Shelter assume my wariness stemmed from guilt? While Louie went up to fetch Alice's bags, I overheard whispered speculations.

Phil Block said, "Dana Travers' is way to small too have killed a jock like Jay Andrews."

"It was blunt force trauma to the head. Even a small person can hit someone over the head with a rock," said my other team-building dinner companion, Maggie Coutts.

Squeezy flouted her newly granted authority, "Do you want me to write up a formal reprimand, suspend her, or fire her?"

Frank Fretz rejected her suggestion with a withering refusal. "The jury is still out, Ms. Quintana. Ms. Travers is off-limits for now. Shelter's interests are our priority." Suzy understood his meaning and acquiesced sullenly.

When Louie came down, I went up to gather my luggage. As I wrapped

Summer in Tellara, I noticed that Juniper, Robin, and Corky were relaxing in the meadow. But now the bench by the stone arch was occupied. There sat Saffron, garbed in amber, proffering heartplums as though waiting to be introduced to good old Inspector Vazquez as my alibi. I laughed in spite of myself. In less than a week I had journeyed from Paradise to Purgatory. Turning the canvas to the outside window where cameras could not observe, I reached in and took the tendered gift and brought forth a small basket of heartplums that I stored in a zipper compartment of my carry-on bag. Once Louie and I had some private time, he would hear all about Tellara.

Since it was framed, I had to check my painting in baggage. With all the insanity about Jay, my overriding concern at the airport was that *Summer in Tellara* might get lost. Frank pretended to give a shit by patting my hand. I abruptly withdrew from his disturbing touch. Frank Fretz delegated Vincent Cretzky to be my 'guardian' in the Chicago office.

He also insisted that the Reptile and I sit together on the flight home. Vincent had difficulty meeting my eyes. Perhaps he had made a muck of his police interview and was feeling guilty about insinuating some untoward business between Jay and me. He had nothing to say that could incriminate me but had probably, in the moment, disparaged my character, just because he was a snake who always took the path of least resistance.

Louie was stuck sitting with Squeezy. She reveled in my downfall. She had nothing substantive to say about me regarding Jay's disappearance, but that didn't stop her gossiping maliciously to the police, colleagues, and now poor, trapped Louie. "I know Jay was your friend," Squeezy counted off her 'Jay theories' on her red-lacquered pointed nails, "but it was a jealous lover, a corporate espionage gone wrong, a pimp or prostitute, a bookie, or a drug dealer." She then counted off her 'Dana theories' with her remaining fingers, "Midnight rendezvous with an old friend, bull shit. It was an assignation with Jay, a gigolo, or a hit man, a job offer from some disreputable company, corporate espionage, a psychotic episode, or murder most foul." Squeezy was running out of fingers.

Louie silenced her with a quelling look and asked, "Suzy, don't you have some puppies to drown?" Then he turned his back. This should have been so much more fun for her.

I hadn't eaten all day, so just after boarding in first class, I pulled a heartplum from my carry-on bag and took a satisfying bite. The flavor transported me back to Heartplum Park and I relaxed a little. The Reptile noticed my exotic fruit and inquired politely, in spite of himself. I grudgingly handed him the smallest heartplum in my bag. He inspected it closely for several moments before taking a tentative bite. "Wow," he exclaimed softly and held his hand to his mouth to capture the juice that escaped his lips. "Where did you get this?"

"It was a gift from Saffron. This is the hybrid fruit that grows in her orchard." For the first time ever, the Reptile looked at me like I was a person. He looked at his heartplum and took another small bite, savoring it slowly this time.

"You say your friend developed this hybrid?"

I said, "Eco-agriculture as opposed to GMOs." I didn't know for sure. I'd have to ask how the heartplum was developed when I returned to Tellara.

"Is she looking for investors?" Leave it to the Reptile. I laughed softly, shaking my head. "No, as far as I know, the heartplum is not a commercial enterprise."

"It should be! It really should." He savored every last bite of the heartplum until there was no remaining pulp. He slipped the pit into his pocket. "So, you really went off with this Saffron person and were given this heartplum?"

"As I said, she's my spiritual mentor."

"She has nothing to do with the insurance industry, then?"

"I have a life, Vincent." I'd called him by his given name. It unsettled me hearing it out loud. I usually called him Mr. Cretzky or Boss to his face.

"Did you show this to the police? There is no other fruit like it. It would have supported your alibi."

"I didn't have any heartplums with me at the police station."

"Frank searched your room. He didn't find any fruit."

"When Frank searched my room, I was still away. Anyway, how did you know what he found?"

"It was discussed."

"That's outrageous. The police weren't involved yet."

"I was concerned for your safety."

"Really?" I was about to say, 'that would be a first,' when the Tellaran artist, Phoenix, walked past me to a seat near the rear of the plane. I rubbernecked him in disbelief and noticed Louie doing the same. Phoenix was dressed in conventional sportswear but still wore his long hair pulled back in a leather thong. He was going to Chicago.

Across the aisle, Squeezy sulked. As the plane took off, she glared at Vincent and me. How dare we be having a civilized conversation? As soon as the captain turned off the seatbelt sign, she was up, demanding that she and I switch seats. As soon as I sat down next to Louie, I gave him a heartplum. I told him about Tellara and the portal to another planet in the painting. But despite the exotic fruit in his hand, my outrageously inventive Louie thought I was withholding the whole truth from him. I couldn't bear Louie distrusting me. "You must come to my apartment to view *Summer in Tellara*. We'll cross through the quantum singularity together."

Louie shrugged noncommittally, "I've seen the painting, remember? I was there when you bought it. Now I understand why you didn't share this so-called alibi with the police. I'm going home to spend the weekend with Hal."

"Bring Hal to my place. We'll go to Tellara together. Hey, that artist, Phoenix, he painted *Summer in Tellara*. He's from Tellara. It's his home world."

"Can he help you with your alibi?" Louie asked.

"We weren't in Tellara together, but he painted the portal with his brushstrokes."

"I think your enchantment with his art is affecting your brain. It's called dissociation." Louie was shaking his head and scowling.

"Thanks for the diagnosis," I said sarcastically; but then asked, "I wonder how Phoenix made it through TSA?"

"He made it through TSA because he's a human being from Planet Earth who has photo ID."

"I never said Tellarans weren't human. I'm disappointed you don't believe me. You're the big conspiracy theorist."

"I believe that humanity has a hidden history, a controlling corporatocracy, and a black ops budget that funds god-only-knows-what technology. Alternate realities are the stuff of science fiction." Louie was being obstinate.

"Well, on Tellara, they know all about our hidden history. I thought you would be excited to hear first-hand of how our planets separated when Atlantis fell."

Louie crossed his arms and said nothing.

"You're angry with me because you think I'm lying about my alibi."

He turned on me, "Don't you get it? You're not the only murder suspect. My interrogation was decidedly accusatory. Sheldon Walters and Frank Fretz are circling like sharks smelling blood."

"I had no idea. God, I'm sorry, Louie."

"You're not the only one without an alibi. I was alone asleep in my room."

"So was everybody else. How does that signify?"

"They are focusing on those of us at Monday's dinner with Jay."

"Alice too?"

"She didn't say and neither has anyone else."

"Our conversation doesn't give us a motive to silence Jay," I replied, hopefully.

"Tell that to Sheldon Walters and the San Francisco Police. Sorry, I'm not in the mood for planet hopping." Louie got quiet and slept fitfully for the rest of the flight. I got up once to look for Phoenix in economy class but didn't spot him. A flight attendant asked me to resume my seat.

At last, the plane landed, and I took a taxi home. That evening, alone in my apartment, I poured myself a glass of chardonnay and hung *Summer in Tellara* on my living room wall. Because my pink robe was grass-stained and covered with heartplum juice, I put on a clean green robe after my shower. I had the weekend to spend in Tellara after I reunited with my dog Rip and talked to my kids. Ruth and I had a short phone call. She was on a date. Jesse came by with Rip and his own mutt, Belle, a collie mix. There were doggie yelps, kisses, and treats all around. The dogs lifted my mood a little, but I still had the blues.

"Jesse, my friend from work, Jay Andrews, was killed in San Francisco this week."

"What?"

"I am exhausted. I want to be alone tonight. Everyone at the conference is a suspect. But me, especially."

"What? Why, Mom?"

"I went AWOL from the conference for a night and a day. While I was away, Jay was killed."

"Where were you? Obviously, you have an alibi."

"Not a good one. Not one I can prove. I need to get back in touch with the people I spent those hours with."

"Who are they and where did you go?"

After Louie's cynical rebuff, I was reticent to share about Tellara, even with Jesse. "Good questions, but I want to reconnect with my new friends and get proof of my alibi before I tell anyone else."

"That's very cryptic, Mother. I want to help you," Jesse pressed.

"You can help me by keeping Rip for the weekend. I need to be alone, at least tonight." After a heart-to-heart about everything going on in his life, he agreed to give me my privacy. Jesse had good news. A big film producer had approached him to illustrate a graphic novel companion to an upcoming science fiction movie. It was a huge career opportunity for him. When he left, the dogs chased him back to his studio, indifferent to any human drama.

The phone rang. It was Javier Vazquez. "Dana, I am calling to make certain you understand the conditions of your release to your own recognizance. Follow your normal routine and notify my office of any deviations. Someone from my office will be contacting you daily, at home or at work."

"I understand."

"Call me if you remember anything about your conversations with Jay Andrews or decide to share your real alibi," he added pointedly.

I was excited to hear his voice at first, but he was so business-like and severe that I felt threatened. "My real alibi? Uh, sure, I already did," was my feeble reply.

After reading my mail, paying some bills, and doing some laundry, I went to bed and switched on the TV. Gemini Dallas, that bland, blonde, salacious gossipmonger, was talking about a scandal in the publishing industry that had escalated into a star-crossed, celebrity murder. I switched channels until I found an old black and white detective film noir that evoked uncomfortable reflections of Inspector Vazquez. I fell asleep seeing his dark eyes float before me in a Tellaran meadow.

Before dawn on Saturday, a knock at my door awakened me. I peered through my window. There stood Phoenix on my threshold. I did a triple take, then opened the door.

"I've come to join you in Tellara," he said.

"I shouldn't be surprised to see you. I saw you on the airplane."

"I must return to Tellara to paint the next canvas for the *Magic Seasons* tableau." I ushered him into my living room and brought him some tea while I donned a summer dress.

"Phoenix, how did you purchase an airline ticket and make it through airline security? How could you obtain valid photo identification from anywhere on Earth?"

"I did not need such identification. I did not need a ticket. I made it through your security lines and onto the plane imperceptibly."

"The flight was full. Did you occupy a seat?"

"I did not need a seat."

"You didn't need a ticket, an ID, or a seat? You're quite the low-maintenance traveler."

"I used Tellaran technology to remain imperceptible as you journeyed home on your petrochemical air ship."

"Louie and I both saw you."

"You were the only ones. Tellaran technology is multi-dimensional as you shall soon discover."

"Can you share your technology with me?" I said, thinking it would help people believe me.

"Soon, we both have imperative missions in Tellara."

"I have to make a call first." I left a pre-dawn message on Javier Vazquez's answering machine. "I'm going on an outing with my artist friend, Phoenix, you know, the one I bought the painting from. I hope to connect with Saffron." I could think of nothing else to say that wouldn't make matters worse, so I hung up. First Vincent, then Louie, Jesse, Javier Vazquez, and now Phoenix, I hadn't had one reasonable conversation since leaving San Francisco.

After you," Phoenix bowed slightly and gestured toward *Summer in Tellara*.

* * *

My entrance through the portal was swift, albeit jarring. I was getting the knack for trans-dimensional travel. My welcome committee consisted of Saffron and Juniper. We moved over to the stone bench beside the trellised arch. Saffron and I sat on the bench and leaned against the wall, Juniper sat on the grass by our feet.

A moment later, the air in the stone wall shimmered as Phoenix emerged from beyond the veil into Heartplum Park. The Tellaran women greeted him warmly.

"Dana," Saffron began, "we have just under a year to acquaint you with the Tellaran world view. This will help you understand what must happen in order for humanity to evolve with ascending Earth."

"I am longing for all the details, but unless I can stay in Tellara full-time, I don't think I can maintain a reliable schedule. I am in deep trouble on Earth."

"How so?"

"When I was here before, a friend was killed. Because I cannot account for my time on Tellara, I am the prime suspect in his murder. My employer would profit from framing me for this crime."

"Profit?"

"Benefit financially.

"Financially?"

"Monetarily, money is power, designated objects exchanged for goods and services. My friend who was murdered was going to expose corruption in our company. I think those whose crimes were going to be revealed silenced him to protect their power. If I can be made to look guilty, their problems evaporate. Getting back and forth through the painting may become problematic. I could be arrested, imprisoned."

"Prison, now there is a concept we know from myths."

"I don't know about crime and punishment in Tellara, but prison on Earth is all too real a possibility for me. Maybe I should just stay in Tellara."

"Tellara is not here to provide a safe haven for you. Your mission is to inform the people of Earth how to live in harmony prior to the planetary shift."

"If people didn't listen to me before, they will scorn anything I say as a murder suspect."

"No one will believe you?" Saffron asked.

"Not so far. But if I can convince them, I hope to bring friends and family with me to Tellara. Is that all right?"

"Of course. No once changes the world alone. A new collective consciousness is built one awareness at a time."

"I will come as often as I can for as long as I am free to do so and bring those I trust with me."

"We must not delay our lessons. Dana, have you studied astrotheology, the science of the stars? It teaches us how celestial events informed navigation, seasons, and archetypes."

"I studied Jungian psychology which describes archetypes, and I took a course in college called 'Physics for Poets.' There was no math involved. But I learned enough to follow the science documentaries on television."

"Television?" Juniper asked.

"Moving pictures with sounds projected electronically onto a screen."

Phoenix added, "I've seen Earth Television. Intriguing. Some programs tell stories, some are informational, and some are musical."

"Your poetical science background is good enough to understand the antediluvian history of Earth and Tellara," Saffron enunciated in her charming Tellaran-accented English. We all shifted in our seats to get comfortable. "As Violet told you, Earth and Tellara were once one planet. Planets evolve in vast cycles. It takes our solar system two hundred forty million years to travel around our galaxy, Sophia's Milk. That is one galactic year. We are at the cusp of Magic Seasons."

I asked Phoenix, "Why do you call the paintings *Magic Seasons*?"

"It is another name for cosmic seasons."

"Cosmic seasons?"

"Yes, did you think that the solar year defined our planets' only cycles?"

"Annually, yes. Four seasons, spring, summer, autumn, and winter."

Clearing her throat, Saffron reclaimed the discourse. "Because we have access to all this ancient data, we know that as Earth travels through spacetime, she passes through cosmic seasons. "I will read from **The Tellaran Chronicles of Science and Spirituality**." Saffron pulled a slim, shiny panel out of her satchel.

A Confluence of Cycles

Solar seasons, spring, summer, autumn, and winter are demarcated by solstices and equinoxes. Beyond that, our planet moves through seasonal cycles on many scales, from the tellestrial, to lunar, to solar, to galactic; even intergalactic progressions. Think of a system of gears of all sizes interpenetrating at demarcated ratios, rotating in rhythm and resonance like an astrolabe. All at different scales, and rates, but each interconnected to all the others, like a vast intricate clockwork. In extraordinarily rare moments, Tellara experiences a confluence of all these intersecting cycles, a simultaneous alignment.

There are other cycles that govern Earth's climate and habitat. Some are solar, some terrestrial, like ice ages. Earth's cycles vary from millions of years, to hundreds of thousands, to thousands, to hundreds, and even to generations of species whereby distinctive memories are retained as myths and stories. Sophia is the conscious blackwhole at the center of our galaxy. Sophia's Milk is our galaxy.

When intergalactic, galactic, constellational, solar, and tellestrial cycles converge, planets enter a rare phase called Magic Seasons. The *divergence of Earth and Tellara happened thirteen thousand years ago. The planetary schism will happen on Earth imminently, and then again in another thirteen thousand years. This twenty-six thousand-year interval that spawns three planetary schisms is a quaternary cusp in our two hundred forty million-year journey around Sophia.*

The term Magic Seasons denotes the rare alignment of cycles that opens portals between dimensions, between our worlds. Light enters through cracks in reality. Leaps to the next scale of evolution are possible. Expand your canvas, jump up a fractal octave. Seeing the resonant pattern in all nature and channeling it, that is magic

The belief in the consistency of planetary surfaces is an error that lulls populations into a false sense of stable habitats. Over galactic cycles, planets are bombarded by widely fluctuating energies, both internally and externally. At the moment, Earth and Tellara are relatively protected in the embrace in Orion's Arm of the equatorial plane of Sophia's Milk. But as we spiral along, moving above, through, and then below the galactic equatorial plane, we are exposed to intense showers of cosmic rays, gamma rays, neutrino emissions, and space debris. It takes millions of years for our solar system to travel from peak to valley of the sinusoidal wave through the galactic equatorial plane

Taken collectively, these cosmic seasons constitute the wheels of time by which we measure the evolution of the Universe.

"I've never heard of constellational cycles. What does that mean?"

Phoenix answered, "Between solar seasons and galactic seasons, there is mid-range cycle. Our solar system revolves within a group of constellations in our spiral arm. In particular, our sun is in a revolutionary pattern with another star in a cycle lasting millions of years."

"You mean our sun is a binary star?"

"Yes, most stars are binaries."

"Do I need to know what these cycles are?"

"You already know some of them.

"Are you describing the mechanistic universe?"

"We see the Universe as consciously directing these cycles in an endless fractal dance from tiniest particles to the edge of the expanding Universe. When all the gears align, there is a harmonic intersection at all scales."

"What happens during these alignments?"

"Data from ancient myth, geology, and other sources suggests that no two alignments affect biomass the same."

Saffron added, "No one, on your world or ours, can predict how this alignment will impact Sophia's Milk or our solar system."

"Is this confluence of cycles part of my message, my dharma?"

"We hope so, Dana." Phoenix hugged me fiercely.

"We don't consider myths to be data on Earth."

"Do you consider memories to be data?" asked Phoenix.

"Interesting question; memories can be accurate or unreliable, although, paradoxically, we rely on them for science and the law. I write things down if I need to remember them."

"What of dreams?" Juniper asked.

"A few scientists consider dreams to contain symbolic data."

"So, symbols are data in some instances?" Juniper persisted.

"That's another gray area. Symbols, myths, and archetypes are studied by scholars but are not used in science or law."

Saffron said, "Galactic movement since ancient of days gave rise to archetypal symbolism we consider data."

"We call our galaxy the Milky Way including the band of stars across the night sky."

Saffron said, "When we're nestled inside our native spiral arm, we're protected from all manner of space debris."

"That's counter intuitive," I objected. "Wouldn't we be more at risk of collision from space debris in the crowded arm?"

"I'm just getting to that. Let's look at another galactic cycle," said Saffron, reading from *The Tellaran Chronicles of Science and Spirituality*.

Confluence of Cycles

Our solar system's natural harbor is inside the Orion spiral arm of Sophia's Milk. We're safe but for the infrequent comet or asteroid. We evolved here. Over cosmic time, our sojourns above and below the safety zone are rare and volatile. We are poised to rise above a peak amplitude where our solar system will be exposed to unfamiliar wavelengths. Since ages immemorial, these external energies have had a profound impact on mass, energy, biology, and consciousness. Living matter, in particular, feels urgent pressure to evolve in form, function, and coherency. Life forms either adapt to new frequencies or go extinct. As new life forms emerge, new paradigms of consciousness evolve to accommodate these nascent biological structures."

A recurring twenty-six thousand-year precession of the equinoxes is called a Great Year and coincides with many of Tellara's histori-cal changes. As Tellara makes a full wobble, constellations along the zodiacal belt appear to cycle backwards through the celestial plane.

My Liberal Arts degree was serving me in good stead. "So, the galactic seasons coincide with events like the K-2 extinction event or the Cambrian Explosion of millions of new taxonomic life forms. Form follows function and function follows form. The Great Year coincides with zodiacal ages like Pisces and Aquarius, which reflect ages of human history."

Saffron continued, "Close enough, Dana. So, you've heard of the precession of the equinoxes?"

"Mostly from popular culture, but I'm tracking your story. Are these long cycles linked to polar reversals, ice ages, and overdue earthquakes?"

"Yes, Dana, geology, biology, history, mythos, consciousness, even civilizations rise and fall with these galactic seasons." Phoenix said. "Thirteen thousand years ago, an alignment occured between the Earth, the Sun, and the center of Sophia. It is happening again in the present galactic season. *Magic Seasons* paintings are being created to coincide with the most direct alignments between our two worlds. During our annual quaternary cusps, the equinoxes and solstices, we are most deeply connected."

I stood and walked around in the meadow, turning to face Saffron and Phoenix. "Are there any other long-cycle catastrophes that might affect Earth's habitat that you want to share with Madam Wayshower?" I bowed ironically.

Phoenix and Saffron exchanged a guarded look, and then he spoke.

"There is an event called a galactic super wave that occurs every twenty-six million years, or so."

"That doesn't sound good. The Earth is 4.5 billion years old. When is the next galactic superwave due?"

"It is a million years overdue."

"Is that all? Well, the Yellowstone caldera eruption is about twenty thousand years overdue, so one imminent disaster to fret about is as good as another."

Phoenix handed me the disc, "Here is a section in **The Tellaran Chronicles of Science and Spirituality** that discusses what we know about this phenomenon."

The Galactic Superwave

The blackwhole at the center of the Sophia is our Central Sun. Like stars and planets, it undergoes periodic pole shifts that are akin to birth pangs. When this happens, Sophia emits a barrage of cosmic rays, charged plasma, electromagnetic radiation, and gravity waves. These travel out in all directions at nearly the speed of light and are incalculably disruptive, causing violent flares in stars, seismic events on planets, and massive DNA mutations in living creatures.

There is no forewarning of the event, just historical evidence in fossil and geologic records.

During the last galactic superwave, Gaia was in nature's hands and the cost was almost total reconfiguration of the firmament. Continents crashed around the globe. Poles shifted. Weather and climate patterns changed drastically. Massive Tsunamis eradicated coastal regions.

Tellara has developed technology to dampen planetary seismic waves in order to minimize quakes and volcanoes while releasing the energy safely into interstellar space. Seismic dampening technology has been sufficient for regular geologic upheavals, but it is unknown if it will prove sufficient to dampen the effects of Sophia's labor contractions, which are now one million years overdue. Tellarans have been preparing to ascend for the last thirteen thousand years in order to face the coming shift as incorporeal beings. We will ride the galactic superwave to our incorporeal ascended state.

I asked, "Since you're going to ascend, I can see why you're not worried about massive death and destruction, but what of the rest of nature, plants, and animals, pets especially?"

"We have set up safe havens to preserve plant and animal life. We have stations in space and on Antarctica where all Tellaran DNA and seeds will be stored until the planet's surface is ready to be reseeded."

"Well, that's swell for you, but we of the non-ascending corporeally-challenged types are going to live through Hell."

"Birth pangs can be painful. As our worlds spiral through the cosmos, our frequency becomes ever more rarified. Gaia evolves."

"Gaia?" I asked.

"Tellara and Earth are two worlds with one soul. Gaia is the Soul Mother of all Earths since primordial times, 4.5 billion years ago." Phoenix answered.

"This is fascinating, but am I going to have to explain galactic astronomy in order to bring my wayshower message to Earth?"

Saffron pulled out flat screen the size of a mouse pad and said, "Dana, all of this is written in *The Tellaran Chronicles of Science and Spirituality*."

Gaia

As Gaia undergoes planetary schism, two collective consciousnesses vie for ascendency over her sentient beings. Gaia herself feels the strain of two frequencies pulling her apart, one the familiar, albeit polarizing, collective consciousness, the other a harmonious unity consciousness in resonance with nature.

Throughout her history, Gaia has convulsed in labor contractions generating geological cataclysms. As this planetary mitosis separated Earth and Tellara, a critical choice was impressed on the psyches all of sentient creatures. Each individual had the free will to go one of two ways in their psycho-spiritual evolution, harmony or duality. The choice we made was encoded in our DNA as we reincarnated.

These vast shifts take up to seven generations to complete. They are believed to occur only at the quaternary cusps in our galactic cycle. Think of Earth and Tellara as sisters with one Mother Soul called

Gaia. Gaia embodies all Earths as her archetypal oversoul. She is
conscious and hosts life throughout her entire depth, from her core
to her surface. As Gaia evolves, she undergoes a recurring process of
labor and rebirth in ever ascending dimensions.

Saffron continued, "Gaia moves along an ascending spiral through spacetime, frequencies, and dimensions. Think of each world as a bead along a coiled strand stretching back to our planet's infancy," Saffron elaborated. "As Gaia evolves, the life forms she nurtures become more coherent in body, mind, and spirit. Tellara is the pearl along this spiral filament that lies nearest to Earth. As another world emerges from the firmament, Earth will divide into Terra Familiar and Terra Nova. Beyond Tellara, many other of Gaia's offspring spin in ever-higher frequencies, each with her own stories, karma, and destinies. On all worlds, life matches the vibrational frequency and heartbeat of its planet. Gaia is the choreographer of her own dance.

"Civilizations on Gaia are cyclic. They rise and fall over eons. Atlantis and Lemuria are but the most recent civilizations that remain in our memory and mythos. But civilizations on Gaia, in myriad variety, stretch back to time immemorial.

"Many ancient civilizations were in a higher vibration to begin with. Other ancient civilizations took millions of years to attain a critical mass of harmony consciousness. And in even more ancient days, Gaia herself had a different wobble. For ages, she was turning cosmic summersaults while her primordial consciousness formed. Millions, even billions of years can pass without a planetary shift. This confluence of cycles is so rare as to be unprecedented. In the age of the Universe, these quaternary Magic Seasons fall within the cusp of the grand galactic cross of the Galactic Year."

"Earth is going to divide." It wasn't a question anymore. I now understood the implications of the impending planetary shift. "It happens cyclically over time." I nodded, following.

"Spirally actually," Phoenix corrected. "Dana, you seem distracted. What are you thinking?"

"Yeah, I'm distracted. I'm caught between two worlds. On Tellara, you're talking end-of-the-world scenarios with me as some leader. On Earth, I'm a pariah with a noose tightening around my neck. So, yeah, I'm feeling the wrench of competing priorities. It's just a question of what happens first, my arrest for murder or being struck by a galactic superwave."

Phoenix ignored my gallows humor, "We're here to answer all your questions."

"Just ask," said Saffron.

"OK, so, were all the Gaia civilizations polarized by destructive forces?"

"Each pearl on the planetary filament has a different story."

"On Earth, divisive leaders pit populations against each other. It creates fear in the masses. Earth has known millennia of wars, slavery, poverty, violence, and exploitation of every imaginable kind. Would these divisive leaders possibly be, um…" I was trembling away from speaking out loud Louie's crazy conspiracy theory. "Umm, reptilians?"

"You know of reptilians then?" grinned Saffron.

"Well, not personally, but my friend Louie has this theory about ancient aliens interfering with human evolution."

"Your friend Louie is partly correct. Some of Earth's leaders are reptilians. They wielded a similar control over humanity in Atlantean times."

I offered the same objection I presented Louie whenever he dove down the rabbit hole. "There is plenty of greed among humans to explain all the suffering on Earth. Many sociopathic humans operate primarily from their reptilian brains. For them it's all about survival instinct with no empathy."

Saffron surprised me. "Not all reptilians are selfish. There are enlightened Draconians living among us on Tellara."

"Some of my best friends are reptiles," Phoenix said with a slight smirk.

"OK, so there are reptiles on Earth and Tellara. I doubt I've ever met any or that they have anything to do with me."

Juniper passed around fruit with cheese, bread, and tea. We munched in silence for several minutes, digesting what Saffron had said.

"It's a lot to take in."

"Dana, when we are confused and answers seem to elude us, we dance," said Juniper.

Saffron agreed. "Yes, let us heartdance."

"There are so few of us," I objected.

"Friends are on the way." A few moments later, the hovertrain arrived at the Heartplum Park station. A group of people disembarked. I recognized the Circle of Thirteen Elders. Violet approached and took my forearms in her hands. "I have lived to see the arrival of the wayshower. Prophecy is fulfilled." Then she hugged me. One by one, all the Elders of Esselen greeted me. From throughout the park, dozens of brightly attired Tellarans gathered creating a festive atmosphere. I recognized Robin in the group.

"Let us circle." Saffron led the way to the center of the field overlooking beautiful Esselen Bluffs. We followed, our arms stretching in circles, whirling slowly, skipping gracefully. Two circular clusters formed, men on the outside, holding polarity, and women inside, balancing.

Men began a complex vibratory attunement chant and drumbeat that gradually settled into a rhythmic, repetitive melody. The pulsations generated by the men's voices evoked a web of ethereal threads that gave an underlying spatial definition among the moving women.

My feet, hands, shoulders, and backbone synchronized with the other dancers as I fell into the dance. I let myself go. Rays of light emanated within and without. At some point, my body found an exhilarating sequence of rhythmic swaying steps. A woven tapestry emerged in the space between dancers. Its threads were made of air and light.

Before us lay an image of a blue-green marble planet. The world revolved, rotated, and wobbled in a dance of its own. The world vibrated in a breathtaking blur, then began to separate into two planets, like a cellular mitosis, each taking its DNA into a new nucleus and reforming into separate integral spheroids. Growing ever more distinct, Tellara formed into greens, golds, and blues. Earth emerged with blues, whites, greens, browns, and grays in an astonishing beauty that was both painful and ecstatic to behold. Planets with their moons danced apart from each other in graceful rotations and aligned in a chain of spiraling, ascending planets. Gaias from throughout the ages floated back into this mist of time and onward toward an unknowable future. I was floating with the planets, dancing between stars and galaxies. The web lingered and coalesced. What had just emerged was a multidimensional, multi-sensory, multihued moving phantasma. Drifting back from my trance, I fell to my knees. The dance slowed, then stopped, as the other dancers collapsed.

I recovered slowly, and Phoenix helped me to my feet. I was parched. Juniper handed me a jar of water that I downed in two gulps. We headed for the train station. I rode down the rail and was made a welcome guest in Saffron's home once again. We ate a dinner, vegetable loaf with dill sauce, wild rice, and asparagus. The flavors exploded on my taste buds. It was as though I had been eating cardboard all my life. The rest of the weekend was brilliant. Juniper regaled me with stories of Tellaran reptiles. Then they took me on a tour of Tellaran art and music throughout Esselen Bluffs. We danced, ate, visited, and slept.

I awoke to birdsong and soft laughter. Phoenix and Saffron escorted me to Heartplum Park where I gathered a basket of heartplums. Air shimmered in the red stone wall. Images of the park lost their cohesion. Through the trees, I saw a blurry image of my living room couch. I was moving towards it without volition. The couch moved up beneath me to catch my weight as I drifted into my condo. I turned to look at the painting and was delighted to see Saffron and Phoenix.

CHAPTER 5

Back to Chicago for another freaking Monday at Sh.I.T. Sighing deeply, I did not want to face the day, and yet, I was armored with Tellaran allies and a grander picture of the world than my own private drama. I braced myself for descent from Tellaran bliss to wage-slave-murder-suspect dross.

I arrived at the office two hours later. The silence was deafening and the gazes critical as I walked the gauntlet. Louie, looking pale, was waiting in my cube. "Where were you? I've been trying to call you all weekend."

"I was in another world. You were invited if you recall."

"A package from San Francisco arrived this morning. It was addressed to you, but Squeezy intercepted it and gave it to the Reptile. I received a similar packet at home Saturday. It was from Jay and contains the whistle blower documents he alluded to," Louie whispered to me. "And now Vincent Cretzky has it."

"The contents of this envelope are probably what got Jay killed," I replied. "Now we're in the line of fire from those who conspired to kill him."

"There's more," Louie said.

"What?"

"I spoke to Alice this morning. Shelter has hired an outside law firm to investigate internal fraud."

"Really?"

"An outfit called Waldo Mannheim & Peters," Louie said.

"Wait? What? That law firm is a silent subsidiary of Shelter's. Maggie Coutts says they are ambulance chasers that target appealing clients in order to subvert their cases. How does that qualify them to investigate corporate crimes?"

"Your guess is as good as mine. Alice has already been questioned."

"If they work for Shelter, they will uncover whatever Shelter wants revealed."

"Or fabricated," Louie concluded. On that happy note, we went to our desks to log in to our computers and start the workday.

My phone rang. It was Inspector Javier Vazquez. He began angrily without preamble, "Where have you been all weekend? My office called you all day Saturday and Sunday."

"I left you a message that I was going out with Phoenix."

"That's not how it works. We need to be able to reach you, not the other way around."

"I didn't realize."

"Of course, you did. There was nothing ambiguous about my instructions to follow your routine and be available for us to contact you 24/7. Where were you all weekend?"

I had been in Tellara with Saffron and Phoenix but couldn't say so. "I was with Phoenix."

"Provide me his contact information."

"I can't."

"Of course, you can't. I should have called the Chicago PD to start a manhunt for you."

"Why didn't you?"

No answer from Vazquez for several heartbeats.

"You stay on the radar at all times, Ms. Travers. Tell me you understand, with no exceptions."

Now it was my turn to be silent for several heartbeats. I needed to be in Tellara as often as possible. How could I balance my urgent competing demands?

"Tell me you understand exactly what I'm saying." I could hear him grind out his words between clenched teeth.

"I understand."

"And you will comply, or you will be upgraded from person of interest to primary suspect?"

"You know I didn't kill Jay."

"Your alibi?"

"Soon." Damn! I'd have to invite him to my house and show him *Summer in Tellara*. What else could I do?

"I'll have your alibi the next time I see you. And be prepared with contact information from your friends, Saffron and Phoenix." We hung up.

Around 11 A.M., the Reptile called me into his office. Squeezy was with him, waiting, pacing, salivating in maroon leather. Now that FrankenFretz wasn't holding her back, she was rabid to fire, suspend, or eviscerate me. I was in no mood for her posturing. Emboldened by my Tellaran mission and threatened by arrest for murder, I was pushed to an adrenal edge I'd never known existed. It was my turn to grind my teeth and explain reality.

"Vincent and I have things to discuss that don't concern you. Please leave us for now." I demanded without looking at her.

"You can't tell me what to do," she sneered.

"Give us some privacy." I addressed the Reptile with my most determined gaze.

"As head of HR, anything that affects Shelter operations is my business." She made herself comfortable in Vincent's second chair, intending to occupy a front row seat at my inquisition. "Besides, Frank Fretz wants me to sit in on all disciplinary hearings."

But Vincent had other ideas. I had called him by his first name again. He was feeling my coolness despite my predicament. "Come back later," Vincent instructed Suzy evenly. She turned red and sat her ground for ten seconds. I stared her down. The Reptile shuffled some papers on his desk. In a huff of red rage, she stormed out.

Alone, I whirled on my boss. "Vincent, reality check. I did not kill Jay Andrews."

"I called you in here to discuss your missed workday at the conference. I am going to have to put a reprimand in your file and dock your pay."

"Fine. Whatever."

"That's all you have to say? This is serious, Dana. It will affect your performance evaluation, future raises."

"Is that the primary concern here? Jay's been murdered!"

"Your missing hours have to be documented in writing. I was ordered to do so by Sheldon Walters himself."

"The police know all about my missing hours. Shelter just wants to highlight them. I don't blame you for doing what you have to." My frustration moved me to blurt tactlessly, "You know, Boss, you're not stupid. You've been unethical and arrogant. But you are not stupid. Don't you see what's going on?"

The Reptile ignored the insults. "I certainly do."

"The police are taking a very close look at everyone at Shelter. Everyone, from the top down." I bit off each word.

"Yeah," he repeated indifferently.

"I didn't kill Jay."

"So, you say."

"Sooner or later, the police will figure that out. Where do you think their gaze will turn?"

"Toward everyone at the conference. I understand your pal Louie is in the crosshairs."

"What would be the motivation of anyone at Shelter to silence Jay Andrews?"

"I'm not sure where you are going with this. You and Louie were the only two from the Chicago office who knew him well."

"Personally, yes. What about his professional business? Jay knew things about how those at the top conduct business. He was concerned about corruption. If he was silenced to keep Shelter interests safe, those parties would stop at nothing to remain protected. They have motive." The Reptile shrugged as if this had nothing to do with him.

"So, let's think about this. If the person or persons who silenced Jay are okay with murder, how hesitant do you think they'll feel about pinning the deed on someone else?"

"You seem to be the scapegoat du jour." His casual indictment was a slap in my face.

"For now. But I have nothing to gain by the loss of my friend. Furthermore, anyone who knows what he knew, won't be safe from the people who killed him."

"Only if Shelter corruption was the motive for his murder." The Reptile's eyes slid to a manila envelope beneath his shuffled papers.

"People at the top, people like Frank Fretz and Sheldon Walters, will make certain that suspicion never reaches their level."

"No one would ever suspect Mr. Fretz or Mr. Walters," the Reptile objected.

"You've just made my point for me. Where do you think suspicion will be directed? They'll scheme to offer up a big fish to deflect attention."

"You can't mean me. Chicago is a long way from Dallas, and Jay and I hardly knew each other."

"Sure, but which Regional Director has a history of denying legitimate claims in order to line his pockets with bonus blood money? Which Regional Director promoted a completely unqualified and undeserving slut as head of a division and looks the other way while she flouts rules and abuses her position? Who works in the same office with Louie and me, the last people to see Jay alive?"

"I'd fire you for saying that if I hadn't gotten a directive from Sheldon Walters' himself to keep you close at hand. For your information, all the claim denials were sanctioned by the top," Vincent objected.

"But who carried them out? Were they within the letter of the law? Your underwriters and adjusters don't think so. It's an internal scandal being investigated by those shysters at Waldo Manheim and Peters who work for Sheldon Walters. Why wouldn't Shelter divert suspicion to perpetrators of a lesser crime in order to sail over the top of the shitstorm?"

"You're suggesting that I'm facing an internal scandal? Go on."

"Did you read the contents of Jay's envelope?"

"Yes."

"Did Suzy?"

"She brought it to me unopened," he said.

"It was addressed to me, and you opened it?"

"Yes."

"Bad move. If it contains the information I think it does, and anyone suspects that you read it, you're not safe. You'd better give it to me."

"It contained coded information regarding the distribution of Shelter assets and information. It's possible evidence in a murder investigation. I should hang on to it."

"Don't make me take back my assessment that you are not stupid."

Vincent blanched. "You go too far."

"I'll spell it out for you. I'm already a murder suspect. You're not. Possession of these documents will make me appear complicit in whistleblowing, but could, however, help clear me with the police. They could also make me a target for whoever killed Jay. Anybody who discovers what Jay was going to disclose is in as much danger as he was. The envelope was mailed to me from San Francisco the day he died. The contents of these documents never saw the light of day. They were silenced along with Jay."

Vincent lifted the manila envelope on his desk. "How do you know this envelope is from Jay?"

"I recognize his writing. He sends me Christmas cards." I did not mention that Louie had received a similar envelope at home and told me it contained the incriminating documents that Jay had found on Sheldon Walter's computer. "Did Suzy know this was from Jay when she brought you the envelope—very intentionally unopened?"

He was looking dubious. "I don't know what she knows."

"Does Suzy know whether or not you read the documents?"

"No, but I have no reason to distrust Suzy or anyone at this company."

"Well, I do. Under ordinary circumstances, you'd happily accept a bribe from the big boys to continue playing the game for your own self-interests. But the police do not see Shelter's business model as entirely legal, and they're not going to go away. We're all going to be under close scrutiny, including from the feds if they suspect Shelter has been flouting insurance regulations. Shelter is not going to let someone in the insider's circle take the fall. Who do you think is the most likely fall guy if I'm cleared?"

"Don't the police look at the spouse?"

"Yeah, and Val's been questioned in San Francisco and Dallas. Not only does she have an alibi, but their marriage was a true and happy partnership."

"They'll focus on your pal, Louie."

"Do you really think Louie crushed Jay's skull because he might be a whistleblower?"

The Reptile's face fell into unattractive creases. I almost felt sorry for him. "No, I don't. Perhaps someone from Dallas. What about Alice Redding?"

"They'll look at her. But aside from her disability, she was Jay's professional ally. I think he was being groomed for a spot at the top and recoiled at what he learned."

"As opposed to me." He tilted his head as if to ask, 'Is that what you're implying?'

"Alice had nothing to gain by Jay's death. She told the police everything she knows."

"I'm beginning to get your drift. They could make it look like I had everything to lose if Shelter went down," Vincent sighed. "Do you have any recommendations?"

"Give Jay's envelope back to me now. Then, make this office squeaky clean, in compliance with all regulations. Have another claims adjuster review all the appealed claims you denied in the last eighteen months. Not me, Louie. Have him do an appeal review and award every legitimate claim. Distance yourself from any breath of corruption. Lose your bonuses if need be."

"Dana," Vincent pulled himself back up to his commanding stature, "I've been following company policy. Mr. Walters himself praises me for my hardline tactics."

"Setting you up is more like it. If Jay's murder can't be pinned on me, Shelter will manipulate Heaven and Earth to deflect suspicion on someone else."

"This entire conversation is insupportable."

"So is Jay's death! We are talking about murder, not some celebrity scandal."

Without answering, he handed me the thick manila envelope. "Anything else?" I was surprised he'd considered my viewpoint so readily, but I'd never been so blunt with him.

"Muzzle Suzy. She's hurting you, personally and professionally. Her position in HR is one that demands sensitivity, confidentiality, and meticulous interpretation of state and federal labor regulations."

"Dana, why are you telling me this? I'm not the fool you think I am. I know you dislike your job and disrespect me specifically."

"I don't so much disrespect you as think you've made a career of bad decisions that have hurt your colleagues and our clients. Now, those decisions are coming back to bite you in the butt. Suzy's only about promoting herself. You're a stepping-stone. Everyone can see it but you. Sorry." I had gone too far, but had nothing to lose. Uncharacteristically, I stuck my neck out further, "Who do you trust?"

Vincent paused a long time before speaking. "My wife, Gwen, once. But she and I haven't had a heart-to-heart in years." His voice broke on his whispered admission.

"I like Gwen. She could be a strong ally. Sheldon Walters has the most to lose and he's a cunning survivor. Like it or not, you and I are in the soup together, Vincent. Louie too."

As I rose, Vincent asked, "How do I know you're not setting me up?"

I looked him directly in the eye with an expression that said, "Are you serious?" He had the grace to look away. "We wouldn't be having this conversation if that were the case. I don't think you murdered Jay Andrews any more than I did, but Shelter's internal fraud investigation will uncover whatever suits Sheldon Walters."

"If I decide to go down the path, you're suggesting..." He trailed off, unable to finish his thought. "I need to think it over, talk it over with... with Gwen," he added, almost as an afterthought. "Do you have any more of those purple fruits from Chinatown?" He thought the heartplums came from Chinatown. Just as well. I took two out of my pocket and reluctantly handed them to Vincent. "One for you, one for Gwen."

Departing his office, manila envelope tightly clamped under my arm, Squeezy and I crashed into each other. She recovered first and darted past me into the Reptile's office. "So, did you suspend her, or do I get to?"

I was not suspended or fired. The reprimand was mild, and Vincent reinstated my docked pay after all. The Reptile gave me a pass. I told Louie I was upgrading him to Rodent. Louie said that was an insult to most self-respecting rodents. But Vincent had heard me out, and I assured Louie that he's not an evil alien overlord. If Vincent was ever forced to become a whistle-blower to save his life, it would cost him his career, his prestige, his squeeze, his illusions about his fast track to the top, and maybe his marriage. The Rodent wouldn't risk his position and comfort unless he was a trapped rat. So, Louie agreed that Vincent Cretzky could be a rat.

Later that day, a stack of two hundred thirty-four claims appeals landed on Louie's file cabinets for review. Louie was thrilled. You might think the mountain of work would distress him, but he'd been requesting this assignment for over a year.

Squeezy was on a bitchin' tear. She made three people cry, two women in human resources and Carmela Benedetto in accounts receivable. She convened a meeting. Her pretext was grief counseling regarding Jay's death. Squeezy was the self-appointed grief counselor. Little Miss 'twenty-six-years-old-got-her-degree-by-sleeping-with-professors-slept-with-two-other-bosses-before-the-Rodent-had-ostentatiously-enlarged-breasts-with-maximum-legal-cleavage-dayglow-whitened-teeth-brassy-highlights-and-the-sensitivity-of-Cruella-DeVille' was to be our grief counselor. The staff was stupefied by her hubris. Only the Rodent was not in attendance. But Squeezy was nothing, if not delusional. She opened the agenda with platitudes of shock and remorse regarding Jay's death, followed by oblique references to petite brunette colleagues with unsavory alibis, while conspicuously eying me.

"You are wasting our time." I declared. I was done being slandered to my face.

"People need closure, grief counseling," Squeezy simpered.

"Not from you. You're out of your depth." I was still in my adrenalin-fueled bravado.

"You realize that I am your superior." Squeezy had overplayed her hand once too often.

"Your job is at a higher pay grade than most of us here. Grief counseling needs to be handled by a licensed therapist."

"You may not speak to me in that disrespectful tone."

"I already have." I stood.

Louie declared, "Well, that's two minutes of my life that I'll never get back." He and three other brave souls stood to depart as well. Then there was a stampede. The room emptied in less than a minute. Squeezy stayed in her office the rest of the day and simmered. She and the Rodent didn't go out for their Monday sushi. She left early and everyone in the building sighed with relief.

Finally, alone in my cube, I looked through the packet from Jay. It contained, as I'd suspected, copies of receipts, emails, transcripts, spreadsheets, phone logs, and other documents detailing Sheldon Walter's activities. The data was encoded. I could not interpret it all, but he appeared to have interfered in elections and possibly cheated, stolen, bribed, and killed to achieve his goals. Alas, there were no clues about why Jay had gone out that fateful night to meet with an unknown petite brunette. I faxed the entire contents of the packet to Inspector Vazquez in San Francisco, hoping it would redeem me for being missing all weekend. He was appreciative and called to tell me to send him the originals so he could test for fingerprints. I promised I would.

Inspector Vazquez informed me that Jay's memorial service was postponed until his body could be released to his family. It was still with the San Francisco Medical Examiner. I had been in contact with Jay's family, sent cards and condolences. Alice was back in Dallas and spending time with Jay's widow, Val, and the Andrews girls. Alice and I spoke daily. She was barely coping herself, but staying strong for Val.

I turned to processing claims to be passed to the Rodent for his signature. Each painted a picture of a unique family who had endured a reversal. I might actually get insurance money to claimants who deserved a settlement. A piece of Tellara sustained a flicker of optimism when everyone in the office expected me to be a trembling mess.

Finally, another Monday was over in the life of Dana Mae Travers. I went home and took my dog for a long walk. Over a roasted artichoke and Chardonnay, I waited for Javier Vazquez to call so I could spend a few hours in Tellara. The phone rang and I grabbed it hoping to hear his voice. It was my daughter, Ruth. She waxed poetic about a guy at work she'd dated a few times. Call waiting never blinked, so I looked for science programs on TV. The History Channel was airing a show about ancient aliens. I settled in.

Tuesday was uninterrupted monotony at the office. I kept my head down and my mouth closed. Squeezy left me alone. The Rat left me alone. Colleagues left me alone. Even Louie left me alone. I processed claims. Vincent signed them.

Wednesday morning Inspector Vazquez called me at home.

"You just caught me; I was on my way out the door."

"I'm flying to Dallas to interview Jay Andrews' wife, family, friends, and colleagues."

"Val's going through a hard time."

"Your concern is duly noted. I'll talk to you tomorrow."

We hung up. Yippie! I had satisfied my obligations to the San Francisco Police Department for twenty-four hours. Tellara beckoned. I called in sick.

CHAPTER 6

Phoenix and Saffron met me in Heartplum Park. Phoenix said, "Dana, since you advised us of your dangerous legal predicament on Earth, we have some Tellaran technology to help you. We'll be traveling north by tram to Shastise, Tellara."

We traveled north along Esselen Coast, what I thought of as California. The geography was the same, only different. All the developments were in harmony with the natural terrain. The landscape was dotted with oscillating statuary and sculpted gardens.

"I'm a murder suspect and a professional pariah. My friends are in danger; they have received not-so-veiled threats. Louie doesn't believe me about Tellara. What if my family and friends can't pass through the quantum singularity? I'll never be able to prove my innocence."

When I was done with my pity party, Phoenix said, "Individuals acting from compassion and who have balanced karma can pass through the dimensional portal. No one ever told you being a wayshower was going to be easy."

"Thanks a lot for that morale booster. No one asked me if I wanted to be a wayshower." I was a wuss on two worlds.

"Actually, I did, and you accepted," Phoenix replied.

"Oh right, thirteen thousand years ago, in a prior incarnation. How could that have possibly slipped my mind?"

"The obstacles you face are part of your saga," said Saffron.

"Cold comfort, that. My children will be worried for me. I expect to lose my career and home while waiting for Shelter to release their stranglehold over me. I could even lose my life."

"Help is at hand," Saffron assured me. We arrived in Shastise, Tellara. It had the same geography as Mount Shasta, California, except the entire landscape was dominated by the construction of a pyramid that rivaled Black Butte in size.

Great red marble stones, quarried from a distant region, floated in the air between three great structures: snow-capped Mount Shastise, Black Butte, her eternal companion, and a partially completed red stone pyramid. The mountain herself had been hollowed out to reveal a subterranean vista.

"How are those huge stones floating in the air?" This panorama of thousands of tons of red marble floating among the mountains and clouds took my breath away. The massive stones were gliding into each architectural niche.

Phoenix explained, "Those crystal-encrusted spheres set between the mountain and the construction site create an alternate gravitational field which attracts and directs the stones."

"Alternate to what?"

"Alternate to the center of the planet," answered Saffron. "Tellaran technology is capable of harnessing the gravity of blackwholes. Using a combination of gravity and cymatics, we can maneuver objects of any weight with negligible force."

Phoenix said, "Our entire civilization was built on the best of what remained from previous civilizations."

"Why is Tellara building a pyramid in Shasta or rather, Shastise?"

"Tellara is reinforcing our planetary grid system in anticipation of the coming shift. We are building pyramids on every continent and uncovering those on Antarctica. Pyramids and other Mesolithic structures along planetary ley lines and nodal points will minimize the impacts of the shift energies as we siphon teratons of seismic and psychic energy from Earth."

"Antarctica?"

"Parts of Antarctica on Tellara are green oases. A century ago, while excavating pyramids, we tellaformed Antarctica and used the melt water to replenish global aquifers. The Antarctic islands will be a stable haven for plant and animal life during and after the shift."

"So that's your Noah's Ark."

They looked at me questioningly.

"From our Bible story, one of the accounts of the flood. A man named Noah saved all the animals on a large ship."

"We will save all fauna, flora, and seeds on Antarctica as well as by preserving their DNA in spaceships."

"Like orbiting arks? But what about Earth? It sounds as though we're in for an unavoidably catastrophic ride.

"You're not wrong. Fortunately, Tellara intends to intervene. Not only will our pyramid grid deflect the solar and galactic waves from our own firmament, but while the portals remain open, we will siphon off teratons of the most damaging of the seismic and psychic waves from Earth. It will be deflected it into the uninhabited space between the spiral arms of the galaxy."

"This is a pyramid scheme I approve of."

"We are building pyramids on every nodal point on Tellara. We will activate the shield in a global heartdance."

I changed the subject, "OK, so why is the mountain wide open to a tunnel? I get that you need a staging ground for all your construction, but why excavate inside Mount Shastise?"

"The inhabitants of Inner Tellara opened the Shastise tunnel to the surface six thousand years ago so that the surface folk and sub-surface population could collaborate on environmental issues."

"The sub-surface population? Are they human?"

"Humanoid. We share most of our DNA. Like humans and reptilians, we can interbreed. They are pale and have nearly translucent skin. They call themselves the Lucents. They live near Tellara's inner ocean beneath Tellara's inner sun."

"I wonder if we have a sub-surface population on Earth."

"I imagine so. The Lucents have been on our planets for millions of years. The only way you could harm their environment would be by contaminating your ground water to the depths of the inner ocean."

"Let's hope we don't frack that deep," I lamented.

"Come, we'll show you." Saffron took my elbow and directed me along a winding path that led up the hillside and into an atrium inside the mountain. We entered a cavern that had been carved out of the mountainside. It was so huge that it could have contained a city. It must have encompassed the entire circumference of Mount Shastise, from floor to distant domed roof. Inside there were gliders and machines situated throughout the depth and length of the cavern above a triangular tunnel that looked bottomless. Gliders entered and exited the tunnel every few minutes. There were mission control panels covered with engravings, crystals, and blinking lights in geometric patterns. Hundreds of people in colorful attire bustled in focused activity; some on the floor, some aloft in lighter-than-air gliders; and others on interconnecting, multi-tiered suspension bridges.

We stopped before an array of crystal-encrusted instruments arranged in a symmetrical formation. They were made of metal overlaid with crystals and etchings. The instruments ranged in size from toasters to smaller than cell phones. Saffron picked up one of the smaller devices and handed it to me. It was heftier than a cell phone but fit into my palm like it was a part of me.

"Hang on to that vox, Dana," Saffron instructed. "It will become an extension of your will. Each vox attunes itself to its bearer's DNA. It's more than a machine. It conducts thought waves."

Phoenix explained, "This device is called a vox, short for voxel."

"What's a voxel?"

"Do you know what a pixel is?"

"Yes, like rapidly moving dots on my television screen that make up the picture."

"Well, a voxel is a volumetric pixel. It fills up three dimensions of space and one dimension of time. Voxels fit together like interpenetrating bubbles in a geometric pattern. In two dimensions, the voxel pattern appears as the flower of life. In three dimensions, they form a star tetrahedron with spheres intersecting each nodal point."

"Can you explain to me how this vox works?"

Phoenix began, "Well, as you know, the Universe is conscious at all scales." Actually, this was news to me. But I nodded.

He continued, "All consciousness is entangled. All protons are interconnected."

"Have you heard of entangled protons?" Saffron asked.

"I think it means that subatomic particles, once paired, then separated, continue to move in tandem? Einstein called it spooky action at a distance."

"Partially correct.

"Each proton is a mini, stable, blackwhole spinning at the speed of light. Every proton generates its own gravitational singularity that connects to the P-soup".

"P-soup?" I interrupted.

Phoenix answered, "Scientists call it the P-soup. Poets call it the Great Mother Sea. It has many names. I'll read you this passage from *The Tellaran Chronicles of Science and Spirituality.*"

The Great Mother Sea

Spacetime only seems empty. It is the field of all manifest creation. We can apprehend and measure spacetime in three dimensions. The fastest velocity in our spacetime is the speed of light. Light is the fastest radiation with the shortest wavelength. The wavelength of light, the radius of a photon, therefore, represents the lowest practical measurable boundary of our Universe.

Below this tiny distance, lies a field that interpenetrates all manifestation. This is the unmanifest field wherein monads, which are sparks of consciousness, are 10^{40} times smaller than photons and spinning at velocities 10^{40} times faster than light speed, at the speed of thought. The monad is to the quanta as the quanta is to the Universe.

The Great Unmanifest Field has many names. On Tellara, poets call it The Great Mother Sea. Mystics call it by many names because during intensely spiritual moments, they apprehend it through their opened third eye. It is known to mystics as The Great Unmanifest, and The Field of Pure Potentiality. Some call it Cosmic Consciousness, others Liquid Loving Light, or Living Water. Some call it Quintessence, The Prima Materia, or The Sea of Infinite Possibilities. Tellaran scientists call it the P-soup for primal potentiality.

Tellaran science understands the geometry of empty space in our three-dimensional manifest Universe. But only mystics who have seen the Great Unmanifest understand its behavior. The geometry in this field is completely foreign to our comprehension of number and shape. Everything is whirling 10^{40} times faster than light in singular, infinitesimally small sparks of consciousness, sparks of love, sparks of light. Each monad is a singularity by our understanding of natural law.

This Great Unmanifest Field is sometimes made manifest to us during the heartdance as images emerge from our collective imagination. We sense that the field is omniscient and omnipresent. Do all monads spin in the same direction? We don't know since even our most sanctified mystics cannot hold the motion in their mind's eye longer than a moment. The monads do seem to cluster in moving, extra-dimensional geometries which also cannot be grasped for longer than a moment. Trying to latch on to rhythm, direction, or flow is beyond both mystic apprehension and scientific measurement. Monadic motion creates a kind of music, inaudible to the human ear, but its vibration causes every cell to tingle in ecstasy.

What we do understand is, that every single monad in the Great Unmanifest Field is in constant contact with every other monad. They move so fast that they are all always touching. The Great Mother Sea is the source of all manifestation, consciousness, spirit, spin, energy, gravity, radiance, love, light, and sound.

"So, as I mentioned, each proton is a stable, mini blackwhole."

I wrote black hole in my notebook and Phoenix suggested I change the spelling, "We call it a blackwhole, one word, spelled with a 'wh,' because it both contracts and radiates mass."

"Radiates? Blackwholes attract, contract, and crush everything around them."

"Yes, they do. All that and more." Once again, Phoenix read from **The Tellaran Chronicles of Science and Spirituality**.

Blackwholes

In blackwholes, mass is continuously created and destroyed, radiated and captured by gravitational attraction. Blackwholes spin. The more proximal to the center of the singularity, the closer the spin velocity approaches the speed of light. Inside the event horizon, where spin velocity approaches lightspeed, the gravitational force is intense, but at even short distances from the event horizon, the force of gravity falls off exponentially.

If mass is flung from the blackwhole at a high enough velocity to escape the event horizon, it migrates out into the Universe, there to find a nascent purpose in the vacuum of space. In this way, blackwholes at the center of galaxies continuously add to the mass and energy in the Universe, which is why the Universe is expanding at an accelerated rate and why space is far from empty.

The event horizon of each blackwhole is relatively stable toroidal structure with poles and an equator. Mass curves in an endless loop from equator to pole, in through the 'north' pole, to the center of the singularity, spun around at light speed, flung back out the equator toward the event horizon, only to curve along the surface of the event horizon toward the 'south' pole and repeat the journey. Picture a three-dimensional toroidal infinity symbol in endless circulation.

Not all mass continues along this recurring toroidal journey. Other coherent vortices of mass pass through the quantum boundary at the center of the singularity and return to the P-soup from whence they arose. Each returning vortex of mass reconnects with all the sparks of primal consciousness in the P-soup, the source of everything, inter-penetrating every aspect of creation.

Spinning jets at the poles draw mass across the event horizon and into the center of the singularity. Mass is both captured and radi-ated in the vast jets ejected from the poles of a blackwhole. Consider a whirlpool of water spinning down a drain; an equal and opposite whirlpool of air spirals outward into the atmosphere.

The Universe is constantly sending and receiving new information and energy. The unmanifest P-soup learns about manifestation from the unique experiences of each returning monad, the ultimate attain-ment of conscious evolution. As each subsequent monad involutes, it brings that additional information to the total awareness of all manifestation.

There is but one fundamental force in the Universe because radiation and gravity are two sides of the same coin. The radiating and contracting coherent vortices constitute the primal matter of the involution and evolution of Universal consciousness.

The information contained on any quanta on the surface of a blackwhole contains the information of the whole. Every P-length quanta on the surface of a blackwhole is in constant contact with the quanta sized squished, interpenetrating voxels within the vol-ume of the blackwhole. Each blackwhole is a hologram. Each quanta throughout the inside and on the surface of every blackwhole is a hologram.

The entire universe obeys the properties of a blackwhole. The Uni-verse is a blackwhole. We live inside an expanding blackwhole that is endlessly learning about itself.

"Blackwholes have poles and equators?"

"A blackwhole is shaped like a torus," said Saffron. I shook my head in confusion.

"Donut shaped," Phoenix said to me. To Saffron he explained, "A donut is a popular toroid-shaped cake in America. Too sweet; I prefer bagels, a toroidal bread."

Saffron nodded.

I added, "Just stay outside of that event horizon if you don't want to be chewed up and spit out," I quipped in order to show I understood. I was writing frantically. "I learned that the Universe is expanding at an accelerated rate because of dark energy."

Phoenix said, "Tellaran science is not acquainted with the concept of dark energy. So, now that you understand about blackwholes and primordial vortices, let's discuss the holo-fractal-graphic nature of the Universe."

"And this will help me operate my vox?"

Phoenix continued. "Do you understand what a hologram is?"

"I've seen the holodeck on *Star Trek*."

"Yes, I like that show, except for the warp engines. That's not how we travel faster than light." Phoenix was becoming pedantic. "Do you know what a fractal is?"

"I used the word to describe your repetitive, pointillistic brushstrokes. Fractals are patterns in nature."

Saffron nodded, "We know it's a lot to take in at once, but understanding how consciousness creates, and that even primordial vortices have a qualitative consciousness, will help you direct your thoughts through the vox. Here, read this." She handed me a small flat screen that contained the entire **Tellaran Chronicles of Science and Spirituality.**

The Holofractalgraphic Universe

Each point, object, and region of space is continuously struck by waves from all directions and at all scales throughout the electro-magnetic spectrum. When waves intersect, an interference pattern is created. These interference patterns gather energy and information from every direction at every point. The information of the whole is contained at every point, thus creating holographic patterns through-out the universe.

A fractal is a self-similar, self-replicating, self-referential pattern that follows the golden mean ratio; like the branches of trees, the veins in leaves, the branches of blood vessels, galaxies, ocean waves, pine-cones, and feathers. Nature uses fractals in harmonic ratios to design minerals, plants, animals, DNA, even solar systems and galaxies. Fractal patterns are self-similar and self-replicating but never exactly alike. Animals are fractals, including people.

The event horizon of every blackwhole behaves like a holographic plate representing all the information within the volume of the black-whole.

Everything that exists has its own sovereign consciousness, from sub-P monads to the Universe itself. All consciousness is entangled. All atoms are entangled.

The flower of life, in three dimensions is made up of inter-pene-trating spherical bubbles that connect from largest to smallest on all scales from the Universe itself to the radius of a photon.

By connecting the centers of all these spheres and petals, a vast interconnected grid of interlocking 64-point tetrahedrons is generated. These tetrahedrons connect on all scales from largest to smallest creating a Universal grid that occupies all of space. Empty space is not empty, rather it has an almost infinitely dense infrastructure that appears empty because it is in perfect balance, perfect isometric vector equilibrium.

The spherical, feminine bubbles interpenetrate every grid point of the linear, angular, masculine tetrahedron grid. The scaled grid structure fits together like nested dolls from smallest to largest. Because the force is the same in every direction, none of the grid lines push harder than any others, so no part of the grid ever collapses. The entire grid is interconnected.

The limit of the expanding Universe and the P-length quanta are the practical upper and lower limits of the manifest Universe. Below this P-length boundary, lies the mysterious unmanifest P-soup, the Great Mother Sea.

I finished reading. "People are fractals?"

Saffron answered, "People come from other people. Our proportions follow the golden mean ratio. We are similar replicates of our parents.

"What is the difference between a photon and a proton?" Phoenix was nonplussed. I considered the old saying that there was no such thing as a stupid question, while Phoenix composed his face. I was sorry I'd asked.

"Only about a trillion orders of magnitude. Dana, you are aware that the speed of light is theoretically the fastest speed measurable in the manifest Universe?"

"I've heard that."

"So light waves are the tiniest lengths we can measure in manifest reality. That means that the radius of the photon is the same as the wavelength of light speed."

"You're talking about that wave-particle duality thing?"

"No, light moves in flowing streams of intersecting spirals."

"Huh?"

"Think of two intersecting jump ropes, swinging in alternating rhythm. When the ropes separate, we see the waves. When the ropes intersect, we see the particle. This light particle is the photon." He waited to see if I nodded my understanding.

"The proton, on the other hand, is trillions of times larger. Remember, you can fit 4×10^{40} photon-sized voxels on the surface of a proton."

I summarized my notes, "You're saying that protons are stable mini-blackwholes, that each is a singularity spinning at light speed creating a gravitational center?"

Here, read this," said Phoenix, thrusting his screen into my hands.

The Tellaran Chronicles of Science and Spirituality
Protons

Every proton is a stable mini blackwhole spinning at nearly the speed of light. This creates a gravitational field in each proton that holds every atom together. Within close proximity, the gravitational force is strong enough to overcome the repellent positive force of other atomic and subatomic nuclear particles, including other protons. At even short distances from the nucleus, gravitational attraction falls of very rapidly in a logarithmic curve.

Consider the flower of life as a thin cellophane shell that wraps around the surface of every proton with each petal the size of the radius of a photon. Over $4x10^{40}$ quantum-sized pixel petals fit on the surface of each proton.

Within the proton, 10^{60} voxel bubbles are packed. Energy with information known as chi or prana is continuously exchanged between the surface pixel petals and the interior voxel bubbles, making every proton a hologram.

Each quantum petal on the surface of each proton generates a vorticular wormhole. In continuous pulses, each wormhole attaches, detaches, and reattaches to the pixel petals on the surface of every other proton in its vicinity ceaselessly exchanging information. Due to the extreme minuteness of each pixel petal, the wormholes are necessarily thin. Due to the fact that each atom is 99.99999% empty space, each wormhole is necessarily very long relative to its petal host.

There are approximately 10^{80} protons in the Universe. This means that every proton in the Universe is in continuous contact with at least half the protons in existence. Each proton has the same information as every other proton constantly, continuously, and simultaneously. Each piece of a hologram contains all the information of the whole, at every scale from the sub-P monads, to the quantum level, to the outer limit of the Universe. In any given instant, the Universe itself is aware of the total information in each individual proton.

Every proton is a mapped mirror of every other proton. The surface boundary of the expanding Universe itself is mapped by the flower of life in quantum-sized pixel petals.

Each proton has a singularity at its center. At the singularity, the infinitesimally small vortex would reach a speed that exceeds light speed; so fast in fact, that to our capacity to extrapolate, the singularity is a point of stillness. Here, particles as small as monads, 10^{40} times

smaller than a quanta spinning 10⁴⁰ times faster than light speed,
are able to slip through the boundary in and out of the P-soup. Each
singularity connects with all the monads in the P-soup, sharing sparks
of consciousness between the manifest and the unmanifest. Through
every proton in every atom in every cell of our bodies, we are in con-
stant contact with the unmanifest P-soup, the source of consciousness,
spin, mass, energy, radiation, gravity, sound, light, and love.

This interconnected entanglement among protons is the reason
that we can experience non-local reality, why paranormal events such
as precognition, telepathy, and remote viewing can occur, the reason
that All is One. The spinning of every proton in every atom in every
cell of our being at the speed of light is the reason we are literally be-
ings of light.

I was getting exasperated. "When I asked how the vox works, I was asking how to use it. What does it do? What buttons do I push, what knobs do I turn? Do I really need to know this Tellaran physics to operate my vox?"

Saffron said, "All Tellaran technology is based on physics significantly different from Earth's science. Our energy is implosive, drawing from the infinite P-soup. It leaves no residue. Your energy is explosive, combustible. It leaves residue."

"You mean pollution and explosions." I nodded, beginning to get a glimmer of why this physics explained the basis for my vox's operation.

Phoenix stated, "Dana, your point is well taken. It is time for a hands-on lesson. As you work with your vox, the protons in its crystals will resonate with the blackwholes in your brain."

"There are blackwholes in my brain?" I was indignant.

"Trillions, throughout your body. There are blackwholes in every proton of every atom of every molecule in every cell in your body. What did you think we were talking about, Dana?"

"The cosmos, inner space, outer space."

"Both inner and outer. 'As within, so without; As above, so below.' It's blackwholes all the way down to the quantum level. The interconnected protons in neuron cells and DNA molecules synchronize vox tools to their individual operator." Phoenix had a way of stating obscure facts as if they should be self-evident to a school child.

Saffron was more patient. "Because the protons in all your atoms connect with each other and the P-soup, the protons within your vox will create fields that generate light, heat, gravitation, levitation, non-local reality, and cymatic cutting, and listening tools. Once you harmonize your vox to your DNA, it will function at the speed of thought."

"Speed of thought? Not light?"

She continued, "Instantaneous for all practical metrics. Dana, your vox will enable you to remote view by accessing non-local reality. You can use the vox to remote listen using cymatics. Remote listening is the most difficult application. Cymatic resonance between two people is the basis for audio-telepathy. It takes practice to synchronize."

I turned the golden vox over in my hands, marveling at the power in this little gadget.

"You can use the vox to generate light as focused as a laser or as diffuse as daylight; heat as focused as fire or as diffuse as a warm hug. You can use it to levitate by creating an alternative center of gravity. You can use the vox to make yourself invisible, inaudible, and chemically undetectable; all but incorporeal as you hover inter-dimensionally. While veiled, you can see and hear beyond the cloak of indetectability."

"Inter-dimensionally?"

"Out of phase with the atoms in this reality."

"Like a cloaking device on *Star Trek*?" I asked.

Phoenix replied, "I like that show. The vox also uses sound waves to manipulate matter. It can cut through rock and even sculpt. I used mine to create my statues." I remembered his beautiful sculptures from San Francisco.

"So, light, heat, remote viewing, remote listening, levitation, material manipulation, and interdimensional cloaking. That's one handy little tool. Does it come with an Owners' Manual?" I didn't have to understand Tellaran science to appreciate that its technology worked. But thinking about aligning my thoughts with the crystals was a stretch.

"We are going to train you to use your vox during the rest of your visit. Each of the crystals rotates, tips, and aligns with the singularity in the center of the vox. Each combination of crystal alignments activates one of the tools."

"Like a Tellaran Swiss Army Knife." They looked bewildered.

Phoenix demonstrated a tool using a sonic beam to slice through granite with a sculptor's precision. "One useful aspect of this sonic blade is that it does not generate heat, sound, or light, just an edge that can slice through matter along a curve or straight-line." He carved a delicate, serrated leaf with veins and vines from a chunk of raw granite the size of a microwave oven.

I marveled, "You have to have considerable hand-eye coordination to sculpt something that detailed."

"Now, using the artificial gravitational center," he pointed his vox at the granite leaf and manipulated a blue star sapphire. "I will levitate it slowly." The stone rose over our heads, spun in a gentle ballet, and nestled into a pattern of organically shaped stones, edging together in an interwoven design. The pieces fit together perfectly on both a large scale and in their intricate details.

"Another medium of artistry. This vine and floral pattern will compose a wall inside the pyramid." Phoenix smiled at me.

"Wouldn't an alternative center of gravity have to be huge to counter the Earth's gravity?"

"No, the vox coheres sufficient singularities to create a local gravitational center." He then showed me how to manipulate a sequence of crystals to levitate. I copied his moves on my vox. "Up you go."

"I'm floating! I'm flying!" At first, I was ecstatic. Then, alarmed, I was drifting, rising, and falling in an aerial free-for-all. "Get me down!"

Phoenix joined me ten feet above the floor and instructed me how to return to the floor with a gentle landing.

Next, he manipulated a combination of crystals and disappeared before my eyes. I could no longer see or hear him.

Saffron explained, "Indetectability is not a simple deflection of light and sound waves. Phoenix is actually hovering inter-dimensionally. He occupies a region of non-local spacetime out of phase with our sensory perceptions. Slide these two sapphires all the way to the top and rotate this rose quartz to the left. To uncloak, do the reverse."

I copied Phoenix's operations as Saffron instructed and found myself surrounded by soft, swirling haze. I saw my environment through a translucent screen. I was hovering undetectably. I manipulated myself back to the visible realm.

Next, my view was directed to the vox's small screen, which displayed images of individuals on whom I focused with strong intent. I thought of Juniper and Robin, my Tellaran greeters. They came into view in Saffron's garden. I thought of my son and saw him riding his motorcycle in cross-town traffic. I thought of my daughter Ruth and saw her in her office in a close conversation with a nice-looking young man. "It works across both worlds," I marveled.

"Yes, the vox is trans-dimensional."

"Non-local reality is an unfamiliar concept for me."

"The vox directs your thoughts through the selected singularities in its crystals. Through your DNA, your vox becomes an extension of your will. The vox does not channel negative energy."

"Meaning?"

"It won't work as a weapon."

"Because?"

"It draws its energy from the Great Mother Sea. Cosmic consciousness is, by definition, harmonious."

"You mean the field you call P-soup?"

"Yes. Each vox is a personalized perpetual motion device. It will function as long as you live, drawing implosive energy for you to direct at will."

"We consider perpetual motion to be impossible."

Saffron shrugged, "That's because your science only looks at the entropy side of physics."

I shrugged.

"Explosive, residue…" She prompted me.

"Oh yeah, syntropy." I nodded. "Could I accidently do damage? It cut right through that stone."

"You will be well trained. The vox harnesses syntropy. It organizes matter and energy."

Phoenix showed me how to manipulate crystals to create a light source. It provided multi-directional soft and bright beams. Another configuration created a warm glow.

"Batteries not included," I was being glib, but felt overwhelmed.

As if reading my thoughts, Saffron said, "When in doubt, dance."

We left Shastise Cavern and dined in a nearby eatery with a view of the mountain and the growing pyramid. We were served family style: beet, seaweed, and endive salad, coconut curry soup, and vegetable quiche. Again, the flavors of Tellaran vegetables burst in my mouth with a sensual rush. We followed our meal with a creamy pudding and marvelous coffee. I hadn't realized how famished I'd been, and devoured the feast before me.

On the ride back to the Bluffs, I asked about something that was on my mind.

"I watched a show about ancient aliens on television this week. Do you really think there are reptiles running Earth's governments and corporations?"

Saffron said, "They certainly ran the world in the centuries leading up to of the fall of Atlantis. This is not to say that reptilians cannot evolve spiritually. The saga of the reptilians is ancient and complex. Although they have fourth-dimensional awareness, most engender heavy karma that keeps them trapped in reincarnational cycles, trapped in duality consciousness.

"Draconians have inhabited the Earthly realm for hundreds of thousands of years. They predate humanity. They predate the shift that separated Earth and Tellara. They consider Earth their province, and humanity their property. The reptilians weren't the only ones here at the beginning. Other non-human, extra-dimensional beings helped terraform embryonic Earth. Whenever a planet capable of sustaining life emerges in the liquid water zone, the entire Galactic Family takes notice.

"This came up on my alien's TV program. We call it the Goldilocks Zone from an Earth folktale, not so hot as to have steam, not too cold as to be a frozen snowball, just right for water to exist as solid, liquid, and gas."

"Eons-long care goes into creating habitat that can cultivate evolving biological forms and consciousness. Most of these ancient beings are benign, but not all. Since prehistory, these non-human, fourth-dimensional beings have both aided and interfered with human destiny, biology, history, and spirituality.

"In ancient civilizations, early Homo sapiens routinely interacted with extra-dimensional humanoid races. Earth humans lost awareness of these interactions during the last shift. Earthborn humanity is a species with amnesia due to the trauma of the last planetary shift. We Tellarans banished those individuals whose agenda was to prevent our spiritual evolution."

"The heartdance," I mused.

"On Tellara, we interact with many humanoid races, including Draconians. There are sovereign races throughout the galaxy that function on the physical plane. Their interests vary from helpful, to detrimental, to curious, to indifferent to the fate of humanity. The helpful watch over, guide, and encourage all Gaia's children. Those indifferent to humanity's fate tend to view Earth's development as a scientific experiment. They're not invested in any outcome. The hostile races have an agenda to keep humanity in slavery and at war. Human misery creates a dense vibration that can be apprehended on subtle planes by these beings. Unevolved reptilians consume fear and sorrow like a drug."

Phoenix explained, "The foundations of your world belief systems are predicated on a colossal lie: that there must be dominant and subordinate strata of humanity; that hierarchy is the natural order, necessary, and inherently good. This is a fundamental aspect of destructive polarization. Hierarchy is the basis for all your worldly 'isms.' Earthborn humans give lip service to the concept of equality, but from what we have seen, it is rare in your world."

"What have you seen of my world?"

"I have been transmitting data from Earth," said Phoenix. "We have accessed collections of your world art, music, religions, film, and literature."

"Not our science and technology?"

"No. Your science is reaching some dead ends. But we especially like your television, theater, and movies."

"Careful there, television is thought by some to be a corrupting influence, a source of propaganda," I said.

"Earth art, music, and theater reveal how you use the arts to diminish the pain of polarity. The hierarchical culture on Earth is similar to what we endured during the final stage of Atlantis," answered Phoenix.

Saffron said, "Reptilians, or as they like to be called, Draconians, are exceedingly intelligent. With access to both the third and fourth dimensional planes of existence, they possess a formidable advantage over humans."

Phoenix added, "They appear human and live amongst your population, often assuming leadership roles in industry and politics."

"How do they appear human?" I asked.

"They use an epigenetic marker on their quiescent DNA strands that they can manipulate at will. It is like an on-off switch that enables them to shape shift and hold their human form."

I shook my head in confused denial. "I have always argued that a small percentage of humans are sociopaths. Due to the fact that they lack empathy or conscience, they either end up in prison or in positions of power. We have a saying: 'the inmates are running the asylum.' Still, my friend, Louie, is going to be pleased to hear the confirmation that reptilians exist. He also tells me about a species called the grays."

"The grays are from the Zeta Reticuli system. The Zetas envy humanity's robust genetic material and harvest it to save their own depleted, over-cloned population. They have also been around since Atlantean times. Meanwhile, other members of the Galactic Family remain behind the scenes and are overwhelmingly supportive."

"So, none of these other Galactic Family species interfere with Tellaran society?"

"Interfere, no, guide, yes. The races that are part of the Galactic Family obey a non-interference pact."

"Like the Prime Directive on *Star Trek*? Score another one for Louie. But the not-so-nice Draconians and Zetas can and do interfere?"

"On Earth, yes; on Tellara, no." Saffron continued, "Now Dana, here is an important concept for you to understand. There are individual reptilians on both our worlds who have evolved into loving, compassionate beings with balanced karma and open chakras. It is harder for reptilians to evolve than humans."

"Why, if they have fourth-dimensional consciousness?"

"Draconians leapfrogged over their heart chakras to engage in fourth-dimensional consciousness. They took a short cut from their solar plexus to their throat chakras. This severed the link between their hearts and minds."

"It also disconnected their hearts from their survival and sexual instinct," Phoenix added.

"Reptilian soul-stuff is much feebler than human. Because of their disproportionate regard for reason to the exclusion of intuition, reptilians are imbalanced in their left brains. They value survival, sexuality, and rationality. But they are disconnected from empathy, compassion, creativity, and sensitivity. Without the balanced integration of all the chakras, spiritual evolution becomes almost impossible."

"Like sociopaths, but I don't think they would see this as a weakness."

Phoenix said, "This is their blind spot and is the reason humans will eventually surpass their controllers. Humans are robust at all chakra levels. Keeping humanity in the dark about your true evolutionary potential is essential to maintain reptilian dominance. Although Draconians would be loath to admit it, humanity is the envy and the cherished younger progeny of the Galactic Family."

I said, "Most people consider this to be a crazy conspiracy theory nonsense about alien abductions and anal probes." I was getting fidgety in my tram seat and turned to the spectacular view of the coast.

Saffron answered, "It may not be nonsense on Earth. The grays are a dying race. They covet humanity's genetic vigor. They cultivate our DNA to create viable, fertile hybrids. So far, even with our cooperation, the gray hybrids on Tellara are sterile. The grays' sexual polarity has grown ever weaker over the eons. This generates frailty in their physicality and fecundity. They are a cautionary tale that exemplifies what happens when a species becomes cerebral to the exclusion of vitality, passion, and sexuality. Their lower chakras have waned."

"Do the Draconians and Zetas on Earth know of their counterparts on Tellara?" I asked.

"Know of, perhaps. Crossing that veil is another matter. It takes a coordinated channeling of both heart and mind to open a portal into our dimension."

"Can non-humans cross through the wormhole?"

"Travel between dimensions is the birthright of all enlightened individuals of any species. Ancient races have lived through and passed through all the challenges humanity now faces. Elders in the Galactic Family have learned to adhere to the Law of One: Service to others is service to self."

"On Earth we call it the Golden Rule, 'Do unto others as you would have others do unto you.' But we don't adhere to it very well."

All too soon, it was time to return to Earth.

* * *

Back in my bedroom, I got about four hours sleep before it was time to prepare for work. Placing my vox on a gold chain under my blouse, I grabbed some heartplums, and headed off to schlepp in Sh.I.T.

Later that morning, Frank Fretz arrived at the office sporting an Armani suit, a glam tan, and a Hollywood smile. He was as handsome as he was horrid. We bemused worker bees all looked up from our honeycomb cubes. Frank gave me a tilt of his head and a knowing look. I couldn't tell if it was meant to comfort or intimidate. He walked past the Rodent's closed door and went directly into Squeezy's office. He shut the door behind him and the two nastiest people I know huddled for over an hour, leaving the Rodent out of the loop. Should someone tell Vincent? Anyone? No one got up from his or her desk or dialed his or her intercom. A pall settled over the hive. Silent worker bees, no buzzing, but plenty of sidelong glances, many directed at me.

I silently Instant Messaged the Rodent, notifying him that Frank Fretz was meeting with Suzy. I could not see the Rodent's face, but I inferred resignation in his reply, 'all in a day's work.' Several minutes passed, and Vincent walked out of his office and into Squeezy's with a jaunty skip. Frank boomed a hearty hello and "just in time, speak of the devil," greeting and Squeezy's door closed again. The three now huddled. Had I been a traitor to the working masses by aiding and abetting the Rodent? Two weeks ago, I would have been too uncertain to act. Now, I had a vast new perspective. The heartdance, heartplums, and vox helped me to cope with the deceit in daily situations.

Shortly, Louie was called into the meeting. They kept him in there for just under an hour. He came out pale. But, to his credit, he was stoic. His posture was erect and his expression serene. That's my boy.

Squeezy called me on the intercom and told me to bring the envelope from Jay into her office. It was my turn to walk into some crappy circle of Hell. Frank Fretz directed the inquisition.

"You were out sick yesterday."

"I was."

"Are you feeling better?"

Oh boy, better than levitating in Tellara? "I'm coping," I answered noncommittally.

He nodded sagely, "A mental health day, sure." He then asked inappropriate, pointed questions about my relationship with Jay. I told him he was interfering with an active police investigation and that I would like to get Inspector Vazquez on speakerphone before we continued. I also told him, as I slapped a tape recorder on Squeezy's desk, that I would be recording the entire conversation. Frank was nonplussed; Squeezy, all squinty-eyed malice; the Rodent, forbearing.

"No, you will not. Today's meeting is off the record," Frank scowled. I made no move to turn off the recorder. After a glance passed between Frank and Squeezy, she triumphantly reached across her desk to turn off the recorder. This was not a situation where I could simply declare, "We're done here," and walk away. I was in no position to snub a Corporate VP who also happened to be head of Shelter Security. I had to stay and endure their questions and innuendos. Squeezy was biting her lower lip to keep a malevolent grin from erupting across her face.

"Well then, I'll take notes. However, under no circumstances will I interfere with an ongoing police investigation. Everything said here is on the record. I'm cooperating fully with the police." I situated a clipboard on my lap and held my pen at the ready.

"As are we all, Dana, Dear," purred Frank. What became clear in a very few minutes was how Shelter was setting me up to be blamed for Jay's murder. My convenient disappearance had played into their hands like a feast on a silver platter. Frank asked me about my alibi. I told him it was all in the police report. He demurred, "I understand that you didn't tell the police everything about where you were the night Jay was killed, but you're among friends here. We're laying the groundwork for your legal representation… uh, should you need it," he added as an afterthought. Among friends! My Aunt Fanny and her hairy hippo! I clammed up and crossed my arms across my chest in a gesture of finality.

Frank was undeterred. Now questions came about that pesky envelope I'd received posthumously from Jay; the envelope Squeezy had intercepted; the contents of which Vincent had read and then returned to me; and which I had read while faxing to Inspector Vazquez. In that envelope, I saw spreadsheets listing currency amounts alongside coded favors from politicians in a dozen countries. There were encrypted spreadsheets that seemed as though they could have tracked money-laundering operations. They listed a variety of international small businesses such as restaurants, dry cleaners, psychiatrists, construction companies, and more. Beside each company, international currency amounts were listed alongside what I took to be bank account numbers. These companies reflected negative cash flow and increasing equity. There were phone logs that indicated dates and times linked to obscurely coded events that coincided with prominent political disruptions and scandals. If Sheldon Walters went down, he'd be taking half of congress, China, and EU politicians with him. If my interpretation of this data was correct, no whistle blower had ever had such a loaded gun as the documents Jay had compiled.

Frank stated, "You received an envelope from Jay Andrews, mailed from San Francisco."

"I did."

"Did you read its contents?"

"Yes, it was addressed to me."

Frank grabbed the envelope out of my hands and perused the documents, "This is a pack of lies, you realize?" Frank menaced. "Did you make copies?"

"No."

"Best forget everything you saw in these documents."

I bowed my head and yearned for Tellara. "I was told to mail them to Inspector Vazquez."

"Leave that to me," he purred. Being of reasonably sound mind, I capitulated. The documents had been mailed to me at work. They were ostensibly work related. Did Frank Fretz know that Vincent Cretzky had seen the contents?

Shelter was arranging circumstances so that if I decided to be a whistleblower, they would frame me for murder or make me look like a nut case. If I decided not to be a whistleblower, they could still frame me for murder. Either way, my best-case scenario would be incarceration. Squeezy was practically bouncing in her chair, a difficult move in her form-hugging spandex. Her cleavage was a sight to behold. All three of us became distracted. It was impossible to look away from her jiggling décolletage. The boys were rapt.

Out of the corner of my eye, I looked at the Rodent. He understood what was happening; and to his credit, he looked abashed. He was being pressured to partake in serving me up for a capital crime that he now fully realized I did not commit. Without explicitly saying so, Frank's slant was that I was genuinely the guilty party and that Shelter was hanging in there, backing me, until they could no longer support that position publicly. They would pay for a lawyer when the time came that I needed one. Ha! This from the team that paid the lawyers on both sides of their cases to ensure the outcome they wanted. I had heard about this tactic firsthand from Maggie Coutts at our teambuilding event in Chinatown. The Rodent was expected to collude with this strategy.

I wasn't nearly as distressed as I might have been. Frank Fretz and Sheldon Walters did not realize the direction of Inspector Vazquez's investigation. I was almost certain that Vazquez would overtly focus on me while covertly building a case against Shelter's top executives. While the boys watched Squeezy bounce and blather pseudo-professional banalities, I adopted a Zen demeanor.

While all the attention was on her, Squeezy asked, "So, Dana, what did you have to do to get this job?" Her question was dripping with innuendo.

"Submit a resume," I replied blandly.

"Is there any history of mental illness in your family?"

"Only in my work family, in the Human Resources Department."

Squeezy looked irritated. This should have been so much more fun for her. FrankenFretz seemed confused by my serenity. I should have been a puddle of tears. The silence grew taut as they ran out of veiled threats.

An extraordinary thing began to happen. Frank's face began to morph in front of me. His pupils changed from circles to vertical slits in oblong irises. His forked, dry tongue flicked across his lower lip. His suntanned skin became covered with shimmering tan scales. A similar transformation was taking place on Squeezy's face, on her arms, and bizarrely, on her cleavage. Her scales were taupe with lustrous green highlights, her vertical irises more malevolent than ever. Her hands were lacquered claws. So, there are reptiles among us! And reptiles have tits! Who knew?

My jaw must have dropped to my knees. Both Squeezy and FrankenFretz were staring back at me agog. My hand flew to my mouth in a gesture denoting my stupefied loss for words. Then appearances slipped back into their conventional visage and I shut my mouth. FrankenFretz and Squeezy were actual reptilians. Wait 'til I tell Louie! Vincent remained unchanged and appeared to have seen nothing amiss. He really was a human. I was glad we had promoted him to rat. How had I perceived their masks slipping? Was it the heartplums? Heartdance? Vox practice? Who else in Shelter was reptilian? How high up the food chain did these psychopathic snakes slither?

"Inspector Vazquez calls me almost every day to make sure I follow my routine," I broke the silence.

"I'll be speaking to him myself later today," said Frank. "What have you told this San Francisco Police Inspector about Jay Andrews' documents?"

I prevaricated, "I'll tell him that I have passed the envelope along to my superiors." Frank Fretz preened with self-importance. Squeezy looked at him with shrewd admiration.

"We're done here," the Rodent cleared his throat and stood. He hadn't seen what I had, but he was man enough to cry foul at what was, for all intents and purposes, a kangaroo court.

"Yes, I think we're all on the same page," FrankenFretz allowed, winking at me. I escaped to my cube, grabbed Louie, and dragged him to lunch at the Noodle Palace. We hadn't spoken more than a few words since Monday morning.

"I have so much to tell you," I said.

"Do you want to relive your inquisition?" he asked.

"Not really."

"Me neither, but I think we should," Louie said. "They wanted to know if you showed me the contents of Jay's envelope. I told them no. But they don't know I received the same documents at home."

"Frank confiscated mine. I'm in the line of fire more than ever."

"You don't know the half of it, Dana. They asked me about your mental stability."

"Ha! Good one; they're laying their groundwork. Don't worry Louie, not yet. The company plans to frame me, but I have some resources they don't know about." Under my sweater, I pressed my vox to my heart.

"Right," he said dubiously. "Dana, don't be a Pollyanna. They offered me money to rat you out."

"Maybe you should take it."

"What? This isn't just a bribe, Dana, it's a whopping severance package in exchange for turning on you."

"Take the money and take a looong vacation,"

"I'll think about it."

"Promise?"

"I'll talk to Hal. Should we head back?"

"Not yet." I drew close and whispered. "I believe you. There are reptilians interfering with humans, trying to run the world. I've seen them. And I have a safe haven where we can be free of their threat while we brainstorm how to defeat them."

"Defeat the reptilian overlords? You just told me to take the money and run."

"Louie, it's all true, reptilians, grays, my alibi on an alternate Earth. Do you remember the painting I bought in San Francisco, from that artist Phoenix who was crushing on me?"

"He was crushing on me, but yes, I remember."

"Well, that painting, *Summer in Tellara*, is a portal to another world called Tellara. Tellara is an enlightened parallel Earth. They even have enlightened reptiles and grays."

"Who are you, and what have you done with my friend Dana?"

"I'm serious, Louie. All your conspiracy theories that I indulged all these years were right. I've witnessed them. Firsthand. At Shelter." And in an urgent whisper directly across the lunch table, "Squeezy and FrankenFretz morphed into reptiles right before my eyes. And there's more."

"So, all this time, I've been telling you how the world really is and you have to go to another world to hear about it from aliens?"

"I haven't actually met any aliens on Tellara."

"Of course."

"I'm glad we promoted Vincent because he isn't a reptile. He's a…"

"Rodent?"

"No."

"Rat."

"No, no, he's a mammal, ah er, a human. Vincent is human."

"But not Squeezy and FrankenFretz?"

"Correct. I saw their reptilian scales and facial features, vertical irises, and everything! I even saw FrankenFretz's forked tongue!" I leaned over, "Louie, I was in Tellara the night Jay was murdered. All those hours you were looking for me, that's where I was, on an alternate Earth that I entered through a quantum singularity, you know, in the painting. That's why I don't have an alibi for the police!" Louie looked pained. "The next time I travel to Tellara, I want you to come with me, see for yourself. Bring Hal. The Fourth of July weekend is coming up. We can go to Tellara for four days."

"Hal and I have our lives to sort out. Remember, I have been offered a large severance package to quit my job and betray you by telling them whatever they want to hear about you and Jay. And you think I should do just that."

I urged, "Come with me to Tellara."

"Not gonna happen, Dana. Hal and I are going away for the holiday. We have life choices to consider."

"I'll prove it to you. I have Tellaran technology!" I withdrew my vox from beneath my blouse. "Look, I can use it to remote view. I'm thinking of Hal." Hal came into view on my vox screen. He was relaxing at home on his day off.

"You have cameras in my house?!" Louie cried.

"I have no hidden cameras anywhere." I snapped. "I'm not lying. I'm not stupid. And I'm not crazy! I'm your friend and I'm telling the truth! I was on another planet when Jay was killed, and I've been back to Tellara twice. I've been trying to get you to come there with me ever since." I got up from the table and walked back to the office alone.

There must have been gossip while we were at lunch. The hive was buzzing. One consolation was that it was no better for Squeezy. FrankenFretz, who was taking the lead in framing me, had yoked her agenda of innuendo. He kept himself occupied nosing in everybody's minutia, generally making the whole office feel like naughty children. It was a dismal day. Vincent took the afternoon off. I fled at the stroke of five.

After Louie's response, I was even less sure about burdening my children with the convoluted circumstances of reptilian threats and alternate realities. I almost felt like calling Javier Vazquez. He seemed to have understood that I was trapped in a contrived web of lies spun by Shelter. But he was a cop and I was a person of interest with no alibi. Besides, what would I tell him? I've been to Tellara and guess what? I work for reptiles.

When I got home from that horrible day at work, Jesse had left a note that he had Rip. I dove through the canvas into Tellara. No one was in the park to meet me, so I rode the train to Esselen Bluffs and walked to Saffron's home. Only Juniper was there.

"Where is everybody?"

"An elder is ascending tonight. Many are attending the ceremony."

"Ascending?" I asked.

Juniper answered, "Over the millennia, as the harmonic consciousness prevailed, individuals opt for ascension as a means to depart their corporeal bodies. An individual can ascend when he or she no longer needs to reincarnate. We dissolve into the rainbow body and become transcendent spheres of light. Violet's ascension is preceding the pending global shift."

"Violet, the Eldest? She's the person ascending to her next energetic state?"

"Yes, Violet. She remained corporeal long enough to meet the wayshower."

"Tell me about the ceremony."

"Ascendance is chosen by each individual as he or she designates his or her time of passage. People rarely die unexpectedly, usually from a fluke accident. But often as not, the individual reincarnates soon and within the same karmic group. When an Elder crosses, it is a festival accompanied by music, dancing, and rejoicing. Violet's successor to the Circle of Thirteen is part of the heartdance ceremony."

"Am I allowed to attend?"

"It must be so, since you are here."

"Who will become the Eldest in Esselen?"

"Buffalo and Tangerine will be our newest Elder. She's only one hundred and twelve years old."

We arrived by the crystal-domed structure in the heart of Esselen Bluffs. It was dusk and the crescent moon was just rising. Venus was visible, but no other stars. A crowd was scattered throughout the labyrinthine gardens surrounding the dome. I nodded to Phoenix. We could all view the Circle of Thirteen through the clear dome where Violet lay in repose. The other twelve elders rose to their feet.

The rolling hills surrounding the city formed a natural amphitheater. Thousands of Tellarans gathered on the steppes. They formed continuous rainbows of coruscating hues across the terrain. In the distant crowd, I saw my first blond and redheaded Tellarans, a smattering of persistent recessive genes among the population. At a great distance across the bay I saw individuals with greenish-gold skin and could have sworn they had reptilian features. I hadn't expected them to be so beautiful. Elephants, horses, cats of all sizes, elk, cows, llamas, birds, and dogs joined the celebrants. Tree branches swayed. Tellara was alive as humanity merged with nature to become overlapping cascades of colors. As flower petals dropped to the steppes, they were crushed underfoot. The entire basin filled with perfumed wind.

Everyone chanted and swayed. The air thrummed with vibrations. Violet glowed, softly at first, then with luminescent rainbow hues. A thirteenth person dressed in Tangerine robes, stepped forth into the circle. A glow filled the chamber, emanating beyond the dome, filling the entire amphitheater. A golden ray filled me with bliss. When I looked toward the dome again, Violet was no more. An orb of light ascended and merged with the night sky. Tangerine and Buffalo stood in the center of the dancers. Dancing slowed. Singing softened. The Elders re-formed their circle.

Outside, the crowds also grew silent. The Elders filed silently out into the deep night. The crescent moon was high in the sky and stars now filled the heavens. The Ascendance Ceremony was over. The Circle of Thirteen was renewed.

It was late and I had to work tomorrow. Phoenix escorted me to Heartplum

Park.

"I don't suppose you could come back with me and provide my alibi to the police?"

"My priority is to get to Giza and paint *Tellaran Autumn*, your next portal."

We hugged. I leapt home.

* * *

We were coming up on the 4th of July. We all had Monday and Tuesday off next week. I was keeping my head down and my mouth shut. I spoke to Alice and to someone from Inspector Vazquez's investigation daily. I hardly spoke to Louie and we hadn't gone to lunch together since our quarrel.

Friday night at home, I took Rip for a long walk. When we got back in, I started chopping vegetables for dinner. To my dismay, my kitchen sink would not drain. It was plugged because the disposer was broken. I called around for a plumber, but due to the holiday weekend no one would come until the following Wednesday for less than a king's ransom. I was reduced to microwaving a pasta dish that promised to make me slender.

A car pulled up. Ruth stopped in to say hello. She was spending the holiday at a cabin in the north woods with her new beau from work.

"I wanted to see you before I went away, Mom."

"And I want to meet this fellow of yours."

"His name's Mick. He's a software engineer with a personality and social skills."

"Well, that's refreshing."

"He's good lookin' too. I'm on my way to his condo now and we're going to drive up to his cabin together."

"I'd invite you to dinner, but my kitchen sink is backed up."

"That's OK, Mom. Mick and I have plans to eat along the way."

Jesse joined us with Belle. He teased Ruth about her romance. "Hey Sis, enjoy the fireworks this weekend."

"We'll be making our own fireworks, Jesse." Ruth retorted. Jesse gave her a nuggie.

"Too much information," I held up my hands in mock protest.

"Mom, my bid to illustrate the graphic novel for the next Shock Wave movie has been accepted. My publisher and I are invited to the director's estate for a weekend house party."

"Who's going to be there?" Ruth asked.

Jesse rattled off the names of some actors, writers, and artists he would mingle with. "He's going to screen the rough cut of Shock Wave for us."

"Jesse, this sounds like the biggest break of your career!" Ruth exclaimed.

"It is, Ruth." Jesse was jubilant. "Mom, I just want to make sure you'll be OK alone if I go away for a few days. I know you have a lot of stress right now."

"Of course. I am happy for both of you. Go, have fun. Can one of you take Rip?"

"Sure, I'll take him up to the cabin. Mick has a dog," said Ruth.

"Mom, does this mean you have holiday plans?" Jesse asked.

"I'm waiting for a call." I didn't mention that the call I was waiting for was my check-in with the San Francisco Police. This was not the weekend to invite my kids to Tellara. We chatted for a few minutes longer, then hugged. The kids and dogs departed for their respective fireworks.

I could have been spending the four-day weekend frolicking across meadows carpeted with flower petals. But nooo, here I sat, home alone, with clogged plumbing, waiting for the phone to ring because 'Mr. Javier the Boss of Me' said he would call. Typical. I'd show him. I'd practice with my vox. When I worked with it in Tellara, the vox tools flowed smooth as silk. But here in my living room my efforts were choppy and intermittent. After bumping my head on the ceiling and thudding to the floor, I remembered Saffron telling me that the vox didn't channel negative energy. It must be those pesky blackwholes in my brain. At length, I gave up and turned on the TV in my bedroom, channel surfing for a distracting story. I found something called Garage Sale Wars where people bought each other's junk and argued about its value. It was horrifying, but I couldn't look away.

Finally, the man himself called Saturday morning. "Hello Dana, how is your weekend going?"

"It could be better, Javier." He'd called me by my first name, and I'd responded in kind, with a measure of irritation. "I could have made holiday plans, but here I sit, no thanks to you."

"Tell me your alibi and you can fly to the moon, Dana." He bit off my name, echoing my irritated tone.

If I answered with the truth, I would sound both insane and sarcastic and I had no wish to piss him off. "I'm going out for a few hours to spend time with friends."

"Local friends?"

"Yeah. By the way, Frank Fretz took my envelope, the one Jay sent me. I can't mail it to you."

"I'll get a warrant for it. If you go out, take your cell phone."

"Sure, I answered sullenly, grabbing my vox. There were lots of places where cell phones didn't work, and I could check in with my vox to see if I had messages on my answering machine. I'd have to return home intermittently throughout the weekend. Damn his eyes. I hung up and crossed through *Summer in Tellara* into Heartplum Park.

* * *

Saffron met me. We traveled by tram to Shastise. Phoenix was drawing on a balcony overlooking the pyramid. I sipped tea while watching him sketch the outlines of the three peaks: Mount Shastise, Black Butte, and the red pyramid.

"Is this my next portal painting for *Magic Seasons*?"

"These are preliminary sketches for your winter solstice portal," he replied.

"This drawing is beautiful, but it looks like summer."

"I will start painting *Shasta Solstice* after the first snowfall. I'm leaving in a few days for Giza to paint *Tellaran Autumn*."

"Giza, would that be Cairo, Egypt on Earth?" I asked.

"The site of the great ancient pyramids is where our next portal will open."

"Good to know Phoenix but getting overseas as a wanted person may present problems for me."

"Tell us what is going on," Saffron urged.

I got right to the point. "Events on Earth have intensified. Two of my professional enemies are actually reptilians. And the only person I've told about Tellara doesn't believe me."

"The involvement of Reptilian Illuminati this early in your mission is a complication. We thought we'd have the better part of a year to prepare you to share our message," said Phoenix.

"Bring your friends to Tellara as soon as you can," Saffron added.

"I'll make it a priority." Would that I could.

Phoenix sketched and painted while Saffron and I strolled through the pyramid construction area designated for visitors.

"Saffron, I am curious, how was the heartplum created? Is it a hybrid?"

"No, it is a newly evolved fruit generated using sonic waves to mutate the black plum's DNA."

I interrupted, "Sound waves alter DNA?"

"Yes, DNA is mostly water. Perturb the water and invoke specific genes segments. Sonic waves heal, manipulate organic matter and, as Phoenix showed you, carve minerals. Cymatics alters the geometry of water, cleanses waste, and restores cells. We use sonic vibrations to direct the movement of the pyramid blocks."

"There are sound waves generated by my vox. Can I use it to heal or alter DNA?"

"A vox similar to yours was used to genetically manipulate the first plum pit to generate the first crop of heartplums. About ten thousand years ago, farmers took the sweetest black plums from Atlantis. They manipulated their DNA, synchronizing gene segments to resonate with the heart chakra and third eye."

"You've lost me."

"When your chakras open, corresponding segments of your quiescent DNA become active and encode for new proteins. These higher chakra protein codes were spliced into the heartplum's DNA. Over generations, farmers sweetened the skin, the pulp, enhanced the crispy texture and juiciness. Heartplum trees were also genetically engineered to be hearty and grow in almost any climate or terrain."

"Genetically engineered? On Earth that means a plant's DNA has been woven through with foreign and sometimes toxic organic material."

"Here, it means a plant's native genetic structure is enhanced, its quiescent strands activated to augment healing and resilience."

"I think we call those quiescent strands 'Junk DNA.'"

CHAPTER 7

We dined at an eatery by the pyramid. Afterwards, Saffron and I headed to the tram station. Phoenix came to the platform to see us off. He embraced me then gave me an assessing gaze. "We found each other across ages and dimensions. *Magic Seasons* called to you. When the time comes, follow the crow. She is a crafty bird that offers psychic protection, and accompanies you into the darkest parts of your soul. You must pass through the darkness to fully apprehend the light." He towered over me, ageless, dark, and handsome. Michelangelo could have sculpted his large, strong hands. His sparkling eyes danced in his chiseled face. He was as much a work of art as his sculptures.

His words were a puzzle. "What crow?" Receiving no answer, Saffron and I boarded the tram. We disembarked at Heartplum Park. "I must stay near the portal so I can go back and forth to check in with the police."

"We'll work by the arch. I never tire of the view of the Bluffs," Saffron said.

I slipped my vox pendant over my head. It felt cool in the palm of my hand. Saffron removed hers from her upper arm. Now that I considered, I had seen voxes as brooches, bracelets, and even belt buckles. Practicing its remarkable functions, I felt like James Bond playing with toys from Q. Little by little, I was mastering them. I viewed Louie clearing out his office. He and Hal loaded their car and headed south, out of the city. So, my long weekend passed, hours in paradise alternating with hours waiting for the phone to ring. Javier called Monday night. I was in a delightful mood and he sensed it.

"Are you enjoying your visit with friends?" he asked.

"I am. How about you?"

"I'm working this weekend."

"On Jay's case?" I asked, hopefully.

He didn't answer me, just said, "Stay safe, Dana. I'll call you Wednesday morning at your office." Wow, he'd freed up my entire Tuesday!

* * *

I returned to Tellara. Saffron and Juniper took me on another tour of the artistic highlights of the region. I was spellbound. Tellaran art was interactive, holographic, moving, and mobile. We moved through it rather than simply viewing it. Juniper told me she had gathered a forum to research Earth art, music, literature, poetry, and films. "The study is based on the digital samples Phoenix transmitted through the portal. Thousands of Tellarans have become swept up in the 'Art of Earth Polarity,'" as she termed it. "So dark and yet so hopeful at the same time. Art is humanity's salvation. Every one of you must be the hero of your own life, destined to slog through the burdens and barriers of your incarnations. For Tellarans, Earth art is a touchstone to our ancient, shared heritage, a reminder not to take our hard-won harmony for granted. We have nothing like your conflicts and abstractions, so distant from nature and yet so inclusive of humanity's highest yearnings."

I was moved by Juniper's assessment. "For me, art both exposes and assuages injustice. Visionary art anticipates our noblest aspirations." As we walked, Saffron and Robin prattled on about cosmology, geometry, and fractals. But Juniper used art to elucidate science so that it bypassed my rational mind and coalesced in my psyche as intuitive realizations.

Later Tuesday afternoon, we watched a Tellaran play in an outdoor amphitheater. An epic adventure depicted the early years after the fall of Atlantis, when Zola the Elder brought forth the heartdance unto Tellara. The play was followed by a heartdance in the park. Actors and audience members partook, and a festival transpired. A feast followed the dance as people spread out food they had brought. I stayed in Tellara until well after midnight, nibbling delicious snacks and listening to haunting, beautiful music. The lights sparkling throughout the Bluffs reflected out upon the ocean that rose up to meet the star-filled, indigo sky. No fireworks display had ever been so evocative. All too soon, the holiday weekend came to an end. With hugs all around, I returned to my gracious, albeit, not so spacious, condo.

* * *

Wednesday morning, I dragged myself to work. I already knew from my vox viewing, that Louie had packed up his office and quit. How was I ever going to get Louie and Hal to Tellara? Big Maggie Coutts, from Eastern Division, who had sat at my table in Chinatown, was sitting in Louie's office. She of the "punish the potato eaters" ethos was going to derail all the claims appeals that Louie had been reviewing.

My cube had been searched over the weekend. It was time to seriously consider my situation. Cut and run would make me look guilty beyond the walls of Shelter. It didn't appear that Squeezy's notion to fire me remained on the table. Shelter was keeping me close. I was being framed for murder and offered up like a lamb for slaughter.

At least Squeezy was enjoying herself. I learned from Carmela, in Accounts Receivable, that Suzy and Vincent were no longer together. "Squeezy traded up the food chain. She's now an item with Frank Fretz."

The merging of the reptiles, "Who ended it, Vincent or Suzy?" I asked, torn between gossip and concern.

"I don't know." Carmela answered. "We've just observed Suzy and Frank Fretz canoodling in the halls, and Vincent is laying low."

"I hope Vincent is reconciling with Gwen." On the few occasions when he

90

did emerge from his office, he looked like death warmed over; a sallow, lifeless shell.

I plowed on with my claims. The highlight of my day was when Inspector Vazquez called to confirm I was still following my routine. I told him Louie had been offered money to leave Shelter and was gone.

"Mr. Robles-Leon had instructions to contact me before altering his schedule," Vazquez said. "Do you know where he is headed?"

"No, but I expect to see him at Jay's memorial, whenever that is."

"Soon; the medical examiner is done with his body. I'll be attending."

We said goodbye. I went to the ladies' room and inside a stall, viewed Louie on my vox. He and Hal were driving along a country road. They passed a sign that read 'BRUNO'S Bait Bullets Bibles Beer.' It appeared they were somewhere in the south.

On my morning break, I stopped by Vincent's office and complained that my cube had been searched.

"I know," he said. "Frank ordered Suzy to do it. He said it was a security measure. I objected, but my input was ignored."

"I'm sure Suzy relished the task," I grumbled. "How are you holding up?"

Vincent sighed, "That law firm, Waldo Mannheim & Peters, has been questioning me about denied claims. Long distance so far, but investigators are visiting the office next week."

"Let me guess. Shelter is indifferent to your situation?"

"They're taking a 'wait and see' stance."

"Which means you're in their cross-hairs. Have you told Gwen?"

"We had our first heart-to-heart in years. She agrees that I'm being set up for professional, if not legal, difficulties. She was remote at first, but gradually, as I opened up, so did she." Was it possible Vincent Cretzky was feeling actual remorse for his decades of institutionalized indifference? I handed him a heartplum. He relished every bite and pocketed the pit.

As soon as I returned to my desk, Maggie summoned me. "We need to talk." She thrust a folder at me. I opened it expecting to see new claims. Instead, it was some of my prior work going back six months. She had highlighted a passage here, a number there, and red-inked derisive comments in the margins. There were no actual errors in my work, just instances where I had followed state and federal regulations to award claims instead of using company policy to deny them. "Were we at the same conference, Dana?"

"This is out of line Maggie. I know how to process an insurance claim."

She snickered, "Frank Fretz didn't think so when I showed him my findings."

"Keep out of my files," was my brilliant riposte.

"No can do," Maggie smiled in what passed as a friendly grin, although one eye squinted, making her face look fractured. "Frank directed me to audit all of yours' and Mr. Leon's files for the last six months."

"And this is all you could come up with? Before you go through my work, speak to Vincent Cretzky."

"I answer to Frank Fretz," she said.

"If you are working on claims in this office, your manager is Vincent Cretzky. Corporate security has nothing to do with claims analysis. You're on shaky ground here, Maggie. Shelter is investigating fraudulently denied claims and you're looking for loopholes to deny legitimate claims. Be careful."

Maggie jumped up in my face. "It's a right-hand left-hand situation, Dana. Who do you think is going to be the final arbiter of claims?"

"Ideally, federal insurance regulators. Has anyone ever told you that you're annoying?"

"No, Dana! You're the first." She punched me in the arm, knocking me off balance and raising a bruise. She hooted, "You're all right kid. You speak your mind. I'll make a competent adjuster out of you yet." I shook my head in dismay. Later, I observed Squeezy entering Louie's office to confer with Maggie. I didn't need my vox to know what they were discussing.

Javier called again in the early afternoon. Jay's body was being released to Val Andrews as we spoke. The memorial was scheduled for this upcoming Saturday. I'd meet up with Louie, Hal, and Alice in Dallas. Vincent thought he should attend as a matter of pro forma. I hoped Gwen would attend with him. Of course, Frank Fretz would go. His patriarchal pandering was company policy. Squeezy announced she'd be attending, but every head in the hive simultaneously swiveled toward her, agape, aghast, agog. Suzy hardly knew Jay, and fallout from her recent grief counseling fiasco was still ricocheting inside our brains. Not that everyone in the office didn't wish that Squeezy would go Somewhere. Dallas, Timbuktu, the far side of the Moon, Anywhere.

A weekend in Dallas meant I couldn't spend the weekend in Tellara. *Summer in Tellara* was too precious to move from my living room wall. I was perversely excited to see Javier, telling myself that his understanding of Shelter's criminal climate could help exonerate me. I pushed down the niggling notion that I wanted to see him for any other reason. Instead, I thought about Phoenix, who seemed to care deeply about me in a sexually ambiguous way. I didn't need any romantic complications. Not on Earth. Not on Tellara.

I flew to Dallas Friday. Alice picked me up and drove me to her home. Louie and Hal were already there. It was a houseful of grieving, anxious friends. Louie and I hadn't had a real conversation since our quarrel. But when we saw each other, our differences melted away and we clung together.

Alice served salad and grilled kabobs on her patio. "We can only speak freely outside." Jay's posthumous whistleblower packet was the focus of our conversation. Louie and I had both read the coded documents that exposed Shelter's criminal activities. His was stashed in an undisclosed safe space, near Hal's childhood home, Hannibal, Missouri. Frank Fretz had mine. Javier had faxed copies.

Alice said, "I didn't receive an envelope. I was the insider that instructed Jay how to obtain the encrypted data from Sheldon Walter's system."

"So, are you in as much danger as Jay was?" I asked.

"Sheldon doesn't know as much as he thinks he does." Alice answered enigmatically.

Louie asked, "How much do you think Val Andrews knows about Jay's whistleblowing activities?" We speculated but had no notion of what had passed between husband and wife before his murder.

"We should tell Val what we think is going on, and why Jay was killed," I said.

"That's for the police," said Hal.

"The less she knows the safer she'll be," insisted Alice. I wasn't sure, but the others were. So, we agreed to keep our own counsel for the present.

We would spend tomorrow at the funeral, followed by a gathering at the Andrews' family home. Alice retired early, apologizing for her aching legs. Hal, Louie, and I settled on the patio to continue our heart-to-heart over red wine and heartplums.

Hal appeared resigned to quitting his job and moving away. Although I didn't see him every day, Hal was my friend. Jovial and flamboyant, he had hosted many parties, shared holidays with my family, and even helped paint my living room. He, Louie, and I had marched together in Chicago's gay pride parades. But things had changed since San Francisco. There was tension between us that had never been there before.

I said, "You two seem safe for the present; better, in fact, than I am. One week without you at the office has been unbearable. Maggie Coutts has your old job, Louie, and she is more intrusive than Squeezy."

"Do you need a rude nickname for her?" Louie asked.

Hal interrupted angrily. "This isn't all about you, Dana! What about my home? My career? This is not the first time I've had to uproot and start over. I had to turn my back on my family and community when I came out. But I don't have a choice about relocating if Louie is going to stay safe."

"You're right Hal. I've been self-absorbed," I apologized.

"Look," he continued. "I don't follow all Louie's conspiracy theories, but I know a threat when I see one. I've learned this much: If you gain access to knowledge the Illuminati doesn't want you to share, they will silence you. If they offer you money, take it and don't look back. If you refuse the money and try to go public with what you know, their next tactic will be to ruin your livelihood, health, relationships, and reputation. If you still don't shut up, they will pull out the big guns. People will die."

"Hal, you're so angry. I feel as though you're blaming me," I said.

"I might as well blame Jay Andrews for being murdered." Hal's words exonerated me, but his tone accused.

Louie said, "Dana, you know that Shelter offered me money to rat you out and to start over in a new community."

"And you took it." It was a statement.

"No, Dana, there was another alternative. I left without accepting a payoff and without providing any false incriminating information about you."

I was stunned. "Does that put you in danger?"

"Not if we never speak of Jay's whistleblowing evidence; not if we lead obscure quiet lives," said Louie.

"We're using our life savings to start over. We're heading to New Orleans," said Hal. Hal was an ER nurse who was in demand everywhere. Louie could find work with another insurance company, ideally, a small, honest one. Hal left us to go shower and get ready for bed.

I whispered to Louie. "I've been back to Tellara since we spoke."

Louie covered his face with his hands. "Dana, your alibi stretches credulity. Don't you trust me with the truth?"

I whispered urgently. "I've offered more than once to take you there. Your skepticism has discouraged me from telling others. Inspector Vazquez insists that I provide my alibi the next time we meet. When he comes to Chicago, I'm taking him to Tellara."

"You're scaring me."

We fell silent and went to our respective rooms to sleep.

The following day, at the funeral, Javier entered the chapel. There he was, in a dark grey suit that matched his eyes. He was here in an official capacity and was made welcome by Jay's greeters. Frank Fretz ingratiated himself into Javier's personal space, hovering, impeding, oozing until Javier's body language forced the FrankenFretz to back off. Although he obliged, Frank was smirking as if he knew something. Javier was working, observing the mourners. His eyes found mine. He tilted his head in greeting. I nodded with a weak smile.

The service was heartbreaking as multiple friends, from his many walks of life, eulogized Jay. The entire Dallas office was present, but Alice was the only Shelter colleague who spoke. Her tribute was eloquent. Louie and I held our peace. Frank Fretz knew to keep his mouth shut. Sheldon Walters was conspicuous by his absence. Vincent and Gwen sat at the very back of the chapel. Wary glances were being directed toward my pew. I was getting used to it.

Or so I thought. At the home reception, I stepped into a minefield. It hadn't occurred to me that my presence would not provide comfort to Jay's loved ones. Because I arrived with Alice, the family received me, but the coldness of their reception was a slap in the face. Jay's mother and father took me aside and tearfully demanded to know why I had come. What purpose could my presence serve? They considered me guilty by innuendo. They physically blocked me from approaching Val and maneuvered me toward the door. Jay's parents turned to Frank Fretz, who put his arms around both their shoulders and escorted them into the living room, where their daughter-in-law sat stoically amid her parents and children. The horror of false accusation settled upon me like a mantle of thorns.

Alice joined me in the foyer. "Dana, Frank Fretz has been poisoning Jay's parents' minds against you all morning. Val doesn't feel that way. She and I speak often. She knows that you and Jay were friends and that you had nothing to do with his death."

I blurted, "What else can she think? We talked about this last night. Either she knows something about his whistleblowing activities, or if not, why wouldn't she suspect me? Everyone else does."

"Not everyone. Not me. Not the real killer. If I had had any idea you were going to be treated like this, I would have told you not to come."

"Thanks for that, Alice, but I better go before anyone else decides to call me a murderer to my face." I was trembling as I walked away from the house.

On the front path, I ran into Vincent and Gwen Cretzky, who were just arriving. Vincent gave me a noncommittal nod. Gwen took my arm and pulled me aside. "I have been wanting to talk to you, Dana. Vincent told me what you said, and I agree, he is at risk."

"I'm glad you're on his side. Shelter doesn't make life easy for its employees."

"You don't know the half of it." Gwen seemed tipsy for early in the day. "Shelter ruined my marriage." I didn't know if she referred to Vincent's affair with Squeezy or his slide into corruption and ignobility.

"Oh, I see what you're thinking. But no, Vincent and I have been sexually indifferent to each other for years. It's the compromise of his integrity that destroyed our marriage. We need to rebuild our partnership if we are to face adversity."

"That's too much information, Gwen."

"I tell you this because we are alike, you and I."

Nothing she said could have surprised me more. I saw no similarity between Gwen's vacant eccentricity and my shoulder-to-the-wheel survival mode.

"We're both dreamers. We don't face unpleasant realities until they're forced down our throats." Much as I hated to admit it, she was right. "Dana, I've always felt we could be friends. But Vincent chooses not to socialize with subordinates."

At that moment Frank Fretz and Jay's father strode down the walkway and physically confronted us, abruptly separating Gwen and me, urging me farther down the front path. "What are you still doing here?" Gwen followed, perplexed and appalled.

"What's going on here?" she demanded in her crisp, patrician voice.

"Stay out of this, Mrs. Cretzky," Frank cautioned. At the curb, my escorts nudged me toward the parked cars. Numbly, I began walking. I didn't have a car. We had carpooled. Louie and Hal ran out to the street to flank me. They had witnessed my humiliating ejection from the gathered mourners. Frank scowled by the white picket fence.

"We'll give you a ride, Dana," Hal offered, squeezing my hand. "It really has been a terrible ordeal for you, hasn't it? It's my turn to apologize." His gentle words after last night's tirade nearly undid me. He walked down the street to his waiting car.

Ignoring Frank Fretz, Gwen called, "Dana, I'll call you. We'll do lunch," I nodded numbly. Gwen rejoined Vincent, and they enter the house.

As Louie and I walked away, we were again waylaid, this time by Javier Vazquez. "Ms. Travers, Mr. Leon, Leaving so soon?"

"I was ejected," I admitted.

Louie said, "Dana is being treated like a pariah, all because you insist on calling her a 'person of interest.' Shelter has persuaded the family to believe the worst."

Javier Vazquez was unmoved. "A more forthcoming alibi would help, Ms. Travers. I can only clear you if you confirm where you were the night Jay was killed."

Vazquez and Louie were eying me intently. Back up by the front gate, so was Frank Fretz. Wasn't I just the proverbial fish in the barrel?

"And you, Mr. Leon, were told to inform me of any departure from your routine. It seems you quit your job and left town."

"It was either leave, implicate Dana, or be implicated myself."

"I still have questions for you."

I interrupted, "You know what? I've got some questions of my own."

"Oh, well, then, by all means, Ms. Travers, ask away."

"Have you learned where and when Jay died?"

"Can't comment on that. Despite pressure from above, I'm no closer to an arrest."

"What were the medical examiner's findings?"

"Since it will be reported in the media, I'll tell you. The cause of death was multiple blunt force trauma to the head."

"Multiple?" The word struck me like blunt force trauma.

"Walk with me," he tilted his head toward Louie and gently guided my arm. We obliged and walked down the manicured suburban road. Inspector Vazquez pulled a folder out of his car. "I received some photographs in the mail the same day I received your fax, Dana. Tell me if you recognize anyone." He showed us a photograph that had been taken outside a San Francisco coffee shop. The photo displayed the storefront window. Phoenix's reflection was visible in the glass. In addition to his reflection, a scrollbar streaming time, date, and temperature reflected a backwards image. It was taken three days before the insurance conference started. There were seven people in the café: Sheldon Walters, a square-faced man seated with him that I didn't recognize, the barista, a petite brunette woman sitting alone across the room, and three teenaged girls engrossed with their cellphones.

"I recognize the photographer. He's the artist whose painting I bought in San Francisco. That's Phoenix!"

"Yes," Louie concurred, "That's Phoenix."

"The photographer? That's who you recognize?" Javier seemed perplexed. "Do you recognize anyone else in this photo?"

"Sheldon Walters, of course."

"Anybody else?"

Louie said, "That husky, flat-faced guy might have been wandering around the Regency during the conference, but I didn't see him speak to anyone. That brunette seems vaguely familiar. I don't know where I've seen her either. The three teenaged girls are unknown to me. No one else, just Sheldon Walters and Phoenix."

The other photo showed the same people only the brunette was handing her business card to Sheldon Walters. "This could help clear me!" I exclaimed. "Who gave you this photograph?"

"It was mailed to me anonymously from Chicago."

"It must have been Phoenix? I'll ask him next time I see him."

"You've been seeing Phoenix?" There was an edge to Javier's question that didn't sound completely procedural.

"We spent Fourth of July together between check-ins with you."

"I don't know what I was expecting from you two, but it wasn't the photographer." He shook his head. "Robles-Leon, have you seen Phoenix since you left San Francisco?"

"Yeah, he was on our flight to Chicago."

Javier turned one of his dark, disconcerting looks on me. "The artist you bought a painting from was on your flight to Chicago and you've seen him several times since? In what capacity are you seeing him?"

"We're just *friends*." I instilled as much innuendo as I could into the word.

Louie glared at me. "You've been seeing Phoenix?"

"Yes, and Saffron."

"Did Phoenix know Jay Andrews?"

"No, Jay and Alice went back to the hotel while Louie and I browsed his gallery."

Louie asked, "Why do you suppose Phoenix took this picture? Why would he give the police a photo that retained his own image?"

"Phoenix took pictures all over the city, like any tourist." But I was perplexed. How many times had he traveled back and forth through my condo.

Javier changed the subject, "Have you heard of a law firm called Waldo Mannheim & Peters?"

"They've been hired to investigate Shelter's corporate crimes," answered Louie.

Javier explained, "Their investigators work up the chain. They flip lower level managers by giving them immunity. Those managers then reveal dirt on upper level executives. The higher the rank, the higher the crimes."

"I thought they were mostly ambulance chasers who represent clients suing over wrongfully denied claims," I said.

Javier nodded, "That's one of their functions. Here's how it works. Waldo Mannheim & Peters are ambulance chasers, not just for clients appealing Shelter, but for anybody with an insurance claim lawsuit. If the claim is with another insurance company, they pull out all the stops to win. Shelter operatives research loopholes to undermine other insurance companies' cases. Then, Shelter gets a cut. When the plaintiff is a Shelter client, Waldo Mannheim & Peters throw the case..."

"Really?" I asked.

"Most of the time. They lose once in a while for smaller judgments. It keeps the statistics tidy. Win or lose, Shelter gets payback on almost every settlement."

"How do you know all this?" I asked.

Javier gave me an exasperated look. "I'm a detective, Dana. In the past, in order to have immunity with the Justice Department, corporations had to waive attorney-client privilege."

"In the past?" Louie asked.

"After a massive lobbying effort by businesses and attorneys, corporations can now hire law firms to internally investigate suspected wrongdoing. Companies decide for themselves what to divulge, and what to withhold, from the Justice Department."

"And they cherry-pick that information," Louie said.

"Indeed," said Javier, "effectively hamstringing the Justice Department, which then settles for fines against the corporation, rather than bringing criminal charges against individual executives. Unless said corporation wants a fall guy."

"Poor Vincent Cretzky," I said.

"Why Cretzky, and not you, Dana?" asked Javier.

"Shelter is doing everything it can to implicate me in Jay's murder. Waldo Mannheim & Peters are investigating Vincent for fraud. He told me so himself."

Louie said, "Inspector, we've been anticipating a federal investigation into Shelter's evading regulations. But even if Shelter is spinning their internal investigation, how does that help solve Jay Andrews' murder?"

"Shelter is looking for PR, not justice. Also, if fraud can be revealed, another possible motive arises… another possible suspect."

"To deflect attention away from the documents that incriminate Sheldon Walters. I suspected something like this when I warned Vincent," I said.

"Do I know you at all?" Louie asked me. "When did you warn him?"

"When we upgraded him from reptile to rodent."

Javier reined us in. "It's a valid theory, but it doesn't clear you, Dana. Sure, Shelter wants to steer the investigation. But if you want to extricate yourself from their crosshairs, you need an airtight alibi."

"My alibi is at my condo."

"In Chicago? Not in San Francisco?" He stepped closer to me.

"At my home in Chicago, I'll show you my alibi there." I backed up until I was against his car.

He stepped into my personal space and I felt flustered and weak kneed. "Then, as soon as I finish here, I'll be coming. To Chicago. To your condo. To obtain your alibi. Understand, Dana?"

"Understood, Javier."

"Will Phoenix be there?" he asked coolly.

"He might be." We were staring into each other's eyes, and this time, I did not look away. I was going to show Javier Vazquez the portal to Tellara.

"I'd like a few words with Phoenix myself," said Louie, disconcerted that I had a social life he knew nothing about, and with the guy he thought fancied him, no less.

Javier and I weren't listening to Louie. "You will show me your alibi, Dana."

"And you can tell me whether or not it's airtight, Javier." I was referring to Tellara, but his pupils dilated, and I realized his thoughts took a different turn.

Before I could fumble my way out of the awkward moment, there was a commotion nearby. Frank Fretz was no longer alone. Two men in black suits wearing black sunglasses now accompanied him. They approached us. Javier stepped away from the car and I sidled up alongside Louie. The men in black whipped out badges and the tall one announced, "FBI. We'll be taking over the investigation of Jay Andrews' murder." Their badges identified them as Agents Contreras and Pandomi.

"Contrary and Pandemonium," Louie whispered in my ear. We anticipated a federal investigation into Shelter's fraud, but I was fairly certain that a change of jurisdiction in a murder investigation didn't usually happen in front of suspects and witnesses. What did I know?

Javier spoke, "Not until I get the documents Jay Andrews mailed to Dana Travers the night he died. Mr. Fretz, I still have questions for you." He handed Frank Fretz what I assumed to be a warrant or subpoena or some such.

"Documents, what documents?" Frank Fretz dissembled.

"Shelter spreadsheets documenting Sheldon Walters' quid pro quos with business leaders and politicians, the documents someone at Shelter faxed me." Frank Fretz shot me a look filled with so much rage that I was surprised my hair didn't burst into flames. Javier didn't miss that furious exchange. "Have you been planning to withhold material evidence from an ongoing murder investigation, Mr. Fretz?"

"Not from the FBI. It's the very evidence you speak of that implicates elected officials that makes this a federal matter." Frank nodded toward the men in black.

"Turn your case files over to us, Inspector Vazquez," said Pandemonium, the short, brutish agent. "Then leave." Turning to Louie, "We don't need you anymore, Mr. Leon. You're free to go."

"Ms. Travers and I are not done with our conversation," Javier objected.

"You are done." We were informed by Contrary, the tall, haughty agent. "Ms. Travers, we would like a few words with you. Now."

"Not without a lawyer present," I balked.

"You'll talk to Vazquez, but not to us?" Pandemonium challenged.

"The lady wants a lawyer," said Javier.

"It's in the Constitution," said Louie. "Look it up."

The FBI men looked like they wanted to push it, but then backed off. Maybe it was because another law enforcement officer was present, or maybe it was because they were stepping on jurisdictional toes. "We'll be in your office, in Chicago, first thing Monday morning. Bring your lawyer." I mutely nodded my agreement.

The men in black walked away with Frank Fretz.

"I'm still coming to your condo tomorrow. If you have a valid alibi, I'll make certain those agents can't bury it." Javier said quietly. I nodded my mute compliance. Once I showed him Tellara, he could corroborate my alibi with Saffron. Tomorrow couldn't come soon enough. We made final eye contact before he walked toward the house to play nice with his FBI counterparts.

Louie and I jumped into the car, where Hal was waiting. I was going to have to find a lawyer. But first, I wanted to get to Tellara and get some answers from Phoenix. We drove to Alice's house, where I grabbed my overnight bag and Hal disembarked. Louie drove me to the airport to catch the next flight to Chicago.

"Louie, there's another petite brunette in Phoenix's pictures."

"Yeah, and a witness saw Jay talking to a petite brunette the night he was murdered."

Javier will see the portal tomorrow. Come to Tellara with us."

"Hal and I don't plan to return to Chicago. Hey, why are you crying?"

My words burst out in one ragged breath. "Jay's dead! Val's a widow. His family thinks I'm involved in his murder. I was physically barred from paying my condolences. My cube's been searched. You left Shelter to protect yourself. The office is filled with reptiles who are rejoicing in my disgrace. FrankenFretz's legal tips are veiled threats. Alice is painfully circumspect about her role at Shelter. Maggie Coutts is gleefully denying legitimate claims. The sad, sick joke is that, in a healthy corporation, the person I would complain to would be the Director of Human Resources. In Shelter's case, that's Squeezy the Evil Lizard Queen. Searching my cube was just the tip of her cold-blooded talons. Vincent is rediscovering his humanity just in time to be the fall guy for all of Shelter's corporate fraud. You disbelieve my sojourns to Tellara and won't even come to my condo to see the portal. Hal half-blames me for upending his life. Javier Vazquez ceaselessly tracks my location, limiting my freedom. My kids' lives are moving on without me. The real killer is out there, and we now know what Jay knew, so we're in as much danger as he was. Men in Black are coming to the office on Monday to interrogate me, so I need to find a lawyer in the next few days. On this side of Tellara, I am destroyed." I paused for a breath. "Except for strange, dubious, medicated Gwen Cretzky, who wants to be my friend because we both have trouble dealing with reality. Not to mention, my kitchen sink is backed up! My world is ripping in half."

Louie took a deep breath, "Jesus, what a clusterfuck. Those weird FBI guys seemed to have an agenda that had nothing to do with truth or justice."

"Tell me about it! You did the right thing by leaving Shelter. But you're wrong to doubt Tellara's existence. When I get back there, I may not return to Earth. Oh, except the Tellarans want me to tell everybody on Earth how we must become an enlightened species in order to survive the pending planetary shift." I snorted between sobs.

"Whoa, what? Wait, planetary shift?"

"Yeah, some big confluence of cycles at all scales is coming and is gonna shake things up big time. End time prophecy stuff."

"Dana, why didn't you tell me before that planetary cycles were involved?"

"I was busy being a person of interest in a murder investigation."

"Shit, you're wearing down my skepticism. I am your friend and I owe you the benefit of the doubt. You've stood up for me when others condemned. I'll persuade Hal to come to your condo." My tears were drying. Louie was getting misty-eyed.

"Remember my Tellaran technology? I haven't given up on trying to convince you, but my vox doesn't work when I'm upset." I gave him a demonstration of its light powers. His eyes on the road, he was underwhelmed by my flashlight. I focused on Saffron. Her image appeared on the vox view screen. "Saffron is in her garden."

"I'm driving," Louie barely glanced. "This could be a video of anyone from anywhere." Arriving at the airport, we pulled into the departure zone. "Let me try," said Louie reaching for the vox.

"It won't work for you. It's attuned to my DNA."

"Of course, it is."

I decided to cloak myself right here and now in the Dallas Airport passenger drop zone. Before I could move the dials, a loud smack on our windshield broke my concentration.

"No parking. Drop off and move along," a security guard shouted and punctuated his order with another loud crack to the car window. Louie and I made brief eye contact, his expression considering; mine, hopeful. I hugged him, stowed my vox, and exited the car with my overnight bag. He drove off slowly, watching me in his rearview mirror until he turned out of sight. "Come to Chicago," I mouthed, half prayer, half demand.

CHAPTER 8

I rebooked my flight from Sunday afternoon to tonight's red-eye but managed to secure the last stand-by seat on a 6:30 flight. That would put me on the ground in Chicago just before 9:00 P.M. I was a wreck on the flight and drove home in a stupor. At least I could spend Sunday in Tellara. At home, I dropped my bags and flopped on the couch. Sitting across from *Summer in Tellara*, I prepared to dash into my trans-dimensional sanctuary.

There were scuffling noises in my kitchen, then gruff masculine voices. I wasn't alone. Two men emerged into my living room. I reached for the vox, thinking to cloak and dive through the painting, but hesitated a moment too long. There stood the flat-faced, burly thug from Javier's coffee shop photo.

"She was booked on the red-eye, Kek," said his skinny partner-in-crime.

"Shut up, asshole," said Flatface. The men wore latex gloves, like what you see at a crime scene on TV. They'd been searching my condo. There was nothing of interest or value except my basket of heartplums and *Summer in Tellara*. But heartplums look like plums and the painting is one of many on my walls. Still, Skinny had a camera around his neck and was carrying stacks of papers from my piles of files.

"What's going on?" I asked nervously.

"Get out," Flatface told Skinny. Skinny fled and I heard a motorcycle rev up. Then Flatface stalked toward me. I backed up until I hit the wall, cornered.

"You can go now," I twittered hysterically. His hands were coming toward me and I screamed for all I was worth. My scream was cut off mid-choke and I slid down the wall to a heap on the floor.

"Bitch!" he whispered, his hot, stinky breath in my face. He wrenched my neck, cutting off my breath. "Tellara!" I thought frantically as my view dimmed. I writhed under his death grip. I thought of my children. I thought of Rip. Even now, I thought I could hear dogs barking. Through the haze of my oxygen-deprived vision, I beheld the face of my killer. His flesh phased out and a scaly reptilian visage emerged. His irises were vertical slits in malevolent eyes.

Dogs *were* barking, and the next moment, I was gulping great, burning swallows of air, gasping while rolling away from the commotion. My assailant was fighting off Rip and Belle. Jesse heaved his largest kitchen knife and stabbed Flatface hard and deep in the ribs. He kicked him there for good measure while yanking the blade out. The reptile stood up and shoved Jesse away forcefully. Belle went for Flatface's throat. Canine teeth drew reptilian blood until Belle was thrown into a wall. Rip barked, growled, and ran circles around Flatface, who was bleeding from the neck and side.

"The police are on their way!" Jesse yelled as he heaved himself onto the bleeding reptile's back and took him down again. Flatface wrestled the knife from Jesse's hands and began slicing the air blindly.

We heard sirens. "Get out," Jesse screamed. Belle recovered and bit Flatface's left calf. While Flatface ripped Belle off his left leg, Rip urinated on his right ankle. I stood, grabbed a ceramic vase, and brought it down on Flatface's head with all my might. He didn't even stumble but turned and slashed the knife at my face. I ducked as he lunged and plunged a vicious gash through *Summer in Tellara*, shredding the canvas in two. I screamed but only a squeak emerged from my crushed throat. The Reptile limped towards the door, leaving a trail of blood on my hardwood floor.

We heard a motorcycle rev up and speed off. How had I not noticed those effing motorcycles? They must have been parked in the shadows while I ambled across my driveway in a fog. I slumped, stunned, on the floor. The dogs licked me. I cried without tears or sobs because my throat was so tight nothing would come. Jesse recovered the paperwork Skinny had dropped. Limping and cradling his ribs, he sat by my side and we looked through my papers together to see what the thugs were after.

The police arrived. There was evidence of violent wreckage all over the living room. They took samples of my assailant's blood. They walked around, looked underneath everything, dusted for fingerprints, took notes and photos, and bagged evidence. They asked if anything had been taken. The answer was an ambiguous no; unless they counted photographs of my 401K, insurance records, credit card and mortgage statements, my children's addresses, all our social security numbers, and my Christmas card mailing list.

They asked, "Why would anybody search your possessions, Ms. Travers? Do you have any enemies?"

I dissembled stupidly, writing—because I was unable to speak, "I'm having some problems at work." I didn't feel like going into the fact that I was a person of interest in a homicide investigation in another state and that I suspected that my company was trying to frame me. But they badgered me until I disclosed all my legal woes.

I wrote, "I am a person of interest in a murder investigation. But the real killer is framing me. I think he was the guy who just tried to kill me." I covered my throat protectively.

"Do you know his name?" one cop asked.

I wrote, "The skinny one called the big one Kek and gave them Javier Vazquez's card. An out-of-town police inspector could explain matters to my local police. The cops said it looked like the intruders had been searching for something they'd not found. They weren't unkind, but they were procedural to the point of indifference. While stretching yellow 'crime scene' tape across my door, they told me to go to the emergency room to have my throat checked out and then find somewhere safe to stay for a few nights. But also, to "keep in touch," those ominous words again. I now had made promises to keep in touch with the San Francisco Police, the FBI, and the Chicago Police. I was a popular girl with law enforcement.

I needed to completely disrupt my children's lives for the foreseeable future. I needed to see if *Summer in Tellara* would still function as a portal. I own three turtlenecks and Jesse had packed them all in an emergency travel kit. I pulled out a wad of bills I kept stashed in my teakettle. Jesse went to his studio to pack his essentials. Then, he called his sister and told her what had happened. "You're not safe at home. We're coming to get you. We'll be there in half an hour. Pack a bag."

Jesse herded the dogs into his car. He threw his backpack and my suitcase into the trunk, grabbed some water bottles and food. We pooled our money. I wrapped *Summer in Tellara* in a blanket and set it in the back seat. We were off. I clutched my vox in one hand and cradled the basket of heartplums on my lap with the other. I sucked the nectar from several heartplums while we drove. I couldn't even swallow the pulp.

I checked myself in the rearview mirror and saw dark angry bruises and red welts swelling up on my neck. My voice cracked whenever I tried to speak. I thought my larynx had been bruised.

"We need to get you to a doctor," Jesse said.

"No Jess," I rasped, "We need to get Ruth and find a secure place to think. The thugs searching my apartment know where you both live. Neither of you are safe."

"Then stop trying to talk, Mom," Jesse admonished.

We arrived at Ruth's condo in Chicago around four o'clock Sunday morning. Had it just been since yesterday morning that my world turned upside down? Had it just been a month ago that my biggest problem was my dislike of my morally ambiguous boss and his cold-blooded, hotter-than-shit girlfriend?

Jesse explained to Ruth what had happened and that we needed time and a place to consider what to do. I wrote a note that the police have no interest in my kids, unless they know you are aiding and abetting me as a fugitive. But the Shelter hit men might come at me through my kids.

"We could call Dad," Ruth suggested.

Jesse vetoed that. "We can't contact anyone in any of our address books." It's hard to come up with an intimate, trusted friend willing to put themselves in danger for you and your family when you don't know them well enough to list them in your address book. Regardless of our destination, we needed to get away from Chicago. "And Ruthie, bring as much money as you can get your hands on," Jesse urged.

Ruth became thoughtful and said, "I have an idea."

"What?" Jesse asked.

"Well, it's against company policy to date co-workers, but I've been seeing Mick on the q-t. We drove out to his family's cabin on the lake last weekend. I think I could find it again. Or we could just rent a cabin in the boonies."

"We need to hoard our cash and we may as well cut up our credit cards." Jesse said. "Your friend's place sounds like a good idea if it's remote from neighbors."

"Yeah, it's remote."

"Well then, let's get going. How much money can you get your hands on in the wee hours of a Sunday?"

"We'll hit a neighborhood ATM, and each take out our limit."

Later that morning, we stopped at an 'ask-no-questions' cash for clunkers' dealership in a shady part of the city. Jesse conducted the negotiation and used up most of our cash to purchase a beat up 1993 green Infiniti sedan with 156,000 miles on its odometer. We drove both vehicles to O'Hare Airport and left my Accord in long-term parking, hoping it would delay people trying to track us down. Law enforcement would probably not be checking for green Infinities. Ruth and I moved all our provisions and the dogs into the Infiniti. We headed out of town on 94 North toward Fond du Lac, Wisconsin. Fleeing with my children would play into my accuser's hands, but I didn't see that we had a choice.

Ruth left a message at work that her mother was ailing, and she needed some emergency family sick time. Jesse could work anywhere with his art supplies. He called his director and said he'd be helping his ailing mother for a while. The way my children described me, I sounded ninety and feeble. I felt and looked like a punching bag that had been dragged over gravel. Sandwiched between the dogs in the back seat, I cradled my rent canvas, my heartplums, and my vox.

At sunrise, my cell phone rang. It was Javier Vazquez. I could not talk, so Jesse put the phone on speaker and spoke for me while Ruth drove.

"Dana, I am at your house and you're not here. We had an understanding."

"This is Dana's son. Shelter thugs choked my mother. Check with the local police."

"Dana, are you all right?"

Jesse bit off his angry retort. "No, she is not all right. A man tried to kill her. He choked her nearly to death. The local police told her to find a safe house."

"Do you know anything about Louie Leon's whereabouts? The FBI let him go, but I don't trust Shelter."

I scribbled on a notepad, "Maybe heading to Chicago, maybe New Orleans."

Jesse relayed the message.

"Dana, get a good lawyer. Since you're not here to show me your alibi, you're going to be charged with murder tomorrow. You're going to be arrested." Silence. "Dana, are you there?" Javier persisted. "Dana, turn yourself in. I can protect you."

"Not gonna happen," I croaked. "You can't protect me!"

"Dana! Is that your voice?" Javier shouted into the phone.

"Yes!" shouted Ruth and Jesse together.

"If you're really not coming back, I can get you to a safe house."

"No!" they shouted together again.

Jesse said, "You're an officer of the law. You can't aid and abet a fugitive."

"But you can?" Javier challenged.

"Mom thinks the thugs who searched her place and assaulted her could try to get to her through us."

"Dana, do you know who attacked you?"

I wrote and Jesse read, "The man with the flatface in your photo."

"Toss your phones and don't use credit cards. Call me in two days. Dana, for what it's worth, I know you didn't kill Jay Andrews. I just wish you could have trusted me with your alibi."

"We're beyond that now," I rasped, caressing *Summer in Tellara*.

"If you turn yourself in to me, I can protect you."

Without answering, Jesse rang off and told us to hand him our cell phones. We obliged. He removed the batteries and put the three dead phones in the glove box. I was officially a fugitive, running for my life and running from the law. My children were aiding and abetting.

It was midday when we arrived at the cabin. Jesse shook me awake. Ruth went off to find the key Mick kept hidden under a rock. We trudged in, carrying our bags and my painting. The dogs raced about our feet, leaping and barking. This was canine heaven. They smelled everything in the vicinity and raced around to share the new smells with each other. At last, we got them inside with the promise of food. Ruth heated up some broth, which I slurped slowly. I could taste blood at the back of my throat. Maybe I should have gone to the hospital.

"Mom, you know we're behind you one hundred percent," Jesse began. "It's time to tell us what is going on."

I nodded and began a combination charades, pictures, and note-writing explanation of my visit to Tellara via the painting, and my incredible alibi. I set the painting on the hearth and tried to enter the portal. Nothing happened. My worst fear was realized. Access to Tellara was cut off. I slipped my precious vox up from under my turtleneck. I showed the golden rectangle to my kids and ran my fingers along the geometric configuration of crystals.

"Please tell me that isn't a cell phone," Ruth groaned.

I wrote: "Technology from Tellara. It is the alternate world I was visiting when Jay was killed. Tellara is my alibi." I gestured toward the painting, *Summer in Tellara*. My kids looked at me with slack-jawed incredulity. Before they could tell me they thought I was insane, I shut their mouths by manipulating a star sapphire and a rose quartz. I levitated several feet above my comfy chair. The dogs barked and raced about beneath me. Jesse and Ruth stood and moved over to touch me. I cloaked and maneuvered myself over by the kitchen counter. I made myself visible again and clapped my hands. They turned toward me, stunned.

"What else does your pendant do, Mom?" asked Ruth.

"It's called a vox, short for voxel."

"Voxel?"

I had to write and mime, "Like pixel, only with volume. It cloaks, or as Phoenix says, makes one undetectable to all sensory preceptors. It levitates people or things. I can glide horizontally, only that's harder. You have to resist the temptation to swim and use your thoughts to propel your body." I mimed the breaststroke, then illuminated the cabin. "It creates fields of light and heat, although I've had little use for those, or for the cutting function. It makes a beam that slices through rock or most anything without generating light, heat, or sound. Phoenix uses it to sculpt. And it remote views whatever you focus on. Apparently, it runs on perpetual energy."

"Can it heal your throat?"

I shook my head 'no' and wrote, "It can't heal the painting either. It does what it does. It's technology, not magic."

"It's one of those sufficiently advanced technological devices that appears like magic to us primitives," quipped Jesse.

Next, I demonstrated remote viewing by focusing on someone we all knew well, my ex-husband, Nick, the children's father. I thought of him rarely and with little intention, but this afternoon, I was able to bring in a clear image of Nate watching a baseball game while sipping a beer. He was alone in the room, his third wife not sharing his interest in sports. The TV screen showed the uniform colors, white with red and blue with red. Braves and Cubs, Jesse nodded. "That's today's game."

Then I thought of Louie. Louie and Hal came into focus. They were driving along a rural mountain byway, through steep, wooded terrain. They were traveling at a good clip past evergreens, cypress trees, small farmhouses, and steep hills. I expanded the vox view screen to a wide radius revealing a parallel road. A car appeared to be shadowing them. I peered into the pursuing vehicle. To my horror, there sat Flatface and Skinny. Jesse recognized Flatface too. After leaving my condo, they had made quick time south. Did Louie and Hal know they were being tracked? Hal drove off-road gravel byways he'd navigated since childhood. His pursuers could barely track their signal much less access these hidden lanes.

I needed to warn Louie and Hal. I swallowed some pain medication dissolved in water, wishing it were a suppository, and found a bed. The kids stayed up and I could hear them talking on and off for several hours.

At first light, I realized that Mick kept a computer at his cabin. The kids had found it the previous night. "Did you go on any social networks?" I wrote.

"No," Ruth told me. "No personal data, email, or Facespace. Just checked out the baseball game and then watched some YouTube videos about alternate realities.

"But we did come up with a good idea for staying in touch. We'll join Facespace with aliases. We'll have no other friends, no pictures, and maximum privacy settings."

I wrote, 'Curly, Larry, and Moe.'

"Good one, Mom," Ruth smiled.

'I call Curly,' I wrote.

"Not fair. I want to be Curly," burst out Ruth. I made a moue that let her know it was too late.

"Fine, I'll be Moe," she conceded.

"And I guess that makes me Larry," said Jesse. So, we became Curly, Larry, and Moe Stooge, with spiffy alias Gmail addresses.

I pulled out my vox and remote-viewed Phoenix's San Francisco Art Gallery. If I could contact him, maybe he could help me get to the next portal in Cairo in time for *Tellaran Autumn* to open. Phoenix's Gallery was not there. The recessed, grated doorway displayed lettering for Taco Palacio, a cozy taqueria with a salsa bar, baskets of chips, and plates of steaming rice, beans, burritos, and enchiladas. I could almost smell the food and hear the fiesta music as gaily dressed waitresses swept past customers. I backed out, viewed up, down and around Union Square; nope, no Phoenix Art Gallery. I kept focusing on Phoenix, and finally, his image clarified in Giza, Tellara. He was painting.

I was stranded Earthside and had to get to Cairo and connect with Phoenix by the *Tellaran Autumn*. That was a dilemma for the day after tomorrow. Today, I desperately needed rest, but could only spare a few hours before driving to help Louie elude Flatface. Ruth wanted me to call law enforcement and tell them that a killer was tracking Louie. But I explained half-pantomime, half-writing that Shelter could twist the truth and deliver Louie and Hal into the arms of Flatface.

Jesse went into the Village and stocked up on provisions for humans and canines. He gave me most of his remaining money, $308. I tried to give him back half, but he reckoned I'd need gas money and my business was cash and carry. I took a long, lingering look at my ruined canvas of *Summer in Tellara*. We'd hung it above the cabin mantel. It dominated the room. Jesse and Ruth would be safest at the cabin for the time being. They'd be stranded until Mick came up. If they came with me, from this point forward, they'd be targets, either for aiding and abetting their fugitive mother or as prey for Shelter thugs.

My throat was a little better. I drank tea and ate some soft oatmeal with lots of butter, sugar, and milk. I could swallow with discomfort, and Ruth made me force down some analgesic tea. I was going to take the only car. I wrote, "Keep the painting safe and transport it to Phoenix's house in Mount Shasta. I'll notify you the exact address."

They were worried about me. But I had a plan and a well-packed survival kit, including heartplums, water, and energy bars. And I had my vox. My plan was to get to Louie and Hal, recover Louie's copy of incriminating Shelter papers, and release them to an independent media outlet. After that, Louie and Hal could hole up somewhere while we plotted our next move. I kissed my children and our dogs goodbye, got behind the wheel of the green Infiniti, and set off for the back roads of Missouri. I feared my flight from the law would play right into Shelter's hands. But, like the song says, "It's too late to turn back now."

Louie and Hal were still driving along unpaved, one-lane roads through the hills, woods, and glens. I was able to zoom in on a road map in Louie's lap and determined they were in the Ozarks. I pulled back, seeking their pursuers. They were parked along a distant, parallel dirt road, analyzing a GPS screen.

It took me seven hours driving to meet up with Louie and Hal. They weren't expecting me, and I couldn't risk calling them and alerting Flatface to another presence in the vicinity. Their pursuers were now within a ten-mile radius, zigzagging through brush in a newly acquired land rover. How did they do that? Reptilian technology? I needed to get to Louie before the Shelter assailants.

I caught up with them along a nondescript dirt lane. Their branch-covered car was parked in the woods. I copied their strategy and covered my car with brush. When there weren't enough downed branches, I cut more using the vox. Grabbing my backpack, I set off on foot. There was no trail, so I stumbled through bramble and brush.

They were moving slowly. I caught up close enough to see that Hal was limping and Louie half-carrying him. I called softly to them with my raspy voice. Louie turned at his name and they halted. I moved into the open near them. He saw me and started.

"I thought it was my imagination," he said.

"I was choked," I rasped. I moved toward them and I lent my support to Hal.

"What happened?" he asked.

I pulled down my turtleneck to reveal the swollen brown, black, and blue bruises. "You're being pursued by the guy that did this. He was the flat-faced guy in Javier's photo. I tracked you with my vox."

"We were run into a ditch by the guy in the photo. We returned the gesture and rammed their car into a ravine. Hal directed me to these remote woods, but they can't be far away." Hal appeared to have bruised or broken ribs, a badly bruised leg, and a swollen ankle. "Hal knows a cave near here. We need to rest and hide. He can't move." Hal was barely conscious.

"Do you have your cell phones with you?" I asked.

"Long since ditched, compliments of your favorite conspirisist," Louie said.

The three of us bundled off to Hal's hidden cave.

Hal said, "I used to camp here as a kid. You have to know the cave is there to find it. A spring drips fresh water down one wall. It drains somewhere underground. Otherwise, the cave is dry and opens into a few back tunnels."

The cave entrance was concealed within the crevice of a moss- and ivy-covered rock face at the bottom of a cliff. Overhanging shrubs and branches drooped to the ground. The opening was at ground level, with a narrow, horizontal entry through which we had to slither. We half-dragged Hal inside. He moaned but assisted us by scooching his butt and pushing with his feet. While Louie laid Hal gently on the rock floor, covered him with a thermal blanket, and did a first aid assessment, I pulled out my vox and searched for our pursuer's vehicle. I located them quickly because I zoned in on Flatface. Their car was still in a ravine, but reinforcements had joined them in a Jeep. A few minutes later, they found Hal's car, but not mine. The little green Infiniti blended into the foliage. No one was looking for me in Missouri, but they'd find it soon enough. We needed to buy time to get Hal medical attention. Flatface, Skinny, and the two other thugs were obviously not expert trackers, despite whatever reptilian senses or technology they possessed. They wandered through the woods. This gave me time to hatch an insane plan.

"Louie, you tend to Hal while I seal the opening to the cave." I directed the cutting tool of the vox at an interior wall and began to cut out rocks to stack, fit and cover the entryway. I fit stones, one upon another, until the deep, narrow crevice was blocked. Then I cut an even larger piece to match the size and shape of the opening. I levitated it toward the stone wall and fitted it snugly behind the smaller stones. From the outside, the stones appeared to be a solid rock wall against a solid moss-covered rock face; at least, so I hoped. I turned and sat with a huff, quite spent from my stone masonry endeavors. Louie and Hal were staring.

"I have a lot to tell you," I rasped.

"I guess," said Louie. "Tellaran technology?"

I nodded, holding up my vox.

Hal groaned. I held the vox as a light while Louie searched through my pack and found some codeine and a water bottle. "I can't tell if there is any internal bleeding. If not, you're banged up, but nothing is broken. You're not concussed."

"You first," Hal nodded weakly toward me. I understood him to mean that we both had news, but their update could wait until I did some explaining about the stone masonry and how I'd found them. My throat had had only a day to rest, but I forced myself to whisper, and rest between words.

"You remember my vox?" I held it up for Hal and Louie's inspection. "It cuts, cloaks, and levitates. I used it to remote view you. That's how I found you."

Louie asked, "That's the technology from the alternate dimension you've been visiting?"

I demonstrated the vox's various capabilities while whispering what happened when I returned home after the funeral. "The reptile who choked me slashed *Summer in Tellara*." I mimed choking and slashing. "The portal doesn't work anymore. Phoenix is painting another portal, but it won't be ready until the autumn equinox and I have to get to Cairo to find him." I handed each of them a heartplum and slowly sucked on one myself.

CHAPTER 9

"Rest your voice, Dana." Louie took over their narrative. "We'd planned for a road trip, with money and camping supplies, leaving Dallas for Chicago."

"Chicago?" I squeaked.

"That's right, I convinced Hal to go to your place to check out your alternate-world alibi. When we got there, we saw the crime scene tape and that your condo was dark and empty, so we turned around and headed south. Soon, we realized we were being followed."

"How?"

"Some guys were lurking at the edge of your property when we got there. They sped off in a little brown turdmobile. We kept seeing the turdmobile and became suspicious. We took a circuitous route to the Ozarks, staying off the major highways. Hal grew up here and spent a lot of time off-roading as a kid. After a while, we thought we'd lost them."

"They killed Jay and framed you." Hal spoke through labored breathing. I held his hand and felt it go limp. Then he passed out. Louie and I fell silent. Hal's rapid breathing was the only noise in the cave.

I used the vox to remote view the woods just beyond the cave. The foliage outside our wall came into focus. Our pursuers stood not ten feet away, looking high and low, separated from us by two feet of solid rock only recently fitted into a crevasse. They brushed aside branches and foliage on all sides of the rock face for a good ten minutes. Then they moved on. We monitored them with the vox. As afternoon turned to evening, they returned to their Jeep.

A few hours later we heard voices and dogs in the woods outside our cave wall. I turned on the vox and we watched in horror as men moved the branches to reveal the solid stone wall I had cut and wedged into the cave mouth. The edifice held up under their inspection despite the dogs' insistence that our scent ended here. After all, a rock wall is a rock wall. The seal was seamless. They knew the region was riddled with caves, and began searching the environs, trapping us while Hal grew weaker. I now feared internal bleeding. All through the night, foliage was ripped and trampled, rocks were smashed. In the morning they regrouped and spent the day mounting some kind of sensor towers throughout the woods.

There were eight pursuers in the woods, all human, except two dogs, and two reptiles, Flatface, and Skinny. I showed Louie his image on the vox screen and he saw the reptilian visage. Louie, who had researched UFOs for years, was horrified at his first real look at the scaly, flat-faced, slit-eyed creep on the view screen. "That's the guy in Javier's photo."

"That skinny guy called him Kek, the one I called Flatface," I said.

Louie exhaled, "I was right. Shelter is run by reptilians."

"He choked me and ran you off the road."

"We need to get Hal medical help. As soon as he stabilizes, the three of us are going to your elusive Tellara."

"I told you, *Summer in Tellara* won't work. Flatface slashed it. We have to get to Cairo."

"Cairo, Egypt? In the Middle East?"

"There's another Cairo?"

"Cairo, Missouri, Cairo Illinois, Cairo, Mars."

"We need to get to Egypt."

"I'm sorry I didn't believe you. Let's assess our situation and resources."

I laid out my pack of survival gear that the kids had helped prepare at the cabin. "The kids! The cabin!" I thought with a start and tuned into them while Louie rifled through my provisions. They were sitting around a cozy fire in the log home. Ruth was working on a laptop, maybe Facespaceing Curly Stooge. I could not reply. Jesse was sipping beer with a dark-haired guy. It must be Ruth's beau, Mick. Watching the guys drink beer made me thirsty, so I filled the water bottle with the cool spring water that seeped over the rocks. As soon as the bottle was half full, I gulped it down and then refilled it for Louie.

While Louie drank, he continued with his story. "When I returned to Alice's house after dropping you at the airport, Hal told me that her house had been searched while we were at the memorial. Hal happened upon them and they fled. So, when we saw your place, we knew they were after Jay's documents. These thugs don't seem to know their right hand from their left. FrankenFretz kicks us out of the memorial and doesn't notify his 'break and enter' crew."

"They thought I'd be on the redeye."

"Maybe there are factions within the reptile hierarchy that don't cooperate. Hal was horrified by this further invasion by Shelter. But they never found my packet. We stashed it, before the funeral, right here in this cave."

"Here?" I was incredulous.

"In a cleft over by that wall." Louie pointed. "Anyone Shelter suspects of having Jay's documents isn't safe, no matter what those FBI jerks said. Shelter wants us dead. Alice and I realized that if we want to live, we'll have to become highly visible whistle blowers."

"My thoughts exactly. Where is Alice?"

"She insisted she'd be safe at home. At that point, I urgently wanted to get to Chicago and your Tellara. When that option was closed to us, we hightailed it for the hills. We've been on the run ever since."

We continued with our inventory. Louie's money belt contained fifty-nine thousand dollars, a reasonable amount of money for three people on the run, but worthless with one of them badly injured, and all of them trapped in a cave for however long. Besides the money, Hal and Louie had camping provisions, including food, blankets, bottled water, and clothing. I had several dozen heartplums and a 24 pack of nutrition bars. I had a first aid kit that contained painkillers, antibiotics, and bandages. I brought a change of clothing, a blanket, socks and underwear, my water bottle, a dispenser of sani-wipes, and a lighter.

We had enough provisions to last for a week, maybe longer if we rationed. The sensors outside our cave wall were ominously unblinking. I shook my head, "We're gonna have to find another way out. I have an idea. I'll find a passage and cloak us. We'll levitate beyond the sensors."

"Maybe it'll work. I gotta tend to Hal, but first I gotta pee." Louie moved to one of the back tunnels to relieve his bladder. We didn't know whether or not to wake Hal to give him antibiotics and water. But a few hours later, Hal wet himself and we became alarmed. Hal was an experienced nurse and could tell us what to do. It took an effort to wake him, during which Louie became frantic.

Finally, Hal was lucid but weak. At first, he declined medication. "Don't be stoic," Louie admonished. "It's not stoicism," Hal argued, but weakly let Louie give him painkillers and antibiotics. "What should we do?" Louie asked choking back tears. "Keep me warm," Hal whispered. "I'm bleeding into my abdominal cavity. I'm a nurse, kids. I know a fatal injury when it happens. If you try to escape and save me, we'll all die."

"No!" Louie argued. "Dana says we can cloak and levitate past the lookouts."

"To where? They'll find us in any hospital. Louie, listen," Hal groaned. "Turn me on my side." We rolled him and propped his back with blankets. He was bloated and now blood was oozing from his bowels onto the ground. I was transfixed with horror.

Louie urged me, "Dana, find another passage. Open a hole in the cave beyond those bloody sensors."

"There is no other opening," wheezed Hal.

Distraught, but grateful to have something to do, I went off to search. Focusing the vox and trying to peer through rocks when I didn't know what was beyond them was challenging. Remembering my lessons, I directed my thoughts through the crystals with the intention of seeking openings at intervals. Above us, bats made squeaky, hissing noises. They must have ways out that we couldn't see. Up I floated, seeking bat doors. Nada. In and out of shallow hollows and narrow tunnels I crept. Every direction led to dead ends backed by solid rock walls, all of which were within the perimeter of the sensor towers. One way in. One way out. Sealed off by me. I returned to Louie's side.

"Our only option is to reopen the cleft where we crawled in. We'll be in sensor range, but we'll be cloaked."

"Do it," Louie said. I went to work levitating stones, slowly, meticulously, silently. Louie lay down beside Hal, indifferent to the blood, and cradled his beloved. He pillowed Hal's head on his arm and held back tears. The couple looked into each other's eyes, spoke softly, sharing tender memories and private jokes.

"Here, suck on this heartplum." Louie held it to his lips and Hal tasted. It did seem to bring him some succor as he drifted in and out of consciousness.

"Louie, let me surrender. We'll be together in the next world. I don't fear death."

"Hush, just hold my hand." They lay together in silence while I cut and glided rocks.

I whispered, "The exit is open. We can move now."

"It's too late," Louie sobbed. "He's fading." Hal was unconscious, his breathing shallow and slow. I felt like an intruder in their grief but raged within; another murder at the hands of Shelter. I joined Louie on the ground cradling Hal on his other side. There wasn't any other comfort I could provide. We made helpless eye contact over Hal's prostrate form. We shifted our weight to hug Hal's extremities, watching his face as his chest rose and fell. At the same moment, we realized that Hal, J.B. Halifax, was not going to draw another breath. A wretched choke escaped Louie's throat. I sobbed as well.

Hal was still warm, and I buried my face in his back and let the tears flow into his shirt. Incapacitating grief overcame me. I wept for Hal, for Louie, for Jay, and for the lives we'd left behind. I wept for *Summer in Tellara*. I trembled because deadly pursuers stalked our threshold, and I trembled because now we were trapped in a cave with a dead body.

Needing to occupy myself, I got up and repacked all our possessions into our backpacks. Then, I viewed outside the cave and beyond. Frank Fretz was in Chicago. Vincent Cretzky sat gaunt, alone in his office. Squeezy was busy busy busy shuffling who-knows-what paperwork. Alice was at work, her routine seemingly unchanged. Sheldon Walters was in his big office in Dallas talking on the phone. Flatface was nearby, walking the sensor tower perimeter. He was on the phone too. My kids and the dogs were chillin' at the cabin. Louie's family looked healthy, but worried.

Returning to Louie's side, I asked, "what shall we do?"

"I want to give Hal a tomb. Can you cut some stones?"

"Yeah. Sure, but with our cave entrance open, we need to work fast." I floated stones and he stacked them in a pile around Hal's body.

"Then let's hurry, I want to hold a service too." Louie started to whisper and was cut off by his own sob. "This cave… was Hal's refuge since he was old enough to drive. We met at an HIV support group in a friend's apartment. I had just started at the Shelter Satellite Office in St. Louis. We compared notes about coming out. Hal talked about growing up gay in the Bible Belt. He never came out, but when he became a 'male nurse' his family treated it like a scandal. Hal never got back in touch with his relatives.

"I told him how being a gay Latino in Salinas was no picnic. It was easier for my family when I moved to San Francisco. Then, I got the job offer in Saint Louis. He nursed several of our friends dying from AIDS. After our friend who introduced us died, Hal wanted to get out of Missouri. I accepted the transfer to Chicago. That was six years ago."

We sat in the silent dark for many minutes.

Then, for the first time, I turned the vox up to full radiance. The inside of this limestone cave had never seen such light. All its secret crevices were illuminated. It had a stark, awesome beauty. Red and orange glimmering streaks interspersed with yellow-white calcium carbonate structures seeping from above and collecting below. The bats twittered but ignored us.

The stones stacked by my side were yellow-white limestone engrained with brown and gray patterns. As I levitated stones toward Hal, Louie lovingly built a sarcophagus around him, leaving his face uncovered until we were both able to bring ourselves to say a final farewell. It was wrenching to call forth the right words to commemorate our murdered friend's untimely death in this strange netherworld.

"Hal recited Emily Dickinson when he worked hospice. Can you inscribe a quote on his cover stone? 'Love is Immortality. J.B. Halifax.'"

I engraved while Louie completed the tomb. Then, there was nothing more to do.

"I guess it's time to leave this hole in the ground," he finally said.

"We can go out the cleft where we came in, cloaked, undetectable to their sensors. As soon as we're clear, we can levitate and glide away."

"Show me."

We huddled together and I manipulated the vox crystals. We rose. I cloaked us so that we were undetectable to all sensibilities, as it turned out, just in time. A dog crawled in through the crevasse. Then another. They were barking wildly. I love dogs, but these hounds were decidedly hostile.

A few minutes later, we heard loud repeated explosions outside the rock wall. "Our provisions! And Jay's papers!" Louie whispered urgently, and we drifted down to hurriedly gather every last item from our survival kit. We re-cloaked and rose back up to the cave ceiling, which set the hounds off in a frenzy of confused barking. We found ourselves in the company of bats, who seemed inquisitive despite our being insensibly hidden, even from their sonar. Beneath our feet was a protruding ledge covered with decades of bat guano.

"That's batshit we're standing on!" murmured Louie. "Move us up."

I did so, and the bats accommodated us by gently shifting on their perches. I remembered that bats can hear shapes. Could they sense us?

Another blast tore open a hole in the cliff. A team of equipped trackers, led by Flatface and Skinny, stormed into the cave. Another team of armed sentries guarded the blast hole.

I whispered to Louie, "We can't move through solid objects, and I can't get around those sentries. We're stuck for now."

The trackers turned on blinding searchlights, which set the bats off in a flurry of screeches. "Those dogs are barking at the bats," said Skinny, pointing up. Whether the bats were detecting us, or reacting to the commotion, I neither knew nor cared. I preferred the company of agitated bats to homicidal reptiles and aggressive hounds. We hovered undetectably, watching our nemeses in action.

Flatface spoke, "Before we blasted in, thermal detectors indicated three human bodies in this cave."

Skinny replied, "Yeah, but now, there's only one recently dead body in a makeshift grave."

"How long has he been dead?" asked Flatface aka Kek.

"Little over an hour." Skinny was holding an intricate blinking detector that looked like a tricorder. "His sarcophagus is ambient temperature, as if it's been here for a long time. But the body is still warm."

"Who is it?" Skinny slid Hal's cover stone. "It's just the boyfriend, not Robles-Leon."

"Search every nook and cranny. Robles must still be here," said Flatface aka Kek. Men and dogs searched in and out of the same tunnels I'd explored with the same empty results.

Bats circled our cloak, squealing little high-pitched bursts, but they didn't give us away. "Bless their blind little rodent hearts," I whispered.

"They're not blind, and they're not rodents," Louie corrected as a baby bat wing almost brushed his cheek.

More searchers came, spelunkers this time. Below, they mapped out the cave, while above, we shook with exhaustion, fear, and grief. Skinny came back from a tunnel and declared that someone had used this hole for a latrine within the last few hours. "What are we missing? Lover-boy dies, Robles takes a whiz, and clears out through a non-existent opening?"

"Not him, them. We found another car, a green Infiniti," said a unibrowed searcher climbing in through the blast hole.

"Test it for DNA."

"Already done using RAT-TRAK; a Shelter employee name of Dana Travers and two relations, most likely offspring; male and female. And two dogs."

Kek railed with frustrated fury. "That Travers bitch is too dumb to die! Make one more sweep of every tunnel, crevice, and crack. Then we are going to seal this godforsaken hole in the ground and salt the earth."

"There's no sign of people or dogs in the search radius," said Unibrow.

Pointing to Unibrow, Flatface aka Kek ordered, "Widen the search perimeter. Put up surveillance towers at thirty-foot intervals in a pentagonal pattern. If they got out, they can't have gone far." Kek raised his voice, shouting to the whole crew, "We've got four people and two dogs leaving this area. They may have split up hours ago. They may be on foot or in separate vehicles heading in different directions. Check roads. Track vehicles. Tap into MODOT. Link that data into RAT-TRAK."

Skinny shook his head, "A coordinated escape would have required advanced preparation. How could they elude us and still have time to bury their dead?"

"We got bad data from that incompetent Fretz," growled Kek. "These insignificant jerks have managed to stay ahead of us since Dallas. They must be getting help. I gotta call Walters."

"Our dogs would have detected other dogs if they'd been in the area," said Unibrow.

"Conduct a final sweep! If those troublemakers are in this cave, this will be their tomb along with lover boy."

"You two," Kek pointed to Skinny and a spelunker, "Cover the ground in detail. Look for caves and brush where they might cover or bury themselves."

"Holes where they could've gone to ground, got it," said Skinny as he departed.

"Leave no stone unturned. Get a bigger crew if you need to."

"What about this dead body? Should we report it to the police?" asked a spelunker.

"Leave him to rot," answered Kek. Spelunker looked askance but did as ordered. These guys weren't exactly boy scouts.

We watched the last of the searchers depart leaving behind interior sensor towers.

"They don't think too highly of Frank Fretz. He didn't inform them I'd caught an earlier standby flight while they were searching my condo."

"Or that Hal left the memorial with you and surprised them at Alice's. Why would Kek rely on Frank Fretz when he's got RAT-TRAK?"

"It supports your right-hand/left-hand theory about the hierarchy."

Deafening explosions cut off our speculations. The bats went batshit. The cave went black as openings were sealed. More massive blasts brought down the entire mountainside over the rock cliff. As we literally felt ourselves being buried alive, I uncloaked the bottom of one foot to kick over and crush the ominous interior sensor tower. While still reeling from the landslide, we viewed the arrival of local law enforcement beyond our grotto. After a venting of harsh words, which we could only infer, Kek and his crew packed up and left. They had broken all kinds of environmental codes and noise ordinances but Kek was a law unto himself. Making certain every sensor inside the cave was inoperable, we decloaked.

The cave was getting stuffy. Without the vox, it was darker than pitch. "They'll be back," said Louie.

"I think so too. Did you notice that Kek and Unibrow are both reptiles?"

"Oh, yeah, when we viewed them through the vox screen. Flatface called us jerks."

"Coming from him, it's a compliment," I said.

"We may be trapped, but we have an advantage those killers don't know about: your Tellaran vox."

"You believe me now, about the alternate world."

"I always half-believed you, but I was jealous. Why did you get to see these wonders before me? I've been researching this stuff all my adult life."

"Oh Louie, we could've been in Tellara this whole time." I said no more. He felt responsible for Hal's death, and I felt responsible for trapping us in this cave.

Louie shrugged. "As far as those thugs are concerned, if we're still in here, we'll die here. You said we couldn't go through solid walls?"

"Not without leaving telltale data. They wouldn't catch us as we escaped, but, Phoenix explained they'd register an unfamiliar signature in the rock wall and detect it if we ever cloaked again. We'd lose our insensibility advantage."

"We have another advantage they don't know about. They're looking for us in the woods and on the roads. They're gonna waste time without finding any sign of us. They don't even know how many people they're tracking."

"Thank god Jesse and Ruth are up north."

"Our only way out is through. Let's cut ourselves a passageway."

"I tried that a few hours ago. You're talking miles."

"We got nothin' but time."

I peered into the lighted vox screen. We concentrated on the rock walls of our subterranean prison. It was difficult to bring anything into focus, much less gauge distances. There were solid dark shadows in every direction. Finally, one direction revealed a pale vein that opened to a narrow tunnel. "It would take weeks to cut through to that crevice."

Louie pointed at the mountain over our heads, and said, "What else have we got to do?"

We moved to the back wall. Using my vox, I cut and levitated stone. Using his hands, Louie guided and stacked. Division of labor was dictated by the vox's attunement to my DNA.

* * *

Work went slowly, but the physical labor helped sublimate our grief. It was neither warm nor cold, and regular movement kept our internal thermostats stable. Time became meaningless. Our sleeping and waking patterns, our dreams and biorhythms equilibrated to extended darkness. Cut. Stack. Cut. Stack. Cut a tunnel. Inadvertently, we constructed a precisely fit stone wall. Hours. Days. Time passed. Dig a tunnel. Build a wall.

We rationed nutrition bars and heartplums. After what we guessed were fourteen days, we had no food left, so we were fasting by default. We sucked on heartplum pits, which seemed to pacify the worst of our hunger pains. There was plenty of sweet spring water.

"You know, if we were on the hero's journey, this would be our passage through the underworld," said Louie.

"The underworld sucks," I rasped.

"Yeah, and it usually comes near the end of the journey."

"This can't be the end. I need to get back to Tellara."

Louie observed, "You know, when a man goes on a hero's journey, he ends up saving the world, like Gilgamesh, or Hercules, Harry Potter, or Jesus, even Neo in the Matrix. But when a female goes on her hero's journey it is usually a prepubescent girl like Dorothy or Alice who returns with a puerile insight like, 'There's no place like home,' or 'I've just had the most curious dream!'"

"The Tellarans keep calling me a wayshower. They seem to think I'm in a position to change the world by bringing a message of planetary evolution. In reality, I'm in a position of digging my way out of a literal hole in the ground."

"The world needs a new mythos. Maybe it is time for a grandmother or a goddess to take the hero's journey."

"I'm neither," I laughed ruefully. "By the way, Louie, the way you are fitting those stones in the wall is a work of art. It curves from the old cave toward our tunnel in a wide arc. This is how they built the pyramids, you know, using an alternate gravity source. I saw it in Shastise, Tellara"

"You still gonna invite Inspector Vazquez to Tellara?"

"No. I don't trust him anymore. He told me to turn myself in even after he knew I was choked almost to death."

"That's as good as signing your death warrant."

"Tell me about it. And I wouldn't have gotten to you. You'd be dead."

Because we were fasting, our underworld passage became a vision quest. My thoughts were otherworldly, yet at the same time, a sharp and penetrating, waking dream. The cave was a womb; cutting and stacking, our gestation; tunneling out, our birth canal. When I slept, I entered dreamtime and had a completely separate life. Sometimes in Tellara, sometimes on a post-apocalyptic island, sometimes I visited with Saffron or my kids. Once, Vincent Cretzky was with me in Tellara. Once, I was in Tellara, remote viewing myself in the cave.

I awoke with a notion and grabbed the vox. Louie watched over my shoulder as I concentrated on Saffron. She came into focus with the Circle of Thirteen. I told Louie their names and ages. They began a heartdance in their pavilion. As the heartdance tapestry emerged, it displayed an image of Louie and me in the cave. "They know where we are!" I said excitedly, hurting my throat. Saffron's eyes locked on mine. We were seeing each other in real time. They were trying to communicate with me. "We are trapped in a cave, pursued by Reptilians," I mouthed. "*Summer in Tellara* is slashed."

Another image emerged on the screen. "That's Phoenix!" cried Louie. The image expanded to include the Tellaran version of Cairo's Great Bazaar, Khan al-Khalili. Hundreds of stalls were filled with an endless array of ceramics, glass, fabric, leather, art, spices, and food. I could almost smell the savory aroma. Phoenix occupied a shop full of original paintings, carpets, and kilims. We were being directed to Cairo once we emerged from the cave. That is where we'd find our portal to Tellara. Would that Phoenix could simply paint himself into the cave and we could depart together for Tellara. That would leave the portal trapped in this buried prison. We had to dig our way out and make our way to Cairo, Egypt, Earth. The vision faded. The screen went dark.

Louie spoke first. "Dana, I'm not planning to die here. We're gonna cut our way out of this hole and get to Tellara, where we can figure out how to defeat those reptilian thugs. Let's get back to work."

I was so hungry I thought my stomach would turn inside out. It had shrunk to the size of a walnut and I was sure any food I ate would be painfully filling, but I craved nutrition in every cell. My brain craved more than oxygen and water. We soldiered on. Cut, levitate, stack, build. Hours, days, weeks, darkness, and biorhythms all melted together. The bats were taking a keen interest in our activity. They fluttered about, getting close enough to air-kiss our cheeks. "Do you think that when Flatface brought down the mountain, he trapped the bats in here too? Or do they have another way out?" I asked.

"I dunno. There's plenty of air, but they certainly seem fascinated by our tunnel."

"Do they even have a food source?"

"Bats eat bugs."

"I haven't felt any bugs," I mused. "Say, do you think we could eat a bat?"

"We could totally eat a bat."

"Do you wanna eat a bat?"

"Do you?"

"If you caught it and killed it, I'd cook it with the vox. We could have roast bat."

"How would I catch a bat? I'm not killin' a bat. You kill a bat with your cutting tool."

"I'm not killin' a bat. You kill a bat."

"You wanna eat a bat, you kill a bat."

"I think I could really eat a bat if you killed it."

"Do you think they'd miss just one?"

"I dunno. Do bats have families?"

"Do bats mourn their dead? I'm not killin' a bat."

Thus, began the irrational phase of our passage through the underworld. We kept each other awake bickering about bats and bugs. A couple of regular Mythic Heroes. Gnawing hunger motivated our pace. Cut, levitate, stack, sleep. We measured time in stones. The tunnel deepened; the wall expanded.

While leaning against the wall in a fugue state, I suddenly heard a hollow acoustic ring followed by staccato breathing. I expanded the vox light in the direction of the inky dark. Black on black separated itself into a winged silhouette. I froze with guilty horror. "The bats heard us plotting murder! Oh wait, is that a bird?" The silhouette called softly, part caw, part trill. It was a crow. Then the bird nudged my cheek and I jumped out of my skin shrieking so loudly I was swallowing knives. Crow shrieked. Bats freaked. Louie shouted my name as his footfalls approached.

Crow heard him and quieted her calls to eerie trills that resembled garbled human speech. "This way," she seemed to say. "This way," she nudged my hand.

Louie took in the scene. "It's happened. We're having a waking hallucination."

"We're both hallucinating a crow?"

"No, we're both hallucinating a raven."

"Well, that hallucination is talking to us."

"Right," Louie addressed the bird politely. "We're listening Mr. Raven." Crow perched on the vox. When she was sure she had our attention, she flew to a ledge and pecked at the wall.

"I remember something... Phoenix told me to follow the crow. It would guide me through the darkest passage. Well, this is the darkest passage, and that's a crow."

"That's a raven, not a crow," he said.

"It's a crow."

"It's a raven."

"Are there ravens in the Ozarks?"

"Are there crows in caves?"

"Well it told us to follow it."

"So, we're just going to follow it?"

"Have you got a better idea? We've no idea where we're going and now we have a guide."

"Fine, Fine. Let's follow the raven."

"Crow."

"And the bats." Bats were gathering, mamas whispering, babies chirping.

I carved at the spot where Crow had pecked at the wall. Another peck, another cut, and another slice of rock fell out. Then another. And another. The wall gave way to a hollow. We couldn't see through the impenetrable dark, but cool, fresh wind caressed our faces. Rushing water from far below serenaded us. I expanded the opening, careful to retain a weight-bearing ledge. Slowly, we crawled through to peer into the inky depths. Crow perched between our shoulders on the overhang. He looked down at the rushing water, then he peered at me, then at Louie, and then back down to the underground river. The vox illuminated a staggeringly huge cavern, carved deep by an ancient, raging, subterranean watercourse. Far below the steep walls, the river flowed into a pool of clear, still, deep water. Crow cawed softly as if to suggest we get on with it. Bats fluttered past our cheeks into the vast cavern.

"How will we get down?" Louie asked. At that moment, Crow flew off the ledge and circled gracefully above the pool, coming to light on a prominent ridge adjacent our tunnel. A series of scalable ledges were carved into the wall, almost like a natural staircase. "We can climb down to the pool. Thank you, Crow," I whispered.

"Yeah, thanks, Raven," Louie seconded. The bird tilted her head, trilled musically, and flew off. I hung the vox around my neck. Louie grabbed our few provisions. We climbed to the edge of our ledge when we realized simultaneously that we were being needlessly foolhardy. "We can levitate!" He used the straps of our backpacks to tether our upper arms together. We drifted down, clinging to handholds and footholds because, even weightless, this was scary, dark, steep business, not to mention that we were weak and disoriented. Settling on an embankment at the water's edge, we clung together in relief.

The pool was cold and vivifying. We scrubbed our skin and clothes and put them on wet. I blasted the heating tool. We basked in the healing warmth of the vox's glow. "This would have made Hal's last moments more comfortable," I lamented.

"We would have been detected."

"I sealed our only escape."

"At the time, you saved our lives."

But I felt guilty. This warmth couldn't have saved Hal's life, but it may have made his final moments more bearable. We followed Crow along the narrow strand and stumbled through soft dirt without realizing it at first. The open air was dark, but we heard familiar sounds.

"That's cricket song," Louie exclaimed.

Starlight broke into our vision. Recognition took several moments to register. "That's the sky," Louie sobbed. I stood on a ledge by his side, peering out in silent awe at the glittering pinpricks of stars. Expanding the opening, I cut and levitated while Louie dumped clumps of dirt onto the subterranean embankment. Once the hole was big enough, we crawled out onto damp earth and lay side-by-side, gasping in the humid night air. We left behind surreal visions, fears, and Hal's cold stone tomb. We had traversed the underworld and emerged into unknown territory, bedraggled and half-starved, but alive and resolute.

Part Two

Tellaran Autumn

CHAPTER 10

Louie and I fell into exhausted stupor until dawn. Birdsong and insect buzzing filled the air. The crow was in a branch above our heads. It trilled, cawed, tilted its head to one side, and flew off. "Thank you Crow," I called. My throat was a little stronger now, although it still hurt to raise my voice.

"Yes, thanks Raven. You're beautiful." Little critters were foraging in the dirt. It felt like the dawn of creation. We were thin, dirty, hungry, and exhausted. I didn't imagine we smelled very good either, in spite of our frigid, vigorous baths. We'd scoped out the lay of the land. The sensors were well behind us to the north, in the thick of the woods. We could hear cars in the distance. We headed downhill, obsessed with food.

"Dana let's think about this. Do we want to be spotted along the road in this condition? Anyone who sees us will call the police and that will alert Shelter. We have to stay cloaked."

"And levitate. We're barefoot. Food, and clothes are our priority. Let's look for a house or building."

"That's almost a plan," he said.

"It is all we've got."

"Where is a raven when you need one?"

"He got us through the dark passage," I said.

"I thought it was a she."

"He," I insisted.

"You can tell the sex of a bird?" We argued mindlessly about the difference between crows and ravens and how to sex birds. Before long, I stumbled. The cloak faded. "I can't go on. I need to rest."

"If we rest, we die, but I am exhausted too. Is grass edible?" We crawled under a shrub and in moments were both passed out.

We stirred at the sound of soft voices. "Lady, wake up lady." Someone was shaking me. Enormous glacial blue eyes were peering down at me.

126

Another voice called softly, "Sir, are you alright?"

I sat up with a groan. "You look like you could use a meal. Here, have some juice." The lady handed me bottled orange juice and I sucked it down greedily.

A handsome, dark-skinned man was giving Louie juice. "Would you like some broth?" asked my savior, opening a thermos. "Here, let me dip some bread in broth and you can eat it slowly." We gobbled. The nourishment hit our cells like lightning strikes. I took a better look at our rescuers. They were two old hippies out for a hike in the backwoods.

"Can we offer you a ride?"

Louie and I looked at each other guardedly and did not answer.

"I am Crystal," said the lady with big blue eyes and white blonde hair. "A Pleiadian."

"I am Cosmo, a Vegan," said the tall, handsome, ebony man. "We'll take you to a safe place where you can recover."

"Are you working for the reptiles?" Louie accused. We turned our backs in a huddle under the shrub and surreptitiously viewed them through the vox. They glowed with vibrant humanity.

"There not reptiles, Louie. He's a vegetarian and she's a plebian, you know, like a labor organizer. Louie rolled his eyes at me.

"We have bananas and yogurt in the van," Cosmo called.

"And peanut butter with rice crackers," added Crystal.

"That, I care about," said Louie. Hunger won out over judgment. We crawled back out into the clearing and collapsed.

The tall blonde woman cradled me while she continued to drizzle broth-dipped bread into my mouth. The tall dark man was similarly nurturing Louie. "Did you two get lost?" she asked.

"Yes, so lost," tears filled my eyes.

"Dana, we have spare clothing in our van. Would you like to put on some sweats?"

"We need food, clothing, and a place to lay low," said Louie.

"Louie, we can take you to Wah'Kon-Tah, our community. It's an off-the-grid sustainable eco village."

"How do you know our names?" Louie challenged.

"You've been speaking to each other for the last ten minutes."

"Oh, yeah."

After I felt rested and revived, Crystal half-carried me to their van. I don't know what I expected, but it wasn't an old Plymouth Voyager painted like an Electric Kool-aid psychedelic van. I was beginning to like old cars.

"That vehicle is going to attract the attention of everyone on the road," Louie protested.

"Everyone hereabouts knows this van, knows we're local, and that we were sent by the Galactic Council."

"Ah Ha! Aliens! I told you."

"Not according to the vox." But, after my sojourns to Tellara and through the cave, I was prepared to consider anything.

Not so Louie. "Galactic Council, eh? Who sent you? Reptilians or grays?"

"Neither, we're here to help humanity and Earth," said Crystal.

Crystal and Cosmo all but lifted us into the back seat, where I relaxed for the first time in a month. We'd been surviving on nerves and adrenalin. But Louie was not convinced we were safe. Crystal handed us each a banana, while Cosmo dug sweat suits out of a backpack.

"Eat slowly, Dana."

"Break your fast gently, Louie." We were too ravenous to consider their cautions and inhaled our sustenance.

"How did you find us?" I asked.

"We were summoned to your side by a raven."

"Ah ha! Raven! I was right. She was too big to be a crow!" Louie crowed.

"It was a male raven from beyond this region of Turtle Island," confirmed Cosmo.

"Ha! Male!" I gloated. Cosmo and Crystal looked askance at us but did not comment.

Cosmo was a very tall, bald, ebony-skinned man. He wore a colorful headband, a patterned jacket, and baggy Thai pants. Crystal was equally tall. I call her she, but she was androgynous, although somewhat more feminine than masculine. She wore an ankle-length flowered skirt, a powder blue blouse, and a clashing orange and brown plaid shawl. Her hair was loose, long, white, and straight. Both were statuesque and gorgeous. Both were barefoot. They were the most unlikely rescuers I might have ever imagined. Two cosmic kooks. But then, the crow in the cavern had been incredible, and so had Tellara. Wherever they were from, they did not seem to be Shelter operatives. That made them welcome, at least to me.

"How do you know who we are or where to find us?" Louie asked.

"We were guided to this spot by an Osage Medicine Woman named Sky Dancer. She obtains her information directly from the Galactic Council, usually through an animal totem that connects to her fellow travelers on the path," Crystal affirmed.

"But Phoenix told me to follow the crow, not the raven."

"Maybe Phoenix knows you can't tell the difference between a raven and a crow," snarked Louie.

"Maybe he knows you have gender confusion about birds," I snarked back.

"Do you two even want to be rescued?" asked Crystal.

"For all we know, you're assassins sent by Shelter to finish the job they started back whenever they started whatever it was they started which ended in murder. Twice."

"Louie, you're rambling," I said, but not ungently. He had a right to be suspicious. We were filthy and exhausted and needed aid and succor very badly. "I think we don't have a choice but to trust these two…"

"Aliens? Did you bring your anal probe?" Louie challenged.

"He's a vegan and she's a labor organizer, Louie." I whispered. "They're hippies."

"We're friends of Sky Dancer," Crystal supplied with a Namasté bow.

"What is today's date?" I asked. This question got Louie's attention. We'd lost all track of time underground.

"August second,"

I let fly a startled gasp. Our journey through the underworld had lasted almost a month. I started shaking and collapsed on the back seat. We had traveled a long way underground to create an egress beyond the range of Shelter's sensors. We were emaciated, but not dead. How had we survived?

Crystal handed me a set of pale gray fleece sweats that felt like divinity against my skin. My hands were shaking so badly, I needed Crystal's help to tear off my soggy, shredded clothes, and don the clean, soft fleece. Louie was changing with Cosmo's help. Then they gave us warm, cushy, high-top fluffy boots that slipped on to our cold, calloused feet with no ties. My feet had orgasms.

"Wah'Kon-Tah will provide good will, a warm welcome, food, clean clothes, beds, baths, phones, computers, healers, privacy, and answers."

"How can an off-the-grid village have power and internet?" Louie asked suspiciously.

"We generate power and have our own tower. We can help you with logistics for your journey."

Now it was my turn to give Cosmo a distrustful glare. How did these vegetable munching labor activists know we planned to travel? Reading the dismay on my face, Cosmo replied, "We know of your quest. Wah'Kon-Tah is a haven on Earth."

"OK," I said warily, deciding for the both of us. "Louie, I think this is where we need to go."

"Will there be toilets?" he asked.

"Indeed," answered Cosmo. That seemed to make up his mind and he settled onto the back seat in his cozy sweats and closed his eyes.

Our new friends were decent enough not comment on our ripe odor. Although we had recently bathed in the cold underground river, the weeks in the caves had taken their toll on our personal hygiene. We traveled south and west, uphill and down through the remotest Ozarks.

We'd been on the road for an hour in the psychedelic van when Cosmo pulled into the parking lot of Bruno's Basics, a rural supply store. The sign in the parking lot announced unlimited supplies of 'Everything You Need: Bait, Beer, Bibles, and Bullets.'

"I've been here before," cried Louie. "With Hal, on our way to the cavern."

"I saw this store from my vox!" Having recently filled our shrunken bellies, Louie and I urgently needed facilities and leapt out of the van. Crystal and Cosmo greeted Bruno fondly while we went off to revel in intestinal exigency in Bruno's outhouses.

When we returned to the storefront, Crystal, Cosmo, and Bruno broke off their friendly conversation. Bruno shared that he could tell by our scruffiness that we'd been through an ordeal. Bruno Barlow was a, mature black man with gray hair and a finely groomed beard. He was tall with wise, gentle eyes that saw more than he shared.

"I have a gift for each of you," Bruno offered with twinkling eyes, "Just the thing that each of you needs the most." Bruno presented a shaving kit full of every personal hygiene product a man could want to Louie. Lucky Louie. I drooled.

To me, he presented a big, black, highlighted, dog-eared Bible. "I need this?" I asked skeptically, embarrassed by my ingratitude.

"You never know when the Good Book might come in handy." Bruno said enigmatically pointing to his family tree. Every name began with a B or had multiple Bs in the name.

"The more Bs the Better!" he grinned. "So, when I met my Abby, I knew everything I needed to know about her when I heard her name. I asked her to marry me that very day. And we've been together forty-five years. Three kids, all Bs: Robbie, Betty, and Sheeba."

"Wonderful, but there are no B's in my name."

"Fair enough, Dana, but you want to consider writin' down your family tree in your own Bible."

"Neither of my children is planning to start a family."

"Life finds a way." Bruno soothed in his resonant baritone. I smiled, in spite of my raw nerve endings.

"I reckon you think youdda preferred a personal hygiene kit." When Bruno smiled, he seemed younger and I caught a glimmer of the handsome youth who'd wood his Abby.

"Kinda, yeah," I agreed, self-consciously. "This Bible you gave me looks very old. It's all marked up and dog eared."

"It belonged to my late, beloved Aunt Babs. It was her Barlow Family Bible. She was the last of her line and wants you to have it."

"How could your late aunt have even known I existed much less wanted me to have her Bible?

"In these hills, you gotta trust, Bruno Barlow knows best." He winked knowingly.

"Thank you, Bruno," I said with heartfelt, albeit bewildered, gratitude. "I'll cherish it."

"Someday, you will." Bruno ushered us to the door of his all-inclusive store. "Now get along to Wah'Kon-Tah's magical hot springs." Hot springs! Louie and I exchanged looks of wonder and needed no prodding to hobble back to the psychedelic Van, where we collapsed into the back seat.

In about thirty minutes, we arrived in a grotto filled with a collection of small log cabins, geodesic domes, and yurts. Small ponds, springs, and gardens surrounded the cabins. About twenty people of all ages and ethnicities were tending to crops, kids, animals, vehicles, and woodwork.

"This way," Cosmo hopped out from behind the wheel and led us to a nearby cabin with a wide back porch. I carried my vox and my Bible. Louie clung to his shaving kit and Jay's tattered envelope. Just beyond the porch was a natural hot spring, a sculpted stone hole in the ground, burbling with steamy water.

"Take a load off," declared Cosmo.

We took more than that off, ripping our clothes from our bones and easing ourselves into the delicious pool. Soap and towels appeared. Crystal began to shampoo my hair and scrub my back. I was too near the edge of exhaustion to give a shit about modesty. I savored the pampering. Louie was getting similar treatment from Cosmo. I could have soaked in that hot spring for hours until I passed out, but nature called urgently, again. I hadn't had solid food for weeks and my innards were turning summersaults.

Crystal wrapped me in a terrycloth robe, led me into the cabin, and stood me before a porcelain flush toilet in a white tiled bathroom. Tears spilled over my cheeks as I closed the door and took care of business in warm, private, clean, hygienic quarters brimming with rolls of soft, quilted toilet paper. I don't recall if I'd ever cried on the toilet before, but this was a luxury I never appreciated so utterly. When I finished and stood, I caught sight of myself in a mirror. The face that stared back at me was gaunt and pasty white. Her hair was a clean tangle of salt and pepper that stuck out in every direction. Recovering myself, I brushed my teeth and tongue and flossed and rinsed. Then I brushed, flossed, and rinsed again. Louie was pounding on the bathroom door. I exited and allowed him entry. In daylight, he looked as unrecognizable as me: always wiry, he was nearly emaciated. His dark complexion had not washed out as much as mine, but he was a pale reflection of his hearty, familiar countenance. Louie had not shaved while we were in the cave and his beard growth seemed gradual in the quiet dark. Now, in daylight, scrubbed clean, his thick dark beard made for a startling contrast.

I needed sleep. But first I needed to send a message to Larry and Moe via Facespace. "Crystal, you mentioned a computer."

"Here," she replied, walking me across the quad to the building she called sky room. I shuffled along in robe and slippers to a great room filled with carpets and pillows, chairs and sofas, tables and benches. There was a piano, a stereo, a library of books and videos, a TV, a game room with a pool table and puzzles, and a bank of four computers.

I logged onto Facespace as Curly Stooge and found twenty-three messages from Larry and Moe. I was too tired to read their messages and just wanted to assure them I was safe.

"It was necessary to go underground," as I put it. "The immediate danger has passed. Shep and I are together in a safe place, but Shep's dearest met the same fate as another friend from Texas." This was a round-about, spur-of-the-moment code indicating that Hal had met with the same fate as Jay. As if they needed reminding that the stakes were life and death. I hoped the kids could read between the lines. I closed, "Safe. Soon. Sleep. Love, Curly." When I got back to the cabin, Louie was snoring. I climbed in the other bunk, pulled a woven comforter up to my chin, and joined my friend in deep, dreamless sleep.

It was morning when I woke up. I reckoned it was the next day and I was right. I'd recovered much of my stamina in just one sleep cycle. Maybe it was something in the broth. That thought made me realize I was famished. I rose, showered, brushed my teeth, and dressed in clothes provided at the foot of my bed: underwear, blue jeans, a hooded sweatshirt, white cotton socks, and my yummy, fuzzy boots. I felt the vox on its chain around my neck.

Louie still slept, being much more emotionally wounded than I. Stepping out into the bright sun, I followed my nose to the kitchen adjacent the sky room. I had tiny helpings of fruit, tea, and taters. The food was delicious; comfort food made to order. But I could only eat small amounts before it went through me like greased lightning. I raced back to the porcelain throne in my cabin and indulged in another blissfully hygienic moment of relief. Louie was awake and dressed when I emerged from paradise. I accompanied him to breakfast and kept him company while he partook of the same marvelous post-starvation meal that had tuned me up good and proper just moments ago. We were ready to face the day.

After breakfast, Cosmo and Crystal appeared. She wore a yellow sundress and flip-flops. He wore a Dashiki print caftan and was still barefoot. By comparison,

Louie and I were the drab duo in denim and flannel. Louie's immediate need was to get a message to his sister. We had to assume her premises were being surveilled and her emails screened. "This is a job for Sky Dancer," we were assured by the Cosmic Kooks, in unison.

Louie grimaced at me. "It's OK," I assured him, feeling anything but confident. We were ushered to a secluded A-frame cabin off the commons. A Native American woman with long gray braids sat on the front porch. She was dressed in jeans, a plaid flannel work shirt, and cowboy boots. She could have been any age between sixty and a hundred sixty. I had grown accustomed to the spry mobility of elders these past few months and took an immediate liking to Sky Dancer. She was weaving a turquoise and black, zigzag-patterned blanket on a vertical loom. The loom hummed in her hands as Sky Dancer masterfully whipped the shuttlecock across the threads.

"Welcome to Wah'Kon-Tah, dear Louie and Dana. I am Sky Dancer of the Galactic Medicine Wheel."

"Thanks for your hospitality."

"Thanks for the rescue," we blurted together, still confused about these people.

"Are you tribal? Is this a reservation?"

"I am an Osage medicine woman. Wah'Kon-Tah means People and Place of the Land, Water, and Sky. We are Wah'kon-Tah. This is an intentional community comprised of people of all ethnicities who are drawn to this sacred space. Together we have built a sustainable lifestyle."

"I am grateful we were drawn here," I replied.

"Shall we talk, Dana? Louie, you wait here in the Sun and let Cosmo know if you need anything." Sky Dancer ushered me into her cabin. Louie, Crystal, and Cosmo relaxed on the porch.

Inside, Sky Dancer cut to the chase. "What are you lying about to yourself?"

"Huh?" was my astute riposte. I don't know what I had been expecting, but it was not a scolding.

"How are you fulfilling your life's purpose?"

"Um, I have this connection to another world in an alternate dimension. I have been designated as a bridge between two worlds, Earth and Tellara." In addition to my role as Tellaran wayshower, murder attempt survivor, and falsely accused perp, I felt I had redeemed myself with my journey through the underworld.

"Did you choose this path for yourself?"

"Karmically, but not consciously—in this lifetime, anyway."

"You have accepted this role with intention and purpose?"

"The role was thrust upon me and I accepted it. It has proven useful to my survival."

"When was the last time you had a dream for yourself, for your life?" Sky Dancer's tone gentled.

"When I was younger, I was a researcher in an economic think tank. I loved that job. I served a wide community. When I became a single mom, my career evaporated, so did my dreams. My purpose was raising my kids and earning a living."

"What purpose do you serve now?"

"My purpose is service."

"To whom?"

"Well, there's the catch. On Tellara, I serve the wayshower mission, which is to bring their message of planetary evolution to Earth. On Earth, my mission has been doing whatever I had to do to support my family. At Shelter Insurance, I tried to serve my clients. But if I did that too well, I wasn't serving my employer. It makes me kinda schizophrenic."

"How do you reconcile this?"

"Not very well. I got in trouble with management."

"Give an example."

"Well, recently, I stood up to my boss and told him that he was doing a disservice to our clients by denying legitimate claims. Another time, I undermined a malicious gossip in a staff meeting."

"What was the impetus for standing up to these individuals?"

"I was falsely accused of murder. Individuals in my company framed me. But I had an escape, my portal to Tellara, a world where my adversaries could not follow." I was filled with righteous justification.

"So, you had nothing to lose and a refuge from harm."

"I wouldn't put it like that," I stammered defensively. "It cost me a fight with my best friend, secrets from my children, someone tried to kill me, someone has killed two of my friends, and I'm wanted by the police and the FBI. Plus, my refuge is now unavailable," I was near tears.

Sky Dancer brought the conversation back to my shortcomings. "Did the families you serve professionally have anything to lose?"

"Oh, you want to go there?"

"Tell me about them."

"Well, Fred Miller was paralyzed from the waist down in a car accident that wasn't his fault. He had major medical, disability, and life insurance. Shelter denied his disability claim, paid only a fraction on his automobile insurance, pennies on the dollar for his medical and rehabilitation bills, and reneged on a re-education clause. Shelter did this all because Fred's teenaged son was in the car and had a small amount of marijuana in his pocket. The police arrested the son and Shelter pressured the police to charge Fred. He could not return to his work as a contractor. The family went through bankruptcy and foreclosure. The only reason they're not homeless is because the mom had a job and friends helped find a tiny rental. Fred's appealed three times, hired a lawyer he can't afford, and his son did time in juvie when he could have been at home helping his family. I could not persuade Vincent to settle the claim." Sky Dancer nodded but said nothing, so I plunged on.

"Another client is a kid named Ken Williams. He needed a treatment for a cancerous tumor on his spinal cord. Shelter's oncology committee said that the experimental drug treatment prescribed by the young man's physicians was unnecessary. Shelter would only cover the costs of step-therapy for other, less costly treatments, traditional drugs, radiation, and surgery. Ken could only obtain the prescribed treatment if the step-therapy failed. His parents couldn't afford out-of-pocket payments. Friends, neighbors, and even the hospital held fundraisers. It was too little, too late. The step-therapy took months. It failed. Joe died waiting for treatment. My boss could have overruled the committee. I asked him to, repeatedly. He didn't, and I had to be the message bearer to the family."

"Dana, why didn't you take a firmer stand against your company's policy years ago and help those families you say you serve?"

I felt stung. "I did what I could. There are practical considerations. Shelter was operating within the letter of the law. Defying my employer would have cost me my job, my home, and my financial security. Leaving Shelter would do no good for anyone. Even though I failed, at least I tried."

Sky Dancer took both my hands in hers. Her hands were warm, large, strong, supple, and dry; a weaver's hands. They enfolded my skinny, cracked hands. "Did staying do them any good?"

"For those families, no. But, over the years, I fought and helped other claimants. After I found Tellara and was falsely accused, I became more fearless and made a difference, at least with one person."

"It took a false accusation for murder and refuge on another world to speak out against these wrong doings."

"You make it sound black and white," I said.

"Dana, it's so easy to see the faults in others. You have real adversaries trying to destroy you. In order to defeat your enemies, you must first conquer your inner demons. That which you despise and fear in others is your own inner shadow."

"I'm no killer!' I erupted. "And I certainly never denied a legitimate insurance claim to collect a bonus! I never slept with someone to get a promotion! I worked for people I loathed in order to take care of deserving people!"

"Why did you loath these people?"

"Not all of them. I have this list of malicious gossips and greedy exploiters, oh, and *killers*," I stressed.

"Fair enough, you don't exploit or kill, and you loathe malicious gossips."

"Oh, I see. You mean the gossip stuff."

"Do you think that if you gossip privately, your words won't hurt you?" Sky Dancer held my gaze until I squirmed.

"I'm not the only person trapped in a hamster wheel, running in circles just to survive because the alternative is two paychecks away from homelessness!"

"And now you are a fugitive from justice through no fault of your own."

"How do you know about that?"

"We get the news here. There's a TV in the Sky Lodge. I know about Tellara because I am a Sky Dancer of the Galactic Medicine Wheel. I dance and weave patterns across the multiverse. It's easy to go for broke when you have nothing to lose."

"I have everything to lose! Jay wasn't afraid and it cost him his life. My children are on the run. Anyone of us could be killed if Shelter finds us. I don't understand why the Tellarans chose me. They must have had some confidence in my abilities."

"Oh, they do. And so do I. The Tellarans chose well."

"I was seriously considering becoming a whistle blower when this all started. In addition to criminal charges, Shelter is warming up a padded cell for me. Anger, gossip, and sarcasm aren't pretty, but they hone my sense of humor. It's a coping mechanism. One person can't fix everything."

"One person can make a difference." Sky Dancers tone changed, and she became nurturing. "You wanted compassion for your ordeals, and you have it." Sky Dancer patted my hand. "We're here to help you with your quest, but time is short and there is much to be done since you lost your portal to Tellara."

"You know about that too?"

"I'm a Sky Dancer," she said handing me an old, large, illustrated book called *World Mythology*. "This has been in our library for many years and has helped students integrate patterns in comparative religions and mythos. You may find it helpful in your wayshower mission."

"Another big tome. Somehow, I must integrate Tellaran Utopia with Earth's Dystopia. Thank you, Sky Dancer."

"Go now, eat, soak, and rest. We'll help you prepare for the next leg of your journey." Sky Dancer stood. I rose and she hugged me while I held back tears. This conversation had been filled with as many shadows as the cave.

Next it was Louie's turn to confer with Sky Dancer of the Galactic Medicine Wheel. Later that afternoon we were both resting in the hot sun in summer clothes. Crystal was trying to force feed us with plates of fruit. I nibbled but grew full after just a few bites. "How'd your interview with Sky Dancer go?" I asked.

"Wonderful! We discussed loss and the stages of grief. I wept and she did some sort of ritual with burning sage and herbal tea. She arranged to have a shaman on the west coast contact my sister and update her on my situation. I haven't felt such peace since Hal died."

"That's nice," I muttered.

"What?" Louie asked, hearing the bitterness in my tone.

"My interview was weird and challenging."

"How so?"

"I don't want to talk about it." After everything that happened to me, I'd hoped for positive feedback from this wise woman. Instead, I felt like she'd excoriated me by pointing out flaws in my character to which I'd remained willfully blind. Sometimes, self-awareness left much to be desired. Why couldn't I get tea and sympathy? I was in a full-blown self-pity party and didn't want to spend time with the Cosmic Kooks when they came around to chat.

Oblivious to my self-indulgent swoon, Cosmo offered to give me a massage. That perked me up. Every bone and muscle in my body ached. Cosmo began to rub my shoulders and neck. "You've had a deep trauma to your neck."

"I was strangled and almost killed."

"Let's do some healing, shall we? I can pour energy into your throat chakra, do some acupressure, Reiki, and give you some Chinese herbs to drink." At last, here was my tea and sympathy! Cosmo set to work while I yielded to his strong, healing touch. I didn't so much fall asleep, as succumb to an induced somnolent state on the massage table. When he roused me, my throat felt better and I even felt a laugh burble up from my diaphragm to my throat.

I checked my messages on Facespace. Moe, a.k.a. Ruth, messaged: *"Glad you and Shep are safe, Curly. There is trouble in paradise. Mr. Wonderful wants us gone. No longer willing to be a supporting player in the family drama."*

I grasped her meaning immediately. Her new beau, Mick, the cabin owner, wanted them out.

"Is situation critical?"

"Situation is heartbreaking. We have car, provisions & money. But I've lost a friend."

"Sorry darling. Be brave and safe. Hugs and kisses." I had no idea what comfort an electronic message could provide to a brokenhearted young woman and did my motherly best. Mick hadn't been a rat, but he'd reached his limit. I reckoned his and Ruth's blossoming romance could not handle the pressure of FBI's Most Wanted Mom. Ruth and Jesse were wanted for questioning in connection with

my disappearance. What could they say? If they told the truth about where they think I went, the police wouldn't believe them, but Shelter's goons would. If they lied, they'd be aiding and abetting. Mick was in over his head. I didn't blame him. Just as well they should move to a new location.

"Do you have a plan?"

"Half a plan. We're moving west in the general direction of your favorite mountain."

I assumed they meant Shasta. "I can't join you. I leave for next portal soon. Stay safe." We signed off with endearments.

I joined the Wah'Kon-Tah residents for dinner. Louie and I were introduced to community members, including Joe Two Feathers, Sky Dancer's grandson. We feasted on spinach-garlic soup, a casserole of vegetables and rice, and hearty grain bread with butter. Carb heaven. I kept my meal down easily and enjoyed my first comfortable interlude of normal digestion. Then we watched some TV. I was still a wanted fugitive, so we turned off the news and watched a popular program. But even that failed to hold my interest. I went to my room and browsed through *World Mythology* until sleep claimed me.

Later that week, we joined the residents of our new community for a gathering in the sky room. Sky Dancer explained, "Wah'Kon-Tah, means the 'People and Place of the Sky, Earth, and Water. We pray to Wah'Kon-Tah, the spirit of the Sky, Earth, and Water. Wah'Kon-Tah is our home and our deity." Wah'Kon-Tah's population was mostly composed of Osage Indians, although there were tribal members from throughout America's First Nations, including Inca, Lakota, Hopi, and Navaho. This was an intentional community, not a reservation. Wah'Kon-Tah's residents also included people of Asian, Eastern Indian, African, Hispanic, European, and Middle Eastern descent.

Then there were Crystal and Cosmo. Cosmo identified himself as a Galactic Vegan. Again, Crystal self-identified as Galactic Plebian. She was Nordic-looking, but I was sure there was some Asian ethnicity in the mix. Despite her platinum blond hair and glacial blue irises, her eyes had a gentle almond shape. Another face I recognized was Bruno, with a lovely African American matriarch at his side who must be his Abby. Louie was one of about eight Hispanic folks. There were numerous mixed-race individuals I couldn't place, and several aging hippies. White Americans were a minority.

Joe Two Feathers ran up to Sky Dancer and gave her an exuberant hug. "Grandmother!" the lad crowed. He was about twelve years old, and shared his eyes, nose, and smile with Sky Dancer. She hugged him back. Joe sat at Sky Dancer's feet, clustered together with his parents and brothers. Others sat on mats or took chairs or benches. We were as far from Shelter as I could imagine. Wah'Kon-Tah was a slice of Tellara on Earth. I clasped Louie's upper arm and we sat together in silent gratitude.

Wah'Kon-Tah welcomed all faiths and ethnicities, but everyone here embraced the Galactic Medicine Wheel approach to life. Sky Dancer rose and spoke. "The Galactic Medicine Wheel is the study of the cosmic seasons of our galaxy and our Universe. We're all on a spiral dance ascending through lives and lessons. When we follow the wheel, there are no leaders or followers, no hierarchy. Contributionism provides us with robust sustainability, even surplus."

She gazed directly at me, compelling me to speak. "Like gears of all sizes and varying rotation rates, with interlocking cogs at all scale ratios from quantum to Universal: These revolving and rotating seasons come into alignment once in every few galactic seasons, bringing all of nature into harmonic resonance."

"Well said, Dana."

"The galactic alignment happened on December 12, 2012," said Louie.

"December 2012 was very subtle," said Abby.

Joe followed this thought with his own, "Many felt the shift. It started slowly and softly. It continues to build… above… below… within… without."

"Really? Most of the world seems oblivious," said a hippie guy.

"Most, but not all. We need a critical mass aligned with and attuned to the emergent collective consciousness," said Sky Dancer.

"Saffron said the same thing."

"That's how a new collective consciousness is born, one consciousness at a time," said Cosmo.

"World events have been spinning out of control. Humanity is evolving a new mythos," said Crystal.

"In order to understand our historical mythos, today we will speak of Creation Mythologies. Next Month we will speak of end time Prophesy. Who would like to share?" Sky Dancer asked the group. There was a general mumbling of assent. People stood and recited the creation stories from their cultures, including many aboriginal cultures. Christian creationism was well represented. Bruno read Genesis beautifully from his Bible. I followed along in the Bible he'd given me.

Joe Two Feathers stood and spoke, "I will tell the creation story of Turtle Island. Turtle Island is the name given to the North and Central America by many tribes. There are variations in the story among tribes, but they agree on several points.

The Sky People lived on an island in the sky. The Earth below was all water and filled with creatures who lived in water. Some breathed water, some breathed air. Sky Woman was pregnant. She peered down through a hole in Sky Island. She slipped and fell. The air breathers and birds recognized that she could not survive without land. She made a temporary dwelling in a great tree. The animals dove as deeply as they could, searching for soil beneath the sea. Muskrat dove deepest and gathered mud into his hands. When he returned to the surface, gasping, he asked, "Where can we put this soil that it may support Sky Woman?"

"Put it on my back," said the great turtle."

"The soil was placed on his back and the turtle has ever since held up the land on his shell."

"Why was the world flooded?" prodded his grandmother.

"Some legends suggest that that is how the world started, a water world and a sky world. Others say that when the sea creatures realized that Sky Woman was pregnant and her offspring would dominate the world, they became angered that they would no longer have dominance over the air-breathing creatures. This disharmony in nature caused a great flood that destroyed Sky Woman's home in the branches, necessitating the search for firmament."

Cosmo spoke up, "Eastern Indians also have a legend that the Earth rests on the back of a giant Turtle. The Turtle is one of Vishnu's incarnations. The Turtle is a link between Heaven and Earth, which makes Turtle divine. His top shell is Heaven. His body is the world, and his lower shell is the underworld. Sometimes, the world is depicted as resting on the back of four elephants on the back of the giant turtle."

"Is that where Terry Pratchett got Disc World from?" asked Louie.

"It is an ancient story. So perhaps."

"So that's why it's turtles all the way down." A light bulb went on in my head.

Louie spoke up, "I will summarize the creation story carved in cuneiform on the Sumerian clay tablets. Similar stories were found throughout Mesopotamia, in Assyria and Babylonia.

> *In ancient days when the world was young, and life was new, there was a war for this beautiful piece of real estate we call Earth. Two brothers of extra-terrestrial origin battled over this planet's resources. They needed gold for their technology. Their race was called Anun-naki and they were reptilian in appearance. Tired of doing labor themselves, the Anunnaki needed a species they could control to mine gold. Using strands of their own DNA, the brothers genetically modi-fied indigenous primates, creating early Homo sapiens. One brother, Enki, took responsibility for his creation. He sought to nurture Homo sapiens along the path of evolution so that humans might ultimately join the Galactic Family. The other brother, Enlil, sought to enslave our race. We were cattle to him. He used his knowledge of genetic en-gineering to block some of our DNA from activating specific proteins. We call this junk DNA. This suppressed our ability to apprehend our divine nature. We're designed to be just smart enough to train and*

work.

 For eons, the selfish brother positioned himself as an angry, jealous god and demanded our worship, praise, and loyalty in exchange for the promise of a better life after death. This further compromised our ability to think for ourselves. Humanity remained an enslaved race, albeit, a race with apparent free will.

 In order to outwit Enlil, the selfless brother, Enki, bred with early human women and introduced genetic enhancements into our species that would breed down through the generations. When these recessive traits express, a handful in every generation is able to apprehend humanity's divine nature."

I asked, "Would this all have been before or after Atlantis flooded?

"Millions of years before," answered Crystal.

Crystal, Cosmo, and Sky Dancer were nodding. I knew Louie was a conspiracist, but with me he'd mostly shared jabs about corrupt world leaders, reverse-engineered flying saucers, and anal probes. "Your story presents an overview of humanity's early evolution, though it leaves out many details," Cosmo said. "But well-spoken, Louie."

"The Bible says the world is only six thousand years old," said Bruno. "Conventional science hypothesizes that the Earth is 4.5 billion years old and that modern humanoids first appeared between two hundred thousand years and a million years ago. Now you're saying there is a story that stipulates our origins millions of years ago?"

"What do you believe, Bruno?" I asked.

"What I believe, Dana, is that world myths contain many answers for many people. The mind of God is so vast that there is room for all realities, all stories. I'm a Christian, but I love all religions, all belief systems, including science. Humans were gifted with curiosity and a deep longing to understand our relation to the cosmos. Every culture has found its own way to describe the meaning of existence. Each is a stepping-stone toward greater understanding."

"So, myths are data?" I asked, recollecting the Tellaran axiom.

Bruno answered, "Ancient myths reveal accounts of our ancestors' experiences. They are not dogma, but symbolic archetypes."

Louie said, "Dogma is dangerous in any flavor, even science. Science evolves one funeral at a time. Scientists livelihoods and reputations depend on their theories being the accepted model. New theories gain traction when there is no one left to defend the old doctrine. It took nearly one hundred years for continental drift to become the accepted geologic model. Since science follows the money, and money has an agenda, scientific objectivity can be compromised by corporate and government interests. Fortunately, a new mythos continuously emerges in our modern epoch as, one by one, we wake up."

"Well, original myths are certainly emerging in our era. I've literally interacted with archetypal villains and heroes." I thought of adversaries and allies, reptilians and humans, on Earth and Tellara.

Louie interjected, "But how does this resolve the dawn of Homo sapiens? How do we wade through the data of myth and science to understand when and how we emerged as a species?"

"That is the material question," answered Cosmo. "Let's harken back to Atlantean stories, from all sources. Atlantis and Lemuria fell in a catastrophe that rent the globe. Plato wrote of the fall of Atlantis in Timaeus and Critias. The Bible records the global flood in the saga of Noah. The Sumerians record it in the chronicle of Gilgamesh. The Vedic account of the flood treats this global deluge as the natural order of things rather than a divine punishment. There was a man named Manu who was advised by the god Vishnu, in the form of a great fish with horns, to build a great ship to save his family and many animals from the inundation. He tethered his ship to the horns of the fish, which pulled the vessel to land after the flood waters receded."

"Is this the same Vishnu that was a Turtle upon whose back the world rests?" asked Abby.

"Yes, Vishnu has many animal guises," answered Cosmo.

"Then I think we are mixing up creation apples and Genesis oranges," I spoke up. "Are we speaking of the creation of the world or the origins of humanity? Some myths blend the two together, like Genesis that takes place all within seven days, and others that spread it out over aeons."

Crystal answered, "Let's agree to accept that civilizations on this planet are cyclic, that civilizations rise and fall. According the Vedas, the Sumerian tablets, and many indigenous myths, ours is the fifth human civilization to emerge on Earth. The Vedas call us the fifth root race, the Hopi, the fifth world. Earth civilizations are periodically thrust back to sticks and stones. The surviving remnants of humanity are left to rebuild, repeating all the discoveries and mistakes, but each cycle takes understanding to a higher octave, a higher frequency. We may be doomed to collapse once again under the weight of our own hubris, the denial of the power of nature, and our polarized imbalance. Or we may figure out what is really going on and transcend our barriers to spiritual evolution.

"Atlantis was only the most recent of civilizations that fell as the planet responded to her inner labor pains. The Atlantean civilization lasted for millions of years and fell asunder in a series of cataclysms spread out over hundreds of thousands of years. This was but one of many cyclic civilizations that rose and fell on Earth, that were observed and interfered with by galactic species with varying agendas."

"There is the mythic Greek story of creation. *In the beginning, there was chaos, all shapeless, inert, and confusing. Discordant atoms warred. There was no light, no earth, no sea. What land there was could not could not be walked upon. What water there was could not sustain a swimmer. Chaos was forever changing, at war with itself. wet fought dry. Cold fought heat. Hard fought soft. Gaia settled all arguments and separated the earth, sea, fire, and air. The subtle and the gross separated and each found their own place in manifestation."* Crystal stopped speaking.

I felt moved to share my experience of Tellara. "I have been to an alternate Earth where the human population remembers the destruction of the Atlantean civilization. They consider mythology to be historical scientific data on par with tree rings, ice core, and geologic strata."

"So did Velikovsky, a Russian-American scientist who wrote *Worlds in Collision*," said Louie.

"Well, Tellarans remember the deluge at the end of the last ice age. During the fall of Atlantis, one component of humanity evolved toward unity consciousness while others, that is to say we, remained invested in polarity consciousness. The Tellarans shifted to a higher frequency planet. We stayed here."

"You've been to another world? An alternate Earth?" asked Joe.

"Yes, it's called Tellara. I travel there via a portal in a painting. On Tellara, humans live in harmony. They work in resonance with nature and the consensus of the people. They have no war, money, or scarcity. Healing is a high art. Service to others, not service to self, is the law of the land. As Tellara separated from Earth, the population of humans who revered polarity rebuilt this world. Left-brain thinkers came to dominate. They repressed indigenous tribes, women and artists."

"And sexually non-binary individuals," added Louie.

I nodded and continued, "Polarity is essential to creation. When rightly used, it is like magnetic poles that attract and create. When used wrongly, polarity is divisive 'us versus them' dynamic.

"The Tellarans told me that Earth and Tellara are part of the same sentient, planetary being called Gaia. The last planetary shift rent Gaia into two frequencies: Earth and Tellara, an octave apart. A segment of humanity on Earth is waking up, craving harmony. Our hearts and minds resonate together. We must see through the contrived 'divide and conquer' mentality that has kept humanity in strife. Wah'Kon-Tah is a model for harmony. It is no accident that Louie and I found our way here as we prepare to travel to Tellara." I stopped talking, feeling exposed by my revelations.

But Sky Dancer allayed my anxiety, "Well said, Dana. You are finding your voice."

Bruno spoke up, "Dana, you and I have different notions of polarity." Then he recited from Ecclesiastes.

> *To every thing there is a season,*
> *And a time to every purpose under the heaven:*
> *A time to be born, a time to die;*
> *A time to plant, and a time to harvest;*
> *A time to kill, and a time to heal;*
> *A time to break down, and a time to build up;*
> *A time to weep, and a time to laugh;*
> *A time to mourn, and a time to dance;*
> *A time to cast away stones, and a time to gather stones together;*
> *A time to embrace, and a time to refrain from embracing;*
> *A time to get, and a time to lose;*
> *A time to keep, and a time to cast away;*
> *A time to rend, and a time to sew;*
> *A time to keep silence, and a time to speak;*
> *A time to love, and a time to hate;*
> *A time of war, and a time of peace. "*

CHAPTER 11

Every day was busy in Wah'Kon-Tah. Sky Dancer's time with disciples was spread thin. She dedicated time each day to weave her intricate tapestries. In addition to gardening, teaching, and stargazing, she managed to fit Louie and me into her routine for a few minutes each day. Louie joined the carpenters crew. I journaled and planted heartplum seeds in a meadow beyond the commons.

We worked at Wah'Kon-Tah, through August and early September. It wouldn't be safe to travel to Cairo until just before the autumn equinox when the portal opened. Cairo, Earth would be dangerous every minute. Shelter Insurance & Trust has a banking headquarters in the Cairo business district. We'd travel directly from the airport to Khan al-Khalili Bazaar, where Phoenix had a stall we'd viewed via vox.

We posted a circumspect message on Facespace to Larry and Moe regarding our travel plans. Louie had joined our Facespace circle as Shep. I read random passages in Bruno's Big Black Bible and highlighted creation and end time passages that I thought would be interesting to the Tellarans. Bruno suggested I read Daniel and Ezekiel. I flipped to those sections and found them heavily highlighted, apparently by Aunt Babs.

Since our first uncomfortable interview, Sky Dancer had been unstintingly compassionate. It was she, herself, who advised us to obtain new identities. For an off-the-grid community, these folks ran a sophisticated technological operation. This legal irregularity concerned me, but Louie convinced me it was necessary. Cosmo and Crystal were put in charge of the task, Cosmo apparently having arrived at Wah'Kon-Tah with 'galactic street smarts,' whatever that meant.

My passport sported a photo of the newly thin, pale, unrecognizable Dahlia Rivers. A salt and pepper pageboy framed my face. My short, brunette bob was history. Louie's photo was printed for the equally unfamiliar Leo Selva, a thin, bald, bearded man. We had Tellaran-sounding names, mine a flower and feature from nature, Louie's, an animal and the Spanish word for forest. Our first names bore a phonetic resemblance to our real names, which would make the transition easier. We looked different from our pre-cave dwelling selves and prayed that we'd avoid facial recognition detection. We were fairly certain Shelter would not be searching for us in the Middle East.

Electronic plane tickets arrived on September eighteenth via email. We'd fly from Atlanta to Cairo via Paris. In another life, this would have been a dream itinerary. But under the circumstances, we were fugitives travelling with assumed names and false IDs.

On the eve of our departure, all of Wah'Kon-Tah gathered in the sky room. "This evening we will discuss end time prophesies from various world cultures," announced Sky Dancer.

Bruno rose. "There are a number of similarities between the end time prophesies of Biblical Revelations and Islamic Day of Judgment and Resurrection. Both warn of great corruption and chaos preceding a great tribulation. Both religions expect Jesus to return and battle evil in the guise of the antichrist. The wicked will be separated from the good. The wicked will go to Hell. The good will be resurrected. On the Day of Reckoning, both the living and the dead will be resurrected or raptured. After the tribulation ends, a time of great serenity and peace will prevail."

Crystal rose and spoke, "Ragnarök is the name of the end time prophesy in the Norse mythic tradition. It means Twilight of the Gods. Ragnarök predicts a great celestial battle that will result in the deaths of many, including the Norse gods, Odin, Thor, Loki, and Freya. There will be many natural disasters, including another inundation by water, after which the Earth will be renewed and fertile. Survivors will repopulate the Earth. Humans and gods will work together to restore civilization."

Louie spoke. "Some conspirisists believe that ETs from the Galactic Family are coming to save us. Millions of Motherships have been watching us since we exploded the first atom bomb. Earth is too precious to allow our species to destroy it. The Universe is teeming with intelligent life. Humans have advocates who are guiding us toward higher evolution. There are also ET species who revel in humanity's ignorance, fear, and suffering. We all volunteered to take part in this duality experiment and a veil of forgetfulness has fallen over our species. Alas, the most polarized among us have usurped the most power, trapped as they are in a need to dominate. The Galactic Family has been warning Earth governments for decades, but those in power have not heeded this guidance. The Galactic Family remains in higher dimensions with the exception of a handful who have chosen to incarnate on Earth as Starseeds and Lightworkers for awakening humans. According to UFOlogists, when a critical mass has woken up to the big picture that we are not alone, the Galactic Family will self-disclose. If Earth is in the throes of catastrophic natural disasters, righteous humans will be offered the opportunity to travel off world in spaceships. We will be transported to higher frequency worlds."

Joe asked, "Couldn't some of the bad ETs deceive us into boarding their ships and make slaves of us?"

"I don't know how we could tell the difference," answered Louie. This is just a theory among conspiracy theorists."

I spoke up, "I don't think anyone is coming to save us. As a species, we are self-destructive. We are cruel to the weakest among us. We are soiling our own den. Sure, a number of us are striving for harmony and compassion, but our voices are drowned out. We have to save ourselves."

"What do they believe on Tellara?"

"That planets evolve, not just the species who inhabit them. Earth is just one incarnation of Gaia, the Goddess of Mother Nature. Gaia evolves in celestial spirals, like pearls along a thread, extending back 4.5 billion years. She has undergone a planetary schism numerous times as she has outgrown lower frequencies and ascends to more rarefied dimensions. When this predicted shift happens, Gaia will undergo great natural disasters. In order to prepare for this, Tellarans will ascend as incorporeal spiritual beings. Earth will undergo a great rift akin to the cataclysm that destroyed Atlantis. Two worlds will emerge. Terra Familiar will remain home to those who cherish polarity as the natural order. Others, seeking harmony will shift to Terra Nova."

"How?" asked Joe.

"As I understand it, it will take seven generations. Either by death and reincarnation on Terra Nova, or, for some very enlightened beings, just a shift with Gaia as she separates."

Joe was curious, "So some folks get to go to planet paradise, while those remaining have to rebuild from sticks and stones."

"Both planets will have to rebuild. But it's not a punishment or reward. It's a choice. People gravitate to their natural vibration."

"So, Dana," said Sky Dancer, "these Tellarans selected you to be The Wayshower?"

"A wayshower. They want more to come."

"And your mission?"

"To tell their stories to people on Earth to help prepare us for the coming planetary shift."

"How's that working out for you?"

"I did it for the first time tonight."

"Thank you, Dana. We can all use a new mythos."

"Science has plenty to say," said Abby. "Between pollution and climate change, we are doing worse than soiling our own den. We are destroying our habitat, poisoning Earth, food, air, and water. The Earth will outlast humanity and hopefully so will many plants and animals that we don't push to extinction."

Joe Two Feathers said, "The Hopi Prophecy addresses some of those issues." And he recited.

> *"You have been telling people that this is Eleventh Hour, now you must go back and tell the people that this is the Hour. And there are things to be considered...*
> *Where are you living?*

147

What are you doing?
What are your relationships?
Are you in right relation?
Where is your water?
Know your garden.
It is time to speak your truth.
Create your community.
Be good to each other.
And do not look outside yourself for your leader.
To my fellow swimmers:
Here is a river flowing now very fast.
It is so great and swift,
that there are those who will be afraid,
who will try to hold on to the shore,
they are being torn apart and will suffer greatly.
Know that the river has its destination.
The elders say we must let go of the shore,
push off into the middle of the river,
and keep our heads above water.
And I say, 'see who is there with you and celebrate.'
At this time in history we are to take nothing personally,
least of all ourselves, for the moment we do,
our spiritual growth and journey come to a halt.
The time of the lone wolf is over.
Gather yourselves.
Banish the word struggle from your attitude and vocabulary.
All that we do now must be done in a sacred manner and in celebration.

For we are the ones we have been waiting for. When the Earth is ravaged and the animals dying, a new tribe of people shall come unto the Earth from many colors, creeds, and classes, who by their actions shall make Earth green again. They shall be known as the Warriors of the Rainbow."

"Indeed, we are the ones we've been waiting for," said Sky Dancer.

Joe continued, "The group said their farewells and good nights. Louie and I were left alone with Sky Dancer. She asked to see my vox. "Call upon your mentor in Tellara." I concentrated and remote viewed Saffron, who was in the Circle of Thirteen. Sky Dancer did not look at my view screen. Instead, she turned her gaze to the stars and described in detail what I was viewing, the expressions, the dance, and the image of the Galactic Medicine Wheel that emerged in the tapestry of the heartdance. Sky Dancer really did have a connection to Tellara without the portals. Louie and I were amazed.

He said, "Sky Dancer, finding Wah'Kon-Tah in the middle of this surreal nightmare brought me back from an abyss of grief. We wouldn't have survived without you. I'd stay here if I didn't fear it would put you all in danger. Besides, I made a promise to Dana…"

Louie would have said more, but I gasped. The image on my vox changed. My subconscious betrayed me. Javier Vasquez's visage cohered. My tenacious tracker was standing inside a room filled with old books, maps, and tapestries. A large, ancient map displaying Earth's lay lines and grid points was spread out on a table before him. Beside him, a petite, old woman was dangling a swaying pendulum that was scrying over the maps. The lines on his map blurred and twinkled in several locations including Cairo, Glastonbury, Mount Shasta, the Ozarks, and San Francisco. Vazquez was sleuthing our whereabouts and getting unorthodox help. If he didn't know our immediate location, he would soon. Our departure became more urgent.

Sky Dancer spoke in riddles. "You're not using all your resources." Louie and I looked at each other in confusion. "This man has traveled your path, always one step behind, covering your tracks."

"Covering our tracks! He wants Dana to turn herself in," Louie exclaimed. "He is leading our killers straight to us, here, to Wah'Kon-Tah!"

I concurred with Louie, "We can't take that chance. If I get arrested, I'll be silenced forever. If Louie is found, he'll be killed by Shelter. We have to get to Tellara."

Sky Dancer looked from the stars to her hands, "The old knowledge runs strong in this man. He knows things you do not. He knows things your enemy does not."

"Sky Dancer, we can't involve a police detective in an unlawful, international getaway. I don't even know how many laws we're breaking. I can't put the same interpretation on his image that you do."

"You're the one who brought his image up on your vox screen," observed Sky Dancer wryly.

"Early on, I thought he was an ally. But even after Shelter's reptile choked me, he advised me to turn myself in, and he knows that's certain death. He said he could provide a safe house, but he can't aid and abet fugitives from justice, even if he thinks I'm innocent."

Sky Dancer shrugged. "You must decide for yourself who to trust." This was her farewell benediction; that, and the dog-eared World Mythology book I'd been reading. I tucked it in my carry-on bag alongside Bruno's well-worn Bible.

At dawn, Cosmo and Crystal pulled up in the psychedelic Van to drive us to Atlanta. There were closer airports, but Atlanta would divert interest away from the Ozarks. We loaded our suitcases. They were filled with a few changes of donated clothes, nothing fancy, but nice enough outfits to travel abroad inconspicuously. I wore a beige skirt and a pink cotton blouse. Louie wore tan Dockers and a blue Oxford shirt. We had our passports, visas, and tickets. I had my vox. Louie had the money belt and we both had debit cards in our new names. We left Jay's packet locked in a safe place at the commune. Joe Two Feathers, Bruno, Abby, and Sky Dancer came out to wave us off. Good old Dahlia and Leo were setting off half-way around this world and all the way into the next.

En route to the airport, Louie asked me, "Why the pyramids? Why the equinox?"

"Phoenix tells me that each portal between Earth and Tellara has to be initiated at the nexus connecting our two worlds, something about planetary chakras."

"I've studied world chakras, ley lines, and grids," said Louie.

"Yes, living planets have chakra systems." Crystal agreed.

"The paintings open on one of Earth's grid points where ley lines intersect," I said.

"San Francisco?" Louie was dubious.

"It's where I was on the summer solstice. Maybe it's an emerging chakra. I am learning all this stuff for the first time. Phoenix says that the portals open on each succeeding solstice or equinox when our planetary gears align across dimensions. The portals open first on the Tellaran side, when Phoenix paints himself into and through the canvas. I'm the only one who can open it from this side. After the portal has been opened in each direction, the painting can be moved to any location. From Earthside, it always opens to the Tellaran vista Phoenix painted."

Our air travel was mercifully uneventful. I read about creation stories in the mythology book. At Orly International in Paris, we ate crêpes and fantasized about taking the Orient Express from Paris to Istanbul like carefree tourists. Instead, we caught a European commuter flight and landed in Cairo.

I dreaded that Egyptian Customs and Immigration would recognize me. Our IDs raised no flags, but the customs officer handled Bruno's Bible with great deliberation. He noted that it was marked up and dog-eared. He flipped through to see which chapters had been highlighted.

"You are a Christian?" His question caught me off guard.

"Umm, I've been reading Biblical scripture lately."

"Old Testament and New?"

"Yes."

"What are your thoughts on Genesis?"

"The creation of the world is a mystery." His look darkened. I scrambled to clarify, "But Genesis beautifully reveals the creation story."

"You'll want to see the pyramids."

"Of course, they're an ancient heritage site."

"The pyramids were built six thousand years ago by the Pharaoh Khufu," he stated decisively.

A light bulb went on in my jetlagged brain. Fundamentalists of all the Abrahamic religions considered Genesis to be the literal creation story. Genesis set the age of the Earth at six thousand years. If alternate archeological or geological data dated the pyramids' construction earlier, then the pyramids would be monuments to heresy. "The pyramids cannot be older than the Earth." Thus assuring the officer of my sincere belief, I gave silent thanks to Bruno for his precious Bible.

The custom officer's demeanor softened. "Are you here for business or pleasure?"

"Tourist."

He smiled, returned my Bible, collected a small cash fee for my tourist visa, stamped my papers, and waved me through. "Enjoy your visit to Egypt, Ms. Rivers."

I grabbed my bags and joined Louie, nearly collapsing with relief.

I told Louie about my strange interrogation, "What was that all about?"

"If the Muslim brotherhood had their way, they would tear down the pyramids, stone by stone. Oh, Dana, I wish we had time to see them."

"We'll see them in Tellara."

"Oh, right."

We changed a bit of money and caught a cab to Khan el-Khalili Bazaar. The colorful variety of the Bazaar took my breath away. I've always had the shopping gene and would have liked nothing more than to stroll at my leisure through the labyrinth of exotic merchandise. Leather goods, carpets, ceramics, copper, fabric, confections, jewelry, glassworks, food, and spice barrels filled every inch of every stall. Handmade items were clustered so closely that it dazzled the senses. We couldn't idly wander up and down the covered streets of this ancient monument to retail therapy. I noticed a forest green purse that was to-die-for. The shopkeeper was at my side in a heartbeat, holding the bag and matching jacket out for my inspection. I whimpered as Louie dragged me away. "I wish Hal were here," Louie sighed. As we moved, shopkeepers zeroed in on us at almost every turn.

Even resisting the temptation to stop and shop, it took us over an hour to find the stall that displayed paintings in the Tellaran style. Phoenix's gallery was filled with fractal geometry canvases and intricately patterned carpets. There stood Phoenix. The months of separation evaporated we embraced.

Then my two friends from opposite sides of the world greeted each other warmly, recalling that fateful night in San Francisco when I'd bought *Summer in Tellara*. A lifetime ago; when Jay and Hal had both been alive; when no one we knew was suspected of any crime; when we both had jobs; when our biggest problems were office gossip and where to eat lunch. Phoenix whispered, "We must hurry." He ushered us to the back of his stall, behind a tall stack of woven carpets. A customer was folding rug corners back through the stack, one carpet at a time. She could be there a while.

In the tightly packed recesses of the stall, mounted on the back wall, I first glimpsed *Tellaran Autumn*. I recognized the pyramids, but little else. The foliage on the trees was gold, brown, red, and orange, a New England Autumn in the Middle East. I stood at Phoenix's side, gazing at the painting. It pictured Giza, Tellara, backed by a glorious red, gold, and purple sunset. There stood the configuration of Pyramids flanking the sphinx. Palm trees encircled the three pyramids, which had never lost their gold capstones. Despite the passing of ages, these magnificent geometric megaliths had not worn to relics. They were covered by pristine, white limestone, red marble, and black obsidian. The Sphinx in the foreground was unmistakable in his majestic repose, but its eyes gazed at the world from below a leonine brow and regal mane. The Tellaran Sphinx had the head of a lion. A great, stone wall stood, as enduring edifice between the megaliths and the escarpment where the plateau dropped. Beneath the plateau was a massive reflecting pool that shimmered with Giza's mirror image. The distance must have been great, for the reflection blended deep into a foreground that converged into a lush park covered with autumn leaves.

"Heartplum trees' leaves turn golden, red, and orange in the autumn,'" Phoenix whispered, intuiting my amazement.

"But, deciduous fruit trees in Giza?"

"Indeed, Giza is a regional fruit basket. Beyond the plateau is lush green jungle. There is no continent on Tellara where heartplums don't thrive."

I continued to gaze at *Tellaran Autumn* while Phoenix spoke. There was one solitary figure waiting for me on a wooden bench. Saffron sat serenely beside a basket filled with fruits and flowers, gazing straight out of the canvas towards me. Our eyes locked.

"Louie, look, there's Saffron."

"She real." He was tearing up.

A breeze rippled across the reflecting pool, adding a dimensional depth to the shimmering surface. The golden leaves fluttered on their branches and danced to the earth, forming a red-gold carpet. "Louie, do you see the leaves flutter and fall?

"Yes, and the wind blowing across the pool's surface, forming cat's paws on the water's surface."

My reverie was interrupted when the woman shopping for carpets asked Phoenix a price. He answered her with scrupulous politeness, but clearly did not give her the answer she'd hoped for. This had the desired effect of making her leave. Phoenix pulled a grate down and locked his stall, earning him odd looks from shoppers and neighboring merchants. We three retreated behind the carpet stack, well concealed from the eyes of passersby.

I stood at Louie's elbow and whispered the instructions for seeing the portal. "See if you can find the movement again. Observe the wind moving through tree leaves, stirring the water's surface." As I described this phenomenon, I became aware of leaves fluttering to the ground. Louie must have seen it as well. I reached my hand into the canvas and saw it disappear into a mist. My hand entered the portal and reached out to enfold Saffron's. The portal was open. Louie copied my motion. His arm followed, then his head, then shoulders. Louie was traveling to Tellara. I saw that he had his suitcase in his other hand. I bent to pick up my bags for the trip across the portal and as I did, a shout drew my eyes to the grated door leading out to the Bazaar.

"Dana!" I locked eyes with Inspector Javier 'the stalker' Vasquez. There he stood at the grate, rattling the metal bars. I was stunned into paralysis until Phoenix shook me.

"Dana! I can keep you safe," called out my relentless tracker.

Shocked, I retreated behind the carpets and dove into the canvas, leaving behind my bags with the coolly unperturbed Phoenix. "Dana, wait! Listen!" I heard his voice recede as I summersaulted into the singularity. Phoenix was going to have his hands full explaining my disappearance to Javier. I hoped that Sky Dancer was correct in her assessment of Javier's trustworthiness, but this wasn't the moment to compare notes. I flew through the portal mists and landed with a thud on top of Louie, knocking him over. Louie was sprawled on his face. I stumbled over him and knocked into Saffron, scattering fruit and flowers about the park. "Fabulous entry, Dana," Saffron was laughing. Louie was looking at me with wounded pride.

"We were followed," was all I could offer by way of apology.

"By?" Louie asked, brushing grass off his jacket.

"Vasquez. I had to leave my luggage behind."

"Oh crap, that guy found us fast," Louie stood and dusted grass off his slacks.

"Saffron, this is my friend Louie. I believe you saw him in the cave?"

"Welcome, you are both expected." Saffron took both Louie's hands in hers and gazed at him with compassion. Her long, white hair was swept up in a chignon covered by a beaded lace snood. She wore a bronze satin sheath with wave-patterned beadwork in various shades of gold and burgundy. The beads formed a graceful spiral from shoulder to sandals. Louie seemed captivated by the deep, still power emanating from her ancient, beautiful face. He made an unrehearsed, elegant Namaste bow. By comparison, I felt shabby in my rumpled travel clothes and clumsy entry.

"Who is this Vazquez person you leapt to avoid?" Saffron eyed me curiously.

"We were followed by the police detective who is investigating our friend's murder."

"The murder you are suspected of committing, Dana?"

I replied, "Yes. I was told by a medicine woman in America to trust him. She is Sky Dancer of the Galactic Medicine Wheel. Maybe you saw her in my vox."

"I did. But you ran away from this man despite her counsel?"

"That man tracking us is a law enforcement agent, and I'm a fugitive from the law. He says he can protect me but wants me to provide proof of my whereabouts at the time of Jay's murder."

Louie said, "Saffron, we've been running for our lives and hiding out for months. Somehow, we found a temporary haven on Earth. The people of Wah'Kon-Tah saved our lives and helped us to get to Tellara, but we're not safe on Earth and neither is anyone who tries to help us. Shelter's deadly tentacles are far-reaching."

"I have no idea what to do about Inspector Vasquez," I wailed.

"He can't find us here. He'll get frustrated and return to the States soon enough," Louie declared with more confidence than I think he felt.

"I left my bags behind, my suitcase and my carry-on. Vazquez will find them."

"Phoenix locked the stall," said Louie.

"Phoenix will handle everything in his own good way," Saffron said mildly.

She gave Louie her complete attention. "Oh, my dear, your grief is palpable." Saffron embraced Louie, who quietly accepted her gentle ministrations. For the second time today, he teared up and could not speak. While she spoke softly to Louie, I gathered the strewn fruit and flowers into Saffron's basket.

She turned to me and asked, "How's your neck?"

"Healing," I replied, holding my hand instinctively to my throat. "I rested it in the cave and had some healing work done at Wah'Kon-Tah."

"We'll continue to heal your wounds while you're here." Saffron hooked one arm in mine and her other in Louie's. We turned to survey the landscape and walked down the leafy footpath out of the park to a domed wooden house overlooking the Nile River. Saffron directed us each to a ground floor room to settle in. After freshening up, we gathered in Saffron's living room. Louie had changed into crisp, clean clothes, but I was still in my wrinkled travel clothes.

"Saffron, do you have any clothes I can borrow?" She gave me an emerald green shift that fell to my ankles. I felt revived by Tellaran silk against my freshly scrubbed skin.

She served us steaming heartplum tea in tulip-shaped cups. It was crimson, sweet, tart, and delicious. "Welcome to the city of Giza, in the Region of Kemet," said Saffron.

"It is beautiful. We call it Cairo, Egypt in Earth's Middle East," I remarked, gazing from Saffron's veranda to the boats on the river and people thronging across the bridge. Seeing the actual Tellaran pyramids took my breath away. With their gleaming marble and obsidian cover stones, white, red, and black, and solid gold capstones that dazzled in the sunset.

"Look at the Sphinx," whispered Louie in awe. Its massively large face with flowing, leonine hair. Earth's Sphinx face must indeed have been carved over by a narcissistic pharaoh, as apocryphal legends claimed. Tellara's Sphinx radiated an unblemished face and uneroded body. Its ancient, wise eyes seemed to follow you wherever you walked. The entire plateau around the Pyramids was resplendent with brilliant foliage. Palms, heartplum, cypress, and olive trees intermingled around the reflecting pool. Grass, moss, and clover covered the ground in a verdant blanket. Louie and I sat and drank in the sight. "Dana, we're not in Kansas anymore."

"I'm just so grateful to be back in Tellara, I could kiss the ground."

Along the banks of the Nile, one family caught my eye. I pointed them out to Louie. "Those people don't look quite human. Remember I told you I thought I saw reptilians here."

"They are indeed Draconian reptilians." Saffron moved to my side. "They live among us openly and are beloved members of our community. Their work is for the common good of all Tellara. That family on the bridge has been reincarnating on Tellara since our rift with Earth, thirteen thousand years ago. They're friends of mine, the Raza Clan. We'll be dining and dancing with them tonight.

"I am through the looking glass," whispered Louie.

"Welcome to my rabbit hole."

"Not to worry, dear," Saffron patted Louie on the arm. "Phoenix and I will be at your side."

"Are we going to heartdance tonight?" I asked.

"Tonight, we will dance socially in a bistro with live music."

"I thought that men and women dancing together was a no-no."

"Tellarans dance frequently for all reasons." She stood. "Let's take a walk." We followed Saffron out the front door. She seemed to be gazing far beyond the pyramids as we strolled.

"Let me tell you a bit about myself. In my mid-twenties, I was a georeader. It's a melding of architectural engineering, feng shui, and sacred geometry. As cities develop, geometric patterns emerge. These configurations are analyzed to maintain balanced, harmonious energy flow in resonance with nature. All human communities on Tellara have their patterns periodically attuned. I'd been invited to balance a region called Comanche along the Gulf Coast of North America. I met and fell in love with a handsome young water whisperer named Heron.

"Water whisperer?" Louie asked.

"Heron spoke to water and water spoke to him. He was gifted at equilibrating water in harmony with the atmosphere, the human, animal, plant, and mineral kingdoms. He developed a theory about replenishing the Comanche aquifer and generating a perpetual water replenishment source. Everyone in Comanche was excited. A community dance was held. The Comanche Circle of Thirteen led the heartdance.

"The results weren't as hoped for. The perpetual cyclic source in Comanche would produce water shortages in distant parts of the world. The project was suspended. Heron was crushed. There was some good feedback. Heartdance imagery illustrated that Heron was on the right track. The six-sided H_2O crystal appeared repeatedly in the heartdance tapestry but became imbalanced and faded. Heron was sure that he could achieve the persistent pattern if he overlaid the geometry of the water crystal over Tellara's grids and lay lines. He worked on his calculations for two years and presented it to the Comanche Circle of Thirteen again. They did not agree to review his plan this time. Instead, they asked two other water scientists to recheck Heron's research. One thought Heron had captured the big picture. The other, Bo Raza, who you'll meet tonight, said Heron was still missing the intention of the water."

I was puzzled. "The intention of the water?"

"I'll let Heron tell you about it when you meet him. You've wondered about crime on Tellara, Dana. I was the young wife of a great man who committed a great crime. You asked me about men dancing and women singing? We dance together socially, but in the heartdance, we work with extremely strong sexual polarities. The magnetism manifests higher dimensional imagery. During these moments of connectedness, we feel each other's feelings and share each other's thoughts."

"Like the tapestry I saw of Earth separating into two frequencies!"

"Yes, the heartdance outpictures the probable fabric of spacetime. It is the basis of our consensus government. The images that emerge cannot help but reveal truth and our collective interests. When there are strong differences of opinion, consensus can take a long time to emerge as coherent imagery. The heartdance may display conflicting images or, occasionally, compromise. We can dance with as many people as will fit under the sky or as few as two."

Louie said, "I can't wait to heartdance!"

I explained, "Men hold space using rhythm and melody on the perimeter.

Within the circle, women feel the sonic vibrations move through their cells and are drawn into synchronistic movements that manifest the threads of the incoming imagery."

"Like human cymatics?" Louie asked.

"I think so," I said.

Saffron explained, "Humans are about seventy percent water. The pulsating vibration created by the heartsong rewires the water in all our cells. We actually become musical instruments conveying messages between dimensions. Individuals of non-binary gender can heartsing or heartdance."

"That would be me," said Louie. "Are there many on Tellara?"

"Many. We begin to lose our strict gender identification as we prepare to ascend into incorporeal beings. But we retain enough to enjoy sexual polarity."

Louie and I got quiet as Saffron continued her story. "Heron was convinced he'd made a breakthrough. He prevailed on a group of friends to repeat the heartdance. I agreed and so did five other friends of Heron's, including his mother. The image we generated showed an endless cyclic of flowing water. A water crystal rotated and revolved through season after season on a gently spinning Tellara. But a blurring and wobbling in the threads occurred and the crystal dispersed. Sadly, we couldn't recommend the project to the Comanche Circle of Thirteen. Heron was angry and hurt. He was especially mad at his mother and me. But the dance does not lie."

CHAPTER 12

Saffron continued with her memories, "I realized, in hindsight, that this was when Heron's intention to deceive began. Unbeknownst to me, Heron decided to listen to water and not heed the heartdance imagery."

"Listen to the water?"

"Water whisperers can see the images in water before they manifest. Heron was one such person.

"On Tellara, intentional lies are difficult to premeditate. Heron had to willfully close off a portion of himself to all loved ones. I was pregnant with twins at the time I felt his withdrawal. There is a ritual heartdance performed by married couples that sanctifies sexual union. It enhances intimacy. If we'd done it, I would have known what he was planning. But he kept his distance emotionally and physically.

"It only took Heron three days to set up the switchover in the pressure cells at thirty aquastations throughout the western hemisphere. It was routine for Heron to give these directions to regional waterworks. He supervised the water grid. But this was the unauthorized implementation of his perpetual cycle theory in several tributaries. The change to the flow rate wasn't dramatic. It took crews months to realize the subtle shift in the H_2O crystal dynamic. Those imbalances were the blurs and wobbles we'd seen on the heartdance tapestry. At first the replenished aquifer was robust, overflowing like a fountain. But within weeks, rivers, streams, and lakes all over the world went askew. Some places were thrown into drought. Flood plains on other continents overran. Heron's bosses stepped in and reversed the pressure flow. It took years to restore that natural balance. Heron was disgraced.

"His trial was a very somber dance. I stood with him, heartbroken and heavy with twins. He was found guilty. Punishment in Tellara takes the form of shunning. The community danced with their backs to him. His energy was cut out of the web. He was spurned from the heartdance and forbidden to work with water ever again. "That's crime and punishment in Tellara, Dana. I did not participate in his banishment dance. I couldn't bear it. When it was over, I went to him and sat with him. He did not have to close off his thoughts and feelings from me now that his scheme was revealed. I could feel the full impact of his shame. A few days later, he told me to divorce him. Reluctantly, I agreed that I would after the babies were born. I tried to engage him in the marriage heartdance ritual one more time, but he refused. Heron and his mother stayed with me until the twins were three months old. Then his mother moved to Avalon. I returned to my family in Esselen Bluffs. Heron moved to a remote village in southern Turkey, where he has spent the last eighty years working as a beekeeper." Saffron's voice trailed off and she returned from her memory.

"As the Shift approaches, Heron and a few other Tellaran 'outcasts' must be reintegrated into the global heartdance. Tellarans cannot bear to think of evolving to our next evolutionary level without every soul karmically integrated for the emergence of our next evolutionary species, Homo spiritualis. Reintegrating the few remaining outcasts will balance the karma of the entire sentient population of Tellara. Collectively, we will experience the permanent opening of our third eyes and join the spheres of loving light who can incarnate and disincarnate at will. We will be able to merge in ecstatic union with all others."

"I've seen those spheres of light in YouTube videos," Louie said. "I thought they were spirits."

"I don't know this 'utube' you speak of. When Tellarans assume this form, it is voluntary and doesn't signify death. Tellara will not be split asunder in the pending shift. For us, the shift will be a unifying event from the surface to the core of our world. Our population is in a state of divine anticipation. Some have already ascended."

"Like Violet?"

"Yes, but we cannot restore the planetary karma alone. You Earthborn souls have a role to play in Heron's rejoining ceremony."

"Oh, Saffron, I had no idea. I just thought Tellara was picture perfect."

We sat in silent reverie until Saffron sighed, "You two must be tired from your travels. Go unpack and rest."

"I have nothing to unpack. I left my bags in Phoenix's stall."

"Phoenix will be here shortly, hopefully he'll have your bags with him. Once he arrives, we'll go out to eat. Let's find you a more colorful outfit, Louie. You'll be meeting the Raza Clan tonight, Tellaran reptiles."

Phoenix arrived a few hours later, bearing my suitcase and several valises of his own. Everything was there except Sky Dancer's mythology book and Bruno's Big Black Bible.

"Vasquez," I said to Phoenix, more a statement than question.

Phoenix nodded. "He searched your bag. He was very interested in your books. He asked who Bruno Barlow was. He studied your notes in the myth book and kept it. He knows he saw you. He was friendly and asked me to tell you that he is available to help."

"Did you believe him?"

"I did. I trust him."

"That makes two of you."

"Well, I don't trust him," said Louie emphatically. "If Dana followed his

159

advice, she'd be dead. And so would I. He's like a stone in our shoe."

"He noticed movement in the painting."

"How? Only individuals with compassion and balanced karma can discern it."

"You've answered your own question."

Louie asked, "Phoenix, how does that portal open between worlds, between dimensions?"

Phoenix answered, "I use the solstices and equinoxes to create singularities in my art."

"You've lost me."

"When painting the *Magic Seasons*, I enter into a meditative state, tap into the Great Mother Sea, the source of consciousness. My fractal brushstrokes align with pure thought, which taps into a dimensional portal."

"Are you some kind of a guru?" Louie asked.

"I am a Tellaran," was Phoenix simple answer.

We fell silent until it was time to leave for dinner. My thoughts about Javier were a muddle. I'd trusted him once. But he threw me for a loop with his insistence that I turn myself in. And now, he'd led Shelter to Egypt!

* * *

We crossed a broad stone bridge over the Nile and joined the promenade through Giza. Lively locals, dressed in colorful robes, saris, slacks, vests, and scarves crowded the roads. I had changed into a coral sari and Louie wore midnight blue silk slacks and an embroidered peasant shirt that Saffron had found for him. We entered a charming eatery called Tulip's. The walls were brick, covered with tapestries and brass sculptures. Mosaic glass light fixtures of every color spanned the ceiling by the dozens. Men in intricately woven vests and women in patterned aprons sashayed around tables carrying trays of culinary delights. Aromatic spices wafted past my nose. Vaguely Middle Eastern-sounding music drifted from room to room. I followed Phoenix toward a back wall lined with couches that rimmed a table set low into the floor. Beyond this recessed banquet table was a dance floor with a raised corner stage.

The Raza Clan was already seated when we arrived. Saffron introduced us: Guna Raza, a mature woman, and Bo Raza, Guna's spouse. Their scales ranged from bronze to dark coffee and, from a few feet away, was as smooth as any human complexion. Upon closer inspection, delicate scales lay in soft geometric fans that had a beautiful iridescent sheen. Their teeth looked human. Their irises and pupils were vertical, dark slits rather than round, tinted disks. They kept their tongues in their mouths, but every once in a while, when they got excited, I could see their tongues forked into two slender reeds. Guna had lovely feminine curves and was elegantly dressed in the Tellaran style.

The Razas were fun and funny and put us at our ease. I was seated next to Bo. Up close, I could see the true humanity in his face. They were a hybrid people. "Yes, we intermarry with humans," Bo spoke, reading my mind. "We can interbreed." I hadn't expected this candor.

"What do you want to know?" Guna asked me.

"Well, what do you know of reptiles on Earth?" I asked. This provoked a laugh from everyone but Louie and me, who exchanged a bewildered look. "It is a multi-dimensional punch line to a very old joke," Saffron explained to the two of us, who apparently "had to be there."

"There are several reptilian species among us. However, here on Tellara, we are species fluid. There is much interbreeding among humanoids."

"It is intensely difficult for purebred reptilians to evolve spiritually. Over thousands of generations, we became left-brained, rational to the point that we became individually and culturally sociopathic. Empathy and compassion were considered contemptible weaknesses. Reptilian souls lack the depth and complexity of humans', despite having access to fourth-dimensional consciousness and more complexly wired DNA."

Guna spoke, "We might be smarter than you, but our higher chakras are less robust, that is to say, reptilians on Earth. On Tellara we've overcome thousands of lifetimes of selfishness to integrate our chakras, to integrate our right and left brains, to learn compassion. Humans are able to evolve spiritually and emotionally with much greater ease. You incarnate for dozens or hundreds of brief lifetimes. Reptiles can take hundreds of thousands of long lives with no incentive to relinquish power. Our collective consciousness is inertial compared to the relatively ephemeral web created by humanity. The Draconian collective mind on Earth is stratified into fear-based paradigms that have been concretized over eons. But when an individual reptile does break through that rock-solid ceiling, evolves out of their exploitive mindset, and choses love over fear, we begin our slow ascent to enlightenment."

Bo took over the narrative. "We originated in a region of the galaxy that is remote beyond reckoning. Draconians colonized and enslaved many planets' native humanoids. It is our natural way. Other members of the Galactic Council opposed us and there were ancient wars for the conquest of worlds. We won on Earth, and the Council was forced to sign a treaty of non-interference. They can guide from a distance, but not interfere. It is up to humanity to recognize their shackles and throw them off. Then the Galactic Council will swoop in to help with the healing and rebuilding."

"Have you heard of the Anunnaki? Enlil and Enki?" asked Louie.

"We're descended from them. Earth reptilians remain one big dysfunctional family. We're so grateful to have migrated to Tellara."

Guna continued, "Now, here on Tellara, we've lived, reincarnated, worked, and played among humans for thirteen thousand years. Tellara is our true home. But there is another side to the serpent, a side that is hidden until the individual decides to follow the path of compassion."

"How so?" I asked as colorfully attired servers brought food. Heaping dishes were spread before us to sample and savor.

"It is the thirteenth path, the path of compassion and healing, represented by the zodiacal sign Ophiuchus, the serpent handler, the healer, and kundalini master."

"We don't have a zodiacal sign called Ophiuchus on my Earth."

"You must. Ophiuchus is the constellation between Scorpio and Sagittarius in the zodiacal belt. The thirteen lunar cycles are a reflection of the thirteen celestial cycles through which our planetary equinox wobbles. It is an essential link to the galactic center, the basis of the council of thirteen elders, the foundation of our thirteen-moon calendar."

"We have a twelve-month calendar and twelve zodiac constellations," I said.

"Improbable," Bo raised his eyebrows. "The natural calendar begins on the new moon of each cycle and lasts twenty-eight days."

Phoenix interjected, "The more you learn of Earth's ways, the more improbable they will seem. I think their calendar was intentionally designed to be counter-intuitive and contrary to lunar rhythms."

I spoke up, "Earth has twelve months, each with a different number of days." I was beginning to think Bo Raza was pulling my chain. But he looked at me like I was teasing him.

"My dear Dana, if your thirteenth sign has been obscured from your calendar, those who did so have hidden the healing capacity of the serpent bearer. That would prevent the means of balancing darkness and light."

"Nostradamus calculated his astrology using the thirteenth sign. In 1582, the church established the Gregorian calendar and removed Ophiuchus," Louie supplied this bit of arcane trivia. While I was busy being amazed, Louie spoke again. "The snake is evil in some Earth mythology."

"Ha!" Bo Raza laughed. "That fits. That's Enlil's legacy. Here, like Enki, the serpent is a healer. Ophiuchus is in direct alignment with the galactic center. It is the fourth element in the great eclipse that was upon us during the last day of Ophiuchus."

"That must have been our December 2012. It was much ado about nothing."

"Only for those who expected nothing. For those attuned to the shift of the ages, there were definite changes in our psyches," this from Louie.

"A few years later, I stumbled into Tellara."

"That is hardly 'nothing,'" said Bo Raza. "You traversed the holofractalgraphic vacuum.

"Holofractalgraphic?"

"Holistic, holographic, thousand-petaled lotus mapped on every proton, creating a fractal reflection of the entire Universe."

"Oh," I nodded recalling my lecture in Shastise.

"Not really thousand-petaled. That's a metaphor. The number is in the trillions. The petals of the flower of life are pixels on every proton. Every proton contains the entire Universe as a hologram."

While I strained to follow the discourse when it turned to science, Louie was rapt, savoring every morsel of Tellaran wisdom.

Guna continued where Bo had left off, "There is a black hole in the center of every galaxy. Black holes create galaxies."

"I don't think our science works that way," said Louie.

Guna said, "Based on the information Phoenix has gathered, your science is twelve thousand years behind Tellaran natural history and technology. Your science has gotten off track."

"I can't follow the theoretical math well enough to understand theoretical physics. But I like the science documentaries on TV," I defended my limited understanding.

"Those presentations are helpful only to a point. The foundational assumptions are flawed. The Universe doesn't need complicated mathematics to be understood. It can be mapped using interpenetrating geometric structures in perfect equilibrium, along the golden mean ratio. That is why we say, 'as above, so below.'"

"We have that saying as well, 'as within, so without,'" said Louie. Guna and Bo smiled and nodded. "How do humans and reptiles interbreed?" Louie asked, changing the subject. "Don't reptiles lay eggs?"

Again, the Tellarans of both species laughed. "We give live birth and nurse our young." Guna replied. "We have hair and homoeothermic metabolism. Our reptilian aspect is in our brain biochemistry, chakras, and genetic heritage. On the surface it manifests in our scales, eyes, noses, tongues, and some facial features. Our DNA is compatible with humans but has different active genomes. On the etheric level we are more reptilian. Our mammalian humanity is more than skin deep. This is the result of natural mutations and genetic manipulation that occurred over hundreds of thousands of years."

"What do you do Guna?" Louie asked.

"I'm a poet."

"What about you, Bo?" I asked.

"I'm a water whisperer," he replied.

"Why then, you must know Heron."

"Heron, Saffron, and I go way back. I believe Saffron has arranged an outing for us later this week to call on Heron."

"Isn't he in seclusion?"

"Self-imposed. But not much longer…we hope. That's the reason for our visit."

"Why on Earth would Louie and I be included in your group?"

"The material question would be 'why on Tellara?' hmmm?"

I smiled. "You're right, that's the question. What is the answer?"

"You'll find out in a few days."

"What happens few days?"

"Have you ever traveled on a Tellaran light ship?"

"You mean the airborne blimps I've seen streaking overhead? No, not yet."

"That is how we'll travel to see Heron. But tomorrow, we have an outing closer to home, here in Giza. We'll visit the research facility, Gray Station. You'll meet the local Zeta Reticuli scientists involved in their genetic revitalization program."

"We are going to meet grays?" Louie was excited.

I mused on this as I savored spicy red pepper, spinach, and feta blended in a filo wrap. Music started on the corner platform. It had a lilting, Middle Eastern quality. We were served a mild alcoholic beverage that tasted like beer.

After we all finished eating, Bo Raza stood and offered me his hand, "Let's dance."

Our entire group stood to dance. What I realized after a few minutes was that none of us was partnered up. It was kind of a free-flowing circle dance where all moved in and out of smaller and larger groupings in serpentine spirals. The spirals opened to larger circles, then collapsed into curved lines, in random endless patterns. People from other rooms in Tulip's Bistro flowed in and joined the dance. Louie was having a good time. I heard him laugh for the first time since Hal's death. He allowed Phoenix to sweep him into the music. We danced, drank, socialized, and laughed into the night. I decided I liked social dances on Tellara. Tellarans know how to party.

After only a few hours' rest, Louie and I were awakened by a beautifully composed Saffron. It was much too early. We shared a light breakfast of bread, cheese, cucumber, melon slices, and tea. Bo Raza and Phoenix joined us in Saffron's kitchen, ready for our excursion to Gray Station. But first, Phoenix had a gift for Louie. Louie opened an embroidered box and lifted out a rectangular, crystal-encrusted, gold rectangle. It was a vox. "You'll be glad to have a vox you can attune to your own DNA." Phoenix explained.

Louie was overwhelmed. "I remember when Dana first showed me hers. I thought it was a gag. But I wasn't laughing when she used it to save our lives."

"Wait 'til your training begins! Ha! You'll learn a new definition of clumsy when you literally bounce off the walls." I hugged Louie and we were off. We rode a train to the easternmost side of Giza and walked a few blocks to a building complex. The complex was wrought of gray cinderblocks. It contained the first buildings I'd seen in Tellara that had ninety-degree corners, flat roofs, and no color. It looked like nothing so much as a warehouse district in urban America. There was no landscaping, just gravel. The entire complex was raw land with covered glass tunnels between the buildings.

Saffron explained, "Grays don't like weather. Any weather. They live and work in the complex and rarely step outside their climate-controlled, hive-like structures."

We were greeted by two grays named Leel and Jeej and a human named Falcon. Saffron explained that all grays' names began and ended with the same consonants. "It is a binary thing they adhere to. They don't run out of combinations because, while humans hear about one hundred vowel sounds, the grays hear several hundred thousand." My first impression of the grays was that they were frighteningly cerebral. Some were tall, others short, but all spindly, thin, pale gray, with big, black, almost insect-like eyes. Most wore dingy gray lab coats. Every once in a while, there was a splash of muted color on one of their smocks. "Those are the hybrids," Bo Raza whispered in my ear. "They use color to identify themselves."

"Welcome to Gray Station," said Jeej. Leel bowed. Jeej wore a gray-green smock. Leel's was mauve-gray.

"Let's head toward the conference room. An orientation is prepared." Falcon directed us to a doorway at his left. The room was filled with gray chairs and a gray table, bland but reasonably comfortable. We took our seats and faced our hosts.

"I'm Falcon, one of the Project Zeta administrators. The grays, as you've begun to see, are brilliant, but not terribly imaginative or creative outside rigorous scientific disciplines. They are rather indifferent to color, music, food, art, and most things of beauty, for that matter." Falcon spoke as if Leel and Jeej were not in the room. Louie and I must have looked embarrassed. But Jeej spoke up.

"We have few feelings to hurt. Our emotional bodies are as thin as paper. This is the aspect of the human quality we are endeavoring to integrate into our genetic code."

"With some success," added Leel. "But Falcon misspeaks. We are not indifferent to music. It translates as mathematical code."

Jeej continued, "We have bred many first-generation hybrids. Several thousand every generation, but so far, all are sterile."

"All of the genetic material is donated by sympathetic human Tellarans. The DNA is never cloned. That is part of our strict oversight. The genetic material is spliced into the gray chromosomes," Falcon supplied.

"We are a dying race," Leel stated blandly. "Over millennia, we became so cerebral that our capacity for emotion devolved. We did not know that it was the emotional vehicle which carried our species' fecundity. Lack of emotions has depleted our physical vehicles."

"We live, we work, but we do not play. We do not create. We do not love. We have something of a hive mind. We have little free will. We are all dedicated to this genetic research. It is our only hope for the survival of our species. We are attempting to recover something that we threw away millennia ago," said Jeej.

Leel said, "The hybrids are the best of us. Fecund human-Zeta hybrids would be the greatest possible outcome to our research."

Jeej took over the narrative, "Hybrids have the rudiments of humor, emotion, and creativity. Hybrids understand color and music. Phoenix was going to bring us some Earth music today. Do you have it?"

Phoenix passed across a box of CDs. It included Mozart, Bach, Gershwin, Coltrane, World Music, Ragtime, some Indian, Asian, Zydeco, medieval chants, and Middle Eastern artists I did not recognize. Phoenix had included Frank Sinatra, The Beach Boys, Muddy Waters, Ella Fitzgerald, some Motown, the Moody Blues, and the Beatles. "Here is a start."

"Why these artists, Phoenix?" Louie asked. "This is so random. No Elvis, no Judy Garland, no Cher?"

"It is as what non-Earthborn visitor could gather for a first collection," answered Phoenix.

Falcon said, "The grays use music to discover unique mathematical patterns in the rhythm, melody, or consonants. You have several scales on Earth, the western octave and the eastern scales with their many nuanced half, quarter, and sixteenth tones. Imagine the tones between the black and white keys on a piano. It's like that vowel thing. They hear many more in-betweens."

"We are hoping that music from another world will help expand our mathematical algorithms."

"How is that possible?"

"We're bored with Tellaran music. It is repetitive. We hope to find new mathematical sequences that we can apply to the geometry of the hybrid genome spiral. Music is math. The DNA double helix is geometry. You see?" Jeej replied as though this information was self-evident.

I did not see. But then, when had I ever studied the human genome project or theoretical math or music theory? This was alien thinking, to me.

"Start with Mozart," suggested Louie. "He's pretty mathematical as is Bach." Leel and Jeej nodded.

Falcon set up a holographic projection regarding Gray Station. It included their mission statement, scenes from their laboratories, the fertilization of hybrid eggs by sperm, pregnant women, both gray and human surrogates carrying hybrids to term, and attempts to breed hybrid sperm and eggs, both in the laboratory and the old-fashioned way. What should have been a much too private coupling was, in fact, dreadfully clinical. Grays did not seem to appreciate the sexual act as intimate lovemaking. They really were missing a chip. The hologram showed newborn hybrids being nursed and raised by their surrogate mothers, and hybrid children in classrooms, where they were exposed to art, music, and games by human instructors.

The hologram demonstrated why the genetic engineering wasn't used with reptilian DNA. Although compatible, reptilian DNA overwrites the Zeta code and does not equip their hybrid offspring with a full emotional palette; nothing beyond rudimentary humor, or survival instincts. Without the fully integrated chakra system, the full range of emotions does not codify in hybrid DNA. The gray-reptilian hybrids were unpleasant and sterile. We saw pictures of several gray-reptile hybrids from several thousand years ago. They were ugly, creepy, and fortunately, the first and last of their kind.

"What's with the anal probe?" asked Louie. "The grays on Earth have a terrible reputation for abduction and invasive medical procedures."

"We don't do that on Tellara. But if our counterparts on Earth still use this technique, it is because we have no emotions of our own. Some hybrids have rudimentary feelings. On Tellara, individuals volunteer genetic material for the grays' survival. On Earth, they take what they want. They need their human subjects to be docile and accommodating. Over millennia, they discovered that invasive procedures induce complete humiliation in humans. The most vigorous and intelligent among you will dissolve into compliant shame when your body is thus abused. The amnesiac procedure performed by the grays is far more effective and enduring when applied to a fearful, infantile, fragmented mind. The gray geneticists recognize this fear but have no capacity for empathy. Here, Tellaran human scientists, like Falcon, oversee our work. Exploitation is not permitted."

CHAPTER 13

Next, we toured the labs and met some of the scientists. One gray, maybe a male, named Shoosh, showed us dozens of embryos that were being prepared for uterine implantation. A human woman would really have to be dedicated to the preservation of these strange Zetas to volunteer her body to their cause. I couldn't fathom it. I understood why, on Earth, this work was conducted covertly, by force, and utilized memory-wiping techniques. Part of me was disturbed by the invasive, clinical aspect of the work. Part of me felt pity for these emotionless, cerebral half-beings. I did not envy their fourth-dimensional minds. I hoped we would not have to be here much longer.

Shoosh stunned Louie and me when he held up a mega-ton power syringe, pointed it at us, and asked to harvest cells from the epithelial lining of our stomachs. "You have evolved on a different world. Although human, your genome will exhibit much more primitive chains. Don't mistake my use of the word primitive for unevolved; rather, raw material without the homogenized Tellaran DNA. Tellarans have become a genetic melting pot over the eons, unlike your Earthborn brothers and sisters who remain genetically diverse." Shoosh spoke like a stilted automaton.

His endeavor to soften his threat with his explanation horrified me all the more. I started to back up. Out of the corner of my eye I saw Louie retreating toward the door. Falcon injected himself into the conversation. "That was badly done, Shoosh. You were told to let the hybrids handle the requests. You lack the communication skills needed interact with human sensibility."

Louie said, "It doesn't matter who asked, or how they asked. The answer is no. I want outta here."

"That is unacceptable," said Shoosh. "Your epithelial cells are required. We only need a little of your mitochondria."

"Bite me, Swoosh." I called over my shoulder as Louie and I bolted for the door. Leel, Jeej, Falcon, Saffron, and Phoenix all followed us into the corridor.

"Apologies for Shoosh's manner." Falcon said.

Jeej spoke in a pedantic manner. "His name is Shoosh, not Swoosh. There would be no need to bite. He has a syringe." I gaped at him as if he had two heads.

I turned on Saffron, "Did you know they were going to ask to harvest our DNA?"

"That was the reason for their invitation. But we anticipated that Leel and Jeej would explain the procedure to you."

"You two are hybrids?" Louie's question to Leel and Jeej was as much accusation as question.

"Our smocks are colored," said Jeej. "We assumed it was self-evident."

"We are so personable. That is why we were selected to escort you," Leel added.

"This is a formal occasion," Jeej replied, as if this explained all.

"Swoosh was the first full-blooded gray we've met today?" Louie persisted. "That binary walking computer?"

"His name is Shoosh," Jeej corrected again as if this was the germane point and Louie was an idiot. "He is my sperm donor."

"Well, he's Swoosh to me," replied Louie indignantly.

I wasn't done with Saffron. "This was unexpected and unappreciated."

"So I see." She did not apologize.

"We are a dying species," Leel commented to Louie and me.

"We are a dying species," Jeej repeated.

"The grays are facing extinction despite the assistance of human scientists and Tellaran human DNA," Falcon said.

"Saffron, Phoenix, Falcon, have you donated your DNA to Project Gray?"

"I have," said Falcon.

"I have," said Phoenix.

"Yes," said Saffron. "I do not share your revulsion at the idea."

"They don't clone human DNA. Our oversight is meticulous. They would splice strands of your genes into hybrid chromosomes," Falcon pressed.

"Can we be done here?" my voice was harsh.

"Will you promise to think about it?"

"No!" I yelled.

"No!" Louie seconded. "That was an ambush."

Outside, I said, "Saffron, that was creepy."

"Creepier than the way the grays conduct their secret, invasive genetic experiments on Earth? Shoosh asked. You answered. He explained how your genetic material would be used and why it was needed. You said no again and left. That's the end of it." Saffron wasn't angry or disappointed. But I felt both ashamed and exploited. It was the first time on Tellara that I'd felt unhappy with circumstances.

I turned to Bo Raza. "Sorry," I whispered. I don't know why I felt the need to apologize.

"Do not concern yourself, Dana Travers."

"And what's up with the names?" Louie asked. "All beginning and ending with the same consonant?"

"The gray's names are sequential by consonants and vowels in their own language. They hear the finest distinctions. They think human names are all out of order and don't understand why we choose to name ourselves randomly."

"Just call me Louie Random-Leon."

Bo Raza said, "Reptilians sympathize with the grays. We also once faced extinction."

"How was that?" asked Louie.

"Our home planet, Nibiru, has a long, eccentric orbit. We are only in your solar system for a few hundred years out of our 3,600-year revolution. We need a greenhouse effect to retain heat. The perfect source is gold that was found in abundance on Earth. Had we not mined that gold, Nibiru's surface would have become a frozen ice ball. As it is, Draconians make their habitat below ground, relying on thermal hot springs to manage our environment."

Louie spoke to Bo Raza, "There are Sumerian tablets that claim Anunnaki reptilians from Nibiru came to Earth seeking gold. If Anunnaki technology is so advanced, surely, they could transform lead into gold. Why go to the trouble of mining it and creating a genetically engineered slave race of humans to do the grunt work?"

"Ah!" Bo Raza replied. "But you see, there is gold for trinkets, gold for technology, and spiritual gold. What Draconians did not understand, and what only a handful of human alchemists ever realized, was that to transform base metal into material gold, they must first transform their souls into spiritual gold, into saints who had no greed, no need to hoard. And in becoming holy, they also transmuted disease, aging, and death. The alchemist himself was the gold, the philosopher's stone, and the elixir of life. But reptiles had no understanding of this concept, much less the patience to practice the art for the decades, centuries, even lifetimes in order to succeed. Mining material gold out of Earth's uniquely rich veins was the most expeditious."

"But again, Bo Raza, why do reptilians still need such quantities of gold?" Louie asked. "Sure, Sheldon Walters wears a Rolex, and probably has a warehouse full of gold ingots somewhere, but what is the necessity for a multi-millennia mining operation?"

"And why pass that covetousness along to humans?" I asked.

Bo Raza answered, "Let us look at the unique properties of gold that make it priceless to the Draconians on Nibiru."

The Tellaran Chronicles of Science and Spirituality
Gold

No gold is formed on planets. Gold is extremely rare throughout the Universe. It's true that we are all stardust, because our atoms were generated in the hearts of stars. Gold and other heavy elements are only formed by the rare collision of two dense neutron stars. The radiation released from this bombardment is a more energetic blast than that of any other emission that occurs in the electromagnetic spectrum. Such a collision occurred around 4.5 billion years ago. The generated gold drifted toward Gaia, congealing in veins and nuggets in her primordial soup. This deposit made Gaia the stuff of avarice. That Gaia was in proximity to Nibiru's orbital path targeted us as the spoils of galactic war.

Gold is incorruptible. It does not corrode, tarnish, discolor, rust, or degrade. Gold is inert. Gold forms amalgams, but not chemical compounds. All the gold that ever existed in ancient times still exists today.

Gold is the most malleable of all metals. It can be pounded down into gold leaf sheets only two atoms thick. Diatomic gold can form the thinnest wires of any metal, which has applications for nanotechnology and microcircuitry.

Gold atoms cluster in isotopes, but do not form molecules. Gold nanoclusters can store short-term energy and electric charges for molecular electronic applications.

Gold has unique thermoelectric effects; it can convert heat directly into electricity. Indeed, it is a top conductor of electricity. Gold conducts electricity 10,000 times faster than any other conductor, with no resistance. This makes it a valuable component of many sources of free, clean, renewable energy.

Gold capstones on pyramids form a global grid that Tellara uses to stabilize seismic disturbances.

Gold is a great conductor of heat, because it reflects infrared radiation. It forms perfect thermodynamic shields, both terrestrial and celestial, which is to say, on spacecraft, space stations, and lunar biodomes.

In the case of Nibiru, a shield of gold surrounding its outer atmosphere retains heat within the planet during its long and distant odyssey from the sun. Draconians' need for a gold shield to maintain their habitable climate would have been strong motive to mine Tellara's gold. First, doing the work themselves, and later, genetically engineering the Adamic race to mine gold for them. To Draconians, gold is survival.

Gold has mystical properties. Alchemists use it to transform negative spiritual energy to positive. In the hands of the uninitiated, it can be misused. There is danger in worshiping gold.

When gold is pounded down to the size of a single atom, it is no longer metallic. It forms a white powder called monoatomic gold, which has inert ceramic properties. Monoatomic gold is a superconductor, even at room temperature. This means it has no resistance. Currents do not degrade over distance. If combined with DNA, monoatomic gold can even be a super conductor in living tissue.

When heated, it becomes lighter, even to the point of levitation.

Gold has healing properties. When injected, it coats and sooths degenerative, rough joints. In minute amounts, monoatomic gold can enhance dreams and help clear the pineal gland. It coats neurons, which helps slow degenerative nerve disease.

Monoatomic gold is the primary element in Draconian technology on Nibiru.

"And probably on Earth as well," I speculated.

"Sure," said Louie, "I bet they use it in their RAT-TRAK for looking around the corners of time. There are Sumerian and Zulu legends that speak of beings who came from the stars and enslaved men to mine gold. Incas and South Africans have megalithic evidence of ancient gold mines."

I mused, "Maybe this is the source of legends of dragons hoarding gold that have seeped into our folktales. Maybe it's why there are stories of quests for El Dorado or the Golden Fleece."

"Dragons also hoard jewels," Louie pointed out.

"That would be crystals," supplied Bo Raza. "Many crystals have technological uses."

"Consider quartz in circuits and filters, in computers and clocks. Not to mention that gold and jewels are pretty," I smiled. "Many beings have hoarded and worshiped treasure and given it monetary value."

Louie concurred, "Diamonds and rubies have industrial applications." He lifted his vox and let the sunshine reflect and refract off its crystal facets."

"Let's train with your voxes until it's time for our next outing, said Bo Raza.

"We will be going to a beautiful place," Saffron added. "Juniper will be joining us for lunch at the reflecting pool overlooking the pyramids of Giza."

Later, at the reflecting pool, Louie stood and pulled out a chair as a lovely young woman approached. "Juniper," I rose to greet her with a hug and a kiss. "Louie, this is Juniper, my first Tellaran friend. She greeted me in *Summer in Tellara* on the hills overlooking Esselen Bluffs."

"Louie bowed, "Greetings Juniper. It's my pleasure to meet you. My name is Louie." She sat and we unpacked our picnic lunch.

"Welcome wayshowers," smiled Juniper. Louie's courtesy charmed Juniper, who had seen little of Earth formal manners. "I like your friend, Dana."

Over lunch, Saffron opened a map. "We will travel by airship to Antalya. It will be good to spend time with Heron and his beehives. Then there will be a Rejoining Ceremonial Dance to balance his karma." She pointed to the city on the map, along the Mediterranean coast.

Phoenix explained, "During the Rejoining Ceremony, many participants will choose to ascend early, as soon as they feel the balanced karma."

"What does that mean, ascend early?" asked Louie.

"When Violet chose to ascend, she made the transition to her spiritual essence and relinquished her physical vehicle. Most Tellaran humans will be making the transfiguration within the year. It is the conclusion of our planetary evolutionary shift."

Bo Raza said, "Not all Tellarans will choose to ascend. Even as our geology shatters, we have shelters for all species of flora and fauna. Some havens are off-world ships. There is a massive plant and animal sanctuary on Antarctica, and more being built underground in inner Tellara. You've seen one shelter under Mount Shastise. Those who choose to remain corporeal will replenish Tellaran land, sea, and skies over many millennia."

Phoenix continued, "Unfortunately, none of the grays can ascend. Their species has so little soul stuff. Until they succeed in vivifying their DNA, they shall remain corporeal. They will continue to conduct their research until they achieve hybrid fecundity." If this was meant to make me feel bad, it did, but not enough to change my mind and run back to Gray Station for the Full Needle Treatment.

"What of Tellaran reptiles?" asked Louie.

Guna said, "We are ecstatically awaiting ascension. It has taken us millennia longer than humans and endless incarnations to attain this level of illumination."

Saffron continued, "Tellara and Earth are both are becoming unstable due to our alignment along Gaia's spiral thread. This alignment causes cascading internal gravity waves that interpenetrate all the planets strung along this multi-dimensional coil."

"Bo, what is it like to ascend?" I asked.

"I will transform into a light sphere with my heart center connected to the Great Mother Sea. Each sentient sphere, like each proton, can be mapped with the flower of life. Trillions of petals will cover each conscious sphere."

"Will you still have gender?" Louie asked.

"Ascended beings are gender fluid. I will transcend the duality of life and death, male and female, but I'll still be me. As a sphere of light, I will be able to interpenetrate with all my loved ones, like merging soap bubbles. I hear it's better than sex."

Juniper interrupted, "Of course, the ascended are not purely incorporeal, they still have atomic structure. Those light spheres are mostly plasma through which electromagnetic, sonic, and gravity waves penetrate."

"When will you ascend, Juniper?" I asked.

"During the final shift. I tend to Tellaran animals. I'm helping to build and populate the Antarctic sanctuary for Tellara's fauna and flora. They must be protected when the shift happens. I hope you will come visit our sanctuary."

"It sounds like kind of like an ark." I said.

"Ark?" Juniper asked.

"Noah's Ark. Noah is Biblical character who saved all the animals, two-by-two, in a boat that survived the Biblical flood. The flood wiped out most of humanity."

"This Biblical myth from your world sounds like the collapse of Atlantis, the great flood that wiped our last civilization."

Louie added, "Our Bible provides just one myth about Earth's ancient flood. Other cultures have other similar myths to describe the global event."

"I brought a Bible with me. But it got stolen on Earth. The Bible is the monotheistic foundation of much of Earth's western civilization."

"I brought some Biblical movies to Tellara in my collection," said Phoenix.

I said, "I'll get another Bible for you to read."

Phoenix made a slight bow. "I would read your Biblical account of the destruction of Atlantis as well as your other Bible stories. I hope you remember our time together in Atlantis fondly. We've been friends a long time."

"Have we? What does that mean?"

"You'll remember our connection soon enough. You and I have an ancient history."

Back at the house, Louie started training with his vox under the tutelage of Phoenix and Bo Raza.

"Not so easy is it, Louie?" I teased as he tumbled around the room in undignified bounces.

"Lateral movement is more difficult than up and down!" he grumbled. "No steering mechanism."

"My brother will be joining us for our trip to Antalya," said Juniper.

"Robin?" I asked, delighted.

"Yes, he is expected to arrive in Giza later this evening. We are eager to visit grandfather Heron after so many years."

"If we are leaving Giza for a few days, I want to return to my side of the portal to communicate with my children. Phoenix, do you have a safe house set up?"

"I do. I have moved *Tellaran Autumn* from my stall in the Bazaar to a studio in the Old City."

"That will be more private, away from prying eyes. Is there an internet connection?"

"Yes. I understand how your computer works." After some discussion, Louie and I decided it would be safe for me to go alone. As long as I did not leave the premises, I would remain undetected. Louie wanted to stay in Tellara and practice with his vox. Bo and Phoenix remained to mentor him. I think Saffron wanted solitude. Preparing to see her ex-husband, love of her life, father of her children and grandfather to Juniper and Robin, after a separation of some eight decades might be fraught with emotion, even for this serene Tellaran Elder.

Saffron walked me to the park bench. I looked into the gloaming until I saw the ripples of moving air. I stepped through and tripped onto the studio floor. Luckily, Phoenix had mounted the canvas low on the wall. The studio was spacious and pleasant. Twelve canvases adorned the wall. There was a couch and a desk. I sat at the desk and booted the laptop. It flickered to life in its own good time and I opened my Facespace account.

There were six messages from 'Larry and Moe.' I messaged them that all was well. "Portal recovered." I told them I'd met new people, danced, and gotten an education. I missed them terribly.

Then my heart did a little flip as 'Larry' popped up in the chat app. "Wassup, Curly?"

"All is well at my end. Are you safe?"

"Yes, we were guided to a safe house in Montana by a little old lady named Minerva."

"How did she find you?"

"Apparently her grandson knew we were in trouble and needed help. She's some kind of Romani psychic."

"That sounds weird."

"Weird, but a reprieve from the road."

"Are you sure you're safe? Why would Gypsies help strangers?"

"Seems like they have little love for the police. We feel very protected in this off the grid community."

"Just like Shep and me. A little bird told me there's safe house ready in Shasta, California although the painting is not ready." I hoped they knew that the little bird was Phoenix Fire Bird.

"It is a long drive from Montana to California. But Minerva knows of safe stops along the way."

I messaged Phoenix's address in Shasta, California to Larry and Moe. He'd leased this house on his first visit to San Francisco back in June.

"Check out your favorite Blog." I found Val Andrews' latest post. It was filled with electronic copies of the documents from Jay's incriminating packet. My jaw dropped as I reread those accursed documents, posted for all the world to see. What followed were documents even more detailed than the ones I had read while faxing them to Javier. There were email memos between Frank Fretz, Sheldon Walters, Senator R, Congresswoman G, and Monsignor M. The messages were obscure. Some referred to a problem with 'damp linen' in exotic locales that was being handled by trusted serpents—not servants, serpents. Others referred to sheep with too little work and too much time on their hands. The sheep needed some E and SC. Another series were about a forest fire in the

Mid-Atlantic States that could be dowsed by K2. There was no fire in the east, so this data entry seemed like a cypher.

There were copies of cashed checks, in the millions, signed by Sheldon Walters, to obscure political action groups and charities of all faiths. There were deposits to a bank in Antigua and the Cayman Islands called Caribbean Fidelity Services. There were dozens of invitations to political fundraisers and insurance lobbyists' luncheons.

A multi-page spreadsheet listed forty-seven U.S. state and federal elected officials to whom Walters had donated money. The spreadsheet listed quid pro quos in abbreviated code, whether or not they had been received, and the timeline for delivery. The second sheet listed the names of one hundred seventeen international leaders, bankers, religious leaders, and CEOs who also had coded quid pro quos and delivery dates by their names. Some of the codes were 'V,' 'E,' 'SC,' 'K2,' 'Blk,' and so forth. There was a column at the far right of each spreadsheet labeled 'consequence' in a tiny, squished font. This column was also filled with alpha codes. Some elected officials had an 'L' in that column. I knew enough about current events to notice that these politicians had lost their most recent elections or were falling behind in the polls. There were some who had the code 'S.' Unless you were living under a rock—hell, I *was* living under a rock for over a month, so even that was no excuse—anyone would realize that the individuals marked with an 'S' had been disgraced by scandal. Some names had a code 'B;' Val's research indicated that they had all faced bankruptcy. 'D' showed up in the consequence column of three individuals who had recently died. One apparent suicide, another a brain embolism that erupted just prior to a crucial senate vote, and another was in a fatal car accident. Alice had been right that night at Casa Italia. Sheldon Walters considered himself above the law; he did control governments of several countries, and he did have wealth enough in offshore accounts to buy several small countries.

Then I read Val's testimonial.

"I am Val Andrews, the recent widow of Jay Andrews, and the mother of his two children. He worked for Shelter Insurance & Trust up until the night of his disappearance and death. As widely reported in the mainstream media, Jay was murdered on June 23rd of this year. At first, suspicion was cast on his colleague, a woman named Dana Travers. Individuals at Shelter Insurance & Trust worked very hard to convince me that Dana Travers was involved in criminal activity that led to Jay's murder. But documents contradicting this supposition have come into my possession. These documents were collected by Jay over a period of six months prior to his death. They are posted here for all to view."

I believe my husband was killed because he intended to leak these

176

> documents. The first time I posted them, I took the precaution of
> emailing the blog link to several dozen bloggers and journalists. The
> documents were taken down and my blog was removed from the
> internet about four hours later. As I'd hoped, the documents I posted
> were read and saved by a handful of journalists. They began inves-
> tigating particular details of bribes, falsified accounts, consequence
> codes, memos regarding illegal insurance practices and political pay-
> backs. Once the media investigation began, I reposted the electronic
> documents to another blog site and emailed the bloggers and journal-
> ists. This time, many were alerted and saved copies of the documents
> to use in alternative news outlets. My second blog was also shut
> down. But I'm gratified to inform my readers that all the information
> that Jay died to reveal is now available to the world, disseminated
> by many sources and being investigated by many others. Note: The
> original documents are no longer in my possession.

I pulled out my vox and remote viewed Val Andrews. She wasn't alone. Alice was with her. Alice was scanning items in a stack of newspapers and magazines. She pointed out items to Val, who nodded and wiped away tears. Alice, it appeared, was the person who convinced Val that I was being framed for the very reasons Jay was killed. They appeared to be discussing the blog and posting additional information. My hunch was proven correct when, moments later, another installment was posted to Val's blog.

> I want to say, for the record, Dana Travers was not involved in my
> husband's murder. Dana, if you read this, I'm so sorry you were treat-
> ed rudely at Jay's memorial. I now believe that individuals implicated
> in Jay's documents killed him to silence him. If my husband thought
> this information was worth dying for, exposure of this information is
> necessary to ensure he did not die in vain.

Alice and Val had risked their lives to become whistle blowers while Louie and I fled and hid. I was then astonished beyond comprehension when Alice's visage blurred and refocused. Alice, dear trusted Alice, was a Draconian reptile. Based on my recent acquaintance with Bo and Guna Raza, I realized that the reptiles have always been here, are our distant relations, are not all malicious, and have the ability to evolve spiritually. If Alice had betrayed the Reptilian Cabal, Sheldon Walters reason to track her every move made sense. Either that, or she had set up Jay, Val, and me.

Squeezy appeared on Gemini Dallas' TV talk show to defend Sheldon Walters. She looked garish but sounded polished and articulate. She dissed Alice and me repeatedly, wiped away a tear for Jay, suggested that Val Andrews had been misled by disgruntled former employees, while repeatedly crossing and uncrossing her legs. Gemini Dallas tried to catch her off guard by asking about her affair with Vincent Cretzky. But Squeezy was prepared and said she was dating another man, and as far as she knew, Vincent was happily married. Squeezy was a sensation. Her interview had gone viral.

Conjecture regarding the meanings of Shelter's codes ranged from 'Vote,' to 'Election,' to 'Exile,' or 'Errand' depending on who you read. 'K2' stood for 'the big one,' whatever that meant. 'SC' might have been 'sex change,' or 'sacrifice,' or 'send cash.' Nobody knew for sure. Speculation regarding conspiracy theory and shadow governments became ammunition for politicians whose names did not appear on the explosive Shelter Spreadsheets, for FBI agents circumventing due process, for talk show hosts, journalists, and comedians. Gemini Dallas was holding on to my disgrace like a rabid pit bull. She had interviewed Squeezy again and the two of them reveled in trashing my reputation. I was an incompetent, bitter ex-employee who might even be a killer. I was still a wanted fugitive, the primary murder suspect of the FBI.

A woman who channeled Pleiadians explained that the time of the reptilian overlords was nearing its end and they were clinging to power in the old Piscean ways. The channeler's YouTube also went viral. My name was invoked right, left, and center. I was everybody's favorite Ping-Pong ball. Val Andrews was revered and reviled. I downloaded copies of the most balanced and the most salacious articles to give Louie a flavor of the drama.

I felt partly responsible for the danger to Val and Alice. My escape into Tellara and flimsy alibi forced their hand. I had a safe haven. Val and Alice did not. They stepped onto the world stage to slay the dragon. I began to understand what Sky Dancer was getting at in our first interview. Javier Vasquez had found us in Cairo. The men in black must be close behind. I posted a message to 'Larry' and 'Moe' to tell them I loved them and that I would craft a reply to the blogs as soon as I discussed matters with Shep. Then, I packed up the laptop and returned to Saffron's via *Tellaran Autumn*.

* * *

Robin arrived and we had a delightful reunion. Saffron's family huddled to discuss Heron's rejoining. But Louie and I were focused on our own Earthly drama. Louie read the news with pretty much the same responses I had had, appalled and relieved at the same time.

"By the way, Alice is a reptile." I opened my vox screen so that Louie could remote view her.

"What does this mean? Is she evolving or deceiving us?"

"I want to give her the benefit of the doubt. She's betraying Sheldon Walters. Let's respond to Val's blog."

"We need to tell the world that Shelter killed Hal," Louie said.

I said, "Maybe we can find a way to get word to Hal's family before the media shares the news that J.P. Halifax, husband of Louie Robles-Leon, died last July from injuries sustained when he was run off the road by Shelter Insurance operatives in their attempt to silence Robles-Leon."

"Shelter won't self-incriminate. They left Hal to rot. His family will find out with everybody else."

"You can't go to his family, Louie. They'd hate you."

"I'm sure they already do. But no, I'm not leaving Tellara. Let's tell the world about Hal's murder in a blog reply." We began our sad task of composing a statement explaining what we knew.

> This is Dana Travers, the woman framed for the murder of Jay Andrews. A man named Kek broke into my Chicago home and choked me nearly to death. I was saved when my son and dogs entered the room and engaged in physical conflict to free me. Kek fled. Chicago police arrived and made a report of the damage to my home and my physical injuries. My children and I went into hiding.
>
> The next day, Kek and companions were spotted in Missouri, in pursuit of Louie Robles-Leon, who was with his husband J.P. 'Hal' Halifax. Kek forced their car off the road, seriously injuring Hal. Louie, who was driving, was unharmed and returned the favor by ramming Kek's car into a ravine, Louie and Hal got away. Hal's injuries proved fatal.
>
> Those of us who have been attacked by Shelter operatives remain in hiding, fearing for our lives. We send our deepest condolences to the friends and family of J.P. 'Hal' Halifax.

"Is it laying low or lying low?

"I don't know. Let the Blog Police sort it out." Louie and I problem-solved our meaningless conundrums with pointless spats.

CHAPTER 14

The next morning, Phoenix and I returned to his Cairo apartment with our response to Val's blog. Louie remained behind to train with his vox. I left him floating upside-down in Saffron's living room.

In the Cairo art studio, Phoenix said, "I'll haul back another stash of art, music, theater, and artifacts that I have in storage nearby. See you in a few hours, Dana." Phoenix gave me a Namasté bow and a wink as he departed out into the streets. I watched him from the roof until he slipped out of sight.

It was thirty degrees warmer in Cairo, Earth than it had been in Giza, Tellara. Early October in Cairo was hot, dry, and windy. Giza, Tellara had been partly cloudy, low sixties, light wind, a perfect fall day. I went inside, turned on the laptop, and contacted my children. The encrypted the message Louie and I composed was uploaded to a private cloud account we'd opened. "The clouds here are beautiful," I posted to the stooges' Facespace. "Share when firewalls impenetrable."

Ruth must have been working overtime on her techno magic. Our statement was posted within minutes and showed up shortly thereafter on Val's blog. "Well done, Curly!"

"Well done yourself, Moe."

Larry posted "We're safe in Winter Haven after a trek though safe houses."

Appreciating Moe's code, I replied, "How did that happen?"

"We had a little help from your friend." I was baffled but decided I could wait for details.

I surfed the internet for responses to our newest posting. Many posters agreed I was framed. Among my supporters were Crystal and Cosmo. Their New Age jargon identified me as a wayshower for the Galactic Council; not a huge help, but well meant. Other posters described me as murdering scum, anti-business, and a communist. There were death threats from folks who thought I was trying to get between insured people and their settlements; accusing me of the very corruption I'd fought against. Shelter's smear campaign against me was in full force. I saved the most relevant articles for Louie.

Phoenix returned to the studio. He wasn't alone. To my shock, Javier Vasquez was with him. They were talking like old pals, each carrying one end of an enormous footlocker. I sat in stunned silence, looking from one to the other. I couldn't believe that Phoenix had delivered my tracker to my doorstep.

"Dana, before you get upset…" Phoenix began.

"I am so far beyond upset that words fail," I interrupted furiously. "You've just signed my death warrant!" I screamed in Phoenix's face. He was undone.

He had only ever seen human wrath in Earth films. Having it directed at him by his pet wayshower was unprecedented.

I whirled on Javier. "How did you find me?"

"I'm a detective Dana. I used your books to track Wah'Kon-Tah. I contacted Sky Dancer who communicated with Phoenix. They both trust me."

"Well, I don't. Sky Dancer doesn't have a phone."

"She has a computer," Javier replied. "In addition to being a detective, I know how to scry. I've been trying to help you for weeks."

"Help me get arrested? Lead Shelter to Wah'Kon-Tah? Lead Shelter to this apartment? You'll get me killed. Like Jay. Like Hal."

"Hal?" Inspector Vazquez asked.

"Louie's husband is dead. Killed by Kek, the man who choked me. Don't you read the Val Andrews' blog?"

"Not today."

"Hal lies dead in a cold stone cave. If I had turned myself in to you, Louie would be dead too because I'd have never found him." I rounded on Phoenix and Javier, "You thoughtless, imbecilic assholes! Both of you!" I was apoplectic.

"Louie's husband is dead?" Javier asked again. Phoenix backed away.

"By tracking us, you lead Shelter to our door. And you're confused about why we're avoiding you!"

"I'm in a position to help you."

"No, thanks."

"The tide is turning. The FBI is starting to doubt your guilt."

"Those two Shelter stooges we met in Dallas? Seriously? Just put a capital 'D' for DEAD in the column next to my name!"

"Not anymore," Javier pressed, "Real FBI agents are convinced you're being framed. Shelter's men in black are rarely outwitted or eluded. You and Louie have become a stone in their shoe."

"I've said the same thing about you. And those creeps don't fail because they're reptilians with advanced technology called RAT-TRAK."

"I suspected as much, although I didn't know they called it RAT-TRAK. When Val Andrews posted Jay's documents, Shelter's tactics went into high gear. They engaged in what we in law enforcement recognize as 'black ops mode,' which is to say, unlawful back door threats. This is what convinced others law enforcement officers of your innocence. I've had Shelter on my radar for years. I know you are not an insider."

"Aren't you sweet? But stupid. They'll have followed you here."

Javier interrupted my rant, "I helped your kids. I tracked them to Wisconsin and drove them to my grandmother Minerva's home."

"Minerva?! The Gypsy fortune teller? My kids mentioned her. How did you track them in Wisconsin?"

"I'm a detective, Dana," he repeated, enunciating crisply. "We prefer Romani. I provided a safe house for Ruth and Jesse. Minerva got them from Montana to Shasta."

"As an officer of the law you can't aid and abet fugitives."

"Your kids aren't fugitives. I'm on unpaid leave," his mood shifting. "Phoenix tells me you have access to a haven where Shelter cannot follow."

"Oh, he did, did he?" Stomping, I turned on Phoenix, who had been struggling to gather his wits after my polarizing tirade.

"*Magic Seasons* are my paintings, Dana, my portals. I created them. I have a say in who passes through," Phoenix asserted. "In thirteen thousand years, when you create portals, you'll get to say who can use them."

Words failed. Eyeballs popped. Fists clenched. I felt like vomiting. "You! You! You…both…"

"Portal?" Javier inquired while I stood in strangled silence. "What kind of a portal?"

"A portal to an alternate world." Phoenix stated matter-of-factly. "My home world, Tellara."

"I guessed it was something like that."

My voice emerged as an incoherent diatribe. "How could you possibly guess something like that? There is no something like that! What other portal into an alternate world were you thinking about? The Matrix? Alice down the rabbit hole?"

"Apparently there is a portal and apparently I guessed correctly," Javier replied. "I have a lot of experience with the paranormal."

"Nobody just guesses trans-dimensional physics!" I ground out through gritted teeth.

"Trans-dimensional physicists do. I call it magic," Javier stared at me. Shades of my own ill-considered fantasy life; I'd been hoisted by my own petard. Not that I knew what a petard was, but mine was up there getting bit on the butt by Javier Vasquez's know-it-all gumshoe gaze.

I whirled on Phoenix. "You trust him!?"

"I do." Phoenix just shrugged. Sky Dancer had told me that I could trust Javier and I'd disregarded her. Now Phoenix said he trusted him. "As long as you keep tracking me, my life is in danger. You believe me innocent, yet you won't leave me in peace."

"Sky Dancer counseled me to help you."

I threw up my hands in exasperation. "I yield. But you two just haven't put together the scope of RAT-TRAK. It's a wonder Louie and I made it through customs, much less through to Tellara."

"Dana, Tellaran technology is thousands of years ahead of this so-called RAT-TRAK," Phoenix assured me.

"I'd like to get a look at Tellara," said Javier.

"Follow me," said Phoenix.

"I'm taking the laptop to Tellara. We don't want the Shelter operatives to recover my hard drive. The Internet won't work, but I've downloaded the latest news including responses to Louie's and my statement about Hal's death."

"What statement?"

I snapped the lid shut as Javier leaned over to read. "It'll still be there in Tellara." I wasn't done being peevish.

Phoenix instructed Javier how to view the painting *Tellaran Autumn* in an alpha state, through half-closed lids. The two men heaved the footlocker up and walked through the expanded canvas into the Giza Park. I followed, sulking.

Phoenix and Javier strolled through the park and along the cobblestone path to Saffron's house, guiding the floating footlocker. Louie was in Saffron's front room levitating books and dishes. When he spotted Javier, his jaw dropped, his vox dropped, books dropped, dishes dropped, and Louie dropped to the floor with an undignified thud.

"My sentiments exactly." I dropped onto a divan.

"Inspector Vazquez, our favorite bad penny, turns up across the Universe," Louie sighed.

"Please call me Javier. I would like to explain." Phoenix offered Javier a seat and a drink of lemon water. Javier accepted both and flopped down beside me, uncomfortably close. I scooched away. "Louie, I explained to Phoenix back in Cairo, that I know beyond a doubt that Dana is innocent. I am glad you made it to safety."

"One of us didn't make it. My husband, Hal was killed by Shelter in July. He was run off the road and bled to death."

"Dana told me. The FBI believed you three were on the run together. You just dropped off the face of the Earth."

"Shelter knows better. They're the ones who killed Hal," Louie corrected Javier.

Javier gave a sympathetic nod. "After I missed you at Khan el-Khalili, I tracked Wah'Kon-Tah using Dana's myth book and Bible. Sky Dancer and I Facespaced each other. Our myths and missions converge; the Galactic Medicine Wheel is part of Minerva's world view."

"Sky Dancer!" Louie cried.

"Welcome to my hissy fit," I said to Louie, giving Javier another lethal glare.

"Romani? Gypsies?" Louie cried again. "This reminiscence is all very sweet, but I would like some answers. How did you convince Phoenix to show you the portal?"

"We spoke at length at the Bazaar."

"He never said that, just that he got rid of you."

"Well, he didn't divulge much. But I realized he knew more than he was saying. He gave me a hint that if our paths were meant to converge, they would."

"You have my myth book and Bible." I stated the obvious. "Can I have them back?"

"They're in the footlocker."

Louie exclaimed, "You'll lead Shelter directly to Wah'Kon-Tah! Those people saved our lives and you'll get them killed. You'll lead Shelter to Phoenix's art studio in Cairo. They'll destroy another portal!"

"I said the same thing!"

"Give me some credit. I've been a detective for twenty-five years and a Romani for sixty."

"Yeah, but our pursuers are reptilians with fourth-dimensional consciousness and technology hundreds of years beyond human science," said Louie.

"I know that too. I was raised in mystical lore. I have some fourth-dimensional allies of my own. I used my animal guide."

"Animal guides!" Louie cried again, leaping to his feet. "Gypsies, Medicine Women, Cosmic Kooks!"

"Not to mention alternate realities," Phoenix said mildly, which ended Louie's tirade.

"What is your animal guide?" I asked Javier, interested, in spite of myself.

"The humble honeybee. I am industrious, but I take time to smell the flowers. I rid the world of annoying insects while pollinating the fruits of Earth. And I live to serve honey to my queen bee. What's yours?"

"Apparently crow or raven, not really sure; cunning, clever, elusive, and daring, refined perception, attracted to sparkly things. Oh, or maybe a bat, but I don't have very good radar."

"No radar? Dana, what do you think guided you to Tellara?" Phoenix observed.

"And yours?" Javier asked Louie.

"Wolf," Louie snarled.

"Maybe Javier is our ally," I relented. "He was able to cross the portal into Tellara and Saffron tells me it only opens for people with compassionate hearts and balanced karma. He says he's trying to help, and we've been nothing but hostile."

"Because he's gonna get us killed, not to mention Wah'Kon-Tah, Jesse, and Ruth. Besides, Dana, can't you see he's flirting with you? Feeding honey to the Queen Bee! What a line!"

"I wouldn't be flirting with Dana unless I knew she was innocent."

"You badgered her for her alibi," said Louie.

"So did you."

"I'm her friend. I'm allowed."

"Nobody is flirting with me," I interjected.

Phoenix said, "You know Dana, maybe you could use some help with your Earthside problems."

"How?"

"I sent Javier some photos taken in San Francisco."

"It was you! Javier, where are those photos you had in Texas?" I asked.

Javier pulled the photos from his inside pocket and laid them on the carved wooden table between us. We had seen these photos at Jay's memorial. It was Sheldon Walters at the San Francisco cafe. And this time, I recognized his reptilian companion. I instinctively grabbed my throat. Louie choked back a sob.

"He's the man that choked me," my voice sounded raspier than it had in weeks, "I call him Flatface. His crew calls him Kek."

Louie said, "He was driving the car that ran us off the road. He killed Hal."

"His name is Marvin Kinkle. He goes by Kek."

"The grays would like that," Louie snarked.

"If you knew his name, why did you ask us?"

"I didn't know it when I asked."

Louie speculated "He was in San Francisco the week of June 21st, during our Insurance Conference. "K-E-K; K2, a Shelter operative who does their dirty work. Did you show this to Contrary and Pandemonium?" Louie was being more rational.

"Who?"

"The FBI men in black."

"That's what you call them? No, I'm on leave from my job. I was told that my investigation exceeded my authority. I've been muzzled by the State's Attorney General at the request of the FBI. So, I hung on to evidence that I thought would clear Dana."

"How does that help me?"

"They're real FBI agents, but that doesn't mean they don't work for Shelter." Javier continued. "Agents Contreras and Pandomi are ten-year veterans. They went from college, to FBI training camp, to various postings around the country. The only potential flag in their service is that they have served together more often than not. They were partners in Baltimore, Boston, Los Angeles, and now Chicago."

"What about the petite brunette in the photo? Do you know who she is?"

"I believe she's an Irish investigative journalist named Shari McCann who's gone missing."

"When?" asked Louie

"Around the time of your insurance conference, around the time of Jay's murder. Her editor said she was researching corporate interference with European elections."

"Jay's documents would have been the motherlode for her investigation," said Louie.

"Am I imagining a motive to kill her?" I handed Louie the laptop with news pages loaded.

Javier handed me my books. "You're not imagining a motive. And Louie's not imagining that I was flirting with you."

I gave him my best quelling look. I wasn't done being annoyed. He smiled crookedly and completely undid my composure. I was as good at flirting as I was at providing coherent alibis. Bringing the discussion back to Earth, I said, "If Kek turns out to be K2, we could link him to Sheldon Walters. In the cave we overheard him say he was going to call Walters."

"How did he not find you in the cave?" Javier asked.

"We were cloaked," said Louie cloaking himself, which startled Javier to silence.

I said, "Public opinion could force a more open investigation. Kek probably killed Jay and that journalist."

While Louie quoted aloud from different blog passages, the three of us discussed the facts we knew and possible strategies we could utilize to clear my name, keep us safe, and bring the murderer to justice. I was dropping from exhaustion and left the room to sleep. But sleep eluded me as I thought over the day's strange events, from the grays' gigantic syringe, to Javier's improbable arrival in Tellara, to his getting my children to safety along some Romani underground railroad, to Louie's suggestion that Javier was flirting with me, and then Javier's confirming it.

* * *

The next morning, we convened at the Giza Air Transit Station. Our party was comprised of Saffron, Phoenix, Juniper, Bo, Guna, Louie, Javier, Robin, and me. This was the first time Javier had seen reptiles and after an initial double-take, he seemed to take them in stride. In fact, he seemed too casual about this whole alternate Earth concept. When I first got to Tellara, I doubted my sanity. Louie had been prepared for the reality of Tellara for months, but Javier just smiled crookedly and said he expected as much.

The airship reminded me of a zeppelin coach. The passenger area was a cigar-shaped lounge. There were no wings. Bo explained that levitation crystals were mounted in a geometric matrix below the luggage compartment where the pilot sat. Other etched crystals generated the propulsion system, which drew limitless power from the vacuum. Javier was intrigued and asked endless questions of an infinitely patient Phoenix.

Once boarded, we seated ourselves in comfy chairs around an oval table built to accommodate groups of travelers. I looked around the cabin and observed other Tellarans; some were traveling alone, some in groups traveling together. Our chairs swiveled, tilted, and had ample legroom. There were no flight attendants. There was a self-serve food and beverage center filled with all kinds of fruits and finger foods and a bank of well-appointed private lavatories.

As we took off, the ship slowly circled the Giza Plateau. We were granted a magnificent aerial view of the gleaming pyramids and Sphinx. All talking ceased as we drank in the panorama. I was seated between Javier and Bo Raza. Were it not for the serious purpose of our journey, this might have been a merry party on a thrilling adventure. Still, we 'Earthborn,' as we were called, had endless questions about our respective worlds. I turned to Bo Raza, "Are there any reptiles on Circles of Thirteen Elders throughout Tellara?"

"We have opted out. We are a very long-lived species relative to humans. We live hundreds of years. I am six hundred fifty years old."

"No!"

"We constitute less than one percent of the Tellaran population, but would end up dominating every counsel, in effect, controlling world leadership. Each of us here surmounted Herculean challenges to relinquish our love of power. Relapse is not an option. We work with the bigger picture. We participate in the heartdance. We collaborate with the Galactic Council. We serve as advisors. When Tellaran humanity attains collective higher-dimensional consciousness, we will incorporate all that love into our heart chakras."

"That doesn't make sense," Javier was now listening to our conversation. "Your species is already more advanced than ours. You have access to non-linear time."

"Not to mention RAT-TRAK technology on Earth," said Louie.

Bo replied, "You are missing something important. Earth reptilians only have access to non-local reality with the aid of technology. They have no inherent sixth sense. You don't realize that humans are the envy of many species throughout the galaxy. Despite your current evolutionary status, you have the capacity to evolve vastly beyond many galactic species. Most Earth reptiles want to suppress your potential; but those of us striving to evolve spiritually are honored to be part of humanity's journey."

"Capacity?"

"Humans are connected to the Great Mother Sea by seven robust, integrated bodies, which are layers of consciousness joined by the chakra system. You possess physical, etheric, emotional, mental, spiritual, celestial, and divine fields of energy. Some Earthborn can apprehend higher aspects of consciousness than we can. In this neck of the galaxy, the Pleiadians, Vegans, Arcturans, and Sirians have gone through the evolutionary phases that began in the biological and attained to celestial. These members of the Galactic Family attained celestial consciousness step-by-arduous-evolutionary-step over millions of years of karma balancing and intentional spiritual advancement. Human destiny is anticipated throughout the galaxy. Reptiles and grays who are wise enough to realize this have chosen to hitch our wagon to your rising star."

Bo continued, "Like I explained to Dana the other night, reptilian soul-stuff is meager compared with humans. Reptilian energy vehicles are imbalanced. The lower physical and left-brain dominate. We small handful who made it to Tellara overcame ages of mental conditioning. We had to reject human misery as a source of addictive energy. We had to escape a concretized hierarchy. Unevolved Earthside reptilians are sociopaths who consider humans to be tools, slaves. My clan feels blessed to be counted as tribe with humans."

"But only if we don't have to listen to you sing," Saffron zinged and all the Tellarans laughed.

"Unevolved reptilian humor can be immature and cruel, although coupled with great intellect," Bo Raza explained.

"Like certain cruel TV talking heads?" Javier mused.

"Do you think they're reptiles?" I was incredulous.

He replied, "That's the image that came to mind. Hate mongers masquerading as do-gooders. Cruelty masquerading as humor."

Bo Raza nodded, "That that would fit the profile."

Louie asked, "What's the difference between the Galactic Council and the Galactic Family. The terms are used interchangeably."

Phoenix answered, "The Galactic Family is comprised of every member of every species in Sophia's Milk that has attained celestial consciousness. Tellarans are anticipating being welcomed into the Galactic Family when we ascend. A few individuals from each star system serve on the Galactic Council for a specified duration in order to guide, keep the peace, and monitor treaties."

I said to Louie and Javier, "He means the Milky Way."

CHAPTER 15

"Javier how is it that you have a connection with the Romani underground?" I asked.

"I was weaned on Earth conspiracy theories," Javier answered. "My grandmother raised me until I was fourteen, Minerva, is a Romani Mystic. She told fortunes and knew family stories going back to Atlantis. She taught me hermetic sciences, lucid dreaming, and claircognizance techniques as a child. She was my mother's mother. My mother, Genevieve, married Zorian Vazquez, an ethnic Basque whose parents brought him to America as a young child. He was a poet, musician, mathematician, and UFOlogist. He had visions. When I was a toddler, my parents left me with my grandmother for a brief visit while they traveled to a sacred site. They never returned."

"They never returned?"

"They went to explore an opening to inner earth civilizations. They were last heard from in Mount Shasta. Minerva believes they encountered a humanoid race that went underground millennia ago. She claims to maintain telepathic connection with my mother. My parents are living in paradise under the Earth's inner sun. I've since read many books about Inner Earth civilizations and ecosystems.

"When I was fourteen, my father's parents came to collect me. I went through a Basque coming-of-age ritual. Both sets of grandparents traced their lineage back to Atlantis. But for all that, there was an ancient family rivalry. Apparently, during the cataclysm, Lavatians migrated to India, while the Basques escaped to Europe. Neither culture integrated well with their indigenous neighbors. Each retained significant Atlantean knowledge but were loath to share, distrusting their distant relations. Each suspected the other of being in league with the very Draconians who had brought about the fall of Atlantean Civilization. Old feuds die hard. But my parents generated a minor reconciliation when I was born.

"My Romani relatives would have me live my life, off the grid. My father's parents wanted me to mainstream, so they sent me to public high school. In college I started out as a philosophy major but got in trouble because I disagreed with my professors about the existence of alternate dimensions. I found one open-minded professor who was willing to accept papers on Earth's hidden histories, but she drew the line at Atlantis. The rest of the department thought that was the stuff of fantasy fiction. So, I switched to math. But my professors refused to even discuss sacred geometry or the meaning of numbers as building blocks of the Universe. 'What came first, numbers or shapes?' But that was never on the test. So, I switched to political science, which worked out all right for a few years. But again, I argued with my professors about exopolitics.

"What is exopolitics?"

"The political theory that we are not asking the right questions about humanity's place in the Universe. Are we alone? Are we being interfered with? Are we being watched? Is a war being waged to suppress the evolution of human consciousness? Most people dismiss this worldview as crazy.'"

"You came to Tellara already knowing more than I've learned," I was intrigued by this side of Javier's life.

He continued, "I finished my B.A. and went on for a degree in law and criminal justice. I clerked for a judge anticipating a career in jurisprudence. But I saw so much in the courtroom that convinced me that I'd make a good street detective."

"You must have been the only Romani-Basque in the police force," Louie mused.

"I passed as Hispanic," Javier chuckled. "Vazquez seeped into Castilian regions centuries ago. I grew up seeing the layers within layers of crimes, people, and motives. That includes criminals, victims, lawyers, police, witnesses, and even judges. I instinctively knew you were being set up the first time I interviewed you, Dana."

"I intuited that you were probing for information about Shelter's top tier. But you kept me on a short leash and made my life Hell. And why did you implicate Louie?"

"Yeah, you didn't suspect me, but implicated me with Shelter!" Louie accused.

"Louie, I did it to keep you safe from Shelter."

"Fat lot of good that did. They killed Hal in their pursuit of me," Louie choked on his angry words.

"If you had confided your escape plans to me, I might have prevented Hal's death."

"I wasn't escaping! I was just traveling! By the time we realized we were being pursued, it was too late," Louie jumped to his feet.

"I knew you were in danger even if you didn't," said Javier.

I added, "You were my pursuer, not my ally."

"I am definitely your ally," Javier smiled.

I ignored his remark, "I had my vox and discovered Louie and Hal were in danger. We didn't trust you."

Javier nodded, "As it is, Dana, I tracked down Jesse and Ruth and arranged your children's safe journey."

"I didn't know."

"You're welcome."

"It was Sky Dancer's notes in her *World Mythology* book that led me to Wah'Kon-Tah. She and my grandmother share a certain shamanic connection."

"This is fascinating," Saffron said. "We've been separated for thirteen thousand years. We know so little of the actual lore that has been preserved on your Earth. What do you know about the history of Earth following the last shift?"

Louie spoke, "There are many myths, legends, and scientific theories. We learned of several in an oral tradition gathering at Wah'Kon-Tah. Some involved turtles, one is based on a paradise called the Garden of Eden, and other myths included ancient aliens. Panspermia is the theory that life on Earth originated from microorganisms in outer space that collided with Earth. Directed Panspermia theorizes that life on Earth was seeded by extra-terrestrials who cultivated this planet.

Javier said, "As to the extra-terrestrials, according to Romani lore, there never will be a first contact. The Draconians, Zetas, Arcturans, Sirians, Vegans, Pleiadians, and dozens of other non-human galactic species have been around longer than humanity."

"Dozens?" I was incredulous.

"Maybe more, but humanity is truly born of Earth. My grandmother did not call them ETs either. She calls them humanoid companions. They watched us evolve biologically from Homo erectus. According to Atlantean lore, these early primates were interfered with genetically. My grandmother believes that ancient reptilians spliced some of their DNA into the primates to create the so-called missing link."

"On Tellara, we know that to be the case," said Saffron. "Your panspermia explanation is correct."

Javier continued, "That would have been about a million years ago. To some humanoid species, humans are experimental subjects; to some, younger siblings in the Galactic Family; to others, genetic material to be harvested; for some, we're food; for the Draconians, we're slaves to be exploited, physically, emotionally, and economically. Humanity has been divided up by treaties among many ancient galactic species. We have been interfered with, protected, guided, exploited, and controlled."

Saffron spoke, "Just thirteen thousand years ago, Tellarans overcame this web of alien interference. Each individual faced his and her own inner demons. Our light and dark side were integrated. We woke up as a species, which made us less vulnerable to manipulation.

"My grandmother would llike you," Javier gave Saffron one of his crooked smiles. I found myself smiling at him. He noticed and bestowed his familiar discomfiting gaze. My smile froze into a stupid grin. Louie groaned. I looked out the window. The terrain was magnificent, green hills, forests, and mountains. It reminded me of California.

Javier spoke, "From what I can tell, the story of Atlantis has parallels on both our worlds—its existence, but not its destruction. On Earth, most consider Atlantis to be a fable. Few consider civilizations to be cyclic. Fewer still acknowledge that we are on the fifth cycle of human civilization."

Louie continued, "Or that civilizations fall because planetary stability is cyclic and humans inevitably create catastrophic imbalance. Right now, on Earth, we are building nuclear reactors on active fault lines and poisoning ground water to release gas for energy."

Juniper protested, "But water is sacred, and energy is free."

Louie said, "Not on Earth. These criminal acts are committed by the wealthy and powerful at the expense of all Earth's creatures. Dana's and my former employer, Shelter, is near the top of that hierarchy and profits obscenely from the exploitation of Earth's resources. These corporations convinced millions that this is their inherent right."

"Tellaran culture is not hierarchical," Saffron commented.

"It's hard for us to envision a paradigm that's not based on hierarchy," said Louie.

"Can't you?" I asked Louie. "Wah'Kon-Tah is consensus run."

"Sky Dancer is the leader."

"She functions as an Elder, not a leader." I countered. "Decisions are based on the common good."

"On Tellara, interconnectedness outpictures itself during the heartdance, an external web of inner reality. It is also, in case you are wondering, how we all speak and understand the Earth languages that you speak. We pick up language in the vibrations."

I withdrew into my own thoughts until I was drawn out by Javier. "Dana, there is something I would like from you that I've been waiting for since we first met."

"Yes?"

"Your alibi."

"I should think that by now it would be obvious. I was in Tellara."

"I'm curious about the details. Were you in Cairo?"

"No, the first time I crossed the portal was in San Francisco. I bought a painting from Phoenix called *Summer in Tellara*. It was a breathtaking landscape of the Esselen Coast. The entire west coast of North america is called Esselen in Tellara."

"Did Phoenix show you how to visualize the portal?"

"No. I figured that out by myself in my hotel room."

"By yourself?"

"I have this habit of falling into art. I soft focused into all perspectives at once and saw sails luffing, leaves fluttering, boats bobbing, and grass swaying in the breeze. Then I saw a mist fill my space and the park in the painting emerged across the canvas right into my hotel room."

"You saw magic because you expected to see it."

"Yes, I need magic in my life to stay sane. That sounds contradictory. Most people would see magic and doubt their sanity. I don't practice magic; I've just felt it around me since I was a child."

"In another culture, you'd have been apprenticed to a shaman. I've been exposed to magic all my life, thanks to my grandmother. I understand perfectly. And now, we're experiencing it here in Tellara."

"Javier, I was going to bring you to Tellara, in my condo in Chicago, the morning after the memorial, just like I promised. I was going to show you my alibi in *Summer in Tellara*. Oh, how I imagined your reaction when I disappeared into the canvas."

"I was distressed when I arrived at your home to discover that you'd run away."

"Along with *Summer in Tellara*. Kek slashed it when he tried to get in a parting kill shot. He split the canvas and closed the portal to Tellara. I went on the run, and you lost my trust when you insisted I turn myself in."

"I would have connected you to Minerva's chain of 'underground' safe houses."

"That would have gotten Louie killed."

Louie said, "There was crime scene tape at Dana's condo, Javier. Didn't you speak to the Chicago police?"

"Briefly, but they knew in advance that I'd been relieved from active duty and provided little information. Shelter works fast."

"Relieved?"

"I am on leave without pay, officially off the Jay Andrews' murder investigation."

Louie asked, "Because Contrary and Pandemonium are the lead investigators?"

Javier replied, "They might be FBI, but they're on Shelter's payroll."

"I'm going to view them on my vox to see if they're reptilians," said Louie.

"Hey! Have you tried a heartplum?" I asked Javier.

"No. That's a random segue."

"Not really. I would have given you one in my living room as part of my alibi. Let's go to the refreshment counter." Unselfconsciously, I took his hand and drew him to his feet toward the back of the passenger compartment. We were still holding hands when we reached the bar and when I moved to disengage, he held tight and wrapped his large warm hand firmly around mine. This time I smiled at him, turned, grabbed a handful of heartplums with my other hand, and released them onto his chest.

He had to let go of me to catch the fruit. We did not pay. There was no way to pay. He bit into his fruit. I watched carefully to observe his response to the rich, robust fruit. I wasn't disappointed. He smiled and slurped and took another bite immediately. He smiled again and nodded in delight. "You've given me a lot Dana, you know that, right?"

"Not sure what I've given you."

He took my hand in his and drew it to his lips. It seemed perfectly natural for him to kiss the back of my hand. But it was unexpected when he turned my hand over to kiss my wrist. I withdrew my hand. We were in public.

"You found this world on your own. You were designated by a whole planet as a wayshower for Earth. Your alibi validates my whole life. I look forward to all you have to show me of Tellara."

"I'm still being shown this world. And don't kid yourself, since I've been designated a wayshower, my life on Earth has been adversity, criticism, and worry. There has been little praise and less advocacy. Saffron and Phoenix made it seem ordained. I'm still growing into the role, and there are growing pains. Every time I move through a portal in either direction, my mission becomes more complicated, dangerous, and thankless. But when *Summer in Tellara* was slashed, I was bereft. It was a thousand times more devastating than my physical injuries and fears for my life." I felt my eyes tear. "I don't think Kek knew what havoc he wreaked when he cut off my escape."

Javier asked, "Do you mean your time in the cave?" I looked at him quizzically and he shrugged, "Sky Dancer told me."

"No, I mean my haven in Tellara, my portal."

Where is *Summer in Tellara* now?"

"With my kids, in Shasta."

"They are safe. Because the petition came from Minerva, they were protected by my clan."

"Why would Gypsies protect a couple of suburban white bread yuppies?"

"The Romani have no love for corporate overseers or their enforcers."

"But you're a cop!"

"I serve justice, officially and unofficially. And now I serve Earth's wayshower, Dana Travers."

For the first time, someone was acknowledging that my role as a wayshower was a burden, not a gift. I felt humbled and embarrassed by my need for strokes. But I let his compliments wash over me without deflecting the praise.

Of course, I was attracted to Javier. He was smart, handsome, strong, wise, worldly, and sexy in a craggy, streetwise kind of way. I hadn't opened my heart to romantic magic in several long years. Romance was harder to believe in than portals to other dimensions.

As we returned to our seats, Javier took my hand and seated me with a slight bow. Louie raised his eyebrow speculatively. The Tellarans made no reaction to Javier's attentions to me. Romantic attachments evoked little interest on Tellara. Maybe it was that interconnectedness business.

We arrived in Antalya just after noon, making connections to a rail tram that would carry us up into the hills to Heron's acres of fruit and flowers. The heartplums would have been harvested by now and the orchards would be dormant. But the landscape did not want for fruit and flower of many other kinds. The rolling green hills were fragrant with grapes, apples, red berries, new mown hay, clover, zinnias, clematis, and Witch-Hazel. It was a magical tableau of blossoming beauty. All my senses were stimulated; all my sensibilities converged in harmony. Saffron had grown steadily more withdrawn during the flight, but now she grew animated. Part of Saffron must be overjoyed to see Heron, part of her apprehensive about their reunion.

We were not met by anyone in Antalya. If Heron knew we were coming, he had postponed the moment of truth. We shared a lunch of kebobs, couscous, fruit salad, and rice pudding in a local bistro. Some aspects of cultural and artistic character seemed to have evolved similarly on both worlds, informed by geography, ancient customs, and regional commodities. The food throughout Giza had been decidedly Middle Eastern. The clothes and merchandise in Antalya evoked themes from Arabian Nights meets Vanity Fair. The design of woven carpets included geometric and floral patterns as well as mythological scenes. Sculpted metal, glass lanterns, and ceramic tiles filled streets, parks, and buildings. Local artisans throughout the area were welcoming. I was in retail heaven and Louie had to drag me onto the tram.

We entered Heron's land via a spectacular carpet of flowers, fruit trees, and hemp fields. The tram slid under an archway with suspended, colorful signage. "It says Sultana Safran. That's the name of this plantation," said Juniper. Then we were at the door of his domed home and he came out to greet us. Heron looked older than Saffron. But like all Tellaran Elders, he carried his age with a spry grace that belied his century-plus years. His skin was deeply tanned and weathered from years spent working in the mountain air. He wore his gray hair in a ponytail. He was dressed in khaki-colored pants that looked like Dockers, and ordinary, laced work boots. Heron looked like an old hippie.

He helped Saffron off the shuttle and gave smiling nods to the rest of us. His gaze lingered on his grand-children, Robin and Juniper. "Make yourselves at home," he indicated his shaded patio with a sweep of his arm. Then he and Saffron slipped into his geodesic dome without another word to the rest of us. We sat and nibbled. We'd just eaten, so we barely touched the refreshments spread on the table, but helped ourselves to a fruity, mildly fermented punch. Louie, Javier, and I might have settled into a typical, Earthborn, stilted conversation about the weather and scenery while we all knew that Saffron and Heron were getting reacquainted, however intimately; but not so the Tellarans; again, that unflappable indifference to other peoples' private affairs. I guess when you live with that interconnectedness all your life, certain intimate details of the human condition are as natural as breathing.

Bo Raza spoke to Juniper about her grandparents. "I knew Heron when he was your age. We worked together at the Esselen and Comanche Water Works. I got out of water around the same time he did. I went to work with vox technology, and he began to raise bees."

"Bees! This is an apiary." Now I understood the acres of flowers and flowering crops. "What does Sultana Saffron mean?"

"Queen Crocus," Juniper answered. It is my Granmama's favorite flower. Saffron comes from the crocus flower. And Granmama is queen bee."

"I thought crocus was sterile and had to be hand-pollinated to produce saffron. Crocus doesn't rely on honeybees." Javier observed.

"That's not the case in Tellara. Look at the acres of autumn-blooming crocus.

"Crocus blooms in early spring," objected Javier.

"Crocuses bloom twice a year on Tellara. The bees are busy pollinating them to make saffron honey." Juniper was right. A sea of golden, white, and purple petals waved in the wind amidst tall sheaths of green. I noticed the musical hum of thousands of little yellow insects making merry over every inch of the floral carpet. "They'll bloom for a while longer. The saffron that the bees leave behind needs to be harvested in the next few days. I've helped do it before, when I was a child."

"You came here before? I didn't realize."

"That I visited Granpapa? Oh yes. My parents brought Robin and me here every harvest. We knew he liked his solitude. But we were too young to understand that he was banished. I was in my early teens before I realized that he never danced. It was confusing. The family still came but stayed for ever shorter visits. Then I think he wanted us to stay away. I haven't been back in ten years." Juniper paused to drink in the spectacular color that draped the mountainside. "I love it here. I hope to come live here after Granpapa balances his karma and rejoins the dance. At least until the ascension."

"Balances his karma and joins the dance. That sounds awesome."

"That is why you three Earthborn are here."

"We don't know what to do."

"You serve as a link in a long chain. Rejoining is so rare." Juniper looked to Phoenix for confirmation.

"I've never participated in a rejoining," Phoenix affirmed. "I don't think Saffron has either."

"I have," supplied the long-lived, deeply thoughtful Bo Raza. "Two hundred and forty-three years ago. This is the final rejoining for this thirteen thousand-year cycle. When completed, the entire Tellaran collective karma will be balanced. The entire population will activate their pineal glands and open their third eyes. The rejoining will usher in a planetary dimensional metamorphosis."

"I'm confused about that higher dimension business," said Louie.

"I'm confused about all of it," I seconded. "Webs and spirals and dances and eclipses and shifts. How am I supposed to explain something I don't understand?"

"Now you have Louie and Javier to help," observed Robin and the guys looked at each other uncertainly.

Bo Raza spoke, "OK, so you think of space as three-dimensional and time as the fourth dimension. You live in spacetime, right?"

"Yeah."

"So, an individual with fifth-dimensional consciousness can move freely through space and time, can experience moments as eternities and events simultaneously. Reptilian Earthborn can 'drop in' on designated moments. This gives my species an advantage over humans. You are already aware that spacetime is curved, yes?"

We three Earthlings nodded.

"Those of us with higher dimensional cognition can follow the arrow of time in both directions. We can view moments in history and probable futures."

Louie said, "This does explain the advantage the Earthborn reptiles have on us."

"Don't confuse access to 5D awareness with greater intellect or intuition. Earthborn reptilians rely on technology. They have no incentive to open their third eyes."

"RAT-TRAK," Louie said.

"What's that?" asked Bo.

I replied, "Something they called their sensor system. We heard them discuss it in the cave."

Bo continued, "Viewing around corners with technology is nothing approaching the ability to traverse time's spiral in both directions. Technology cost us right-brain functionality. Intuition atrophied. Also, because of the rigid hierarchy among reptiles, many pivotal points along time's spiral are blocked."

"But Tellaran reptiles have genuine intuition?"

"Ours is a hard-won recovery. Especially cherished during the heartdance."

Phoenix added, "Tellarans retain this temporal awareness for varying durations; some have permanent 5D consciousness, others glimpse it during the heartdance."

"Like certain saints and yogis on Earth," speculated Javier.

"Very likely. And soon, this higher state of consciousness will be the natural condition for all Tellarans," said Phoenix.

"Once Heron rejoins the dance," said Bo Raza.

"Which will be very soon," said Saffron breezing into the patio arm in arm with her ex-husband.

"Have you two heartdanced?" Bo Raza directed his question to Louie and Javier. They shook their heads no. "We've been busy. We just got here."

"We'll prepare tonight. Afterwards, it will be easier to understand how the heartdance opens our higher perceptions."

"When I dance, I see imagery and feel ecstasy. Is that my third eye opening?" I asked.

"The image we conjure during the dance is a slice of the spacetime spiral. Eternity intersects tangentially in the moment. A non-localized event becomes actualized, so yes, you experience a moment of higher-dimensional awareness." Louie and Javier looked intrigued.

"Let me show you all around the ranch," Heron offered. We rose to walk. Moving felt good after our travels and feasting.

CHAPTER 16

We walked together around the land and arrived in the heart of the apiary. The fields, covered with hundreds of hives, spread out in great coils, flanked by flowering crops on all sides. Each field was a hexagon, creating a honeycomb pattern throughout the acreage. Heartplums, apples, almonds, melon, vanilla, and crocus surrounded us, growing over the hills and dales. The harvest perfumes of fruits, flowers, grass, and honey were intoxicating.

Javier took my hand and led me away from the group. We strolled through the orchard. He leaned me up against a tree and then we were kissing. I hadn't quite considered if I wanted a romantic entanglement, but here I was, melting into his embrace. I'd forgotten the wondrous flush of new love; how giddy hormones turn everything on its head. His strong arms felt wonderful as his embrace tightened. I didn't even know where my arms were when I noticed my hands were full of the hair at the nape of his neck and I was pulling his mouth ever more deeply onto my own. I must have been breathing, but I don't know how. At some point I realized we were lying on soft grass at the base of a heartplum tree. Our kissing had progressed to a full-length body press and I eagerly met his every rock n' roll. Face to face, heart to heart, my cells came alive over every inch of my skin. I loved the feel of his weight from head to toe, along my breasts, torso, and hips, and the sensation of molten liquid that filled my abdomen and melted my limbs. The moment lasted an eternity.

I heard my name. Javier's voice was husky; my ears were filled with distant fog. We both came up for air. I think I said his name aloud. Then, neither one of us could think of anything else to say and we were kissing again. We were rumpled, with limbs entwined, when the rest of our party arrived on a hilltop above the orchard. This time voices penetrated my fog and the good Inspector's as well. We rolled apart and sat up. I was covered in leaves and began to primly adjust my sarong. Javier chuckled at my genteel affectations but helped me to my feet with a crooked smile and a wicked gleam in his dark eyes. We walked up to join the others hand in hand. We were both smiling unselfconsciously, and everyone greeted us with Tellaran indifference. Everyone except Louie, who tilted his head and eyed me like a crow. I wanted Louie to be happy for me. He'd lost so much so recently. Of course, my happiness mattered to him. None of us were kids, and in this season of my life, there was no point in being disingenuous. I was lucky, surprised, and happy to have rediscovered the romantic side of my soul. It felt glorious to have this mature Romani pursuing me. I didn't know if this was love, but for the nonce, Javier was a priority. Time with him was right up there with 1) clearing my name of murder, 2) whistleblowing international corporate crimes, 3) keeping my loved ones safe, and 4) saving two worlds.

By the time we arrived back at Heron's dome, it was late afternoon. The air was cooling, and a slight breeze stirred. Heron offered a light repast. Saffron advised us to eat a very light dinner, as this evening's ritual was going to be deeply meditative. We nibbled on fruit, veggies, cheese, and bread. Juniper sat next to her grandfather and Heron spoke.

"I know that Saffron has filled you in on my story. But it's important that you hear from me why I've waited so long to rejoin the dance. Eighty years ago, I committed a crime; I altered the water balance of the western hemisphere without consent of the Comanche Circle of Thirteen Elders. Because of my shunning, I hold the tension for Tellara's entire opposing polarity. Like a rubber band stretched taught to the Nth degree, Tellaran consciousness is waiting to spring forth and equilibrate a planet's worth of karma. To overcome my banishment, all I ever needed to do was ask to rejoin the heartdance. I could have done so many decades ago. But while I was out there alone, extraordinary knowledge was revealed to me."

"By whom?" Juniper asked her grandfather.

"By Nature, Gaia, Tellara. When I rejoin the dance, our entire population will experience a collective reverberation. Between tomorrow and the moment of the ascension, if anyone commits a crime, any crime, no matter how trivial, our group karma will be unbalanced again, and we will not collectively evolve to 6D consciousness. Opening of the third eye means activation of the pineal gland, another sensory organ. We'll be able to apprehend more information along the electromagnetic spectrum. New colors that contain emotional content will become perceptible."

"All Tellaran sentients will partake," said Bo. "And the information we apprehend is the color of love."

Javier spoke, "We have a description of something like this on Earth. The alchemists called it the Prima Materia. The holiest individuals, whose third eyes opened, apprehended this radiance. They say there were no words to describe the experience. Seeing and feeling loving light is incomparable." Again, Javier amazed me with his knowledge of the mystic philosophies. I must remember to thank Minerva.

"Even more than that, the entire planet, Tellara herself, will attain higher consciousness."

"Do you know the Gaia theory?" Phoenix asked us.

"Yes," Javier confirmed, "The Earth is a living organism whose whole is greater than the sum of its parts."

"Not just living, but self-aware down to every cell of every creature and every atom of every jot and tittle. From her core to the edge of the solar system, all Tellara is alive, sentient, and vibrating in ecstatic anticipation of her global ascension."

"Even though it's bound to be rife with violent geological upheavals that will kill many creatures?" asked Louie.

"Don't confuse shifts with chastisement. Cycles are inevitable, natural, and evolutionary," said Saffron.

"During the shift, Gaia-Tellara will experience union as a single sentient being, but only if there are no remaining polarized outliers. Once I rejoin the dance, the entire planet becomes critically interdependent as never before. I held out rejoining the dance in order to spare every Tellaran this possible fate."

"Kind of like a Bodi Satva," supplied Javier.

"What does this mean?"

"On Earth, in Eastern traditions, a Bodi Satva is an enlightened individual who commits to remain among the masses of humanity in order to help balance their karma, even at the delay of his or her own ascension."

"There are many Tellarans who make this sacrifice," said Heron.

"I meant you, Heron, holding space for every Tellaran."

"Well, that is an honorable way to look at it." Heron looked away.

Then Saffron said, "We have much to do. There are only a few hours of daylight remaining to prepare."

"Too bad you don't have Daylight Savings Time on Tellara," Louie commented.

"What is Daylight Savings? How does that work?" asked Juniper, intrigued.

"Oh, twice a year we reset our clocks to change the hours of sunrise and sunset."

"And you call this Daylight Savings? Why?" Bo Raza chuckled.

"Well, we coordinate clocks with events—like work and school hours, mealtimes, that kind of thing." Louie looked around to see if the Tellarans followed. "We synchronize our clocks with solar noon. Daylight Savings shifts our schedule during seasonal changes. During the warm seasons, it stays light later. We use less energy."

The Tellarans began giggling and repeating the phrases.

"Daylight Savings."

"Saving daylight by changing the clocks."

"It stays light later!" someone snorted.

Now they were all laughing, faces red, tears spilling down cheeks, snorting, and slapping their knees. The tension in the room had been so taut while Heron spoke; I guess this release was needed. Still, this seemed an overreaction. Sure, I'd always found Daylight Savings an outdated, inconvenient nuisance, but it never gave me a giggle, usually more of a groan, especially in spring when I lost an hour of sleep on a Monday morning. I said as much out loud and was greeted by gales of uncontrollable Tellaran laughter. Dignified Saffron sputtered juice out her nostrils and didn't even try to cover her indelicacy. We Earthborn found ourselves joining in, simply because of the merriment of the moment. "Glad I could provide you with a home-grown punch line," Louie quipped as order was restored. The occasional guffaw escaped from one of the Tellarans and they all started up again.

Javier said, "Native Americans say that 'only the white man would think he could cut a foot off the bottom of a blanket, sew it onto the top, and declare it to be a foot longer.'"

"So not all Earthborn are so foolish," said Phoenix.

Later that afternoon we sat with Bo Raza and Heron.

Bo spoke, "As you know, tomorrow's ceremony is a dance to reconcile Heron's karma with the rest of sentient life on Tellara and to equilibrate all the water on the world."

I looked at Heron. "Saffron told us you used to be a water whisperer."

Heron said, "Once a water whisperer, always a water whisperer. Water is just no longer my vocation. Now, I am a bee whisperer. Before I was shunned, I studied everything about water, from its chemistry, to its crystalline geometry, including its memory, anticipation, thermodynamics, and its role in the creation of the Universe and here on Tellara."

Javier probed, "I've heard that water has memory, but not anticipation."

I said, "Saffron mentioned that water has intention."

"Water both remembers and plans. It transmits information via its shape. Here," He handed us a flat screen and recited from memory as we followed along from **The Tellaran Chronicles of Science and Spirituality.**

Water

Water has so many anomalies compared to other molecules, that it defies complete understanding. The secret to water is self-love, which gives it almost mystical sentience. Every water molecule loves itself. Every water molecule loves every other water molecule. Science chalks up water's anomalies to its polarized covalent bonds and hydrogen bonds, but these features only describe water's tangible properties.

Liquid water is composed of pre-crystalline matrices called clusters. Factors that influence water's crystalline structure have to do with its history, where it's been and what it's been mixed with, the shape of its conduit, its flow, the intention, emotion, sound, and vibrations in its vicinity. Clusters work as memory cells. The cluster itself can remain cohesive for long periods of time. This is how water records, stores, and shares information. Its molecular clusters form encoded structures that function like, a malleable codex.

Water molecules are very social, bonding endlessly with one another, forever dancing together, combining, separating, and recombining. Moving water molecules make their own music. They remember every dance partners and geometric choreography they've shared. They remember the chemicals and life forms they've partnered with, the substances they've dissolved and mixed with throughout the ages. Water molecules remember the past and anticipate the future. Water communicates with itself and in a way, all the water in the world is engaged in an endless heartdance.

Free oxygen atoms are slightly positively charged. Free hydrogen atoms are slightly negatively charged. Oxygen has 6 electrons in its outer valence shell. Oh! It longs for 2 more electrons to feel complete. "Please grant me 8 electrons," it prays. Along comes a hydrogen atom with one lonely electron, aching for another. Then along comes another free hydrogen, also longing to bond. Each hydrogen atom shares 1 electron with the entreating oxygen. Two covalent bonds are formed. A water molecule is created. Nature rejoices.

Not long after this happy union, a magnetic attraction grows within the water molecule. The hydrogen's negatively charged electrons try to get as close as possible to the positively charged Big Oxygen. They glide so close, that after a time, there is a phenomenal exchange of magnetic charge. The oxygen atom becomes slightly negative; the hydrogen atoms become slightly positive. Each water molecule becomes a magnetic dipole.

Now out in the world, on land, sea, and air, even interstellar space, these negatively charged oxygen atoms become oh so attractive to the positively charged hydrogen atoms in other water molecules. Intrigued, they move towards each other, slowly at first, then, in a passionate rush, the O- connects with the H+ in a satisfying, gratifying hydrogen bond. More and more water molecules cluster together, each bringing its memories and hopes.

The polarized covalent bond between the hydrogen electrons sharing the valence shell with oxygen electrons is a tight, albeit, polygamous marriage, two H's for every O.

If the covalent bond is polygamous, the hydrogen bond is polyamorous. Twenty times weaker than the covalent bond, hydrogen bonds are tough, but not unbreakable. These fickle flirts makeup and breakup in the presence of heat. Water has the greatest heat capacity of any liquid. This means it is a heat reservoir: much heat can be added without raising the temperature. But, when water reaches its melting or boiling points, those hydrogen bonds get restless and randy. They promiscuously mix and mingle with every available oxygen *atom in the vicinity.*

Meanwhile, back in oxygen's outer valence shell, the original 6 electrons are jealous of the tight polarized, magnetically sexualized covalent bonds. The original 6 electrons form 3 lonely loner pairs. They repel the hydrogen electrons, pushing them as far away as possible. This molds each water molecule into a V-shape with an asymmetrical charge. This V is the foundation of water's nascent lattice structure. Keep this V-shape in mind. The angle of the V, or angle of incidence, is key to information sharing between these shameless social creatures.

Water freezes at 0ºC. Water is densest at 4oC. Herein lies the mystery of why ice floats in liquid water. Unique to H_2O, its solid form is less dense than its liquid. When water cools to freezing, oxygen's jealous loner electron pairs repel the hydrogen electrons to their maximum possible distance, narrowing the V angle to its tightest, densest configuration possible. Water loves to hang out at 4ºC. In this snuggest, happiest cluster, maximum information is shared. Every molecule communicates its memories, love, and now, intentions.

If ice were heavier and denser than liquid water, lakes and oceans would freeze from the bottom up, not the top down. Once frozen solid, bodies of water would rarely, if ever, thaw all the way to the bottom. Life, as we know it, could not have formed on Tellara. The dense water forms a liquid layer beneath a protected ice cover. Because water sinks as it cools, the bottom layers remain oxygenated. Fauna and flora thrive through the winter only to surface again in spring as the ice cover melts.

The detailed structure of water molecule clusters in liquid water can actually be observed using X-ray diffraction. No two clusters are alike, although they all are similar. The more molecules and clusters in proximity, the more rapidly they mix, mingle, and exchange information. As these molecules cool to freezing, these pre-crystalline gatherings collaborate on their nascent lattice structure. Clusters of molecules use shape to embody a memory codex of each molecule's individual history, where it's been and what it's mingled with. These pre-crystalline clusters also contain information, the source of waters' ability to anticipate the shape it will assume if frozen.

Every water cluster is comprised of a unique combination of molecules. As water cools, each unique cluster shrinks, their V-shaped lattices reorganize themselves: pushing, pulling, deforming, and rotating in all directions to design its nascent matrix. Here is where the individual molecules cooperate together where the dance will take them. The love story of every water molecule desires to embed itself into a distinctive hexagonal crystal. Each pre-crystalline structure imagines the unique matrix its components will form, each molecule contributing its history, emotions, and aspirations. At the moment of freezing, the dance stills and the hexagonal crystal solidifies.

Every snowflake is different because every snowflake is composed of a unique cluster of H_2O molecules that have never combined before. For any water molecule, the snowflake is its most ecstatic embodiment of perfection. Every snowflake is in a state of orgasmic bliss.

Another anomaly is, that, unlike every other fluid, the denser water gets, the faster it moves. (Consider traffic jams to visualize how all other fluids slow down in heavy traffic. Alternatively, think of how white water rapids form when watercourses narrow.) This is true in pipe flow and in nature. Around icebergs, ice caps, and ice flows, dense liquid water molecules rapidly dance around buoying up the frozen ice.

All living things are basically water containers. Every living cell contains water molecules that bond in single file or in clusters. These molecules travel, inform, and communicate with each other.

Most of the DNA molecule is water. The DNA nucleus impresses its code on the surrounding water. Gene pairs dictate what protein will be formed, while water, the ultimate shape shifter, wraps itself around the organic compounds to fill available space within the double helix. The shape of the amino acid deforms each water cluster. Water clusters partner with amino acids to carry information from cell to cell.

Most of the human brain is water. Neurotransmitters deform the water clusters in our synapses. The deformation of these shape-shifting geniuses alters the angle of each V with respect to its neighbors in the microcluster. Water partners with neurotransmitters to carry information throughout the brain and body. Water is the vehicle of consciousness.

Water forms a partnership with plants. Evapotranspiration is the process whereby water is released from the top of plants into the atmosphere. Water being expelled from the surface of leaves creates a vacuum in the tops of plants. This pressure difference draws water upwards from plant's roots. Water molecules inside narrow capillaries form into chains held together by climbing hydrogen bonds. (Think the eensy weensy spider.) The upward force generated by these single-file molecules in collaboration with the vacuum formed by evapotranspiration is stronger than the force of gravity. The xylem draws water up from the soil to the top of the tallest trees. Upon reaching the tops of trees, water is used: 5% for photosynthesis, 10% for nutrition, and 85% for evapotranspiration, returning those molecules to the hydrologic cycle.

Water in plants also affects seedlings. When seeds first bud under-

ground, their stems contain enough water to reach 400 atmospheres of pressure. This is why even tiny sprouts can break through solid rock, forming all the soil on the planet.

When frozen water melts, its memory is erased. When liquid water evaporates, its memory is erased. This self-cleansing process removes all information from water molecules except how to sustain life. Keeping water clean is crucial to life. It is very rare to find pure, distilled H_2O in nature. Water, the universal solvent and ultimate shape shifter, always partners with its neighboring substances.

Water is very cohesive. Liquid water has the widest temperature range of any liquid on the planet. A fluid won't boil until its pressure is the same as the air around it. Water just doesn't want to let go of itself, slow to freeze and slow to boil. Tellara is bathed in liquid water. Water is the only substance to naturally occur on Tellara as solid, liquid, and gas. Tellara is the perfect distance from the sun to be predominantly liquid water. Farther away, Tellara would be a snowball. Closer to the sun our world would be a steam bath.

Another paradox: Hot water freezes faster than cold water. This has been observed since ancient times. As the liquid warms up, the molecules vibrate faster and move apart. The hydrogen bonds relax and stretch. The hotter the water, the wider the V is in the polarized covalent bonds and the weaker the angle of incidence. In very hot water, the covalent bonds become weaker than the hydrogen bonds. But in the instant when the rapidly vibrating, heated molecules meet a frosty blast, the hydrogen electrons rush to the embrace of the oxygen nucleus, clinging for emotional and magnetic support. As the polarized covalent bonds quiver in anxiety, energy is rapidly released causing rapid cooling, rapid freezing.

In nature, water follows the beds that it carves through the terrain. Water loves to carve curves in the landscape allowing natural clusters form and thrive. Water shape-shifts to fill whatever vessel it enters. When pumped through pipes, water is pushed with high pressure along strait channels and 90° ducts. This breaks down the natural, pre-crystalline clusters, depriving water of its rich history, symmetry, cohesion, memory, geometry, and beauty. On Tellara, we learned long ago to propel water through curved, spiraling channels, and to return it to the hydrologic cycle after use. This is why communities have curved inflow conduits and circulating outflow ponds. We call swirled water vitalized water. It maintains the sovereignty of clusters, prevents corrosion, and promotes healing.

Viscosity, cohesiveness, and surface tension all describe water molecule's magnetic desire to cluster together. Water has the highest cohesiveness, viscosity, energy density, and surface tension of any non-

metallic liquid. It is called the universal solvent because it can dissolve almost any substance and retain the H_2O molecules' sovereignty. The chemistry doesn't change, rather, the V angles shift at the molecular level. Water loves to bead and clump across distances to form ever-larger beads. Falling water drops are so cohesive they sometimes even bounce. The surface tension on still ponds is so cohesive that insects skate and lily pads float across the top.

Water feels thoughts and emotions. Send water love, compassion, and kindness before you drink it or bathe, and you will infuse yourself with positive vibrations. Conversely, when water is exposed to negative emotions, it is the same as being exposed to chemical toxins. It pays to love water, the substance of life. All the water on Tellara is vitalized. This means it flows through natural conduits free from toxins and filtered through charged crystals. When you mix Tellaran water with any other water, it transfers its purified vitalizing qualities because all the new water molecules fall in love with the vitalized bonds.

I was afraid Heron was going to read more, and I was already reeling from information overload. I knew water was miraculous, the stuff of life, but all these anomalies were swimming in my brain, literally. Thankfully, at that moment, Saffron appeared and told us it was time.

"We need to prepare for tomorrow," Saffron announced. "Ladies, you are with me."

"What do you mean?" I asked.

"We will be sequestered tonight. The men have their ritual preparation and the women have theirs."

I looked at Javier, who was looking back at me in disbelief. The same thought must have been running through both our heads, "I finally find a romantic connection, and now I have to do some same-sex ritual! I don't think so!" Javier and I stood and held hands and made to move off together.

"Dana, please wait," Saffron held up a delaying hand gesture. "Our preparation is about planetary polarity."

"Oh, well when you put it that way," I grumbled.

Before she could continue, a group of people arrived on the patio and there were introductions all around. Neighbors, children, and elders from Giza, Comanche, Iroquois, Europe, Asia, Africa, and Esselen arrived. I recognized Buffalo, Tangerine, and Ivy from the Esselen Elders.

There was shared chatter about Daylight Savings Time. Newcomers cracked up as the joke was repeated. There were about thirty people milling about, all planning to migrate to their gender-respective retreats. From the ridiculous to the sublime, the preparations for the rejoining dance were being taken seriously and the hour was nigh. Javier and I hugged and kissed longingly, completely indifferent to our public display. No one cared. Reluctantly, we pulled apart when we heard Saffron speak.

"Those of you who are gender fluid, feel free to choose your retreat location, as long as you define your polarity tonight in preparation for the rejoining dance." I realized that Phoenix, Louie, and some of the new arrivals experienced sexual polarity differently from the preponderance of individuals. "I'll stay with the guys," Louie said, and Phoenix nodded. Gender bending, androgyny, and sexual orientation were natural and open on Tellara.

An elder named Jasmine lived on the neighboring land. There was no ownership per se, but stewardship. "It is my honor to host the feminine retreat." Jasmine and Saffron led the women onto a footpath over rolling green hills. I turned back to see Javier and Louie looking after me, Louie with mischief, Javier with frustration.

We walked to Jasmine's property and into her lovely, ranch-style home. Another several dozen women of all ages were there already. Young girls sang and played together in a nearby gazebo. Inside and out, the grounds were covered with tents, domes, tables, mats, and pillows. When we arrived, each woman assumed her position on one of the mats. I chose a mat near the door, secluded yet sheltered.

We quieted and Saffron spoke. First, she introduced me as the Earthborn wayshower that many had wondered about. Of course, my pale skin, blue eyes, and short stature made me stand out. As usual, I was greeted with gentle acceptance. This was a planet that had not known racial bigotry for thousands of years, so I didn't feel awkward because no one else did, either. The children asked questions about Earth, but Saffron hushed them, explaining that these questions could be answered tomorrow after the rejoining. But now, it was crucial to understand the role Louie, Javier, and I were to play as links in a karmic chain spanning worlds, cycles, and souls. It was daunting and humbling, but I just sat there and allowed everyone to look me over until their curiosity was satisfied. More women arrived. There were now nearly fifty women, children, gay couples, and reptilians, including Guna Raza. We exchanged warm greetings. The atmosphere was expectant, reverent, and festive at the same time.

From a distance, we could hear the men's drumming and chanting. Cups of tea were passed around and each woman sipped. "You don't have to drink the tea, Dana. It contains plant medicine that expands the mind. The children drink a separate brew."

"When in Rome," I replied, and sipped just a little.

We closed our eyes and got comfortable. Saffron led us in a guided meditation that got very deep very fast. I entered an altered state of consciousness onto a carpet of moss, clover, and grass as soft as down. Luminescent green beings fluttered around me. Tiny lightening balls with adorable faces and leaves for wings. "Are you fairies?" I asked.

"I am a clover deva," sang a tiny creature in a melodious lilt. Then dozens more of the glowing green orbs erupted from the clover beds surrounding me. They were accompanied by grass and moss devas, each with its unique winged configuration, color patterns, and faces. The moss devas were covered with stems and caps that effervesced intermittently and tinkled like bells. The leaves on the grass devas were of mixed lengths, long and sleek, short and hearty. They whispered with wind of their own creation. The plant devas fluttered around me producing an unbearably sweet, soft air.

Then, what I could only describe as soil devas, emerged from the ground. Red, brown, and golden grains woven with grassroots floated among the green plant devas. Bubbles of air and water fizzed while microbial particles popped. The soil added a bit of percussion to the serenade. From beyond our immediate locale, thousands more devas arrived to accompany nature's symphony.

Devas from heartplum, apple, almond, melon, vanilla, and crocus plants joined insects, birds and bees to regale us. At length, a golden silence blanketed the countryside. I hovered in this euphoric stillness for ages. I felt warmth on my face that I gradually realized was sunshine. Around me, others were stirring. Each woman present was arising from her vision into the breaking sunrise over the Antalya hills.

Bliss and beauty aside, I had to pee. Just like every ladies room on every alternate Earth, there was a line. As I emerged from my turn on the commode, Juniper handed me a cup of tea. "Same brew as last night?" I inquired.

"Just some black tea with grated orange rind, and a splash of fresh cream."

"Ah, Earl Grey, my favorite." I slurped. Juniper had loaded the tea with cream and honey. It was the perfect way to break my fast. Food that locals had been preparing for days in anticipation of the ceremony was being laid on tables. I helped lay out a buffet of warm bread, butter and jam, eggs, cheese, fruit, nuts, olives, cucumbers, and tomatoes amidst aromatic dressings. Ceramic carafes held juice and tea. The food was light and rich at the same time. I ate my fill, savoring every morsel. I could have stuffed myself, but forbore, heeding Saffron's caution that we wanted to enter the day's ritual with clear minds and bodies. After cleaning up all the food and dishes, many of us collapsed back onto our mats for a mid-morning respite. We shared stories of our collective vision of Gaia's auditory and visual fantasia. I may not have made love last night, but the bliss I'd experienced had sated me, body and spirit.

At noon, we headed for the large meadow adjoining the properties of Heron's and Jasmine's spreads. Every woman dressed in spectacularly bright colors.

Sarongs, caftans, and robes of every manner billowed in the breeze. I wore a turquoise and silver Grecian-styled gown. The men were walking towards us, equally colorful in their ceremonial regalia, nearly floating as they came. The field was filled with hundreds of men, women, and children, human, reptilian and, I guessed, Pleiadian or Arcturan or Sirrian—I wasn't sure—tall blondes, and taller, ebony, androgynous individuals. Leel and Jeej were there with Falcon. We'd been joined by stakeholders, local and remote, all with a profound interest in the outcome of today's rejoining ceremony. I don't know if they all realized the stakes as Heron had explained them to us yesterday, but no one was unmindful of the enormity of the moment. I spotted Louie and Javier. They smiled and nodded at me but remained within the cluster of men.

Two concentric circles formed, the men outside the women. The women formed a spiral from the perimeter to the center, arranged from oldest on the inside to youngest at the edge.

Heron sat alone in the center of this cluster of humanity. Men began to chant, drum, and strum. I felt as though I was vibrating inside music.

The men's simple circle began to migrate, altering its shape into an infinity symbol, which bisected the women's group into two separate, enclosed spirals. The figure eight intersected at the very center where Heron sat cross-legged. The men paced the contour of the infinity figure. The women spiraled into the center of their teardrop and back out again. A single thunderous drumbeat resounded. Music reached a crescendo. At this signal, everyone began singing and dancing.

Instead of one heartdance image coalescing in a single circle, two images emerged, one in each teardrop of the infinity symbol. In our circle, the image of a whirling, spiraling double torus emerged. It was composed of flowing water, draining endlessly down waterfalls to a central singularity, and then rising at the outside in continuous fountains.

I felt myself float above the pulsating infinity symbol, outside my body. From this vantage, I could see the entire dance.

The image in the other teardrop was of Tellara convulsing in planetary labor contractions. Volcanism, quakes, tsunamis, thunderclouds, sandstorms, and cyclones the size of hemispheres blanketed Tellara. Massive amounts of Earth, Air, Fire, Water, poured forth over Tellaran creatures that writhed in agony and ecstasy. One by one, each creature yielded to the elements and collapsed into singularity.

I felt myself expand to the size of Tellara. I apprehended colors I'd never seen before and knew that this was the radiant darkness the mystics spoke of when one's third eye opened. Luminous orbs swirled around me.

Our massive collective aura was joined by swarms of bees, other insects, birds, fish, mammals, reptiles, and all animals, like a phantasmagoric, extra-corporeal Noah's Ark. The dance was joined by flowers, trees, and all manner of green plants; and then by dirt, lava, rocks, crystals, water, fire, and wind. Elements, devas, and creatures swirled together. Boundaries dissolved. Other heartdances were happening all over the planet and we all shared collective, loving light. For the third time in two days, a single moment stretched into eternity. This was my best "now" ever.

Snippets of others' breathing and shifting limbs filtered into my awareness. I was back in my physical body, lying on the grass. I was wrapped in someone's arms. I opened my eyes. Javier and I were in a loving embrace. Our eyes locked. We kissed, unmindful of the other waking beauties strewn across the hillside. Young and old were clustered together in piles of laughter.

It began to rain, lightly at first, but harder within minutes. Water had joined the ceremony. The entire group praised the water and got soaked like little children. We gradually collected ourselves and drifted away in the miraculous downpour. Heron was back in the heartdance and all was right with the world. Water had blessed our ceremony. It was time to share, to prepare, to serve, and to savor a feast.

Rain blessed us on and off for the next several days. Heron was over the moon. Louie, Javier, and I were feted because we were links in the karmic chain between Earth and Tellara. The hundreds of questions the children had held back yesterday poured forth in a torrent of curiosity. Louie, Javier, and I answered until we were hoarse. Then Juniper had the brilliant idea to show some Earth movies to the group and nagged Phoenix to share his stash of artifacts. I chose *The Sound of Music*. It gave a false sense of how humans break out into song during especially dramatic moments, but did dramatize our polarized population, our warlike nature, our frailties, jealousies, religious contradictions, and conceits.

The Tellarans loved it and learned the songs swiftly. The hills were alive. When it was over, Phoenix selected Slumdog Millionaire, a film that vividly portrayed the best and the worst of the human condition. The Tellarans were appalled by the caste system, as we explained it, and were unable to comprehend non-consensual sexual acts, nor women as sexual objects and children as slaves. We tried to explain these parts of the story, but they were utterly foreign to the Tellaran mind. Louie explained that most adults wouldn't allow younger children to watch this movie, which just led to questions about why sometimes erotica was naughty and sometimes it was nice, why sometimes violence was considered entertaining and sometimes horrific. There were no good answers to satisfy the Tellaran sensibilities.

Leaving Louie and Phoenix to field questions, I put on Pleasantville and slipped out with Javier. Heron had considerately made up a space for us in a yurt beyond the apiary. The past two days of heightened receptivity enhanced all connections, not the least of which was Eros. Mystical levitation turned out to be my new favorite foreplay. Javier had an effortless seduction. Add to that the fact that the guy had artistic, talented, beautiful hands, an accomplished, tantric knowledge of a woman's body, and a sensuous, generous mouth, I melted into him. When he entered me, my entire being enfolded his and drew him deeper within. We made love for hours. My multiple orgasms stretched on and on and extended through every cell in my body. I could tell Javier was experiencing the same ecstasy as his orgasms climbed chakra by chakra from his shaft to his throat. A guttural groan escaped from both of us simultaneously.

We were both in a state of euphoria when I remarked, "Clearly, you're not a virgin."

"I've never been married but never lived as a monk. I almost married. I was with Trina for six years."

"Why didn't you marry?"

"She's clan, Romani, lives with Minerva. She wouldn't marry a cop."

"Clan?"

"Distant cousin. Minerva is the head of an extensive Romani clan with kin across all continents. I was not the only orphan she raised. Trina would hardly consider marrying outside our culture. Marry a Basque half-breed? Never gonna happen. She wanted her kids raised in the old ways. Trina and several other cousins all live in a rural neighborhood in the vicinity of Minerva's house. It is the house I grew up in. Your son and daughter met the clan when they were on the road."

"Ruth and Jesse's safe house?"

"The very one. My people understand under-the-radar road trips."

"Why did you ever become a cop?"

"Insatiable curiosity. And an ancient, almost genetic, hatred of injustice. Believe it or not, I didn't fit anywhere else. I tried academia, but my ideas were unpublishable."

"The other cops must have noticed that you were a square peg in a round hole."

"They noticed, but I solved crimes no one else could. I discomfited the great and powerful. I broke scandals and crimes the others wouldn't touch. I dare say, I was as much reviled as respected. No one will mourn my retirement."

"You're retiring?"

"I may be forced to if Shelter has its way. I've disturbed a nest of vipers with deep tentacles."

"Aren't you mixing metaphors?"

"Several." We kissed again.

CHAPTER 17

Javier and I awoke the next morning and lingered in our private cocoon for several hours.

"What did you do during the men's preparation ritual?"

"We did a heart dance."

"With no women? How?"

"We all took turns holding polarity. Phoenix and Heron thought Louie and I should heartdance at least once before the rejoining."

"What image emerged?"

"Gaia stretched out along a spiral of many Earth-like planets, like pearls on a string."

"Beautiful. No special tea?"

"There was food and beverages."

"But no special tea?"

"You mean like special brownies?"

"Yeah, only with significantly more kick."

"Nothing like that, but believe me, that heartdance was beyond psychedelic."

"So was the rejoining. Now, that was mind-expanding."

"Magical Mystery Tour. I gotta say Dana Travers, your alibi does not disappoint."

"I'm glad you tracked me down to get it."

"Not mad at me anymore for being so relentless?"

"Your tenacity is growing on me. Among other things…"

Around noon, we joined the others in Heron's kitchen.

Apparently, everyone had slept in. The others in our party were clustered in a friendly hub. They took little notice of our arrival. Louie and Phoenix stood shoulder to shoulder; arms wrapped behind each other's backs. Louie looked at me knowingly. He looked happy for me. He looked happy for himself. He disengaged and walked over to hug me.

He had spent the night with Phoenix. I felt a surge of mixed emotions. No one could ever replace Hal, but Louie had found solace.

"You found romance," he kissed me on the cheek.

"So did you, apparently."

"I found respite from my grief, but no; Phoenix and I were loving, but not lovers."

"It's not my business, but that makes me feel close to Hal."

"I merged with Hal's spirit during the rejoining when the wolves came to the dance. Hal used to tease that we were both wolves. Wolves mate for life, so now

I'm a Steppenwolf, a lone wolf of the steppes who had lost his soul mate. But my heart is at peace for just this moment."

"If any creature could resurrect your wolf spirit it would be a rising Phoenix. Maybe you were right, back at the art gallery in San Francisco. Maybe Phoenix was checking out you and not me."

"You're right too. He was checking us both out."

"Still, my rendezvous with Phoenix kept you and Javier guessing while you were waiting for my alibi," I teased.

"Did I hear my name?" Phoenix joined us. Then Javier was at my side, smiling. A brunch buffet had been laid out and we all nibbled on the leftovers.

Many of the dancers left the area the day after the rejoining, but all who remained spent the next two days harvesting saffron. Heron stored the precious spice in soft hemp cloth bags. He gifted each of us with a small sack of golden saffron as a memento of his stunning rejoining ceremony. We all spent time around the bees and collected honeycombs filled with saffron honey. Honey from the crocus flower has no equal on Earth. Louie and Phoenix were exchanging saffron recipes that I couldn't wait to try.

Our final day at the farm began with an early wake up knock on our door and a holler to pack for the road. Heron was returning to Giza with us. We traversed our tram path in reverse. It was melancholy to be passing through the landscape for the last time, but the weather was beautiful, and all Antalya was on autumnal display. We had an hour to pass while waiting for our airship connections. To our delight, we were met in the city by a group of locals, many of whom had attended the rejoining dance. Jasmine was there, several local elders, Falcon, Leel, and Jeej. There were hugs, laughter, and tears all around.

They surprised us Earthborn visitors with individual gifts. No wrapping paper here in Tellara, although there was a bit of ceremony. I received a beautiful, forest green purse. It was oversized, hobo-style, made of soft, supple leather-like fabric, almost identical to the bag I had admired at the Khan el-Khalili in Cairo. "It is a hemp blend," said Phoenix. They could not have picked a more perfect gift. "It's a hobo bag! I love it!" I gushed.

"Don't you mean Bo-Ho bag," asked Louie, my fashion-conscious friend.

I answered, "Both are correct. It means a bag made from one single piece of cloth, the shoulder strap and pouch are one continuous weave, and look, mine has a secret compartment woven into the strap."

Louie was given a caftan of black satin with silver trim. It had a geometric mandala pattern that spiraled from front to back. Louie put it on over his jeans and t-shirt and looked like a native-born Tellaran. "I'll be metrosexual stylin' in Giza," Louie preened, clearly delighted with his gift.

Javier's gift came in an etched wooden box. He opened it to view his own vox. Javier could not have been more pleased. Now all three of us had our own Tellaran tools. Our complicated lives were just a bit safer, if not saner. I could tell the fellows thought I'd gotten a poor deal with my big green purse, its wide shoulder strap and fancy compartments, but men simply don't understand purses, not even Louie, although he totally gets shoes. I stuffed my saffron, honeycomb, and pocketbook into my green bag along with my embroidered turquoise gown and was ready to travel with one lovely carry-on bag.

Leel and Jeej joined us for the return trip wearing powder blue smocks. We were a merry crew as we boarded the airship and took our seats in a conversational salon large enough to accommodate all members of our party. I sat between Javier and Bo Raza. Phoenix and Louie sat across the table from us.

A few minutes after takeoff, Louie reached out to me, took my hands in his, and called my name rather formally. "Dana, Dana," he repeated. "I've come to an important decision." I waited, not knowing what to expect.

"I'm going to donate DNA samples to the grays. I want to help this race to survive." Louie nodded toward the gray hybrids. Leel and Jeej stood and bowed to Louie, then sat again in silence.

"The grays are a species worth saving. I realized this in the rejoining ceremony. The Tellaran grays seek to restore their fertility by reactivating their lower chakras. In order to attain their higher, finer emotions, they will have to travel through their darker shadow emotions. They need to do this to understand how they arrived in their barren quandary. I comprehended their collective will in the dance. The grays want to recover love, integrate their hearts and minds. I want my DNA to be part of their legacy." There were unshed tears in his eyes.

"Louie, I'm so proud to be your friend. I sensed the same thing. Our own species is rushing headlong towards its own destruction. The grays unintentionally gave up their birthright to evolve. We're not so different, we're just making different mistakes."

"Exactly, but we'll face a similar crisis if we destroy the very planet we call home."

"Louie, I will also give the grays samples of my DNA. The goal is evolution, for all of us."

Leel and Jeej stood and bowed towards me. "Count me in," said Javier, not having been faced with the chainsaw-sized power syringe thrust at our bellies by Swoosh. Leel and Jeej turned to bow at Javier before reclaiming their seats.

"Give my regards to Swoosh," Louie nodded to the grays. They spoke among themselves and then said in unison,

"Do you mean Shoosh?"

"Right, Shoosh. Sorry. I got the wrong name stuck in my head."

"Since this is a time for disclosing realizations from the dance, I want to tell you all that I felt a connection with the honeybees that joined us," said Javier.

"Connected with the bees?"

"Their group mind; they understand the plight of the bees on Earth and they want to help. The bees in Antalya are robust, genetically diverse bees from the seat of two civilizations. Some of them will travel back to Earth with us through the portal."

"Exactly how will they travel? Fly through in a swarm?"

"Heron brought along two hives in carrying cases. I will transport them to America."

I protested, "Javier, this is a potential ecological disaster. A parallel Earth is bound to have a similar, but ever-so-slightly different microbial regime, for which its counterpart has no defenses. Your Tellaran bees will never survive the diseases and toxins propagated on Earth's hives."

Heron explained, "There will be some die off. The DNA of Tellaran bees is enhanced because they have been pollinating heartplums for millennia. Some of the Tellaran bees will have immunity to Earth's contaminants. Enough will survive to regenerate hives and ultimately hybridize with your bees, enhancing their immunity. It is a long-term project, requiring patience."

I asked Javier, "You have the logistics for this covered?"

"I'm still working on that. I was hoping that together we could figure something out."

"Well, one thing we have going for our bees is that we've started a heartplum grove in Wah'Kon-Tah. That's where we should take the hives."

"Speaking of hives, you should hear this." Louie took both of my hands in his. "I've made another decision, Dana. I have nothing to return to, Earthside. I'm marked for death by Shelter. I won't ever be with Hal again, but I think I could find peace in Tellara."

Heron and Saffron remained silent. Louie turned to Phoenix. "You brought me back from despair. I would like to join you in your mission to create the remaining portals between our worlds."

"Louie, you are a chosen wayshower. Alas, cannot remain on Tellara."

"What do you mean? Can't remain? Why not?" Louie turned to Saffron.

"Louie," Saffron began gently, "I fear we failed to impress upon you the significance of balancing our planetary karma. The karma of every soul, living and dead, including every incarnation going back thirteen thousand years, has been balanced. You are not part of Tellara's group soul. You are not indigenous to this world. You're a link in the karmic chain that connects Tellara and Earth. Were you to try to join us in our final heartdance, you would be left out of the great collective. You would be left behind for thirteen thousand years. For the same reason, Phoenix cannot go with you to Earth to stay. The short time he spent on Earth engendered no new karma. He is integral to our world soul. As the time of the shift approaches, next spring, we must all migrate to our home worlds." Louie was near tears. He turned away from the rest of us.

"However, Louie," Phoenix began gently, "you can stay with us until the very last minute, in late spring. You can help me work while I complete the two final paintings *Shasta Solstice* and *Avalon Equinox*. Meanwhile, we can help figure out how to transport the bees to Earth."

Louie sounded reconciled. "We can move the hives to the next portal in Shastise, Tellara. Dana and Javier can pick them up Earthside and transport them overland. Crystal and Cosmo could use the Electric Kool-Aid van."

"Why can't we all travel to Shastise in Tellara and cross over to Earth together?" I countered.

"Dana, the portal must be opened from each side by the original wayshower from each planet. I open each portal from Tellara to Earth. You, in turn, open it from Earth to Tellara."

"Louie crossed over before me into *Tellaran Autumn*."

"After your DNA penetrated the mist into the Tellaran landscape."

"Oh," was all I could think to say. I had not considered my return trip through customs and immigration.

"Can't we take *Autumn* with us to Shastise and cross over there?" asked Javier reasonably.

"The painting is Earthside. I wouldn't risk passing a singularity through another singularity. There's no way to predict what would happen. You will have to transport *autumn* back to America on Earthside."

"But you brought it through once?" Javier probed.

"I paint myself into and through the painting as a character in the foreground as the portal manifests around me. Until Dana opened *Summer in Tellara*, I was trapped on Earth."

"Stranded?! I never knew that."

"You wouldn't have; I'm only a figure in the painting 'til I emerge through the portal the first time."

"What if we'd never met? You'd have been stranded on Earth!"

"The portal was drawn directly into your path. I paint myself into the picture last. The portal opens as I complete the details of my features. It is at this moment our singularities intersect. You discovered how to perceive and cross the threshold. Dana, you and I have been linked for thirteen thousand years."

"I felt the magic building before I arrived in your San Francisco art gallery. I felt a connection with you when we first met, like I was inside your paintings."

"And so you were."

217

"Could I create a portal on Earthside?"

"You'd have to master trans-dimensional physics and integrative art. In thirteen thousand years, you'll need to do it from Terra Nova to connect with the next wayshower in Terra Familiar."

"It may take me all thirteen thousand years to learn that."

"I have four opportunities to integrate the portals into my art, one at each quaternary seasonal date of this pivotal year. The intersection of our planetary singularities holds the portals open. Another wayshower might use music, poetry, architecture, or even a garden."

"You're saying the portals are singularities?" Javier asked.

Phoenix laughed. Saffron, Heron, and Bo Raza smiled. "Where did we leave off with our multi-dimensional physics lessons?"

"You mean on the way to Antalya?" Louie rejoined the conversation. "You left us with our heads spun around backwards and up our butts so far that we were inside out."

"Very well," Phoenix plunged onward. "The Universe is made of an infinite sea of singularities. Our worlds, Earth and Tellara, each have a central singularity, which is to say a blackwhole, at their hearts. An event horizon lies deep within each planet's core, creating a region of hollow Earth.

Javier objected, "That sounds like the opposite of a black hole. Black holes are not stable, they violently attract and crush."

"Blackwholes both attract and radiate. Many are stable, especially protons," said Phoenix.

I groaned, as Phoenix opened his silver disc to a folio about Planetary History. "You have that journal with you?! Here we go again."

The Tellaran Chronicles of Science and Spirituality
A Bit of Planetary History

Thirteen thousand years ago, our planets shifted onto two separate frequencies. Our planets are moving along vast, out-of-phase sine waves that intersect every thirteen thousand years. The last time was at the advent of the Holocene era, near the final destruction of the Atlantean age. When the sine waves cross, the singularities at the centers of our planets intersect. We don't share spacetime, but our fifth-dimensional spirals overlap.

This intersection occurs during the cusp of ages, the few years before and after the galactic eclipse. A lot of stuff happens during this intersection, the polarity of each planet reverses, consciousness expands, and seismic activity erupts, which can alter the planet's tilt and spin. Wayshowers can open portals between our worlds.

We are in a period known on Tellara as the Magic Seasons. This is a twenty-six thousand-year cusp in the our two hundred forty million-year revolution of our solar system around the center of our galaxy. The era originated during the great geologic upheavals and floods that destroyed Atlantis and Lemuria. We are approaching the next planetary schism which will impact both Tellara and Earth. Tellarans will ascend into incorporeal beings of light. Earth will split into Terra Familiar and Terra Nova at two separate frequencies.

This planetary schism will happen again thirteen thousand years hence as the Earth completes her precession of the equinoxes back to the cusp where the Magic Seasons all began, between Libra and Virgo. There have been civilizations on Earth prior Atlantis and Lemuria, but they rose and fell hundreds of thousands, even millions of years ago.

Louie said, "On Earth, we have two competing geologic theories about how planetary changes happen. The prevailing view is called Uniformitarianism, sometimes called gradualism, meaning steady processes like erosion created all of Earth's geologic features. The other is Catastrophism, which means that Earth's geologic features were caused by short, violent events, possibly worldwide in scope."

Phoenix answered, "Both are true."

Javier asked, "Has this intersection of planetary singularities happened more than once?"

"The intersection of sine waves and singularities yes; Normal planetary upheaval, yes; Planetary schisms, no. Dimensional shifts we're living through are extremely rare." Phoenix answered and continued reading.

There are other galactic seasons that impact Sophia's Milk in our two hundred forty million-year sojourn around Sophia. We pass through vast cycles, solstices, and equinoxes. Only as our souls evolve can we begin to comprehend how vast galactic and intergalactic forces impact planetary surfaces and the life they support.

Sixty-five million years ago, Gaia became interesting to reptiles and grays. The Galactic Family didn't join the party until after the grays and reptiles started engineering human DNA, evolution, culture, and civilization. There were frightful territorial wars throughout the solar system back then. The Galactic Family came along to negotiate the peace and enforce the treaties. From that time forward, Earth's sentient creatures have faced a choice in how to direct their evolution. After several hundred thousand years, the "Two Paths" bifurcation emerged as the recurring paradigm for our planet. The split is consciously directed by Gaia herself. She is running the show. Tellara is utterly unanimous in its will to continue together onto the next evolutionary step.

Earth is one fractal octave behind Tellara in its evolutionary scale.

There is a critical mass of Terran creatures on Earth who wish for unity consciousness, balance, harmony, and peace. The job of the wayshowers is to demonstrate how to unite these global aspirations. Those that don't join will continue on pretty much the same, divided by polarized thinking. They won't participate in the shift in consciousness. All Terrans will notice massive geological, climatological, political, and economic transitions, including wars, pestilence, disease, fire, and flood.

"But now there are three wayshowers," Louie exulted.

"Indeed," Phoenix affirmed.

"Take this cup from my hands," I said to Javier and Louie.

"Excuse me?" asked Bo Raza.

"It is a quote from an Earth parable. Dana would prefer that this responsibility did not fall to her. She's glad for the support."

"It may feel like a burden, Dana, but you volunteered for it thirteen thousand years ago. I was there. I remember."

"I wish I did."

"You will," stated Saffron, "if you choose to go through your Chakra Ceremony next spring in Avalon."

"How's that?"

"The spring painting, *Avalon Equinox*, will emerge at the site of Blue Henge. It is there where we hold the Chakra Ceremony."

"I'll be with Dana," Javier squeezed my hand and I felt cheered.

"Then you, too, are welcome to participate."

"I don't have a choice, do I?"

"The ritual is a blessing. All Terrans should welcome the experience of the Chakra Ceremony," said Bo Raza.

"Why do you sometimes call us humans and sometimes Terrans?" I asked.

Bo Raza answered, "Because Homo sapiens are not the only sentient humanoids indigenous to Earth. Draconians, Zetas, and Lucents have been native to Earth for thousands of generations. Terran is an all-encompassing humanoid term."

"Zeta Reticuli, technically live off-planet, but have been in Earth space for thousands of generations," said Leel.

I changed the subject. "I have to travel back to America using my fake ID, then on to Shasta, California to open the winter portal."

"Yes, but then finally back to Tellara for our winter solstice celebration," Saffron reassured.

"And you can't make another painting at another location, say at Wah'Kon-Tah in the Ozarks?" Louie asked. He'd asked me this on the plane and I'd told him to ask Phoenix because I wasn't sure.

Phoenix answered, "The locations are determined by the planetary gridlines and nodal points. The groundwork is laid in the singularity where the centers of our planets intersect. The portals pre-exist in spacetime, dictated by geophysics."

"San Francisco is not a grid point on Earth's ley lines," Louie objected.

"It will be after the shift," answered Phoenix.

"Once we open the portals in both directions, we can move the paintings anywhere on Earth, right?"

"Yes. And *Shasta Solstice* is almost done. I named it for your mountain on Earth."

Javier used the lull that followed to outline our logistics. "So, Phoenix, you and Louie will travel to Shastise in Tellara. You'll transport the beehives and ready the portal on the Tellara side. Dana and I will return to Earth via *Tellaran Autumn*. We'll fly back to the states, bringing *Autumn* with us. If we're safe and alone, we can come back to Tellara before winter using *Autumn*."

Phoenix confirmed, "Yes. We'll rendezvous in Shasta with Dana's son and daughter. They should be at my safe house by now."

"They are," I said, and we all nodded at each other as if it would be that simple.

CHAPTER 18

By the time we arrived in Giza, my head was spinning. I felt an aching need to hug my kids. Louie, Javier, and I huddled together in Saffron's garden and peered into my vox screen. Ruth and Jesse were in an attractive house in the hills outside of Mount Shasta. There was a picture window and patio with a view of the mountain. The dogs were sleeping together in the sun. Ruth was reading. Jesse was online. I peered over his shoulder. There were several Facespace posts from 'Larry and Moe' that I could read but not reply to. They knew I was safe and would contact them when I could. The laptop was in Tellara and for safety's sake, should remain here. I was still wanted by everybody for 'questioning,' including Interpol at this point. There was nowhere safe Earthside to stash the laptop. Internet cafés would have to do for the nonce.

Next, we viewed Alice. She was at work at the Dallas Shelter Office. Alice had a private office framed with glass walls to ensure lack of privacy. She was at work on the computer and had a stack of files on either side of her desk. Shelter was still keeping her close. They must know of her involvement with Val as a whistle blower. Why was she still free to walk around and work? Val was at home with her kids. She was cooking and yelling for her daughters to turn off the TV and get to the lunch table. Val and Alice seemed safe enough for now.

Javier was stunned to see that Alice was a reptile. "What's going on here? Whose side is she on?"

I said, "That's the sixty-four thousand-dollar question. She's helping Val expose Shelter corruption, but instead of silencing her, she's waltzing around the Dallas office like she owns it. Sheldon Walters talks to her daily."

"Yeah, but don't forget, she's the one that hacked the data for Jay so he could download his documents." Louie countered.

Javier retorted, "That's what got Jay killed. And it didn't bring down Shelter."

I answered, "You begin to see why we haven't been able to trust anyone. One thing we can probably count on is that Shelter operatives thought Jay's documents would never see the light of day."

We viewed the Shelter Regional Office in Chicago. It was business as usual. Vincent was in his office working. He was organizing papers into several stacks and labeling file folders. Maggie Coutts from back east was in my former cube. Louie's office was empty. Squeezy was in Frank Fretz's office. They were having sex. Nice. We did not linger for two reasons; one, because none of us were voyeurs and two, because naked, Squeezy and Frank were revealed in all their reptilian, scaly, clawed glory. I felt a twinge of guilt as an image of Bo and Guna Raza flitted through my frontal lobe. Surely reptilians were entitled to intimacy.

I was wrong to judge. It was speciest of me, if that was a word. Nevertheless, I simply could not believe that there was an iota of true affection between the two opportunistic lizards sprawled across Frank Fretz's desk.

Our view moved to the lobby. Gwen Cretzky arrived in the elevator and made her way to Vincent's office. It looked like they had a lunch date. I recalled that Gwen had tried to make a lunch date with me at Jay's funeral. That ship had sailed. As Gwen and Vincent were waiting for the elevator, the doors opened and Tyrannosaurus Rex himself, Sheldon Walters, flanked by a small entourage of hefty lizard thugs including Kek, Skinny, and Unibrow, disembarked. Vincent remained long enough to shake hands and present Gwen. The thugs waited off to the side. We could see the thugs' reptilian features via the vox screen. Their pale scales lay slack below their fleshy visages and the pupils in their sallow yellow irises narrowed to vertical slits. Walter's entourage headed down the hall toward Frank Fretz's office, where the carnal act was still in progress. We couldn't help ourselves. We peeked.

Walters et al. entered. Frank and Squeezy finished their business with casual indifference. Walters and his thugs sat and waited. This made us uncomfortable

"This is really an alien sensibility," said Louie. Squeezy and FrankenFretz have no concern for discretion."

"Tellarans seem indifferent to public displays of affection," I said. "Is that a double standard?"

"Change the view screen," said Louie.

We turned back toward Vincent and Gwen. They were holding hands in the elevator. This cheered me. "They look reconciled."

We tuned our view to Louie's sister's family. His sister and brother-in-law were at work, their kids in school. Things in her family appeared stable, normal, and safe. Then we viewed Hal's family. There was nothing to see really. Only Louie knew them slightly. They didn't appear to be grieving. We were sure they knew of Hal's death because I had blogged about it. But their lives seemed business as usual. Louie was over it.

"I'd like to view my grandmother," said Javier. Minerva was at home in the room full of books where I had once spied Javier scrying for me. She looked studious and preoccupied. Javier smiled.

Next, we looked at Javier's office, his chaotic San Francisco police precinct. His police buddies were talking across their desks, drinking coffee, handcuffing two men to chairs, typing, and pointing to a wall map of the city. Javier's desk was unoccupied. Apparently, I was the only one of us who had been replaced at work. Somehow, this didn't bother me. I felt relieved.

We turned our attention to Wah'Kon-Tah. Crystal was in the apiary tending to the hives, hand plucking mites from the bees' fuzzy backs. This got Javier enthused and we watched for several more minutes before turning our attention to the main compound. Cosmo and Bruno were pulling up in the Electric Kool-Aid Van with a load of hardware. Joe and Abby helped them unload pipes, widgets, and gadgets.

Sky Dancer was alone but for a raven that perched on her porch railing. She was rocking with her eyes closed. It appeared she was meditating. We were going to tune out and give her privacy when suddenly, she opened her eyes wide and peered directly at us. There was no question that she saw us as her focus narrowed. Then she smiled and raised her hand in silent greeting. I waved back. Sky Dancer mouthed a message across the worlds. "We're waiting," she seemed to say. She placed her hand on her heart, closed her eyes again and withdrew her attention.

"Wow," said Louie.

"Yeah," said Javier.

"Wow," I said.

"Yeah," said Louie.

"Maybe you could use your vox to find your parents," I suggested to Javier.

"I will when I learn how to use it. When does our training begin?"

"Louie said, "I need more lessons."

Dinner was just the six of us, Louie, Phoenix, Heron, Saffron, Javier, and me. We shared a delicious stew that we put over buttered, home-baked bread.

"Bo Raza said he worked on voxes. Maybe he could train us."

"Bo invented the vox," Phoenix corrected.

"Invented it? I thought it had been around since forever ago," I said.

"Forever ago? Is that like Daylight Savings?"

"No, it's a colloquialism that I just made up."

"Dana, you can't just make up a colloquialism," Louie corrected. "By definition they've been around since forever ago."

Bo came over after dinner and I settled in to observe while the guys trained. He started with a passage from *The Tellaran Chronicles of Science and Spirituality.*

Entangled Protons in the Voxel

The vox crystals use human thought waves to draw monads from the P-soup into manifestation. Monads are directed into the voxes functional operations, such as levitation, cloaking, heat, light, mom-local reality, viewing, vibrational cymatics, inner hearing, and sonic carving. Since the source of the vox's power comes from the P-soup, its energy is inexhaustible. Voxes function until their operator dies or ascends.

The vox crystals have all been spun in sixth-dimensional fields, four axes of space and 2 axes of time. These crystals have high-

frequency, radiative properties that are stepped down from higher dimensions and transmit at the speed of thought, 10^{40} times faster than light. Each proton is a hologram of the entire Universe. Each voxel in each proton contains all the information in the Universe. The vox crystals use this principle to channel the operator's thoughts through selected protons, atoms, and molecules.

Your vox will begin to work once you attune it to your consciousness. Clusters of water molecules in your brain contain memory and intent. These resonate with crystalline vertices, edges, and faces inside the vox. Manipulation of the surface crystals activates the inner crystals, which will become attuned to your specific thought patterns. Water clusters in your DNA will harmonize with your vox so that only you can use it. If your intent is compassionate, your vox will align with your will at the speed of thought. If your intent is self-serving, the vox tools won't work.

Then Louie and Javier got down to business, starting with the easiest tools. Both were keen to levitate and cloak. At that point I jumped in as assistant coach. After several hours, Javier asked, "Bo! You invented the vox? Can you add tools to it?"

"What do you mean?"

"For instance, could I project a holographic image across a room?"

"Or better yet, into another room?" asked Louie.

"Could I transport myself across distances?"

"Could you modify it so we that when we're cloaked we can glide through solid walls without leaving a trace the reptiles can detect?"

"Could we beam through walls!?"

"Beam me up, Scottie!"

"Could it be used to heal injuries?"

"Could it make fire? Wind? Water?"

"Oh, how about food? Like the replicator?"

"On *Star Trek*? Yeah, yeah! A replicator, a transporter, and a holodeck? Can you make the vox do those things?"

"How about using it to project images like the heartdance tapestries and show us possible futures in the view screen so we can peek around the corners of time?" Louie and Javier were talking faster than I could think. They were having a total guys' moment celebrating their new techno-toys, practically jumping up and down with excitement at the possibilities.

"Slow your speech," said Bo. "I don't understand all your words."

I interrupted the tool time, "It never occurred to me to ask that the vox provide additional tools. I was satisfied with the tools I was given. I still haven't mastered inner hearing so we can use the vox screen like Facetime or Skype.

Apparently, inner hearing is the precursor to audio-telepathy."

"We're asking about the possibilities," said Javier."

"I asked about moving through solid walls, but Phoenix said it would leave a signature the reptiles could detect, voiding our cloak."

Bo addressed us, "You know that there really is no such thing as solid matter. Matter is 99.999% empty space. The space between atoms is vast. But moving through solids increases your probability that out-of-phase subatomic particles might collide. That would create the disturbance that would leave a trace of your passing. You could slide through a solid object once, but even cloaked, you'd activate Shelter's sensors. From that time on, they'd know to search for that signature anomaly. You'd be exposed."

"RAT-TRAK," Louie confirmed. "Our enemy's technology."

"The vox is a tool, not a weapon," said Bo.

Louie asserted, "We're talking protection, not aggression."

"Defense, not offence," seconded Javier.

Bo explained, "If you ever project hostile thoughts through the crystals, you'll fall flat on your face."

"Yes Bo, but we live in a hostile world, and have deadly enemies," said Louie

"My priority is to keep Dana safe." Javier's protective comment warmed my heart. My boyfriend was a wayshower.

Bo said, "I am going to have to think about this. When I invented the vox, I foresaw no need for the tools you describe."

"But are they doable with Tellaran science?"

"Hypothetically."

"Can we help?" asked Javier.

"We'll get some *Star Trek* episodes from Phoenix and show you what we mean," Louie said.

"Make it so." I rolled my eyes.

"This would have been so useful in the bat cave!" Louie exclaimed.

I was impressed in spite of myself. "You know what, you guys are on to something. But right now, I'm tired and I'm going to bed." I heard the guys talking excitedly for a while longer, then Bo Raza bid good night. Shortly after that, Javier joined me.

The next day Louie, Javier, Bo Raza, and Phoenix raptured about techno-toys. True to their word, the guys selected specific *Star Trek* episodes to illustrate transporters, replicators, and holodecks.

Bo Raza said, "I know what you want tools now. The problem is fitting the mechanisms into a device as small as the vox. Crystals have to be micro-etched and integrated into precise geometric relationships. Don't forget, the vox draws energy from the P-soup. It is perpetually powered by source energy. Internal components need to endlessly spin."

"We can't wait to help!" said Javier. And they were off, drawing schematics, charts, and geometric designs.

Saffron and I spoke of recent events. We spoke relationships in a girl-talk kind of way, rather than mentor to student. We compared Tellaran views of romance with Earth's. I recounted how Earth's views of love and marriage had changed over the centuries, how some cultures still had arranged, and in some cases, forced marriages. That led to conversations about mythological love stories. I got out Sky Dancer's mythology book and we compared Earth's myths to Tellara's. It was a relaxing, happy day.

"Tomorrow we go to Gray Station," Saffron told me. That kind of brought me out of my reverie, but I was up for it. I was just hoping Shoosh could find a smaller needle.

***

The next day it rained.

"How can it rain in Giza? Where is the Sahara Desert? Why is it so green and lush along the pyramids?" asked Javier.

"Our global water is balanced," was Heron's simple answer.

The gray skies matched the gray cinder-block compound that Leel and Jeej called home. I wondered if they were glad to return home after their sojourn to the hills of Antalya, which had exposed them to days of golden weather, blue skies, and a downpour. We rushed through the windy rainfall toward the doors of their lobby and were met by Leel, Jeej, and Falcon. There was little formality in gray culture. We were escorted to the laboratory and asked to don gray hemp-cloth vests. They meant for us to remove our tops and don the vests over our bare skin, but no private space was provided to change.

Javier and Louie changed in the lab, but I waited in silence until Leel inquired as to the reason for my delay.

"Where's the changing room?" I asked.

"What's a changing room?" asked Leel.

"I need a screened enclosure to change."

"Why?"

"Because I am a human female from the planet Earth. It's our way. Do you have lavatories in this building? Toilets." Leel let me to an oddly deep, narrow bowl in the hall. No doors. "I am requesting privacy to undress." Actually, the grays didn't care a whit about naked bodies, and I'd been naked with Javier in bed, and with Louie in the cave, by default as our clothing unraveled. I changed in the empty hall and returned to the lab in my vest. Still, I wasn't comfortable open to the cold in a room full of clinical observers. Perhaps Tellaran woman donors were less modestly inclined.

Shoosh, Lil, Jeej, and several grays who'd not been introduced were in the room. Then there was Javier, Louie, and Falcon.

"Do we need an audience for this procedure?"

Falcon replied, "These are clinical observers."

"What can they learn from watching us be probed? Is one abdomen not like another?"

Shoosh answered, "All the difference is in the epithelial cells in the stomach lining."

"The ones you can all view after they're extracted?"

"Yes."

"Then I would prefer privacy during my procedure."

Louie intervened, "Privacy seems to be a concept that the grays don't understand, much less value."

"Well, they better figure out how to value privacy if they want my stomach cells." Why was I making such a big deal out of this? I'd decided to provide cells to help save this species. I just didn't like being treated like lab animal.

Javier addressed the grays, "Humans from Earth value a concept called dignity. Tellarans take it for granted because it is freely given and never denied. Which of you actually need to be here to conduct these procedures? Just Shoosh, and one assistant, right? The rest of you, leave now."

"Very well, we will watch from the observation screen and film the procedure," agreed Leel as if that resolved matters.

"No, you won't," Louie declared, getting testy himself. "Look, Leel, Jeej, you're hybrids, right?"

"Yes," they nodded, with a tinge of what might have been pride.

"Supposedly, you have rudimentary emotions."

"We do," Jeej replied, with a tinge of what might have been wounded pride.

Louie continued, "You're undertaking this research to save your species. You've made a connection between emotions and fertility, correct?" Leel and Jeej nodded.

"Then pay attention to Dana's emotions. Understanding these very sensibilities is what is going to restore your emotional bodies, activate your lower chakras, and ultimately make your species fertile again. The part of humanity that Dana is expressing is the very part you've lost." Louie was eloquent.

Javier spoke up. "You want our cells; these are our conditions. Everyone leaves but Shoosh and one assistant. No observation rooms, no films."

I said, "I want Javier to stay with me." I wanted one human in the room. Falcon coordinated the exodus and promised to see that the grays would abide by their agreement. Leel and Javier stayed with Shoosh.

"Stand here," said Shoosh pointing to a wall. Shoosh placed his hand on my ribcage, and selected the injection site. His hand was surprisingly warm and soft. I think this was the first time I had been touched by a gray person. That is how I now thought of the grays now, as people. I watched as a smaller and saner syringe was injected into my solar plexus and dark red epithelial cells were withdrawn. It wasn't painless, but it wasn't agonizing either. There was a melancholy intimacy to Shoosh's extraction of my core bodily substance. He was receiving something primal, ancient, and purely mine, but he expressed no feeling response. I bled from the injection site. Javier found a cloth and made a small pressure bandage. Shoosh didn't give me another thought. He had his prize.

Louie rejoined us. Falcon came in with Louie and provided chairs. I slumped down to wait for the guys.

"Want me to wait in the hall?"

"Don't bother."

Next up was Javier. He withstood the procedure valiantly but bled more that I had. He made his own pressure bandage from a scarf I gave him.

Louie gave up his cells with poise. He didn't bleed at all.

When the three of us had completed our donations, Shoosh and Leel bowed in unison. Then it was over. The entire process was clinical to the last, the sad, small, brilliant, hopeful gray people. We bowed back at them and departed Gray Station. Pulling my blouse over the gray smock, I wondered if I would ever see any of them again, knowing as I did, their distaste for the outdoors.

"Let us know if there is a way we can share your findings with the Earthside grays," Louie offered as we walked back out into the driving rain. I waved at the gathered gray folk. None of them waved back, but I thought I noticed Leel make a slight inclination of her head. That was it.

Warm soup, fire, and cozy company were the agenda for the afternoon. We ate, sitting on pillows and wrapped in blankets before a roaring fireplace in Saffron's vaulted living room. The rain pelted heavily against the windows over the churned-up Nile. After lunch, Bo Raza arrived. We resumed vox training. For the next several weeks, vox practice, design, focus, and alas, physics lessons dominated our schedule.

After bumping off the walls repeatedly while attempting to levitate and move forward at the same time, Louie erupted in frustration. "I'll never attune these pesky protons to my brainwaves!"

"That's because you're not taking spin into account. Remember everything is spinning."

Louie objected, "I learned that the Universe began spinning at the moment of the Big Bang and is still spinning from this initial impulse."

Phoenix explained, "That would mean there is no friction in the Universe, which is not the case. Here, read this passage."

229

The Tellaran Chronicles of Science and Spirituality
Spin

The Universe is a vast superfluid, which is to say that the Universe obeys the laws of fluid dynamics. This superfluid is inconsistent in its density and composition. This inconsistency causes density gradients in spacetime topology, much like the hills and vales of Tellara's surface and the waves and currents our oceans. This superfluid is not frictionless, nor is it lacking in viscosity. Although molecules in intergalactic space and within galaxies are widely separated, they interact with each other. Deep space is not a true vacuum.

Spin fluctuations give rise to co-moving systems within spacetime. As these systems become more coherent, synchronized, and harmonized, they give rise to matter. Matter is spinning systems in spacetime, the result of coherent fluctuations. These self-organizing systems entrain spacetime from their vicinity into larger, more stable patterns, gaining energy and information as they grow.

Gravity is a force resulting from the curvature of spacetime in the presence of mass. This curvature is often represented graphically as a ball resting on a trampoline surface which depresses, forcing the ball to roll down in a spiral. As the density gradient (slope) increases, the curvature of space-time increases, gravity increases, and spin increases. The stronger the density gradient (or steeper the hill) the tighter and faster the spin. We call this torque.

As Above, so Below:

The Universe is rotating. Galaxies rotate within the Universe. Star systems rotate within galaxies. Planets rotate within solar systems, fluids on planets rotate, atomic and sub-atomic particles rotate. The original impetus for spin in the Universe emerges from monads emitted from of the P-soup. Each spiral interacts with other spirals at all scales, increasing and decreasing along the phi ratio (golden ratio) in a never-ending confluence of cycles from the Universal to the quantum (P-length).

As within, so without:

Nature abhors a vacuum. In the presence of a near vacuum or low-pressure center, surrounding matter will rush in to try to fill the void. As matter converges, the superfluid around it rotates. This causes a displacement of the converging matter, deflecting it into a spiral. This deflection is called the Coriolis Effect. On our rotating planet, the Coriolis Effect gives rise to cyclonic weather systems like hurricanes and tornadoes. Coriolis affects spin at all scales.

In the macrocosm, because the Universe itself is a rotating superfluid, the Coriolis Effect defines the shape of galactic spirals as star stuff converges toward the spinning blackwholes at the center of galaxies, including our Sophia's Milk.

On the microcosmic scale, Coriolis defines the shape of spinning protons, electrons, and sub-atomic particles all the way down to the quantum level.

Size defines Speed:

The Universe is perpetually spinning and expanding because quantum vortices are endlessly emerging from the P-Soup, creating new matter. This maintains a balance between the organizing-gravitational-contracting effect of spin and the expanding-radiating-dissipating effect of entropy. Gravity balances radiation. Contraction balances expansion. Syntropy balances entropy. Every vortex approaches the speed of light as it converges toward the vacuum at the center of the quantum singularity.

In the macrocosm: Density and speed decrease proportionately in spacetime topology as mass expands toward the outer limits of the Universe.

In the microcosm: Density and speed increase proportionately toward the lower limit of spacetime, the quantum level. This is called conservation of angular momentum.

While we cannot measure what is happening in the P-soup, it is the highly organized source of all spin, mass, energy, consciousness, and spirit. The P-soup is all around us, interpenetrating all creation. The singularity at the heart of each vortex connects it with the sub-quantum P-soup, the Great Mother Sea. This includes the singularities in the atoms in the all cells of our bodies. In deep, meditative states or during the heartdance, we can apprehend the structure of this formative substance. To mystics whose third eye has opened, sub-quantum vibration is perceived as Loving Light.

The vortices emerging from the P-soup are the building blocks of the Universe. They cluster and nest geometrically in ever increasing scale following the golden ratio, along the 64-tetrahedron grid and flower of life. The smaller you go, the tighter the spin, until mass merges into the P-soup. Primordial Spin is the causal, organizing principle of our 3-D reality.

Louie asked, "What about the God particle that we just found on Earth? It's the smallest particle, the smallest building block of mass. Have you found that?"

"We aren't looking for it because there is no smallest particle. Coherent spin in spacetime is the source of mass."

In our final week in Tellara, we heartdanced together with friends and acquaintances from all over Giza. The heartdance was held in the park by the reflecting pool, amidst the fall foliage.

Heartdance imagery materialized. A blue green Earth emerged from deep interstellar space. Earth rotated to a familiar aspect. A great volcano centered in North America erupted, spewing molten lava and ash deep into the atmosphere and beyond, into space. Continents upheaved violently. Tsunamis broke across the Atlantic, Pacific, and Indian Oceans in recurring vertical walls of water. The Gulf of Mexico surged north until the Mississippi overflowed her banks all the way to the Great Lakes, creating an inland sea.

Earth shuddered and contracted. Two distinct globes emerged, connected by threads of molten rock, water, air, fire, and dust stretching between the spheres in a planetary mitosis. The spheres coalesced into two distinct worlds and slipped apart along a spiral thread, one ascending, the other holding its place in the celestial firmament.

On the lingering world, chaos reigned. Psychic energy crashed, generating more fiery seismic activity, warfare, and waves of destruction and death. The planet that slid up along the spiral thread settled into an easy rotation that reflected the spin of our rhythmic, spiraling dance. Colors softened, skies cleared, land turned green and a rush of fruitfulness blossomed on every continent. Neither world resembled my familiar home.

Tellara moved into the web. The pas de deux became a pas de trois. Tellara drew into focus, revealing an intricate tapestry of people living stories, nature exuding glories. Even as Tellara was rent with geologic cataclysms, her atmosphere blinked with billions of points of light. These points of light absorbed the seismic shudders and glowed all the more brilliantly. Tellara experienced no birth pangs and contractions. She remained intact, luminescent, whole.

Tellara drew close along the golden coil and became a magnet, drawing away Earths' murky seismic energy, dissipating it into billions of harmless dust clouds that dissolved across the Universe. Tellara mitigated the worst of Earths' destruction by siphoning off seismic and psychic waves. Earth still split asunder, but as soon as the geologic violence subsided, planetary healing began. The dance wound down as, one by one, the women sat, and the men stilled their voices.

"Saffron, it looked as though Tellara saved both Terra Familiar and Terra Nova from complete destruction."

We were a pensive dinner party. Farewells were said, plans devised, and promises of winter visits made. Our spirits rose when we listened to a combination of Earth and Tellaran music. Javier and I demonstrated ballroom dancing to Big Band music. Our Tellaran friends joined in with great enthusiasm. They didn't have an equivalent to Rock n' Roll or Blues, so the Rolling Stones were a revelation. We danced into the night, our gaiety masking our preoccupation. The imagery from the heartdance was never far from our minds, nor was the onus of the tasks that lay ahead for all. That night, I fell into the dreamless slumber of reluctant heroes.

The next morning it was still raining. Louie wore a purple velvet kimono over black harem pants and Phoenix was dressed in midnight blue of the same style. The beehives were loaded into the back of a shuttle that would take them to the Giza Air Station and then off to Shastise, Tellara. There was no great rush; there was a bit of time before they were to depart.

"Hey," said Louie, "do we have time to read some Earthside blogs? Or watch some TV news?"

"Good idea," replied Javier, proudly powering up his vox. He tuned in C-Span and found a monitor with closed captioning. Congress was in session. Among our elected representatives in the House of Representatives were four reptiles. Two of them were representatives named on Jay's documents, Congresswoman Gnositall, and Congressman Kaoz. Despite being implicated, Senator Rockbottom was leading the inquiry in the Senate. Around the chamber, various congressional aids scurried about delivering papers and messages. About a half-dozen of these underlings that really run the show were reptiles.

Congress was holding testimonies about the Shelter Insurance and Trust criminal fraud. Sheldon Walters was on the hot seat. Gnositall and Kaoz were lobbing softballs. Other Congressmen were trying to make serious, hard-hitting inquiries, but were consistently derailed by Gnositall and Kaoz. It made me cringe to watch. But then, a Congresswoman from Illinois named Vera Wayne stated flatly that 'Kaoz and Gnositall must be on the Shelter payroll, but it doesn't matter because the investigation will continue with or without Walters' cooperation.' On that note, Javier turned off his vox screen.

Louie hugged me and said, "I have my vox, Dana, I'll keep you in my sights every day."

"Me too," I sniffed. Then everybody was hugging, even those of us who were going to be together another day. We escorted Louie, Heron, and Phoenix to the Giza air station and watched our guys climb into a blimp filled with baggage and bees. My dear friends were traveling to the other side of this world as I prepared to travel to the other side of mine. I don't think 'farewell' quite covered the depths of our parting pangs.

The next morning, we received a telecall from Louie and Phoenix informing us that they were in Shastise, that the painting of the mountain was ready and hanging in a pavilion by the glistening red pyramid I had watched being built. All that remained was for Phoenix to paint himself into the foreground come Winter Solstice. The three peaks, the marble red pyramid, Black Butte, and snowcapped Mount Shasta, were behind our guys. They looked hale and happy.

So, that was it. It was time for Javier and me to return to Cairo via *Tellaran*

Autumn. We were traveling from Cairo, Egypt to Atlanta, to Shasta, California, America, the Earth, the Milky Way, the Universe, Home. That was the plan.

I left Sky Dancer's book of World Mythology, my Bible, and my laptop with Saffron. They were possessions that could provide clues as to the location of Wah'Kon-Tah. Saffron, Bo and Guna Raza escorted Javier and me to the Reflection Pool Park where we'd entered Giza. It was just daybreak. The rain had stopped, but the fallen leaves were thick with dew and the damp soil beneath our shoes smelled of loam. I wore my travel suit from the flight over, the inconspicuous beige and pink togs Crystal and Cosmo had once upon a time provided to Ms. Dahlia Rivers. Going on Javier's advice, I would again be traveling under my assumed name. Dana Travers had never departed the United States, had never passed through Customs and Immigration into Egypt. Dahlia was returning to the U.S. of A. After that, we'd make our way west, ideally via Wah'Kon-Tah. I had packed my few items in my oversized, green hemp hobo bag from Antalya.

I wasn't ready to leave paradise, but it was time. Javier and I held hands, looked into the undulating air, stepped forth into the mist, and through the singularity. We emerged in Phoenix's Cairo art studio. Everything here seemed shabby, with sharply contrasting edges and noisy street sounds. At first, we just collapsed on a sofa and hugged each other in silence. The reality of our road ahead weighed on us like lead. I was still a fugitive. I had to overcome the conspiracy against me to get a message of hope and harmony to our wounded world. I didn't feel remotely fit for the task, despite all the pep talks from my cheerleaders on two planets.

When I did finally move, I rose and walked over to the wall of paintings, intending to cut them free from the frames and roll the canvases into tubes. "Better we take a couple of Phoenix's landscapes," I mused.

"Yes," Javier agreed, "one of many is less obvious when you go through customs. We don't want to call attention to the significance of the portal painting."

The rolled-up paintings fit neatly into a cardboard tube, one of several stacked in a corner. The tube fit into my green bag if I didn't close it all the way. The paintings lay alongside my saffron, honey, travel kit, turquois gown, and clean underwear. I was traveling light, but oh so heavy.

Part Three

Shasta Solstice

CHAPTER 19

Javier and I grabbed a taxi to the airport from outside our Cairo apartment. I was traveling as Daliah Rivers. He was traveling as himself. I used an airport public computer to message Larry and Moe. "All's well. Homeward bound."

Although we had time for a nice meal in the airport crêpe place where Louie and I had dined. We shared a spinach, mushroom, pepper, and Gruyere-filled entrée and a strawberry blintz for dessert. The security check was uneventful as was the flight itself. We made our connection in Paris. Once again, I lamented that we were unable to spend any time in Paris. We had to travel as expeditiously as possible to California via Atlanta and hopefully Wah'Kon Tah. On the long flight we slept, held hands, shared ideas, hopes, and dreams, and feasted on onion soup, quiche Lorraine, fruit salad, crème brulée, and champagne.

At U.S. customs, I declared my two rolled-up paintings, honey, and saffron. While flying, Javier had advised me to bury my false I.D. and resurrect Dana Travers as soon as I was back on American soil. In a bathroom stall, I stowed Daliah Rivers' documents in a sealed hidey-hole in the wide strap of my hobo bag and went to wait for Javier at our prearranged rendezvous by the car rental counter. Time passed. He didn't come. I returned to the ladies' room and from the privacy of a stall, viewed Javier on my vox. He was being questioned by Agents Contrary and Pandemonium, reptiles both, as if I should have been surprised. Apparently, Shelter's surveillance had caught up with us. Javier stonewalled them until he was forcefully hauled away to a Department of Homeland Security van on the tarmac. He was being detained and I could not guess why or for how long.

We had no Plan B for Javier's detention; all our concern had been for my detection. We'd neglected the danger to him. Time stretched. I grew frantic. I paced, thinking, holding back tears. After an hour I exited the terminal to breathe some fresh air. I searched the sidewalk up and down, where transportation was coming to pick up passengers.

A stretch limousine pulled right onto the curb, blocking my steps and abruptly cutting off my thoughts. Sheldon Walters emerged. I could have sunk through the sidewalk. He called my name cordially, "Dana Travers, or is it Daliah Rivers, come join me." I backed away. The uniformed security types who patrolled the loading and unloading zone disregarded my plight. Kek and Unibrow exited the limo from either side and flanked me. I recoiled from Kek. He leered. My throat began to close off protectively. This wasn't an invitation.

I was shoved into the back seat and prepared to meet my doom. But what transpired is what would pass for a cordial conversation with Sheldon Walters. Had I not previously viewed him through my vox and seen his reptilian features, I would have considered him a debonair, mature man-about-town. Kek sat in the back with us while Unibrow drove.

"So, Dana Travers," Sheldon Walters began smoothly, "You have been one very elusive lady causing many people great inconvenience."

"I've been somewhat inconvenienced myself, Mr. Walters."

"Please, call me Sheldon. We're going to be friends."

"Doubtful. People I love have been killed. Let's neither of us pretend you weren't behind those crimes."

"I must admit that that whole Hal business was handled very awkwardly." He looked at Kek with an arched brow. Walters had referred my friend's murder as 'that Hal business.' This set my teeth on edge, as I remembered how Hal had bled to death in a cold, dark cave. I had never understood before what the expression meant: 'teeth on edge.' Mine were vibrating in ice-cold rage.

"Yes, yes," continued Sheldon Walters silkily, "Frank Fretz overstepped his authority with that matter."

Had I heard right? Had he just implicated the FrankenFretz in Hal's murder? That could not have been unintentional for a mind as sharp as Walter's. "It was Kek who killed Hal and tried to kill me."

As if I had not spoken, Walters continued, "We don't really want to keep chasing you from Kingdom to Come, Dana. We quite missed you on your way into Cairo; clever traveling as Dalilah Rivers. We weren't looking for you in Egypt. Shortly after your arrival, the facial recognition software identified you. Our crew scoured Cairo and parts beyond. Wherever you hid, we'll find out eventually, along with Robles-Leon and his contraband. Congratulations on your weight loss, by the way."

I made no reply.

"So, you left the country with Robles-Leon, and returned with Inspector Vazquez. Interesting collaborators. It's time you stopped running. Thanks to me, these ludicrous suspicions against you have been cleared. There's a place for you at Shelter Insurance and Trust, not to mention a promotion, with a corner office, and view of the city."

I was nonplussed. Return to the cesspool? Become a literal wage slave for Sheldon Walters so that he could watch my every move? I would not be free to be myself, much less some karmic end-time wayshower. How would I get to Shasta? Reunite with Javier? As I sat there, disintegrating into a puddle, Sheldon Walters casually reached across the limousine and plucked my green bag off my lap. He proceeded to paw through my possessions.

"This one little carry-on bag is all your brought?" First, he pulled out the saffron and honey. He sniffed both and then set them on the seat between himself and Kek. "You brought perishables overseas?"

"Honey doesn't spoil and the saffron is packed in an airtight container. Customs let me keep them." Why was I explaining myself to him?

"Customs had orders to clear you." Next, He looked at the tube with the paintings in it, pulled off the cap, and unrolled two visionary landscapes. "Do you have receipts for these paintings? Did you declare their value?"

"How dare you? These were gifts from the artist." Both had been painted by Phoenix, but only one of them was a trans-dimensional portal. Walters peered over each painting in thoughtful silence but appeared to notice nothing significant. Even if he didn't appreciate the art, it was impossible to miss the fractal geometry and tessellated brush strokes. Any higher dimensional creature would know that geometry is a language. Kek peered at the canvasses over Walters' shoulders.

Kek snorted, "I've seen work by this artist in her condo. I slashed it a good one." Could they detect Phoenix's singularity? Walters rolled the canvasses up without comment. He then methodically raked through the rest of the pockets in the bag, but none of my sundries interested him. He looked through my wallet and passport.

Finally, he tossed my purse back to me. I reached forward to collect my belongings. As I leaned, my vox swung forward, and Walters reached out. To my horror, he yanked the chain from my neck and grasped my vox. He held it in his hands studying it intently. He manipulated the crystals like keypad buttons. Nothing happened. He twisted the surfaces trying to pry open the inner workings, but the vox gave up no secrets. Near as Sheldon Walters could tell, the vox was a clunky pendant. I sat mute.

Kek grabbed it, "What is this? An ugly gewgaw from an antique shop? Or a relic from Granny Travers? Real gold but worthless crystals in a chunky design." I could contain my revulsion no longer. I swooned forward and vomited on my captors' laps, spraying technicolor French cuisine across the limo.

Kek roared with disgust. Walters shuddered and flinched. The limo screeched to a stop. I grabbed my vox from Kek's sticky, stinky hands as both men erupted from the vehicle at light speed, leaving me alone to repack my belongings. The limo was parked in front of a small, white, private jet on a private tarmac. In only moments, Sheldon Walters reappeared from the plane impeccably groomed, sporting an expensive gray linen suit. He held open the limo door for me. I exited shakily, my knees barely holding me up.

"So, what have you to say, Dana? The charges against you have been dropped."

"I was never actually charged with anything."

"No, you left before that could happen, and now, it never will," he said with an unctuous smile. "Are you ready to return to work?"

"Not for you."

He ignored me. "We've created a new position for you. How does Appeals Manager sound?" Sheldon Walters asked, wiping his hands with a white linen handkerchief after touching me. Flanked by Kek and Unibrow, I couldn't use my vox. I was going to have to go with him. "We're not driving back to Chicago. We'll be much more comfortable in my private jet."

Kek was still hopping around in a filthy rage shaking my vomit from his skin. He had stripped to the waist and thrown his shirt and jacket across the tarmac. "Go on board and change, Kek," Walters ordered impatiently. After Kek entered the plane, Walters ushered me up the stairs to the jet cabin by pushing me at arms-length ahead of him. I was certain that Kek was K2 from Jay Andrews' documents. I was glad I puked on Kek. I would have to remember that human vomit is a potent repellent to Draconian sensibilities.

There was no way I was going to be able to reconnect with Javier today. Still, the reptiles didn't know everything about me. They knew nothing of Tellara, my vox, or Wah'Kon-Tah. But they knew enough to waylay me and detain Javier, a tactic that successfully separated us. I hoped that by finding nothing after several hours, Contrary and Pandemonium would let him go. At the moment, Javier did not appear to be anyone's priority, just an inconvenience. Sheldon Walters had spun his web and I'd neatly stepped into it.

Kek emerged from a back room, showered and dressed in an impeccably tailored black suit and leather boots. I resigned myself to a lonely flight back to Chicago in Walters' private jet, curled up in my own stink by a window seat. No one offered me a shower or clean clothes. Thoughts of my recent airship travel from Antalya to Giza aboard a cozy cabin with loving friends contrasted horribly with this grotesque first class prison.

In the late afternoon, we landed on a private airstrip in Chicago, one I'd never heard of. A limousine was waiting to deliver me home. Kek made a move to usher me off the plane. He did not try to touch me but used his body language to direct me where to move. I stuck my finger down my throat and mimed gagging. Kek recoiled. Sheldon Walters actually laughed. I moved away and took a parting shot at Sheldon Walters. "I may be trapped in your schemes for now, but I refuse to ever be in the same room again with your murderous pet lizard!" I held Walters' gaze and spit out the last word like it was dirt in my mouth.

"I'm nobody's pet," hissed Kek. He looked like he'd like nothing better than to kill me with his bare hands. If looks could kill, I'd be ashes.

"You're no T-Rex," I countered looking directly into Walter's eyes. Both men glared at me, wondering, I'm sure, if I were invoking a turn of phrase or telling them that I knew exactly who and what they were.

Sheldon leaned over me, his imposing height dwarfing my small frame. "You'll work for me until I say you don't. I'll give you a free hand with appeals. You'll answer only to me. And Dana, we'll be watching you and your loved ones."

Silently, I moved away from him toward the limo.

"By the way, where is your pal, Louie Robles-Leon?"

"Louie and I got separated in Cairo." I shrugged. Why didn't Walters just kill me? What did he need from me? He had a dangerous ulterior agenda. Like Alice, he was keeping me close. He'd had Alice under his heel for decades, maybe her entire life. Somehow, I had to get to Shasta, California and from there to Tellara. At least I had my vox, and first chance I got, I would view Javier, Jesse, and Ruth. I seriously needed to learn how to use the audio-telepathy tool so Javier and I could speak.

Delivered to my door, I showered and changed, unpacked, and wiped down my vox. The sealed paintings remained in their tubes. Everything else went into the wash. I could only assume my home was bugged with state-of-the-art RAT-TRAK. I didn't dare use the vox, computer, or telephone to locate loved ones. I puttered around the house in frustration, without even my dog to keep me company. Getting to Shasta had gotten complicated. Javier would view me on his vox when he got the chance. He could contact Jesse, Ruth, and Sky Dancer. I'd have to make the best of my position as a pawn behind enemy lines.

I turned on the television. I hadn't seen any American TV for months. There was my own face. Gemini Dallas, in her bland blond glory, was proclaiming my innocence and announcing my return to the 'sheltering arms of Shelter.' What I encountered all over the news was my new, thin face, my salt-and-pepper pageboy, my now-prominent cheekbones and slimmed neckline. Everybody was being apprised that I was no longer suspect in the murder of Jay Andrews. The police had moved on to other leads. I was returning to my job at Shelter Insurance to the delight of all concerned. Or so Gemini Dallas declared with an artificial smile. She seemed almost disappointed that I was innocent, causing her exploitive story to run out of juice. If I told her who the real killer was, she'd be in danger. She was better off being a media shill spouting corporate propaganda ad nauseam until it became de facto truth.

I knew the background of the Shelter scandal as it impacted me and mine. But I hadn't paid close attention to other global events. Gemini Dallas' face was replaced with a Ken Doll look-alike. While in Tellara, I had missed wild fires, pandemic riots, hurricanes, floods, droughts, shootings of civilians, and massive die offs of fish and of fowl.

Shelter was going to have massive insurance claims and appeals. My position as Appeals Manager of a huge multinational insurance agency, already in the spotlight, would be extremely visible. I would still be a lightning rod for the media. Was I being hung out to dry? A corporate scapegoat?

At least my kids would be aware that I was no longer a fugitive, that I had been waylaid by Sheldon Walters, and that I was returning to work at Chicago Sh.I.T. I opened my painting case and unrolled Phoenix's canvases before taking myself off to bed.

The next morning, I woke up and prepared for work. Of course, it was a Monday. In a surreal daze, I found a plaid wrap skirt that I could cinch. How would my colleagues react if I showed up in an embroidered caftan? Gravel crunched as I crossed my driveway on that chill November morning. There sat my little white Honda that I'd left at the airport when I went on the run. It had been found and so thoughtfully returned. With a resigned sigh, I began my commute into rush hour traffic.

Stepping off the elevator and into the heart of Sh.I.T., I crashed landed on Earth with a stupefying thud. Only days before, I had been levitating with friends, rolling in flowers, and dancing with the birds and bees. Now, I trudged into a soulless, industrial carpeted, cube-filled, colorless office at the dark end of the Universe. There was no gun to my head, but defiance of Sheldon Walters meant that I would jeopardize the safety of my loved ones.

Frank Fretz and Vincent Cretzky greeted me, Frank appraising, Vincent genuinely pleased to see me. He must have actually missed Louie and me. Why not? We worked so hard it made him look good. All eyes were on me as Sheldon Walters himself ushered me into Louie's former corner office. Oh, it had windows all right, overlooking the Chicago skyline, but it also had glass walls open to the office interior. Everyone could watch me at my desk. The looks I got from people ranged from envy, to awe, from goodwill, to resentment, and even to resignation that this plum position had been created and I had fallen into it.

"Travers, you have all the luck," said big Maggie Coutts.

"You can have the effin' job and the corner office with my blessing," I told her.

"What's your damage, Travers?" She was confused by my attitude.

Ignoring the stares, I settled in and logged on to the computer. Within moments, there was a knock on my door and Squeezy, in a shocking purple mini dress, entered without waiting for my response. She wasn't happy to see me, but she didn't seem pissed off either. She looked at me appraisingly. Something was on her mind, "Well, Dana, you've managed to skate through all these travails unscathed."

I just shook my head. "Suzy, people I love are dead. I was with Hal when he died. I've been on the run for my life for months. I'm scathed."

"Nevertheless, you have HR paperwork to fill out. I've brought it with me." She plunked a stack of forms on my desk. "I need you to fill out and sign these docs. We're going to put you back on payroll at a higher pay grade. You're management now," she gushed. "You're only subordinate to Vincent Cretzky in this office. Although, you answer to Frank when he comes to town and I speak for Frank when he isn't here."

"I'll keep that in mind." I didn't bother to correct her that I had an understanding with Sheldon Walters. Like Alice, I was subordinate only to him.

"You do that." She left with an authoritative clickety-clack of her savagely pointed toes preceding skiver heels.

I began working with Vincent. We reviewed sixty appeals together and I made recommendations for those claims that I thought we should approve and settle. The clients had waited a long time for money that was rightfully theirs. To my surprise, Vincent let me decide each appeal without debate. I couldn't tell what was going on in the office dynamic. Vincent didn't answer to Frank. Suzy didn't answer to Vincent. Vincent only answered to Sheldon Walters. I cooperated with Vincent, answered to Sheldon Walters, and gave a nod to Suzy to stroke her ego. The rigid hierarchy of Sh.I.T. had become weirdly ambiguous. Why was Vincent being such a positive professional about paying out appealed claims? I didn't argue. We were doing good, important work.

Meanwhile, FrankenFretz, the security chief, came to the Chicago office on Tuesdays, Wednesdays, and Thursdays. The rest of the time he was in Dallas groveling to Sheldon Walters. Everyone assumed Fretz was trouble-shooting Shelters' internal fraud investigations being conducted by Waldo, Manheim, & Peters. Their auditors met with Fretz and Vincent once each week. Even if Frank Fretz didn't know, I knew that, even though he was a reptile, he was a pawn in Sheldon Walters' game. Just like his boss, Frank flaunted the glam-tan, well-dressed, cosmopolitan look. He and Suzy were an item, and they were sickening together. Nobody else on the planet cared, but everybody on the planet had to witness their baby talk and googly-eyed glances.

After three days, I didn't think I could stand the confinement one minute longer. Then, through the glass walls of my so-not private office, Javier step off the elevator. Just like that, he waltzed openly into my life. He saw me. I stood. Just as he reached my door, FrankenFretz body-blocked him from stepping toward my office. Fretz said loudly and in no uncertain terms, "This is a private place of business. Travers is no longer a suspect. The San Francisco Police have no jurisdiction in Chicago."

I threw open my door and said, "Javier is my lunch date." Frank turned to me, his jaw dropped. It was good to see somebody else dumbstruck for a change.

Suzy came around the corner to see what was going on and looked from me to Javier. "You can't be here, Inspector Vazquez. Security will escort you out of the building," shaking her razor-sharp nails in Javier's face.

Turning on his lover, Frank Fretz ground out through gritted teeth, "I am security, you nitwit." Suzy looked abashed and gave him a scornful look. Was I the cause of their first fight?

Javier elbowed his way passed the quarreling lovers and kissed me full on the mouth, lingering, slow, and deep. I kissed him back with gusto. Javier's greeting spoke volumes to everybody who was wondering what the San Francisco cop was doing here. If Frank or Suzy found our public display of affection unprofessional, they were muzzled by their own inappropriate exhibitionism. Arm-in-arm, Javier and I strolled into the elevator and left the hive buzzing.

In the elevator, we clung together for the ride from the fifteenth floor to the lobby. We made it to my car, drove home, and enjoyed my lunch hour getting reacquainted. Food was involved at some point. I asked, "Why did Contrary and Pandemonium detain you at the airport? I watched on my vox until I was abducted by Walters and Kek."

"They were speculating that I was still investigating Jay Andrews' murder."

"Aren't you?"

"Not officially. But they knew I was traveling with you and drew their own conclusions. Even though they're really FBI agents, I knew they were reptiles sent by Walters and had no federal report to file. I stonewalled them. At some point, they must have gotten the all clear to release me."

"Yeah, once I was safely in Walters' captivity."

"They kept my wallet and passport, so traveling became problematic, hence my delay getting to Chicago."

"You're here now." We kissed.

Javier drove me back to the office and kept the car. He said he was going to run some errands and would pick me up from work at 5:15. That afternoon was the longest I'd ever spent behind a desk. It was also the happiest and most productive. Files floated through my fingers.

Once again, I was the object of gossip and rubbernecking, only this time the speculation wasn't murder and mayhem, just spicy romantic rumors. I'd gone from fugitive prey to paramour of my predator, not to mention Appeals Manager. Conversations ceased whenever I entered a room. Alas, without Louie to confide in, Sh.I.T. was shit. I spent the rest of the week reviewing appeals, making recommendations, and notifying the disbursement office of the checks I wanted them to send to claimants. I put a report together to submit to Vincent and present at the next managers meeting.

During the day, Javier researched evidence relating to all things Shelter. Each evening, he picked me up after work and we rushed home together. He prepared wonderful meals. We read and watched documentaries about conspiracy theories, alternate history, and archaeology. Javier filled in the gaps with his endless knowledge of mythology and ancient civilizations. He gave me books to read. I used burner phones to contact Jesse and Ruth. They might be somewhat safer since my return to the fold, but the Shasta location had to remain shielded.

Javier and I had circumspect conversations about how we would get away. Our lovemaking had gone undercover, literally based on our assumption of hidden surveillance. Javier could find any conventional bugs, but as I learned in the cave, reptilians had technology beyond our ken. So, we played our cards close to the vest. Post cuddle, I often journaled while Javier scanned his crime files.

One night, we turned on the TV for a few minutes before sleep and there was my face again, this time on a late-night comedy show. People were still taking an interest in my return. It was actually pretty funny to hear Trevor Noah call Shelter Insurance and Trust Sh.I.T. and Stephen Colbert speculate about the codes in Val Andrews' blogs. I was still the joke du jour, but nobody knew whether or not I was a villain or a victim. So, they turned me into a pretzel. Gemini Dallas had wanted me to be guilty so badly that she tried to make my relationship with Javier into something sordid. I viewed Ms. Dallas through my vox; nope, not a reptile, just a mindlessly malicious mammal.

We spent Thanksgiving with Alice, Val, her daughters, her parents, and in-laws. I didn't want to return to Dallas, but Val literally begged me. She was relieved that I'd been cleared, and the police had new leads. We dared not travel to Shasta, nor use the portal to Giza. So, missing my kids and dogs terribly, Javier and I flew to Texas. Shelter would be gratified that they could keep us on their radar.

We stayed with Alice. Val hosted the feast, but we all pitched in. Jay's parents fell all over themselves, apologizing for my treatment at his memorial. They had acted on prejudicial information provided by Frank Fretz. I shared a sanitized version of Hal's death and Louie's and my time as fugitives. When the children were in bed, Val pressed for details, hoping I could shed more light on Jay's murder. "Jay's and Hal's deaths were connected by Shelter's operatives. I think Kek killed Jay. I know he killed Hal and tried to choke me to death."

"What about Louie?" Alice asked.

"We got separated while on the run," I answered obliquely. "Shelter hasn't found him."

Javier showed Val his photograph of Sheldon Walters and Marvin Kinkel, a.k.a. Kek in a San Francisco café eyeing a petite brunette. This image appeared on Val's blog the next day motivating investigative journalists to ask, "Where is Shari McCann, the missing Irish journalist?"

The first of December, Javier's extended leave-of-absence ended. We dreaded becoming a long-distance couple. Knowing RAT-TRAK, we dared not even move the paintings to another location until we made good our getaway. Louie, Phoenix, and Saffron would have to suss out our Earthly predicament via their voxes. Louie and I tried and failed at the audio-telepathy vox tool. Direct contact was not an option.

December was a long, lonely month. Javier's was back to work in San Francisco. He was assigned new cases while covertly investigating Shelter. Before he left Chicago, he helped me hang *Tellaran Autumn* in my living room. The portal was there in case of a dire emergency. If I had to dive through to save my life, I could, although, it would give away our trans-dimensional haven. One solace in having the painting in sight was visits from the other side. From time to time, the Giza park bench was occupied by Saffron, Juniper, Bo, Guna, Heron, Louie, or Phoenix. I could see but not touch or hear my friends.

CHAPTER 20

Law enforcement was no longer looking for my kids. Jesse remained at the Shasta safe house with *Summer in Tellara* awaiting Phoenix and the winter arrival of *Shasta Solstice*. Ruth returned to Chicago to resume her job and hopefully to reconnect with Mick. But Mick had left his job. She gave up her apartment and moved in with me. "I don't want you to be alone Mom."

"I'm not alone, Ruth,"

"How's that?" Ruth inquired.

"I told you on Facespace. I have a man in my life."

"I thought that was code."

"Code for what? I have a lover. It's serious."

"Where is he now?"

"In California."

"Then how exactly is he in your life?"

"We're working on it. Long distance relationships suck. He's a detective from San Francisco. Don't you watch Gemini Dallas?"

"That journalistic hack? Hey, is it the same San Francisco cop who guided Jesse and I to Minerva's?"

"Yes, Javier Vazquez." Ruth and I were both biding our time, pining for absent loved ones. She viewed *Tellaran Autumn* with me and finally, truly understood that the painting was a vibrant, living artifact. She recognized Louie when he came to the park. "You really have traveled to an alternate reality," she whispered outside one morning when we both felt a safe distance from prying sensors.

Vincent chaired the weekly staff meeting. The business-as-usual agenda covered new regulations, new policies, new claims, and ongoing appeals. I was last on the agenda. "I have approved seventeen of twenty appeals," I stated. "Let's start with the Terrence case." I began enumerating my cases and policy rational.

"Seventeen out of twenty is too high," Squeezy interrupted. "Especially if you exceed allotted funds."

"It's not the percentage that matters; rather, the case-by-case merit of each appeal," I countered.

"Not according to Frank Fretz. We have to limit our quota of approved appeals to conform to Shelter's business policy; a case in point, the Terrance claim would be a settlement in the millions. That's unacceptable. You could use his drinking as a loophole."

"I could not and would not. Mr. Terrance was clean and sober the entire year before the incident. He tested clean. Besides, this is my call. Your opinion is noted but my professional judgment is final."

"You could approve two of the smaller appeals and deny Terrance. That way you'd get a higher approval percentage and a lower dollar distribution."

"During an audit? You're missing two points. First, appeals are evaluated on case-by-case merit. That is our only criteria. Second, no one from Human Resources has justification for interfering with Claims. Your meddling in case files is unethical, bordering on illegal."

"Frank Fretz doesn't think so. He wants me to keep my finger on the pulse of the entire office."

"Frank Fretz's interference in Claims is inappropriate." So is office dating. "Does Shelter have a policy about that?"

"It was tried once at headquarters, but it didn't take."

"Because the corporate leadership wanted to keep their options open without worrying about sexual harassment?"

Squeezy sneered condescendingly, "Think what you like, Dana."

"It's worked out for you, hasn't it Squeezy?" The silence in the room was thunderous. I had called her Squeezy to her face, in front of a dozen colleagues. It wasn't enough that I'd implied that she was sleeping her way to the top, I'd revealed my own gossipy condescension. There was just no way to soften this blow or back-pedal. So, I groveled. "That was very unprofessional of me, Suzy. And unkind. Please pardon me." Mortified, I bumbled through the rest of the appeals. Suzy was uncharacteristically silent. Finally, Vincent put us out of our misery and adjourned.

To my mortification, my faux pas had a positive effect on morale. Suzy did not retaliate. As the butt of an office-wide joke, she had no choice but to rise above it. My private, disrespectful nickname for Suzy Quintana was now public domain. I received winks and thumbs up from colleagues all day. There were giggles and muffled whispers in every corner. I missed Louie!

I got a call later that afternoon from Sheldon Walters. He thought my gaff was a hilarious joke at Frank and Suzy's expense. He even called her Squeezy and asked if I had a nickname for anybody else.

"I called you T-Rex once."

He laughed, "So you did. Good work, Dana. Glad to have you back aboard." People high and low in the company thought my faux pas was a refreshing jest. Poor Squeezy. I had to stop thinking of her that way. Suzy was a perfectly respectable name for a woman of any species. I also felt a glimmer of understanding of the seductive nature of praise for bad behavior. Sheldon Walters' snake oil charm could seduce a good person down a spiral of entitled indifference to the suffering of others. Indeed, Vincent must have once been a decent man. Was he praised for denying claims? Was the suffering of clients ridiculed? Was his bad behavior rewarded with praise, money, promotions, and invitations into the senior circles of the power elite?

Days passed and the incident lost its sensational edge. Work continued. Vincent and I worked together to restore insurance payouts to rightful claimants. A family got a disability payout and found affordable housing. A disabled client could afford to go back to school to study computers. A kid with leukemia got an experimental bone marrow treatment. A single mom got a new car. The Terrence family got a one-point-two million-dollar payout. There was resistance to this new premium-versus-claims benefit ratio from other regional managers. Vincent shielded me and took the brunt of criticism himself. He explained to the other managers that this was about PR. Shelter was dealing with federal investigations and internal audits. The house had to pay out the occasional justified claim to stave off findings of fraud and class action suits. There was grumbling about lost bonuses and tort reform, but Vincent prevailed, for the present.

On Thursday morning I received a phone call from Gwen Cretzky, inviting me to lunch. "I promised you in Texas that I'd call you so we could catch up. I've been remiss. I'll be in to pick you up at noon and we'll go to the Union Club."

"The Thai Noodle place is just around the corner and very good."

"Nonsense, you'll love The Union Club. The artwork is to die for and so are Chef's Thursday French specials. I'll see you at noon. Plan on a long lunch. Vincent will approve."

I hung up, bemused. I had to admit, I had always wanted to see the art collection at the Union Club. Gwen arrived in a black and white Chanel with red trim. Her red hat, shoes, and purse offset her perfect blond coif. She looked twenty years younger than the last time I'd seen her. Maybe she'd had some work done. Or maybe she'd stopped self-medicating. She noticed my weight loss immediately.

"Dana, you're so thin and lovely," Gwen gushed. "However did you do it?"

"A month-long fast in a cave."

Gwen tittered. "Precious. Is that what you call your Spa? Vincent came out to greet us when he overheard his wife's laugh. He was cordial and charming as he escorted us to the elevator. Gwen and I got looks from every corner, including Frank and Suzy, who stuck their noses out her door to gape and glare. I had a detective boyfriend, a new management position, a corner office, a direct line to Sheldon Walters, a collegial relationship with Vincent Cretzky, and now, a social outing with his wife. Wasn't my life just picture perfect?

At the restaurant, we were seated by a window overlooking the city, across the room from a half-dozen canvases of portraits, landscapes, lake views, and bucolic hunting parties. I ordered French onion soup, fromage blanc soufflé, and ginger ale. Gwen ordered asparagus, vichyssoise, roasted veal chop with morels, and a bottle of Dom Perignon. The sommelier poured us both a glass even though I was sipping ginger ale. Gwen was certainly right about the cuisine. It was to-die-for. I could have eaten another bowl of soup but saved room for soufflé and crème brûlée. Gwen ate and sipped champagne, polishing off the whole bottle, save for my glass.

As Gwen descended into her cups, she grew loquacious. "Vincent and I are a team again. Of course, our estrangement was mutual. I've suffered from severe depression and acute anxiety for years. Decades, really. Oh, I had such hopes and dreams. I thought Vince would run for office, state senate, governor maybe. I'd be a political wife, envied and in the public eye. I was brought up to it. Oh! Don't worry. We were Democrats. Mother was friends with Adlai and Ellen Stevenson. Do you remember them?" I nodded, but Gwen was lost in her memories and continued as if I weren't there.

"Mother and Daddy approved of our match. But Vince was seduced into corrupt acts early in his career. Daddy's attorneys advised me immediately. I still loved him then. I was bitterly disappointed by my lost dreams of being an influential political hostess. I thought about divorce, but Father forbade it. No Delaney had divorced in recent memory and Daddy needed the appearance of a stable, happy family. He was running for office. Mother and Daddy entertained lavishly. My sisters and I even came out at balls. That's my maiden name. Delaney. You may have heard it."

"I grew up in Chicago. Everyone's heard it. Wasn't your dad the State's Attorney General?"

She nodded, "Before getting into politics, Daddy was a corporate lawyer who worked for Sheldon Walters. After several years, for some reason, Daddy wanted out. Walters doesn't let go. When Daddy was elected, there was some worrisome quid pro quo between them. Sheldon Walters was invited to our wedding. Did you know that?"

I shook my head no.

"Walters offered Vincent a job. But there was a darker implication I didn't understand as a young, pampered debutante. I finally realized that Daddy wanted Vincent and me to stay married to keep us safe. By then, Shelter had entrapped Vincent. There were veiled threats. Daddy knew something he took to his grave. Vincent and I stayed married and he stayed at Shelter. We stayed safe. That's our Faustian bargain. I started to drink. My promised destiny turned out to be a life of vain regrets."

"Vain as in vanity or as in ineffectual?"

"Both," She giggled again, a brittle titter.

"Gwen, I am sorry about the adversity in your life. But you're revealing some pretty personal information. I'm not sure why."

"I told you. We're alike, Dana."

"You said we're escapists."

"That's part of it. Sometimes I live in a state of such extreme intensity that I could punch a hole through this reality and into the next."

"Oh," I was at a loss for a comeback.

Gwen's story took a circuitous route to get to the point. "I was a magical child. I was ridiculed into conforming. Mother's nickname for me was Inside-Out-Upside-Down-And-Backwards. That's how I functioned in the world. Mother said I did it to get attention. But I was just trying to fit into an insane world. I conformed by becoming extroverted and popular. It took all my energy to maintain that mask. Vincent saw through my facade to the whimsical introvert." Gwen was getting drunker and weirder. "I write fairy tales. Did you know that? I've never submitted them for publication. They'd reveal my madness."

I sputtered ginger ale across my plate.

Gwen ignored my breach of etiquette and continued. "I believe in magic. You do, too. That's another thing we have in common," Gwen swayed her index finger back and forth between us like a wand casting a spell. "In one story, a kingdom has a treasure beyond measure on a mountaintop. All who find the treasure return to lives of poverty and madness."

I settled in to enjoy the tale of the **Treasure Beyond Measure.**

"One day, a princess decides she will quest for the treasure and sets off with all the worldly provisions she can carry. Along the way she has vision quests, animal guides, and plants that open to reveal her trail. When she arrives at the mountaintop, she finds a niche in the rock face that holds the treasure. She puts in her hand and pulls out a simple stone. She is expecting a jewel, but it's an ordinary gray rock. But the rock speaks to her. "The mineral kingdom is the oldest kingdom on the Earth. All Earth's creatures except human still listen to the wisdom of living rock. The mineral, plant, and animal kingdoms have important wisdom for the human species, but you've tuned us out. Unless you pay attention, the Earth will cease to be habitable for all life. All creatures will pay for humanity's crimes against nature."

So, the princess realizes that the ability to hear minerals, plants, and animals is the treasure beyond measure. She replaces the stone into the niche for future questers and returns to her kingdom to share the message from Nature. She is met with derision and ridicule. She realizes that her predecessors on the quest chose simplicity and humility. Their poverty and apparent insanity reflected their sagacity, not their failure.

As a princess, she couldn't assume the role of humble hermit. She marries, becomes a queen, and has babies. She tries all her life to bring the messages from her mountain quest to her people. Politics and affairs of state interfere. Still, the queen sets up a foundation to finance individuals from all kingdoms who wish to undertake the mountain quest. Little by little, wisdom in the land grows to include the voice of nature.

The queen insists that each of her children make the quest when they come of age. Her husband, the king, does not understand, but he goes along because it's important to his wife, and he likes her, and it was her money and throne that he married. So, each of the royal children makes the quest. Other noble families see this quest being endorsed and rewarded by the royal family. So, they begin to send their children on the mountain quest as well. But many of the youth return to become renunciates who forsake their family business responsibilities. There is a backlash.

The kingdom becomes polarized. Civil war is threatened. The queen and her children suggest that some elder statesmen undertake the mountain quest. But the old guard ridicules the questers for listening to a rock. The Queen has her supporters, but the pragmatic king withdraws his support. He becomes estranged from his wife. Civil war is averted.

Still, in every generation, a handful of folks undertake the mountain quest and discover the treasure beyond measure. They listen to messages from Nature and share the lessons we need to hear if we are to survive. Their voice is quiet compared to the posturing politicos. But it is ceaseless."

"Thank you for the story, Gwen."

She droned on. "Yes, after Vincent was drawn into the maw of the beast, I withdrew into alcohol and fantasy. I banished Vincent from the marriage bed. I got pissed at God. The bad guys run the world." Gwen was tracing her fingertips over her collarbones and sculpted chin with graceful sensuality. I realized there was more than touch of Blanch Dubois in Gwen Cretzky. "Say, I have an idea. Let's go get our fortunes told. I know this great tarot card reader named Clover."

"Gwen, I have to get back to the office."

"I told Vincent I was keeping you for the rest of the day. Besides, I've yet to ask you about yourself. You must have a story. You must have been at a spa, right?"

"No, Gwen. I was on the run for my life. I went weeks without food. I lived in a primitive survival environment." I didn't want to go to a tarot reading with her, but her story about Shelter got to me. Their tentacles were far-reaching. Was I positioned at Shelter to have access to information that would help in my role as a wayshower? Here was information presenting itself to me. It was an opportunity, perhaps as important as processing appeals.

"A tarot reading?"

"Yes, let's settle up and head out." Gwen paid the bill and we exited to the cloak room, walking slowly to appreciate the fabulous private art gallery.

I said, "I'll be the designated driver." It was fun driving Gwen's Mercedes. Heading uptown in blowing snow and icy roads, we pulled onto an attractive residential side street near the lake and parked in front of a two-story brick house. Clover welcomed us in a flowing green velvet skirt and embroidered blouse. She had neat, short gray hair and wore no makeup. Clover was tall, smooth-skinned, clear-eyed, athletic, and in her early sixties. Her living room was filled with books from floor to ceiling along three walls. There were comfy chairs and love seats circling a coffee table. She offered us tea as we sat. I realized we were expected. Gwen had planned this reading and made an appointment well in advance. I surrendered to the moment.

I drew my cards and Clover remarked that she couldn't recall ever having seen so many Major Arcana Keys in one spread. "Dana, you have a global mission, a karmic dharma. You must face terrible foes and journey through dark passages in order to find your voice. And find your voice, you must. I don't understand this part, you have a haven in two worlds, but that will not be enough to protect you or serve your mission. The good news is that you don't have to do it alone. You have allies, young old, male, female, again, in multiple worlds. But before you complete your mission, you will experience agony and ecstasy. Still, you will prevail in ways I cannot comprehend. You have a still-small inner voice that will enable you to face your darkest shadows. Heeding this voice will give you the courage to speak your truth." Gwen was writing things down for me.

"Do you understand these two worlds I speak of? Is it perhaps your professional and personal lives? Or internal and external worlds. It's very esoteric."

"That sounds about right." Clover was more spot-on than she imagined.

Gwen drew her cards and Clover grew quiet for a long time. "Gwen, you have good news and bad news. Which do you want first?"

"The bad news," Gwen was resolute.

"Well, you have lost your path for a good number of years. You came into this incarnation to make a difference, but lost focus and hope."

"Vain regret," Gwen whispered to herself.

"There is a way out of this unhappy paralysis. You are going to reconnect with your partner, perhaps even renew the dream you once shared. The good news is that you are going to get a do-over. I cannot see what form it will take. Something will befall you that will seem like the end of the world but will be a miracle. Something that caused you pain is going to bring renewed purpose.

If you give help, you will receive help from unexpected sources." Clover bit her lip, hesitating. "I cannot see beyond that. There is a shadow." Gwen was listening and writing. She seemed reconciled to what she already knew.

It was clear from my Tarot reading that these women believed I had a mission to be some kind of spokesperson against corporate corruption. Gwen determined it was her purpose to assist me in any way she could. "We connected for a reason, Dana. I felt it ever since that night Vincent came home and told me how you gave him a piece of your mind. You became my ally."

"I honestly don't know how you could help, Gwen." I shrugged. "We're both trapped in our present predicaments." Once I got to Shasta, I would free myself from Sheldon Walters' bondage. Due to Shelter surveillance, vox technology was not enough. Help had not yet come from Wah'Kon-Tah. Crystal and Cosmo had been off the radar. Javier was figuring out his career trajectory in San Francisco. Jesse remained in Phoenix's Shasta safe house. Ruth was my only ally in Chicago. Except now, apparently, so was magical, escapist Gwen Cretzky.

Gwen gushed, "I have money. Lots of money."

"Money is good," I allowed, "but not a solution to our immediate problems."

"I know powerful people who do not genuflect to Shelter. Dana, I have waited for a means and opportunity to untether Vincent's and my affairs from that."

"Cesspool?" I suggested.

"Yes." She took a deep breath and looked at me with solemn eyes, "I need to know that what you are doing is real. Then I will know that I'm not insane."

"My mission is real enough, Gwen. And dangerous; you don't want to cross Sheldon Walters."

"Sheldon Walters fucked up my life decades ago. Living well, far away from his influence will be my revenge."

"Then perhaps we can help each other," I nodded, and Gwen smiled.

Gwen dropped me at my car in the Shelter parking lot and I headed home to my quiet condo, my art, tea, and slippers. Ruth wasn't there. I hoped that meant good things for her love life.

It was Friday which meant that Frank Fretz would not be lurking in doorways, flicking imaginary dust off his Armani sleeve. But I wasn't prepared for Suzy's tirade. Her cloying perfume and minty fresh breath assaulted me as soon as I exited the elevator onto the fifteenth floor.

"You did not return to work after lunch yesterday afternoon. Would you mind explaining why not?"

God, she was relentless. I didn't answer to her. Maybe if she'd asked me nicely, I'd have told her that I had Vincent's permission. I didn't explain long lunches anymore. But I needed to clear the air. So, I followed her to her office, where we sat facing each other.

"Suzy, I don't owe you any explanation for yesterday afternoon. But I do owe you an apology for my remarks in the staff meeting earlier this week. I have disdained your arrogance and what I considered your unprofessional behavior ever since you were hired."

"This is an apology?" her gaze narrowed.

"I realize that my contempt for you was a mirror for my own arrogance. I was a self-righteous gossip. But, to be fair, you are such an easy target. Your indiscretions are so blatant. I got so used to thinking of you by a derisive nickname that I blurted it out unthinkingly. Even a hate-mongering lizard like you doesn't deserve to be belittled. I owe it to both of us to confront you honestly and to your face. I should have done it years ago."

Suzy sat flummoxed for several heartbeats. Then she spoke slowly and softly. "You call me a hate-mongering lizard in the middle of your so-called apology? That negates your intention."

"I do not use the term derisively. I use it literally. Your humanity is only skin deep, and your genetic code is different from humans. Your species are hate-mongers because human misery fuels you like an addictive aphrodisiac. But it doesn't have to. You can rise above these darker impulses and evolve into a compassionate, enlightened being. Some of your kind have done so."

"This is insufferable."

"For a fourth-dimensional being, you're pitifully narrow in your life experience."

She stood and faced me with stunned surprise that I knew these aspects of her culture. "I *am* a fourth-dimensional being, you stupid cow. You are part of a slave sub-species whose purpose is to serve my kind. How dare you presume to educate me?"

"I presume to clear the air, Suzy. I want us to understand each other. You may not appreciate my honesty about your character flaws mirroring my shadow back to me, but there it is. I learned something from you. Though not the lesson you intended me to learn about my place as your inferior. I'm telling you this because perhaps you will use this opportunity to learn something from me. You are a caricature of the worst of your species. Sheldon Walters considers you a joke with your garish makeup and slutty outfits."

"Vincent and Frank both love that I'm comfortable with my sexuality."

"You're dressing for men and not yourself. Look at the most successful corporate women. They wear refined designer outfits with tasteful hair and makeup. Google it."

"You insult me while presuming to apologize?"

"My bad. I have sort of given myself a pass with reptiles. It is hard to see the good in individuals who profit from others' suffering and who manipulate circumstances for their own advancement at the cost of other people's lives and livelihoods. But I am trying to see the good in you."

"Does Sheldon Walters know that you can recognize reptiles?"

"I imagine he suspects. I called him T-Rex to his face when he dragged me back to work with deadly threats."

"You didn't return of your own free will?" Suzy was flabbergasted. "I thought you begged for your job back!"

"Return to this cesspool intentionally, when I could have been free? Living with Javier in San Francisco? Not at all; but I'm here now and doing some good work. The policy changes I implemented in appeals are helping deserving people."

"You're not the nice person you pretend to be. Maybe that's why Walters thinks he can use you. I'll ask him."

"Whatever you say to Walters won't alter my arrangement with him. You're as much a pawn to him as I am. And you're right; certain people bring out the worst in me. A lot of them work at Shelter."

She spat. "Big, stupid, meaningless words. I'll just call you Dana Dimbulb. Maybe it will catch on."

"Fair enough." If she had hoped to get a rise out of me, I was over it. We had descended to name-calling. And I had started it. "Can we be done now?"

"Get out of my office." Suzy snarled.

CHAPTER 21

Early Monday morning of solstice week, Jesse called from a burner phone in a Northern California town a day's drive from Shasta. There was a new development. "It's snowing," Jesse declared without preamble. I understood this to mean that *Shasta Solstice* was now on Earthside. Phoenix had painted himself into the foreground and emerged in Shasta, California. Phoenix couldn't return home until I arrived to open the portal to Tellara. He was stranded. Travel plans took on urgency.

He continued, taking his time and speaking carefully. "Are you expecting snow in Chicago?"

"No, no snow in Chicago." In other words, do not bring *Shasta Solstice* to Chicago!

"Okay. Well then, we should spend the holiday together in California." I understood. Then we then spoke of mundane things in case his disposable phone was not secure. Jesse was incorporating visionary fractal geometry into his graphic novel. The dogs loved the foothills.

Everyone at Shelter had two long weekends off for Christmas and New Year's. The first thing I did, after speaking to Jesse, was request extra days off so we could arrive in time for the solstice. Vincent approved it without comment. An hour later Suzy stalked into my office and said Human Resources couldn't approve any extra days off. I'd given short notice during a busy time. I shrugged. "I can complete all those older files after the first of the year."

Suzy added insult to injury, "Sheldon Walters wants a skeleton crew working Christmas week. The company needs to process as many claims as possible before the end of the year. Our audit isn't going well. Shelter is being tried in the media and might be tried in actual courts. Walters wants a show of good faith, with you at the helm, Dana. You're management now. Step up."

"Not gonna happen. I'm taking vacation days to spend with my loved ones."

"I speak for Sheldon Walters. This is his decision." Suzy said.

"It's not my job to make Sheldon Walters look good. He calls me himself when he has something to say." I returned to my files, fuming. It would be easier to beg forgiveness than ask permission. Firing me over disputed vacation days would invite bad press, something Sh.I.T. wanted to avoid. If I quit, Walters would find another, less savory, way to confine me. I might hate working for Sh.I.T., but I hated being a falsely accused fugitive even worse. Sheldon Walters could maneuver me behind bars or into a padded cell with one phone call. He could have me killed with a glance at Kek. He could arrange accidents for my loved ones. He wanted to keep me close in order to figure out how I had eluded him all those months. He and I were trapped together in Chinese handcuffs. But that would change when I got to Shasta.

Ruth had left Chicago in mid-December and was staying with Minerva at her Romani enclave. I called Alice and Val to invite them to join my family for Christmas. Val was spending the holiday with her family. It would be their first Christmas without Jay and there was a melancholy resignation in her voice. Alice, however, made plans to meet Minerva in Montana. Our conversation was circumspect. "I'll make my travel arrangements though Shelter's business office. California here I come."

"Is it OK to use company means for private travel?"

"Walters is very generous with me. He always keeps tabs on my whereabouts to make sure I'm safe."

"Lucky you! My friends will meet you at the airport." Crystal and Cosmo would pick Alice up at the Dallas airport before she boarded. Once in the van, she would be obscure from RAT-TRAK as they drove to Montana and then Shasta.

When Javier and I spoke on the phone, we kept our conversations mundane but endearing. We practiced clandestinely with our voxes, endeavoring to develop our audio-telepathy tool. At appointed times, we entered random public buildings, usually with high ceilings, found empty bathroom stalls, and cloaked. Exiting to open spaces, we hovered above the madding crowd. We usually returned to the lavatories and visibly exited the buildings just to satisfy our RAT-TRAK snoops. They must have thought we had the strangest bathroom habits. Activating the audio-telepathy function on our voxes was indeed difficult. In order to hear each other, we had to simultaneously attune the water in our brains by vibrating the same note. Javier had perfect pitch. I could carry a decent tune within a narrow range. Directing my hum at the rose quartz on my vox, I waited until the Javier's rose quartz vibrated in resonance. After weeks of practice, on my last night in Chicago, we could finally 'hear each other's words in our heads. Magic!

The eight passenger Psychedelic Van would transport Sky, Joe, Alice, Minerva, and Ruth to Phoenix's Shasta safehouse. They would be there before me. "I'm amazed that Sky Dancer is willing to leave her community to spend time with our families during this holiday season," said.

"Mount Shasta is one of the chakras of the Earth. Sky Dancer and Minerva consider this trip a pilgrimage. It's time for the Grandmothers to activate Earth's planetary grid. Working their magic during the solstice will be especially powerful."

"Phoenix mentioned that the Earth had chakras."

"Earth's chakras are vortices where spiritual and psychic energy concentrate, centers of magic and power. Giza, Haleakala, Uluru, Glastonbury, Mount Shasta, Teotihuacan, and Tibet, to name a few."

"Three of the grid points coincide with portal locations," I said.

"We'll be on one soon enough. Dana, go home and pack *Autumn*. Stay invisible as much as you can. You have a coach reserved on tonight's California Zephyr."

Our vox connection ended. At my condo, I silently, invisibly, lifted a window I'd left cracked open. Leaving all the lights off, I retrieved *Tellaran Autumn* from my living room wall and rolled it up inside my coat. Getting in and out quickly, I lowered the window. Decloaking in Jesse's vestibule I walked openly to my parked car wondering what my observers would make of my errand. I drove to a part of town closer to the bus station than the train station and parked near a noisy sports bar named The Watering Hole.

Entering, I ordered a Bloody Mary, took a few sips, went to the ladies' room, found a vacant stall, cloaked, and returned to the busy room. There, I hovered by the door, waiting for it to be opened by another patron. Two women in black entered. They moved with stealth, suspiciously eyeballing every corner of the room, Shelter operatives, for sure. While the door behind them slowly closed, I swiftly exited, hovering inches above the ground, leaving no footprints in the snow. I watched with rapt guilt. One operative, a blonde, planted herself by my abandoned drink, the other, a brunette, moved towards the ladies' room. When she came out scowling, they searched the entire bar, patron by patron, ungently pushing and pulling chairs. Their lack of subtlety irritated several customers but was taken as a come-on by two inebriated fellows. A fracas ensued as the womens' retreat was blocked by the disappointed Lotharios.

"Baby, I'll buy you a drink," said one, reaching for the blonde's hand as she swiveled his chair. Blondie sprained his thumb. He howled.

"Come sit on my lap and get to know me better," said the other drunk, running his hands over the brunette's ass, pulling her down. She spun, hissed, and knocked over his chair. "Bitch!" he screamed. The bartenders watched indifferently, all in a day's work.

It was December nineteenth, two days before solstice. I was facing a long, cold trip to the train station, so floated away from the lizzies-meet-jerks tableau. I ascended above traffic and moved as the crow flies toward the train. I floated to a bus stop, and while the bus doors opened, I floated aboard a local to the train station. My vox lit up in transit. Javier displayed a berth number. As easy as that, I made my way to a private, cozy berth. I cranked up a wall heater. Moments later, Javier joined me on the California Zephyr to Sacramento.

Breathless with joy, I asked, "How long have you been in Chicago?"

"I arrived just this afternoon." We were alone, really alone, for the first time since we'd arrived on U.S. soil from Cairo.

We passed a nervous hour waiting to depart, followed by a nervous encounter with the conductor who took our tickets and gave us the friendly once over. Cradling my vox in my palm, I viewed the 'women in black' who had torn apart The Watering Hole in pursuit of me. They were getting a tongue lashing from Kek. I viewed my condo. Jesse's and my places were crawling with searchers. I recognized Unibrow and Skinny from the cave. Javier recognized several of their faces and said he had files on them. They took all my paintings and stashed them in a van. I mourned for my art.

Cityscapes whizzed past our window and gave way to farmland. Fallow farmland gave way to snow-covered red rocks and then snow-covered mountains. We laughed, loved, talked, walked, and ate. We viewed our loved ones via our voxes. Louie and Phoenix viewed us back and we showed off our sonic skills in idiotic renditions of *Louie Louie* and *By the Time I get to Phoenix* that would resonate in their heads. Phoenix's house in Shasta was getting crowded. The place was filled with food and cheer. Everyone was waiting for us, for me to open *Shasta Solstice* to Shastise, Esselen, Tellara.

"Javier, I've never really understood what Phoenix and Saffron meant by my mission as a wayshower. I'm not in a position to disclose the Utopian nature of Tellaran society without exposing the *Magic Seasons* portals. Shelter reptilians would stop at nothing to block our access to Tellara."

"Our access to Tellara is our greatest asset."

"All this creeping around and hiding in the shadows. I am not accomplishing anything. I'm not doing anything proactive."

"Except being a fugitive, a media darling who was famous for fifteen minutes, and presumably, at some point, a potential corporate whistle blower."

"Alice and Val's bravery has reconciled me to blowing the whistle on Shelter. But Jay's documents have been circulating for months and aside from some embarrassing media moments, no one has been indicted. The congressional hearings went nowhere. And it would be madness to out Walters and Kek as evil reptilian overlords trying to control the world."

"Don't forget, I am gathering background information on the reptilian players in this game for global dominance. I have been for almost two decades. When you appeared in my office as a suspect served up by Frank Fretz, I had the break I'd been looking for, a crack in their secretive shield. You were a gift in my life with your crazy nonexistent alibi."

"Yeah, dancing in Tellara. Good one."

"You should have told me the truth that day."

"What if I had told you I found this portal to an alternate Earth. I was dancing with the elders and learning about Atlantis."

"Your alibi would have fallen on receptive ears. I'd have put you in touch with Minerva."

"I didn't know that at the time."

"I dropped enough hints over the weeks."

"Your hints were obtuse and as threatening as they were reassuring. Louie thought so too. It took Sky Dancer and Phoenix double-teaming me to trust you."

Javier said, ""Frank Fretz despised me, that should have counted for something."

I replied, "Frank Fretz despises everyone. The unctuous little weasel even hates those he grovels to."

"I knew from the beginning of my investigation that Shelter insiders were framing you for crimes they had committed."

"I had an inkling, but I couldn't rely on it. I'd never been interrogated before. I don't know from felonies. My friend was dead. I was grieving and a suspect. You told me to turn myself in. You hounded me at home and work. Do you know how vulnerable I felt? If it hadn't been for Tellara…" My voice trailed off.

"I was giving you time and space because I liked you so much."

"I liked you too, but you intimidated me."

"Dana, I am sorry if I had a blind spot. Of course, you were terrified. People were trying to kill you. You were running for your life. When the time comes that I have enough incriminating evidence to bring Shelter leaders to justice, I will act."

"Meanwhile, I sit at Sh.I.T. a working drone."

"Albeit a drone doing good works for humanity. Shelter is trying very hard to reform its image by paying out claims to the flood and fire victims. You're leading the charge."

"Millions of others are doing good works in their careers, like you, being a detective, and catching bad guys. My job has little or nothing to do with the planetary shifts Saffron described. Surely, working for Shelter was not the intent thirteen thousand years ago when I agreed to this wayshower gig."

"Your job places you at the nexus of global corruption and global healing. Like it or not, your job at Shelter makes you a player."

"Being in the public spotlight has not been complimentary. I've been asked to give an interview with Gemini Dallas." That made us both laugh out loud.

Javier teased, "You could make unsupportable accusations about Sheldon Walters. You could publicly point your finger at Kek as the corporate hit man who killed Jay and Hal. You could share your understanding of the hidden history of our world."

"No, no, and no. Not helpful." We both laughed uncomfortably. "Thanks to Tellara and you, I know more now than I did a few months ago, but I'm no authoritative researcher. I've read a few books, listened to some lectures on YouTube, and danced the heartdance. What would an interviewer ask me anyway? Who's been helping you? Where is Louie? How did you and Inspector Vazquez get together? Where did you hide while a fugitive? Did your children aid and abet you while on the run? Are you grateful to Sheldon Walters for giving you your job back? Nothing I want to answer."

"But just because you don't want to answer those questions doesn't mean you don't have something to say. I wouldn't mind hearing how, thanks to you, Shelter has provided unprecedented aid to the millions of people suffering from the recent natural disasters. And, what are your ideas for how much more all segments of government and industry could be doing to help society recover."

"Global recovery is not salacious enough. The media wants scandal."

"You could blog or vlog like Val. That would be proactive." Then he kissed me, and we stopped talking.

In the privacy of our scenic cocoon, in the afterglow of lovemaking, while sipping champagne, Javier said, "Marry me, Dana."

I was completely in love and I knew he was too, yet I hadn't seen a proposal coming. We'd only been together for a few months. We'd met because of a murder. We'd consummated our love in Tellara under ideal conditions. We'd been separated and reunited twice. I stared mutely for several long seconds, having long since been gun-shy about matrimony. My first one didn't take. I understood perfectly well what a lifelong commitment was and what intimacy was all about. I had everything I wanted or needed already with Javier.

"Javier, we met because someone I cared about was murdered and I was suspected of having something to do with his death."

"Jay gave his life to expose evil. And he exposed plenty, albeit, posthumously. Shelter is on the defensive. Our friendship confounds them further. We're on the same team, Dana. We're dimensional travelers and reluctant wayshowers. We're better together."

"All true," I knew I was going say yes before the word was on my lips. "I think I've known since the moment we met that we belong together."

"You eluded me across two worlds, Lady. You're not getting away again."

"I thought you were trying to bring me to justice."

"Oh, there's gonna be some serious justice between these sheets." After a fabulous session of Tellaran Tantra, Javier spoke again.

"Didn't you wonder why Sky Dancer helped me? You have no idea how much I worried about you until I learned about the portals. She knew before I did why I was pursuing you."

"It seems as though everyone knew before I did." We kissed. We cuddled.

I cried and sighed and smiled. "If you like, we can get married this week in Tellara."

"I like." Javier ruffled through his jacket pocket and pulled out a small box. "I bought this for you in Giza, Tellara side."

"Bought?"

"Resourced," he corrected himself, remembering that no money is used in Tellara. He held out a small, pentagonal, gold-colored jewelry box. I opened it and beheld a gold, open-style band studded with sapphires, rose quartz, and amethysts. The design took my breath away. I sighed when Javier put it on my finger. I held it up to the light and cried happy tears.

"The stones match my vox."

"I know. That's why I picked it. The jeweler was thrilled it was going to one of Earth's wayshowers."

I savored the moment, gazing from my guy, to my ring, to the sun rising over the Rocky Mountains. Life on Earth could be as beautiful as life on Tellara.

We disembarked in Sacramento mid-morning. Javier had left a false trail of breadcrumbs for our pursuers. If his ruse worked, they would be waiting to pick up our trail in San Francisco. Javier and I were blanketed by our insensibility cloaks. Jesse and Ruth were there to pick us up.

"Jesse, we're here," I whispered through a small vent I opened in my cloak. "Open the car doors for the dogs. We'll slide in. Head east."

"What the?" Jesse exclaimed.

I said, "If they can't see us, they might not follow."

"I get it, we saw you cloak at the cabin."

Ruth and Jesse escorted us to a car I didn't recognize, an ancient brown rambler that was old before Jesus was born. Javier checked the car for a tracking device, found one on a rusty rear bumper and loosened it so it would fall off as soon as we pulled out. Shelter worked fast. Javier worked faster.

"How long have you been here?"

"About thirty minutes."

"And in half an hour they managed to stick a tracking device on your bumper? Is it possible they put the device on your car in Shasta? Could they know the location of the safe house?"

Jesse shook his head, "I just bought this car an hour ago here in Sacramento."

"They might have viewed ahead on RAT-TRAK to see where you'd be."

"RAT-TRAK?" Ruth asked.

"Reptilian spyware. I bet they're staking out Chicago, Sacramento, and San Francisco. They probably thought they hit pay dirt when you and Ruth drove up to the train station." Javier and I slid in the back with the dogs and stayed cloaked. "But, as far as they know, we never disembarked from the train."

"If Ruth and I drive off alone, hopefully, your trackers will assume this was a diversion."

Javier checked every inch of the interior for listening devices and found none. "The Shelter guys only had time to install one device on the exterior of this car. The inside is clean."

He waited and watched as Jesse pulled onto the freeway. When he reckoned it was safe to speak inside the car, he said "Hello."

"Jesse, Ruth, this is Inspector Javier Vazquez, my fiancé."

"Fiancé! When did this happen?"

"Last night."

"We've spoken," Jesse stated. "I recognize your voice."

"Yeah, when you and your mom were first on the run, up north. We talked on the phone."

Ruth said, "You directed us to Minerva's house in Montana."

"That was me. Stay east and turn south on five."

"'Til when?"

"I'll let you know."

Ruth said, "Minerva is at the Shasta house now."

"I can't wait to see grandmother again," said Javier

"I can't wait to meet her. I owe her for your lives," I said.

"I can't wait to see your fiancé's face," said Jesse."

"It's a good face," I told him.

Javier interrupted, "Jesse, pull into this motel. Ruth, take the dogs out for a walk in that field. Leave the doors open for us. Jesse, go inside like you're going to book a room. Buy something from the vending machine. Come back and close the doors to this car. Walk around behind the building like you're going in a room."

"This place may not allow dogs."

"Doesn't matter, we're not staying. You'll find a silver Subaru Forester parked in front of room eighteen. It's open. The keys are under the mat. We'll be there waiting. Jesse, get in the Subaru alone. Open the passenger door. There is a baseball cap with a curly wig inside. Put it on and turn your jacket inside out. Ruth, you duck behind an SUV and pick up one dog, Dana, pick up your dog and cloak him. Ruth, I'll cover you with my cloak. Get in the car and stay low. Jesse, open the back of the Forester station wagon and make like you're loading and moving stuff around. Leave it open for us to crawl in. After I tell you, close the hatch, close the passenger door, get in the driver's seat, and drive away. You'll look like a guy alone with no dogs. Any questions?"

There were none. The plan worked. Jesse merged onto the highway solo.

Back in the parking lot, all slouched and disheveled, a man in a black coat was crawling under the Rambler. Another exited the office and shouted something. Both looked around, but our Subaru was just one of dozens of cars in holiday highway traffic heading in every direction. Invisibly, I gawked at Contrary and Pandemonium as they quarreled and smashed the old beat up Rambler with their fists. I could imagine them demanding to know how we had eluded them again. A middle-aged woman, I assume the desk clerk, came out to the parking lot yelling at them to move their car if they weren't going to check in. Then, all three were screaming and gesticulating at each other, the reptilians shouting that they wouldn't be caught dead driving this piece of shit or staying in her seedy fleabag. They didn't show their badges.

I was giddy to have a sexy cop on my side. He'd outwitted reptilians in black.

Jesse warned us, "They'll tow the car. Will they be able to figure out where we're going?"

Javier said, "Possibly; they'll use reptilian forensic science. Particles from your clothing might lead them to Shasta."

Ruth said, "They don't know what car we're in now. The Rambler has never been in Shasta."

"How much time do we have?"

Javier answered, "Even with reptilian technology it will take months. All they will have to go on is our DNA; No soil samples, fauna, or flora."

"How do you know all this stuff?" Ruth asked

"I'm a detective," was Javier's now familiar refrain. "By the time they find the exact location, the safe house will be empty, and the paintings will be on their way to Wah'Kon-Tah."

We climbed from the rear of the car to the back seat and decloaked which thrilled the dogs. "North to Shasta?" Jesse asked.

"North to Shasta!" I replied, overjoyed to be able to hug my kids.

"Dude, you make one hell of a first impression," said Jesse to Javier. "Great escape plan, you cooked up."

"It was a good plan, Jesse. But it wouldn't have worked without Tellaran technology. We got lucky."

It was just as well that no one else had come to meet us at the train station. Keeping Louie's whereabouts secret was crucial to keeping him alive. Keeping our allies from the Ozarks off the radar maintained a haven for our expanding tribe. Keeping Minerva out of the picture was Javier's priority. Once free of the Shelter goons, ours was a merry road trip with stories to exchange.

"You've been to Tellara?" Ruth asked excitedly.

"I have indeed," replied Javier.

"Is it everything Mom described?"

"All that and more."

"I can't wait to go!"

Driving along the clear, dry highways of Northern California was a delight after the icy, slushy, dirty winter streets of Chicago. After a few hours, we entered mountain country. Snow was back. It covered the hills stretching to the horizon. We all got out and put chains on the tires while sipping cocoa from a thermos.

We exited the highway and took local streets onto a steep, winding road into a pleasant subdivision. There were old growth trees mixed with seedlings spread over raw land all around the houses. Jesse pulled into a driveway in the shadow of Mount Shasta and Black Butte. Phoenix's rented house had a Tudor old-world look to it. We parked alongside the psychedelic mini-bus in a double-wide garage.

Arriving on the eve of the winter solstice, we spared a glance at the scenery before hurrying inside. The mountain rose from the level ground straight up into the sky, a brilliant, snow-covered pyramid alongside its black, pyramidal companion. Louie was waiting in his black and silver caftan, his jewel encrusted vox hanging on a heavy gold chain. His hair had grown out; so dapper, so handsome, my Louie. We clung together in joy and sorrow, joy to be together again and sorrow that I was back at the job that had destroyed so many lives.

Then Alice saw me and joined our hug. Knowing that she was a reptile who had broken the chains of heartless duality in order to evolve spiritually made me admire her courage beyond measure. "I'm going to start calling you Alice Raza." She looked at me quizzically.

"You'll see soon enough," said Louie.

Sky Dancer's eyes beamed approval and I got a lump in my throat. Javier embraced Minerva; the woman who had raised him after his parents disappeared. He brought her to meet me. She must have been close to a hundred years old. She was tiny and frail-looking but keen intelligence shone from her sparkling black eyes. Her hair was still gleaming black, tucked in a loose chignon. Her skin was deeply lined and crinkled when she smiled, which was often. We chatted for several minutes until Minerva faltered a little. We all felt like idiots for keeping her standing, but she waved us off and found a comfy couch cushion next to Joe Two Feathers, who had become her new best friend.

I greeted Crystal and Cosmo. They had been here for two days and were helping assemble and stack rooms full of canvases, books, DVDs, CDs, statues, and artifacts of every medium in preparation for transport where they would be digitized for Tellaran posterity. The room was filled with happy chaos as people and dogs cuddled. Wonderful smells of cider and cinnamon filled the house. I realized I was hungry.

Then Phoenix stood before me. Our greeting was almost solemn; my relief at seeing him was palpable. We could hardly let go of each other's hands. He pulled me from the melee and asked, "What has changed?" His warm large fingers brushed over my left ring finger and his eyes sparkled. "I was with Javier when he selected your ring." He took my hand and escorted me to the dining room where we viewed *Shasta Solstice* together.

It had evolved since I had first viewed his preliminary sketches last summer. Mount Shastise on the canvas was painted from the same perspective as from our dining room window. The red pyramid stood completed and gleaming with a gold capstone. Hundreds of trees surrounded the triplet pyramids and grew partway up to the natural tree line. The evergreen boughs were heavy with snow. Higher up the mountain, branches swayed. I could hear the whispering pines. Midnight blue sky was pierced with twinkling stars. It was snowing in the painting. Snowflakes glittered, illumined from all directions at once. Near the base of the mountain stood rustic log buildings. Their windows glowed golden. Near the door of the largest lodge, a small group of winter-clad hikers hovered.

I was drawn into the snow flurries of that winter midnight. Snowflakes landed on my cheeks and eyelashes. Wind caressed my face and hair. My hands felt the chill breeze. Snow gathered in my palms. My hands, my face, my arms, and finally my whole body disappeared into a now-familiar mist. I had crossed into Tellara. The portal was open.

People were hiking toward me from the log building. It stood alongside the meadow where we had danced that long-ago summer afternoon, when I traveled by train from Esselen to Shastise. That was the day I had been gifted with my vox. I recognized Saffron, Heron, Robin, Juniper, and Corky. My friends were waving and stomping their boots in the snow. I took a step forward and found myself embraced by Tellaran friends.

"How long have you been here?"

"On and off for two days. We've been staying at the log lodge since Phoenix transferred the painting to Earth."

Bo and Guna Raza followed along from the trail behind the mountain. There were more hugs and welcomes.

I heard noise behind me. "Hi Mom!" Ruth and Jesse entered Tellara for the very first time and looked around in wonder at the red pyramid. "This is amazing." My kids were followed through the portal by Rip and Belle. The dogs leapt enthusiastically into the snow. Of all the trans-dimensional scenes I'd ever imagined, none surprised me more than my dog frolicking in Tellaran snow. Robin's dog, Corky, bounded up to greet his canine counterparts. A multi-dimensional doggy sniff-fest got underway.

Javier came through, escorting Minerva, who was wrapped in a heavy afghan and sporting thick, fuzzy boots.

Saffron kissed Javier's cheek and lead our group into the log lodge. The room was warmed by a blazing fire and filled with comfy chairs, love seats, couches, and rough-hewn tables.

One by one, each of my Earthborn friends and family entered Tellara through *Shasta Solstice* and followed the hikers into the log lodge. Louie and Phoenix waited to escort Alice through the portal. Passage through the portal to Tellara was her ultimate test. We had been taking it on faith that our friend loved and trusted Alice. This was my call.

But Alice sailed through the portal, a born wayshower. Her eyes immediately fell upon the exquisite face of Guna Raza and, close by her side, Bo, who was laughing and clapping Louie on the back. Alice's eyes locked on Guna, drinking in her reptilian splendor. Tears filled her eyes and spilled unchecked down her cheeks. Bo and Guna, openly reptilian, conversing in easy friendship with humans, presented a sight Alice had never dared to dream. Guna was elegant in a blue and silver kaftan. Her hairless scales shimmered from her face to the back of her scalp, which was adorned with rivulets of concentric silver ornaments. The scales that shaped her facial features defined exotically symmetrical eyes, cheeks, lips, and sculpted brow.

Guna noticed Alice staring at her and in a moment saw through Alice's mammalian features. Guna and Bo rushed to greet Alice. Thirteen thousand years of Tellaran harmony stunned the sensibilities of an Earth-bound reptile longing to break free. Alice was dazed with hope and wonder. Guna embraced her as she sank to her knees. Bo flanked the ladies and whispered to Alice, "Can you release the visage?"

Sobbing, Alice nodded. "It takes focused attention to hold the mammalian features."

"Then let go, child," Guna cooed. "You are safe. You could not be here if your heart was not pure and your karma balanced." Alice gazed upon Guna as a lost child who at long last has been reunited with a searching parent.

"Dana, Louie, we did not realize you had reptilian friends on Earth." Guna's words were almost an admonishment.

"We only recently learned it ourselves with our voxes."

"And did not think to tell us?"

"It is Alice's revelation to share, not ours," said Louie.

"Well, it's true," declared Alice. Standing and gathering her composure, she addressed us. "I am a Draconian. I would never have voluntarily shared my reptilian nature with my human friends. I could never have dreamed I'd be believed or accepted."

"You are in Tellara now, Alice, and we all think you are beautiful," said Bo

Raza. This made Alice cry again. "My name is Bo Raza, and this is my wife Guna Raza."

"And now, I am Alice Raza," Alice declared. "Thank you all for bringing me to Tellara."

"We are tribe, said Louie."

"Is there somewhere we can get inside?" asked Louie. Together Bo and Guna guided Alice to a back room in the log lodge. Her eyes met mine as she passed and I remembered our dinner the night before Jay's murder, her face in my vox as she made the fateful decision to post incriminating evidence about Shelter, and now her glorious transformation, flesh morphing into shimmering scales. With a decisive tilt of his head, Bo closed the door gently but firmly conveying Alice's need for privacy. I turned back to the room filled with Tellaran and Earthborn loved ones. The first face that found my gaze was Louie's. How could we have seen this coming, and yet, how could we have not expected it? We were all overwhelmed to witness Alice's 'coming out.'

CHAPTER 22

"Let's sit," Saffron gestured to the array of comfy chairs, couches, and love seats. We sat around the stone fireplace and introduced ourselves: Saffron, Phoenix, Heron, Juniper, and Robin from Tellara; Joe Two Feathers, Sky Dancer, Minerva, Ruth, Jesse, Louie, Javier, and me from Earth. Bo, Guna, and Alice just a room away. Cosmo and Crystal said they'd be along later after taking care of a few things. Hal was gone but still present in our hearts. For Ruth, Mick's absence was a void. Jesse put his arm around his sister. Corky, Belle, and Rip curled up on a rug by the hearth.

Ruth was still heartbroken about Mick's absence in her life. She'd had hopes for a long-term, serious, committed relationship. It would probably have happened had Sh.I.T. not torn our family apart. She didn't know if they would ever see each other again. Her trust and his boundaries had been shattered.

Saffron asked, "Is Winter Solstice a big Earth holiday."

"Louie said. "Not as big as Christmas, along with Hanukkah, Kwanza, Las Posadas, Yule, and Saturnalia. We light candles, decorate our homes, wear festive clothing, exchange gifts, and have a feast. Many people worship in church or temple."

"Church?" Heron asked.

Louie answered, "Most Earthborn people pray in buildings designated as sacred spaces."

"Like the pyramids?"

"No, but often with spectacularly beautiful architecture including domes and stained-glass windows."

"Do you ever worship in Nature?"

Louie said, "A few do, but not so much in modern times, especially not in winter. Churches, mosques, and temples come in many shapes and sizes. Worship on Earth takes the form of prayer, sermons, songs, lectures, and chanting. Sometimes kneeling, sometimes wailing, sometimes celebrating, and sometimes, even dancing."

Minerva said, "Our rituals vary from culture to culture. Some are very esoteric and mystical. We offer blessings and gratitude."

"Celebrating gratitude with others is wise," affirmed Heron.

Louie said, "We do that at an American holiday called Thanksgiving. For that holiday, we mostly celebrate four days off work and a traditional feast. Many folks travel to spend time with loved ones. The story of Thanksgiving goes back three hundred years. The story of Christmas goes back two thousand years."

Saffron said, "Solstice goes back thirteen thousand years, ever since Gaia equilibrated in this axial orbit."

Phoenix nodded, "Solstice happens four days before Christmas. Tomorrow, in fact."

I said, "We look forward to celebrating a traditional Tellaran Solstice."

"And your Christmas holiday in a few days on Earth," Juniper said, locking eyes with Jesse who blushed to his roots.

"Not Guna and I," Bo said as he had exited the back room.

I was disappointed. "Oh, I am sorry; why not join us?"

"You see our faces, Dana. You are used to our reptilian features. You even find us attractive."

"You are beautiful," I nodded.

"Well, Dear, no force in any Universe could persuade Guna or me to enter a dimension where we had to conceal our true identity. We went through Hell to rise above that oppressive behavior."

"Like an addict who has struggled a lifetime to maintain sobriety." Louie offered.

"Multiple lifetimes," Bo corrected.

Guna Raza took my hands in hers and said, "The time has passed when I could take on the guise of human flesh or even want to. My reptilian features are the best part of me. I worked hard to grow my heart, and establish positive karma. From what Alice has told me, I don't dare risk showing up in your world with these scales, even in a private home. You have enemies pursuing you. You're in the public eye and under private surveillance."

Our holiday gathering wouldn't be the same, but I understood.

"I am not going back to Earth either," Alice entered the great room with quiet dignity. She stood erect in a shimmering ruby red gown. The flesh of her arms, shoulders, and face had been replaced with glimmering coffee and bronze scales. The back of her skull was covered with a jeweled headpiece. Her face was defined by a prominent brow, high, prominent cheekbones, and a narrow, receding chin. Her nose was very small and her nostrils vertical holes. Her pupils opened as vertical slits in golden irises. Her transformation took my breath away. The entire group fell silent in her presence. "I have an opportunity here to learn about the possibilities for my species. You cannot imagine how isolated we are, we few reptiles seeking Individuality. I will remain in Tellara until the last possible moment. Then, I will come home and teach."

She still limped from her old injury, and still carried extra weight. But she now possessed grace when she moved. Alice was at home in her own skin. An occasional tear still slipped down her cheek, producing a sparkle of iridescent scales. "Reptilians represent the worst of the left-brain, domineering conquerors who colonized, oppressed, and killed the indigenous tribes of Earth. My friends in the Reptilian Individual Movement seek to balance the hemispheres of our brains even as we balance our karma."

Sky Dancer said, "Your transformation reminds me of a story. Remember the Hopi saying? 'We are the ones we've been waiting for.'" Joe picked up a drum from along the hearth and began to beat a slow, steady rhythm. Heron found a drum of another timbre and began to beat a counterpoint. Voices grew still.

"This is **The Legend of the Eagle and the Condor**," Sky Dancer spoke in her deep contralto.

>"Once, on Turtle Island, the Eagle and the Condor flew side by side in friendship. Turtle Island is North America. Turtle Island is home to many creatures and was unbroken for millions of years. There was no man-built canal to disrupt its magnetic flow. Humans lived in harmony with the land, the water, the plants, and the animals. Humans lived in harmony with the seasons. They planted and hunted and harvested according to Mother's cycles. The indigenous peoples were one with nature. The indigenous people of the world live a heart-centered life. Tribal peoples care for the Earth for the next seven generations. The indigenous peoples of North America are the Condor.

>"Then came the Europeans. The genocide of the Native Americans began. The Europeans saw the gentle, natural, harmonious ways of the Indians and called us primitive savages. They did not understand our connection to nature. With the arrival of the Europeans came the dominance of the logical, rational, western, hierarchical, mindset. The Western, left-brained consciousness is the Eagle. When Europeans arrived on Turtle Island, they undertook to intentionally destroy the peoples' way of life. The eagle and the condor no longer flew together. The Turtle was rent asunder from her brother the Crocodile, South America, when the Panama Canal split the continent."

>"Some European leaders were reptilians who understood only too well the danger posed by the right-brained, intuitive, tribal people with their shamanic connection to nature spirits. Europeans had long since wiped out the intuitive, feminine, matriarchal aspects of their culture using the patriarchal authority to designate wise women as witches. The genocide and forced assimilation of the indigenous peoples was ongoing and sustained, an intentional strategy to enslave humanity in a system of rigid hierarchy.

>"The good news is that the Western imperialists were not completely successful in their agenda to annihilate the indigenous ways. The Condor was driven almost to extinction. Then, in an ironic twist, western biotechnology brought this magnificent bird back from the brink. Western science used left brain science to heal what they them-

selves had almost destroyed. All over the world, the western mind is turning to the indigenous mind to understand our relationship to the planet.

"Eagle is keenly intelligent and productive. Condor is ancient, nurturing, and creative. Both are needed for humanity to survive, to evolve. Together, the integrated left and right brain hemispheres make a balanced humanity. Soon Eagle and Condor will fly together again, and Turtle Island shall be healed. Western peoples are waking up to the wisdom of indigenous elders who are now sharing our wisdom to all seekers. This is the formation of the Rainbow Tribe. According to prophesy, when the eagle and the condor fly together, the human race will finally have the wisdom to overcome the problems of its own creation."

The drumming slowed and quieted as Sky Dancer sat back, crossed her arms, and bowed her head.

Ruth said, "Humans, in and of themselves, are greedy and selfish enough to destroy our Planet. We don't need the reptilian agenda to explain how we've sown the seeds of our own destruction."

Alice said, "That doesn't mean Draconians weren't there the whole time, facilitating divisive hierarchy and undermining cooperation."

Saffron spoke, "Terrans are close to where we were at the time of the collapse of the Atlantean civilization. For all the interference by reptilians, you're not without support. Elder brothers and sisters from the Galactic Family provide guidance to humanity."

Just as Saffron spoke, Crystal and Cosmo entered to log lodge. "Galactic Family?" Ruth asked.

Crystal answered, "species from alternate dimensions, and star systems, who serve all beings' highest evolutionary aspirations."

"Dana, why did you not tell me that you were working with Avatars?" Saffron asked me pointedly.

"Avatars?"

"We are Avatars from the Galactic Family who have clothed ourselves in human guise over our light bodies. We live among you to serve and guide humanity."

I addressed Crystal and Cosmo. "You told me you were part of the Galactic Family, but I was never sure what that meant. I thought you said you were a plebeian, you know a regular hands-on working gal and that Cosmo ate a vegan diet," I mumbled, embarrassed.

Crystal and Cosmo laughed softly. Then everyone laughed at me and I had the grace to smile while blushing.

Cosmo bowed and said, "Vegan, from a planet that circles the star you call

Vega, here to guide Terrans."

Crystal spread her arms and said, "Pleiadian, from a planet that receives her light from both Electra and Maia. I am here to serve."

"Louie," I asked. "When did you figure out Crystal and Cosmo were actual star people?"

"When they introduced themselves to us."

"Why didn't you tell me?"

"It was self-evident. I didn't realize you were confused."

"You should always assume that I'm confused," I mumbled.

Cosmo rose and expanded to his full height of nearly eight feet tall. His luminescent ebony skin gleamed. Crystal also stood and assumed her full height. She was shorter than Cosmo, but still over seven feet tall. Her skin glowed with a white halo. The whole room basked in the loving light they radiated.

Sky Dancer said, "I've been a contactee since childhood. Many Sky People have been similarly contacted and instructed. We are shamans, medicine men and women, teachers, inventors, storytellers, alchemists, scientists, healers, artists, and now, wayshowers. Crystal and Cosmo have guided me all my life, and my ancestors before that. They established Wah'Kon-Tah long before the arrival of Europeans."

"They're older than you?"

"By eons," Sky Dancer answered.

"We can do tasks with you, but not for you," said Cosmo. "We guide and advise."

When there was a lull in the conversation, Robin said, "Tell us of your winter Earth myths."

Ruth shared the Nativity story, which was received with appreciation for its universal, archetypal themes. Then Joe explained about Santa Claus, the North Pole, the sleigh, and reindeer in lavish detail.

"Both these myths celebrate the same holiday?" asked Juniper.

"It wouldn't be Christmas without Santa bringing his bag of presents down the chimney." The Tellarans were baffled, but we Terrans just laughed.

I said, "Santa has some sacred aspects to his story, but yes, Christmas has become commercialized."

Cosmo rose and said, "Hanukkah is another midwinter holy celebration. It is based on the miracle of Jews who kept their candelabrum lit for eight days with oil sufficient only for one day." He then gave a beautiful, detailed rendition of the Hanukkah story, almost as if he'd been there.

Alice said, "A more recent winter celebration to migrate from Africa to America is called Kwanzaa. It is a Pan African celebration commemorating the first fruits of the year. Africa is a warm continent. Prior to colonization and slavery, Africans harvested abundantly all year round. Kwanzaa is both sacred and secular, marked by both prayers and gifts. It was revived in the New World by African-Americans seeking to honor their roots." When Alice finished, we fell silent for many moments, then adjourned for our respective sleeping quarters on our respective worlds. We'd gather tomorrow morning to celebrate the shortest day of the year.

At first light, we assembled in the log lodge. The Tellarans taught us their Winter Solstice ceremony. We made prayer flags using different materials, including fabric, paper, sheaves of grass, woven twigs, and anything else that would burn. We poured our hearts' desires into our prayers. We were allowed to include as many wishes and messages of peace and good will as we could integrate into each flag. We went outside and built a campfire in the snow-covered meadow. We learned a Tellaran mantra that we all chanted phonetically. Saffron translated:

> Gaia's heart beats endlessly
> In synchronicity with Sophia, Sol, Luna, the planets, and stars
> Blessed Darkness gives way to Blessed Light
> Our hearts are warmed
> Our hearths are abundant
> We await the return of the light
> The longest night has come and gone.

Many other families sat around nearby fires and did their own fire-dance ceremonies. One by one, we tossed our prayer flags into the fire, sang, and danced. The ceremony lasted until late afternoon. We were still warm from dancing around the fire. Spontaneously, Louie and Javier broke into song with White Christmas. The rest of the Earthborn joined in. At first, we sang only secular tunes, not wanting to impose an Earth religion on the Tellarans' sacred festival. But, having heard the nativity story, they wanted to hear more, so we sang religious carols as well. The Tellaran families in the area were delighted with our songs and joined our fire. I must own that among our group of Earthborn carolers, none of the Travers family possesses a polished voice. But Javier and Louie made up for it; Javier with a beautiful baritone and Louie with a soaring tenor. Phoenix joined in some of the refrains with an easy, Earthy familiarity. The families on the meadow clustered round us and we sang and danced 'til dark.

Then we adjourned to the log lodge for a zesty feast of bread, baked squash with nuts, beets, beans, and greens, ordinarily not my favorite combination, but tonight, the meal melted in my mouth. From somewhere, Louie procured eggnog laced with rum, which was shared with delight by all the adults. Ever resourceful, Louie got Phoenix to help him locate Christmas-like decorations, lights, candles, bells, ornaments, and carvings of people and animals that he arranged like a nativity. He brought in branches from outside and spread an evergreen garland across the mantle over the great stone hearth. After dinner he brought in a living potted tree that we all decorated together. It was the best non-Christmas-Christmas I had ever celebrated.

Phoenix spoke, "Dana, before it gets too late, let's go hang *Tellaran Autumn* and get both portals open. We've got a lot of material to transport for storage in the Tellaran archives." So, we headed back to the crossroads marked by a labyrinthine stone design. The air rippled in now-familiar undulating thermal shimmers. One-by-one, we crossed back to Earth, all but Alice and the Raza Clan. All three dogs leapt through the portal with the holiday revelers.

I pulled Phoenix's precious canvas from my green bag, which he mounted it on a wooden frame. We hung *Tellaran Autumn* alongside *Shasta Solstice*. Jesse came in and saw the two paintings together, both pulsating with internal fractal vibrations. He disappeared for a moment and returned with the damaged *Summer in Tellara*. Jesse hung it alongside the other two canvasses, *Summer, Autumn,* and *Solstice*, three *Magic Seasons* now assembled.

I said, "*Summer in Tellara* seems sadly still, but is it my imagination, or do I see a tiny fluttering of fibers at the edge of the gash?"

"Magic springs eternal," Phoenix answered enigmatically.

On the Tellaran side of each portal, teams were ready and waiting to ferry copies of Earth's greatest art works which Phoenix had gathered over his many months' sojourns to Earth. Receptacles were waiting to digitize and archive Earth's art. The repositories were shaped like interlocking star tetrahedrons. Crystal and Cosmo were ready in the dining room and began a human chain to pass boxed and wrapped art works into the waiting hands of Saffron, Bo, Guna, and Alice in Shastise, and to Jasmine, Falcon, Leel, and Jeej in Giza. Soon, we were all busy conveying precious bundles through portals. Someone put on Christmas classics and we fell into a dancing rhythm that went on late into the night.

* * *

At one time, I took a break and crossed into Giza to greet Leel, Jeej, and Jasmine, who showed me how the star tetrahedrons interlocked into three-dimensional containers. The art was being transformed into a database that the Tellarans would access even after ascension. I caught glimpses of exquisite copies of Botticelli's *Venus*, Van Gogh's *Sunflowers*, and Kandinsky's *Yellow-Red-Blue* as they zipped through my visual range. Thousands of images had been scanned, digitized, and stored. The next day, December 22nd by Earth calendar we were going to have a wayshower summit to brainstorm our strategy of bringing Tellara's message to Earth while eluding adversaries.

Phoenix said, "Both summits and festivals are enriched by the heartdance. But you are right about having work to do. Now that the portals are opened, transporting Earth's artistic artifacts into Tellaran storage is just one priority. Strategizing how to keep our wayshowers safe and launch their mission on Earth is the other."

"Voxes all around," suggested Louie.

"Vox training."

"Heartplums and bees."

"Heartdancing."

"And don't forget that pesky Tellaran science," I grumbled. Ideas flew faster than I could assimilate.

Every Earthborn was gifted with a vox, and Bo Raza declared he would conduct training. Joe, Sky Dancer, Minerva, Alice, Ruth, and Jesse marveled at the amazing tool they'd seen me use. Crystal and Cosmo declined, stating that they had natural faculties that had served them for ages. It was time to get some sleep.

* * *

Part of me was looking forward to the summit, to problem solve together, but part of me just wanted to be on vacation. The morning after Solstice Festival, we joined elders from Esselen, Giza, and Comanche at the red pyramid. A round table, flanked with dozens of chairs, occupied the center of the room. We took our seats and introduced ourselves.

The meeting room was a sanctuary taking up the entire ground floor of the pyramid. Carved pillars held up the high ceiling. Translucent crystalline reddish bricks let in filtered daylight that dappled the bas-relief wall carvings of the cavernous room. The sculpted columns displayed winding, spiral chains of DNA covered with vines, leaves, flowers, planets, stars, galaxies, animals, and faces ascending from the tiled floor to a flower-of-life pattern engraved in the ceiling.

The early part of the meeting resembled a plenary session at an international conference. We brainstormed about how Earthborn wayshowers could orchestrate our David versus Goliath, whistle-blowing exposé of the reptilian hierarchy in time for the planetary shifts. This conversation was way overdue, but, to be fair, we had been delayed behind enemy lines.

Minerva recounted ancient lore from Romani stories that dovetailed with the ancient planetary schism. Joe chimed in with the Hopi prophesy of two worlds emerging from one. One by one, we recounted our understanding of where our worlds had been and where they were going, and how, on Earth, we had been deprived of humanity's true history and archaeology. We spoke of how our life paths had brought us to Tellara and what we saw as our wayshower roles as part of a rainbow tribe. For the benefit of the new wayshowers, Buffalo recounted the schism of the antediluvian world into 3D Earth and 5D Tellara.

Phoenix spoke up, "Dana, it has always been important that you gather an Earthborn team around you. Once all four *Magic Seasons* portals are completed, our work together will be nearly done. As Earth shifts into separate planets, each person will make a choice to ascend to 5D Terra Nova, or to remain on 3D Terra Familiar."

Saffron spoke, "To some, good and evil, life and death, wealth and poverty, a creator separate from the creation, masculine and feminine, free will and determinism, hierarchy; all pairs of opposites make sense, are the natural order, mutually exclusive, and inherently good."

"Whereas we see these opposites along a continuum," said Louie.

Phoenix continued, "We are all moving in the same direction, each at his or her own pace, evolving into vehicles capable of holding higher vibrational frequencies and more coherent consciousness. Our free will determines the rate of evolution. The path is in no way linear. Not one of us has followed the paths of involution and evolution along a smooth curve. Make no judgments for those who will disagree with and even oppose you."

Saffron spoke again, "There will be many who are receptive to your message, individuals who long for civilization in resonance with nature and a resource-based economy."

"Is Tellara ascending also?" asked Jesse.

"Gaia Tellara will attain 6D consciousnes, but will not separate into two planets," answered Bo Raza. "She will stabilize. The humanoid Tellarans will attain 6D consciousness adn become ascended beings in the vicinity of Gaia Tellara. Our position along Gaia's spiral was established when Atlantis rent our firmament asunder. Tellara will face geological upheaval, but nothing on the order of magnitude that could cause a planetary rift. Earth is the planet facing the extraordinary schism. Those who migrate to Terra Nova will be its architects. You will develop art, science, technology, culture, ideology, and all things that make up a global village. "Terra familiar will rebuild on the remnants of your collapsed civilization."

Saffron spoke, "When we ascend, we will attain incorporeal vehicles."

"Like those spherical balls of light hovering among us during the heartdance?" Louie asked.

"Yes," replied Bo Raza.

I said, "I remember seeing a luminescent sphere emerging during Violet's ascension."

During the shift, "Tellarans will ascend en mass to this incorporeal state."

"Will you lose gender and sexuality?" asked Jesse who was obliquely eying Juniper.

"Not altogether. Sexual polarity is the creative life force of the Universe. Attraction is the organizing principle. Gravity is metaphysical love. It attracts mass into coherent design. But in the higher, rarefied frequencies, attraction between polarities expresses itself with exquisite subtlety. We won't be missing physical intimacy, if that is what you are wondering about. Conscious spheres of light can interpenetrate. That is an orgasmic experience that I'm looking forward to." Bo Raza finished speaking and Jesse was blushing scarlet. This was more information than he bargained for.

I spoke, "So, our mission is to bring a message to the world: during the planetary shift, we can follow our natural resonance to a higher frequency or remain in our comfortable duality niche."

"Free will," said Javier.

"Easier said than done," said Louie. "Give us an update about what's going on Earthside, Dana."

I shared events at Shelter and in the media. It was important for the Tellarans to understand that some of us couldn't labor in obscurity and were closely watched all the time, while those in the Ozarks, had much more freedom to act.

Louie said, "I never asked, how is Wah'Kon-Tah obscured from Shelter trackers?"

Cosmo answered, "We impose a deflection scheme. People notice our colorful van on the road. They notice the narrow bridge leading toward Wah'Kon-Tah. But as soon as they observe, they lose interest. Their focus moves on. We delayed our arrival in Tellara to put the same deflection scheme on the Shasta house."

"These aren't the droids you're looking for," joked Louie.

"The Jedi mind trick," laughed Joe.

A consensus emerged which led to logistics and an action plan. Sky Dancer, Joe, Cosmo, and Crystal would transport *Tellaran Autumn*, a stockpile of heartplum seedlings, crocus plants, vitalized water, and beehives from Shasta to Wah'Kon-Tah, which would be our home base. Crystal and Cosmo would amass Earth art in Wiltshire, England, in anticipation of the spring portal *Avalon Equinox*.

Alice declared, "I'm remaining on Tellara with Bo and Guna until the spring portal opens. On Earth, I am never free from Shelter's net. When I do return to Earth, I'll bring a message of hope to reptiles seeking to be part of the Individuals Movement."

Louie said, "I'm remaining in Tellara until the equinox, also. I understand there's a chakra healing ritual in Avalon. I have nothing to go back to."

Phoenix said, "Next week, I move to Avalon to begin painting the next portal."

Minerva wanted to stay in Tellara. "I've heard all my life about the Romani's connection to Atlantis. I want to see for myself what memories have endured. Saffron informs me that treasures of the Atlantean Romani survive on Tellara, Antartica to this day. According to our lore, Gypsies migrated from Atlantis to India prior to the last shift. On Earth, our treasures have been lost or destroyed as our people were forced to scatter. I am the keeper of a legacy going back thousands of years. I have tangible proof to give to the clans."

"How do you know that Antarctica covers the remnants of Atlantis? On Earth, that's just fringe speculation."

Saffron answered, "Atlantis was a global maritime culture, an epoch, not just a single location. In the Atlantic Ocean, there was a central island chain named the Atlas Isles with a capital city on the big island named Atlantis. When the glaciers melted, coastal cities worldwide were flooded, and the world's surface weight was redistributed. This caused an axial pole shift and crustal displacement."

Minerva asked, "What is crustal displacement?"

Saffron answered, "Continental plates don't just drift slowly over geologic ages. They are floating because the crust is detached from the mantle. During violent pole shifts, the equator realigns. Crustal plates can migrate precipitously to different parts of the world. Of course, this would cause greater cataclysmic inundation of all regions and violent wobbling until the surface weight distribution stabilized. In the case of the Atlantean islands, they were completely flooded. They didn't so much sink as migrate from the semi tropics to the south pole."

"How do you explain mile thick ice?"

"The water covering the islands froze rapidly. Each year, it snowed over the Antarctic. Year-after-year, the snow never melted. Over ten thousand years, the buildup of snowfall compressed into miles of compacted glacial ice. We've spent the last two hundred years excavating Atlantean relics, uncovering pyramids, recovering verdant flora, and using polar ice to replenish aquifers on every continent."

"I want to stay in Tellara, Grandmother," Joe Two Feathers said to Sky Dancer.

Sky Dancer said, "I have to go back Joe, but you don't. There are natives in Osage territory that need refuge from hate crimes. I must guide them to Wah'Kon-Tah as I have done for decades."

"Joe could stay with me," offered Minerva. Sky Dancer agreed, and so it was arranged, Sky Dancer would return to Wah'Kon-Tah with Crystal and Cosmo while Joe remained in Tellara with Minerva.

Javier asked, "What about the portal paintings? Shall we leave one in Shasta or transport both to Wah'Kon-Tah?"

I said, "Take *Tellaran Autumn* to Wah'Kon-Tah so Joe and Minerva can travel back and forth anytime they please. Keep *Summer in Tellara* and *Shasta Solstice* here with Jesse for now. If either safe haven is breached, we'll have portals in two places."

Jesse said, "Javier, you warned us that Shelter would be able to trace the location of the Shasta house given enough time."

"That's been taken care of with our deflection scheme," said Crystal. "Shelter operatives might find Shasta, the subdivision, even the road, but they will drive by the house a hundred times without noticing it."

Louie asked, "So your Galactic technology must be impervious to reptilian tracking."

Cosmo answered, "Deflection isn't technology. It's concentrated thought."

"So, it really is a Jedi mind trick!" laughed Joe.

Javier said, "I plan to retire as soon as I return to San Francisco. I have some loose ends to tie up including collecting the last bit of evidence from Jay's murder investigation. I'll join you in Chicago as soon as possible."

"Chicago! I want to stay in Tellara!" I declared but was overruled.

Saffron said, "You have unfinished business with this Shelter organization."

Sky Dancer said, "You need to split your time between Earth and Tellara."

Phoenix added, "You are in a unique to position to learn what Sheldon Walters plans next."

"I can do all that with my vox from here," I whined.

Phoenix said, "This is the karmic assignment you agreed to thirteen thousand years ago."

I remembered Gwen's notes from Clover's tarot reading, "*Dana, you have a global mission. You must face terrible foes to find your authentic voice. You don't have to do it alone. You have allies and havens in two worlds.*" I was reminded that Gwen Cretzky had offered to be my ally, had even offered to put herself in Shelter's crosshairs to help me without understanding my role as a wayshower. We had agreed to help each other. I reluctantly decided that I must descend back into the snake pit.

Jesse said, "I'm going to need money. Before Louie and Phoenix showed up, I could barely afford toilet paper."

Louie reminded Jesse, "You can get whatever you need from Tellara. You don't even need to leave the house, the now deflected house."

Juniper said, "Come through the portal whenever you please. I'll be here."

Ruth wanted to return to Chicago. "I'll stay with you Mom, until Javier arrives. I was lucky to get my job back. My boss is a big fan of Val's blog." I knew she still hoped to reconnect with Mick. As long as I minded my Ps and Q's at

Shelter, Ruth should be safe. Besides, she had a vox now.

Jesse said, "I might not need money now, but I'll need gas money in order to rendezvous with the rest of the tribe." I emptied my pockets and gave him several hundred dollars. Others chipped in to make sure he had enough money to reach Wah'Kon-Tah in the silver Subaru Forester.

Louie explained money to the Tellarans. "On Earth, we need coins and bills for simple necessities, for survival."

Phoenix chimed in that he had been forced to learn about buying and selling as an alien visitor. Seeing capitalism through Tellaran eyes was disconcerting. But it did not negate our need for funding. We'd all need to quit our jobs this spring. We needed supplies for Wah'Kon-Tah, escape plans, seeds, art, and whatever expenses arose in our mission to explain Tellara's message about the planetary shift.

Saffron explained the basis for a resource-based economy to us Earthborn. We were supplied with, precious trinkets that could be pawned or auctioned on eBay. We felt embarrassed to take these freely given gifts, but pragmatism overruled our sensibilities.

I said, "We have a rich benefactor in Chicago, Gwen Cretzky." But when I said her name aloud, Louie and my kids flinched.

"You can't trust a Cretzky!" Louie cried.

"Gwen's different." I defended.

"Yeah, She's crazy!"

"In a good way. She wants to help. Very soon, we're going to share our experiences as alternate world contactees. How will we know when it's the right time to whistle-blow on the deadliest corporation in the world? To disclose humanity as a slave race? The planetary shift?"

"We'll all figure it out together," answered Javier.

"That's right, Mom, we're a team of wayshowers with voxes," seconded Ruth.

"In need of training," said Louie.

The discussion veered into communications. Javier said, "We need to devise a new way to stay in contact with each other. We'll be separated and vulnerable. Due to its tentacles in intelligence agencies around the globe, Shelter overhears everything we share via phones, social media, and Skype."

"Javier and I got our audio-telepathy tool working for the first time just before we arrived. It took weeks of practice."

Jesse said, "It's time to dispense with the Three Stooges alter egos. If that alias hasn't been penetrated, it will be soon."

"The Three Stooges? What's that?" asked Robin.

To my chagrin, Javier, Louie, and Jesse launched into a painfully accurate spontaneous impersonation of Moe poking out Curly's eyes and Curly slapping himself in the face yelping nyuk! nyuk! nyuk! Then Moe held Larry in a headlock and inflicted a series of painful nuggies while Larry howled a high pitched whoot! whoot! whoo! I regarded the Tellarans, mortified. The Tellaran women stared in bewildered disgust. But the Tellaran men were laughing, even the elders. What Y-chromosomal, lowest common denominator had we wrought? Even on Tellara, men thought the Three Stooges were funny and women were repulsed.

Later in the morning, we were surprised to be honored by the elders for our contributions to Tellaran Society.

"What contribution?"

"Earth Art," said Buffalo.

I objected, "Phoenix collected the art over many months. We only formed a human chain for a few hours to transport the artifacts to Tellara. Tellarans in Shastise and Giza helped to organize store the massive collection in the geometric constructs."

"It was a joint effort and more fun than work," said Joe. But the Tellaran elders were emphatic regarding the priceless gift our world had provided.

Buffalo said, "The conflict-ridden polarized mindset is staggeringly eye-opening. We had no idea polarity could produce such virtuosity, so painful and beautiful at the same time."

Juniper said, "Competition in sports, wars, religions, and politics baffles us. But we recognize that not everything about duality is corrupt, it is the source of humor, genius, agony, and ecstasy."

"Beautifully stated!" said Javier. "And good to hear that Earth has something to offer Tellara."

"But not your best news today, is it Javier?" Jesse nudge his elbow.

All eyes turned to Javier, who looked at me. "Dana and I have an announcement."

I moved next to Javier, held up my ring finger, and displayed the brilliant crystals for all to see. "Dana and I are getting married," my fiancé announced gently. The room buzzed with congratulations and questions.

"When do you plan to marry?" Ruth asked.

"This week," Javier replied.

This news brought an explosion of excited comments.

"In Tellara?" asked Juniper.

Minerva announced, "I brought the traditional tsweeka to celebrate, homemade plum wine."

"Since Bo, Guna, and Alice will not cross to Earth, why not marry in Tellara?" asked Louie. "Everyone you love best is here."

"In the Pyramid?" prompted Saffron.

This notion stimulated another outburst of ideas. "Men and women dance together at weddings!" said Heron, still euphoric over his recent rejoining.

Saffron said, "There is also a private Tellaran Wedding Dance Ritual that the bride and groom do on the first night of their marriage. Heron and I can coach you."

"We have the log lodge reserved for the next five days," Saffron offered. "Most of us could stay there."

"We planned all along to marry in Tellara," said Javier.

"Mom, you could find a Tellaran wedding dress! I would love to find a Tellaran caftan for myself."

"Let's go upstairs and see the chamber where you can marry," said Saffron. "We can heartdance."

We ascended spiral staircases to the next floor, Javier levitating Minerva. The second tier of the pyramid was taken up by another chamber, smaller than the ground floor, but still vast. It was decorated with rippling bas-relief walls of sculpted glyphs, mosaics, and tile floors in geometric designs. The men formed a circle around the outer perimeter, the women gathered in the center. The chanting and drumming began. The dancing began. Images emerged on the fourth-dimensional tapestry. It was Earth's most magnificent artistic glories, ancient and modern, paintings, mosaics, photographs, sculptures, film clips, dances, songs, and instrumental musical compositions. The imagery formed a kaleidoscopic, symphonic web of moving images from humanity's artistic legacy. The heartdance lasted almost an hour and left us breathless with ecstasy.

The summit ended just after noon. The discussions had been draining, the dance vivifying. Before leaving, we climbed to the third tier of the pyramid and spent quiet time in the meditation space. Four alters flanked the perimeter in cardinal directions. Each alter dedicated to offerings of water, the land, the sky, and the stars; the four elements, water, earth, air, and fire. A central alter was devoted to the fifth element, the quintessence, the liquid loving light described by mystics and poets. Golden sparks swirled from the alter to the apex of the golden capstone. As we meditated, a joyful reverence closed our ceremony.

On the walk back to the log lodge, Louie told me that when he had to depart Tellara for the final time, he planned to settle in Wah'Kon-Tah and be a beekeeper. "We all have to end up somewhere. I'm not going to go back to Chicago. I'm not going to New Orleans without Hal. I'm not ready to start over in a new city and certainly not in the insurance industry. I think that the nearest place for me to call home on Earth is with Sky Dancer in the Ozarks. I understand why Heron found peace with bees and flowers during his years of isolation."

"That's where I'd go if I didn't have to return to Chicago." We hugged.

We spent the rest of the day in the log lodge training with our voxes. Louie had become very advanced and helped Bo and Phoenix coach. The newbies made repeated mistakes, bumping off walls and laughing together. But we all practiced the cloaking tool with deadly solemnity. I said, "When Louie and I were trapped in the cave, and the Shelter goons were looking for us, we had to hover, cloaked for hours."

Louie elaborated, "But the sonic cutter, heat, and light tools were every bit as crucial to our survival."

Phoenix warned the new wayshowers as he had once warned me, "You can penetrate and cross through solid objects when cloaked by your vox. But, the instant you do, you will leave a quantum residue that reptilian RAT-TRACK can detect. From that point forward, they will relentlessly seek your vox signature. Your lives depend on each other's caution."

***

It was December 23rd. I had a wedding to plan, a dress to find, and Christmas gifts to resource. We looked around Shastise for gifts and clothes. Unlike resort areas on Earth, Shastise did not double as a boutique gift center. There was no actual town. The region was a wild nature preserve. We forgot about shopping and savored the unspoiled beauty of this region. Hiking in winter mountains is easy with voxes. We stayed warm and levitated over gnarly obstacles. We also entered the excavated opening to the mountain and peered down the bottomless shaft, imagining the world of Inner Earth. That evening we returned to the lodge elated but empty-handed.

"It's too late to shop anywhere tonight," said Ruth.

To which Juniper replied, "If it's evening in Shastise, it's morning in Giza."

"And Giza is filled with clothing outlets of all kinds!" I declared.

"Christmas Eve in Giza it is," said my groom.

"We can get there through the dining room!" said Louie, and we all got our second wind. Traipsing down to the winter portal, we crossed into the Shasta, California dining room, then hopped back through *Tellaran Autumn* to park lands alongside the Nile. Minerva remained behind with Saffron, Cosmo and several Elders in the Shastise log lodge. It was winter in Giza, but the ground was dry and the sky clear. Retail heaven awaited; no, make that resource heaven. My groom and I kissed and bid each other adieu, promising to meet up for a late lunch at Tulip's bistro.

Ruth, Alice, Sky Dancer, Crystal, Juniper, Guna, and I set off toward the far end of the Nile Bridge. Javier, Louie, Jesse, Phoenix, Joe, Robin, and Heron entered a men's emporium center filled with caftans, turbans, and sultan-type pants and vests.

Our merry party entered a ladies' dress boutique filled from wall to wall with racks of designer dresses. Ruth and Alice went nuts and even Sky Dancer, the no-nonsense matriarch, got a twinkle in her eyes. To my surprise, Crystal got into the spirit of dressing up. The proprietress approached. "You are the Earthborn wayshowers, are you not?" Our light skin and diminutive sizes gave us away anywhere on Tellara.

"Yes. I need a wedding dress and my friends need formals."

"Formals?"

"An Earth term for the fanciest you've got."

"We have a wonderful new line of Earth Movie dresses."

"Really? Why?"

"Oh, Earth movies are the absolute rage on Tellara. Your movies arrived just in time for the ascension and we have all gone rapturous integrating the wonders of duality into Tellaran designs. Come, see for yourselves," said the woman, who told us her name was Acacia.

Ruth and Alice were rhapsodic over the myriad Tellaran caftans, but I found myself drawn to the beautiful, film-fashion, hand-sewn, Hollywood knockoffs. I pulled out about ten dresses in my size to try on. The dressing rooms were a colorful chaos of 'oohs and ahs' as we took turns modeling our finery. Acacia brought us tea and more selections she fancied.

Sky Dancer looked regal in a deep plum caftan embroidered with birds in flight, their feathered wings, a multi-hued array of finely woven threads. Alice selected an iridescent, silver and white caftan with matching headdress that accentuated her cocoa complexion. Guna chose an amethyst and silver chiffon Earth Movie design that I thought I'd seen on the red carpet. Ruth chose a floral fuchsia and black geometrically cut, clingy sari with a slit nearly to her hip. It was slinky and sexy. She looked hot. Juniper tried on several Earth Movie dresses. She moved like Cyd Charisse in crimson. Crystal asked if I minded if she wore a crystalline white, beaded dress. I told her I didn't, because I would not be wearing white.

I selected a pale periwinkle chiffon with pastel blue silk lining. The bodice fell into crisscrossed ruching embroidered with tiny white primroses. It flared slightly to an A-line skirt with a layered, fluted hem. Diaphanous cap sleeves fluttered to my elbows. The dress shimmered, flattered my figure, clung, and moved with me. Like a star out of a 1940's movie, I had been born to wear this dress.

Most of us selected headpieces as well, but Ruth convinced me to just weave some flowers into my hair and wear it down and curled. She would style it for me. On Earth, almost no one could pull a wedding off in one day. But the pyramid temple had been reserved for our group for this weekend well in advance. Saffron assured me that food and flowers would not be a problem.

Saffron, herself, would officiate. She had given Javier and me a book filled with Tellaran poetry from which to select our vows.

It was time to settle up with the proprietress, an awkward point in a resource economy. But Acacia put me at ease immediately. She happily piled the carefully selected accessories on her counter and began expertly packing dresses in wardrobe bags. "The key to a successful resource-based economy is to never take more than you need. Everyone gives. Everyone shares. Everyone works. Our payment is friendship."

"We don't feel we've given our fair share. We're visitors on your planet."

"Nonsense! Not only has your art infused our culture with untold riches, but you've shared your very DNA!"

"You know about the DNA?"

"Everybody knows about the DNA! We are all over the moon with hope for the little Zetas!"

"I'm glad. I didn't realize it was so widely known."

Acacia laid her hand on mine and delayed me as I prepared to pick up my packages. "I have another boon to ask of you in exchange for my merchandise, wayshower."

"Name it."

"I'd like to attend your nuptials tomorrow." I was charmed. Acacia had been so disarmingly genuine and friendly. On Earth, her request might have been unseemly. On Tellara, it was an acknowledgment of community. "You are most welcome to join us."

"Then, I'll see you tomorrow in Shastise," Acacia smiled.

We left the store and rummaged through several crafty outlets for Christmas gifts. By late afternoon, we'd been shopping for five hours of colorful chaos. It was time to retrace our steps to Tulip's bistro where we'd dined, the night I met Bo and Guna Raza. The menfolk were waiting for us in the brick and tapestry back room. So were Saffron, Cosmo, Buffalo, and Minerva. Middle Eastern music was playing, and an array of spicy, aromatic appetizers was spread across the long dining table. I took my seat at Javier's side and we greeted each other warmly.

"Merry Christmas," toasted Javier as we raised our glasses of mulled wine.

"Yuletide Blessings" said Jesse.

"Matunda ya Kwanzaa!" said Alice.

"Happy Hanukkah!" said Crystal. "Cosmo and I honor all holy days."

Javier looked over my load of packages and asked, "Are you ready?"

I smiled and whispered, "This is going to be interesting." Just like that. Our Christmas Eve Rehearsal Dinner began. Ruth told everyone that Acacia had been invited.

Javier shared "That's good because I invited Leel and Jeej, along with Tulip and Ibis, the owner of the Men's Bazaar."

Our waiter, Elk, remembered Louie from previous visits. Elk offered to give us the "royal treatment," and laughed uproariously at his own joke, which, he explained, was the new 'Earth slang.' He was still laughing when he returned with a pitcher of amber ale. "There is no royalty on Tellara," he chortled to himself as he moved around the table.

"That's delightful, Elk. It's nice to see you again," I said.

"I'll see you tomorrow at the wedding," he replied. "Tulip and I are catering!"

"Wonderful!" Javier and I declared together.

"Royal treatment. You crazy Terrans!"

Ruth asked, "What's this about sharing DNA, Mom?" So, Louie, Javier, and I explained to our tribe about our trip to the Gray's Laboratory and our tour of their genetic project.

After dinner we went our separate ways. Most of the Earthborn returned to the Shasta house to wrap presents. Tellarans didn't have giftwrap, but we used pretty paper and colorful fabrics to craft our own designs. That night in bed, neither Javier nor I could sleep. "This is the strangest, fastest wedding plan I've ever heard of," I sighed.

Javier replied, "Saffron, Heron, Louie, and Phoenix say they have it all under control. On the day after Christmas, we'll have the ceremony in the Red Pyramid and the reception in the log lodge. In addition to Elk, locals are bringing food and are included on the guest list."

"The wedding guest list is getting crazy. By Tellaran custom, everybody who helps is invited, so everybody wants to help. Oh, God, tomorrow is Christmas!"

"And you wanted simple. Well, Dana Travers, Wayshower of Worlds, nothing is simple anymore." After snuggling with both of us for several minutes, Rip settled in a comfy chair on my side of the room and began to snore contentedly. Javier and I cuddled and slept.

＊

When I awoke, the house was bustling. Louie had a crew busy in the kitchen and others were intermittently ferrying art to Tellara. Javier sat with Sky Dancer and Minerva. I joined them with a tray of coffee and fruit. After breakfast, we all crossed to Shastise and hiked across the snow, our arms laden with gifts and pastries. The Tellarans were up and waiting, the Christmas tree ablaze with lights, ornaments, and glass icicles. Beneath the tree were dozens of gifts, wrapped, beribboned and tagged. The gift exchange was a melee of fascinated exclamations, while Christmas carols filled the air. Tellarans had no one holiday where there was an all-out gift exchange among this many people. I kept my giving simple. Everyone except Javier received a stained glass, star tetrahedron Christmas tree ornament handmade by a Giza artisan named Persimmon. I gave Javier a masculine gold ring embedded with blue sapphires and lapis. I received gloves, a stuffed white toy rabbit, a miniature Christmas tree, Tellaran lace, a carved wooden dog that resembled Rip, a few crystals, sapphire earrings to match my ring, and from Phoenix, drawings of people and places we'd visited together. The Tellarans were delighted with the music, giftwrap, and gift exchange.

We got our cameras out and took photos of the group. The entire gathering posed between the Yule log and Christmas tree: Nine Earthborn: Ruth, Jesse, Javier, Louie, Minerva, Sky Dancer, Joe, Alice, and me; Seven Tellarans: Saffron, Phoenix, Bo Raza, Guna Raza, Heron, Robin, and Juniper. Later, Leel and Jeej joined us. Minerva was unfazed to see the gray aliens, but Ruth and Jesse were astonished. And there stood Crystal, in her illumined Pleiadian glory, and Cosmo, the magnificent giant ebony Vegan. We were truly a galactic family.

"Joe asked, "Do you think you'll use gift wrapping paper next year?"

Phoenix answered gently, "We won't be corporeal next year." That made us all get quiet.

Saffron asked, "Do you cut down a precious tree every year for every household?"

"No," I answered, "It's not like that. Not everybody on Earth celebrates Christmas. Trees are grown on vast Christmas tree farms for this annual harvest. But many families use artificial trees, made to look real; they last for years. Only a few families still cut trees from the wild forests. Many people use living trees in pots that can be planted outside in the spring. I buy a living tree every year that I donate to a conservation group. Earth wastes many things. Earth deforests huge swaths of precious woodlands. But there is a growing consensus that conservation of trees is a vital part of our survival."

"We know that trees talk to each other," Joe added.

"This tree is going back into the hillside in a few days," said Guna Raza.

"Good to know," said Javier.

"Why don't you grow more hemp? It's the best construction material on Tellara," said Heron. "You wouldn't have to cut down trees."

"Complicated story," said Javier.

"This lodge is made of hemp logs," said Heron, which caused us all to look at the walls in wonder.

Louie announced, "I'm heading back to Shasta to prepare a traditional Christmas and Thanksgiving menu rolled into one with vegan options. All are welcome to help and to dine."

"None of the Raza clan are attending," lamented Robin.

"Don't you have leftovers on Tellara? Alice teased.

When I returned to the Shasta house, Christmas carols and aromatic fragrances permeated every room. Phoenix asked us to share our favorite Christmas movies. We watched *It's a Wonderful Life* together and the Tellarans loved it. They loved George Bailey and Clarence the Angel. They roared at the dance scene over the swimming pool. They marveled at Uncle Billy's Crow. They cried when the bank examiner tore up his warrant and joined in the carols. They fretted when Mr. Potter did not get his karmic comeuppance but speculated about his next incarnation.

All afternoon, we transported art to Tellara while listening to carols in the dining room. Tellaran friends came and went throughout the day. The work of transporting art could have gone faster if all three portals were open. Our day was filled with good company and an endless stream of roasted chestnuts, stuffed mushrooms, rum balls, and eggnog. In the afternoon, Leel and Jeej entered our dining room.

"Welcome to Earth." I said. "Do you eat?"

"We are hybrids," they declared in unison, as if this explained all.

"OK, two more seats at the table."

Robin announced that he wanted to learn more about Earth culture and civilization. "I have found that the best way to learn about people is through their stories, their art, and their rituals." Joe offered to be Robin's guide. The two boys decided to learn about parades, ball games, movies, and, later, parlor games, if anyone was up for a challenge. Heron decided to spend time in the TV room with his grandchildren. Juniper joined in, followed by Jesse. Javier took Minerva to rest before dinner. Sky Dancer and Ruth joined Louie in the kitchen. Javier and I set the table and then took the dogs to Shastise for a romp. No one stepped outside the house in Shasta, California.

Howls of laughter erupted from the small TV room. I peeked and observed a scene from the zany movie called *Bill and Ted's Excellent Adventure*. This is, apparently, what Joe and Jesse thought would help explain life on Earth to Tellarans. I was dumbfounded. But Joe explained to me that the characters in the movie were trying to do the same thing as the Tellarans by meeting historical characters from Earth. The Tellarans wanted to understand human humor. They had wearied of trying to understand football. The glories of competitiveness were lost on the Tellarans. But comic movies had an engaging appeal.

A scene came on where Napoleon visited a water slide amusement park and went crazy on the slides. Heron laughed so hard he fell out of his chair. Heron, the water whisperer, was watching a bully playing in water with children, splashing and carrying on with such abandon that he lost himself in the silly scene. Saffron stood beside me, unshed tears filling her eyes. "I haven't heard him laugh like that since we were newly married. There must be something to this Earth humor that is born from the pain of duality." She shook her head and walked off to see if she could help in the kitchen. But everything was ready, and Louie intercepted us.

"Dinner!" Louie called. Louie, Sky Dancer, Phoenix, and Ruth had been cooking for two days. A feast of traditional fare and vegetarian delights was served. Dinner conversation took a convoluted path as each of us disclosed our latest adventures.

Robin explained his understanding of Earth drama and comedy that brought howls of laughter from the rest of us. Juniper enchanted Jesse describing Tellaran art. Jesse was eagerly anticipating moving statuary. Ruth listened quietly with a whimsical smile but said little. Louie caught us up about his intercontinental travels on Tellara. He'd gone native. Life had regained some of its harmony for my grieving friend. Leel and Jeej ate sparingly and seemed to like the sweet potatoes best.

Javier said, "The beehives are in the garage being kept warm under thermal blankets. Sky Dancer will transport them to the Ozarks and nurture them until spring, when the bees emerge naturally."

Sky Dancer brought up an issue Louie and Javier had discussed in Antalya, "If these newly introduced Tellaran bees follow typical adaptation patterns, they will die off when exposed to Earth's colony collapse disorders. Wah'Kon-Tah is remote enough that we have acres of wildflower fields to nourish our remaining hives, but we've lost thousands of bees to monoculture, GMO's, and toxic insecticides."

Heron said, "Many Tellaran bees will die, but not all. And those that survive will thrive. Once a Tellaran bee becomes a queen, her hybrid workers will be robust. In a few years, when the heartplums and crocuses blossom, apiaries will revive regionally, then around the continent, and around the world as migrating birds deposit heartplum seeds abroad."

"This spring will be a perfect time to expand the heartplum orchard that we started last summer. Bees love the heartplum blossoms. They also love the fertile Tellaran crocuses."

We were all too full to eat dessert. Ruth had baked two pumpkin pies, two apple pies, and a rum cake. There was vanilla ice cream, Irish coffee for the hearty, decaf, whipped cream, and fruit. The Tellarans were delighted with our meal. Phoenix had sweet potatoes and dressing for dessert. I packed up oodles of leftovers to deliver to the Raza Clan.

Javier said, "Growing up we played games after a holiday diner, usually Charades or Pictionary."

Jesse said, "That might not work with an interplanetary group just learning about each other's art forms. After today, they know of *It's a Wonderful Life*, but what about *Sponge Bob Square Pants*?"

"You just gave away my idea!" Ruth joked.

"We'd need objects common to both worlds that can be drawn or pantomimed. After much discussion we made up a game. Each player would pick a drawing of a common object and stick it on their forehead without looking. On your turn, the others would give any kind of clue, from pantomime to verbal clues, anything but say the actual word.

I gave an example. "I might have a picture of a mountain on my forehead with the word written below. I wouldn't see it. You all would. Someone could make a peak with their arms." I demonstrated. "Others might say, a tall rock formation covered in snow. It has a tree line. We can see one from our window. Like that. I would guess until I got it." Everyone seemed to grasp the rules.

We divided into two teams mixed with players from each planet. Each team drew pictures of common objects on sticky papers and wrote the name beneath.

Ruth was up first. She had a picture of fluid waves with the word 'water' printed below.

Louie made wavy motions with his hands.

Leel guessed, "internal gravity waves."

"Leel, it's not your turn to guess."

Jesse said, "wet."

Jeej guessed "geophysical fluid dynamics."

"Jeej, Ruth is guessing. But those are good clues."

"It comes in faucets, lakes, and rivers," hinted Javier

"Water," guessed Ruth and we all clapped.

Javier, having given the winning clue stood to take his turn.

Jeej objected. "Why did you continue playing when we guessed correctly the first two times?"

Ruth answered showing her card, "Jeej, the picture was waves and the word was water."

Jeej objected, "Internal gravity waves and geophysical fluid dynamics obey the same physical laws as water."

"Right you are. That's a point for Leel, a point for Jeej, and point for Javier," Louie said cheerfully. Javier is up," We clapped for Leel and Jeej and told them, "Great job."

"Don't I get a point?" chuckled Ruth.

Javier pasted a card to his forehead. It was a picture of a tight spiral with the word 'coil' written below.

Jeej said, "Solenoid DNA.".

"Less specific, more generic," said Javier.

"Nautilus shell," Phoenix said making a narrowing circle with his hand.

Javier guessed, "Spiral."

"Red shelled cochlea," said Leel.

Javier said, "coil," and we all cheered."

"One point for Javier and two points for Leel and Jeej. Are you sure you haven't played this before?" said Louie our unofficial scorekeeper as we all descended into giggles.

Now, Phoenix, a Tellaran was up. Let's see how well our instructions translated. Phoenix drew a card. It was a picture of a rain cloud with the word 'raincloud' written below.

Jeej said, "Hydrologic cycle."

I said, "Precipitation from the sky."

Phoenix guessed rain. He was partly right and was told to keep guessing.

Javier said, "overcast."

I said, "cumulonimbus."

Phoenix guessed, "rain cloud."

"You didn't get any points this time, Jeej."

Jeej protested, "The rain cloud is part of the hydrologic cycle."

"We needed a specific answer," said Louie. It was interesting to see Jeej almost pout. He wasn't passionate nor was he competitive, but he was confused as to why his perfectly accurate answer didn't earn him a point.

I was up with a post it on my forehead.

Leel's guess was as good as a clue, "instrument in the heartdance."

"Drum," I guessed.

Ruth moved her fingers as if playing piano or typing. I guessed keyboard and won a round of applause. The game went on. Despite the fact that we'd made the game as simple as possible, it still got chaotic. Leel and Jeej never got the concept that only the player with the post-it note was supposed to guess. But their guesses worked as clues, and Louie kept giving them points. Everybody got a turn. We kept playing because despite the lack of coordinated rules, this was fun and funny.

Jeej went last. The picture and label on his sticker were of a dancing woman.

"Heartdance," said Leel.

"Leel, don't use part of the word as a clue," Louie explained. "Jeej, here's another clue, Dana, Ruth, Alice,"

"Terrans," said Jeej.

"Saffron, Guna, Juniper."

"Now you're mixing up planets," Jeej objected.

Ruth stood up and danced a little provocatively. Everyone clapped.

After several more clues and missed guesses, Leel spoke up, almost agitated.

"You are trying to get him to say he is a dancing woman and he is neither!"

Jeej was almost indignant, "I am not female, and I don't dance." He took his sticker off and sat in as near to a huff as an unemotional Zeta could.

Louie said, "Yes, but you got the most points, Jeej, so you're the all-around winner." We all applauded Jeej who seemed mollified.

After games ended, we all turned to our respective beds. Heron, Saffron, Juniper, and Robin departed through *Shasta Solstice* to the log lodge. Leel and Jeej went back to Giza via *Tellaran Autumn*. Joe negotiated a sleepover from his grandmother and joined Robin, along with Corky and Belle. Rip stayed with me.

CHAPTER 23

It was my wedding day. I was up at six, the same time I arise for a normal workday. Those of us who stayed in the Earth house took turns in the shower and in the kitchen, snacking on leftover goodies. Late morning, we set off through *Shasta Solstice* to Shastise, Tellara. I stood alone for a moment in that pristine winter field. Aromas of smoke and coffee arose from the lodge. In daylight, I could see acres of snow-covered, tree-filled landscape dotted by dozens of geodesic domes. It wasn't snowing, which was strange, because it was always snowing in the painting. It was always midnight in the painting. Why didn't the painting change with the time of day and weather? I thought of *Summer in Tellara*, the sunlit meadow where it was always dawn. What happened when it rained? Magic was confusing.

Lost in thought, I heard someone call my name. Bo, Guna, and Alice approached from the log lodge. Alice looked happier and better rested than I'd ever seen her, proudly displaying her mahogany-and-bronze scales, kohl-delineated eyes, and emerald attire.

"We missed you last night. We would have moved the party to Shastise, but Saffron said not to."

"We were busy. Thank you for the feast, by the way." Alice hugged me and said, "I had the best night of my life!"

"You look magnificent!"

"My transformation has only just begun!" We chatted excitedly about all things Tellaran as we made our way toward the lodge.

I was ushered to a small geodesic dome off to the side of the lodge. It was set up with a vanity, a closet, and bathroom. Alice and Ruth kept me company as I prepared. We hung our dresses in the closet and Ruth began weaving small white and purple flowers into my hair.

There was a knock at the door. Leel and Jeej entered. I could tell they were dressed for the occasion because they wore slightly colorful tunics. Leel's was cream with blue smudges. Jeej's was blue with gray splotches. On Earth, these would be a wardrobe malfunction, but for Zetas it was an improvement over their gray on gray. Jeej clutched a metallic case that looked suspiciously like a medical supply kit.

"Jeej!" I demanded, "Did you bring syringes to my wedding?"

"Of course," he replied in his near monotone. "Javier told us not to bring them to the holiday meal, so we waited until the nuptials ceremony."

I groaned, "Oh Jeez!"

"Not Jeez, Jeej," Jeej corrected me.

"Not Jeej, Jeez!" I corrected him.

"Jeej," he countered.

"Jeez. Jeez. Jeez Loueez! Jeezy Creezy Japaneezy Easy Peazy! You don't bring syringes to a wedding!"

"Your biological offspring are here, correct?" asked Jeej.

"Yes."

"They share your mitochondrial DNA, which is passed solely through the mother's chromosomes, correct?"

"Yes."

"This provides us with a genealogical link for your phylogenetic evolution. This is a signature genetic tracer. The tiny lady with dark hair is the maternal grandsire of Javier. Yes?"

"Yes. Er, no. Sire applies to males. What's the female equivalent?" I asked Ruth. "Grand-mere?" she shrugged, jabbing a hairpin a little too hard.

"They, too, share the mitochondrial genealogical link. Like us, you are a genetically engineered species. Your mitochondria are so much more robust."

"Yes, yes, but…" I trailed off.

"And the one called Sky Dancer is maternal grand-mere to the boy, Joe, yes?"

"Grandmother, yes," I was getting the picture.

"Another invaluable mitochondrial link for our database. We brought the syringes to extract epithelial cells from the stomach linings of your Earthborn human wedding guests." Jeej opened his case, extracted a long, thin syringe and started walking determinedly toward Ruth. She whirled to face him, brandishing a curling iron.

"Jeej, please!" I interrupted, "Why are we discussing mitochondrial DNA on my wedding day? You cannot take medical samples from wedding guests at the ceremony. It's just not done."

"But that is to be a meal. How is that different than the holiday Krizmizz meal? We assumed the nuptial ritual would be more structured."

"Structured for non-medically invasive procedures. There are other priorities today."

"Not for us," said Leel. And for a moment, I saw a hint of forlorn fatigue cross the countenance of these single-minded creatures.

"Save the syringes for the reception. I promise to bring up DNA sampling during my toast. Listen, are you two even here for the wedding? Would you rather just get your samples and leave? Or do you want to join in the day's celebration?"

They were quiet for many seconds, then Leel answered, "We are part human. We prefer to be included rather than excluded in milestone rituals. We are trying to integrate our humanity."

"Then you need to get gussied up!" Ruth proclaimed, interjecting a festive note into the strained conversation, and deflecting Jeej's syringe back toward his case. She rummaged through the closet and pulled out whatever colorful accouterment she could find. "Jeej, put that away for now. Leel, come here." Leel obediently approached Ruth, who stood her before the vanity mirror and adorned her head with a filigreed silver tiara. She draped a delicate, glittering silver necklace over Leel's shoulders, covering the top of her tunic. Then it was Jeej's turn. Ruth tied an elegant burgundy and gold cravat in over Jeej's smock. It draped to his waist. We dug up a burgundy felt cap for Jeej. It might have once been a woman's hat but covered his dome with a certain panache. Then Alice turned the two Zetas to view themselves in the full-length mirror. Leel and Jeej stood side-by-side viewing their reflections. A look approaching confusion crossed Leel's face. Jeej looked almost annoyed.

"Adornments," stated Leel flatly.

"They serve no purpose," said Jeej. I think he felt betrayed. They had arrived with the simple expectation of gathering stomach lining epithelial cell samples from wedding guests and gotten themselves bedecked in pointless non-utilitarian finery.

"It's fun to get gussied up every once in a while," explained Ruth.

"Fun?" asked Leel.

"Gussied?" asked Jeej.

"Beauty is its own reward," Alice offered. "Why didn't you come earlier? The summit would have been the perfect occasion to collect DNA samples."

"Our presence was not requested. We were invited for yesterday and today. So, we thought this was our opportunity."

"Why weren't you included at the summit? Who should have invited you?"

"Anyone."

I said, "I apologize. From now on, you have a standing invitation to partake in our group activities whenever I'm in Tellara." Leel and Jeej looked at me, looked at each other, and looked at me again, I think signifying their acceptance.

"Now, you two go find some seats in the temple. We'll be along shortly," said Ruth, ushering the two grays to the dome door. They exited just as Guna Raza entered in all her reptilian finery. She was draped in a richly iridescent amethyst gown with matching bejeweled headdress.

"We are gussied," said Leel apologetically to Guna as she and Jeej shuffled off morosely, Jeej clutching the precious medical kit to his cravat-covered chest. The words "part human" and "prefer to be included rather than excluded," reverberated through my thoughts.

Ruth took me by the hand and led me back to the vanity table, where she resumed weaving flowers through my hair. It struck me that these odd but brilliant grays, these Zeta Reticuli, were our own distant cousins. If Tellaran lore was to be believed, I too, was "part human," and part of many other galactic cousins. We are all hybrid humanoid races throughout the Galactic Family. And in that Galactic Family of shirttail DNA relations, there were the inevitable family alliances and feuds. Looking at Alice, I understood that it was up to each sentient being to choose how easy or difficult their evolution was going to be.

"What are you thinking about Mom?" Ruth asked

"Whatever any bride daydreams about right before her wedding: galactic evolution." Ruth tugged my hair and Alice laughed out loud. She emerged in her lustrous silver and white caftan with an elegant flowered headband. Ruth was stunning in her flowered fuchsia caftan with shimmering black trim. She topped it with a bright pink fascinator suitable for a royal wedding. Then it was time to help me into my dress. I felt like a vision in periwinkle. Ruth had been right about weaving flowers into my hair. Facing the winter chill, draped in fleece from our shoes to our crowns, we levitated together from the dome to the pyramid.

Javier and I had discussed and planned a small wedding. But the Pyramid Temple was packed with Esselen, Comanche, and Giza Elders, Earthborn loved ones, Saffron's extended family, the Raza Clan, Jasmine, Elk, Tulip, Leel, Jeej, Falcon, Acacia, Persimmon, Ibis, and Shastise locals. There were nearly one hundred colorfully garbed guests in attendance. Everyone who had helped in any way to prepare for the wedding was an invited guest. In charming irony, many of the younger Tellarans had opted for Earth-style formal fashions and the Earthborn had all opted for Tellaran draped fashions. I was glad I had selected my periwinkle and blue gown when I saw Javier in his top hat and tails. Like me, he had selected elegant, traditional American apparel. Weren't we just Fred and Ginger?

We gathered in the vast gold-tiled temple. Somewhere from within the walls, Pachelbel's Cannon was being piped. Javier had picked it. The Tellarans hearing it for the first time were enraptured. There was no aisle, just a circular gathering with bride and groom in the center. We exchanged vows selected from Tellaran poetry, listened to Saffron chant while others intoned softly. She then spoke, "I have selected a passage from Gaia. For the gathering of wayshowers, it is especially relevant."

The Tellaran Chronicles of Science and Spirituality
A Message from Gaia

Thirteen thousand years ago, I, Gaia entered the age of Leo. The ice age ended, and glaciers melted, causing a global flooding. This cataclysm was recorded in my flora, fauna, and mineral remains as well as worldwide myths of inundated civilizations. Surviving humans were reduced to sticks and stones.

But some survivors remembered the antediluvian world and codified their knowledge of planetary cycles in megalithic edifices. We are living in a time where there is a confluence of prophecies, calendars, mythos, scientific discoveries, and inner voices urging us to pay attention to terrestrial, lunar, solar, stellar, and galactic seasons.

The planetary shift is upon us. Sentient beings in my dominion have free will and all eternity to decide their rate of evolution. I am your mother. Your health and well-being depend on my health and well-being. I won't wait for you to decide. I am ascending with or without you. What has happened before is happening again. There is nothing new under Sophia.

Javier thanked Saffron and said, "It's time for humanity to create our own harmony and write our next mythos." A nuptial heartdance followed, which levitated participants into swirling spirals. After drifting back to the floor, we moved out of the pyramid and across the snow-covered alpine meadow.

En masse, we entered the log lodge for our reception. Everyone gathered at tables. There was some confusion that no food was laid out, despite extravagant preparations throughout the day. Leel and Jeej, bedecked and beknotted elbowed their way forward to stand at Javier's and my side. It was now or never, time to honor my second vow of the day. I began uncertainly, "On Earth, it is customary to give wedding gifts to a newly married couple. I don't know if this is also a Tellaran tradition, but Javier and I have a singular request for our Earthborn family and friends. We want to give a gift to Tellara."

Javier picked up my narrative, "Tellara has given us so much. Tellara needs something that only Earthborn humans can provide. The Tellaran Zeta Reticuli are cousins to the extraterrestrial race known as the grays to Earth UFOlogists. Both species are in a race against time to breed fertility into their offspring. Zetas share their ancient genetic antecedents with Homo sapiens. On Earth, the grays take whatever biological samples they want. Their human donors are abducted. There is speculation that an ancient pact gave the grays permission to harvest human genetic material from some families."

I spoke, "Here on Tellara, the human gene-pool has become homogenized over the past thirteen thousand years. Many Tellarans have contributed their DNA to the Zetas. But it has not been enough to revivify their species. Earthborn humans from different lineages provide the best hope to generate the mitochondrial DNA that will save the Zetas. This is part of our collective legacy."

Javier took over for me, "Dana, Louie, and I have all donated cell samples. We thought about our decision long and hard. Our DNA will be spliced into hybrid human-Zetas, just like Leel and Jeej." Leel and Jeej bowed to the guests. Jeej started to open his med kit, but Javier restrained him with a gentle hand.

"The Tellaran grays need the help of our other Earthborn guests. Those of you who are willing, please consider it a wedding gift for Dana and me. Your DNA will help create a viable Zeta race here in Tellara."

"It's kind of a slightly invasive procedure." I added ruefully.

Things appeared promising. But then, of course, Jeej had to open his big mouth and his big metal case. "There will be very little abdominal cramping if we extract your stomach lining epithelial cells on an empty stomach. The syringe is self-cauterizing." Jeej whipped out the jumbo syringe from his med kit and brandished it like a switchblade at our stupefied wedding guests. "You'll feel a little pinch at first, but you'll be able to eat and drink within fifteen minutes of the procedure."

"Let's move into the adjacent dome, for privacy," declared Leel, looking directly at me. Jeej took Ruth's hand and lead her to her appointment with genetic immortality. Ruth had known this was coming from our pre-wedding confrontation, so she had had time to consider. She flung her dark curls and shot an "I dare you" look at her brother. Jesse gaped from Ruth, to me, to Louie, and then to Javier, all of whom nodded or shrugged. Joe studied his shoes. Sky Dancer looked unflappable. Minerva grinned.

"It's up to each of you," I announced. "I am sorry you didn't have more time to consider. But, for what it's worth, I donated my DNA, and it wasn't so bad." Javier was at Minerva's side telling her he understood if she didn't want to. But she shooed him away. "Miss a chance to breed Romani DNA into a hybrid extraterrestrial race? Never." And Minerva rose to her four-foot-eleven inches of golden garbed pride and followed Ruth into the back room. One-by-one, Jesse, Sky Dancer, and Joe entered the adjacent dome to donate stomach cells to the humorless hybrids who had made us laugh so hard just last night with their incongruous party games. Jeej still wondered when he was going to get his points.

Crystal and Cosmo hung back. "The Zetas have had Pleiadian and Vegan cells for thousands of years. As beings of light, our DNA is incompatible. We no longer sexually reproduce. We phase in and out of physicality."

"Music," declared Javier and Louie's pre-recorded tape began to play.

"Food!" declared Saffron. And mountains of prepared dishes were carried out of the lodge kitchen and loaded onto the dining tables. There were green soups, fruit salads, garnished vegetables, curries of red, yellow, and green, cheesy potatoes, puddings, cakes, and pies. "How did you manage all this food? I asked, amazed. "Do you have house elves?" Saffron looked at me blankly until I admitted, "It's a cultural reference."

"Dana, dear, we need no such helpers. Everyone contributed."

"On Earth, we call it a potluck."

"'Potluck,' I like that."

Louie's compilation of Big Band and Rock 'n' Roll played in the background. Sinatra was singing *The Way you Look Tonight*. Javier led me to the dance floor. We were still dancing as Ruth and Minerva reentered the room and took seats near the dance floor. There was no head table, just a collection of round tables with no seating chart. Everyone mingled. The Tellaran guests wanted to sit near the Earthborn. They were eager to discuss movies, theater, literature, music, comedy, and war.

Jesse danced with Juniper all night. Louie danced with Ruth, Alice, Guna, Tulip, Jasmine, and finally the bride. We toasted with Minerva's Tsweeka, a homemade pear wine with a wicked kick. We drank a sparkling Tellaran wine called Pezza. We danced, ate, and drank long into the night. I was floating with happiness. Tellarans were floating literally. They loved Sinatra. They loved the Beatles, and Rhythm and Blues. Louie even threw in some Disco. The Tellarans were utterly delighted with our partnered dancing style. They'd seen it in our movies and were eager to try ballroom dancing. They loved to spin each other. Since many of them were at the cusp of ascension, their spinning became ethereal, slow-motion, airborne twirls as Frank sang *Come Fly With Me*. I asked Jeej to dance. He declined, but I told him he was not allowed to say no to the bride. Chagrined, he permitted himself to be dragged to the dance floor and did a binary two-step until I released him from his agony. Javier danced with Leel with similar results. The Zetas were agile but had no rhythm.

As the music struck up Billie Holiday singing *I'll be Seeing You*, I got kind of choked up. Seeing these harmonious humanoids, Homo sapiens, Zeta Reticuli, Draconians, a Vegan, and a Pleiadian was wondrous to behold. Cosmo expanded to his giant 8-foot tall ebony luminous body. Crystal, nearly as tall, and just as radiant danced with him. Phoenix took photographs of everyone.

Would that I could freeze this moment for an eternity. Forks clinked on glasses, drawing me out of my reverie. Javier dipped me and planted a massive kiss on my mouth. I kissed him back eagerly. The Earthborn howled and cheered. The Tellarans caught on and joined in the spirit of romantic manipulation of bride and groom. We celebrated knowing that tomorrow would begin days of work, clean up, travel, and farewells. But tonight, we 'Flew to the Moon' with Frank and twirled 'Here, There, and Everywhere,' with the Beatles, 'Shook, Rattled, and Rolled' with Bill Haley and his Comets, 'Rolled on the River' with Creedence, and 'Hallelujahed' with k.d. lang. When Muddy Waters 'Dusted his Broom,' Louie and Ruth took over the dance floor with a down and dirty boogie that could only have arisen on polarized Earth.

Saffron whispered to me, "I don't think we need to teach you the Tellaran Wedding Dance Ritual."

CHAPTER 24

The next few days flew by. Jesse, Rip, and Belle settled comfortably into the safe house with *Shasta Solstice* and *Summer in Tellara*. Juniper was back and forth helping Jesse download art for Phoenix. Crystal, Cosmo, and Sky Dancer loaded *Tellaran Autumn,* heartplum seeds and seedlings, crocus bulbs, vitalized water jugs, and beehives into the psychedelic van and took off for Wah'Kon-Tah. Javier and I stayed on in Shastise until the last minute. Alice, Louie, Joe, and Minerva waved adieu to us from the base of the snow-covered mountain. They stood alongside Saffron, Heron, Phoenix, Bo, Guna, and Robin.

I didn't like the notion of being in Chicago without a portal, but I was under constant surveillance. The others were shielded by Crystal and Cosmo's deflection scheme. Whatever I had to do at Shelter, I planned to get done quickly. But when I thought of that pesky wayshower's mission, I would be in harm's way wherever I went. The center of the storm was as good a place as any to anticipate our karmic dharma.

Ruth and I traveled with Javier as far as San Francisco. He dropped us at the airport before we could get emotional. We flew back to Chicago while he headed to his precinct to officially retire and peruse old case files. Travel was uneventful and my apartment was quiet. We turned in almost as soon as we walked in the door, anticipating any conversation would be overheard. I slept alone and didn't like it. Ruth and I both had work the next day.

I returned to the office on January second with a stunning blue sapphire and rose quartz ring on my finger and anxious concern. I needn't have worried. No one said a single word about my extra, unplanned days off. Frank Fretz surely knew I was in town but was relieved I had voluntarily returned to Shelter.

In our last conversation, Suzy had rejected everything I told her as meaningless drivel of an inferior subspecies, but after the New Year, changes in her affect were strikingly apparent. She came into the office with a complete makeover. Gone was the garish, thick makeup. Her human visage was clear and smooth, her lips pale pink. She wore a pale rose and beige high-collared print dress that swirled above her knees with a lovely matching pink blazer that offset her flushed complexion. Her hair was light brown with blond highlights, no brassy streaks, no teasing in the short, silky coif that framed her face. She wore the cutest pink sling-backs I'd ever seen. She nodded curtly toward me. She smiled at Maggie. And when she entered the Human Resources wing, I heard her wish her 'team' a Happy New Year. Some even said it back to her. I knew that her outer changes did not reflect an inner conversion. That I had called her a caricature of the worst of her species and declared her behavior blatantly distasteful must have struck nerve.

Vincent returned from the holidays in good spirits. He and Gwen had spent time with their estranged son, Raymond, and done some family healing. Vincent was laidback with the staff. He waved off a mistake that Maggie made and told her that everyone needs an occasional do-over. Suzy spent the whole first week back with her door closed, delighting everyone with her remoteness. The relaxed mood was disconcerting. Only FrankenFretz was his same-old smarmy, albeit well-groomed, self, which maintained some of the familiar office dynamic. Frank had switched his days in Chicago to Mondays, Tuesdays and Wednesdays.

On the second Monday in January, my favorite 'men in black' entered the office. Contrary and Pandemonium marched in breezy unison down the hallway as if they owned the building. Everyone stopped working to stare at the unexpected drama. Frank Fretz greeted them and sent Suzy off with a dismissive nod. She looked rebuked but did not protest. Contrary and Pandemonium huddled with Frank behind closed doors for forty-five minutes. When they came out, they went into Vincent's office. Loud, angry voices emerged. The argument continued for half an hour and I heard my name mentioned twice. Not really thinking of the consequences, I called Gwen and told her what was going on. She was out running errands and made a quick U-turn toward the Shelter Building.

Gwen stepped off the elevator in time to see Vincent being arrested for conspiracy, fraud, and embezzlement. He was handcuffed and escorted out of his office on a needless walk of shame. He and I made eye contact for a moment, then he shifted his gaze to Gwen. An understanding passed between them. Suzy looked on from her office door with unblinking, narrowed eyes, pursed lips, and clenched fists. I could tell from her expression that she had not foreseen this development, nor had she been included in the loop. She might still have feelings for Vincent Cretzky, despite his reconciliation with Gwen and her affair with Frank Fretz. Could she feed off the misery of a human she cared about.

My dislike for Vincent "The Rodent" Cretzky had waned, thanks in a large part to his loopy wife. I knew he had nothing to do with Jay's death. Conspiracy for what? Murder? He'd never killed anyone—those ill-fated insurance claimants whose settlements he'd denied, notwithstanding. Neither had he embezzled. The so-called fraud he'd committed was company policy. I knew a scapegoat when I saw one. Gwen went into Vincent's office and started making phone calls, presumably to lawyers. Frank Fretz entered, wrenched the phone from her hand, and roughly dragged her out into the hall. "This office is locked out. Its contents are evidence." Gwen avoided making eye contact with Frank. She caught Suzy watching her and stared back until Suzy turned away. Bravo Gwen.

Gwen came and stood at my side while newly arrived women in black, Blondie and Brownie, strung yellow police tape across Vincent's office and proceeded to box up the contents of his files. Before leaving, Gwen whispered to me, "We have business to discuss. I'll be at the Ravenswood Bar at 5:15 tonight." Without a backwards glance, she walked to the elevator.

I arrived at the bar, spotted Gwen at a corner table and sat down. "You know we're being watched. We huddled at our secluded table. Gwen pretended to cry. We both got drinks and, through her tissue Gwen spoke urgently. "Vincent hid some documents in the conference room files. These documents will incriminate both Fretz and Walters and will exonerate Vincent. He's been copying and saving files since you warned him that he might be a fall guy."

"I didn't think he took me seriously."

"He didn't, at first, but I did. Remember, Sheldon Walters' history with my father. We've anticipated this arrest since last summer. Vincent realized he could never get anything out of the building, so he hid his evidence in plain sight. Can you get it?"

"Me? I am under as much surveillance as Vincent." But even as I protested, I knew I could use my vox to cloak this stealthy operation.

"He trusts you, Dana. He heard the higher ups talking about it when you were on the run. They think you've got some allies in high places. So does Vincent. So do I." Gwen sobbed convincingly in her tissue as two unfamiliar gentlemen moved in to occupy the table next to us.

"Can we buy you ladies a drink?"

"No thanks." I was polite but knew perfectly well they had been sent to eavesdrop. Gwen snuffled outrageously into her hanky. I patted her arm reassuringly. We moved to the bar to order another round, leaving our frustrated followers to sip their drinks. At the bar, Gwen spoke again, this time while holding her glass to her mouth. "The security code to the conference room is 3739*. Once inside you'll see a bank of file cabinets that covers the entire back wall."

"I know it."

"Second drawer from the bottom, second cabinet from the right. Find a simple manila envelope with the word 'Settlements' written on it. Get it and get out. Vincent and I will rendezvous with you tomorrow morning, right at the time you would be going to work. We'll be at the gas station at the corner of Westchester and Robles."

"Louie would have liked that."

"That's why Vincent chose it. We can't go back, Dana."

"I know, but how will Vincent be with you? He's been arrested."

"His attorney is getting him out on bail as we speak. Really, so far, they've only been able to drum up white-collar accusations. The conspiracy thing will never stick. The judge is a dear friend of my father's. Remember the Delaney name? Shelter isn't the only one in this state with connections."

"Shouldn't you be with him now?"

"I'm following our plan. I'm here with you. We prepared. We need the original documents before they are missed. Can you do it Dana? Will you? I know it's a big ask, but we don't know where else to turn, and already you've outwitted those Shelter devils for months. Vincent's docs include memos directly from Sheldon Walters detailing how to 'legally' circumvent state and federal insurance and banking regulations, so long as certain state and federal politicians played along."

"I can help, Gwen. It would be my pleasure to stick it to them. The more incriminating stuff we can get on Shelter, the harder it will be for them to crawl out of the hole they've dug for themselves."

Gwen squeezed my hand in gratitude. Our unwelcome reptilian pick-ups now flanked us at the bar. "You sure you ladies wouldn't like to join us for a drink?" One of them beamed a charming, come hither grin. Still in character, Gwen sobbed loudly and drunkenly, into her hanky, "hfffff fffff wawawawa fff."

"I have to get my friend home, family issues," I whispered to our would-be dates. We left together and Gwen took me back to my car at the Sh.I.T. parking lot.

CHAPTER 25

Gwen sped off, sober as a judge, presumably to meet up with her recently released husband at their upscale Chicago estate, there to wait until our morning rendezvous, maybe even to get some sleep, trusting his wellbeing to me, his insubordinate subordinate. In order to help Vincent out of serious trouble, I had accepted a dangerous job. Was this part of being a wayshower, or just plain foolhardy? Instead of getting into my car, I walked to an unfamiliar neighborhood building, slipped into an alcove, and emerged cloaked, insensible. Once outside, I levitated a few inches so that I would leave no footfalls in the newly fallen snow.

Waiting for someone to exit, I slipped through the open doors into the vestibule. It turned out to be Maggie Coutts, hurrying home after an intense day at work. She looked shaken. To Maggie, Shelter Insurance and Trust was an enduring pillar of capitalist righteousness. Seeing Vincent arrested unraveled her world.

I sailed up the stairs and flitted into my floor behind a janitor. The office was deserted. Maggie must have been the last to leave for the day. The key code Gwen had given me worked perfectly. I entered the dark conference room and went directly to the file bank. Second drawer from the bottom, second cabinet from the right, all the way to the back in a nondescript manila envelope with the innocuous label "Settlements," hidden in plain sight. I stuffed the envelope into my bag and closed the drawer silently. I turned to survey the room. Nothing was disturbed. I prepared to leave as imperceptibly as I'd entered, when voices in the hall deterred me. I levitated myself on top of the cabinets, scooched into the corner, and sat cross-legged.

Fluorescent light flooded the room. Shelter's finest entered the room. Frank Fretz and Sheldon Walters led the way, followed by Agents Contrary and Pandemonium. Kek, the K2 killer, entered, elegant in a black leather jacket. He removed it to reveal black turtleneck, black slacks, and a black beanie pulled over his forehead and ears. He wore a shoulder holster that packed a magnum, and he had a Bowie knife sheathed at his belt. I imagined he carried other weapons. No one noticed me, cloaked in the silent, still shadows.

Walters declared, "The others will arrive via chrono-filament at any moment."

To my amazement, two translucent people appeared at ceiling level, descended down invisible cables, solidifying as they landed in the opposite corner. I recognized Senator Oral Rockbottom and Congresswoman Fanny Gnositall, two movers and shakers from Washington D.C., ostensibly on opposite sides of the bipartisan divide. Then, Chicago's own Monsignor Muncher slid into the room in ebony Jesuit robes. This demonstration of reptilian technology stunned me. They could not only peer around corners in time, they could slip in and out of moments in spacetime. How far was their reach? How advanced was their technology?

Frank was pouring expensive brandy and Suzy came carrying a steno pad. One by one, the human facades dropped and were replaced by scales of various shades. Sheldon Walters was magnificent, tall, and shimmering with white scales and cream highlights. Unmasked, he was clearly the alpha male, or should I say, Alpha Draconian. Kek was equally commanding with scales of white with ice blue highlights. After experiencing the beauty of the Razas, I had to admit that these two creeps exuded stunning animal masculinity. During the commotion of the greetings, settling onto chairs, stowing coats, dissolving flesh faces, and filling glasses, I silently viewed the tableau before me in rapt horror. Sheldon Waters was clearly running the show, T-Rex indeed. He got right to business.

"Rockbottom, what's up with the Andrews' dossier?"

"Buried in committee, it'll never see the light of day," said the Senator.

"Except for the contents that were posted to the World Wide Web by Andrews' widow and Alice Redding," said Kek. "How did the widow get hold of the documents?"

Suzy answered, "Either her husband or Alice Redding."

At the mention of Alice's name, Sheldon Walters clenched his jaw. "We'll get to Redding later. The Andrews' blog is hearsay. What do we know about the other dossiers?"

Suzy sat at a table, reading from notes, "Andrews sent one to Robles-Leon and one to Dana Travers. The Robles-Leon packet is still AWOL. The Travers file is the one we've buried."

Kek said, "But not before she faxed copies to that police Inspector in San Francisco. Keep the originals buried. Online investigators might uncover some information about the Trust side of the house."

Pandemonium spoke up, "Both Redding and Robles have disappeared off the face of the Earth."

"Which leaves the Travers woman. It always comes back to her," said Flatface Kek making a disgusted expression, no doubt recollecting my vomit. "We picked up her trail when she departed Cairo. She'd eluded our sensors for a month. She brought a hemp purse, two paintings, honey, and spices into the country. We're having trouble locating the spice merchant. The saffron tested doesn't come from any crocus farms we can identify in Asia Minor. We've been keeping her under constant surveillance since her return."

Walters screamed, "But we haven't had her under constant surveillance! She disappeared over the winter holidays. For twelve days!"

"But she came back, subservient as ever," Frank Fretz stated.

Kek said, "She disappears from time to time and we can't track her. She disappeared in San Francisco the night Andrews took a fall. Then again in Cairo, and twelve days over winter. She bought a painting from the same artist in Cairo that she met in San Francisco."

"Where are the paintings now?" asked Walters.

"We took all her art. But two by her artist friend are missing," said Pandemonium.

"Those paintings mean something. This artist, what's his name?" asked Walters.

"A pretentious, one-word name: Phoenix. There's no background on him," Contrary grumbled.

"Dig deeper. Burgle her house again. Take everything. There must be some clues in there. Get the hemp bag while you're at it."

"She brings it to work every day," offered Suzy.

"Good, arrange for her to lose it," Walters said to Suzy who grinned eagerly.

My forest green hemp hobo bag from Tellara! I don't think so!

"We got hold of the beat-up rambler her son was driving and traced microorganisms to a Shasta, California subdivision. We surveilled every house. If they were there, they're gone now." My heart missed a beat.

Kek said, "We've got her home, car, daughter, and work under surveillance. Her son is still a no-show. But he's not important. Probably following his dick around California."

"We keep track of everywhere she goes and listen to everything she does," said Contrary.

"Where is she right now?" asked Sheldon Walters.

"Right now?" Pandemonium and Contrary exchanged guarded looks.

"Right. This. Minute." Kek said savagely.

"She went for drinks with Gwen Cretzky after work today. We tailed her, but we lost her when she came back for her car. Her car is still here, but she's not. We searched the entire property."

"So as of this exact moment, she is off the grid? Is that what you're telling me? How is that even possible? Look ahead to nodal points in the grid. Use RAT-TRAK."

"Sir," said Contrary, "We already have. Travers eludes us sporadically. We don't have an explanation unless she's getting help from, well, an outside source." These reptiles knew I was getting help, but their hubris persuaded them that they could always stay one step ahead of me using their tried and true technology.

Sheldon Walters bit off, "So, as of this moment, we cannot track the whereabouts of Alice Redding, Louie Robles-Leon, Dana Travers, her son, or her daughter. Do I understand correctly?"

Pandemonium didn't answer but said, "She's fucking that police detective from San Francisco, the one we kicked off Andrews' murder investigation."

"She married that cop over Christmas!" said Suzy. "She's got a sapphire rock on her finger the size of the moon."

This was clearly news to Sheldon Walters. "Married? To Vazquez?"

"Yess sir," hissed Suzy.

Walter's asked, "Where is the good detective right now? Or have we lost him as well?"

"On a flight to Chicago from San Francisco," answered Contrary. I already knew this from my vox.

Kek asked, "Why would that cop want to fuck a middle-aged frump like her? He's still a put-together dude. Send some tight pussy his way. Who are you fucking this week, Squeezy?" Kek asked. There was crude laughter throughout the room. Suzy glared at Kek.

Frank Fretz said, "That's uncalled for, Kek."

"Ms. Quintana, thank you for your services," Sheldon Walters nodded to Suzy who understood that she was being dismissed. Silently, she picked up her notes and left the room.

"That was beneath you. She's a valuable resource," Frank Fretz said.

"Fine," said Kek. "Fucking you makes her feel important. She thinks she's traded up. But she's tasted mammal meat. She's spoiled goods. Why not send her to fuck the cop?" Frank Fretz stood up and faced Kek with his fists clenched. Frank scales were not white or cream or even golden brown. His scales were army green with gray bands.

Walters cut in sharply, "Gentlemen, enough. Have Vazquez met at the airport by one of our elite female operatives. Seduce that cop away from the Travers bitch."

"What if the cop is really into Travers?" this from Pandemonium. "He married her."

"If we can't seduce Vasquez away from Travers, kill him. Set her up to take the fall. We can always keep track of her in prison." This was Kek, who obviously had the authority to give orders to kill.

"Done," answered Contrary.

"And find her!" blasted Walters.

"We can always use children and pets to manipulate the mammals," said Kek.

"Find and detain the daughter. Find the son. Find Travers. Contreras and Pandomi, you lost them, you find them."

Pandemonium said, "Dana Traver's car is still in the parking lot of this building. Her daughter's car is at her mother's condo. But neither are inside those buildings."

"Ssslipped away again! How doesss she do that?" Kek literally hissed.

The 'men in black' squirmed in unison. It was good to see these two creeps on the hot seat.

"Find out!" Walters bit off each word. "Who is watching her home now?"

"Two of my best."

"Any activity?"

"Not human; but all kinds of unusual animal activity; ravens, raccoons, deer." Animals did not interest Sheldon Walters, but I knew Sky Dancer used animals as guardians and messengers.

"What about Cretzky?" asked Contrary. "He's already out on bail." Mercifully, the conversation steered away from me.

Frank Fretz answered, "That was to be expected. He lawyered up quick. Cretzky nearly crapped in his pants when we arrested him. He never saw it coming. His dumbstruck wifey was there to witness his humiliation." This proclamation was followed by raucous guffaws at Vincent's fall from grace.

But I knew otherwise. The Cretzkys had prepared for this contingency. Vincent had seen the writing on the wall since last summer when I'd confronted him about his vulnerability as a scapegoat. He'd spent months laying groundwork for his defense, procuring evidence, depending on Gwen, getting legal help, stashing cash, preparing his escape, and courting an ally—me—to secure exonerating documents. His 'dumbstruck wifey' had skillfully played her part. Bo Raza was right about Earth's ruling reptiles. They relied utterly on their technical tools, the chrono-filament and RAT-TRAK. The intuitive side of their brains was dormant.

When the laughter died down, Frank Fretz said, "The fraud charge is a sticky wicket. Too many bonuses for claim denials might lead back to corporate. Also, it's a leap from embezzlement to conspiracy to commit murder. We need a fall guy to connect Cretzky to Jay Andrews' murder. Ideally, that would be Alice Redding."

Kek replied, "Jay Andrews got what he deserved. Alice convinced us we could cultivate him as an asset. Instead, Andrews was spying to be a whistleblower. She had to have known. Alice misled us, betrayed us, and disappeared."

Walters said, "Does anyone have a theory about who's helping Travers' pathetic crew evade us?"

"It might be Alice, I know you keep her tethered, but she has a history of betrayal from that other incarnation..." Contrary trailed off.

Pandemonium said, "There are unsubstantiated rumors of a Reptilian Individual Movement, reptiles who want to break free of the hierarchy."

Sheldon Walters declared, "Unsubstantiated is right. Every Draconian is addicted to human misery and there is an endless supply on Earth." He could not imagine the evolvement of the Raza Clan. Our cohort of insignificant wayshowers had thrown a monkey wrench into the smooth operation of the reptilian cabal.

Sheldon Walters spoke thoughtfully, "The Travers woman mentioned our reptilian nature several times. She called me T-Rex. She called Kek my pet lizard."

Others laughed, but Kek quelled them with a nasty hiss, "She'ss getting non-terresstrial help."

Monsignor Muncher spoke for the first time, "Not from the Galactic Council. They play by the rules. We've questioned our informants. No one has broken any treaties."

Pandemonium said, "Gwen Cretzky has gotten cozy with Travers. That bothers me."

Kek ordered, "Arrange for Gwen Cretzky to have an accident. Blind her."

Frank Fretz said, "Val Andrews has done more actual damage to Shelter than anyone else. Couldn't we at least hobble her?"

"Leave Val Andrews alone for now," Kek replied with a hiss, "She'ss too vissible while her husband'ss killer hasn't been brought to justicsse. Anything happens to her, it's a lightning rod to corporate." I got the impression that when the Draconians hissed, they were losing their cool.

Frank Fretz said, "We opened files on everyone who posted favorable input on Val Andrews' blogs while Travers was a fugitive. We singled out all the new agers, in case they would lead us to any yogis, gurus, or saints who might have opened their third eyes in this incarnation. There are a handful in every generation that we have to monitor. Nothing. The few enlightened sages we found did not post to any Internet blogs."

Contrary said, "There were two hippies who posted to Val Andrews' blog from an Internet café in Atlanta. Both were strikingly attractive. A tall fair blonde woman and a tall black man."

"Could they be renegades from the Galactic Family who are working outside the Council?"

"Nothing they did suggested they were anything but human. We tracked them to a health food store where they bought seeds, herbs, incense, and food staples. They paid cash. According to the clerk, they show up in the city a few times a year to run errands for some commune in the hills. We haven't found the commune and they haven't been back to Atlanta since Dana Travers returned to Shelter. They don't seem connected to Travers except for their ideology. The clerk said they were airheads, but he was, too."

"Why can't we find this commune? It should be easy enough to track a couple of hippies from Atlanta."

"As I stated, the Atlanta connection seemed insignificant. It's a long shot."

"But it's our only shot. Follow it," said Walters. I knew the commune, Wah'Kon-Tah was almost eight hundred miles from Atlanta, but shivers ran down my spine.

Walters asked, "So, Louie Leon-Robles, what about his family? Anything there?"

"He has a sister. No contact since he went on the run with his dead lover. Little contact with his parents since he came out decades ago. His family has more questions than answers."

"And the dead fag, Hal?"

"Nothing. Disowned decades ago."

"Who the fuck are these hapless brain-dead nobodies?" Walters was screaming, spittle frothed at his lips. His sinuous forked tongue wiped the spit from his chin.

Pandemonium said, "Travers' first hideout was a cabin in Fond du Lac, Wisconsin. They stayed there for several weeks. The daughter's lover boy, a computer geek named Mick Silas, kicked them out when he found them there. He gave them wheels and money but sent them away, presumably to Shasta."

"Does this Mick know anything?"

"Just what he saw on the news. Nothing else. He freaked when he realized that Dana Travers was his slut's mom. We turned him over to the grays for an anal probe and a mind sweep. He's still with them but they have nothing to report," said Kek.

I was appalled! Poor Mick! All he'd ever done was have feelings for Ruth. And now he'd been abducted and tortured by the grays of this world who were indifferent to human suffering.

Frank Fretz said, "OK, so Cretzky takes the fall for what? Embezzlement, insurance fraud, money laundering, obstruction of justice, and whatever else we can make stick. But we can't pin the Andrews murder on him. He has an alibi."

To which Kek sneered, "Cretzky's alibi is Squeezy, and she'll say what we tell her to say."

Frank Fretz shook his head, "Suzy already spoke on the record with the San Francisco police. If she recants now, things could get more complicated. All the white-collar stuff could go away with a good lawyer and an honest judge. Only conspiracy to commit murder will get him behind bars."

Walters spoke, "Fair enough, Frank. Explore how we can concoct a murder motive for Cretzky, and then come up with an accomplice, ideally Alice Redding. Don't frame the Travers woman just yet. We need her to lead us to the allies helping her slip off the grid. Separate her from her crew by any means necessary."

Contrary asked, "Do we need Cretzky behind bars? Isn't it enough to ruin his life and deflect all suspicion of wrongdoing away from Shelter's corporate executives?"

Kek answered, "Alice knows too much about Shelter Trust. She might share it with others besides Jay Andrews. We've got to plug all the leaks permanently. Prison or death."

Walters turned his attention to the politicians and the other items on his agenda. "Armaments?" He directed this to Senator Oral Rockbottom.

"Hardware is on track for Afghanistan and Saudi Arabia."

"When?"

"Ten days, via Pakistan to Al Qaida, ISIS and the Saudi royal family. Twelve intelligence operatives, all serpents, all deadly."

"Plutonium?"

"Already on site. Concealed from satellite surveillance by chrono-filament drop-zone. The North Koreans won't know what hit 'em. The Americans will shit themselves trying to avoid international condemnation," said Rockbottom.

"Gold?"

"Enough bullion in Venezuela, Shanghai, Cairo, and Zurich to strangle the global market any week we decide to move."

"Seeds?"

"We've covered the entire Middle East, India, and Pakistan with genetically modified seeds. We used the U.S. military to do it," Rockbottom guffawed.

"Any dent in China?"

"Not with seeds. But with pesticides."

Congresswoman Fanny Gnositall, the only female participating in this summit, took over the narrative. "They'll produce fruits and vegetables, but the second-generation seeds are sterile. Everyone in the cradle of civilization will have to buy seeds from us. In eight generations, the sterile seeds will have cross-pollinated with enough global agriculture to make us the only source of food for the leaf-munching mammals. The bees are critical. Another good dose of pesticides and we'll have global famine in fourteen years. The pisser is, they'll all know it's coming and won't be able to do a damn thing about it."

"If we do our job right, they'll all blame each other," said Senator Rockbottom.

"How you gonna disperse the stuff?" asked Kek who by now, I gleaned, was Walters' peer.

"Chemtrails," said Gnositall. We'll do the first big distributions over the most liberal and most conservative counties in America. Somewhere in Texas and somewhere in California. We'll start a rumor in California that the chemicals were spread by the shadow military government that wants to weaken our immune systems. In Texas, we'll suggest that the chemtrails are a liberal plot to dumb down children."

"I love it when the rabble gets roused." Kek was cackling.

"They'll blame global warming," laughed Frank Fretz.

"They'll blame Planet X, the Taliban, and Santa Claus." Everyone snickered at their leader's clever jest.

"They'll think it is Armageddon and rush back to Mother Church," opined Monsignor Muncher.

"And you, Monsignor, how are plans coming along for our One World Religion?" asked Walters.

"As you know, the Pope has eliminated the honorific title Monsignor."

"The Pope will do what we tell him, as did his predecessors," this from Kek. Kek could tell popes what to do? I was astonished.

"Yes well, the Jesuit antipope is an apologist for the New World Order. He will play his part in bringing about the fulfillment of the third prophesy of Fatima, chastisement of the holy and unholy alike. When Rome is a charred ruin, when global pandemic kills half the clerics in the Holy City, and the Vatican crumbles under the weight of its own corruption; that will be the time to declare the advent of the new One World Religion. It will be patriarchal and monotheistic. All the children of Abraham will unify under the masculine external deity and pledge obedience, loyalty, Jihad, and worship. Pedophilia rings and Satanic ritual sacrifice will be integrated into the mainstream. Women as property in need of subjugation will be restored. Present company excepted," the monsignor said with a nod to Congresswoman Gnositall, whose noncommittal expression spoke volumes to me but seemed to sail over the heads of the men in the room.

"There is one thing we have no control over." Sheldon Walters stood and paced.

"Just one?" Kek asked, sarcastically.

Walters ignored him. "If the galactic superwave pulses before we consolidate our stranglehold on global power, we'll have to go into our underground network of survival chambers. We'll have to wait out the climatic upheaval; for who knows how long?" These reptilians knew of the long cycles of evolution and extinction, of planetary shifts and could no more control or predict them than the Tellarans. They only know the galactic superwave was overdue and would be nearly instantaneous. They had contingency plans of their own.

Walters lamented, "We can't predict if the wave will scorch planets or bring on another ice age. Below ground, we'll be safe and retain our technology. But when we emerge after centuries, we will have to start over. The surface dwellers will be smashed back to sticks and stones. But they will be much more spiritually advanced, attuned to nature, like the indigenous cultures we worked for centuries to wipeout. Instead of using religion, media, and curriculum control, we would have to dominate them violently in order to conquer a race of frightened primitives."

"What's a little genocide among friends? Our weapons will be a thousand years beyond their slings and arrows," observed Kek.

Sheldon went on, "But if we complete our orchestrated visions for the New World Order before the shift, before the galactic superwave, the unwashed masses will willingly enslave themselves, forsake spiritual evolution in exchange for survival. We will own Earth and all her creatures for a million years."

The priest stood and paced, "You can't see these galactic superwaves coming. They travel at the speed of light. Every twenty-six million years or so, there is a galactic pole reversal that causes a core explosion in the black hole at the center of the galaxy. Powerful pulses of radiation cause biological evolutionary explosions on the structure of DNA throughout the galaxy. Stars flare and go nova. Shockwaves form at the bow wave of our solar systems, trapping cosmic rays that battle solar winds. Planetary magnetic fields are disrupted. Gravity waves cause seismic events on every planet. Cosmic, gamma, and radio waves follow. Every band on the electromagnetic spectrum would inundate every solar system in the galaxy. Earth would be unrecognizable."

"Tell uss ssomething we don't know," hissed Kek.

Senator Rockbottom said, "Massive seismic events would be our signal to get into the reinforced underground survivor bunkers."

The Jesuit continued, paraphrasing my Tellaran lessons. "Galactic core explosions seem to alternate between evolutionary and extinction events on Earth. As it happens, we are scheduled for an evolutionary burst on the scale of the Cambrian explosion that generated millions of new species in the blink of a geologic eye. This event would coincide with the foretold shifts predicted by Eastern Vedas, Mayan Baktuns, Theosophical Rounds and Races of involution and evolution, Biblical Revelations, and aboriginal end time prophesies from around the world. We've worked successfully to bring about the sixth extinction event so that we could successfully undermine an evolutionary leap to these hairless mammals with their stupid fucking heart chakras."

"As long as they live in scarcity consciousness and survival mode, we own them." Senator Rockbottom growled. "This is the job of governments and the corporatocracy."

"I am the corporatocracy," snarled Walters. "From where I sit, our work is being undone by a band of inconsequential sheeple."

Frank Fretz yelled, "We must ensure our domination on human consciousness before any planetary shift can facilitate human spiritual evolution."

"Famine, war, and disease will make the Black Death look like a tea party." Kek laughed coarsely.

"They'll work for water," sneered Frank Fretz importantly.

The Reptiles were laughing, drinking, and very relaxed as they strategized the enslavement and genocide of all creatures great and small. Javier, Ruth, and

Jesse were in deadly peril. So were our dogs. Alice and Louie had been wise to remain in Tellara, beyond the reach these malignant misanthropes. They eavesdropped on my love life, intended to kill my loved ones, and planned to steal my forest green hobo bag! Enough was enough!

Sheldon Walters spoke, "Keep all the media attention focused on Shelter's Insurance side of the house. Make sure Shelter Trust is never investigated or people in this room will wish they were dead. Assets will be found and frozen, even in Russia. Poverty is not an option. Shelter Trust controls the World Bank, the Federal Reserve, and every currency in every country except the handful of terrorist outliers. Fretz, throw a few red herrings into the mix on the Insurance side of our operation.

FrankenFretz replied, "I'll implicate Alice Redding before we find her. She's the insider most likely helping Travers, just like she colluded with Jay Andrews."

Walters said, "If anyone, and I mean anyone, spots Dana Travers, seize her and bring her to me. Get the word out to every operative."

"What about Squeezy?" asked Kek. "Has she outlasted her useful purpose?"

Walters replied, "I like her. She's a born chaos creator. Keep her around."

To Senator Rockbottom and Congresswoman Gnositall, Walters said, "Keep a lid on Congressional committees and the media."

To Fretz he said, "We need another celebrity nip slip. Who's fucking who in Hollywood? Drug an ingénue and get her to jump naked in a fountain. Then have her murdered by somebody famous. We need a salacious trial. Feed the lead to Gemini Dallas."

These Draconians had global plans to reshape Earth using the planetary shift as a catalyst to mold events to their own vision, and I was a stone in their shoe. Good. I had felt pressured to return to Shelter and now I knew why. Hearing this monstrous conversation and gathering Vincent's documents fulfilled this phase of my Mission. They never considered the possibility of a web of higher consciousness, the evolutionary tool the Tellarans used to break the reptiles' power thirteen thousand years ago. They didn't realize Tellara existed. They must not realize that Gaia herself evolved. They liked conspiracy theorists for their entertainment value. When something authentic was uncovered by researchers, they sent in disinformation specialists. They didn't guess that light workers and wayshowers had tools to foil their grandiose schemes. They were utterly confident. I knew more now than I did an hour ago, but they had centuries of strategy on their side. I was on information overload.

"If that's all our business, it is time for obeisance," declared Kek. They all stood. The men remained as Congresswoman Gnositall opened the door to leave. Having no desire to witness reptilian obeisance, I flitted out the conference room door, above the fray.

Congresswoman Fanny Gnositall walked to Suzy Quintana's office, where Suzy sat sulking. I couldn't resist the opportunity to eavesdrop. Suzy hissed, "I know I was ridiculed by the boys. It's all that Dana Dimbulb's fault. She humiliated me."

"Frank stood up for you. It wasn't that bad, Suzy. Only Kek said anything derisive and he said it in front of you. Walters wouldn't allow anything else said. He said he likes you and wants you around."

"They all laughed at me."

"Frank insisted that you are a valuable resource," Gnositall assured Suzy.

"It doesn't matter what they said. You don't understand. Vincent Cretzky was my ticket to ride," Suzy was pacing.

"That makes no sense. Suzy, he's a human." Gnositall replied. "You'd have risked all your credibility."

"I was planning on conceiving a child with Vincent to start my dynasty. That Dana Travers was right about one thing, womankind is rising. They don't talk about it, but the patriarchy will crumble under the weight of its own hubris. It won't be a man's world much longer."

Gnositall objected, "The hierarchy won't give up power without a world war."

"Who cares if the human race blasts itself back to sticks and stones? I've been patient for millennia. When humanity rises from the ashes, humans will look to women the save their pathetic species."

"That's an insane ambition, Suzy. But I'm listening. Go on."

"It's that Traver's woman's fault. Somehow, she contrived to get Vincent back in the sack with his insipid wife. Travers got away with murder. She's a spoiler who needs to die." Suzy was resolute. That incensed me. I hadn't committed murder, but here Suzy was rehashing old grudges. Also, I had no knowledge of Vincent and Gwen's intimate life. As if?!

"Careful Suzy, I fear you overreach," cautioned Fanny Gnositall.

"I have a plan," Suzy insisted.

"So did Alice Redding."

"Alice Redding was foolhardy. She's chained to Walters. They'll find her. She can't take a piss without him yanking on her choke collar. She's trapped in a job she hates, to a man she loathes, lifetime after lifetime. She acted precipitously. I won't."

"Then let me give you one piece of advice. Do not discuss your ambitions with anyone else, not even Frank Fretz."

"No, never Frank Fretzzss," Suzy hissed. "Men are useful, but not trustworthy."

So, reptilian women had ideas of their own. Could they be any worse than those planned by the men?

CHAPTER 26

I floated out of the office clutching Vincent's envelope inside my precious green bag. Remaining cloaked, I drifted out with the cleaning crew. The predawn air was damp and frigid. I couldn't go home. I had to rendezvous with Vincent and Gwen in the morning. One by one, I viewed my loved ones via my vox. Ruth was at the condo, cloaked and avoiding Shelter agents. Jesse was driving toward Chicago in the silver Forester.

Javier's redeye landed at Chicago O'hare. In baggage claim, he was accosted by his would-be seductress seeking help with her luggage. It was Blondie done up as a lovely ingenue while seething with a hint of untapped lust. Always the gentleman, Javier aided her with a luggage cart and then brushed past her to hail a cab. Blondie race out after him. Brownie pulled and they tailed Javier. One disadvantage of the vox was that it didn't ring. I hummed middle C at Javier, then Ruth, then Jesse, but their sonic crystals did not activate. I was on my own. We all were.

I floated along at a loss for where to wait until my rendezvous with the Cretzkys. I thought of Sky Dancer. She could track me with animals, but I couldn't understand their messages. Then it hit me. I did have one friend who had fourth dimensional consciousness who could see around the corners of time. ALICE!! She only needed to contact me once via some future moment. If, perchance, she and I ever saw each other again, I could describe this moment to her and request help.

Levitating along with a flock of birds, I came upon the AllNite Coffee Shop in a part of town I rarely visited. There were about ten customers drinking coffee and eating breakfast. I entered a nearby dark alley and decloaked. Trying to look inconspicuous while entering the coffee shop, I took a counter seat away from the windows. Two gentlemen I didn't know flanked me. The one seated to my right said, "Call me Huckleberry." The other said, "Call me Finn. Alice Raza sends her regards." I could have cried.

"Can I buy you a cup of coffee, Dana Travers?" asked Huckleberry.

"Coffee would be lovely."

Huckleberry was over 6' tall, lanky, and sporting tawny brown curls. While not exactly handsome, he had an agreeable countenance. Finn was shorter and stockier, but more handsome. His physique was all muscle and no fat. He had curly brown hair, and despite their height difference, the two could have been brothers.

Finn said, "Alice isn't the only one who wants to climb out the primordial ooze. Let's get you warmed up and take you to a safe house. We can help you strategize your plans."

"I have a rendezvous in just a few hours with some friends in trouble."

"Then let's finish our coffee and go." Huckleberry settled our tab and the three of us left the diner. We climbed into an all-wheel Jeep and headed for the Chicago burbs.

I was toasty warm by the time we arrived at an old farmhouse south of the city. Huckleberry led me inside, while Finn parked the car in a barn. The house had been restored to its early 20th century architecture, with modern amenities, but scant furnishing. Huckleberry showed me to a back bedroom furnished with a queen-sized memory foam bed. "We'll handle your rendezvous with the Cretzkys," Finn said. I couldn't help it; I fell asleep before my head hit the pillow.

Voices woke me. Then Javier was cuddled next to me and we slept again until more voices penetrated our dreams. When I awoke, I realized Javier was beaten black and blue. I dressed his wounds while we spoke.

"What happened?"

"Minor altercation."

"With whom?" I pressed.

"Ladies in black."

"I call them Blondie and Brownie. Walters sent them to seduce you. They hurt you."

"I hurt them back," Javier almost laughed, but winced as it made his lips crack.

"How did they find you?"

"They surveilled me from the airport."

"When did you cloak?"

"After I got to your condo. Jesse and I took the offensive. But we didn't want to give away Tellaran technology. So, we used the old-fashioned advantage of surprise. Believe me, they were surprised."

"Jesse's here already? Is he alright? What about Ruth? Couldn't you just get away?"

"Jesse's in better shape than me. They were ransacking your condo and planning your abduction. There's a prize for the operative that takes you to their leader. Others are searching for the Cretzkys."

"They're waiting for me at the corner of Westchester and Robles."

"Not anymore. Ruth met with the Cretzkys. They're on their way."

"So, Ruth got out of the condo safely." I breathed a sigh of relief. "What car did she use?"

"Crystal and Cosmo picked her up in the Electric Kool-Aid van."

We joined our new companions in the kitchen. I hugged Jesse who was bruised and bloody but smiling. He handed me *Shasta Solstice* and *Summer in Tellara*. We had a portal again. Crystal and Cosmo parked their psychedelic van and entered the kitchen. "Hello friend," Crystal hugged me.

"How did you know to come here?" I asked.

"Sky Dancer visited Alice in Tellara via *Tellaran Autumn*. She directed us to Huckleberry and Finn's safe house. Everyone's gathering here to strategize the next stage in your mission."

Huckleberry and Finn introduced themselves as members of the Reptilian Individual Movement. "What's next?" Javier asked Huckleberry.

Huckleberry replied, "We need to conceal Vincent and Gwen Cretzky from Shelter and the Chicago Police until we can present his exculpatory evidence."

"I went into Shelter's file room and appropriated the evidence that will clear Vincent and implicate Sheldon Walters. Does that make me an accessory after the fact?"

Javier replied, "No. Vincent Cretzky was framed. He's out on bail and not a fugitive unless he jumps bail."

"Too late," said Ruthie's voice from the door. She entered with Vincent and Gwen Cretzky in tow. The Cretzky's looked like refugees, wearing layers of clothing and carrying several packs each.

I handed Vincent the packet I stole for him. He tore it open and laid out the contents. It contained a file folder and a thumb drive. There were memos, from Sheldon Walters to Vincent Cretzky, instructing him that he would earn a 10% bonus on the amount of every claim over one million dollars he was able to deny, and a 5% bonus on claims denied below one million dollars. There were several annual memos singling out Vincent Cretzky for his mastery of the black pen stroke and for finding quasi-legal loopholes. These included check stubs bearing Walter's signature.

Javier set down the documents I had faxed him from Jay Andrews' files. Together, we perused the evidence that would clear Vincent and incriminate Shelter executives and their collaborators. Terrorism, bank fraud on a global scale, drug trafficking by intelligence renegades, the overthrow of governments in order to ransack banks and museums of priceless artifacts, assassinations, stockpiling weapons, torturing 'disappeared' individuals, triggering earthquakes, floods, droughts, intentional famine, weapons of mass destruction in private hands—Sheldon Walter's hands—trillions of dollars in gold bullion in Sheldon Walter's hands. What court in the world was high enough to prosecute? What nation or international body could outmaneuver this corporate leviathan? Sheldon Walters, Alpha Draconis, controlled the world.

"Vincent, when I picked up your file at Shelter, I overheard an explosive conversation among the senior reptiles. Did you know they can slide up and down, in and out of places on an invisible strand linked to other places?"

"Yes, said Finn, "The chrono filament. We use that on a limited basis."

Well, Senator Rockbottom, Congresswoman Gnositall, Monsignor Muncher, and Suzy joined Walters, Fretz, Contrary, Pandemonium, and Kek. We're all marked for death, imprisonment, or scandal. They know about the impending planetary shift but cannot predict the exact timing of the galactic superwave. Their agenda is to consolidate their stranglehold on global power before the shift hits so that they can emerge on top after the cataclysms."

"How so?" asked Ruth.

"A combination of chemtrails, GMO seeds, insecticides, privatization of water, fomenting war, assassinations, propaganda, hoarding gold, and I don't know what else. I also learned that there are no women in the upper echelons of reptilian power, which vexes Suzy no end."

"Reptiles?" asked Vincent.

"Sounds chillingly organized," said Ruth.

"Yeah, banks, corporations, some governments, the media, and terrorist groups are all involved. The Vatican and maybe some evangelical groups too. Apparently, the Trust side of Shelter Insurance and Trust is orchestrating it all and may be the key to deciphering those spreadsheet codes. Oh, and Kek might be senior to Walters. Walters deferred to him more than once."

"Weird," said Vincent. "Planetary shift?"

After discussing the implications of the powder keg, we were sitting on, the conversation moved to how to keep the evidence safe until we could get it into the hands of those who served justice and keep it away from those who abrogated justice. Publicizing the evidence was paramount.

"First we upload it to the web, then take Vincent's evidence to Tellara for safekeeping," said Ruth, gesturing toward *Shasta Solstice*.

Gwen and Vincent watched, perplexed as to why we attributed as much significance to these paintings as we did to the incriminating evidence.

Gwen asked, "How can a painting help exonerate Vincent?"

As she spoke, *Shasta Solstice* shimmered and expanded magically. Louie and Phoenix emerged, bearing baskets heartplums.

"Leon!" exclaimed Vincent, agog, as he witnessed his long-lost colleague emerge from the portal of an alien landscape. "What the Hell? You've been missing for months. I thought you were dead."

"No such luck, Vincent. Nice to see you too. Have a heartplum." We all shared a group hug while Vincent and Gwen looked on, astounded.

"Dana, not that I'm ungrateful, but what is going on here?" asked Gwen.

"You're the one who told me you believe in magic. Well, you are witnessing it. This is a safe house, Gwen. Tellara is a safe world. It lies through a portal in that painting. My guides from our sister world have been assisting us."

"Assisting you to solve crimes?" asked Vincent, flabbergasted.

"Among other things," Javier nodded politely to Vincent and Gwen.

"I was in Tellara the night Jay was murdered," I said.

Gwen said, "Your alibi was in a painting?" It was more statement than question.

"That was not our original purpose in contacting Dana Travers," Phoenix addressed the Cretzkys. "But, as you are beginning to realize, there is no such thing as a coincidence." Phoenix handed heartplums to the assembled group.

Gwen slumped against the wall and Vincent caught her in his arms as they slid to the floor together. We all sat on the floor in the unfurnished room, munching and thinking aloud while Vincent and Gwen played catch up.

I sat next to them. "This must be a scary time for you. But there is a way through. Is your primary objective safety or truth? We can help you either way. Tell me now, Vincent."

"I'd give all I am to keep Gwen safe."

"And I'd give all I have to know the truth," Gwen countered.

"Give the lady whatever she wants," said Vincent.

I asked, "Vincent, what is your middle name?" This wasn't a random segue. It was prelude to apology for Reptile and Rat.

"Raymond, my grandfather's name, my son's name. It means wise and strong protector. Why do you ask?"

"For a long time, I made up snarky middle names for you. Vincent Raymond Cretzky."

Vincent looked abashed and turned to Louie. "I heard about the death of your husband, Louie. I am so sorry. We didn't know him, but I knew you had a happy homelife."

"Thank you, Vincent. He was murdered by Kek." Louie got a little choked up. "Now, brace yourselves for an epic story."

I spoke, "There is a confluence of events on two parallel worlds, Earth and Tellara. We used to be joined, one planet, but thirteen thousand years ago at the end of the last ice age, there was a shift that resulted in a great schism. It's recorded in myths like the Fall of Atlantis and Noah's flood. Some of humanity took the high road to compassion and cooperation; others took the familiar path to conflict and competition. We, here on Earth, are all descended from people who took the easy, path."

"Except Phoenix, who is Tellaran," edited Louie. "And Crystal and Cosmo, who are...never mind. That part of the story can wait. Dana, you were saying?"

"Our friends on Tellara remember us and care about our survival during the impending planetary shift. So, they found a way to enter our world and bring us wisdom and technology. Tellaran technology seems like magic to us but is really possible because their science is so advanced. They can bend light, and levitate and..."

"Help you lose weight?" Gwen asked breathlessly.

"Not so much," I grimaced. "Events on Earth must play themselves out according to karmic dynamics and free will. Each individual life is a reflection of what is happening on the world stage. Macrocosm, Microcosm. As above, so below. As within, so without. Some people have kind of intuited this all along. We don't fit in because we know the world is a pack of lies. Our internal truths make sense. But if we talk about it too much, we are considered nuts."

"But I like this kind of nuts," said Gwen

"I married this kind of nut," said Vincent, hugging Gwen.

"Me too," said Javier.

"I heard you got married. Congratulations." Vincent shook Javier's hand and said, "Dana, all those years in the office, you kept your light under a bushel. Gwen saw it before I did."

"Just trying to do my job," I explained to my former boss.

"We all knew Louie was the conspiracy nut!" Vincent said, shaking his head.

Louie spoke, "It's right and proper that many people find truth in the unseen, unknown, and unrevealed. Tellarans are still building pyramids. Look, here is a painting of one in Mount Shastise that they just finished. Cool huh?"

Louie continued, "Tellara is going through a shift also. But they are one octave higher than us. Their shift will be very different from ours. Tellarans will ascend to an incorporeal dimension. In the heart of both our planets, we share a central singularity, a single heart. We are like a string of worlds made up of Gaia in all her manifest natures, worlds without end, always moving toward higher coherency, as we transcend each dimension. As Gaia ascends, sentient species choose more coherent and rarified patterns.

"Not everybody wants this. Lots of people only understand strife and scarcity. Haves and have-nots make sense. The ends justify the means. We don't have to stay locked in this polarized collective consciousness. The more of us that understand service to others is service to self, the more of us that can join in that higher frequency Gaia, Terra Nova."

"Yes, I see," nodded Gwen.

"I remember this fruit. You first gave me one on the plane home from San Francisco." Vincent mused. These came from Tellara?"

"I remember that flight. Jay was dead. I was a suspect. I'd been to Tellara. I'd met Javier. Suzie was obnoxious."

"I ridiculed you. Then you gave me this fruit. I could eat this fruit every day of my life. Here Gwennie, have another."

Phoenix interrupted our reminiscence "These are heartplums. They activate dormant DNA and one's heart chakra. The longer they're in your system, the more compassionate you become. Heartplums are a hybrid fruit."

"How do you know you're not being brainwashed by GMOs?" asked Vincent.

"We'll all find out together when we ascend," smiled Phoenix.

"Yeah but what if the ascension doesn't happen?"

"It is already happening. It has been happening for decades. Our ascended friends float among us all the time. They are in the state they choose. Tellarans have overcome the veil between life and death."

"Delicious," commented Gwen. "This fruit really aligns and open chakras?" I nodded.

"Dana was the first wayshower," said Louie. "I was the second."

"Wayshowers?" Gwen asked.

"Now they include Javier, Ruth, Jesse, Alice, and others from Wah'Kon-Tah." Phoenix was still reciting names, "Sky Dancer, Joe, and Minerva. Soon, Huckleberry and Finn and then you two. Once you cross to Tellara and begin your mentorship, you will be part of the wayshower mission to advise humanity of the need to align with higher frequencies before the coming shift."

"Alice Redding? Alice from Dallas who's been missing since Christmas?" cried Vincent.

I nodded. "She was at our wedding and decided to remain in Tellara. She's happy and safe. And soon, you will be too."

"Let me get this straight, Alice Redding is living in Tellara and that's why Frank Fretz is going mad trying to figure if she had a copy of Jay's documents. She has her documents in another world. I love it." Vincent began to laugh.

"No. Actually, Alice never kept copies. She helped Jay download and disseminate them. If she ever had any, Val has them now."

"What was your original purpose for contacting Dana?" Gwen asked Phoenix.

"Dana is known as a wayshower for Earth. I am the wayshower for Tellara. Our connection is ancient and karmically ordained to heal Gaia. In vast cycles, Gaia connects with her counterparts along her spiral. During these confluences, it's possible to open portals between the worlds. We call this twenty-six thousand-year cusp galactic magic seasons; thirteen thousand years ago, now, and thirteen thousand years hence."

"These times they are a'changin'," sang Louie in his lovely tenor.

Phoenix said, "Tellara is helping Earth. No one on Tellara is indifferent to Earth's dilemmas. We are learning everything we can about your culture in order to assist."

Vincent protested, "Yeah, but, what if you're making mistakes and don't know it? Leading us down a dead end?"

Phoenix explained, "We follow the geometry. The patterns of the Universe are written everywhere in nature. Just follow the fractal trails of the flower of life, the seed of life, the tree of life, the fruit of life. It is written in your DNA. The Universe is organized along these fundamental paths. Sacred geometry is the structure of existence. It includes behavioral as well as physical, emotional, mental, biological, and spiritual motion. It is the pattern of consciousness, everywhere in nature. The more we follow it, the more in harmony we are with ourselves and others."

I addressed the entire group. "Phoenix, there is more to consider regarding Earth's destiny. I must share with you everything I learned while cloaked in the den of reptiles. I entered the conference room to procure Vincent's file, but before I could leave, a cadre of people entered. After a minute, they dissolved their human visages and revealed their reptilian scales and flat facial features."

"Reptiles?" Vincent asked again.

"Shelters corporate executives," I repeated what I had overheard in the reptile summit, and what plans were being implemented. Javier was writing it down, making yet another document to add to our database.

I concluded, "This threat is intentional, ongoing, and calculated."

Louie said, "We can't just choose to play nice. We have pushback from those who would enslave us. We all need to go to Tellara."

Jesse objected, "That's great 'n' all, but who's gonna remain Earthside to get these paintings to Wah'Kon-Tah?"

"I cannot remain Earthside. My priority is to create the portal in *Avalon Equinox*," said Phoenix.

Jesse asked, "What about Ruth's idea to pull *Summer* and *Autumn* to Tellara through *Shasta Solstice*? That would keep them safe."

Phoenix objected, "I advised previously against pulling a singularity through another singularity. The fractal brushstrokes are meticulously applied. The singularities would cancel each other out. The portals would close. Once a painting is Earthside, it must remain Earthside. It is up to you wayshowers where to assemble the whole *Magic Seasons* collection. Once all four are together, they will connect."

"Connect? How?"

"The singularities in each painting will merge."

"Previously, we kept the paintings separated so we'd have several points of access in case our safe spaces were penetrated. Wah'Kon-Tah is the most protected place on Earth. We should assemble them there."

"We're in agreement," said Louie as Crystal and Cosmo nodded.

"So, we have two logistical issues," stated Jesse. "Transporting these paintings from Chicago to the Ozarks; Opening *Avalon Equinox* in both directions after Phoenix finishes painting it; Getting Mom to England without her being apprehended by Shelter agents; and finally, getting *Avalon Equinox* back to America and to Wah'Kon-Tah from England."

"That's four issues," sniffed Ruth.

Javier objected, "No, it's three. Sheldon Walters has put a contract on all our lives. Even cloaked, Dana can't stow away on a transatlantic flight." My groom defied anyone to contradict him.

"Walters wants me alive. He wants the rest of you dead."

"OK, Mom," Jesse agreed. "We still have to get someone to England to bring *Avalon Equinox* to Wah'Kon-Tah so mom can open it."

Ruth addressed Phoenix, "Could you open *Avalon Equinox* on the Tellara side, have Mom will follow you through to Glastonbury, and we'll find out together if she can open the portal from Earthside."

"Would this work?" Jesse asked Phoenix.

Phoenix replied, "Unknown. If it's ever happened before, it would have been millions of years ago, during the magic seasons last cusp."

"Even if Dana opens the portal in both directions, she still can't transport *Avalon Equinox* from England to America. Not with every Shelter operative in the world hunting her," Javier said.

"Agreed," said Jesse. "Who can?"

"Someone has to travel from England to America?" Ruth reasoned. "I suppose could."

"No! You can't." I insisted. "That contract means you're all targets."

"Crystal, Cosmo, could you?" asked Louie. "You two guided us to Wah'Kon-Tah under Shelter's radar. And I don't think Shelter knows your faces."

"Actually, Contrary and Pandemonium noticed them in Atlanta."

Crystal replied, "We've said before, as guides from the Galactic Council, we can do things with you but not for you."

"We do nothing to engender karmic ties on Earth. The paintings will have to be transported by Earth natives."

"Finn and I are of this Earth," declared Huckleberry. "Bred and born."

Finn confirmed, "Our ancestry goes back millions of years and thousands of incarnations on this planet. The Individual Movement may be young, but Draconian reptiles are ancient Earthlings."

"That's right, Bo Raza told us you were Terrans."

"Not only that," said Huckleberry, "We've got a few tricks up our sleeves. Like safe houses that Shelter cannot find, and circumspect ways to travel."

"We can navigate around RAT-TRAK and the chrono filament," chuckled Finn. Our two reptilian hosts were very pleased to offer services to aid in the wayshower's mission.

"Huckleberry and Finn, that is a wonderful offer. You'd be taking a profound risk." I said.

"Not really, but we do want something in return." They were nodding and smiling.

"What?"

"We want to come to Tellara!" They were so excited they were practically hopping. "We want to see Alice again and meet the Raza Clan!"

"Yes, to all you request!" I gave Finn a high five and Javier clapped Huckleberry on the back.

"You're reptiles?" sputtered Vincent, who seemed to be losing his composure.

"We are Draconians," said Finn with a slight bow.

"Good reptiles," explained Louie.

"There's more than one kind of reptile?" Vincent asked skeptically.

Huckleberry replied, "A handful of us have determined to serve the highest good for all species. It is called the Individual Reptile Movement. Alice started it in a prior incarnation. That is why she was kept in bondage by Walter's. She couldn't access RAT-TRAK herself, but saw to it that we got our hands on it to reverse engineer their technology."

"RAT-TRAK?" asked Vincent.

I answered, "reptilian technology. Very advanced, but strictly mechanistic. No use of intuition to direct its purpose. Unlike the voxes, designed by the Raza Clan. The Tellaran tools that we use." I held up my vox and levitated a few feet in the air.

Louie said, "The Raza Clan participated in the ascension of Tellara all those eons ago, when Atlantis underwent its downfall."

"The Raza Clan? Who are they?" asked Vincent.

"They're spiritually evolved reptiles who are assisting Alice so that she may return to Earth openly as leader among our people," said Finn.

"Alice Redding is a reptile!?" Vincent was crazed. "Who else is a reptile?"

"Sheldon Walters, Suzy, Kek, and Frank Fretz, to name a few. And that's just in our office," Louie said matter-of-factly."

"Reptiles running Shelter?" Vincent roared, throwing up his arms.

"Real reptiles?" marveled Gwen.

"Trying to run the world since ancient days," said Javier.

Ignoring this byplay, Phoenix addressed our hosts, "Of course, you would be the perfect choice to transport the *Avalon Equinox* from England to Wah'Kon-Tah."

Finn turned to fully face Vincent and Gwen. Huckleberry stood across the room from all of us. Both morphed. Their smooth flesh turned to patterned scales. Finn's were tawny with tan highlights. Huckleberry's were tawny tinged sienna. Their noses and eyes recessed into slits. Phoenix bowed to them and they bowed back. We all bowed. It seemed like the thing to do at the moment. Then as swiftly as the morphic phase began, they were restored to fully human.

"How do you do that?" asked Vincent, bewildered.

"It's an epigenetic toggle that we consciously control," replied Huckleberry.

"Please don't ask for more information," I pleaded. "You'll get a lecture."

"Not human? Reptiles? What else?" asked Vincent.

"Vegans," Cosmo bowed. "From Vega." As Cosmo spoke, he expanded to his full gigantic height and glowed loving light.

"And Pleiadians." Crystal's silver light body expanded. As swiftly as the morphogenesis began, their otherworldly impressions passed.

Vincent and Gwen sat in stupification.

"Technically, Vincent, we're all Terrans," I said. "That's an inclusive word for all humanoids on Earth."

"By the way, how is Alice?" asked Finn.

"Alice is enjoying herself in Tellara," said Louie.

"I could view her with my vox," I suggested.

"Better not," replied Louie. "Her training with the Raza Clan is intensely private. Everyone has been asked to leave her alone this last month."

"Wait," cried Vincent. "I'm still having trouble tracking this conversation. I get that Dana was in this land of Tellara when Jay died. Now you're saying she had some role in opening a doorway between worlds?"

"Yes, Vincent, Tellara and I are connected through these canvases. Four paintings form a collection called *Magic Seasons*, like the galactic cusp. Two of the four are here on the wall. A third is in the Ozarks. The final one is not yet completed and needs to be opened on the spring equinox in Glastonbury. Glastonbury is called Avalon in Tellara. The two planets have similarities but have evolved separately for the last thirteen thousand years. Phoenix and I both need to be together to open the portal. He brings each painting through to Earthside. I open it back to Tellara, creating a two-way portal."

"Crossing to Tellara helped Dana elude the Shelter Illuminati," said Javier.

"Were you in Tellara when you said you were in the cave?" Gwen asked.

"No, we were really in the cave all those weeks. We didn't discover a safe haven till we dug our way out. Crystal and Cosmo found us and took us to Wah'Kon-Tah."

"You dug your way out of a cave? How?" asked Gwen.

"The cutting tool on my vox" I answered.

"We're overlooking the most material point," stated Vincent, regaining his composure. "We need to release all the evidence from my files. And fast. It's not just about exonerating me anymore. It's about crimes against humanity. There's proof that Sheldon Walters masterminded the Barlow bank fraud that collapsed the economies of six nations. He sold nukes and chemical weapons to terrorists. He has his finger in the pot of no fewer than eight environmental crimes that have collectively killed millions of people in six different African nations. And worse, he is a major player in the global slave trade of children. The pretty ones become sex slaves. The unattractive young people are worked to death work in mines and cacao fields. Between Jay's files and mine, Sheldon Walters, Kek Kinkle, and Frank Fretz can be tied to weapons of mass destruction, international terrorism, and the escalation of the drug trade. The murder of Jay Andrews can be laid directly at Sheldon Walters' door."

"Vincent, when and how did you gather this data?"

"You're not the only one who can eavesdrop, Dana."

"But they sweep for surveillance."

"Vincent answered enigmatically, "Frank Fretz has a way of not looking where he suspects nothing. He's always considered me beneath notice."

"So, who would you suggest we turn these documents over to, Vincent?" Javier asked.

"We should post them online ourselves. How safe is this safe house if we go online?" Vincent asked Finn.

"This house is off the grid, but we have powerful Undernet access. We have our own server in the back room."

"How is that possible?" asked Gwen.

Finn shrugged, "Reptiles are technologically inventive."

"This place is safe for you to post your documents," confirmed Finn.

"Let's get started," said Vincent.

Huckleberry called from the other room, "Hey, come watch this." He had turned on the television. Gemini Dallas was having a rant about Vincent Cretzky, the now-missing fugitive. Pictures of Vincent and Gwen were being splashed across the screen. Gemini was interviewing their son, Raymond Cretzky, who had little good to say about his father and nothing at all to say about his mother, except that he couldn't understand why she stayed with his father as long as she had.

Next, Gemini Dallas interviewed the Shelter spokesperson, Suzy Quintana, petal perfect in lavender. She declared that Shelter had proof of Cretzky's embezzlement and hidden offshore accounts of over one billion U.S. dollars in Shelter assets.

Vincent protested, "We have the savings Gwen managed to squirrel away— nothing approaching billions. We're innocent and on the run." He and Gwen were holding hands.

"Been there, done that," I shrugged, a little unkindly. Vincent had the grace to look sheepish. "Congratulations, Vincent, you're now officially a fugitive." I shook his hand.

Gemini and Suzy went on with their salacious innuendo for a few more minutes before Gwen could stand it no more and turned off the TV.

"I know a frame when I see one," declared Javier. He and Vincent made eye contact that broke off when Vincent shook his head in frustration.

Ruth spoke, "As soon as we get all your new evidence posted, we'll pass the file and thumb drive to Tellara for safekeeping. Vincent and Gwen should go there as well. It's not safe for you Earthside. You can return to Earth in Wah'Kon-Tah when the time is right."

"How do these paintings tie in to Shelter's crimes?" Gwen asked.

"Timing," stated Louie. "It all started with Dana's alibi."

"You've all been to Tellara?" Vincent asked.

"Everyone here but Huckleberry and Finn. And you two."

"Do you mean to tell me that this lame-o crew is all that stands between global dystopia and Earth's emancipation from corruption?" asked Vincent, reverting to form before catching himself.

"Yep," replied Louie, "Welcome to Tribe Lame-o."

"I apologize," said Vincent, "You pulled our fannies out of the fire at risk to yourselves. If we succeed, nations will charge Shelter with crimes against humanity. Congress won't be able to shield him. Walters, Fretz, and Kek could be tried in an international criminal court, maybe the UN or the International Court of Justice in Den Hague."

"But not Suzy Quintana?" Gwen asked peevishly.

"She's not implicated in any evidence I've seen," Vincent answered.

"Or in the meeting I witnessed. She's evil all right, but on the outside looking in." I declined to mention Suzy's insanely ambitious plan to take over the hierarchy and breed with a human male who could stand by her side as consort, but never usurp her authority. Or that Vincent was her intended sperm donor.

Vincent said, "Let's start scanning and uploading this evidence now. We'll need journalists and investigators to follow up on every lead until we can get the originals to a source that has not been corrupted."

Remembering the reptile summit, I said, "Point investigators to the Shelter Trust banking interests. Suggest that all Walters' assets should be found and frozen. He'll think there is a traitor in his inner circle."

"Do you happen to know any detectives?" Javier raised his bruised eyebrows peevishly. I kissed his forehead and said, "Go for it."

Jesse summarized, "When we get everything done here, Huck and Finn will leave for England and set up a safe house in Glastonbury. The rest of you will cross through to Tellara. Crystal, Cosmo, Ruth, and I will gather *Summer* and *Solstice* and head for Wah'Kon-Tah."

"But not in the silver Subaru. Travel with Crystal and Cosmo in the psychedelic Van," I cautioned needlessly.

"Mother, do you know how many cars I've abandoned in the last six months?"

"Leaving the car here in the barn is not the same as abandoning it."

Phoenix said, "The portal between the worlds will be at its strongest when the fourth painting is activated. All the paintings need to be together to complete the *Magic Seasons* tableau before the planetary shift. Together, they will merge into a megaportal that will help save Earth by siphoning off teratons of seismic and psychic energy."

"Planetary shift! Teratons?" Exploded Vincent. "What the?"

"Yes, Dear," Gwen said serenely, patting his arm. "Now I understand. This mission isn't just about corporate whistle blowing. We're on a planetary deadline. Isn't that right Mr. Phoenix?"

"Yes. The final connection between our worlds will dampen the geologic cataclysms that erupt during Earth's shift. However, resolving any criminal, political, or economic cataclysms on Earth is up to you." Phoenix swept his arm to indicate all present.

"Get started blogging. I'll organize a meal," declared Javier.

"Can we really go to Tellara?" Gwen pointed to *Shasta Solstice*.

My fingers caressed the painting and set off shimmering ripples across the canvas. "As soon as your evidence is launched on the web, we'll go together."

"After we've eaten," Javier mentioned food again.

Vincent addressed Finn. "Social media worked well for Val Andrews. Her blog is now a vlog with video postings of her revelations."

"We need a media blitz," said Louie, "bigger than a single podcast, no matter how effective."

"I can help," offered Jesse, who joined the techie fest.

Javier and Gwen cooked. Crystal packed the van. Phoenix and Cosmo downloaded and transported art to Shastise. Huckleberry, Finn, Vincent, Louie, Jesse, Ruth, and I went to the back room, and got busy matching every piece of spreadsheet data with Vincent's thumb drive key. Finn launched a website on his secure undernet server. Vincent directed. I scanned. Louie digitized. Just like old times. Jesse created short, colorful memes. Ruth uploaded data to sites around the world. Huckleberry shielded the undernet from hackers as we worked. The task took hours. It was stressful and mentally taxing. Vincent, Louie and I reviewed each detail and decided in which criminal category to list it. We realized that Vincent's thumb drive held a key to decode the spreadsheets. We could've used Alice. We could've used Jay. The material appeared on multiple websites, vlogs, podcasts, news outlets, and social media simultaneously.

In addition to notifying Val Andrews, Ruth had posted to several investigative journalists, mainstream and alternative media outlets, law enforcement agencies, intelligence organizations, and sovereign nations' governments. Sheldon Walters had access to more information than the NSA, the CIA, Interpol, Mossad, the FSB. In fact, Sheldon Walters could undermine facets of global black ops with a few keystrokes. The facts were out, and no amount of scrambling could put the genie back in the bottle. No spyware could penetrate Finn's Undernet firewall. Jesse said he'd never see its equal and that the programming code was stunningly impenetrable. We were, indeed, playing on a much larger canvas than previous generations had imagined. The world stage was in our living room.

We didn't have to wait long for reactions. Before we even sat down to food, our evidence had gone viral. Justice, including proof of Vincent's innocence, was now in the hands of 'We the People of the Planet Earth.' It wasn't long before counter threats from the African and European Unions began flying across social and mainstream media alike. Some Congressmen and Senators were running for cover. Others were making sanctimonious statements. The White House was uncharacteristically silent.

Someone turned on the television. There was Gemini Dallas, salivating over the scoop of the millennium. She got her facts right this time. The story itself was so sensational; she didn't need to use her trademark hyperbole. First, she interviewed Val Andrews, who shared how she had known for a while that the real executioners of her husband had been the Shelter higher ups whom Jay had planned to expose. Now, she was deeply worried about her friend Alice Redding, who had been missing since Christmas. I wished I could reassure Val.

Next, Gemini Dallas interviewed Raymond Cretzky again to see how he now felt about his father's guilt or innocence. Raymond was a prig. He reminded me of the old, arrogant Vincent as he said he couldn't begin to guess where his father's misdeeds ended, and Sheldon Walters' began. "My father may not have committed the crimes he's been charged with, but that doesn't make him a good father." Gwen teared up watching her son condemn his father.

Gemini asked, "Your mother is standing by your father. They are on the run together. What do you make of that?"

"My mother always had more compassion than good sense," answered Raymond.

Gwen turned to Vincent, "Raymond doesn't know all the facts."

Vincent replied, "I'm glad to hear him publicly denounce me. As long as we're estranged, he's safe from Shelter."

Gemini Dallas turned to insider expert, Suzy Quintana. In a sky-blue designer dress, and coiffed in golden curls, Suzy knew just enough to sound like a cheerleader for the good guys. She was horrified to learn of the scope and scale of her employer's crimes. She came across as erudite and judicious. Again, it was Gwen who shut off Suzy mid-sentence.

Tantalizing aromas from the kitchen distracted us. Whistle blowing was hungry work. We were a boisterous group at a table of salads, pastas, veggies, sauces, and breads. As usual, Crystal and Cosmo drank little and ate less. There was a combination of giddiness and solemnity as we finalized our logistics.

It was time to make our next move. Gwen and Vincent were strangers in a strange land. They seemed to be enjoying themselves, although they kept making sidelong glances at Huck, Finn, Crystal, and Cosmo. I had to remind myself how I behaved at the beginning of my sojourn into alien territory.

"Let's all visit Tellara together and deliver Vincent's evidence to safekeeping. Then, we'll go our separate ways to gather people, places, and paintings. Does everybody know where they're going?" Louie asked. We all mumbled our assent. "Does everybody know where everybody else is going?" We all mumbled our confusion. "Another successful summit by Team Lame-o!" Louie cheered.

After cleaning the kitchen and gathering our possessions, not the least of which was my green hemp hobo bag, we faced *Shasta Solstice* together. Louie was the first to leave. "I will see you in Tellara, friends." Vincent and Gwen gawked as Louie shimmered through the painting into the alien landscape. Even Huckleberry and Finn were impressed.

"All right, Vincent, Gwen, let's get those documents through to Louie," Phoenix held up his hand, and *Shasta Solstice* shimmered and expanded. He passed through the files and the thumb drive to Louie's waiting hands. For several moments we made eye contact in two worlds.

"You're up, Vincent," Phoenix said. Vincent stood before the shimmering portal. Louie held out his hand. Vincent moved forward to grasp it. Vincent stumbled into the wall and banged into the canvas. The portal closed and would not reopen. We were all silent. "Try again." But try as he might, the portal wouldn't open for Vincent.

"You try it, Gwen," he said to his wife.

Gwen stood before the painting and we all focused on the snow-laden branches swaying in the winter wind as a thousand fractal snowflakes drifted downward. Gwen moved toward the ripples. Louie reached out to her. They clasped hands. Louie's hand dissolved. Gwen grasped thin air and bumped into the wall.

"In order to cross through the portal to Tellara, your karma must be balanced and your heart light." Phoenix pronouncement was non-judgmental, but still stung.

Gwen sighed, "We can't go to Tellara."

Vincent clutched her to his chest and kissed her tears. "It's all right, Gwennie. We'll get away. We've told the world our truth. The evidence is out of our hands." The Cretzkys took the disappointment with stoic resignation. "Plan B," said Vincent with forced joviality.

"Maybe we should turn ourselves in," Gwen whispered. "The evidence against you is being discredited. You jumped bail, but you're innocent."

"It won't matter. Our danger is from Shelter, not the law."

"Besides," Javier interrupted, "a few in law enforcement work for Shelter."

"Remember Contrary and Pandemonium?" I asked. "Those men in black who came to Jay's funeral and then arrested you in our office?"

"Yeah."

"They're both reptiles."

"The Illuminati are interconnected, globally. Until Walters and his partners-in-crime are brought to justice, you should lay low," Javier advised handing them each a heartplum.

"I led us down this path. I was a fool." Vincent half-choked out the words.

"You did what you had to, every step of the way. And when it was time, you woke up. There is no shame in your story. Do you think none of us has made terrible mistakes?" said Javier to Vincent, clasping his shoulder.

"There is no need to turn yourselves in. Let's revise our plan." Cosmo spoke, "Jesse and Ruth planned to travel with us by van to the Ozarks. Now, Ruth and Jesse, accompany your mother to Tellara. Vincent and Gwen, maybe you cannot cross through *Magic Seasons*, but your evidence is safe in Tellara, and you can transport these paintings to Wah'Kon-Tah with me and Crystal."

"Yes!" I exclaimed, "Crystal and Cosmo drive a van that eludes Shelter's surveillance. You'll be off the grid as you travel."

"You mean that old hippie van we came in? Vincent asked.

Cosmo said, "As guides from the Galactic Family, we'll transport you to Wah'Kon-Tah. You won't be our first refugees." He winked at me reminding me of Louie's and my bedraggled rescue from the cave.

"We will be honored to transport these paintings to safety. It's the least we can do for all you've done for us," said Gwen. "No more vain regret."

Crystal said, "Another small act of courage to help balance your karma. The police are looking for a man and a woman, probably in a newer model rental car. We will be two couples, one interracial, the other, aging hippies, traveling in what Dana calls the Electric Kool-Aid Van. We will not be of interest to law enforcement or Shelter operatives."

"How can you be sure?"

"People smile at our vehicle as we pass by, then quickly lose interest."

Vincent said, "I have barely begun to come to terms with my arrest. My attorney doesn't know where I am. Thanks to Gwen's foresight, we have a fair amount of cash, but no access to friends, family, bank accounts, or familiar haunts. Despite the evidentiary upload, it may take weeks, even months to clear my name. I had to risk it all to expose the enormity of organized exploitation. Now I'm a burden."

I said, "You're not a burden. You're fighting back."

"We are tribe," replied Cosmo.

"The rest of us must all cross to Tellara before you can take the paintings off the wall," said Jesse.

"Then let's depart."

"Take care of each other," was all I could think to say to Gwen and Vincent. Ruth crossed next, calling to Rip, who leapt through the canvas in doggie delight. Next, Jesse and Belle slid through the shimmering ripples. Phoenix bowed and melted into the canvas.

Gwen was holding back tears as she watched this magical pageant from which she was excluded. Vincent looked both yearning and resolved, longing to see utopia and determined to do whatever he must to bring justice to our own beautiful, flawed, violent Earth. Javier hugged Gwen and kissed her on the forehead. He shook Vincent's hand.

Then Javier turned and planted a quick kiss on my lips and whispered, "Soon."

Vincent and I embraced. "We'll be together again in Wah'Kon-Tah. It's a little slice of Tellara on Earth."

"Thanks Dana, we owe you our lives. I'd be languishing in prison for years without your help."

"Here, take the basket of heartplums with you." I let go of Vincent and Gwen. Crystal and Cosmo stepped up behind. "As soon as I'm gone, take the paintings down, wrap them up, and load the van."

"We know what to do." Crystal replied with an almost human impatience.

"Get going, Dana Travers," Vincent said gruffly.

"We'll meet you in Glastonbury," said Huckleberry. He and Finn each kissed me on the cheek.

Crystal and Cosmo flanked Vincent and Gwen. Huckleberry and Finn stood off to the side. "Fare thee well," I said in a quaint turn of phrase that just burbled up from somewhere inside me.

I turned toward *Shasta Solstice*. The wall shimmered. Saffron grasped my hands and pulled me through. "What the heck kept you Dana?" Saffron approached and I embraced her, still emotional. "They couldn't cross, Vincent and Gwen."

"I heard. It's all anybody is talking about." We turned to where the portal had recently shimmered with life and saw the ripples in the warm afternoon air diminish to stillness. I brushed the air with my hand, and nothing stirred. *Shasta Solstice* was down. I faced Saffron, Heron, and Javier.

"Where is everybody?"

Heron answered, "On their way to Avalon." It was late winter in Shastise. The snow was melting. Green was poking out all over the landscape, although the mountaintop was still white. "Let's catch the next airship." Within hours, we arrived on a grassy plain dotted with beautiful, massive stone edifices and statuary. Stone Henge stood in its original, unbroken resplendence. Across the field stood another, smaller henge. It was built of blue marble and granite walls and pillars. A distinctive multi-faceted crystal dome covered it. Our tribe was gathered there, gazing at the henges and watching Phoenix paint.

Phoenix's smock was covered with dabs of pigment. His brush strokes were swift, tiny, bright, thick, and sure. He painted the texture of the Blue Henge and grassy landscape onto the canvas so that the images rippled with life. Plein air meets fractal geometry. The painting was coming to life before our eyes; golden sun, azure sky, verdant grasses, fuchsia heartplum blossoms, and the interweaving blue veins of the marbled henge temple swirling together.

Phoenix took a break and cleaned his brushes. "On the eve of the vernal equinox, while the rest of you dance, I will activate the singularity by painting myself into the canvas. Meanwhile, we have the entire spring to pass together in Tellara."

Part Four

Avalon Equinox

CHAPTER 27

Reunited with my fellow wayshowers, we rested in Avalon for a day, then checked on our Earthside counterparts. Thanks to Crystal and Cosmo, Vincent and Gwen made it safely to Wah'Kon-Tah. With the helping hands of Sky Dancer and Joe Two Feathers, they were hanging the *Magic Seasons* canvases in the sky room. After a hearty meal, Bruno and Abby escorted the Cretzkys to a cabin. Huckleberry and Finn had landed at Heathrow and cleared customs. They were driving a small hired Mazda east, out of London, presumably toward Glastonbury. Stage one of our plan seemed to have worked with no casualties or leaks. I could turn my attention to springtime in Tellara.

Saffron explained, "Dana, this region of Britain is ripe with ancient power that predates the shift. Henges, temples, and labyrinths have been built here and used for rituals since time immemorial."

Louie said, "There's a Blue Henge on Earth too. Its buried ruins were recently excavated. On Tellara, it is used for ritual ceremonies."

"What kind of rituals?" I asked.

Saffron answered, "Blue Henge is the site of a profound ritual called the Chakra Journey. It is a rite of passage that ushers you through each of the spinning energy vortices that connect your physical body to the Great Mother Sea. The chakras align along the spine from the base to the crown and connect internally with our endocrine system. The ritual reveals which energies dominate each chakra, from the root to the crown and even beyond into the higher chakras that connect to our subtle bodies."

"I've heard of the chakras. You're saying that they connect our bodies to the P-soup?"

"What Earth science refers to as the sub-Plank field," supplied Louie.

"Blue Henge is a seven-sided temple with an inner chamber and outer altars. Each of the seven sanctuaries contains energy from one of seven chakras. In each sanctuary, the seeker can experience previous lifetimes or life circumstances that were dominated by that chakra energy." To better prepare me, Saffron read from her screen, *The Tellaran Chronicles of Science and Spirituality*:

Chakras

The first chakra, the root chakra is located at the base of your spine. Its color is red. Its element is earth. It is the seat of survival and vitality. It is blocked by fear. It is paired with the adrenal glands, which trigger fight, flight, freeze, and panic.

The second chakra, the sacral chakra lives above the genitals. Its color is orange. Its element is water. It is the chakra of sexuality, pleasure, tribe, and creativity. It is blocked by guilt. It connects with ovaries in woman and testes in men.

The third chakra, the sun chakra is centered around the solar plexus. Its color is yellow. Its element is fire. It is the center for will-power, ego, ambition, and identity. It is blocked by shame. It connects to the pancreas.

The fourth chakra, the heart chakra, is centered around the physical heart. Its color is green. Its element is air. It is the center for compassion and love. Grief blocks the heart chakra. It connects to the thymus gland.

The fifth chakra, the throat chakra, lives in our physical throat. Its color is blue. Its element is sound. It is the center of truth and self-expression, where one hears her authentic voice. It thrives on truth and courage. It is blocked by lies and denial. It connects at the thyroid gland.

The sixth chakra, the third eye, is centered in your forehead, above your two physical eyes. Its color is indigo, deep bluish purple. Its element is light. It is the center for self-awareness and insight that all is connected. It is blocked by illusion, the greatest of which is the illusion of separateness. It connects to the pituitary gland.

The seventh chakra, the crown chakra resides in the crown of our heads and is the highest of the physical chakras. Its color is violet. Its element is thought. It links to the collective consciousness. It is blocked by Earthly attachments. The activated pineal gland opens a new sensory organ that perceives living loving light.

Beyond the physical chakras are subtle chakras attached to your rarified bodies, not all of which can be apprehended while still in your physical vehicle. Some teachers say we have as many as twelve chakras, waiting to be activated as consciousness evolves.

Saffron stopped reading. "Inside the temple, the journey through selected lifetimes will give you access to memories of the lives that shaped you into the individual you are. Some situations will be painful, others pleasurable; all will be illuminating and healing. Time will be fluid. Are you ready to enter, Dana? I'll hold you vox for you."

"I can't take my vox?"

"You won't need it. We'll be waiting for you here when you emerge."

"I'll follow you in a few hours," said Javier.

"I'm not sure I'm ready."

Embracing me gently, Louie said, "I've done the ritual. It is life-altering, healing, and illuminating."

"Easier than our journey through the underworld in the cave?"

"Easier isn't the right word, but well worth the journey."

Dubious, but buoyed by Javier and Louie's enthusiasm, I announced, "Ready as I'll ever be." I approached Bluehenge Temple and faced its azure pillars and towering entryway, feeling dwarfed, humbled, and excited. Entering, my slippers rustled on the white tile floor. The stones underfoot and along the walls rang out with sonorous vibrations. A woman in a white robe and turban ushered me into an alcove to my left.

First Chakra ~
Vitality, survival, earth, red, blocked by fear

As I passed through the archway, the space around me was suffused with a curtain of red light. Crimson waves rippled throughout the temple. Deep in the alcove stood a small altar and a cushioned chair, but no other furnishing. The walls were red rock. The tile floor was an undulating pattern of reds: blood, crimson, burgundy, floral, and fruit. As I stepped along the rippling stones, vibrations erupted in every cell of my being.

I was plunged into the Great Mother Sea as a whirling point of consciousness in unmanifest unity. A question was posed by the collective thought of all monads, "Who wants to go for an ultimate and unique ride called creation? No two journeys alike." Trillions of monads volunteered for the adventure. I was one of them. The Primal Sea ejected us with a fateful admonition, "The path to evolution begins with involution. You can't fall out of the Universe."

In the moment of my emergence, duality was born. Self and not self. I was rocked by the sensation of separation, my first thread of sovereign consciousness. From the unmanifest sea of bliss, to a fragile, solitary vortex, separation was both blissful and terrifying. The only way back was forward, onward through the mysterious, tangled current.

For time without end, I was subatomic, then atomic, molecular, then mineral. After an indeterminable time, I realized I was corporeal. I had mass, which over ages became more coherent. I metamorphosed from mineral to organic molecule, to a protoplasmic blob, and eventually a seed. Proto-senses emerged, touch, light, sound, the passage of time, distance, and balance. I sensed the chemicals around me and reacted. I swayed in the water, wind, and sun. After eternity relishing my floral iterations, I had a face, then claws and jaws. I ate. I mated. I migrated.

At length, I was in an adult, humanoid, female body. I was surrounded by people, all sleeping together in a huddle to ward off the chill outside our cave. My belly was full. Someone snored. Someone farted. A child fussed and was silenced on her mother's teat. A familiar hand grabbed my breast and pulled me into an embrace, initiating sex. In this press of human flesh, there was no privacy, but there was vitality. And for this moment, there was the peace that came with knowing my tribe was safe.

A rush of energy swept away the cozy tableau. Painful new surroundings emerged. I was in chains, being dragged. Why had the ritual brought me to this miserable incarnation? I dropped to my knees and vomited, purging the darkness until a red whirlwind swept through the sanctuary. When the wind cleared, a tableau of misery appeared. Slaves by the thousands were chained together at the neck, hauling stones. We were building the Great Wall of China. I was a slave, a female chained together with a dozen other women. My neck chafed and my hands and feet bled. At dusk we stopped working and were given rice and water. One of my keepers singled me out and raped me. The women to the right and left maintained stoic indifference to my plight. When he was finished, my keeper let fly a few lashes of his whip for good measure. Our eyes locked for a moment. My tormentor was the man I knew in this life as Vincent Cretzky.

A crimson whirlwind whipped away the scene and replaced it with another tableau. Another chain gang of slaves, only this time, I stood with the whip. I was a man and my slaves were men and women together. There were a few slaves in my charge that I delighted in tormenting. Their suffering made me feel powerful and important. It aroused me sexually. The anticipation of brutally beating one of the pathetic captives and torturing her before I mounted her and released my seed was intoxicating. I saw my quarry. She knew I had singled her out for a night of torment. Our eyes met. My victim was Vincent Cretzky.

Lifetimes drifted by, revealing vignettes where survival at all costs dominated. Slavery, rape, murder, brutality, cannibalism, the kidnapping of women and children, and slaughter of men from rival tribes were the custom. Marauders raided villages, sometimes for pay, sometimes for a perceived cause, but mostly for food. Back and forth, the whirlwind ripped me between scenes of perpetrator and victim.

These horrors were interspersed with respite lifetimes in peaceful tribes. We cooperated to survive. We fed and healed each other. We created primitive music and dance. We told stories and drew images of hunts and rituals. Our wisest members settled squabbles. When someone misbehaved, that tribal member was punished and humbled proportionately. Every person was valued. I interacted repeatedly with prior incarnational personalities of people with whom I had relationships in my present lifetime: my parents, my children, my ex-husband, Louie, Javier, and again, Vincent. My soul yearned for the peaceful, cooperative lifetimes. Collaboration as the basis for survival began to dominate my karmic options of where and when and with whom to incarnate.

The whirlwind cleared the tableaus and I was back in the red temple. My breathing was ragged as if I had run a marathon. I'd faced my emotional wounds and my capacity to inflict cruelty. I had come face-to-face with my darkest, ancient shadow. There was more to life than just surviving. I wept with gratitude for my modern, complicated life and ached for a hug.

Red light washed over me. My root chakra spasmed with urgent life force. Primitive music filled the temple. Ancient wind instruments, drums, and strings vibrated from the soles of my feet to the crown of my head. I danced without inhibition. A snake at the base of my spine uncoiled, empowering my life force as my Kundilini rose. I felt freed from the wounds in my root chakra.

Second Chakra~
Sexuality, pleasure, tribe, water, orange, blocked by guilt

An orange light glowed. As I crawled toward it, the light grew warmer, more vibrant, immersing me in healing waters. My crawl became a breaststroke, carrying me forward in rhythmic contractions that guided me into a cosmic womb. Warm fluid gushed between my legs. I was pregnant with myself, giving birth to myself. My body emerged, naked and panting. A thousand orange suns heated my flesh. My womanhood was aglow with menstrual sensations, mildly erotic, wet, and warm. Was this the afterbirth of my own labor contractions? My blood was healing and purifying.

I loved being a woman in this incarnation. I felt many years younger than my near-sixty Earth years. I felt like a new young mother who had sailed through childbirth with ease and pleasure. Childbirth had restored my body and spirit. I wondered what Javier would feel in his second chakra. How would the warmth of a thousand orange suns nurture a man's birth pangs?

I dragged myself onto a thick carpet of ginger, tangerine, and golden petals, woven together in a fabric. I draped it sarong style. An orange comfy chair sat to one side of the alcove. Long-lost trinkets, crystals, dolls, and pictures were arranged on an altar. Candles and incense burned with sweet woody fragrances. Statues of goddesses and gods flanked either end of the petal-strewn dais. I had been here before, when? Then, it came to me. This was my private altar in Atlantis, when I had been a temple priestess. A curtain of soft orange swept across the alcove and revealed a tableau from an Atlantean incarnation. A woman entered my room; my sister. Her name was Selena, but I recognized her as Louie.

In this tableau, she is much older than I, my revered elder sister who serves the goddess as a High Priestess. I am proud and humble to be her acolyte. Today, we are meeting important business and political leaders from the village. There is urgency about this gathering. Atlantean scholars have forewarned that a series of catastrophic quakes and floods will soon be upon us.

Atlantis' best and brightest, carrying precious artifacts, are being transported to distant lands where our civilization will be preserved and restored. There is a place on a boat departing today that will carry Selena safely east. She tells them she will only go if I accompany her. I feel so grateful when the captain says yes, we can share a cabin. We grab our few belongings and follow the leaders quickly to the harbor. The waterfront is bustling with ships and refugees. It is pandemonium. Men appear and shepherd Selena onto a gangway, bound for a grand ship. They leave me behind in the mob. I cry out for them to wait for me. Selena cries out for them to bring me. Neither of us is heeded. We are separated and hysterical. Her boat is launched while I stand clutching my small packet of possessions. She calls that she will return for me. But we both knew she will not, cannot return.

I return to the temple. Before my familiar altar, I curl up into a fetal position and weep myself dry. When there are no more tears, I go back to work, maintaining the candles, incense, prayers, and flowers. I am just going through the motions of being alive, as are the others left behind to die.

It was only days before the quakes started. At first, the tremors were mild and manageable. As they escalated into mega-quakes, volcanic eruptions, and tsunamis, the temple floors splintered in heaving rifts. My fellow acolytes and I became stranded on fragmented slabs. The tremors reached a crescendo that shook the firmament to dust. I survived long enough to see a wave the size of a mountain sweep the golden-domed temples out to sea before engulfing me in its watery depths. I died feeling bitter, broken, abandoned, and betrayed.

The glowing orange curtain swept across the scene. I was living in Atlantis again. It was thousands of years later and great cities had been rebuilt along the emergent coastlines of this maritime civilization. Scholars advised us that another, greater geologic cataclysm was coming. There were reports that survivors from the first wave of our dying civilization had reached lands to the east, where they had built stone edifices that mathematically encoded Gaia's Galactic Seasons.

In this incarnation, my name was Janka; I was a gifted songstress who had married a successful merchant named Solan. I recognized him as a prior incarnation of Buffalo. I didn't love him. I was an opportunist who had seduced him into marriage when I was young, beautiful, and desirable. He'd made the best of it and was always kind to me. Selfishly, I had denied him children. Feeling betrayed and bitter from the abandonment by my sister in a prior incarnation, I felt the world owed me. In the upcoming exodus, I would have a guaranteed berth because of my fame and Solan's fortune.

Solan was on a committee to determine which fleets would carry Atlantean art, science, technology, literature, music, and spiritual teachings to distant lands. The most seaworthy vessels would be outfitted with the best seamen. Solan secured us a berth on the Helios. When I boarded the ship, I complained that my berth was too small and stark. Captain Zalko was indifferent, bordering on contemptuous of my vanities. I resented him. I recognized Captain Zalko as Phoenix.

I made the worst of a good situation, whining to whoever would listen. Singing at night to pass the hours, my beautiful voice mollified the resentful mariners and scholars. I oozed pretentious pride because, in my heart of hearts, I felt guilty about my position in this noble quest. Everyone else had long since dropped any pretense of status. Finally, after a quelling look from Captain Zalko, I kept my peace.

We were headed west. The crew on this ship was charged with building temples and pyramids that would teach the natives celestial science. Our scrolls contained knowledge that would be encoded in stone edifices to last throughout the ages. When another generation of humans faced cyclic planetary changes, our Atlantean messages would forewarn them.

On our tenth night at sea, our ship was beset by a terrible hurricane. We had outrun Earth-shattering quakes and tsunamis and were in sight of Maya, only to be dashed against the rocks by something so mundane as a tempest. We grabbed everything we could carry and headed for lifeboats. Even I, in a frantically unselfish moment, abandoned my fineries in order to preserve scrolls sealed in airtight ceramic jars. I carried six in my tunic. Solan tied another eight to his smock. He and I were on a lifeboat with twenty other survivors. The small crafts were seaworthy, but the storm and the rocks overwhelmed us. We crashed into headlands and our lifeboat was dashed to splinters. I grabbed floatation planks from the boat's remnants. So did the others. Solan was injured. His head bled and his left arm hung at an impossible angle. The scrolls he carried weighed him down. Solan was in deadly peril. I swam to him in the stormy waves, dragging boards along. He could barely cling to anything. One arm was useless, the other embracing the blessed ceramic urns. "Save these scrolls," he cried to me in the din. I heaved his jars onto our makeshift flotation, relieving him of the weight and freeing his good arm.

Solan, this husband of mine, a man I had selfishly manipulated and used, needed my help to survive. He clung to the planks, weak and shivering. I held his face above water, using all my might to keep us close to the timbers. Heaving him onto the raft was beyond my strength. In this moment of mortal peril, I realized what I had wrought. "I've cheated us both out of a lifetime of love." I called to Solan above the storm.

A section from the Helios' cargo hold, containing a crate filled with scientific instruments, drifted by. "Grab those artifacts, Janka," Solan rasped in my ear.

"Can you hang on without help?"

He said, "Yes," but we both knew he was lying.

"No, I'm staying with you." My tears mingled with the sea spray.

"Save Atlantis, Janka. We are mere transmitters of our legacy. It is my dying wish, the reason you were given a berth on the Helios." This last statement cost him much strength and filled me with guilt; selfish to the last. His body was dead weight. While I secured his right elbow and wrist over a plank, the instruments were drifting away. Releasing him was the only way to recover the artifacts. He would live if only I could get him to shore. Against my own best interests, I heeded his wish, let go, and swam toward the retreating cargo. I reached this second float and kicked back to Solan with all my strength, planning to tether the planks together into a makeshift raft. In the violent waves, I found our floatation boards, but Solan was nowhere to be seen. Calling his name, I cursed the gods. Exhausted, I climbed onto the planks in the stormy dark and clung to them. Many hours passed until, at some point, all was darkness.

By daybreak, the waves had died down to crests and troughs that permitted intermittent visibility. No land was in sight, but other lifeboats and rafts dotted the sea to the horizon. Clinging for my life, my arms, hands, and feet had become paralyzed with cramps. Thirsty, alone, and adrift, I could never maneuver these loaded wooden floats to an unseen shore. Solan had died for nothing.

Cheeps and squeaks disrupted my wretched stupor. A pod of dolphins appeared. Nudging my hands with their noses, they broke my grip, forcing me to let go of the planks. Two dolphins buoyed me up on their backs. Others steered the wooden rafts with their precious cargo. They steered me away from the rising sun, a giant neon orange ball, guiding us further west. The dolphins stayed with me for two days. At times they were swimming so close and fast that I was propelled effortlessly by a slipstream the pod generated. At length, we reached a tropical storm-swept beach strewn with cargo, debris, and people that I recognized from the Helios.

Men waded out to relieve the dolphins of their cargo. Women hauled me up to my feet in chest deep waters. Fresh water was ladled down my throat. I clung to my savior cetaceans until Captain Zalko disengaged me and dragged me through shallow waves to warm golden sand. Falling to my knees, I rocked and cried, calling Solan's name in the vain hope that someone would tell me that he'd been found and saved. Alas, no such news came.

The crew of the Helios left me alone in the hot sun for several hours until Captain Zalko approached and spoke. "Solan was a fine man. He was the reason you were included on the ship's passenger manifest. The scrolls and instruments you saved are among the most valuable Atlantean relics. Solan's faith in you was justified." I peered into the Captain's nonjudgmental face and felt guilt for my previous behavior. But at that moment, I would have traded all the treasures of Atlantis for Solan's life.

"Get some food and make yourself useful," he directed gently and left me alone again. I heeded his instructions and found myself welcomed by my fellow survivors, no longer the useless prima donna, but an integral member of a group with a momentous mission. The aroma of baking food filled the air. Native Mayans were cooking a meal of fish, corn, and beans over red-hot rocks, our first feast together.

I had been a cold wife to Solan, but in our confined shipboard berth, in the aftermath of our terrifying departure from inundated Atlantis, we had come together as man and wife. Now, I found myself shipwrecked and pregnant, but not alone. Nine months later I gave birth to twins, a boy and a girl. In the years and decades that followed, I found my place as a temple priestess. I anointed altars, watched the stars, taught the scrolls, chanted prayers, swam with dolphins, and grew old. I never remarried. My son married a Mayan woman. My daughter married a Mayan man. They had many children between them.

Captain Zalko and I were the last two elders of a lost civilization to have made their way to this part of the Americas. We hoped there were other Atlanteans, elsewhere, on Earth's enduring continents. Captain Zalko, my revered, ancient Phoenix, was dying. We were on the same beach where we had made landfall from the Helios' shipwreck decades earlier. He told me a story of how he had been anointed as a wayshower for a planetary schism. The cataclysmic upheaval we had lived through had split our planet into two.

Zalko spoke, "While in the temple of the oracle, Gaia herself instructed me that our planet is entering a twenty-six thousand-year period she calls magic seasons. It takes Gaia between two hundred forty million and two hundred sixty million years to complete one revolution around Sophia. That is a galactic year. The magic seasons are a transitional cusp we transit through in this part of the galaxy. In thirteen thousand-year intervals, Gaia will undergo planetary schisms and rent our one planet into two planets at different frequencies, one in harmony consciousness and the other in divisive consciousness. The first rift is the cataclysm we lived through when Atlantis was inundated, and the world flooded. The next will happen thirteen thousand years hence. There will be a third and final schism in twenty-six thousand years. Many Atlanteans and Mayans will transcend to the higher-frequency world. I am one of them, but many people will remain behind."

"Behind?"

"Here. This familiar Earth will continue much as it always has, with families, farms, commerce, technology, flawed governments, and struggling spirituality. In thirteen thousand-years, Gaia will need another wayshower."

"I don't understand," said Janka. But, I Dana, observing this lifetime tableau, understood with fatalistic clarity, absolution for my guilt.

"An individual who will help the next phase of humanity to find their way to a more evolved spirituality, so they can survive the shift and reincarnate on the next higher frequency phase of Gaia. Will you be that wayshower, Janka?"

Another dying wish! I reluctantly nodded my acceptance. "I really want to go to that harmonious place."

"You'll have help. I'll be there to guide you." Captain Zalko, my Phoenix, died in my arms, our hands gripping fast to each other as I watched his final breath leave his body and waited for the inhalation that was never to come. I sat with him for many hours. Years later, I died in the temple at Coba, the last survivor of the Helios. I exhaled my final breath as the sacred chanting of my many Mayan progenies reverberated within the stones and through the jungle.

A bright orange, curtain closed the tableau. The second chakra alcove emerged from the mist. I climbed into the orange, comfy chair as the serpent stirred within gut. It rose from my womb on my inhalation, hovered on my exhalation and rose to my solar plexus with my next breath.

CHAPTER 28

Third Chakra ~
Solar plexus, will, ego, fire, yellow, blocked by shame

I rose and followed a rippling yellow curtain as it swept through the temple. As far as the eye could see, yellow grass and golden wildflowers waved in the gentle breeze. Another adventure through Karmaland. A crow cawed. Two black birds landed, flanking my shoulders. One was a crow and the other a raven. They reminded me of Heckle and Jeckle, mischievous cartoon birds that I'd watched as a child.

"Are you ready for a game?" Jeckle the crow asked, while Heckle the raven heckled.

"Game?"

"Round One!" cawed Heckle. Golden grass rippled toward the sky. A tableau appeared before me.

I was six. My parents were quarreling in the kitchen because my mother suspected my father of infidelity. I didn't know what that was. Mother scolded me for carrying too much on my plate. Startled, I dropped my food. Milk and jelly flew everywhere. My mother screamed at me. My father did nothing to stop her. After a time, he cleaned up the mess while Mother stood fuming. He did not comfort me but gave me stern looks of reprimand. I felt shame and apologized. Mother told me to go to my room, where I cried myself to sleep feeling unworthy.

The next day, at school, Jimmy, a boy from my street, was getting bullied. The big boys made him cry. He wet his pants. He must be unworthy too, must deserve to be harassed by these other boys, who seem to know. No one raised his or her voice in his defense. If I did, they might target me. This persecution happened to Jimmy a lot after that first time. In tenth grade, Jimmy killed himself. I felt somehow responsible.

I went to his funeral. Standing on a hilltop, I watched my younger self with the other mourners. Jimmy's spirit came to stand by my side. "Sorry, Jimmy, I never stood up for you. I was never a good friend. I was afraid of those bullies, so I kept my silence and let them tear you apart."

Jimmy said, "You were a kid, Dana. The teachers didn't do anything either. They considered bullying part of life. My parents finally moved me to another school, but by then, I was destroyed. My suicide seemed like the only way out at the time. It means a lot that you came to my funeral."

"Can you forgive me?" I asked.

"Always," was his compassionate reply. "Can you forgive yourself?"

"I don't know. I once ridiculed a girl at school. I played a horrible trick on her and made her cry in front of the whole class. Why did I do that?"

"Because she reminded you of the part of yourself you hate."

"I wish I could ask for her forgiveness." And then she was there, a girl named Rita, now a woman. She got up close in my face and looked long and hard.

"I want to ask your forgiveness, Rita. I am sorry from the depths of my soul for being cruel to you when we were schoolgirls. I can't use youth as an excuse. I was old enough to know better."

"I hate you," she replied. "I do not forgive you. I want everyone who ever hurt me to suffer." Then she walked away and disappeared into the group of mourners at Jimmy's gravesite.

"I deserved that," I lamented to Jimmy.

"It doesn't matter what she feels about you," he replied. "Sometimes people have to experience being targets to learn compassion and forgiveness."

Heckle and Jeckle fluttered around me, "Round Two," they cawed in unison as thousands of yellow flower petals fluttered across the tableau.

I saw myself at my first job after college. There was a woman in the office named Marta. We took an instant dislike to each other. She was competitive and thought everything I did was designed to undermine her. In turn, she tried to undermine me every chance she got. I was conscientious and accountable, but I couldn't stay out of her way. An incident occurred, Oh! I remembered as the scene played out before me. A sensitive document that Marta had produced contained an unauthorized, politically inflammatory statement. Our manager accused Marta of inserting it. I knew she didn't because she would never antagonize an important client. Ambitious to a fault, she was all about boot licking her way to the top. I also knew that the statement was opposite of her politics. I realized that a malicious copy editor who hated her had done the deed. He couldn't take his gloating eyes off the train wreck he'd caused. Marta was reprimanded. I held my silence and let her take the heat, not because I enjoyed her pain, but because I just wanted to stay below the radar. She was sure I'd done the misdeed to get her in trouble. She fumed at me, stepped up her tactics, and became her own worst enemy. She was soon fired. I had neither lied nor sabotaged her. But I had watched her take the fall and breathed a sigh of relief, taking the path of least resistance.

"I wish I could tell her I'm sorry," I told Jeckle who was distractedly scratching the dirt, looking for worms.

And up the yellow grassy meadow walked Marta, prematurely aged, gray-haired, with bitter lines etched in her face. "I lost everything when I lost that job," she sniped. "That was my golden ticket. You destroyed my career!"

"I didn't write the words that got you in trouble," I lapsed into our bitchy bickering from all those decades ago.

"But you knew who did and said nothing!"

"True. I did not defend you when I could have."

"Bitch."

"I am sorry you never recovered professionally."

"It's all your fault."

I didn't know how sorry to feel. Marta provoked such antipathy. I'd committed a sin of omission, but she'd stewed in her own juice for all these years and never stopped blaming others.

"Round Three," cawed Heckle. Marta melted into the tall yellow meadow.

A new scene wove its way up through the golden blades of grass. I was married to Nick Travers. I'd just learned he'd cheated on me. Ruth and Jesse were toddlers. I was accusing him of infidelity. He shrugged and said he was ready to leave. We blamed and ridiculed each other. The children cried. Facing my role in the dissolution of the marriage, I forgave both of us. But I still didn't understand where my critical nature came from or why I believed that relationships aren't safe. I'd stopped trusting him before he became untrustworthy. We had both sabotaged our marriage from the start. There was no one to blame, only lessons to be learned. I wished I could say I did not ridicule anymore, but I recalled my recent professional gaff, calling Suzy 'Squeezy' in a staff meeting. That blew up in my face.

I turned to Heckle, "I am so glad my children are still close to their dad. They can do better in relationships than I did before I met Javier."

"Round Four!" cawed Jeckle. A yellow curtain of flower petals swept by.

I was at my new corner window office in Shelter. Jesse was there. He had brought Shasta Solstice from California. This was all wrong! Jesse shouldn't be at Shelter with the portal to Tellara. He hung the painting behind my desk so that it was visible beyond the glass walls. Colleagues stepped into my office to view the painting.

"Oh look, I can actually see snow flurries in the canvas," said Carmela Benedetto from Accounts Receivable.

Suzy entered. She had reverted to femme fatale mode in leather and leopard. "It's not snowing in a picture, you nitwit. Get back to work," Suzy snapped at Carmela, who rushed off. "Mr. Walters is in the building. He will want to see this painting."

I exclaimed, "Jesse, take the painting down and get it out of here, now!" I moved to take the painting off the wall. But Jesse stayed my arm with his hand. "Mom, you have to face this."

"What?"

Suzy was yammering into her cell phone as Sheldon Walters barreled toward us. In my office, standing next to Suzy, the two of them peered at Shasta Solstice.

"That ninny in Accounts Receivable thought she could see it snowing in the canvas."

"Rubbish," he barked. "But that fractal geometry embedded in the brush strokes is a code. That's how these troublemakers are passing messages. We'll take it to study."

"This painting is not yours to take!" I cried in alarm.

"You really don't understand anything yet, do you, Dana Dimbulb?" sneered Suzy. "We just let you have the illusion of ownership. When we need something, you don't get a voice."

"The painting is in my stewardship. I will protect it with my life if I must."

"Stewardship, now there's a hollow word." Walters was using the mocking tone Suzy had used.

"I'm keeping this painting." Walters bore down menacingly, pulling out a vicious serrated blade. He was going to slash the canvas as Kek had slashed Summer in Tellara. I stepped in front of the painting, taking the full force of Walters' blade through my belly. My solar plexus was slashed. I fell backwards through the portal and landed on the golden hilltop in my solar plexus chakra, safe in Temple.

"Game's over," cawed Heckle and Jeckle in unison.

"That was no game. That was a nightmare," I retorted.

"How is your wound?" asked Heckle.

I felt my torso where the blade had carved me open, and found it was whole. In fact, ecstatic sunlight radiated from my solar plexus. Basking in the golden rays, the birds fluttered their wings, blurred, and phased out. Where each black bird had stood, two new large and majestic birds emerged, eagle and condor. Taking flight above the meadow, raven and crow were no more. The eagle and the condor flew off to distant horizons, first north and south, then east and west. They looped back, intersecting at the center of a vast infinity symbol they had traced across the sky. Colliding in a fiery conflagration of flame-gold feathers, a phoenix firebird emerged from their ashes.

The phoenix landed at my side. She was as tall as I was, with a vast wingspan and billowing orange-gold feathers. "Call me Goldie. Let's see what happened in an alternate multiverse where you learned to trust more and fear less. Round One Redux," announced Goldie, as a blazing yellow curtain swept the scene.

I didn't help Jimmy, but I told my parents how he was being treated at school. My emotional vulnerability gave my parents an opportunity to comfort me in that moment when they were not preoccupied with their own anger. My sense of unworthiness diminished. My need to protect myself by ridiculing others diminished. I did not play a mean trick on Rita. For karmic reasons that I could not fathom, Rita had been a magnet for many acts of cruelty. Her life played out much the same in both realities. In this one, she didn't even remember who I was.

"*Round Two Redux,*" crooned Goldie.

When Marta was accused, I spoke up in her defense. I told my boss that she was not easy to work with, but she would never sabotage professional documents. Later, Marta got fired for other reasons, but didn't blame me. She got her career back on track. It was never the career she had hoped for, but she became a nicer colleague. The copywriter who sabotaged her had no apparent difference in his life. For reasons known only to him, he never sabotaged anyone else.

"Round Three.."

"I know, redux." I interjected. "But this feels more like a do-over and do-overs aren't real."

"They can happen in the chakra ritual," Goldie replied.

In this do-over, I still married Nick Travers. We wanted babies, and Jesse and Ruth were born in the first three years of our marriage. I did not drive him away and he did not cheat. We outgrew each other. Instead of a series of trophy wives, he found happiness in a second marriage with a wonderful woman. It was Carmela from Accounts Receivable who'd seen snow flurries in Shasta Solstice.

Goldie did not show me a do-over of Round Four, the painting debacle at Shelter. She just told me, "Ya done good, kid. You stepped aside from your little ego in order to embrace your higher calling."

Relief washed over me. I'd forgiven those who'd wronged me, but more importantly, I'd forgiven myself. When I hurt others, I hurt myself more. "Still, all these tableaus are from my current incarnation, Goldie, and imaginary do-overs don't count."

Goldie replied, "Healing one aspect of your soul heals multiple souls. Ancestral wounds are healed by clearing epigenetic tracers which no longer perpetuate to progeny. Waking up is not as fun as it sounds."

"It doesn't sound fun at all."

"Humans dislike those who reflect the qualities you avoid about yourselves."

I nodded, "It's called denial and it has long been my familiar companion."

"The solar plexus protects these hidden wounds. Your sun center should be the seat of ecstasy and brilliance. Instead, most of humanity holds the shame of many lifetimes in this chakra. To compensate for your shadow, humanity craves material comfort and generates chaos."

"For a so-called wayshower, I'm pretty slow on the uptake."

"Shamans, saints, artists, poets, and healers are visionaries who see utopian possibilities." Goldie nuzzled my shoulder, helping me to accept a compliment.

"Some visionaries are ordinary office workers who believe in magic."

"But still," I objected, "Reality has a powerful way of pushing back."

Goldie soothed, "The parasites who think they run the show have been scheming to control humanity since before the advent of writing. But the Universe is vaster than their most elaborate ambitions. They can't plug all the cracks."

"Like the song says, 'There are cracks in everything, that's how the light gets in.'"

"The key is to reconcile opposites: free will and determinism. Evolution is inevitable, new generations, new ideas. Our free will choice is whether to evolve purposefully or dragging our feet."

"I guess I've been a foot dragger for many lives."

"Those who choose an accelerated path expedite free will. When souls slog through countless incarnations because they are comfortable with the status quo, even on the bottom rung of life's ladder their lives are ever more dictated by external, deterministic circumstances. These souls seek to punish those who do not share their beliefs."

"We call them fundamentalists on Earth. They come in all flavors. But I don't agree, Goldie. Life on Earth is tough for everybody regardless of their beliefs. Everyone faces traumatic ordeals in every lifetime: scientific rationalists, religious fundamentalists, saints, and sinners. Life is beautiful and messy. Free will sometimes takes a back seat to another person's will."

"Souls on fire incarnate into a spiritual hot house which may contain terrible tribulations, forcing one to processes frequent lessons."

"Some troubles are meaningless, with no one to blame, no lesson to process."

"Didn't we agree that waking up is hard to do?"

"Waking up ain't for sissies." The tall golden grass rippled across the windswept meadow.

Then Goldie segued absurdly. "Which came first, the phoenix or the egg?"

"I give up."

"Neither, the phoenix rises from its own ashes. It doesn't lay eggs."

"Is this a riddle or a joke?"

"Knock Knock."

"Who's there?"

"Phoenix."

"Phoenix who?"

Phoenix rises from its own asses."

"Goldie that's as moronic as it is crude," I objected, laughing in spite of myself.

"Do you want to hear a poem of my own composition?" Goldie asked.

Glad for the distraction, I replied, "Yeah, sure."

Preening like a diva, Goldie recited:
"A phoenix' life's made in the shade
Something about lemonade.
The fire's orgasmic.
The ashes fantasmic.
Sometimes a bird wants to get laid."

"Something about lemonade! That's a terrible line. And I don't think fantasmic is even a word!"

"Everybody's a critic! I couldn't find a word to rhyme with orgasmic, so I had to make one up. There should be a word that rhymes with orgasmic," declared Goldie haughtily.

"You're right about that," I agreed. "There should be many words that rhyme with orgasmic."

"Hellooo! It's an important word and belongs in many poems."

"No argument here."

"Yourgasmic," Goldie sang.

"Moregasmic," I quipped.

"Roargasmic"

"Fanfuckintasmic."

"Yes!" Goldie rejoiced. "One should shout these words loudly during the moment of sexual ecstasy. And I would, if I could have sex!"

I laughed at the thought. "I'll remember that when I see Javier."

"Your husband?"

"Yes."

"Tell me all about his lovemaking."

"I think not, you dirty bird," I reprimanded primly.

"Not at all. I am an immortal, ancient, asexual creature," Goldie replied. "I've watched people and animals dance the fandango for ages and I want to know what all the fuss is about. Would you give up sex for immortality?"

I countered with a non sequitur. "Something about Lemonade?"

"I suppose you could do better?" Goldie challenged.

"Lemonade, made, shade, raid, afraid, unafraid.. of blank blank we are blank unafraid."

"Of poop we are never afraid!" exclaimed Goldie dramatically. "Phoenixes neither eat nor poop."

"For a creature that doesn't have bodily functions, you have a scatological turn of mind."

"One's interests can range from the bawdy to the sublime."

"So I gather."

"Of blank we are never afraid. Of germs we remain unafraid," Goldie conjectured.

"Of death we are never afraid," I supplied.

"Perfect," Goldie spread her wings, made a pirouette, and recited theatrically:
> *"A Phoenix' life's made in the shade.*
> *Of death we are never afraid.*
> *The fire's orgasmic,*
> *The ashes moregasmic,*
> *Sometimes a bird wants to get laid."*

Clapping, I asked, "What happened to fantasmic?"

"I liked moregasmic better. It implies more orgasms. Thank you."

"You're welcome."

"It is a brilliant collaboration between a mortal woman and an immortal bird. I will share credit with you."

"Please don't. I couldn't take credit for that, uh, poem," I protested.

"Oh, but you must!"

"No, really!"

"I insist."

I gave up, "OK, fine. Thanks for sharing the credit."

"Our illustrious verse will be remembered long after we're both gone."

"You'll be around forever."

"I was trying to soften the blow."

"Tell me, when you are consumed by flames and reborn from ashes, how does that feel? Is it a painful death? A difficult birth?"

"No, it is exquisitely pleasurable, my favorite part of immortality."

"Well, there's your answer, Goldie. Sex and death are two sides of the same coin. Your fiery death and rebirth are your orgasm and your moregasm."

Goldie's feathered face rubbed against my cheek and her soft voice was a whispered kiss. "I'll see you again, Dana." She extended her wings to their full span, threw back her long neck, and burst into flame as her entire body was engulfed in a fiery conflagration, all the while exulting, "Fan-fucking-tasmic!" until only a pile of smoldering ash remained.

I contemplated the snake in my navel as it uncoiled and rose to embrace my heart.

CHAPTER 29

Fourth Chakra ~
Heart, compassion, love, air, green, blocked by grief

The light gradually ripened from gold to green. Leaves unfurled into a thousand shades from the softest sage to the deepest forest. My body was swaddled. I could only open my eyes a sliver to blurry images. A fuzzy emerald surface resolved into focus. Strong, warm arms enfolded me in a green baby blanket. Focus clarified; my own mother gazed upon me with all the love in the world. I was a newborn babe, cradled in her arms, and could only gaze back at her with infantile awe.

Unaccountably, I remembered this moment, this moment of absolute unconditional mother love. Mother's face morphed and was replaced by the face of another loving mother. I was another infant in another lifetime. Mother's face morphed again. I soaked in the beauty of infinite mother love through a thousand incarnations. Her hair flowed blond, then red, then black, then wavy, then straight, then curly, then canine, then scales, then feathers. Her beauty merged into the face of Divine Mother; a face so radiant that it was unbearable to behold

I had not known that joy could be so intense that it hurt. My heart ached and little infant whimpers escaped my throat then roused into a gusty wail. Her brilliance subsided a little and I could bear her visage again. Despite my helplessness, this moment was perfect.

Mother reverted to my own very dearly beloved and recently departed Mother, Gayle. It was a younger version of Mom and a toddler version of me. We were in a room I remembered from the first house in which I ever lived. The green walls were illuminated by soft morning light. My Dad, Frank came into the room, young, skinny, and handsome. I was their only child, and this was a happy memory. I was safe and loved. Mother and Father were giddy with affection for me, still basking in wedded bliss.

The walls receded and were replaced by a wooden hut. I was with the same parents, except, this was a medieval incarnation. My parents could barely afford to keep me alive in this painfully indifferent world. Poverty was a harsh master. Fast forward, as a young man, I joined the priesthood, trying to fill the void in my heart and the ache in my belly. But while the church fed my body, it did not nourish my spirit. I expected to serve God's flock; instead, I was trained to use the faithful to service the Church's interest. Several more lives in medieval Europe passed before me in which the Church dominated my circumstances. I was a self-righteous inquisitor, a woman burned for heresy, a nun, and an abandoned orphan.

In one tableau, I was a peasant farmer during the Medieval Inquisition in Southern France. I was poor, dirty, ignorant, religious, and content. I had a nice wife and two sons who had grown to manhood. I had a hound dog named Pierre in honor of all the rocks in my miserable plot of soil. In our village there was a humane count, Raymond, and his good wife, our Countess Elaine. Both were kind and friendly. Her charitable works brought light to our desolate lives and made festivals happen.

One winter, Inquisitors came to town. Our beloved Countess was accused of heresy and tortured to death. Count Raymond was offered his life in exchange for relinquishing his land, title, and wealth and departing on a pilgrimage to the Holy Land. Heartbroken, he complied and left our village forever. His daughters were sent to convents. His sons accompanied him to the Holy Land. I knew Count Raymond as Vincent. I knew Countess Elaine as Gwen. A new count and countess were appointed to govern our feudal village. They were dour, joyless, pious, heartless, ambitious folks. I recognized them as reptilians, Senator Oral Rockbottom and Congresswoman Fanny Gnositall. The Church got most of Raymond's wealth when King and Pope endowed our new lords. We accepted their rule, but there was never another village celebration. We shrank into our hovels and worked ourselves to death. That was our righteous and holy obligation.

The sorrow of all the loss of these harsh incarnations was assuaged when I incarnated as a nun who ran an orphanage, and then as a privileged nobleman who offered largess to his small feudal community. As I viewed this parade of past lives, I experienced the joy of selfless service to others as the remedy to grief.

There was a presence at my side. I turned to see a tall, striking, dark-scaled reptile beside me. She looked very different, but I knew it was Alice.

"Welcome down the rabbit hole," she whispered jubilantly as if this was her domain.

"Alice! You look beautiful!" We hugged and danced in each other's arms.

"Welcome yourself! What's up with your makeover?" Alice had previously stood my height, five foot three inches tall. Now she was a statuesque six-foot Amazon. Her facial features were unchanged but stretched over an oval rather than a round face. Her neck had lengthened as well. She was dressed in a stunning red and gold dashiki dress with matching red and gold headdress.

"Is this you in a prior incarnation?"

"No, Dana, this is now. Reptiles can metamorphose their appearance. We do so very rarely. It is painful, time-consuming. Few who have done it once ever do it a second time. Most would rather cross over and reincarnate into a new body. But I have imperative work for the Individual Reptilian Movement on Earth, which necessitated a transformation that would make me unrecognizable to the Reptilian Hierarchy. Bo and Guna Raza guided me through this metamorphosis. I have been with them in Tellara these many weeks since your wedding. Once the transformation was complete, I traveled to Blue Henge Temple to share my story with you."

"You are as beautiful on the outside as you are on the inside, living proof that every soul can spiritually evolve."

"You recognized me, instantly. Others will not. Call me Alice Raza."

"Oh, Alice!" We hugged again, and she began her story in a powerful contralto.

"For many lifetimes, I was a reptilian enforcer. I hunted and killed humans like animals. I was good at what I did and reveled in it. The men who you know as Sheldon Walters and Kek Hammer were on my team. We had different names and faces in those incarnations, but we three dominated the apex of the Hierarchy. We Draconians are longer-lived and have greater past life recall than humans. Because of this, most reptiles do not recognize humanity's vastly greater evolutionary potential. Reptiles think of the soul as a pathetic human fabrication designed to ease humanity's meaningless existence. You are useful for labor, entertainment, sex, and sometimes food.

"Alice, how did you change your mind?"

"Not my mind, Dana, my heart. It was a slave raid in West Africa near the end of the eighteenth century. In that lifetime, my guise was that of a Portuguese mercenary. I captured tribal people and herded them onto slave ships bound for the Americas. The Reptilian Hierarchy's agenda was to dominate Africa in a multi-century strategy: first, the slavery holocaust; second, the economic holocaust which exacerbated tribal wars and promoted colonization; third, biological warfare by the introduction and promulgation of diseases which kept the population orphaned and hungry; and fourth, the devastation of fresh water sources. Slavery, colonization, disease, war, drought, famine, all an intentional, multi-pronged agenda. The Bible was our greatest weapon."

"Why? For God's sake?"

"The continent of Africa holds ancient relics and riches from Earth's prehistory that its tribal people have protected, and reptilians have coveted for millennia."

"Riches?"

"Archeological evidence of the seeding of life on this planet by ancient galactic species."

"Oh, that fits with Louie's theory of panspermia," was all I could think to say.

"In a slave raid, in what would be present-day Angola, I was horribly wounded. My fellow raiders left me for dead. The very people that I hunted carried me deep into the interior between Angola and the Congo where they delivered me to the hut of their Witch. They called themselves the Children of the Moon. The first thing the Witch did was use her magic to strip me of my human facade and expose my reptilian visage. I was too weak to resist.

"Her magic?"

"Herbs, chants, rituals."

"What was her name?"

"Reva. She manipulated aboriginal powers in resonance with nature that reptilians have actively suppressed all over the world. Crushing the right-brained, intuitive aspect of human understanding was a major motivation of colonization and religious conversion by European powers."

"Including the Church?"

"And other western religions."

"Please continue with your story."

"We reptiles are a vigorous species, but my convalescence lasted months. I was fed strange plants that gave me surreal waking dreams. I languished between life and death in the sweltering heat, assailed by altered states of consciousness. An endless stream of tribal ancestors and ghosts of the Moon Children visited me. They showed me their stories, their joys and sorrows, their ceremonies, deaths, births, and trauma at having their families ripped apart by this evil slave trade.

"Outside my hut, despite the terrible sorrow of kidnapped young people, life went on. Daily activities were punctuated with ceremonial music, dancing, chanting, animal noises, bone flutes, strange twanging string instruments, and ceaseless drumming. In my drugged state, this backdrop of rhythmic tribal life became normal. My consciousness was cracked open by psychedelic plant medicine from the iboga tree. To use a modern expression, Reva was deprogramming me. Between the ancestral visitors, the drumming, and the hallucinations, I apprehended the triumph of the human spirit due to your open hearts and robust souls. This realization caused agonizing, incapacitating pangs of conscience. I resisted the healing. I went mad. You can only imagine how much I hated this transformation at first. Had I not been so weak, I would have torn that jungle apart destroying every living thing I could reach. That primeval, psychoactive plant made me ache for love, an utterly foreign concept.

"The iboga plant medicine worked differently on my reptilian physiology than it does on humans. I already had fourth-dimensional consciousness, but my newly opened heart chakra was raw, evoking the emotional and psychic pain of every injury I'd ever inflicted. The disincarnate Children of the Moon ancestors bore witness to this dark purge, sometimes in silent witness, sometimes screaming out the voices of the voiceless, sometimes dancing and chanting reenactments of my brutal crimes. There was no escape. These so-called primitive tribespeople had saved my life and inflicted an all-consuming cleansing of my soul. I could not regain the amoral high ground nor my reptilian arrogance. I screamed and ranted but, debilitated, I could do little more than crawl out to the fire. The Children of the Moon chanted and danced my heart awake. They formed a circle around me. My name was a repetitive incantation that was both scolding and merciful. I cried for the first time.

"After many moons, the drumming ceased, the chanting stilled. I lay as a lump in the dirt, not knowing if I was living or dead. I was dragged to a pond and dunked into cool water. The village women washed my wounds. I was exhausted and starving. Small amounts of food and water were fed to me. I craved meat but was allowed none. Later, I became aware I was no longer in the pool, but seated on a mat in Reva's hut. Pond, hut, pond, hut, I crawled between the two locations for an indeterminate time while the powerful drug worked its way out of my system.

"I was as helpless as a kitten, a word I use intentionally, I felt like a pet. I, who had mercilessly traded slaves, was now property, or so I thought, not understanding that I was an adopted tribal member. I spent my days learning how to walk, talk, and discern unbidden flashes of compassion in my nascent heart. I laughed with humor, not cruelty. I cried when others suffered. Irrational creative thoughts entered my consciousness, so I began to carve wooden talismans. The children included me in their sports, including the stone games where my clever patterns delighted all players. Never to be trusted with weapons, I was forbidden to hunt. Time passed. I had been living with the Children of the Moon for two years.

"Reva, ancient and terrifyingly beautiful in her primal paint and animal garb, was my savior. Prior to my confinement, I'd have considered her a primitive joke, fit only to be worked to death. Now, I considered her the most glorious creature on Earth. Her power and magic shamed me. We reptiles can see around the corners of time, but Reva could swim in temporal currents and channel the flow. She could call in rain and beasts of prey. She could camouflage herself as a tree. She used this technique to evade slavers and to shield others.

"Reva had a young acolyte named Chanda, who was my caregiver and teacher when Reva was busy with other tribal matters. Chanda weaned me off the ibogaine and helped me understand that the drug was a healing ritual, not a punishment. She was just past puberty, vital, and talented in the magical arts. Chanda was Reva's protégé. Dana, you were Chanda."

"What?! I was a medicine woman in Africa?"

"That is where we first met and learned to honor each other. When I finally took human form again, I modeled myself after Reva. In this lifetime, Kek and

Walters cannot fathom why I choose to incarnate as a short, disabled, black woman in the American South, having once been a macho warrior. I tell them I am on a mission to learn more about our burdens as custodians. They accept this preposterous explanation because changes in loyalty among Draconians have been incomprehensible since time immemorial."

I interrupted, "But we both know that it's happened before, and that brilliant reptiles live here on Tellara."

"Kek and Walters don't even entertain the possibility. I am an enigma that must be scrutinized. Meeting the Raza Clan has affirmed my deepest aspirations for the Reptilian Individual Movement on Earth."

"So, you remained with the Children of the Moon?"

"Not much longer. One morning, slavers attacked our village. I fought side by side with my tribe; a wild jungle lizard standing upright and shredding slavers with claws and teeth. Most backed off, but one among them was a reptile enforcer that I knew. He did not recognize me. My newly darkened scales had transformed my appearance. Nevertheless, he knew me for a traitor to the Hierarchy, and struck a mortal blow.

"Nearby, Reva was veiling herself by dissolving into the trunk of an iboga tree, shielding Chanda with her branches, but to no avail. Chanda and other Children of the Moon youth were tethered and dragged off into captivity. I saw Chanda... you... Dana, dragged off to a life of slavery. I witnessed the magical legacy of the Moon Children slip away for generations as my own lifeforce waned."

"So, I was a slave?"

"In a sense, we both were. Hovering between life and death, the disincarnate tribal ancestors surrounded me. I was granted the opportunity to break out of the concretized Reptilian Hierarchy permanently. This awakening, that humans seek as your birthright, is an abomination for Draconians. Our fourth-dimensional experiences are limited to the physical, sensual, and mental. Compassion, creativity, and intuition are unnatural. Our DNA precludes it. Using free will to break out of my species' fixed mentality transformed my cells at the molecular level."

"I felt connected to you the moment we met, Alice."

"I lost track of you for many lifetimes, Dana. But when I encountered you at Shelter, my heart soared with joy," Alice reached out and took my hand in hers.

"What an extraordinary journey."

"The goal of the Reptilian Individual Movement on Earth is to reach critical mass in our numbers. The good news is that once Individuals have exercised compassionate free will, it is easier for us to recognize each other. We will eventually connect collectively and be a genuine challenge to the Hierarchy."

"Like the hundredth monkey effect?"

"Yes, the Hierarchy has a blind spot to love. I recruited Huckleberry and Finn as children, two orphans longing for mother love. Thanks to Reva and Chanda, I know how to awaken compassionate hearts."

"This would probably be a good time for me to tell you about the time I needed rescuing and Huckleberry and Finn found me in the AllNite Coffee Shop."

"Yes, even though I know they rescued you, recount the particular details so I can peer around the corners of time and arrange the connection."

I did so, and we reminisced for a while. "Alice, your story is a revelation. Since going through your metamorphosis on Tellara, you've become a statuesque beauty."

"I choose this attractive guise for my return to Earth. We reptiles are a vain species."

"We humans are too."

"We've noticed and exploited that trait for centuries. Vanity, thy name is Homo sapiens." We both laughed as the deep green horizon glowed pink with sunrise. A dog barked. Then another. Rip came bounding up to greet me. So did Pierre, the hound from my medieval peasant life. "This is very trippy, a living mutt and a departed dog together in my heart chakra." Soon dogs I had known and loved in many incarnations surrounded me, rejoicing in our reunion. "All dogs do go to Heaven!" I exclaimed.

Alice spoke, "Animals embody unconditional love. You have loved many pets and never intentionally harmed an animal." With that said, two friendly fat pigs, numerous horses, donkeys, yaks, cats, and a crow burst through the green thicket. Affectionate animals nuzzled me as I recalled their names.

Goldie, my fine-feathered phoenix friend, glided gracefully into the love fest. "I told you I'd see you again, Dana." I introduced the fantasmic phoenix to the resplendent reptile.

"Goldie, meet Alice Raza." The two bowed deeply to each other.

Alice rose to her full height and fixed me with an inspirational gaze. No more the weak, wounded wallflower, Alice wordlessly announced her departure from my ritual. Twelve pink lotus petals radiated from her heart, expanding until she dissolved into a celestial starburst. Pink lotus petals enfolded all the animals in a whirling flowerstorm. I was alone with Goldie.

The sun rose higher, unveiling clear azure skies. Below, aquamarine waves lapped at our ankles. I waded to the water's edge and climbed onto a large flat boulder, warming in the morning sun.

Simultaneously, we spotted a large blue caterpillar inching its way over the smooth rock surface. Goldie plucked it up with its beak. The caterpillar bellowed with great indignation, "Let me go you fowl feathered beast! I am the storyteller here in the throat chakra sanctuary!"

The Fifth Chakra ~
Throat, voice, truth, sound, blue, blocked by deceit

Goldie dropped the caterpillar back onto its rock, burst into flame, cried out "Moregasmic!" while consuming herself. The caterpillar disdainfully crawled away from the smoldering pile of ashes.

"It'll be back, and I'll have to scold it all over again." the caterpillar grumbled. "Let's move inside, shall we?" he asked hospitably.

"Lead the way," I accepted. He climbed onto my forearm, lifted his body to an upright bearing, and turned his face toward the west. We entered an enchanting lakeside cabin.

"Do you have a name?" I asked.

"My name is Sapphire, but my friends call me Sapphy. I have been awaiting you Dana Travers. How have you enjoyed the panoramas you've faced so far in the chakra ritual?"

"I would not use the word enjoy."

"Lessons?"

"That's more accurate, and right now I could use a respite from lessons."

"Were you told that if you align all seven chakras, you would have an opportunity to access your higher chakras, those beyond the body in the etheric field?"

"Not interested. This has been a difficult passage."

"Then how about a story? I am a renowned raconteur. Come, sit, relax."

Sapphy led me to a comfy couch overlooking blue water and azure sky. The room was filled with stacks of books. The walls were covered with shelves lined from top to bottom with volumes, photographs, and art. I recognized titles, faces, and scenes from many lifetimes, some of them my own. I nestled into the couch. Sapphy perched atop a stack of books and took his place beside my ear. "Look to your left. There sits a freshly steeped cup of heart blossom tea." I saw the steaming brew and took a satisfying sip while Sapphy munched a handful of heartplum leaves.

"Best to begin at the beginning, don't you think?" Without waiting for me to answer, Sapphy assumed an oratory posture. "Once upon a time, you thought you knew the story, but the story of reality is oh, so much bigger than you realize."

"I glimpsed a bigger story when I came to Tellara through a portal in a painting."

"Well, Dana, expand your canvas, because the story is always bigger and more mysterious than you think it is. No matter what you think is going on, there are intelligences beyond the boundaries of your comprehension that are orchestrating vaster mythos."

"I hope so, because in my planetary narrative, the bad guys are winning. We fight endless wars over contrived motives. Good people suffer while the wealthiest control our resources. We are destroying our habitat. Earth is becoming dystopian."

"And Tellara is Utopian?"

"Relative to Earth, I think so."

"But you're in a position to change that?"

"So they tell me."

"Consider that no one is in control. Beyond the boundaries of the known scale of reality we follow fractal pathways to our next octave of experience. You have an opportunity to use your voice to steer your planetary narrative to the next level."

"That sounds like a bumper sticker from the sixties, 'What is Reality?'"

"Reality is scale, Dana. Reality is what you are aware of from the smallest to the largest aspects of perception. In your case, from the Earth's surface to the sun, your ecosystem, biology, and weather. Although you know that subatomic bits and galaxies exist, do they impact your daily life?"

"Not until recently, when I passed through a quantum singularity; but in general, no. My daily life defines my reality: my health, my activities, the people I interact with, my environment."

"When you expand your canvas, reality expands along spiraling fractal pathways to ever vaster experiences."

"I know about fractals, self-similar, self-replicating patterns in nature."

"Patterns in spacetime. Hence, stories are fractals. So are lifetimes."

"No!"

"You keep repeating similar patterns until you've learned the lessons."

"Spare me from repeating patterns!"

"Plants and animals are fractals," Sapphy continued as though he had not heard me.

I replied, "I've seen the phi ratio in a tree's branching system. That's a Fibonacci fractal pattern."

"People are fractals."

"So, I've heard."

"People come from other people, replicating and similar but not identical. All your organic systems follow the golden ratio, skeleton, blood vessels, DNA, even family resemblance."

"Hmmm… I've seen those golden proportions in Leonardo's Vitruvian Man."

"Ah, Leonardo," Sapphy sighed rapturously. "We are all spiraling through the

Universe, moving ever onward in a cosmic loop, originating in the Great Mother Sea, involuting through the stages of matter and awareness, and evolving back to the her. As we leap to each successive octave, the vehicles we design become ever more coherent to house our evolving consciousness. We each bring our unique experiences back to the whole. Infinite variety in perfect unity."

"According to my lessons with Saffron, we created our world collectively."

"You all agreed to accept Earth's reality as the correct, inescapable world. But this consensus reality comes from centuries of programmed beliefs. It is not the end of the story."

"I get what you're saying. For instance, Louie thinks there is an ancient space war going on for the sovereignty of Earth. Evil reptilians are battling the enlightened Galactic Family over humanity's right to self-determination. Even if this is true, it doesn't impact people's daily lives. But if this hypothetical battle were to somehow be disclosed, all of humanity's realities would bust wide open."

"As would your reality 'bust wide open' if any mythic prophecy came to pass."

"Like Revelations," I nodded, thinking about the end time myths we shared in Wah'Kon-Tah.

"And beyond these space wars and mythic prophecies?" Sapphy prodded.

"Ever vaster stories, lessons, lifetimes, and realities?" A light bulb went on, "Like Tellara ascending."

Sapphy counseled, "Buckle your seatbelt, kid. It's going to be a bumpy ride back to the P-soup."

"Sapphy," I asked, "What manner of creature are you?"

"My taxonomic designation is Nymphalidae Galactica. But I prefer the generic Imaginal-Celled Raconteur, at your service." Sapphire executed a gracious bow and handed me a small bouquet of heartplum blossoms and kept the leaves to munch.

"A raconteur with many hands."

"I like to multi-task, eat, read, write, paint, arrange flowers, and dust all at the same time."

"You are a very talented fellow. Is Tellara your home?"

"No, I am an inter-dimensional visitor.

"What brings you to my throat chakra?"

"The experiences you undergo in this journey are of your own design. I must be here because you drew me into your orbit."

"Well done, us! What does it mean to be inter-dimensional?"

"I travel along thought waves. I remember the future as well as the past. I read the Akashic Record."

"Sounds like magic."

"What do you think magic is?"

"Well, an imaginative man from Earth once said, 'Any sufficiently advanced technology is indistinguishable from magic.' Voxes seems like magic to me."

Sapphy crawled off the stack of books and moved to an enormous open volume on the floor. Flipping through pages, he found a passage, "That imaginative fellow was named Arthur C. Clarke. It's right here in my Earth Lore text. Here's a quote from another ingenious Earth human named Nicola Tesla. 'The day science begins to study non-physical phenomena, it will make more progress in one decade than in all the previous centuries of its existence.' You see, Dana, ninety-six percent of the Universe is imperceptible to human sensory organs. The non-physical infrastructure of so-called empty space is the implicate order of existence. Your Earth science studies only the perceptible, measurable four percent of all manifestation, the explicate order."

"Well, we have hypothesized dark matter and dark energy to fill in the empty space." I defended what I thought I understood.

"I wouldn't invest any of my leafy greens in a search for dark matter or dark energy."

"But apparently you have a better notion of what's out there in the vacuum?"

"Tellaran science is based on it."

"Do Earth scientists know that they are leaving out the ninety-six percent of everything?"

"Yes, but they ignore it. You see, the density of empty space is virtually infinite."

"Virtually infinite? What does that mean?"

"When measured in Earth units, the density of so-called empty space is 10^{93}gm/cm^3.

"That's a big number."

"Infinite and organized. The implicate order appears empty unless you know what to look for. In order to solve theoretical equations, physics has renormalized the density of empty space to zero. It is a veritable vacuum catastrophe." Sapphy shook his head and his antennae quivered.

"From infinity to zero, that's one hell of a paradox," I said.

"It is so inconvenient to have infinity on one side of the equal sign in an equation. Infinity equal to anything else just doesn't compute. Not to mention the peskiness of having infinity on both sides of an equal sign. Infinity equals infinity. Every other term becomes inconsequential." Sapphy chewed thoughtfully on his heartplum bouquet.

I thought about this for a minute and said, "At least this renormalization helped establish boundaries so science could calculate about the four percent. We're even searching for the tiniest theoretical God particles."

"Remember what Tesla said about studying the non-physical phenomena? Instead of looking for a fundamental particle, Tellarans study the fundamental structure of space. Space is infinitely dense because it has an internal geometric structure that is perfectly balanced in every direction and at every scale. This forms the most stable shape that can exist, the nested cube octahedron." Sapphy flipped through his Earth Lore text. "Another of your brilliant Earth scientists, Buckminster Fuller, named it the isometric vector equilibrium."

"Another highfalutin' term for whatever you just said. Except, those vector lines can't all be the same length if this grid exists at all scales." I thought I had him there.

"Those geometric shapes, like cube octahedrons and star tetrahedrons, are nested, like your Russian Matryoshka dolls, in precise ratio along the golden spiral. Each geometric structure can be divided and subdivided from the outer limits of the Universe to the tiniest quanta, always along the exact Fibonacci fractal scale. At intersecting points on the linear infrastructure, spheres interpenetrate the grid, like bubbles. From quantum foam to the Universe's boundary, bubbles spinning, interpenetrating, vibrating, and sliding along the grid in a cosmic dance."

"That's what you're calling the implicate order, this invisible configuration of lines and circles?"

"Look here, your Galileo Galilei said, 'Mathematics is the alphabet with which God has written the Universe.'"

"There must be people on Earth who study this ninety-six percent of everything! It's mathematics, geometry, numbers, and shapes, all vibrating at every frequency."

Sapphy flipped through the pages. "Dear me, I see that on Earth this entire branch of study is mostly unfunded and ridiculed. Your science has its prejudices. The technology of the explicate leads to entropy, combustion, explosions, and depletion of resources. The technology of the implicate leads to organization, syntropy, and perpetual energy."

"On Earth, science follows the money. Funding sources must be invested in the explicate order, like petrochemical energy. We call the implicate order paranormal, supernatural, or metaphysical. The phenomena arising from these events are dismissed as non-scientific superstition."

"To be fair, some of your scientists take the concept of nonlocal reality seriously. Everything is entangled and connected. That's why the Universe is holographic, fractal, and filled with perpetual energy."

"Einstein called nonlocal reality 'Spooky action at a distance.'" I remembered that from the Discovery Channel.

"This brilliant quote by an Earth bard named Shakespeare says it all. 'There are more things in heaven and earth than are dreamed of in your philosophy.' Not so much spooky as magical." Sapphy crawled over to a potted plant and picked himself a bunch of leaves.

"What do the laws of nature have to do with magic?" I asked.

"You said it yourself. Vox technology utilizes non-physical, conscious, syntropic, nonlocal, vibrating, and spinning perpetual energy. It is therefore indistinguishable from magic."

I helped myself to another cup of heartplum tea, while observing, "Sapphy, you nibble those leaves constantly."

"Feeding my imaginal cells," he answered munching a mouthful.

I mused, "Living in my imagination has brought me both joy and sorrow. It got me to Tellara, but all my life, I've randomly daydreamed when I'm supposed to be attending to business."

"One woman's daydream is another woman's doorway to new worlds. The entire Universe is a design of consciousness. The linear aspects of the 64-tetrahedron grid constitutes the masculine, rational qualities of mind, the yang. The spherical bubbles that interpenetrate the grid points comprise the feminine, creative, intuitive mental qualities, the yin."

"And that geometric infrastructure is the foundation of creation? Is this the P-Soup?"

"No." Sapphy was adamant.

"Don't tell me there's more invisible stuff out there."

"You already know about it. The 640tetrahedron grid makes up the vacuum of spacetime. The P-soup, the Great Mother Sea is made up with monads 10^{40} times smaller and faster than light. The speed of thought drives your vox.

"Sapphy, I really can't visualize what you're talking about."

"Well then, let's visit the quantum vista together, shall we?"

"What? How?"

Sapphy crawled over to a bookshelf and, using his many appendages, rummaged through their bindings until he found a massive black volume and gently slid it onto the floor. Opening to a page filled with drawings and symbols, he invited me to come close and read over his shoulder. As he recited in his singsong lilt, my focus contracted and together we merged into the parchment. My scale of reality swiftly shrank as planet-sized atoms whizzed by us. We glided along gridlines and rolled over spherical slides; down, down as countless moon-sized whirlwinds danced around us. Down further still, we descended through a spongy layer of roiling froth, to find ourselves at last motionless in a sea of liquid, loving light.

"Is this the P-Soup?" I was wonderstruck by the beauty filled with blinking sparks of inconceivable colors and a background hum of pure music.

"Welcome home to the omnipresent Great Mother Sea." Then Sapphy struck a professorial pose and recited, while I watched the panoply of creation.

Original Spin

Beneath the quantum boundary
Lies the Sea of Pure Potentiality
Source Field, P-Soup, Cosmic Mind
Where every notion is designed
Prima Materia, Protosea
Mother, Father, Gravity
Zero-Point, Vacuum, Levity
Primal Possibility
O Great Mother, O Great Sea
Bosom of Eternity

Proto-matter of creation
In endless organized gyration
Creates mysterious geometries
With staggering velocities
In exotic rare dimensions
That defy all known conventions

Particles tinier than the quanta,
Spinning faster than they oughtta
So swift as to appear motionless
But they are not emotionless
Spiral whirling with delight
Living Liquid Loving Light
Each monad spark of consciousness
Has urgent longing to express

Some monads bathing in original spin
Have journeyed there and back again
Billions of years, myriad incarnations
Untold limitations ineffable vibrations
Each thread in Universal history
Weaves through Akashic tapestry
From perfect unity to infinite diversity
Monads rejoin Great Mother Sea
As each entangled spark returns
Sharing all that it has learned
Ancient cosmic law demands
Universe gains wisdom as she expands

Nascent sparks in Cosmic Sea
Bathe in monadic ecstasy

Yearn to take the Hero's Quest
Cry out in foolish innocence,
Enthusiastic Yes! Yes! Yes!
To involute and then evolve
Each unique aspect to resolve
These spinning vortices galore
Seek to experience
More! More! More!
Little knowing what's in store
O, bring me home Great Mother Sea
Bosom of Eternity

"Sapphire, I love all those other wonderful names for the P-soup, especially the Great Mother Sea. It evokes the authentic union of science and spirtualty. I know of another name for this omnipresent sea. A master named Obi-Wan Kenobi called it the Force. He said it surrounds us, penetrates us, and binds the Universe together."

"I'd like to meet this Obi-Wan Kenobi."

I smiled. "So, would I. Sapphy, this vista reminds me of the tableau in my first chakra. I was a monad volunteering to jump off that great precipice into the unknown, believing nothing could hurt me. I was advised that you can't fall out of the Universe. What a feckless, fearless fool."

"Incarnating ain't for sissies, Dana. It's a good thing we're all in the soup together."

"I'm glad you used poetry to describe our vista. Phoenix drags me through tedious lessons."

"Nymphalidae Galactica are born raconteurs." We began to float towards the fuzzy boundary that surrounded the Great Mother Sea. We were the size and shape of quantum petals sliding through gauze designed like the flower of life. From beneath, the pattern looked like a flat membrane of finest lace, but as we emerged into that effervescent foam, I could see tiny tangential structures jutting into tetrahedrons that interconnected in perfect symmetry, ascending like myriad ladders into vaster, distant panoramas. We slid in and out of the quanta-sized openings.

"Welcome to the quantum foam," pronounced Sapphy. Spinning monads emerged into our space. Some escaped upwards and found a niche within the lattice. Others retreated back through the petals into the Primal Sea. Some dizzyingly fast sparks flew up and away, far beyond our field of perception. I had to tread water in order to keep my balance in this spongy foam while brushing swirling bubbles off my face. Beyond this quantum foam, I could apprehend the ever-expanding architecture of the Universe. Translucent beams, pyramids, and spherical bubbles intersected at grid points. Some vortices spun far up the lattice, along fractal tendrils following the golden mean ratio. Other voxel vortices whirled and coalesced into ever-more defined particles. "I feel a poetic moment coming on," Sapphy said. As he recited, I watched, mesmerized, as the voxels scattered through the quantum foam, converging into organized patterns all over the architecture of the Universe.

Syntropy

We've heard of chaotic entropy
Diffusing mass and energy
For entropy to disperse organization
Presupposes harmonized configuration
Resonant concatenation
Within the fabric of creation

Consciousness drives syntropy
Using quantum gravity
To sculpt regular polyhedrons
Like octagons and tetrahedrons
Isometric vector equilibrium
Quantum gravity is quantum love
As below, So above
As voxel vortices emerge
Geometric forms converge
Syntropy sculpts proto-matter
On holofractalgraphic ladder

Spongy fuzzy foam surrounds
The Primal Sea's upmost bounds
  From our scale of reality
  This tiny quantum boundary
Is finer than the finest mesh
Within a frothy frizzy mess
  Flower of life weaves delicate lace
  Petal portals launch time-mass-space
Each voxel vortex emerges to be
Mass in our reality
As matter or as energy
  Through roiling boiling quantum foam
  Burst forth in air and sea and loam
Monads emerge with relentless insistence
Dancing the Universe into existence
  Extraordinary Big Bangs, infinite tiny bangs
  Continuous creation, perpetual birth pangs

When negatively unstable voxel ascends
Thru quantum foam she then descends
   These gentle ephemeral vortices
   Elude internal gravity forces
She collapses back into the P-Soup
To rejoin her proto-matter mother group
   If this monad gets her way
   She'll rise again another day

Whence emerges vortex with stable thrust
Onward piercing quantum crust
   Whizzing past minuscule photon
   To arise as stable blackwhole proton
A cosmic truth is then revealed
Protons occupy unified field
   In a moment of entangled elation
   Exchanges Universal information
   Each center of gravity
   Joins its atomic family
The proton exults in its Universal sharing
Nonlocal cosmic love and caring
   Fundamental particles of existence
   Engaged in primal cosmic dance
Spinning at light speed, cohering mass

Whence the positively unstable voxel
Explodes through portal petal volatile
   Erupting through the vortex door,
   Disrupting quantum foam galore!
   Eagerly accruing mass
   Solid, liquid, plasma, gas
   Drawn from singularity
   Still linked to Primal Mother Sea
   Blackwhole shapes a galaxy
   Using quantum gravity
   Or should I say negentropy?
Our heroine is not yet done
Attracting matter farther flung
   Galactic heart, crucible of creation
   Continuous matter generation
   Her poles erupt galactic geysers
   Innumerable exploding stars
Our esteemed blackwhole attracts and expands
Ejecting massive spiral bands

Galactic arms of ringing flow
Along the golden ratio
Along event horizon mold
Toroidal field's arms so enfold
She spins and grows with causality
In violent graceful choreography
Conscious causative mystery
Of every spiral galaxy

"Sapphire, you've just given me an astonishing insight." I called him by his proper name after this poetic display. He bowed graciously. "I hadn't realized why understanding Tellaran physics would maximize my vox's capabilities. Now, I can visualize proto-matter voxel vortices rising at the speed of thought. Javier and Louie asked Bo Raza if he could tweak the vox to function as a replicator or a transporter like on Star Trek. Bo told us that it wasn't the technology that needed changing, but the operator's thoughts. Sapphy, I can channel my thought waves through the vox crystals to direct those tiny sparks of proto-matter as they zip through the quantum foam, while they're still undifferentiated and directionless.

"I could manifest a heartplum, an apple, anything! Food. Blankets. Clothing. Gasoline. A car for that matter. I can transport objects from here to there. Not sure about living tissue, people, or pets!" I was getting ahead of myself. "We won't need money! This is access to pure energy! We could irrigate fields! Turn bullets into flowers. This is real power!" I paused, overwhelmed. "This is real magic!"

"I am pleased to see you take the next intuitive leap, Dana. Go on, what else?" We were still in the quantum foam, where I had to tread froth and blow bubbles off my face.

"The vox is short for voxel, the volumetric quantum pixel. It channels thought waves through its tiny interior crystal facets. I wonder, do the reptilians on Earth have technology this advanced? I've seen them do amazing things like blink out of a room. But Bo Raza invented the vox, and he insists Earthborn reptilians cannot access its tools."

"And why would that be, do you think?" Sapphy probed as I pondered the continuous creation before my eyes.

After a thoughtful pause, I answered. "Because quantum gravity is quantum love. The Universe is a sea of spinning SpaceTimeMass. The building blocks are monads of love that emerged from the P-soup. The vox operates using positive thought waves and compassion. It can never be used as a weapon or to channel negative thoughts or feelings." I paused to breathe. "Reptiles don't consider compassion useful."

"Yes, they consider frequencies of love and mercy to be noise." Delighted, Sapphy clapped six pairs of hands. "Shall we return to the library?"

I nodded and we floated upward and onward, passing lattices, vertices, bubbles, and whirlwinds. We emerged out through the page of the massive black book, expanded to our full size, and rolled onto the floor of Sapphire's cozy lake front cabin. "That was astounding, Sapphy."

"It's one of my favorite journeys. Floating in the Great Mother Sea always restores me to perfect harmony."

"It was blissful beyond reckoning."

"You got to see how the Universe continuously dances itself into existence."

"The Holofractalgraphic Fandango," I quipped.

Wisdom and wit lit his eyes. He flipped through the big volume of Earth Lore and quoted, "According to another sage from your species called Oliver Wendell Holmes, 'a mind expanded by a new experience cannot return to its old dimensions.'"

I kissed him on the cheek, nearly causing him to tumble, but his multiple feet kept him balanced on the massive book. "Beholding the source of all love, all consciousness, and all spin answers so many questions."

Sapphy took a dignified nip of leaves. "Which reminds me, I need to get spinning myself. I have a date with my imaginal cells."

"You mean… it's that time?" I trailed off thinking of cocoons.

"I'm almost done eating leaves."

"Will I see you again?"

"Depend on it, Dana Mae Travers. Don't you know? The caterpillar always has the last word."

"And what would that be, my friend?"

"Butterfly."

And with that, Sapphire spun out of the room in a flash, leaving me alone with my thoughts. I leafed through books and photos in the library, finding written passages and images depicting moments from many previous lives.

My kundalini stirred, coiling from the base of my spine along my backbone to my throat. The snake squeezed along its length and wound upwards from the back of my neck to my forehead, activating brilliant sounds and colors, scents, and sensations. As it ascended, it changed colors from deep sky blue to indigo, my own personal Rainbow Serpent.

Sixth Chakra ~ Third Eye
Expanded vision, self-awareness, light, indigo, blocked by illusion

Following the deep indigo night sky, I was propelled into starlit space. The Universe conducted a grand symphony that resounded in perfect harmony. The undifferentiated pure music of the Great Mother Sea separated into distinct strands, comingled melodies of the world's most beloved music of every genre. They resonated together in one magnum opus. I was inside music, spiraling ever onwards, floating through star clusters and nebulae. Iridescent colors flew by me in coruscating waves. I finally nestled in a pulsating mandala of sound and color.

"Welcome to the galactic core," said a rich feminine voice. A translucent woman in gauzy white floated along beside me. She appeared to be made from fluidic stardust that wisped like wind, waves, and feathers.

"You must be Sophia. Tellarans call our galaxy Sophia. On Earth we call you the Milky Way because of the beautiful white bands of stars that stretch across our heavens."

"Yes, and the Tellarans call those white bands Sophia's Milk."

"On Earth, you are the Goddess of Wisdom."

"That is one of my designations, but I am more ancient than your oldest myths, older than Gaia by billions of years. I am the galaxy. From the Great Mother Sea, I brought forth and designed all the mass and energy in my spiral arms and celestial bodies, including the bio-matter of my galactic children. As each DNA seedling took root, an experiment began on each planet. I watch you all from my exalted perspective." Her sheer image fluttered and flowed.

"If this is the galactic core, we must be inside a blackwhole. Why don't I get sucked in?"

"You are woven into a very stable mandala at the edge of the event horizon. It's anchored to your third eye chakra."

Within the mandala, I observed the endless panoply of humanity throughout the ages. Entwined images moved through stories, inhabiting different incarnations, landscapes, rhythms, breaths, and deaths. Images wove through cycles within a celestial astrolabe, like a cosmic heartdance. "What am I viewing? What am I hearing and experiencing?"

Sophia answered, "This is the Akashic record. Mass makes an impression on the fabric of spacetime as it spirals along."

"I've heard something to that effect."

"As your solar system revolves around Sophia's Milk, Earth and all her creatures leave behind permanent grooves. Your DNA etches its experience into an individual furrow, all the way back from the present moment to your conception. Beyond that point your parent's DNA carves channels back until their conception, and so on back through countless ancestral generation. Nothing is lost. Experiences follow patterns that repeat throughout millions of lifetimes in each individual, family, and karmic group."

I allowed the impressions to wash over me, bathing in the comprehension that lifetimes follow fractal patterns. We do not just reincarnate, we repeat form, function, experiences, and relationships on ever-escalating spirals that leave permanent impressions in spacetime. The panorama of historical vignettes danced around us accompanied by the galactic symphony.

Sophia enfolded me in her vast fluidic wings and said, "Come let's leave this event horizon and slide along the Orion spiral arm of your solar system." Just like that, we were sliding along an Akashic groove towards the outer edge of Sophia's Milk. I could now see events as they were unfolding in real time and even probable futures. This was remembering the future, like Sapphire said he could do, the future retelling itself with endless permutations. Some future memories were wonderful family gatherings at Wah'Kon-Tah and loving moments with my loved ones. But other future memories disturbed me: confrontations with Sheldon Walters, courtrooms, blood. "I don't want to see this anymore," I cried out.

Sophia gently released me to the cosmos. The rainbow serpent spiraled from my forehead to my crown, shifting from indigo to violet. Rays of light beamed in all directions from my head forming a wreath of violet.

Seventh Chakra ~ Crown
Violet, collective consciousness, expanded sensibilities, thoughts, and feelings, blocked by Earthly attachments

I floated beyond the edge of the Milky Way, or as I now thought of her, Sophia. The mandala was revolving around and through other galaxies and nebulae in our galactic cluster. Alone, I reached the edge of the Universe, floating along the rim of a vast double torus, near the equator where the two toroids met. The double torus was like a three-dimensional infinity symbol. Everything was expanding at an alarming, incomprehensible speed. I remembered Phoenix telling me that the radius of the Universe was ninety-one billion light-years across. From this perspective, I could see this part of the galaxy was expanding, while near the poles, matter was contracting, sliding inward to the center of the Universal singularity. Blackwholes all the way up and blackwholes all the way down. These quantum singularities were the building blocks of the Universe.

The entire pattern depended on every individual component. Saffron's words came back to me with haunting clarity: "Each consciousness is a thread in the vast tapestry. Pull out one thread and all creation unravels." Each of us is a cell in the mind of God. God did not so much create the Universe, but is the omnipotent, omnipresent, omniscient Universe itself, expanding as each individual "I AM" arises from the Great Mother Sea. The creator is the creation. The architect is the architecture.

A galactic-sized yin yang appeared in my vista. It took the form of a three-dimensional rotating double torus. The dark petal broke through its balanced boundary and crept over the light petal. Darkness spread, consuming the light.

Imbalance prevailed. For endless moments, I could do nothing but watch in awe. Then, the tail of the white petal pierced the black petal, expanding into a glowing white ball. Balance was restored, the eternal yin-yang, dark-light, projection-reception, masculine-feminine. Oneness swept over me in orgasmic convulsive waves of bliss. Who knew that the Universe had sex with itself all the time?

I laughed at the dawning of the answer to the age-old question, "Is there sex after death?"

Ha! Existence is sexual union. Creation is sex. This was Moregasmic. Goldie, my fine-feathered Phoenix, would enjoy this. And just so, Goldie flitted by, singing and reciting doggerel. She perched on a nearby nebulae. "This bliss is our birthright as conscious beings. The obstacles foisted on us by our own folly only delay and deter, never deny our return to Source."

I asked Goldie, "Why would any sentient creature want to deny other conscious beings this blissful birthright? How and why has our species been so duped for so long?" The scale of the manipulation staggered me.

Some answers danced in the mandala. Goldie said, "Look, there are permutations in the pattern. Those cause temporary imperfections that must be balanced out. The Universe is a self-correcting closed system." We watched the yin and yang petals and spheres continued to summersault around each other in an endless ballet. "Despite its apparent stranglehold, domineering power is temporal and, by design, ephemeral."

I must still have Earthly attachments if I was not an enlightened master walking around with my third eye open and cosmic consciousness filtering through my daily thoughts. I was not ready to give up on romantic love, sexuality, and sensuality. I was still passionate about Earthly justice and not patient to wait for karma to work itself out over lifetimes. I craved living in a warm, comfortable, safe home.

I was more than ready to release my snarky sarcastic wit. That was fair. And I've understood this entire incarnation about the shades of gray with respect to gender fluidity, doing the right thing for the wrong reason, and forgiving my enemies. But if ascending to Terra Nova was as far as I got in this corporeal template, I was more than satisfied with that. Saffron had hinted, and Sapphire had told me, that if I aligned my chakras in the journey, I might glimpse those higher, rarified, incorporeal chakras that only enlightened masters apprehend. It could happen here in the Blue Henge temple. I wasn't ready to see beyond the edge of the Universe, but my rainbow serpent had other ideas.

Eighth Chakra ~ Ultraviolet

I don't know where the seventh chakra left off and the eighth began. The kundilini snake had slithered beyond my brain. I had no choice but to go with the flow. Drawn upwards and outwards, I floated about eight inches above my head as a glowing monad of consciousness. The multi-dimensional, musical mandala still pulsated, vibrant with color, sound, and fragrance. In a disembodied dance, I spiraled beyond any recognizable frame of reference amidst millions of glowing monads. Was this tableau universally vast or infinitesimally small?

Crystal and Cosmo appeared. "Thank God you're here. I'm losing my mind. How do you stand it out here, unmoored from all familiar landmarks with no corporeal handholds?"

Cosmo said, "This is where we live Dana. This is the natural habitat of light beings. We've told you that we only clothe ourselves in coverings of flesh to interact with humanity, and that our luminous 12-strand DNA can no longer integrate with 3D biological species like Homo sapiens and Zeta Reticuli."

"Did it ever? What of those mythic stories about angels or watchers breeding with human women?"

"We weren't there in Ancient of Days when carnal procreation transpired. We're only about ten thousand years incarnate. That interbreeding era occurred over a million years ago. There is still controversy regarding whether it was done to control or liberate nascent 3D Homo sapiens."

I asked, "So, if humanity is ascending from 3D to 5D on Terra Nova, and Tellaran consciousness is ascending from 5D to 6D, where exactly do you find your stable home in this disconnected disembodied corner of spacetime?"

Crystal answered, "We are in your eighth chakra, Dana, in your 8D rarified body." The tangible loving light they radiated soothed my disquiet.

Cosmo said, "In the 8D realm, the veil between life and death dissolves and pairs of opposites are reconciled." Disincarnate loved ones emerged from the sea of monads. I recognized my mother Gayle, and my father Frank as sparks of light. We danced, laughed, and wept together by interpenetrating. Other ancestors joined me, spiraling back in geometric progressions through generations; from grandparents to great grandparents and beyond. The hopes, blessings, healings, and responsibilities of my ancestral lineage enveloped me.

Hal and Jay joined us. Communication was instantaneous. We all simultaneously grokked that Kek had killed both Jay and Hal. My friends were at peace, waiting to incarnate on Terra Nova. Other souls who had been murdered by Shelter joined us, including Gwen Cretzky's father, the late lamented politician and Shari McCann, the Irish investigative journalist. There was a consensus that Hal's murder was egregious collateral damage. Shelter usually silenced their enemies with surgical precision. They tried to make my lack of alibi play into their hands, but my Tellaran odyssey continued to foil their well-calculated strategy. Without warning, all the other monads dissipated, leaving me alone and untethered.

The pulsating mandala became a swirling sea of interlocking jigsaw puzzle pieces, each holding the holofractalgraphic imagery of an entire epoch, its stories, sceneries, and souls. This churning panorama was magnificent but terrifying. The Great Mother Sea had said that I couldn't fall out of the Universe, but I was isolated from everything tangible and familiar. Who was I? I had vague recollections of having a body, a name, memories, but these were fleeting external concepts. Pushed to the brink of insanity, my identity was slipping away. To be alone, incorporeal, out here in the center of everywhere and nowhere triggered panic. I had no mouth and yet I screamed, "I want to go home!"

CHAPTER 30

At last, I felt a physical sensation: warm water was pouring over my face and body. Face? Body? I had to ponder the meanings of these abstractions. I was receiving information via my physical senses. Whispering voices filled the air. I felt breath fill my lungs. Strong soft hands massaged my scalp, my feet, and my hands. Aromatic scents filled my nostrils with wondrous associations of fruit and flowers. Then, I tasted something hot and sweet. Tea drizzled into my mouth. I gulped and sputtered, but finally allowed the tea to roll across my tongue. One more cough and my eyes opened. I was restored to consciousness, not quite awake, but fairly functional.

Juniper and Jasmine, dressed in short white shifts, were giving me a Turkish bath, pouring basins of warm soapy water over my prostrate form and sluicing me off with clear steamy water. I lay still and indulged in their ministrations. They would have continued, but being back in my body, I realized my bladder was calling. I pulled myself up to sitting and announced my need to use the toilet. I was as weak as a kitten, and simultaneously, as strong as an Amazon. They pulled me to standing and guided me to a private stall constructed of warm marble walls that stretched high above my head and opened to a skylight. It was dawn. It had been dawn when I entered the Blue Henge. How long had I been in the temple?

I was suddenly anxious to dress and see my loved ones. I exited the stall, supported by Juniper. She dressed me in a white terrycloth caftan and slid on matching fluffy, white slippers. She brushed my hair and pulled it behind my shoulders. It was now long enough to stay back by itself.

Juniper asked, "How high up in the chakras did you ascend, Dana?"

"I think I stopped at the eighth. I got scared, and something brought me home."

"There's no place like home," Juniper quoted as she escorted me out of the temple into the waiting arms of Ruth and Jesse.

"Mom! Your hair!" Ruth cried.

"I know! It's wet."

"White."

"What?"

"White."

"Wet!"

"White!" Ruth and Jesse shouted at me in unison. Ruth pulled a tendril of my long locks forward and dangled it before my eyes. Snow-white tresses, glittering with sunlight, drifted through Ruth's fingers. Unrecognizable locks settled on my shoulder.

"How long was I in the temple?" I asked, stunned by this physical transformation.

"Two days, Mom."

"It felt like two years." So many ideas and memories swirled through my mind. Lifetimes, events, sounds, faces, laughter, and tears all merged in an inarticulate sputter. I sat in the grass, still feeling weak as a kitten and strong as an Amazon. Alice joined us.

"You were in there with me, weren't you, Alice?"

"Yes, I joined you for a few hours in your heart center," Alice smiled.

"It felt longer."

"Look." Alice held up a hand mirror. I still looked like me, but I had taken on that ageless look I'd seen in Tellaran elders. Any of us could be anywhere from forty to a hundred forty years old. We wore something besides our age on our faces. We reflected wisdom, love, power, joy, and suffering. If anything, my laugh creases were deeper, which added to their compassion. My hair was snow white and ten inches longer. The mantle of elder had settled on my shoulders. "I know what my wayshower's mission demands of me."

Ruth asked, "What is that, Mom?"

Before I could answer, Javier strolled out of the temple, escorted by Buffalo and Phoenix. He too, had gone through a physical transformation. Dark wavy hair still covered his crown, but his gray temples had expanded to frame his entire face in a silver halo. His face also had undergone the age-defying transformation that deepened its texture but added to its sweetness of expression. We hugged. "Wow," he said, tugging my white hair.

"Wow, yourself," I said, stroking his silver temples.

"The tribe is assembling, Dana." Louie exclaimed, running up to me with outstretched arms.

"Oh, Louie, I got to spend time with Hal," I whispered. "He is at peace."

"I know, I spent time with him in my heart chakra. But look at you! Dana the White Witch."

"Yeah," I chuckled. "Look at me."

Heron, Robin, and Joe Two Feathers approached from Stonehenge with Rip, Belle, and Corky. Despite my changed appearance, Rip recognized my scent and ran rapturous circles around my ankles while I tried to scratch behind his ears. Bo and Guna Raza approached from the other side of the meadow. Saffron, Sky Dancer, and Minerva joined our gathering.

"Are we all here?" asked Saffron."

"All but Vincent and Gwen," I answered. "They are part of our tribe."

"They are safe in Wah'Kon-Tah, learning sustainable living skills." The speaker was Cosmo. He and Crystal emerged from a Tellaran Airship much like the one we had traveled aboard in Giza. They were followed by Huckleberry and Finn, my rescuers from the Reptilian Individual Movement, the underground organization founded by Alice.

Javier spoke, "I thought you were heading to Glastonbury to set up a safe house in England for *Avalon Equinox*."

"We've been there and back again," Finn answered. "All is in readiness for the spring portal to open."

"We wanted them here," said Crystal.

"We, meaning the Galactic Family," added Cosmo. "We brought Huck and Finn to Wah'Kon-Tah and they entered through *Tellaran Autumn*. The greater the collective mind, the easier it will be to create the peaceful world you envision."

Javier replied, "Buckminster Fuller said: 'You never change things by fighting the existing reality. To change something, build a new model that makes the existing model obsolete.' I learned that from an elegant Queen Bee named Aldora."

"Bucky also said that love is metaphysical gravity," said Louie. "A grasshopper named Sage taught me that."

"Bugs on this planet sure know a lot for creatures with such ephemeral lifespans," observed a puzzled Finn.

"Wait 'til it's your turn," teased Alice, poking him in the ribs.

Huckleberry and Finn embraced Alice, marveling at her reptilian grandeur, and then approached Bo and Guna Raza. Alice made the introductions. Huckleberry and Finn shed crocodile tears to meet their enlightened Draconian counterparts. They dissolved their mammalian visages to reveal their tawny scales.

Crystal spoke, "Gwen and Vincent were successful in transporting *Magic Seasons* from Chicago. *Shasta Solstice*, *Tellaran Autumn*, and *Summer in Tellara* now hang in the sky room at Wah'Kon-Tah. You will be gratified to know that in the proximity of its companions, *Summer* is slowly reweaving its fibers."

"How can a canvas repair itself?" asked Jesse, who had carried the rent canvas of *Summer* across the North American continent twice.

Phoenix replied, "*Magic Seasons* are more than canvases and pigment. The portals grow stronger with number and proximity. When all four paintings connect, a megaportal will emerge."

"Mega?"

"Connect?"

"Yes, when *Avalon Equinox* joins its fellow portals, *Summer in Tellara* will be fully restored."

I asked Crystal, "You've been with Vincent and Gwen. How are they really?"

She answered, "It's bittersweet. They are grateful to be safe but viewing themselves in the media is harsh."

"I remember. Let me see for myself." Launching my vox screen, I concentrated on the Cretzkys. Vincent was in a meadow filled with busy Tellaran bees. Gwen was nearby, planting heartplum saplings.

Louie peered over my shoulder at the screen and smiled ironically. "Vincent Cretzky. Who'd have imagined this a year ago? We were still calling him rude nicknames."

"Take a look at Sheldon Walters," Louie suggested. "The net is closing around him."

"All right," and I pulled the Alpha Draconis up on my vox screen. So did Javier and Louie, because this image drew a cluster of viewers. Walters was alone in his fancy office. He was tearing it apart, smashing furniture; breaking everything he could lay his hands on. Kek entered and was pelted with a glass decanter for his trouble. Then Suzy walked in, demure in pale peach. Walters ceased his tirade. Turning to Suzy, we saw his lips move. Using our collective focus, we hummed, evoking audio in our vox crystals. "I want them all dead," were the first words we heard.

"They're all still missing!" hissed Kek. "Gemini Dallas has been inviting them to be interviewed on her show if they have nothing to hide. No nibbles so far. On the night of Jay Andrews' disappearance, Travers claimed to be on a spiritual retreat."

"Is that where you think they are now? Kek, this motley crew of cretin mammals? Howling at the moon on some mountain top in Tibet?" Walters snarled sarcastically. "You're friends with the Travers woman, right Suzy?"

Suzy looked scandalized. "Uh, sort of."

"Good. The next time you see her, kill her."

"Yes Sir!" Suzy bolted, smirking her most exultant 'I get to kill Dana!' look. I'd seen enough.

Ruth probed, "Mom, you said that you realized what you must do to launch your wayshower mission."

"Yes, sharing the message of thriving with harmony consciousness is more important than Shelter's contract on my life. I'm going to become Shelter's worst nightmare, the whistle blower from Tellara. People need to know about the impending planetary shift and the urgency to make sustainable, compassionate choices. I'm going to disclose my time on a parallel world, and what I've learned from Tellarans, emissaries from the Galactic Family, enlightened reptilians, and ethical grays. It's time to take my show on the road and speak in live venues, shoot the moon and damn the consequences."

"When are you planning to start, Mom?" Jesse asked.

"As soon as we open *Avalon Equinox*, in a few weeks."

Louie cautioned, "Dana, consider. We Earthborn can only remain in Tellara until the summer solstice at the latest, the anniversary of your opening of the first portal."

"It's been less than a year? So much has happened."

"Some of us just arrived in Tellara," protested Huckleberry.

"We want to spend time with the Raza Clan and undertake the chakra journey," added Finn.

"I want to spend time in the Osage region on Tellara," said Sky Dancer.

"I have more to learn of Tellara's Romani heritage since our migration from Atlantis," said Minerva.

"Juniper has promised to show me more Tellaran art," Jesse said ardently.

Phoenix said, "I'm still transporting Earth art to Tellara. Crystal and Cosmo have offered to help."

"Robin has promised to show me the animal sanctuary in Antarctica," said Ruth.

"We all have so much more to learn here," entreated Joe Two Feathers.

Javier addressed me, "Dana, I spent time with my parents in my heart chakra. They're in inner Earth where Tellara and Earth overlap in the planet's central singularity. I want you to come with me to the cavern in Shastise so my parents can meet my wife."

"One woman, alone against Shelter?" asked Alice. "What say you, Dana?"

I faced my tribe. There were now eight human wayshowers: Louie, Javier, Jesse, Ruth, Sky Dancer, Joe, Minerva, and me; three reptilians: Alice, Huckleberry, and Finn. And there was Cosmo, the Vegan and Crystal the Pleiadian. That made thirteen in all, twelve of whom appealed to remain in Tellara for as long as possible.

I said, "Since my first visit to Tellara, I have been impressed with the urgency of my wayshower's mission to share Tellara's message with Earth."

"*Our* wayshower mission," Javier emphasized.

I looked into the faces of my loved ones. I shared their desire to remain as long as possible but had another concern. "The *Magic Seasons* all have to be together before the planetary shift. After it's opened, *Avalon Equinox* must be transported to Wah'Kon-Tah from England. The four paintings together will create the megaportal that Tellara will use to siphon off and dampen teratons of seismic energy that will be unleashed during the shift. What if we're not on Earth when these geological cataclysms begin? What if the paintings haven't been brought together? What if *Summer in Tellara* hasn't had time to reweave its canvas fibers?"

Javier spoke, "There's another consideration, Dana. While in my chakra journey, I was shown secrets that will help enhance our vox tools. I want to practice replicating and transporting."

"Me too," said Louie. "I've been practicing manifestation. It's amazing, but still unstable." He tuned his vox, held out his hand, and a heartplum materialized for about ten seconds, then faded away.

I answered, "You're right. You're all right. More vox training would give us an important tactical advantage." We seemed to be at an impasse.

But then Saffron resolved our dilemma with a simple suggestion, "When in doubt, dance!"

Women circled and musical instruments were gathered. Drumming and chanting began. A haunting flute melody wafted evocatively. Nearby, cattle lowed, horses nickered, dogs fell silent. Women swayed and moved in syncopation. Our arms and legs coordinated as percussion, woodwind, and strings reached a crescendo. Threads of a multi-dimensional tapestry emerged. The image cohered of Earth, Sol, and Luna. The full moon rose over North America and hovered over the Ozark Mountains. Luna then revolved through her phases as, all the while, Earth rotated from day to night. We were seeing the passage of time. Again, the full moon rose over Wah'Kon-Tah. Again, Luna revolved swiftly through her phases and the Earth spun from day to night twenty-eight times. A third time, the moon rose over Wah'Kon-Tah. This time she ceased revolving at her half-moon phase. The Earth began to tremble, but after a few minutes, subsided. Luna revolved for fourteen more days. By the next full moon, Earthquakes became violent beyond reckoning. The tapestry drew back to a great distance, revealing Earth's planetary schism. Although I had seen this image in my first heartdance, the magnitude of the disruption was shattering to behold.

The image receded to a vast distance. Tellara phased into our dimension, almost on top of Earth. A stream of raw energy burst from Wah'Kon-Tah and was drawn forth through the megaportal. The energy stream was diverted, beyond Mars, beyond the Solar System, and into deep space between the spiral arms of the galaxy. We watched in wonder as deadly seismic energy dissipated into harmless ripples across interstellar space. Even as Terra Nova was vibrating away from Terra Familiar, Tellara, our elder sister, was saving Earth from obliteration. Three embodiments of Gaia hovered at different frequencies as the tapestry dissolved.

The music quieted. Our dance steps slowed. The imagery faded. We sat with our thoughts for several minutes. Then Louie spoke, "We have ten days until March 21st, the spring equinox, when the portal opens. One lunar cycle beyond that takes us to April 18th. The second lunar cycle takes us to May 16th. The third lunar cycle arrives on June 13th, prior to summer solstice. During June, Earth will be seismically active, but not cataclysmic."

Jesse took over. "But by late July, the geologic upheaval will induce the Earth-shattering shift."

I added, "We must return to Earth by early May if we're going to have a reasonable amount of time to take our show on the road and still return to Wah'Kon-Tah for the megaportal."

"Two months here. Two months there," said Joe. "A fair compromise for all wayshowers."

Ruth had a great idea, "Just because we're in Tellara doesn't mean we can't create podcasts revealing everything we want to disclose. There's no reason to delay the mission. The messages can be filmed here and posted from Wah'Kon-Tah."

Javier spoke, "You know, that seismic activity occurred very near Wah'Kon-Tah, over the Madrid fault line. Not Yellowstone, not San Andreas, not Vesuvius, not the Pacific Rim."

"Meaning?" Sky Dancer asked.

"If Tellara were not there to siphon off the seismic energy, the entire region would be…"

"Kablooey," Joe supplied, his arms gesticulating.

"Yeah, so why do we want to be in the epicenter of the planetary shift?" Javier asked.

Saffron said, "To hold the megaportal open. Wah'Kon-Tah will be in the eye of the storm."

Phoenix added, "There won't be any safer place on Earth."

"Your thoughts, Dana?" asked Louie.

"We decided together to move *Magic Seasons* to Wah'Kon-Tah. That can't be a coincidence."

Louie agreed, "We do this for Terra Nova and Terra Familiar."

"No reason to return to sticks and stones if we don't have to," said tiny Minerva, leaning on Javier's arm. "I've had vivid psychic revelations of Earth's last schism. It took thousands of years to rebuild civilization."

I confirmed what we had seen in the heartdance. "We can safely stay in Tellara until the 16th of May." There was delight among Terrans and Tellarans alike. Everybody had exciting adventures planned.

Phoenix said, "Before we go our separate ways, while you have Bo Raza here, why not develop these new vox functions together?"

"Good idea," said Javier. "Let's stay in Avalon until the equinox and figure out manifesting, transporting, and audio-telepathy."

After we'd all rested and broken bread, we gathered around Bo Raza in the Avalon meadow and took out our voxes. Bo said, "Louie, demonstrate your manifestation technique again and tell us how you developed it."

"I did the Chakra Ritual several weeks ago and have given this a lot of thought. In my heart chakra, I met with a marvelous grasshopper named Sage. She told me about morphogenic fields."

"Me too," said Alice, "from a cricket named Buddy."

"What are morphogenic fields?" asked Ruth.

Louie continued, "According to Sage, 'Time cannot be separated from the objects that fill it.' She meant that in order to manifest an organism, genes are not enough. There must be an organizing field for the organic molecules to fill. The more stable the field, the easier for the proteins to find their niche. The proteins in our hands and feet are the same, but what tells each molecule where to go and how to fill each pattern?"

"What about inanimate objects?" asked Ruth.

"Likewise, the atoms and molecules need a receptacle to fill, a preexisting field." answered Louie.

Ruth mused, "Manifesting an inanimate object must be easier."

"You'd think so, but surprisingly, it's not," said Louie. "With fruits, the DNA does most of the work to organize the molecules."

I spoke, "I have an idea. My caterpillar, Sapphire, showed me the primordial substance of the Universe. It's made up of teeny tiny voxel vortices, burbling undifferentiated from the P-soup. Using our thoughts, we could direct these primal voxels onto the framework of the envisioned field; first the atomic structure and then up the chain to molecules, crystals, or cells."

"Would we need to know chemistry and the periodic table?" asked Louie.

"I don't know. So, let's start with a stable element. Think of something gold with a definite shape."

"How about a gold ring?" suggested Joe. Louie nodded.

"OK, Louie, close your eyes, travel with me to a layer of quantum foam that is releasing trillions of infinitesimally tiny vortices. In your mind's eye, use your vox to draw these vortices toward you while holding the image of a ring in your other palm. Let the voxels organize themselves into gold atoms. Don't tell them how, just let them apprehend the image." Louie concentrated and, in several moments, a gold ring appeared in his palm. We were all amazed. But again, like the heartplum, after about ten seconds, the ring dematerialized, and we all sighed with disappointment.

"Still," said Louie, "That was my first success with an inanimate object."

"I might be able to help," Javier offered, "I learned something from Aldora, the queen bee. Natural laws are entrenched habits. They can change over time if we rethink imagery in advance. Aldora said that: 'Time cannot be separated from the events that fill it.'"

"Both events and objects are inseparable from the spacetime they occupy!" Jesse exclaimed.

"So, objects and events have duration. As does behavior,'" said Alice. "Habits feel compelled to fill familiar morphogenic fields as we flow through time. These fields can become stable, even concretized, making behavior hard to change, habits difficult to break." She winked at Huckleberry and Finn.

"Especially for reptiles," grumbled Finn.

I said, "Hey, Louie, think about how bats can hear shapes. Maybe that will help."

Bo Raza coached, "Louie, this time, when you visualize the ring, see the morphogenic field before you as a catcher's mitt to mold the atoms, and picture the ring as an unbreakable pattern in spacetime. Let shape fill time as well as space."

Pushing up his sleeves and closing his eyes, Louie declared, "Here goes nothing!" It took a little longer, but the gold ring appeared in his palm. And this time, it remained. After about thirty seconds of gawking, we passed it around, handing it to one another, trying it on our fingers, holding it up to the light.

As Louie slipped the gold ring on the third finger of his right hand, Bo Raza declared, "Well done, Louie! Let's all practice this manifestation for the rest of the day. Tomorrow, we'll begin to work on relocation and audio-telepathy communication." For the next ten days, vox training was our intense focus. We broke into groups and practiced new skills. Bo Raza called it relocation, but we all called it the transporter beam. It was more difficult than manifesting, because we didn't always hit the right spot. We joked about needing transporter pads. But, finally, after a clarification by Bo Raza on nonlocal reality and morphogenic fields, we got better and began transporting inanimate objects, fruit, and living plants.

"We need to practice on a live animal," said Alice.

"Not a dog. That's for NASA and cosmetic laboratories," said Ruth emphatically.

"What about a bug?" suggested Finn.

"I just became friends with a magnificent grasshopper," said Louie. "Not sure I consider bugs a lower form of life anymore."

Jesse cautioned, "Transporting is much harder than manifesting. The atoms aren't undifferentiated. They're already in someone's body and brains, fit together, and alive. We're setting ourselves up for an epic transporter malfunction."

"Splinching," said Joe.

Bo Raza solved our problem by volunteering. "I am certain of how relocation works. No harm will come to me." Bo beamed himself from the meadow to Blue Henge and back again.

Louie asked, "If you have this technology, why don't Tellarans relocate all the time? Why bother with airships and trams?"

"Who's in a hurry?" Bo answered. "There is so much beauty to see."

We took turns transporting ourselves and each other. We kept the distances short at first, but gradually, as our confidence grew, we beamed each other out of sight, and back to the meadow. We beamed ourselves cloaked and then levitating.

"What about a disguise?" asked Joe. "Isn't that kind of like manifesting?"

"Meaning?"

"Suppose I'm being chased, and I want my pursuer to think I'm a big grizzly bear?"

"Joe, there are no shortcuts to shamanic shape shifting," Sky Dancer admonished. "That requires cooperation with your animal totem. And we don't use our voxes as weapons." But I liked Joe's idea and wished I could have manifested a grizzly bear in Kek's face during his murderous attacks.

Activating the vox audio-telepathy tool remained the most difficult mental discipline to master. We had to generate cymatic patterns in the water in our brains that translated into sound vibrations, words. Javier and I had managed a brief breakthrough during our long-distance relationship, but our thoughts had synchronized. The entire group agreed to hum middle C. It resonated with at least one crystal on each of our voxes. The more we hummed, the greater the clarity. The more of us who attuned, the sharper the acoustic focus inside our heads. We got better, but audio-telepathy remained an intermittent skill.

All the Earthborn wayshowers underwent the Chakra Ritual in the next few days. The Razas and Alice shepherded Huckleberry and Finn through the Blue Henge. It was a far more severe passage for the ancient, recovering Draconians than for we short-lived humans, though truth to tell, my journey was unbearably intense at times. Huckleberry and Finn took days to recover but returned to vox training with renewed spirits. Vox training, heartdancing, chakra rituals, Tellaran lessons, filming and posting podcasts were fruitful ways to pass the time until the spring equinox, but at last, the day came.

* * *

Tellarans from far and wide came to join in this momentous heartdance. Hundreds in colorful regalia chanted, played, and danced while Phoenix painted. We all heard the rhythm and thrum created by the outer circle. Women took our places in concentric circles, creating a geometric pattern of intersecting webs. Once again, we became threads in a multi-dimensional fabric, every thread an essential part of the pattern in myriad interpenetrating designs. Stories overlapped like those I had witnessed in the celestial astrolabe in my crown chakra. As our ecstatic dance reached its climax, many of the singers and dancers underwent an amazing transformation. Their physical bodies began to glow and, like Violet when she had transcended, their bodies morphed into luminescent orbs. They floated among us by the hundreds, drifting on the wind, then floating away. As the music subsided, the orbs vanished from sight. Many Tellarans ascended, while many remained behind.

After the heartdance ended, we gathered to watch Phoenix put the finishing brush strokes on *Avalon Equinox*. Finally, he pulled off his paint-spattered smock to uncover a burgundy caftan underneath. He had painted a final character, a dark-haired man facing into the canvas, dressed in the same burgundy caftan. His outline was vividly defined. As I gazed at the final canvas in the *Magic Seasons* collection, the brush strokes blurred. Dancing figures blurred. Figures of drummers and musicians phased. The canvas expanded. Phoenix on the grass merged with Phoenix on the canvas. The painting shimmered and rippled. Then, Phoenix was gone and so was *Avalon Equinox*. He had painted himself through to Earthside, and the painting went with him.

"You're up, Dana," said Louie, as Javier nudged me forward. I had never crossed through a portal in this direction prior to opening it from Earthside, and none of us knew if it would work. But I had to try. I gazed into the meadow, seeking the undulating atmospheric ripples that indicated a quantum singularity. Moving into the shimmering ripples, radiant flashes momentarily blinded me. When the lights cleared, I was in Merry Old England, The United Kingdom, Earth. The painting, *Avalon Equinox*, now Earthside, was held taught between Phoenix's firm hands. He dropped the painting and I did a little happy dance. His gaze was fixed on Earth's familiar, ruined Stonehenge. It was surrounded by busloads of tourists. Phoenix stood gawking at the remnants of the magnificent edifice. I comforted him, "We love our Stonehenge, in all her crumbling glory."

"It retains its dignity. But where is Blue Henge?"

"Lost to the ages, reduced to rubble." Our poignant musings were interrupted. Immediately behind us, the painting shimmered to life and we had to grapple to pull the corners taut. Huckleberry emerged, and then came Finn.

"Reporting for duty." Finn bowed deeply to us. "Shall we go to the safe house?"

"Is it near?"

"Walking distance," Huck said.

I asked, "When we are all ready to return, will you be flying back to America? Did you fly here legally?"

"Even without our voxes, we have our ways," winked Huckleberry.

Finn said, "Let's head to the safe house together so you can open the portal in privacy, Dana." The four of us walked together for over a mile when I asked, "Can't we use our voxes to transport?"

"In this wide-open space, filled with tourists and cameras?" Finn shook his head. "We're lucky to have crossed over without attracting attention."

"We're almost there," soothed Huckleberry. And so we were, as Finn unlocked the door to a small cottage with an overgrown garden.

Phoenix mounted the canvas on an interior wall. I peered at the brushstrokes, willing them to move in the familiar fractal dance that signified the opening of a singularity. In moments, I saw movement on the canvas. Dancers swept gracefully across the meadow, branches swayed in the breeze, and there they were, the rippling mists that drew me forward across the dimensional portal. I emerged onto the Avalon meadow.

"What took you so long?" exclaimed Javier.

"We had to walk to the safe house. *Avalon Equinox* is hanging in the Amesbury cottage, waiting to be transported to Wah'Kon-Tah."

"And the others?"

"Present," laughed a delighted Huckleberry as he stepped into the meadow, followed by Finn and Phoenix. "And ready for our next adventure as soon as we transport the paining to Wah-Kon-Tah."

Alice said, "Stay with us until we figure out our logistics."

Jesse asked Saffron, "You told us that Tellara has made provisions to preserve all your life forms. How so?"

She answered, "There are spacecrafts in orbit that contain all the genetic material of your millions of species.

Heron said, "They'll remain in orbit until Tellara's continents restabilize enough to support sustainable ecosystems."

"An orbital Noah's Ark," Jesse mused.

Heron continued, "In addition, we have Tellaformed Antarctica as a living sanctuary. The Island chain now consists of rolling green hills, savannas, meadows, lakes, rivers, and mountains. It is a haven for Tellaran fauna, a botanical garden for Tellaran flora. Our current south pole will gently pivot toward a temperate Pacific latitude. A handful of caretakers, mostly grays, but some humans, will remain corporeal in order to tend the flock."

"The grays can't ascend," explained Juniper. "They haven't hybridized enough to activate all their chakras. They are relocating to Mount Zola on Antarctica in order to continue their genetic research and manage the sanctuary during and after the shift. It's a way for them to learn about service."

"And the humans choosing to remain behind?" Jesse asked.

"Some who love tellestrial nature want to shepherd in the new era," answered Juniper. "They'll ascend after Tellara stabilizes."

We Earthborn wayshowers held another of our wonky summits that never turned out as intended but gave us a sense of focus. In the remaining weeks, we all wanted to see as much of Tellara as possible.

Louie said, "Practicing your vox skills is paramount!"

I said, "Especially audio-telepathy for one-on-one and group contacts."

Jesse said, "We don't need to know where everybody is every minute, we can keep in touch with our voxes."

Ruth argued, "Yes, but I don't want to be viewed in private moments."

Jesse answered, "Maybe we could have designated times to simultaneously activate our audio function?"

Ruth said, "But we'll all be in different time zones."

Louie said, "Let's master the audio-telepathy tool locally before we start launching global conference calls."

"Aren't we going to Antarctica?" Joe implored impatiently.

"At some point," Sky Dancer explained to her apprentice shaman, "I want to tour Osage country on Tellara to see what remains of Wah'Kon-Tah prior to our forced evacuation."

"I want to see that too, Grandmother," Joe replied to Sky Dancer.

"I want to revisit Mount Shastise, where I encountered my parents during my heart chakra ritual," said Javier.

"And where we got married," I smiled.

Now everyone was talking at once.

Minerva wanted to seek sites of Romani lore which she thought would be on Antarctica, the remains of Atlantis.

Jesse wanted to see and record as much Tellaran art as possible.

Others wanted to visit the orbiting space ark that carries Tellaran DNA, seeds, and digitized Earth Art.

"Don't we all want to see this Antarctic zoological and botanical sanctuary?" Joe asked again.

"Since we all want to see it, let's go there first," said Ruth. We agreed to start our Tellaran tour together and then go our separate ways until it was time to return to Earth.

I said, "Wherever we all go, we all have to be back to a portal site on May 16th, by the Earth calendar. Shall we rendezvous here in Avalon." There was a general consensus.

"Finn and I will return to Earth today and transport *Avalon Equinox* to Wah'Kon-Tah. We'll return to Tellara and meet up with all of you in Antarctica. It won't take more than a few days with our voxes and the chrono-filament."

"So, does everybody know where they're going?" Louie asked.

"Yes," we all mumbled."

"Does everybody know where everybody else is going?"

"Antarctica!" This time we all knew. There were fond farewells to Huckleberry and Finn along with our felicitations to the Cretzkys.

* * *

"Your ship awaits," announced Heron. We boarded a comfortable Tellaran airship and were taken on an aerial tour of Tellara. The ship coasted at a low altitude from Avalon, across Europe, then zigzagged from the west to east coast of unspoiled Africa. Jessie filmed everything. We finally came to land on the northern slope of Mount Zola, the Tellaran name for the highest peak on the Antarctic island chain; named for Zola the Elder, initiator of the heartdance.

We disembarked to a commanding view of the largest Antarctic island. It was cool and windy, and in early April, we had clear skies and oblique sunshine as Tellara slid toward its southern winter. Below us were open expanses of grasslands and woodlands filled with roaming animals. There were pyramid complexes near the South Pole. There were mountains with tunnels that opened to inner Earth, like we had seen in Shastise.

"You're looking at seven hundred thousand square pars of animal and plant sanctuary," boasted Heron.

"Pars?" I whispered to Javier and Louie.

"I dunno, acres, meters, miles?" said Louie

"Whatever the measure, it's vast," said Javier.

"What happened to all the tons of ice?" asked Joe. "How did you green this land?"

Bo Raza answered, "For over two hundred years, we have been relocating Antarctic ice to replenish aquifers around the planet. Water on Tellara is plentiful and vitalized. Farms are irrigated in resonance with nature. Sea levels are stable, keeping coastlines pristine and ocean currents steady. That's why regions like Comanche and Giza are green oases and not dust bowls or deserts."

"Yes, but how did you transport all this ice?" Joe, the youngest among us, was asking all the questions, but we were all like curious children, giddy to learn about this wondrously transformed continent.

Bo Raza answered, "That's why I invented the vox two hundred years ago. Voxes were first used to cut and redistribute immense blocks of ice around the planet."

"Voxes are also used for the construction of pyramids to connect the planetary grid. The pyramidal grid is the mechanism we use to mitigate global seismic activity," explained Guna Raza. "When the ice was removed, ancient Atlantean relics were uncovered, not just the pyramids, but cities containing pavilions, amphitheaters, henges, temples, thoroughfares, plazas, habitats, human and animal fossils, and everyday artifacts, all flooded and fast-frozen. Many relics have been restored in situ. Others are housed in a museum at the base of Mount Zola."

As we scanned the Atlantean ruins, Minerva declared breathlessly. "The original Gypsies came from here. Of course, the Romani migrated to India thousands of years before the Basque migrated to Europe."

"Heard it all before, Grandmother," Javier sighed under his breath.

"The others haven't," Minerva sniffed.

"I have another question," Joe said, pointing to the east. "You are housing prey and predators in the same regions. Look, there are bison, sheep, and elephants together with tigers and jackals. Is that safe?"

"All the creatures have the right to survive in a balanced ecosystem. There are thousands more prey than predators. Both populations are kept in check. None go hungry. None overbreed. All migrate, eat, and drink freely. This is a maintained habitat. Later, after the shift, animals will be redistributed around the globe, and over time, nature will reassert her own balance."

"It's like Eden," Minerva said.

"Eden at twilight," sighed Sky Dancer wistfully.

Descending the slope, we were surprised to encounter a square concrete edifice that could only house the Zeta Reticuli compound. Here however, walls were covered with vines, flowers, and ivy, mitigating the industrial starkness so favored by the grays. Leel and Jeej emerged to meet us.

I greeted them, "I understand you will stay and work with animals and plants here on Mount Zola."

Leel said, "Dana, it is not a choice. We won't ascend. We cannot breed. We will age and die. At least we can be caregivers for life."

Jeej continued, "We infertile hybrids are no longer needed in the Zeta Reticuli fertility project. We are needed to ranch and farm. Any Zeta hybrid capable of breeding will remain in the fertility project."

"Wait!" cried Louie, "Some of you are fertile? Since when?"

"Since Dana and Javier's wedding. Since the collecting of Earthborn kindred mitochondrial DNA and earth music. Our newest hybrid clones show every sign they will ovulate fertile eggs and ejaculate fecund spermatozoa."

"That's wonderful!" "Fantastic." There was a general murmur of delight from all present. This was big news even for the Tellarans.

"It will take many generations to stabilize our reproductivity, but our race is going to survive."

We gave the little grays big hugs, which they barely tolerated and did not return. "Here, try this, it's like a hug only not so invasive," Joe taught Jeej how to high-five and Jeej reciprocated tentatively. "Or try this," Joe demonstrated a fist bump with Minerva and turned to Leel. "C'mon, make a fist. Now bump me, bump me." She got the gist of it and bumped Joe who whooped his delight.

"Mount Zola will be our home for the foreseeable future," Leel explained. "Most of us want to work with heartplums, but we'll be rotating assignments. My first project will be animal husbandry in the climate-controlled African savanna. Oh, the sunlight, dust, and wind! So much weather!" Leel and Jeej joined our party as we ambled down wooded paths trod by a pack of wolves and a family of chimpanzees, all well-fed, all indifferent to humanoids and only mildly curious of each other.

Our first stop was the Atlantean Museum. We spent two days there, and Minerva did not want to leave. She expressed amazement at etched gold encasing jewels, beads, bangles, and bells in settings she recognized from ancient tradition. "On Earth, this crest has been lost and stolen over thousands of years, since before the diaspora of the Domari, Lomavren, and Romani. It reduced our history to folklore. The loss of these insignia relegated so many clans to nomadic poverty and so many queens to chattel. We were once a great matriarchy. We weren't always called the Romani. We were the Lavatlans, the Lava-initiated Atlanteans. Because we were warned by our soothsayers, ours was the earliest exodus. The Lavatlans departed Atlantis during the first wave of volcanic eruptions, long before the final inundation. We relocated to northwestern India for thousands of years. We didn't split up until we became outnumbered by regional tribes who feared our magic. They attacked, killed, and robbed us. The nomadic diaspora began."

"And the Basque? What were we called?" Javier asked.

"Your people were always called Basque or Vasque. They came millennia later to Western Europe and stayed isolated. Both Romani and Basque can trace their ancestry to Atlantis, but epochs apart. That's the source of our rivalry. Not that your parents cared." The delighted Tellarans gifted her with a collection containing rings, earrings, necklaces, bracelets, belt buckles, a gold medallion, a jewel encrusted crown, and a scepter from an unidentified Atlantean clan. Minerva was beside herself. The authenticity of these artifacts was a million times more valuable than their weight in gold.

"Some jewelry imprinted with this insignia was uncovered when the Nazis stole our treasures, but they did not recognize its significance and melted down the gold and extracted the jewels. Same with Ceausescu in Romania; and before that, the Muslims in India and Asia Minor, the Zoroastrians in North Africa; even the Christians in Europe, Bah! Always trying to convert us. Always forcing us to flee!" Minerva exclaimed as she adorned her diminutive figure in gold and jewels.

"Grandmother, this is a common logo. It's a goddess with lions alongside, revering her. We've seen this goddess from the Far East to North Africa and every ancient pantheon in between." As he protested, Javier helped Minerva don some of the jewelry and put one ring on his own right pointer finger.

"Look closely, Javier," she insisted. "It is subtle, but not if you know what to look for. The lions are female and marsupials. This goddess is the Atlantean antecedent to all those pagan pantheons. She was never really lost but transmuted to Egyptian and Hindu deities long after the great shift. Javier, these relics prove our matrilineal ancestry."

"Marsupial lions are extinct," objected the museum curator.

"But our lineage isn't. This marsupial goddess insignia is known only to a handful of Romani Elders in every generation. Our heritage will be restored just in time for the End of The World. Ha!" Her cry was part triumph, part lamentation. Seeing petite Minerva shout while crowned in royal gold was a revelation. "We need to get to Shastise to see your mother!" She shook her bejeweled finger in Javier's face as her bracelets jangled authoritatively.

Javier turned to the museum guide. "Surely, we cannot keep all these precious artifacts."

The curator said, "It's Earth's heritage as well. Your grandmother, Minerva, has told us more about the origins of these Atlantean relics than we ever knew. We've excavated many similar pieces. These keepsakes deserve to survive the shift on both our planets. Marsupial lions are long extinct on Tellara and we never made the connection to the goddess. Perhaps this will help restore a lost culture."

"A lost matriarchy!" declared diminutive Minerva, who despite the weight of the jewelry, bore herself regally. She used the scepter as a walking stick while Javier carried a small but heavy sack of treasures.

"Let's go look at some animals, Queen Minerva," he said, taking his grandmother's arm and ushering her out of the museum.

We observed most of the vista from cable cars that carried us from one vast enclosure to the next. We traversed gargantuan climate-controlled pavilions housing every manner of beast and bud; prominent among them, dormant heartplum orchards preparing for Antarctic winter, while in another pavilion, heart plum trees were bountiful with spring blossoms. Bison filled great plains. Wildebeest and elephants migrated along African-like savannas. Flocks of tropical birds fluttered through a rainforest jungle. Polar bears accompanied seals, walruses, and penguins on oceanic icebergs in freezing enclosures.

Juniper pointed out that every enclosure was also a vast farm for all the flora native to each region, and food was being cultivated among native plants; a cornucopia for humans, grays, and animals to share. We were spellbound, but poor little Leel and Jeej shivered, shook, and huddled in response to the swiftly shifting weather patterns. I could have stayed in Antarctica for the rest of our visit, others had other places to visit and we were preparing to go our separate ways.

On the last night of our visit, Huckleberry and Finn arrived just in time for a savory meal of African stew. We were staying in a parkland filled with domes and A-frame cabins. We heartdanced and then sat around a bonfire and shared stories. Animals hovered nearby, listening to the soft drumbeat and plaintive flute. We heard loud purrs from wildcats, lonely wolf howls, and the soft lowing of cattle. The dogs sat near us, watchful, but relaxed.

The next morning, day we separated. Sky Dancer and Joe Two Feathers went off to the Comanche-Osage region of North America with Heron. Huckleberry, Finn, Alice, and the Raza Clan went on a world tour of all Tellara's ancient megaliths.

* * *

A group of us boarded an airship for Shastise. Javier, Minerva, and I were accompanied by my kids, Saffron, Louie, and Phoenix. "Grandmother, I don't expect us to encounter M'dya and Pai in the mountain, but I would like to share the experience we had in the heart center with Dana." Javier turned to us and said, "Although Minerva and I did not undertake our Chakra Rituals at the same time, we converged in our Heart Centers deep inside Tellara's Mount Shastise. The tunnel leads to Inner Tellara. On Earth, the tunnel entrance is concealed high above Mount Shasta's tree line but goes all the way to Inner Earth. Earth and Tellara share a central singularity, a central sun, Pol. Pol rotates, yet never sets in the Hollow Earth, but there are clouds, rain, winds, and snow that buffet its three continents, Hyperborea to the north, Shambala around the temperate and tropical zones, and Agartha to the far south. Time passes very rapidly in the underworld. In the forty years that my parents have been gone from my life, four hundred years have passed for them. But they have not aged."

Minerva spoke, "Were they to try to leave, they would age and crumble to dust upon hitting the surface atmosphere."

"Like Lo-tsen leaving Shangri-La in Lost Horizon," Ruth speculated.

Minerva replied, "Yes, apparently there are portals between the Earth's surface and Inner Earth around the world: in the Himalayas, the North and South Poles, Mount Shastise, Avalon, Giza, El Dorado in the jungles of South America, and others both fabled and real. The Earth is honeycombed with vast tunnels at all depths leading deep into the planet's center. These domains are occupied by several Terran species, giants, blue people with multiple limbs, and non-Draconian reptilian humanoids. Interior radiant rocks provide life-giving light to thousands of miles of fauna and flora. At the very center, live the

Lucents, highly evolved translucent beings of light."

Javier took over, "So, in my and Minerva's heart centers, we descended into the tunnel at Mount Shastise and my parents ascended. We could speak to and touch each other, but they could ascend no higher into our atmosphere. It was a bittersweet reunion. I told them of my life with Minerva since their departure, of my education and career, of meeting my beautiful but slightly kooky wife. They approved and expressed their desire to meet you. Shambala is their home and it is populated with surface humans who have found their way to Inner Earth over many millennia, going back into lost prehistory. They live among the Lucents in a peaceful, robust culture of surface expats."

Minerva nodded and spoke, "The Lucents have almost no pigment and silvery hair. They are very large, twelve to fifteen feet long, but float like fish in the sea. They have arms, legs, and beautiful faces. They only eat fresh fruit. The Lucents never need to escape the sun's rays as the surface émigrés do. Javier's parents live in a well-appointed cave that shields them from the unrelenting sun, Pol."

Javier picked up the narrative. "My parents are happy and safe. They missed me terribly and tried to return to the surface of Mount Shasta, to the opening they had stumbled into. But years passed and I was no longer a child. They were too old to survive on the surface. The Terrans species throughout Inner Earth are not worried about the pending planetary shift. It will be stable at their depth. Our reconnection via the Chakra Ritual was a gift for all of us. It could only have happened on Tellara."

Minerva interrupted, "We don't know that. We could find the opening on Earth when we return and join them in Shambala!"

"Grandmother, what do you want? To reunite with your daughter or to restore the Lavatlan dynasty?"

"I want to see my daughter, your mother, Genevieve and your Basque of a Father, Zorion Vazquez. I will introduce Genevieve to your *gordjer* wife and her children. After I return to Earth, I will reunite all Lavatlan Clans."

"I want that too. But we may not be able to make contact outside the Blue Henge Temple."

"I'm not a child, Javier. And I'm not stupid." Boy, Minerva could whip herself into a frenzy.

"Well," I broke in, "I'm not so settled as you presume." I objected to the pejorative term that meant 'one who stays under one roof.' "I am a traveler of worlds, planetary wayshower."

"Which is why you are worthy of Javier, and why I helped your fleeing children elude Shelter thugs."

"You saved our lives, Minerva," said Jesse. "We will never forget your hospitality or the secret back roads route you provided us with."

Our airship landed in Shastise and our somewhat frazzled party disembarked. "Before we enter the mountain, shall we break bread together?" Saffron suggested, gesturing to a restaurant overlooking the vista. Phoenix, Saffron, and I had eaten here a lifetime ago, on my second visit to Tellara, when I had viewed an incomplete pyramid and received my vox. Everyone enthusiastically agreed and after a short hike, we sat down to a meal of salads and stews.

I sat next to Louie. "Dana, I wanted to share with you my heart center experience. It was nothing so dramatic as Minerva's inner world odyssey, but it meant the world to me. I was with Hal. We relived lifetimes we'd spent together in all our gender and relationship roles. We planned our next lifetime together on Terra Nova."

"I'm so happy for you. I was with Hal briefly in my Third Eye. He was so kind, so wise, and so serene." I was tearing up. So was Louie. We hugged deeply, oblivious to the rest of the table conversation, thankful to our souls for the depth of our friendship. "And you know I spent time in my heart center with Alice."

"Yes," Louie replied, "She shared so much with me during those months you were trapped at Shelter while we were dancing here in Tellara. I feel a verse of *Side-By-Side* coming on." He actually began to sing, "Oh, I ain't got a barrel of money..." others around the table heard and joined in, remembering the occasional lyric. The tension broke as we Earthborn wayshowers warbled the familiar ditty.

"Your Earth songs are so sweet," sighed Saffron. After lunch, we descended into the tunnel via a lengthy elevator ride, passing through layers of multi-colored, phosphorescent strata. We disembarked on a well-lit landing. The ceiling was high beyond reckoning. The tunnel opening below us appeared as glowing, red, molten rock. But the landing we stood on was covered with a soft, thick moss and we made ourselves comfortable.

"This is where we met my parents," said Javier. Javier's parents, Genevieve and Zorion, did not materialize. Minerva went into a deep trance, received a very powerful psychic transmission, and was profoundly satisfied.

Upon rousing, she spoke a language only Javier understood and then told us, "Although Genevieve and Zorion could not be with us physically, they were with us in their subtle bodies by astral projection. They saw all of you and approve of Javier's new family."

"Since we're in the neighborhood, I'd like to take the tram to Esselen Bluffs."

"Wonderful!" declared Saffron.

"What's there, Mom?" asked Jesse. "That's where Juniper and Robin said they would meet us."

"I hope Corky is with them," said Ruth, petting Belle and Rip.

"Let's go." Our spirits were revived as we set off. We disembarked in Heartplum Park, my old stomping grounds. Juniper and Robin were there to greet us. The dogs frolicked around the orchard. I turned and looked deeply toward the site of the original singularity, *Summer in Tellara*'s portal opening. The original *Magic Seasons* had not yet rewoven its canvas enough to reopen. Phoenix gazed with me at the motionless air and shook his head with resignation.

"What is this place, Dana?" asked Louie.

"I recognize this scene," said Jesse. "Turn around everyone. This is the view of Phoenix's first painting, *Summer in Tellara*." Everyone turned to view the rolling green hills that lead down to the beautiful seaport.

"What exactly are you showing us, Dana?" asked Javier.

"My alibi. I was in Heartplum Park when Jay Andrews was murdered." Everyone looked at me. "Juniper, Robin, and Corky greeted me on this very spot. They took me by tram to meet the thirteen Elders of Esselen. Saffron fed me, trained me, and taught me the heartdance. I returned to the hotel in San Francisco to a nightmare world of false accusations. But Tellara never deserted me. Tellara called me back and brought every one of you with me."

Jesse said, "We're all wayshowers, fired in the crucible of Blue Henge and bathed in the vitalized waters of Tellara."

Ruth said, "We know what our wayshower mission is, and how little time we have to accomplish it," said Ruth.

We took the tram down to Esselen Bluffs and visited the crystal-domed pavilion of the thirteen elders. We retraced my steps as the confused acolyte. We then traveled by air to points far and wide, including Osage country so dear to Sky Dancer and Joe. We met up with the Raza clan, which now included Alice, Huckleberry and Finn, at the Pyramid of the Sun at Teotihuacan in Mexico and traveled with them to Machu Picchu and Uluru. Jesse and Juniper went off together on a whirlwind tour to record Tellaran art. The rest of us actually took a trip to one of the orbiting arks that housed Tellaran seeds and DNA samples. The technology involved in this immaculate storage facility was breathtakingly advanced.

* * *

"It's time to return to Avalon, and then to Earth," said Louie sadly.

Ruth replied, "At least Wah'Kon-Tah will provide us with a soft landing. I've never been although I've heard so much about it."

"We have a few more days until May 16th," said Javier. "Time enough to make another podcast."

At last the moon told us it was time to rendezvous with our fellow wayshowers. Last to arrive were Jesse and Juniper. When we were all there,

Phoenix announced that the transfer of Earth art to Tellara was as complete as could be. All our Tellaran acquaintances and friends were here with us. The farewells caused unprecedented chaos and lasted for hours. We had each made multiple connections. Restaurateurs, museum curators, dressmakers, beekeepers, dancers, storytellers, artists, grays, humans, reptilians, animals, young, and old assembled to bid us farewell, collectively and individually. There were endless group hugs. Jesse and Juniper were inseparable, kissing, hugging, and crying. Louie and Phoenix held each other, hands to elbows, gazing into each other's eyes soulfully. We did a final heartdance, but the images were fleeting and wispy. Our hearts were all so sad and conflicted.

We packed up our keepsakes and it was time to go. Standing together, watching the rippling air, an opening emerged through which we could see the familiar walls of the sky room in Wah'Kon-Tah. One-by-one, my fellow wayshowers crossed the dimensional portal to be greeted by Crystal, Cosmo, Bruno, Abby, and the Cretzkys.

"Will we ever see each other again?" I asked Saffron tearfully.

"When *Magic Seasons* opens the megaportal between our worlds, we will see each other across the dimensional divide."

"For the last time." I sobbed." I tried to memorize every beloved crinkle on her beautiful, ageless face.

CHAPTER 31

"The last to depart, I fell through the quantum singularity into Gwen and Vincent's waiting arms. The sky room was filled with friends and residents. Friends on Tellara had had time to adjust to my altered appearance, but Vincent and Gwen were startled to see my long white hair and serene bearing. Gone was the pudgy, timid brunette who sulked and skulked around the office. In her place stood an ageless force of nature, not much bigger than Minerva.

We'd all been transformed by our sojourn. Louie's hair was long, salt and pepper, and held back by a hemp strap. Almost all of us had more grey or white hair, all of us but Queen Minerva, who's black, flowing locks retained their ebony sheen beneath her golden tiara. We were all wearing Tellaran-style caftans, saris or harem pants. We carried hemp bags filled with voxes, evidentiary documents, and Tellaran mementoes, not the least of which was Jesse's computer filled with images of art, geography, biodiversity, dance, and music from every Tellaran continent.

Vincent gave me a crushing bear hug. "Did you see how much art we sent over?"

"Yes, indeed. All of Tellara is thrilled."

"Are any of the Tellarans visiting with you?" asked Gwen looking past me to the paintings.

"No, we returned to take care of urgent business. We must spread to word of the impending planetary shift and humanity's need to get into harmony with nature. We hope the podcasts helped lay the groundwork."

"Your last podcast was a lollapalooza!" said Vincent. "You should see the blowback."

"Any signs of intrusion through the deflection scheme?"

"None, all's copacetic in our neck of the woods. Wah'Kon-Tah is Heaven on Earth."

"Are you still a wanted man?" Louie asked.

"Only by Shelter, not any law enforcement agencies."

Louie said, "Shelter is a primary source of greed. They held humanity back from enlightenment during this last epoch."

Jesse said, "Our goal is to prevent them from carrying their power forward."

Sky Dancer said, "Wah'Kon-Tah is our home base, but the mission is global. We want to hear about everything that is happening on Earth."

As we dined on cornbread and veggie stew, Vincent said. "While you were away, the global criminal implications became so convoluted that Congress is at a bipartisan impasse. There are resignations, firings, apparent suicides, independent counsels, bank scandals, and business collapses. Politicians and billionaires are moving to Paraguay. There have been surgical drone strikes all over the map. Some think the Illuminati are cleaning up loose ends. Subpoenas have been issued by the European and African Unions. Sheldon Walters' hope of keeping the 'Trust-side' of the organization out of the investigation went south when eight countries, four European and four African, issued arrest warrants against him for crimes against humanity. One of those warrants is for the murder of an Irish journalist named Shari McCann. She went missing in San Francisco the same night Jay was murdered. You remember, the woman who resembled Dana? All eight countries are requesting that Shelter senior executives be tried in an international criminal court. Their assets have been frozen."

Javier said, "I seem to remember a television somewhere in this room." The television was rolled out from a closet and tuned to an all-news channel. Just our luck, Gemini Dallas was yammering on about Shelter's crimes. The net around Sheldon Walters was tightening. Words like treason, murder, genocide, and crimes against humanity were being bandied about. News outlets from the mainstream to independent gadflies were uncovering Walter's dirtiest linen. Speculation on the codes in Shelter's leaked spreadsheets was rampant, terrifying, and, according to Alice, mostly accurate.

"Dana Travers and her motley crew are brave enough to release incriminating podcasts, but not brave enough to come on my show for an interview?" Shelter wasn't the only one scouring the globe for our tribe. Gemini Dallas taunted, "Where in the world is Dana Travers?"

"Getting ready to take her show on the road," quipped Louie, giving me a thumbs up.

We watched for a few minutes until speculation about indictments began to repeat; different talking heads, same conjecture. At length, Javier suggested, "Let's see what we can pick up on our voxes. Before scheduling a lecture tour, we need to know what Shelter knows." It was time to put our vox audio-telepathy training to work. Humming in harmony while aligning our vox crystals, we huddled together in the sky room and concentrated on Sheldon Walters. Vincent and Gwen peered over our shoulders; eyes locked on our vox screens.

Walters came into focus in his office. As we snooped, Kek entered Walters' office and the two Draconians brainstormed about how our ragtag team of mammals was still eluding their surveillance. Walters wanted Vincent Cretzky, Alice and Louie as badly as he wanted me. Kek was apoplectic, "Our technology is a thousand years ahead of theirs. They must be getting help."

Walters ignored his outburst, "Status report."

Kek launched into his account. "We badgered Val Andrews, but she retaliated with an immediate vlog that put some of our operatives at risk. After the release of the ragtag team's last podcast, Pandomi and Contreras were crucified in the press."

"Good. It took the pressure off me for a few days," Walters snorted.

Kek continued, "We grilled the boyfriend's clan and Robles-Leon's families again. Hal's years of estrangement from his family led to dead ends. Louie's sister is frantic to know his whereabouts. The Cretzky's son has no information as to his parents' whereabouts, or so he told Gemini Dallas on her talk show. Oh yeah, he met Squeezy on Gemini's set and is enamored with her. I think they're screwing. Like father, like son."

Vincent had the humility to look abashed. Gwen remained stoically expressionless.

"What kills me is Alice Redding eluding surveillance that I installed. It's worked for decades, lifetimes, and now, it goes silent just as that damn Travers bitch gets involved!" Kek finished on an explosive note.

Walters replied, "That's the strangest part of this whole cluster fuck. Alice has been in my back pocket for lifetimes. She can't go anywhere without triggering a blip on my radar."

"We lost track of her in Shasta, California last Christmas. It took us from December to late February to identify their hideout. Empty now, but covered with DNA, food, fur, fibers, garbage, and forensic evidence from all the people and dogs that Travers associates with."

"After months of searching, you found that house within days of Cretzky's arrest and disappearance. None of this is a coincidence."

Kek was losing it. "They're getting help! There's no other explanation. There were traces of humanoid DNA we could not identify. There were traces of Zeta DNA, but not like any we've ever catalogued. One of the Galactic factions must have violated their treaty."

Walters replied, "That would be unprecedented in over a million years."

"Have you got a better explanation?" Kek argued.

"No! The rules of the game are changing, and I'm the one who makes the rules!" Walters said through gritted teeth.

Kek continued, "We found Travers' apartment in Cairo right after we picked her up in Atlanta. But there were no leads as to how she's been evading our surveillance. We found human DNA and art supplies. We retrieved all the paintings from her condo except one that I gashed last summer. When she fled, she took that one ruined canvas, nothing else. We're searching for her artist friend, 'The Phoenix.'" Kek made air quotes. "He's mixed up in this somehow.

Some of the DNA we found at both sites is of 'unknown origin.'"

We paused in our vox viewing. "Wow," said Jesse. "They found the Shasta safe house right after I left. I got out just in time."

"They didn't recognize the Zeta DNA from Leel and Jeej," said Louie. "Tellaran grays mutated differently from Earthside grays."

"And they stole all my art!" I lamented.

Javier said, "But not the portals, they're safe here in Wah'Kon-Tah."

"And they'll remain here while you travel," Sky Dancer confirmed.

We were going to stop viewing, but something caught Jesse's eye. "Look at this."

"Here comes the Goon Squad," said Louie, as FrankenFretz, Suzy, Blondie, Brownie, Pandemonium, and Contrary entered Walters' office. It was the first time we'd seen the killer goons all together. It was gripping to hear them receive eviscerating reprimands for allowing us to get away.

Walters berated Suzy for letting Vincent and his ditzy wife out of her sight. "You were authorized to use chronovision to peer around temporal corners, and you still lost them right here in Chicago?!"

"They dropped off my surveillance at the corner of Westchester and Robles," she whined.

"Robles, huh? Well, that's a deliberate slap in the face!" growled Kek, referring to Louie Robles-Leon. Louie chuckled and gave Finn the thumbs-up. Frank Fretz was put in charge of the thankless operation of tracking us all down under threat of disembowelment. I almost felt sorry for him until Kek spoke up. "Save the Travers kill for me."

All present at Shelter morphed to reptilian visages. They hissed their words as though spitting sparks. They suspected we had a hideout in the Chicago area, but thanks to Huckleberry and Finn's rigged RAT-TRAK, the farmhouse eluded them. Kek's thugs had ravaged the entire Ozark mountain region, but thanks to Crystal and Cosmo's deflection scheme, Wah'Kon-Tah also remained undetectable to Shelter's surveillance. Frank Fretz said, "Alice might have passed along RAT-TRAK to some conspirators."

"That's it!" declared Kek pounding his fist so hard that Walters' desk shook. "Somewhere along the line, Alice Redding got her hands on RAT-TRAK." Kek was partially correct. In addition to Huckleberry and Finn's modified RAT-TRAK, Alice was safely in Wah'Kon-Tah viewing her persecutors with vox technology that was both physically and metaphysically beyond Shelter's scope. Huckleberry and Finn gave each other a high five.

Walters said, "I contacted the Zeta Reticuli Hive Hierarchy, and demanded information on the activities of the Galactic Council. I told them we need whatever information they have for the 'stability of civilization.' They insist no treaties have been broken. The grays turned up nothing useful, not even the unidentified DNA. In thousands of years, I have never been so stymied by these sheeple."

"They ain't seen nothin' yet!" declared Louie closing his vox screen.

I faced Huckleberry and Finn. "We all owe you an incalculable debt of gratitude. You've saved our lives. You transported *Avalon Equinox* from England to Wah'Kon-Tah. All four Magic Seasons are together and *Summer in Tellara* is reweaving her canvas so rapidly that we can observe the fibers merge with a magnifying glass."

"Whatever we did for you has been repaid many times over. You gave us Tellara. I am Finn Raza, Master of the Chakra Ritual. It was traumatic. We were trapped for many weeks in our lower chakras, feeling the persecution we'd inflicted throughout many lifetimes. But once in our hearts...." He trailed off, choking on his words.

"Yes," said Huckleberry, "Opening our heart centers was painful, but enriching beyond measure. Our lower chakra energies don't dominate our sensibilities anymore, don't leapfrog up to our third eye. Compassion, forgiveness, courage, and empathy are integral to our character."

"Speaking of courage," Alice broke in, "I know what every code on those spreadsheets stands for and I'm willing to testify. Before my sojourn in Tellara, I dared not come forward."

Louie asked, "Will the courts recognize Alice Raza as Alice Redding? Here." Louie opened his hemp satchel and pulled out all of our original documents and data that incriminated Shelter in general, and Sheldon Walters in particular. "We know Shelter operatives have scoured the globe to eradicate whatever copies of evidence they could find and crash every website that posted theories against them. But this original evidence must get into the hands of an untainted international criminal court."

We were interrupted by a low-pitched rumble that grew steadily louder. The Earth began to shake; mildly at first, and then more forcefully, shaking furniture and upsetting our balance. After we spent about a minute stumbling and clutching door frames, it ceased. "That was the warning we got in our final heartdance," said Louie. "We have six weeks before the planetary shift."

"Turn on the television," someone said, but it was already on. One epicenter had been in Japan, there had been another at Mount Aetna, and yet a third beneath the Yellowstone Caldera. A sonic boom had rung like a gong deep in the Earth and traveled through molten layers around the entire world. Although of low magnitude and brief in duration, this unprecedented quake had been felt across every continent.

We all began talking at once, but Ruth shouted over the din. "We've got to start our wayshower lecture tour now in order to share Tellara's message with Earth. I'll be booking our itinerary. We're going to speak at colleges and in conference rooms around the world, starting in North America."

Louie said, "We'll transport collectively by vox, just like we practiced in Avalon. No movement that Shelter can track."

"Who all is going?" asked Javier. Everyone but Sky Dancer, Vincent, and Gwen raised their hands. Sky Dancer said, "Joe and I have work to do at Wah'Kon-Tah." Joe looked disappointed but lowered his hand. Vincent said he and Gwen would come forward when it was time to testify. Crystal and Cosmo said they would join us intermittently, but Wah'Kon-Tah had always been their priority. With voxes, we didn't need the psychedelic van to conceal us anymore.

Alice said, "I'll contact Val Andrews and see if she wants to join us."

Jesse said, "I'll be recording and posting the talks to Facespace; hopefully staying ahead of Shelter's disinformation campaign."

Ruth got on the computer while the rest of us watched earthquake news on TV. After a few hours of work, she announced, "We leave at first light for Dallas, then Phoenix, Mexico City, Los Angeles, and San Francisco. I'll book a city per day as we go and post the promotional announcements on social media several hours before we arrive in order to keep it word-of-mouth."

"Honestly, Ruth, I don't know how we are going to be able to afford accommodations on this ambitious tour you've arranged. None of us have jobs anymore. My passport is back in my condo, if the goons didn't take that too."

"Mom, for someone so bright, you're not getting the picture. These are paid gigs! You are going to get money to speak in nice rooms filled with people who want to hear the most significant whistle blower of all time. People are waking up to the criminal inequities of the Corporatocracy that is keeping humanity in scarcity. They think you have inside information that can blow the lid off the Illuminati. And, you do."

"We'll be using our voxes to replicate food, and water," chimed in Javier. "We'll cloak, travel, and even keep track of the Goon Squad. We could return to Wah'Kon-Tah every night if we want to."

"Is that our wayshower's mission? Corporate whistle blowing?" I questioned.

"That's why people will come, at first," said Huckleberry. "Politics is often the gateway for people waking up to a larger reality. When the average person realizes that their entire government is a lie, they begin to question everything. They discover that the rabbit hole is very deep indeed."

I was nonplussed. Paid gigs? Whistle Blower? Bring down the Corporatocracy? Expose the Illuminati? Prepared remarks? Suddenly, the newly minted fearless wayshower was tired. "Vincent, may I see my room please?" Vincent and Gwen escorted Javier and me to a cabin. The Cretzkys walked arm in arm. They were enjoying a respite from the insane chaos of world events. Our respite was over. We were about to go on the offensive.

While we had been traveling and training in Tellara, Wah'Kon-Tah folks had been busy. The tribe had organized itself into a coherent community that functioned with rhythmic precision. Everyone had tasks, but no one seemed to need a boss. Crystal and Cosmo had been seminal in the consecration of this region before white man ever set foot on American soil. Wah'Kon-Tah, the People of the Sky, River, and Land had always been a haven, a node where supernatural crosscurrents intersected, creating a beacon to the Galactic Family. Locals beyond Wah'Kon-Tah were being drawn to the vibration of the intentional community. Our population was growing; cabins and domes were being erected, infrastructure and utilities were being installed, and farmland expanded. A Tellaran-like haven had emerged in the heart of Osage territory.

***

Huckleberry said, "We've stayed off reptilian detection for decades. They can't RAT-TRAK us. Reptilian technology may be a thousand years ahead of human engineering, but it's still thirteen thousand years behind Tellaran technology which is based on compassion."

Louie said, "We can arrive undetected at our speaking destinations. Our audiences will be notified via the blogs of allies. We have another advantage. We can track them, but they can't track us."

Our travel was made all the easier because Walters and Kek had their hands full deflecting investigations into their crimes. Despite our advantages, we had two close calls. The men and women in black arrived in our auditoriums in Phoenix and LA but didn't approach closely enough to commit televised mass murder. They must have been waiting for their opportunity, but we came and went so surreptitiously that we were gone before they blinked. Our lectures were packed. People came for the corporate whistle blowing and stayed for the planetary shift warning which had been previously disclosed on our podcasts. We linked the two topics. Corporate greed was designed to instill fear and scarcity consciousness in humanity, expediting conflicts.

Val Andrews joined us in Dallas, and any harm that came to her would point directly back to Sheldon Walters. Val's blog now detailed the suspicious disappearance of two other investigative journalists besides Sheri McCann, one in Egypt and one in the Central African Republic. All three had been researching Shelter's activities. The evidence was circumstantial, but still, very incriminating. For a few days, news of the journalists' linked 'disappearances' eclipsed other headlines. I could just see Sheldon Walters breathing fire over these nuisance hits. Even if he was cleared of all other crimes, he'd been tried in the press just as he was ramping up the business of enslaving humanity.

As long as the criminal investigations didn't look too closely into Shelter Trust where behind-the-scene banksters were manipulating the global economy and resources, Walters would skate through any allegations. But thanks to Alice's accurate and specific interpretation of the spreadsheet codes, heads of state, bankers, business leaders, and politicians from many countries were being connected to Shelter's wrongdoings. While we were in Denver, Sheldon Walters and Marvin 'Kek' Kinkel were formally charged with eight counts of crimes against humanity and genocide by a coalition of European and African nations. They forced the convening of the International Criminal Court at den Haag against Shelter's top executives. Resolving to stay in America where the court could not reach him, Walters was enraged to learn that the FBI was preparing charges of fraud, embezzlement, murder and treason against him and Kek. All of Walters' friends in high places could not protect him from the indictment and pending prosecution

Shelter had masterminded the bankruptcy of individuals, families, businesses, regions, countries, and now a continent. African regions were suffering drought because Shelter had privatized their aquifers and modified weather patterns. This had started water wars in sub-Saharan Africa between nations and warlords. Millions were dying. Famine was spreading. People were appalled to learn that Africa was not suffering a natural disaster but intentional environmental destruction on an unimaginable scale. The rest of the world was taking action to provide unprecedented aid. Sheldon Walters had gone from being an invisible mover behind the shakers to the lightning rod for the one percent of the one percent. Undaunted, he continued to dress like a fashionista and behave like a rock star, at least in public. In private, we used our voxes to view his tirades. Walters didn't think he'd committed any crimes. Everything and everyone on Earth were under his province. He was remaking the world in his image and culling the population of undesirables, from traitorous whistle blowers to inconvenient populations. It was his birthright, the inherent natural order, and the culmination of millennia of design.

Our speaking tour was interrupted. Louie and I were subpoenaed to testify in front of the tribunal of international judges at den Hague Peace Palace. We were going to the Netherlands. Ruth canceled speaking engagements in Central America and booked flights for Amsterdam. Huckleberry, Finn, and Alice returned to Wah'Kon-Tah. We would no longer be traveling shielded by our voxes. The eyes of the world were on us. All the original documents that incriminated Kek and Walters, and exonerated Vincent, were concealed by my vox and would be turned over to prosecutors once we arrived to testify. Shelter would not be able to bury the evidence, but I would have to admit that I stole it.

There was a subpoena for Vincent Cretzky. The Europeans and Africans wanted his embezzled Shelter funds to pay for restitution. Vincent would be making an appearance at some point, although the money he was accused of stealing was still in Sheldon Walters' back pocket. There was a subpoena for Suzy, the media darling and righteous insider. Frank Fretz would testify for the defense. I was dreading my testimony. It was one thing to speak in front of a receptive crowd hungry for my side of the story. But I would be facing adversarial cross-examination.

Fortunately, Suzy took the stand the day before me. She looked sophisticated in a conservative navy-blue suit. All her answers were ostensibly framed in defense of her esteemed employer rather than as a witness for the prosecution which confounded the court. Brilliantly playing both sides, she managed to be shocked by the recent accusations against her boss, all the while positioning herself as the logical candidate to restore ethics to Shelter for the good of the order. If only she had known the scope of the crimes sooner! Meanwhile, the Shelter Board of Directors was running scared, so if Suzy wanted to step up and become the new face of Shelter, she was welcome to be their next scapegoat.

The next day, it was my turn on the hot seat. "How did you come to possess the material Jay Andrews stole from Shelter?" asked a favorably disposed prosecutor.

"He mailed it to me on the day he died."

"But you turned the original documents over to Frank Fretz, is that correct."

"Yes, but I have another packet of the original documents."

"Where?"

"Here, with Louie Robles-Leon." Louie was sitting in the front row. There was an uproar in the court the defense protested, spectators speculated, and the judges banged their gavels. Arguments followed as to whether or not these documents could be admitted. The tribunal of three human judges took the packet and indicated that they would hand down a decision after reviewing the evidence.

The prosecutor continued. "How did you come to possess the evidence Vincent Cretzky stole from Shelter?"

"Vincent collected it in a file, and I removed it from the office after he was arrested."

"How did you come by your conjecture of the spreadsheet codes?"

"A lot came from the internet which was proved accurate by criminal investigations." At Shelter's lawyers' table there was an outburst of whispering and objections that were overruled. They objected to Cretzky's documents being submitted. They were overruled. Shelter's lawyers objected to everything I was asked and every answer I gave, but we got through the testimony. I didn't mention Alice but worried her name might come up in this afternoon's cross-examination. They'd question the content of the podcasts that revealed I was a contactee and use it to shred my reputation. They'd realize that I was disclosing the actual source of our technical support but twist it into something vile. Walters glared at me with those malevolent eyes, willing me to choke.

When the prosecution lawyers were done, a guard ushered me into a witness waiting room. The room was empty when I arrived. My advocate was nowhere in sight. I was startled when an icily familiar female voice rasped, "Hello, Dana Dimbulb."

"Suzy!" I whirled to face her. "What do you want?"

"The hierarchy opened a conduit into this moment in spacetime so we could meet privately."

"You mean the chrono-filament?"

She applauded condescendingly. "Excellent, Dana. We misunderestimated you."

"There is no 'we' in your species." Suzy was as youthful as I was ageless. To the world, she and I were whistle blowers on the same side of justice. Nevertheless, she had been assigned to kill me the first chance she got.

"The hierarchy takes care of its own," Suzy scoffed.

"If you're male. I heard them speak of you as a vulgar joke, damaged goods. Your sexual partners were assignments. You peaked professionally when you took a human lover."

"I don't think Frank Fretz would agree with you," she replied with coy confidence.

"He was uncomfortable having an affair with a discard who 'fucked mammal meat.' Their words, not mine. Fretz considered you a short-term investment. He can't stay with you if he wants to ascend in the hierarchy."

"Where are you getting your information?" I could tell that this struck a nerve. She, too, must have wondered how I eluded the Reptilian Cabal. "You know nothing of the hierarchy."

"I know there are no women at the top. They call you lizzies, like fillies. I know that the hierarchy is crumbling because there were no oversights to runaway greed. Your leaders will be victims of their own success. By channeling all the money into the hands of the few, the hierarchy killed the goose that lays the golden egg. Money is meaningless if billions have none and owe trillions to few. And we 'unwashed masses' are beginning to recognize that fact." I made air quotes.

Suzy scoffed.

I continued. "The more power you accrue, the more energy it takes to maintain your human visage. For this reason, many of your species stay out of the public eye. Members of your species can and do evolve spiritually. The oppressed recognize their status long before the oppressors realize that, they too, are in bondage. Women must ring out a clarion call to restore the natural world. That includes Homo sapiens, Draconians, Pleiadians, Zetas, Vegans, Arcturans, and other Terrans currently incarnated on Earth."

"What did you do? Watch and episode of Ancient Aliens?" Suzy sneered.

"Suzy, we are on the brink of a galactic event horizon. The Divine Feminine will be restored. Women will usher in the next age. You have the ability to evolve spiritually with the shift."

"Tell me something I don't know." She tapped my chest with a manicured nail, "You're getting multi-dimensional help. Which of the species in the galactic family broke their prime directive and interfered?"

I said, "I work with individual reptiles who have broken clear of the hierarchy and seek spiritual evolution."

"Reptilian Individuals? That's a myth."

"You asked. I answered."

"I want names."

"They're not mine to give. Why be loyal to the patriarchy? They are taking the planet Earth straight to Hell. I know you loved Vincent. You could seek individuation. You don't have to kill me."

Suzy got a calculating look on her face. "I am here on an assignment from that so-called obsolete hierarchy." She threw back her head and called out to the vaulted ceiling, "We're ready, Gentlemen!" The air shimmered. Kek and Walters descended along invisible filaments, materializing on the carpet from a moment around the corner of spacetime.

I said, "reptilian technology at its finest."

Kek sneered, "You know too much. Good thing you're going to be dead before you can reveal any more secrets." He hefted his lethal blade, curved like a scimitar and serrated on both edges. I recognized the brutal weapon that had slashed Summer in Tellara. Walters stood arms akimbo, serenely confident. Kek raised his arm to strike a blow across my neck, but Suzy stayed his arm.

"May I," she smiled at Kek. The creep was charmed in spite of himself. "So, you want to draw blood, do you, Lizzie?" he hissed.

"Yessss," Suzy hissed back. "This is my kill!" Slowly, Kek handed his blade to her. I stood transfixed as she allowed her human mask to dissolve. Beige and emerald scales framed flat nostrils and vertically slit pupils. A thin forked tongue flicked over her bloodless lips. No choice, I was going to have to use vox technology to escape. Instantly, I cloaked and levitated. Kek and Walters' eyes were riveted on the place from where I had just vanished.

Kek snarled, "Hey!"

Simultaneously, Walters howled "She..." and pointed to my previous position.

But Suzy had her back to me as she cradled the knife and hissed a dark, terrible cry before whirling and slicing deep across Kek's neck, decapitating him in one swipe. Blood was erupting from the remains of his neck. In a heartbeat she turned on Sheldon Walters.

Sheldon Walters saw the blade coming and began to ascend the invisible chrono-filament. But not fast enough. Suzy's deadly blade severed both his legs just below his groin. "Bitchsss!" he hissed, crashing to the floor in a bloody heap.

As he lay bleeding out, Suzy snarled, "Be smart and reincarnate as a female if you ever want a job on my world. It's my turn to rule." Sheldon Walters was still pointing at the spot where I had disappeared and moaned, "Travers…" But Suzy wasn't listening. The palatial room was transformed from a royal showplace to a gory horror show. Her suit, hands, and hair were drenched with blood.

She whirled toward me hissing, "Thank you for your advice, Dana. Now take mine."

But I was gone, cloaked, and hovering in the vaulted ceiling.

Enraged, she stood over her handiwork for a second and just for good measure, plunged Kek's blade deep into Walters' heart. She summoned the chrono-filament and shimmered out of the room.

An instant later, Suzy returned through the main door with Frank Fretz, Contrary, and Blondie. She had looped around time and space faster than humanly possible, appearing in an identical pristine Navy-blue power suit. She scoured the room with her eyes, but my cloak was impenetrable.

"What went wrong?" Frank asked. "Where is Travers' body? Why are Kek and the chairman dead?"

"Plans change. You all work for me now."

"Not bloody likely, lizzie," Frank sneered. At his sexist slur, Suzy's eye's narrowed cunningly.

"Couldn't we frame Travers?" Contrary asked. "She was supposed to be here."

"We can't frame her if she's not here, you dolt," replied Frank.

"Frank, you have a genius for stating the obvious." Suzy ripped the bloody knife from Sheldon Walters' chest, whipped it toward Frank Fretz, splattering him with fresh arterial blood as he reached out to deflect it. With that final calculated maneuver, Suzy summoned her pre-arranged chrono-filament, and shimmered out of the room. As she rose, the goons fled, leaving the blood-stained Frank to fume while he attempted to link to an expired chrono-filament. He was blood-spattered and stranded. How could I have possibly imagined that Suzy would choose to evolve based on a few upbeat words from me?

I glided out the opened door behind Contrary and Blondie and overheard their plan to reenter in moments to catch Frank in the act. Cloaked, I maneuvered above the crowd and out through the open doors to the surrounding gardens, decloaking among tall shrubs. Entering the building, I went through security, and wandered into the crowd. Ruth pulled me into a quiet alcove, "Mom, where were you? We were told to wait for you in the witness room at this end of the building."

"I was misdirected. I'll tell you everything later." This explanation would have to suffice for now. We were in public and could easily be overheard. Once again, I did not have an alibi for a murder I did not commit. Normally camera shy, I stood my ground and fielded questions from a cluster of reporters. Javier, Jesse, Louie, Val, and Ruth at my side. While speaking, I saw Suzy join the crowd. For the second time today, she gave me the derisive, sarcastic applause. If anyone noticed, they would think she was lauding my testimony since we were both witnesses for the prosecution. I ignored her.

"Tell us about your physical transformation, Dana," called a reporter who used my first name. "How did your hair turn all white?"

"This has been a challenging year. It aged me." My voice quavered. My unease was perceived as understandable nervousness for this afternoon's impending cross-examination by Shelter's finest. Lights, cameras, and microphones were shoved in my face. The whole world was watching. Questions flew at me about my roles as a whistle blower, but I realized that this was a global opportunity to reveal my role as a wayshower and share my Tellaran message.

"My hair turned white because I've been on an intense journey across two worlds. I've been asked to bring a message to the people of Earth, not just of corporate corruption, but of planetary shift. These times we are living through have been prophesied." A collective groan arose from the reporters, but I pressed on as Louie and Javier stepped up to flank me with their voxes held in the replicator position.

Louie whispered, "Speak of Tellara and we will project images."

"Shelter Insurance and Trust is but one notorious example of the divisive hypocrisy of this age as it draws to an end. A new age is upon us. I'm not a prophet or a religious zealot, but I have been mentored to be a wayshower by more evolved humans on an alternate world called Tellara. Tellara is a planet with rules but no rulers. The residents obey the law of one; service to others is service to self. There is no government, just heartdances that reveal the outcomes of proposed activities. These events range from the personal to the galactic. One revelation was of Earth's impending planetary shift. Only a few Tellarans ever visited Earth, although I am delighted to share that Tellarans adore Earth art, music, literature, fashion, and, especially, movies."

The crowd was breaking up. I was losing them, but Javier, Louie, and now Jesse, triangulated their voxes and projected the image of planetary schism. I narrated, "The Earth will be rent asunder, splitting in two, one Earth ascending to 5D at a harmonious vibratory rate and another remaining in place and being covered with lava and volcanic ash, much of the surface turning into a scorched wasteland."

"This is a holographic special effect," called one reporter, "impressive but hardly inexplicable."

"There's more," I declared. Tellara has vitalized water. They've learned to balance their global watershed to sustain all creatures. Louie and Javier projected an image of a great iceberg calving off Antarctica. Tellarans teleported it to replenish a dry aquifer in the Sahara Desert and the land above blossomed with overflowing life. "We've brought back some of this vitalized water from Tellara." A fountain emerged in the middle of the great hall and clear water poured forth. People tentatively drank from the fountain and declared it the sweetest, purist water they'd ever tasted. "We've brought back revitalized bees and this wonderful fruit called heartplums. "Baskets of heartplums emerged all over the tiled floors. As people sampled the unfamiliar fruit, they declared that this was bursting with exotic flavor.

"Here are some images from Tellara," Jesse said, and a scale model the beautiful red pyramid emerged in the midst of the great palace hall nearly scraping the vaulted arches. The pyramid was solid. Reporters and onlookers surrounded and touched the red marble edifice in wonder.

I continued, "We provide these manifestations to help you understand that Tellara is real. We're using Tellaran technology. Thirteen of us have been through the portal to our evolved sister planet, some for many months, all of us learning how a society can function for the greater good. Tellara's warning of the planetary shift is real. If you want to ascend to the higher frequency, harmonious Earth, Terra Nova, now is the time to get right with nature, get right with your neighbors, practice the golden rule, be of service to others, engage in prayer or meditation to still your mind and open your heart. When humanity was given dominion over the Earth, it was not to exploit it, but to be good stewards so that nature would bring plentiful life for generations to come.

Louie took over, "It's a choice between unity consciousness and polarizing consciousness. It is not a judgment so much as recognition of your nature. If the reconciliation of opposites makes no sense to you, if mutually exclusive polarities seem inherently good and natural, then be in peace on Terra Familiar. The status quo will remain. Resentment of people different from you will continue unchanged. There will always be someone else to blame." There was a commotion at the far end of the hall, yelling, running, and slamming of doors. Louie finished speaking as all the vox projections faded. "Those of us who have been to Tellara have been designated wayshowers. We will be presenting our message in detail at venues across the globe once these legal proceedings are finished."

A hoarse cry arose followed by alarms and sirens. The mutilated bodies of Sheldon Walters and Marvin 'Kek' Kinkel had been discovered. Most of the reporters turned away from our implausible sideshow and ran to cover the sensational bloodbath. Two journalists remained, one to ask about Tellaran technology and the other about details of the prophecy.

As it turned out, I didn't need an alibi. Suzy feigned terrible shock and reported to the palace guard that, just a few minutes ago, Frank Fretz had given her the brush off in order to enter the witness room for what he described as "something that did not concern her." Naturally, this had hurt her feelings because she knew as much about Shelter operations as he did. Since she'd become a whistle blower, their romance was on the rocks. If he hadn't excluded her, this might not have happened!

Contrary and Blondie backed her story. Ever pragmatic, the cold-blooded reptiles gave up one of their own and closed ranks to protect the hierarchy. Only now, it was a herarchy and Suzy was letting her kind know that she was the Lizard Queen. Take a good look, world.

The press migrated away from me and began interviewing Suzy Quintana, the dutiful, photogenic, heartsick Shelter manager. Her boss and his bodyguard murdered by her lover. Oh, the tragedy of it all! Suzy Quintana would have no choice but to take on the mantle of leadership in the rudderless corporation. She knew enough about the business to hold it together for the stockholders, for the board of directors, and for the clients. Suzy Quintana would steer Shelter back to corporate accountability. In the wake of recent global earthquakes, insurance claims were unprecedented. Suzy would see to it that all were evaluated fairly, case by case, with no quotas.

The den Hague Peace Palace murders created an international sensation. Frank Fretz's arrest was swift, his conviction a foregone conclusion. The spin emerged that Fretz had seen the photo of Walters and Kek in the coffee shop with Irish journalist Shari McCann. He realized that Andrews had turned over incriminating documents to McCann and that Kek had murdered them both on Walter's orders. Frank blackmailed them. Walters and Kek threatened retaliation. Frank somehow found the ancient blade inside the palace and struck in self-defense. The holes in this spin were colossal. Conspiracy theorists went crazy with speculation. My name never came up. And Suzy, inundated with attention and publicity, left our feud for another day.

Louie's and my remaining testimonies were taken in deposition without objections. Crimes of the dead were stipulated to. Walters and Kek were convicted posthumously for crimes against humanity and genocide. Settlements were made to the European and African Unions from Shelter's deep pockets. Investigations into the disappearance of journalists in Africa escalated. Frank Fretz, the blackmailer-murderer was behind bars, keeping his mouth shut, biding his time. Financial restitution, water restoration, insurance payouts, and small business bailouts ensued with stunning alacrity making Suzy a global heroine.

The new women-led regime at Shelter Insurance & Trust was a public relations triumph. The glass ceiling had been shattered. Suzy presented herself to the world as a feminist's wet dream. But serious sums of embezzled money remained hidden. Vincent Cretzky was at large, and although cleared of all charges, was suspected of knowing the location of a fortune in stolen currency.

Our small group accepted speaking engagements throughout Europe, Turkey and Africa. Our presentation consisted of corporate whistle blowing in the morning and planetary shift forewarnings in the afternoons. Although alien disclosure damaged my credibility with some, sharing our Tellaran experiences was our wayshowers' mission.

***

We returned to America for our final few presentations before the shift. One cold, wet spring day, less than a month before summer solstice, we were back in Chicago. We presented mostly in small theaters and campus lecture halls, but today we found ourselves in a fancy hotel ballroom. This was a homecoming of sorts for our itinerant tribe during Imon. A young man I did not know approached our table. I took him for a lecture attendee and greeted him cordially. "Did you enjoy this morning's lecture?" I asked graciously.

"Thank you, ma'am, I did." But he was not looking at me. He was gazing at Ruth. Jesse stood and reached out to shake his hand. Then I understood. This was Mick, the man who had helped hide my children and then sent them away when the situation became too dangerous. Mick was handsome in a nerdy sort of way. He had a long and lanky build, curly brown hair, wore clunky glasses, an argyle sweater, and a bow tie. But his deep resonant voice made him come across as decidedly masculine. Ruth remained seated; her eyes locked on his.

"Mick."

"Ruth."

She said, "Have a seat." He pulled over an empty chair and joined us.

"I must thank you for helping my children in our darkest hour."

"I did what I could."

"You helped until too much was asked of you, and then, you wisely set boundaries. You had no way of knowing whether or not I was a murderer."

"I knew you were Ruth's mother."

"Why are you here, Mick?" Ruth asked with a catch in her throat.

"To ask you if there is a place for me in your life."

"Much would be asked of you now. We're infamous," Ruth said flatly. I could see on her face a mixture of love, hope, and wariness.

Then I remembered, Oh! God! The grays! Sheldon Walters had set the grays on Mick to extract information from him regarding my kids' whereabouts after they fled the north woods. What had happened to him? Even though Walters was dead, my issues with him remained unresolved. Just as these reflections crossed my mind. She entered the restaurant.

Of course, Suzy would have known I was in Chicago. In a forest green designer pantsuit, she radiated power. She'd gone from femme fatal to ingenue to corporate leader in less than a year. An entourage that included Gemini Dallas, Maggie Coutts, Agents Blondie and Brownie, and Congresswoman Gnositall accompanied her. Suzy approached our table. Cameras flashed around the room. This was our first public encounter since Den Hague.

Ever undiplomatic, Maggie addressed Louie first, "I hope you don't want your office back, Leon. It's mine now."

Louie sputtered his coffee. "Keep it. It's yours."

Then Maggie turned to me and declared, "You left too soon, Dana. Shelter has a new woman-led culture."

"I'm glad things are going well for you, Maggie," I replied noncommittally. I was thinking 'murderer-led culture.' But then, there was nothing new about that.

Suzy cut Maggie off with a glance and addressed me directly. "Dana, how are you?"

I could not give her a straight answer. I watched her calculatingly kill two of her own and then frame her lover for the deed. I looked from Blondie to Brownie, whose real names I never knew. Contempt must have shown in my eyes. I looked back to Suzy and noticed that now she, Blondie, and Brownie were staring at Alice. Did they recognize her?

Alice rose to her magnificent height, the embodiment of the Reptilian Individuals Movement.

Comprehending Alice's metamorphosis, Suzy said, "So, the snake has shed her skin."

Alice tilted her head ever so slightly. She had no fear of Suzy.

"Alice Redding, you are full of surprises."

"My name is Alice Raza."

"Well, Alice Raza, there is a place for you for in my women-led organization."

"I must decline," Alice demurred. "I will be presenting on the wayshower panel this afternoon. You may be very interested in my Tellaran experiences. All will be revealed."

Suzy's eyes narrowed. Alice had directly challenged her. Alice would be a more formidable adversary to Suzy than I ever dreamed. I was always skittering away cloaked, but Alice stood unbowed and let Suzy know that she had as much knowledge and power regarding the Draconian agenda as anyone living. And now, she had Tellaran technology. Suzy turned back to me, as if to speak.

"Is that all?" I cut her off. Suzy looked around the table assessing each of us. No one addressed her entourage, although Gemini Dallas kept filming. We resumed our meals. Everyone seated at our table (except Mick) knew that Suzy was a cold-blooded killer. To the rest of the world, Suzy Quintana was a champion.

Ever after a story, Gemini Dallas addressed me, "May I conclude from your silence that you will not be supporting Ms. Quintana in her bid for the Senate?" My jaw dropped. All our jaws dropped. Suzy was running for elected office. My stupefaction must have shown on my face. Louie laughed so hard he nearly fell out of his chair. His reaction was perfect. I laughed too, right in Suzy's face. Then everyone at my table laughed. Even Suzy laughed. We were all in on the joke.

After several sputtering attempts, I found my voice to answer Gemini Dallas with a non-sequitur, "Vincent Cretzky did not embezzle money from Shelter Insurance & Trust. He was framed by Sheldon Walters, just as I had been."

Gemini Dallas pressed. "Will you be campaigning for Ms. Quintana, your former colleague and fellow whistle blower?" Gemini's cameraman was in my face, her pen was scribbling, and listeners were gathering. I had to put a stop to this.

"Vincent has millions of dollars. It is his wife's money. He has nothing approaching the billions or trillions Sheldon Walters stole. Sheldon Walters died knowing where those funds were stashed." I looked directly into Suzy's eyes as I stated this fact. Her eyes lit with my next words. "Dig deep enough into Shelter's business and maybe you'll find a trail to that money."

Sitting down, Alice sighed loudly. "If only you knew someone who could decrypt every remaining code in Walters' database, the person who developed his software for decades, someone who administered the RAT-TRACK and chrono filament inventory, someone who knew the whereabouts of offshore accounts, someone Walters trusted implicitly because she was bound to his will for lifetimes and disabled to limit her autonomy."

Suzy exhaled steam. Sheldon Walters and Kek might have been in denial regarding the magnitude of help we were getting from Tellara and Alice. Suzy had no such illusions. We were armed with technology beyond her ken. Our little team could derail her grandiose plans if she didn't finesse her every move, her now, highly visible professional and political moves. We all knew time was short.

I replied to Gemini Dallas, "When Walter's embezzled money is returned to its defrauded victims, we'll talk politics." Suzy understood. She had killed Sheldon Walters without knowing where his trillions were stashed. Alice might know, but Alice was playing for the other side. It gratified me to point out the obstacles that Suzy had strewn on her own path. Her lethal agenda was not going to delay our wayshowers' mission. It was time to reveal that I had witnessed Suzy murder Walters and Kek. We were at a stalemate, Suzy 'The Lizard Queen' Quintana and Dana 'not-so-dimbulb' Travers. Suzy tipped her head to me in a nearly imperceptible bow that said, 'well-played.' Then she and her entourage moved on. Agent Blondie spared a longing, lingering backwards glance towards Alice.

Mick leaned over toward me and confided, "I have a message for you from the Zetas. We had a most illuminating encounter."

"Do tell!" Louie gushed.

"Do you want everyone to hear?" asked Mick.

"There are no secrets at this table." I assured him. "Did they torture you?"

"They came for me, the grays. They told me the reptilians had sent them to abduct me. But the Zeta Reticuli aren't subservient the Draconians and resent their presumption of control. There is a treaty alliance among the ET humanoids going back hundreds of thousands of years. None of these species like being called Extra Terrestrials or Aliens. They were here for millions of years before Homo sapiens or even Neanderthals."

"We call them Terrans," Ruth interjected.

Mick continued, "The work the grays do with abductees is an endeavor to revitalize their race. They didn't conduct any tests on me. They only work with individuals of their designated lineage and have done so for many generations. I was shown around their facilities and had my questions answered. They consist of multiple sub-species ranging from very tall, pale, cerebral grays— the masterminds; the short, large-headed grays who do the genetic research; and biomechanical, drone-like worker grays who take care of all the mundane chores. Then, there are the hybrids in various stages of human integration. They all tap into the Zeta Reticuli hive mind."

"Brave New World meets the Borg," said Louie.

"The best way for me to help both our species is to join your mission." Mick turned to look directly into Ruth's eyes.

Ruth whispered, "I accept your offer, Mick. Welcome through the looking glass."

"Devil's advocate moment," Javier interrupted. "Suppose Mick's been messed with hypnotically or with mind-altering alien technology?"

"What if he has?" Louie replied. "We've all been hypnotically messed with since we were kids, by the media, advertising, by the politically-motivated curricula, and religiosity. Do you think we could be in any more danger? Ruth will keep him in line."

"Would you like to meet some grey hybrids?" Mick asked.

"We have," said Louie and Ruth in unison."

"Where? When?"

"On the higher dimensional planet we've visited."

"There are gray hybrids among us," Mick said.

Alice said, "They must be perfectly humanoid in appearance to avoid reptilian detection."

"The hybrid grays are indistinguishable from humans. And they don't care what the reptilians think."

"It sounds as though the grays on Earth have made more progress than the grays on Tellara, genetically speaking," speculated Louie. "On Tellara, the grays only use DNA from volunteers, not from a designated genetic lineage."

"Tellara," said Mick. "I saw your disclosure in Den Hague."

"You will hear more about it during our afternoon presentation. We are all contactees," Ruth said.

Javier laid his hand on my forearm. "It's time."

I looked at the clock and saw that it was time for the afternoon session. Attendees were milling about the threshold of the ballroom. We headed to the podium while Ruth and Mick lingered and were lost in the crowd. Suzy's entourage sat in the back row.

Chapter 32

My morning talk had been the retelling of my experiences with Shelter Insurance and Trust. People thirsted for the whistleblowing details. I discussed: Jay and Shari McCann's murders, the misery of being falsely accused; Kek's attack in my living room; Hal's murder; life on the run; my marriage to the detective investigating the murders; and my involuntary return to Shelter.

Javier summarized the tribunal at Den Hague and how the murders of Sheldon Walters and Kek Kinkel led to the conviction of Frank Fretz. But he hinted ominously, "There remained many unanswered questions in this case. There are global implications."

Val spoke of the connection between missing journalists and missing money. Her blog had incited a revolution that broke the back of corporate media. There were slides from her website that included police reports, Phoenix's photos, and Shelter documents.

A woman called out, "Val, your blog was like David's slingshot. You brought down Goliath!" Val was applauded as another global heroine.

Someone commented, "Dana, you have an angel on your shoulder, or you'd have been killed three times over."

Another called, "Val, Dana, and Suzy! Women really are showing us the way to heal the world!" I blanched. Val bowed her head. People applauded.

"Why isn't Suzy Quintana here? She's your fellow whistleblower and now, leading the reformed corporate model." More people applauded, but the panel remained silent.

So, the morning talk was old news. Alice and Louie defended Vincent and suggested that not all the codes on the Shelter spreadsheets had been cracked. Some might lead to offshore bank accounts.

We had disclosed our Tellaran sojourn in podcasts, at Den Hague, and in previous presentations. When we began the 'Alternate Earth' portion of the presentation, some audience members walked out, but more stayed. Today, Jesse would be filming and uploading to the Internet in real time. The moment had come for 'full disclosure.'

I stood at the podium. "I have visited another planet, a sister Earth in a higher dimension called Tellara. I spent much of this last year in that other world while a fugitive from false murder accusations. To say Tellara was a haven would be an understatement."

"How did you get there?" called out a questioner.

"The Tellarans opened a portal between dimensions. At first, I went through alone. Later, loved ones followed. Meet the other members of our Tellaran wayshower team: Louie Robles-Leon, a man of many talents. Louie stood and bowed with a sweeping gesture. "My daughter, Ruth Travers, is running the slide show. Javier Vazquez, the determined detective who sought justice for all is seated by his grandmother, Minerva Regina, matriarch of her clan." Javier and Minerva waved and nodded. "Alice, Finn, and Huckleberry Raza shared our adventures and have their own stories to tell. Crystal Electra and Cosmo Vega were mentors to all of us. And in the back, recording us, is my son, Jesse Travers. Several members of our team remain behind organizing a sustainable community."

I continued, "The Tellarans taught us that our history and science here on Earth contain age-old lies. We've been brainwashed. You might say that in Tellara we were deprogrammed. Tellara and Earth were once one planet. Thousands of years ago, our worlds split into two planets. Tellara evolved into unity consciousness at 5D while Earth remained in duality consciousness at 3D. Tellarans no longer divide and conquer. They use no money. Commerce is based on contributionism. They don't have war or governments. They rule by consensus doing a community heartdance. Their land and water are pristine, and their plants and animals thrive in unspoiled habitats.

"Our planets share a singularity at their cores, each of which is an embodiment of Gaia. Gaia is Mother Earth, Mother Nature, sentient. Tellarans described Gaia's structure as pearls strung along a spiral filament from the densest to the most ethereal. At 3D we're the lowest on this evolutionary spiral. We are in an era the Tellarans call Magic Seasons. This period is the cusp between galactic seasons in our two hundred forty million-year galactic revolution around the center of the galaxy. Magic Seasons is a twenty-six thousand-year interval bracketed by three cataclysmic planetary schisms, each thirteen thousand years apart. The last was recorded in mythic records as the Biblical flood and the inundation of Atlantis. Another schism is imminent, and the final one will happen thirteen thousand years hence.

"This planetary schism will cause the separation of Earth into Terra Familiar at 3D and Terra Nova at 5D, two entirely separate embodiments of Gaia. Terra Nova inhabitants will be in the infancy of creating a society based on harmony consciousness. Terra Familiar will rebuild this world with the same duality mindset in which we now all live. Both Earth and Tellara are home to multiple humanoid species besides Homo sapiens. I've met them, lived with them, and worked with them. This makes me an alien contactee, not an abductee, mind you; rather, a student.

"We're going to break down our Tellaran lessons as they were presented to us. Initially, our mentors spent a lot of time teaching us unfamiliar science. I found this irrelevant until I understood how the unified fields of science and spirituality were the basis for their technology. On Earth, there is a disconnect between the very tiny quantum mechanics and large-scale astrophysics. Tellaran science has unified space-time-mass using geometry based on the flower of life and nested star tetrahedrons from the quantum to the Universal."

I locked my knees to keep them from shaking and began. "There are several species of aliens among us, although they do not like to be called aliens or ETs since they populated this solar system for eons prior to Homo sapiens." Ruth posted a slide. I narrated, "Here is a photo of a Zeta Reticuli or gray, a Draconian or reptilian, a Pleiadian, and a Vegan." It was Jeej, Bo Raza, Crystal, and Cosmo. In the photo, Crystal and Cosmo had shed their human skins and shone in towering luminosity. "This photo was taken at my wedding. These friends were among our guests." The next slide showed the bride and groom and extended wedding party with multiple species gathered in front of the Red Pyramid of Shastise. This disclosure was met with murmurs of surprise, disbelief, and a smattering of applause. Val and Mick were both moved by this image. Suzy did a double-take, recognizing pre-metamorphosed Alice, proof that she had hidden on another planet. What Walters wouldn't have given for this information!

"Here are the lessons the Tellarans bestowed on us over a period of many months."

"First: Earth became interesting to several highly advanced galactic species around the time of the Cambrian explosion, five hundred sixty million years ago. Billions of new taxonomically unique species appeared overnight on a geologic scale, which is to say, over the course of seventy million years." A slide of hundreds of unique, ancient, colorful, distinct sea creatures appeared; then another slide displayed the timeline of species evolution in an artistic spiral from Precambrian to the Holocene. Life-sustaining planets are highly prized throughout the Milky Way. Patient caretakers cultivated the fledgling biota on Earth.

"These ancient races oversaw the genetic engineering of our species. Humans are a hybrid race and our role on this planet is intensely contested. Are we livestock, food, slaves, servants, property, genetic raw material, prospective members of the galactic family, or potential gods on a larval rung on the evolutionary ladder? The latter possibility is the reptilian hierarchy's greatest fear, their motivation for keeping us oppressed.

"According to Tellaran natural history, Homo sapiens is a hybrid race genetically engineered by elder races to our current evolutionary level. The designers had distinct reasons for doing this and their objectives varied according to each species' motivation. They manipulate circumstances to create fear and suffering because they feed off negative emotions. And yet species are simply here to observe us, like subjects in a grand experiment."

I received a question from the audience, "Are you saying there is a cover-up regarding aliens visiting Earth?"

I was finding my stride, "I know there are non-Homo sapiens humanoids on Earth, but I do not know who masterminds their cover up or why."

Louie, in an elegant silver caftan, stood and spoke, "There is no one answer to your question. Some members of the Galactic Family want to keep their presence a secret from humanity until we have evolved spiritually. Others have tried to contact us and been shot down. Some ETs contact persons individually, to provide lessons. One species abducts humans for their own purposes. Several species are getting bolder about revealing themselves openly. They fly their ships in formations mirroring their home constellations so that we might deduce where they're from. Some elite humans on Earth serve Draconians. These human leaders, calling themselves the Illuminati, seem to hold all the wealth and power. They are, in fact, slaves, themselves, to beings whose interest is keeping humanity in the dark about our origins and destiny. The Draconian agenda is opposed by the Galactic Council, which would like to facilitate humanity's advancement.

"The Galactic Council is comprised of members of the Galactic Family who serve and protect ancient treaties among stakeholder races. They don't interfere with human development, like the prime directive on Star Trek."

"Are there any humans on this council? It seems we should be represented," called an audience member.

"We're not yet members of the Galactic Family, but we may have a seat at the table. The Galactic Family is waiting for us to wake up to our potential." The slides were scrolling through images of various non-human Terrans.

Louie sat back down. I spoke again. "My second point: Tellarans taught us that there are vast cycles within cycles in the Universe that our science disregards. On Tellara, it is understood that very long terrestrial, solar, stellar, and galactic cycles drive Earth's ages. Sometimes these cycles force changes on celestial bodies, both catastrophic and gradual." The slide forwarded to an image of the Milky Way with an arrow pointing to the Orion spiral arm with the caption, 'You Are Here.' "Now, as much as some species like to think they're in control, everything on Earth is subject to indeterminant, cyclical forcing factors. The Tellarans figured it out because they can interpret signals beyond human sensory perception in their heartdance. Some cycles are thousands of years long, others are hundreds of thousands of years long, millions, and billions of years long. Earth is entering a confluence of long and short cycles. Louie's going to guide us through these wheels within wheels, when cycles at all scales align." A slide popped up of cogs and gears intersecting on an assembly of astrolabes at all scales. Louie stood at the podium and I sat.

"Let's start with the vast and telescope down to the short. Just as larger objects influence smaller objects, longer cycles impact shorter cycles. There are Galactic Cycles:

"The Universe is about 13.7 billion years old. The Earth is about 4.5 billion years old. Life began on Earth about one billion years ago. It takes our solar system two hundred thirty to two hundred fifty million terrestrial years to revolve around the galactic center. This is one galactic year. Our solar system is near where we were during the Cambrian Explosion. This is a little disingenuous, because the Cambrian Explosion lasted seventy million years. But bear with me, this just means that the cusp of this galactic ages is very long.

"As our solar system revolves around the galactic core, it inscribes a sinusoidal spiral along the plane of the ecliptic. That means it goes up and down as it moves forward. It takes sixty-four million years for the solar system to crisscross from one amplitude peak to the next." A slide went up of the sun spiraling up and down along a sine wave in an out of the plane of the ecliptic. "The plane shields our solar system from cosmic radiation. Every thirty-two million years we depart our protected field into no-man's-land, above or below our spiral arm; above and below being relative terms." The visual was of the sun revolving around the galactic arm, slowing rising and falling in an endless spiral as the planets trailed in their circular paths. "When we leave the safety of our spiral arm, we encounter cosmic rays and dust clouds. Some of those dust particles are the size of small planets. Not the kind of stranger you want to meet in a dark interstellar corridor." There was a small ripple of gallows laughter.

Louie continued as the slide changed. We were looking at the super massive blackwhole at the center of the Milky Way. "Tellarans call the blackwhole in our galactic core Sophia. They call the Milky Way 'Sophia's Milk.' They call black holes 'blackwholes,' one word with a 'W.' Sophia both contracts gravitationally and expands by radiating mass from the P-soup, what we call the sub-Plank field for the scientist out there. Every galaxy has a blackwhole at its core, which generates all mass and energy in continuous creation. The blackwholes at the core of all galaxies are their causal sources and are very stable."

A question flew up from the audience. "I thought black holes formed when stars collided."

"That is one cause. Blackwholes emerge continuously from the P-soup. If a galactic core is a positively unstable blackwhole, the galaxy continues to expand. If the core reaches dynamic equilibrium, the galaxy remains stable in size. If the core becomes negatively unstable, the galaxy will begin to contract, consuming itself. Every galaxy has a unique life cycle. But let's stay in the Milky

Way."

"About every twenty-six million years Sophia undergoes a pole shift which generates a galactic superwave. The superwave discharges intense cosmic and gamma rays. This cosmic wind impacts every celestial body in the galaxy, including our sun, which, in turn, generates a solar wind, which disrupts every layer of the Earth. Based on geologic strata, we're about a million years overdue for this superwave. So, we have that to look forward to." Louie got another small laugh for his wry observation. "It would be nice to get some core samples from Mars. Maybe we could compare cosmic and gamma wave events in the strata to determine our relative geologic time scales."

The slide changed to an artistic rendering of a shower of comets bombarding the Earth. Louie continued, "There is a thirty-one to thirty-seven million-year periodicity in major comet bombardments in our solar system. If this comet bombardment were to coincide with our rise above the galactic plane, outside our protective spiral arm, it would increase our chances of getting struck by a comet by several orders of magnitude. Considering that this comet bombardment is millions of years overdue, and that we are currently nudging our way beyond our safe harbor, well, you do the math. These kinds of prognostications don't scare me, because the notion of planetary stability is erroneous. The biosphere is built on shaky ground.

"Moving on, let's look at some Solar Cycles." An image posted of our sun with violent sunspot eruptions. "Short Solar cycles have a twenty-two-year periodicity, which is expressed in eleven-year sunspot cycles and magnetic pole shifts. The sun has an internal calendar driving its magnetic and radiative ages. Tellarans think that there are longer solar cycles that coincide with Earth's magnetic field and glacial ages."

The slide forwarded to a binary star system: Sirius A and Sirius B. "There is a theory that our Tellaran teachers consider highly probable. Our sun might be part of a binary star system."

"Most stars are binary," called a man in the front row.

Louie nodded, "Can it be that so much time has elapsed since our sun's partner reached its apogee that it wouldn't have been observed since the advent of mankind's current civilization?"

"You can't find something you're not looking for," called Louie's fan in the front row.

"Don't rule out serendipity," Louie beamed. "Tellarans use mythic data as well as geologic strata."

Javier stood up and Louie stepped aside to let him speak. "This concept crosses over into some metaphysical territory, which I would like to address. The Vedic scriptures measure very long periods of time called Yugas. Yugas last millions of years. A version of these texts on Tellara suggests that when Sol and its companion star are moving apart, times on Earth are filled with escalating tribulations as distance increases, culminating in the collapse of civilizations. When the stars start traveling toward each other, Earth becomes more peaceful, building toward a golden age."

"Thanks, Javier, your long-view is an antidote to my catastrophic forecasts." Javier smiled as he sat, and Louie resumed. The slide changed to show images of Mars from decades ago to the present. "Notice that the polar ice caps on Mars seem to be melting or perhaps sublimating since the polar ice on Mars is CO2. Is it possible that global warming is occurring on other planets in our solar system? Can this be attributed to a solar forcing factor or an internal planetary cycle analogous to our Terrestrial cycles? Another possible cause of planetary climate change is the one hundred thousand-year recurrent fluctuation in the eccentricity of Earth's elliptical orbit around the sun. Right now, we're in our tightest elliptical orbit."

An audience member asked, "Is this eccentricity in orbit true for Mars? Venus? Saturn?"

"I don't know," answered Louie. "Is there an astrophysicist in the house?" He paused for audience muttering to die down. "Again, core samples from Mars' ice caps would be intriguing to study. Even if these astronomical factors are influencing climate change, man-made pollution is exacerbating and accelerating global warming. Tellarans think so. They are not experiencing global warming, floods, fires, droughts, or other anomalous weather patterns."

"Don't Tellarans control their climate?"

"Yes, but always in resonance with nature as revealed in heartdances. Altering the natural balance without compensation can cause problems that take years to rectify. We learned of one such occurrence during our stay. The whole planet danced together to rebalance nature."

Louie continued, "This brings us, finally, to some biological cycles."

"What do these cycles have to do with aliens or alternate worlds?" called front-row man.

"The diversity of species on Earth waxes and wanes in approximately sixty-two million-year intervals, about twice as long as that overdue comet bombardment. Evolutionary explosions and mass extinction events seem to alternate with a regularity that science does not explain. Darwin, himself, thought there must be other evolutionary triggers besides natural selection, some from cosmic, external influences and some from internal biological processes. One selection criterion he posited was beauty, another was adaptability. A critter may not be the most alpha, but he may have a wider internal thermostat enabling him to survive heat waves or colder winters. Darwin left it for future generations to theorize about possible evolutionary mechanisms." Louie paused. "If I may editorialize for a moment: Instead of looking for other evolutionary forcing factors, capitalists embraced survival of the fittest in order to justify Social Darwinism. This is an academic way of saying the rich deserve to be powerful because they are better adapted. The rest of us, not so much." Louie shrugged to a few ironic groans.

There was another question from the audience. "Where are we now on this evolutionary timeline?"

"We are due for an evolutionary explosion, an increase in the number and viability of organisms as we return to the scene of the Cambrian explosion. However, due to man-made impacts, we are in the midst of Earth's sixth mass extinction. This current, interglacial epoch is called the Holocene. But some scientists think that man-made impacts have altered Earth so extensively that we should call this the Anthropocene."

"Would the sixth mass extinction be happening if man were not around to alter the Earth's ecosystem?" asked a woman.

"I don't think so. Extinction is not happening on Tellara, even though Tellara's position in space-time is basically identical to Earth's. In fact, a mass spiritual evolutionary leap is taking place. Tellarans are ascending—by choice—into incorporeal spheres of loving light. Tellarans have stored seeds and DNA to preserve every species."

"Tell us more about life on Tellara," called a woman.

"Well, it's a utopia compared to Earth. Our guides insisted that we need to understand our history from a galactic perspective if we want to build a harmonious, sustainable civilization. Other galactic species know about our true history even if we don't. Tellarans have had this knowledge since the last planetary schism, which coincided with the melting of the glaciers and the Biblical flood."

A slide popped up of the Earth tilted at 23° axis relative to the sun. The axis extended to the stars in our celestial sphere. Louie gathered his thoughts, "Here's a terrestrial cycle that many of you know about, the dawning of the Age of Aquarius. The Earth wobbles on its axis of rotation. The precession of the equinoxes sweeps the axis of rotation through the zodiacal belt. It takes twenty-six thousand years to complete one Great Year, and about two thousand one hundred years to advance from one zodiacal age to the next. The age takes its name from the constellation in which the sun rises on the Vernal Equinox."

Javier stood, "We've all been alive during the transition from the Piscean Age to the Aquarian Age. We've seen the advent of flight, transmission over airwaves, telephones, radio, television, computers, the Internet, satellites, social media, all in the last hundred years. The age of communication is Aquarian energy. Because these ages last thousands of years, the cusp between them can last decades, a century, a lifetime."

Louie said, "There are just a few more cycles left to look at. Aren't you all glad to be living in an interglacial interval? Glacial ages last approximately one hundred thousand years, around the same length as Earth's orbital eccentricity. The advance and retreat of glaciers changes not just sea level, but wind and weather patterns. Axial Pole shifts seem to coincide with the advance and retreat of glaciers. Glacial ice redistributes the weight on the planet's surface. This can tip the Earth's tilt and rate of rotation, causing seasonal changes. The equator has been known to drift. Days could get longer. Climate zones could migrate. Why, for instance, is there lush greenery beneath Antarctica's ice caps? It was once a temperate garden. Where was the equator then? Tellarans measure not just continental drift, but crustal displacement.

"The Earth's magnetic poles have shifted one hundred seventy times over the last one hundred million years. We have a pretty good handle on this pole reversal due to sea floor spreading and plate tectonics. Core samples from the mid-Atlantic ridge show that the Earth's magnetic alignment alternates north to south, at approximately six million-year intervals. We seem to be living through this magnetic shift currently. The poles are weakening and migrating thousands of miles. The north magnetic pole is sliding towards Siberia. This is happening on Tellara as well. Their theory is that the magnetic field will go to zero, and then re-emerge at opposite geographic poles. Again, let's look at Mars, no magnetic field and no atmosphere. Core samples would be so helpful. Incidentally, this reduction in our magnetic field coincides with the current solar minimum in sunspot activity."

"So, a magnetic pole shift would be gentler than an axial pole shift?" asked an audience member.

"Ostensibly, yes, no flipping of continents, but we can only guess how technology might be disrupted if Earth had no magnetic field. This reminds me, we all recently lived through an anomalous global seismic event. Earthquakes with multiple epicenters occurred simultaneously. Every continent shook. So did every sea floor. It was a relatively mild event on the Richter scale, yet there was an unprecedented sonic wave deep below the Earth's surface in her molten layers. As one scientist put it, 'the Earth rang like a gong.' Volcanoes, earthquakes, and fault lines around the globe are overdue for what geologists call mega events. These include Vesuvius, the New Madrid Fault line, the Pacific Rim, and the Yellowstone Caldera. Mega quakes cause mega tsunamis. Mega tsunamis rock the Earth.

"Folks, we're looking at lots of overdue cataclysmic events, from the cosmic to the geologic, to the synoptic weather outside your window. What if these wheels within cogs and gears aligned concurrently? How often might this confluence of cycles have happened in Earth's 4.5 billion-year history? In galactic history? Tellarans theorize that ancient memory is encoded in our biosphere's shared DNA. DNA is a cosmic library dating back to the primordial soup. Maybe answers are coded in our so-called 'junk' DNA, maybe in the DNA of frogs or trees or ferns or algae. What are we losing as we destroy our ecosystem? Who could possibly gain from the annihilation of this ancient record just as humanity is cracking the genetic code?"

Louie was drawing to a conclusion. "I don't want to end on a down note, so let me share that this time around the big wheel, our species is waking up. Let's not allow a handful of self-selected ruling sociopaths decide our future. A planetary rift is coming. It will impact our geology, biology, and consciousness. If large objects impact smaller objects, and long cycles influence short cycles, large masses of woke people could give rise to hope in all humanity. See y'all back here in a few million years to compare notes!" Louie bowed to heartfelt applause. In the back row, Suzy examined her nails.

Javier spoke next. "Now that we've gotten all those scary cycles out of the way, let's discuss a little Tellaran natural history. This is the third message from Tellara to Earth: "Civilizations on Earth are cyclic. They rise and fall over many thousands even millions of years. Earth is currently interglacial, not too cold, not too hot, not too dry, not too flooded. Just right. Ours is not the first advanced human civilization to rise from sticks and stones to the space age. The most recent was known as Atlantis and is described in various accounts: Plato, the Sumerian tablets, the Biblical flood stories, in Vedic verses, and indigenous myths. Atlantis was a global maritime civilization. As the glaciers melted, coastal and island communities were flooded leaving archaeological relics submerged. Our ancestors who survived the collapse built megalithic monuments to enshrine information vital to our survival. Megaliths are clocks and calendars with messages mathematically encoded. Knowledge of prior cyclic civilizations is understood by galactic species who helped cultivate Earth's biosphere. Either our species was so traumatized by this catastrophe that we have collective amnesia, or, these memories have been intentionally discredited by centuries of programming. Certain less-than-altruistic species use this to their advantage.

"Tellarans consider the Universe, itself, to be a conscious living organism, and each of us a cell in the Universal mind. If we scale the Universe from its outer boundary to the quanta, the midpoint of this comprehensive metric is biology. From the Blue Whale to a single cell, biology is the event horizon between the cosmic and the quantum. Human consciousness is the event horizon between expanding Universal consciousness and the tiniest nascent particle emerging from the P-soup or sub-Plank field."

"Does our consciousness limit the upper and lower boundaries of our reality? Or do these boundaries define the limits of our perception?" asked a woman.

"That's a chicken and egg question that I cannot answer. Reality is the limits of perceptible scale. This leads into our Fourth point. Some of you have heard the expression that we are co-creators of our own reality. There is another part to this equation. We live in a consensus reality that participates in our creation. We experience reality through the filter of our beliefs and attitudes, many of which arise from generational media, educational, and religious messaging. None of us is an island. We share what Jung called the collective consciousness. Earth's collective consciousness is inertial and entrenched with ancient lies."

Javier was going to continue, but Minerva Regina rose in all of her 4'11" grandeur, bedecked in Lavatlan jewels, a pendant, a scepter, and a crown. Javier bowed to his grandmother as she approached the podium. He adjusted the microphone to her height. "My grandson has yet to mention that we can only be fed lies for so long before the center will not hold. The story of our reality is fracturing. Who among us does not recognize that, as a species, we have entered uncharted territory?" This got a murmur of assent from the audience. "As a result of humanity waking up, there are two collective consciousnesses vying for predominance. The traditional collective that tells us that God is external and masculine, that we were all born naughty, especially women; that war, disease, and hunger are an inevitable part of the human condition; that hierarchy is the natural order and inherently good despite the fact that this stratification gives rise to slavery, racism, sexism, classism, and all the other isms; that rational, left brained thinking is exalted, that imaginative, right-brained intuition is tolerable only in small doses among artists, bohemians, and inane females; that only God can save us from ourselves; disobedience to external authority needs must be punished; and that nature is ours to dominate and exploit.

"There is an emerging collective that integrates the heart with the head, the intuitive with the rational. This evolving collective echoes the mindfulness of global indigenous peoples who live in resonance with nature. If I harm the environment, I harm myself. If we do not solve our problems together, no one is going to consider us a species worth saving. We are the ones we've been waiting for." Minerva was a masterful orator who punctuated her remarks with her scepter. "Our collective consciousness, ingrained though it may be, is a mere bubble in the galactic mind. This truth has been trained and blamed and shamed out of us by generations of authorities who were themselves trained, blamed, and shamed. We do not need an intermediary between ourselves and universal mind. Everything in the Universe is capable of evolving, is in fact, inexorably evolving." Minerva echoed the Hopi prophesy. "Like all pairs of opposites, free will and determinism lie along a continuum. This time of great transition is like a swiftly flowing river. It is so great and swift, that there are those who will be afraid, who will cling to the shore. They will be torn apart and suffer greatly. The river's destination is inescapable. You will get there whether you fight and cling to external, deterministic forces, or chose accelerated evolution. The Romani rejected external authority thousands of years ago." As she mentioned Romani, she displayed the insignia of the marsupial lioness to the camera for several long moments, then resumed her seat as though mounting a throne.

When Javier was certain his grandmother was done speaking, he resumed. "Here's the Fifth point in our wayshower revelations. Our exposure to Tellaran science and technology was mind blowing. They are thirteen thousand years ahead of us." This provoked an excited murmur from the audience and a shrewd glint from Suzy. "The good news is that, on the home front, there is a revolution happening on the vanguard of science, medicine, engineering, the arts, and the humanities. The unifying thread in each of these breakthroughs is consciousness. Researchers working in these innovative areas often toil in small groups, which are rarely well funded, and often face scorn from the establishment. If scholars inside academia pursue these revolutionary theories, they commit professional suicide. Funding sources dry up; tenure and livelihoods are threatened."

A man interrupted, "The hallmark of scientific rationalism is open mindedness."

Javier replied, "Science is attached to accepted theories, regardless of inconsistencies. If the data doesn't fit the theory, the evidence must be discarded. We can't find dark matter or dark energy. We don't understand the source of the strong and weak nuclear forces. We can't find the missing link. The so-called God particle didn't match its predicted radius, charge, or duration, but was embraced to validate the cost of CERN. Evidence of human settlements in America have been dated as ancient as two hundred thousand years old. Because that dating contradicted the twenty thousand-year-old Bering Sea land bridge migration theory, all the evidence was scuttled, and archeologists' careers were ruined. Scientific theories are tenacious, bordering on dogmatic." Javier paused for a breath, "As Louie said, let's end on a positive note. Free energy technology is emerging at light speed, and the public is soaking it up via the internet, self-publishing researchers, and alternative news." We were actually manifesting our wayshower mission. It was time for questions. We all sat at the panel and passed the microphone around.

"What does Shelter's criminal activity have to do with extraterrestrial disclosure and intersecting cycles?"

Louie answered. "Good question. Sheldon Walters was highly placed reptilian overlord in the cabal that controls our planet. So was Kek Kinkel. They knew of these impending planetary shifts and had an agenda to consolidate their stranglehold over humankind before any of these long cycles aligned, before a critical mass of humanity could awaken."

"And join that emerging unity consciousness?"

"Yes," answered Louie.

I spoke, "Others in the Shelter Insurance and Trust are part of the reptilian conspiracy, including Suzy Quintana." The audience stirred uncomfortably. Suzy seethed in the back row.

"You must hate reptiles, Dana."

"Not at all, some of my best friends are reptiles. They protected me while I was a fugitive. Sheldon Walters and Kek were two horrible individuals, by any standards."

"Then Frank Fretz did the world a favor by taking out two evil reptilians."

I resolved, once and for all, to expose Suzy's calumny. She could not be allowed to run for office. "Frank Fretz is also a reptile. And he did not swing the deadly blade. It was…."

Surging through the crowd, Suzy leapt on stage, and ripped the microphone out of my hand. "Enough!" she screeched. "Dana Travers has had a psychotic break with reality. This so-called alien disclosure is rubbish."

"That is not true," called a serene voice I recognized as nearer and dearer. Alice rose from her seat on the panel. "Every species in the galaxy is capable of living by the Law of One: service to others is service to self. I am living proof." Alice dissolved her human visage to reveal her shimmering bronze and coffee scales. There were gasps from the audience.

"You mean The Golden Rule," called someone.

Alice projected her rich contralto as she glided across the stage in reptilian grace. "It is much more difficult for reptiles than for humans to evolve spiritually because our heart chakras are atrophied. Our species empowered intellect to the exclusion of intuition and compassion. We forced this dualistic paradigm on a young humanity. It was a brilliant tactic but contained the seeds of its own undoing."

A man in the audience stood. "You could be wearing a costume. We all have a reptilian brain. Maybe sociopaths operate from their survival instinct and don't develop empathy. We don't need aliens to explain man's inhumanity to man."

Suzy shoved me aside and took my microphone. "You're exactly right, sir. This presentation is not disclosure, it's a hoax."

Alice continued graciously, "I am a Draconian Reptilian. So is Suzy Quintana, the real killer of Sheldon Walters and Kek Kinkle."

An audience member called out, "Then she's an evolved reptile too. She took out those monsters who were enslaving humanity."

"Yes," called another. "She's more humble and courageous than we knew, keeping her heroism anonymous." Everyone on stage was struck dumb by this curious twist, even Suzy.

Crystal joined us. She opened her arms and expanded in a radiant glow, revealing her seven-plus-foot-tall Pleiadian aspect. "I am no hoax," her voice reverberated. "My species evolved on a planet in the Pleiades. I incarnated on Earth eight hundred years ago as a being of light. I have revealed my presence to a handful of sages in every generation. Now, I reveal it on the world stage." Audience members basked in the glow of her spiritual luminescence.

Suzy still had my microphone. "Thank you for all your support. I never intended for my valiant act to influence my election campaign or sway efforts to pardon Frank Fretz. That recording equipment contains privileged information!" She glared triumphantly at me before waltzing offstage. This round went to Suzy. Not so to her ham-fisted entourage. Agent Brownie bashed the camcorder Jesse was operating. Jesse, the tripod, and camera crashed in a violent cacophony of cracking plastic, metal, bones, and glass. Brownie emerged with the digital drive in hand and ran to catch up with Suzy.

Javier rushed to assist Jesse. Cosmo got there first. He used his palms to project a light-healing beam on Jesse's broken arm. A squad of men and women in black surrounded them. "Don't try to hurt anyone in this room." Cosmo declared, standing to his towering height. Alice was tall. Crystal was taller, but Cosmo was a giant. Now, this was Disclosure. They both radiated luminous blessings that filled the room with grace.

"Stand down," Suzy commanded. Her entire entourage swept out of the room as she called to me, "We're not done, Dana Travers."

"I'll getchu my little pretty," Louie snarked under his breath. Suzy was gone, but Blondie expression was haunted as she gazed back toward Crystal, Cosmo, and Alice.

A questioner called, "So, we're not alone. And we've been engineered and interfered with since time immemorial?"

"Cultivated is a better term," said Cosmo.

A woman called, "Dana, your son wasn't the only one filming this afternoon's presentation. It's already gone viral including the giant who healed your son."

"Vegan, at your service," bowed Cosmo.

"What about the gray aliens, the ones who abduct people?" called a man.

"I can answer that," Mick climbed onto the stage. A striking woman accompanied him. She was not quite human, had an exaggerated Audrey Hepburn appearance: very pale with a long neck, slender, elongated limbs, a tiny waist, a mere hint of a bosom, and large, dark eyes glistening in an oversized head. She wore a headpiece, so we couldn't tell if she had hair. Mick said, "Meet Viv, my genetically engineered Homo sapiens-Zeta Reticuli guide."

Viv said, "My egg donor contributed 80% of her hybrid DNA and my human sperm donor provided 20% of his DNA. I am not human enough in appearance to live among you, but others of my kind can and do. We are saving our species by cross breeding with humans."

"I'd fuck you," a college student called out. There was nervous laughter as Viv assessed the young man as to his worthiness to breed. Her calculating stare made him squirm. I had to admit, Earth's gray hybrids were more attractive and engaging than Leel and Jeej. We did one thing better than Tellara and it was due to abduction and defilement.

Draconian, Pleiadian, Vegan, and Zeta flanked us on the panel. They were the real story now. Cameras clicked. Questions flew. Alice, Crystal, Cosmo, and Viv told of their history and purpose on Earth. A few audience members asking about their abduction experiences thronged Viv, whose patient answers evoked tears. Around eleven that evening, the last person filming announced he was out of memory and batteries. The hotel manager asked us to vacate the room. We retreated to a private hotel room away from curious onlookers.

Jesse's cell phone rang. It was his father, Nick Travers. Nick had seen Jesse get assaulted and then healed by light beamed from a giant alien. It took Jesse and Ruth half an hour to peel their father off the ceiling. Collectively, we received an audio-telepathic message from Sky Dancer, "Summer in Tellara has completely rewoven itself and all the Magic Seasons brush strokes are undulating in strange synchronized ripples. I think you need to return immediately in case the megaportal is opening." Wah'Kon-Tah tugged at our hearts. Alice voxed Val to her kids with a promise to join us soon. Mick hugged Crystal and Cosmo transported her to the Zeta home ship. Ruth conveyed Mick to Wah'Kon-Tah. Gathering our gear, the rest of us manipulated our voxes and transported to the Ozarks.

* * *

We entered the sky room and were greeted by Gwen, Vincent, Huckleberry, Finn, and Joe. They chorused together: "We saw your presentation." "It's all over the internet." "Viv and Alice were beautiful!" "What are you going to do about Suzy?" "Minerva, you stole the show!" Sky Dancer entered and said, "Good timing." In moments, Alice arrived with Val and her extended family. Crystal and Cosmo materialized, apparently from the orbiting Zeta ship. Bruno and Abby entered together. She said, "We've stored survival emergency kits throughout the region."

Just as Sky Dancer had said, *Summer in Tellara* was completely restored and all four paintings were almost dancing together as brush strokes tessellated in syncopation. They hung in a tight semi-rectangular arrangement, *Summer* and *Autumn* on the left, a little above *Solstice* and *Equinox* to the right. Countless Tellarans appeared in all four vistas: elders, mentors, friends, dancers, strangers, and animals filled the canvases. We saw the heartdance before we heard the chanting and music. All of Wah'Kon-Tah's residents, old and new, crowded into the sky room to witness *Magic Seasons* take on a life of its own.

Landmasses from adjacent canvases merged, scenery blended in fractal spirals. Seasonal weather patterns of clouds, leaves, flower petals, and snowflakes flowed across canvas boundaries. Branches shed snow, buds emerged, blossoms burst forth, fruit appeared and ripened. Gray skies turned blue and then orange as the sun set and rose. Wind blew through varied terrains, commingling color and texture. The portal, no longer confined by four flat canvases, was a spherical montage that expanded to encircle us. The sphere filled the room, its edges shimmering with white-gold flame. It expanded to fill Wah'Kon-Tah and then the entire Ouachita-Ozark interior highlands. It was midnight in the Ozarks. It was midnight in Tellara.

"This is the megaportal!" cried Joe. "The shift is starting!" We were in the Ozarks and in Tellara simultaneously. People and animals throughout Missouri, Arkansas, and parts of Oklahoma were enfolded in this window between worlds. All traffic stopped. All eyes lifted to familiar stars in overlapping skies. A veil of Tellaran geography overlay Earth's terrain. Tellarans, both corporeal and ethereal heartdanced and chanted among awestruck local folks. In sympathetic cadence, everyone in the vicinity began vocalizing and dancing along. Millions of voices on two worlds sang a hymn to the Universe.

En Masse, Tellarans shed their bodies and transformed into orbs of loving light. Heron and then Robin transfigured before our eyes. Glowing orbs danced across the sky in this unprecedented portal between worlds. Guna and Bo Raza came forth and reached out to Alice, Huckleberry, and Finn, who clung together until their hands dissolved in luminescent swirls. Finally, only Juniper, Saffron, and Phoenix remained in their physical bodies. Reaching across the chasm, Saffron and Phoenix pressed their palms to our palms, each of us in turn. They included Vincent and Gwen in their benediction. They wept openly. The Cretzkys had finally entered Tellara. Jesse and Juniper clung together until the firmament beneath them spread asunder. Phoenix grasped Louie's hands and their tears streamed across worlds. Saffron clasped my hands in hers and I both felt and watched her dissolve into radiant mist as she shed her body. Phoenix shimmered as I called out his name. He morphed into an ecstatic white-gold swirl, his face lingering for several precious moments until my revered wayshower was corporeal no longer. The entire night sky was aglow with millions, maybe billions of ascending, radiant orbs, elating many locals who sensed angelic blessings. This was our destiny, some of us a mere thirteen thousand years behind the Tellarans.

The firmament began to tremble. "This is it!" cried Louie. Intense quakes struck Earth and Tellara simultaneously. The New Madrid seismic zone was shifting. Gravitational disturbances knocked everyone down where we cowered together in a protective huddle. It took several interminable seconds to coordinate protective shields with our voxes. Beneath us, the floor buckled in undulating upheavals that tore the foundation apart. The ground below became an unstable liquid. Together, we levitated. Rocks and dust funneled through the crumbling sky room. A supersonic wind howled through Wah'Kon-Tah. Even cloaked, it seemed to rip through our very cells. Debris screamed across the dimensional opening in earsplitting seismic, psychic, and sonic currents. I squinted against the tumult and saw cascading whirlwinds of energy churning beyond Tellara into interstellar space. It was dazzling and terrifying at once. After a seeming eternity, the cataclysms subsided, and the spiraling torrent diminished to a roiling rivulet. The Tellaran landscape gradually came back into focus. My gaze lingered upon the receding orbs as they ascended towards a distant celestial light.

The portal closed. It shrank back to four separate canvases crumpled in the remains of the sky room. There was no more than a pinprick of starlight in the indigo sky of Shasta Solstice. Then, that infinitesimal light blinked out. I reached my hand to each painting and caressed canvas and brush strokes. No singularity, no portal. The vital, beautiful utopia that had been part of our lives for a year closed with Magic Seasons. The Era of Tellara was over.

This had been no ordinary quake, nothing near the six or seven magnitude event predicted for the New Madrid fault. For one thing, it had lasted seven minutes. We endured an endless trauma, huddled at the epicenter between dimensions, witnessing teratons of destruction sucked beyond worlds. It could not have been local. Even with Tellara's mitigation, this was the genesis of the planetary rift. The land around us shuddered as it settled into altered topography amid toppled structures. Earth had been spared from obliteration, but who knew what wreckage lay beyond our region? Miraculously, there were injuries, but no deaths. We slowly gathered our wits, performed triage, and attended to the business of survival. A good number of our emergency kits were intact past the boundaries of the main compound. But even without them, we at Wah'Kon-Tah were singularly blessed. Thanks to our voxes, we had been spared the worst of the cataclysm, and now, would be able to manifest survival necessities.

Satellites were still operational, so some news got through. Massive Earth changes continued, as aftershocks reverberated for weeks. Later, more detailed news reports said the New Madrid fault had shaken at a magnitude 7.7 for an unprecedented seven minutes, an eternity while it was happening. Geologic shifts had happened on several continents. Vesuvius had erupted. Most of Italy had been evacuated in a drama that had consumed Europe. Japan had sustained a mega quake. The Pacific Rim experienced tsunamis that impacted coastal communities around the entire Ring of Fire. The upheaval along the New Madrid dampened the strength of Yellowstone Caldera. It was not the cataclysmic eruption anticipated by geologists. Yellowstone had released a pyroclastic burst of ash, gas, and debris into the atmosphere that Tellara had siphoned off. What volcanic dust remained covered North America in a nonlethal layer. The Mississippi, Ohio, and Missouri Rivers flooded to form an inland sea that extended from the Great Lakes to the Gulf of Mexico. Cities and farms were wiped out in one geography-altering deluge.

Wah'Kon-Tah was now an island chain in an inland sea. We had thought that the megaportal would be world-shaking news, but the spectacular otherworldly event, although discussed locally, was a mere blip on the media's radar. Mainstream news was doing all it could to keep up with the updates on global geologic cataclysms. It seemed that only Ozark witnesses realized that damage to Earth had been minimized. Tellara's mitigation had restored stability to Earth months before the aftershocks would have subsided naturally. Otherwise, Earth would have tumbled into a new orbit with bizarre polar alignments, forcing continents to summersault into each other across tsunami-wasted ocean basins. Earth had been spared annihilation, even as she rent into two planets. Still, the damage was more than enough to bring civilization to a standstill as humanity slowly picked up the pieces.

CHAPTER 33

We began rebuilding and reinforcing our community. Much of the work was facilitated using voxes to manifest supplies. Farming, electricity, carpentry, plumbing, hauling water, food, and supplies took every hand. We were divinely grateful for the hot springs and soaked our exhausted bones together in the evenings after meals and before ceremony. Each night we gathered around a fire for stories, songs, and chanting prayers. Sky Dancer led the spiritual side of life and, against all reason, Vincent Cretzky emerged as the pragmatic manager of day-to-day operations.

Throughout the region people began to refer to the inland waterway as the Mizzippi Sea. Bruno's bridge still stood, a two-lane wood and concrete engineering marvel that we reinforced with vox-generated rebar. The so-called creek that flowed beneath the bridge was now a torrent of white water. Flooded and collapsed roads throughout the region were slowly being restored. Rebuilding was going on everywhere on Earth. Despite the widespread destruction, life in many places returned to a semblance of normalcy as people from all walks of life pooled their resources. Many locations on Earth remained in chaos. Millions needed food, water, and blankets more than they needed answers. There was a secondary die-off as survivors with minor difficulties and isolating complications could not find infrastructure to feed, aid, and heal. We helped as much as we could, using voxes to travel abroad and manifest subsistence supplies for desperate survivors. There were so many of them and so few of us, but Huckleberry and Finn were always deployed. Months passed. Volcanic dust continued to spread and settle. Limited telecommunications resumed, including parts of the Internet and Wah'Kon-Tah's Undernet. Regional commerce recommenced. Military planes were flying. Animals migrated and those who survived were gradually adapting to new habitats.

Wah'Kon-Tah was no longer off the map. The diversionary scheme erected by Crystal and Cosmo had disintegrated during the planetary shift. Wah'Kon-Tah became a kind of Mecca throughout the region. To help evacuees find us, Crystal and Cosmo did not restore the sheltering shield. Pilgrims of every age, gender identification, race, religion, ethnicity, and ideology continued to arrive on our island community. One was my now-single ex-husband Nick, who had been conveyed by Jesse and Ruth. His congratulations to Javier and me were as sincere as his gratitude for finding a port in the storm. Mick and Ruth had accelerated their timeline from first date, to break up, to makeup, to living together, to starting a family. Val and Jay Andrews' extended family found musical and mechanical ways to contribute. Louie invited Carmela Benedetto, from Shelter's Office of Accounts Receivable. He'd viewed her on his vox being berated by Maggie Coutts and asked if she wanted out. She accepted his offer in a heartbeat and he transported her here. Carmela was captivated with our island settlement. Nick Travers was captivated with Carmela. It wasn't long before they were a couple. Unbelievably, Shelter was still operating; Chicago, overlooking the northeastern shoreline, and Dallas, the southwestern coast of the Mizzippi Sea. Insurance was meaningless in a post-apocalyptic world, but Shelter offices served as Suzy's governmental headquarters.

There were over a thousand of us living on Wah'Kon-Tah now, up from two hundred just one year ago. We worked hard, laughed, soaked, sowed, reaped, shared, and cared. Life had assumed a different rhythm since the changes. No matter one's ideology prior to the shift, contribution and cooperation were our unifying principle. No money changed hands. We didn't need to barter since our resources were communal. We all worked several hours per day, each according to his or her gifts.

A smattering of news got through. Suzy's propaganda machine kept Gemini Dallas on the air: "North America is now geographically divided into three regions. The Eastern American Seaboard stretches from Newfoundland to Georgia. Florida is gone. The Central North American Region is divided by an inland sea. It stretches from Hudson Bay to the Gulf of Mexico and west to the foothills of the Rockies. The Western Region is now known colloquially as the Wild West. It extends from British Columbia to what's left of Southern California and inland to the western slope of the Rocky Mountains. Ham radio operators have received only sketchy news from the Yukon and Alaska. The American and Canadian Rockies have become a no-man's-land. For your own safety, citizens are advised to stay out of the Rocky Mountains. Armed mountain men are hotly contesting election results in the Wild West.

"On a positive note: Fanny Gnositall, former United States Congresswoman, survived the geologic cataclysms and is now the Governor General of the Eastern American Seaboard. And just yesterday, Suzy Quintana, the heroine of Den Hague, was elected Governor General of the American Central Region. Quintana won in a landslide by basing her campaign on feminism and Illuminati bashing. In the Wild West, the former governor of British Columbia, Stormy Pettifogger has assumed the role of Governor General. The Rocky Mountain Men are up in arms, demanding an American man assume control.

"Very little news is available from Asia, Africa, or Europe. South America is fairly stable, geographically, if not politically. We heard unsubstantiated reports of a deadly swine flu outbreak in China and increased locust swarms in Sub-Saharan Africa. According to Undernet sources, countries are merging borders. Others are Balkanizing. Women are coming to power and fighting less over territories and more over water and seeds.

"In another story, an idiotic faction is endeavoring to restart the drug trade to North America. But connections have been severed. Many addicts died or detoxed in the aftermath of the geologic upheavals. Meanwhile, marijuana is proliferating all over the western hemisphere. Wherever there's sun and water, there is hemp. No one in power cares. People are farming hemp for fiber, fuel, and building materials; not to mention medicinal and recreational purposes. Stay safe Earthlings. This is Gemini Dallas signing off."

Throughout the Ozarks, bicycles and horse-drawn carts were everywhere. Donkeys were prized possessions. Breweries and distilleries were up and running in no time and proved to be a valuable trading commodity. We had our own microbrewery and drank Bruno Beer as we sat around the nightly fires sharing stories. The heartplum seedlings we transplanted on Wah'Kon-Tah produced fruit its first year. Thanks to the birds, heartplum seeds propagated to thousands of acres beyond our islands. Tellaran and American bees crossbred and flourished in the absence of pesticides. Birds from all over the continent flocked to our island to nest in the diverse woodlands. In addition to Bruno's Bridge, we now had a small harbor filled with boats of all sizes that had transported settlers from across the newly formed shores of the Mizzippi Sea. We had solar panels storing energy, water wheels turning, and windmills spinning. We had a granary milling flour. We had a thriving dairy and kept our cows happy enough to produce all milk we needed. Except for the chickens, most of our animals had the run of the main island. Farm animals returned to the compound because there was food, safety, and affection. The crocus crop was in full bloom, producing saffron. We used hemp for almost everything from fiber to lumber. We even had patches of cotton and flax from which we spun and wove cloth. Wah'Kon-Tah was trading saffron, honey, and heartplums to towns along both coasts. We were self-sufficient with tools and building supplies. Mostly we were rich with fresh clean water, seeds, and labor. We almost didn't need our voxes. Almost.

We all found useful new vocations. Joe and I gardened and cooked. In the garden, my specialty was pulling out dead plants and live weeds. Joe had the green thumb, so I assisted him. In the kitchen, I was a savant with whatever we harvested each day. So, Joe became my apprentice chef. Javier worked with the bees. We had a surplus of honey and beeswax. Vincent oversaw our reconstruction, often as not, harvesting hemp stalks. Sky Dancer and Alice served as our ceremonial elders. Minerva traveled between Romani clans and Wah'Kon-Tah providing wisdom and resources. Gwen and Vincent were like a couple of kids in love. Gwen became our favorite fireside storyteller. She had found a niche for her kooky imagination and was no longer self-medicating. One night, Gwen told us this parable:

"*A Pleiadian, a Medicine Woman, a Monotheistic Messiah, and a Polytheistic Guru are standing together at the summit of Mount Illumination. They look down over the four cardinal directions and observe the masses of humanoids scaling the mountain on their individual paths. At the bottom of the mountain, great barriers separate seekers. Miles of solid rock divide them. Their beliefs are polarized, mutually exclusive dogma.*

Along the way, seekers can make a choice regarding what route to take: 'Shall I be my brother's keeper?' 'Shall I keep that which my brother needs?' Or even, 'Shall I destroy my brother for my own gain?' These are free will choices. One can take as few or as many detours as one chooses. One can stay near the bottom of the mountain for many lifetimes, reveling in polarizing concepts. Or, one can be a soul on fire, yearning to ascend and join with Illumined Ones near the top. Seekers ascend by choosing compassion.

As seekers ascend, their paths converge. The distance between their ideologies narrows. People begin to see things from each other's perspectives. As each seeker attains the summit, all barriers dissolve. There is no judgment from the masters on Mount Illumination, only infinite patience for each soul.

The paths are many, the Truth is One."

Gwen worked with Jesse to keep a record of our progress using photography, journals, illustrations, and videos that were posted on the Undernet. Bruno greeted newcomers and helped them get settled. Huckleberry and Finn ran our trade operation with off-islanders and transported much needed resources to struggling communities far and wide. Ruth and Mick operated a greenhouse for medicinal plants using our repository of Tellaran seeds. In addition to breeding new strains of healing herbs, she was breeding my first grandchild. And Louie, well, Louie went off by himself for days at a time, still wearing the gold ring he had manifested on Tellara on his right hand, and Hal's wedding band on his left.

Joe spoke to me one day in the garden, "Dana, do you remember when I spoke of the Hopi end time prophecy?"

"Yes, when Louie and I first came to Wah'Kon-Tah."

"When the Earth is destroyed and the animals are dying, a new tribe will emerge comprised of all races. They will call themselves Rainbow Warriors and will restore Earth to Paradise. I think we could do this on Wah'Kon-Tah."

"Joe Two Feathers, so mote it be." Above us, ravens and crows circled.

***

Another year passed as we settled into our subsistence rhythm. One misty autumn morning we were awakened by disturbing metallic and automotive noises. Bruno's Bridge groaned as massive convoys crossed from the mainland to our village. There was shouting, then gunfire and explosions. Javier and I rushed from our cabin to encounter a surreal horror. Suzy had shown up with a uniformed company of soldiers. She was dressed in a khaki camouflage mini-dress with plunging neckline. Her high-heeled combat boots had pointed steel toes covered with spikes. Agents Contrary and Pandemonium were in command of the so-called Governor's Guard. Suzy's favorite media darling, Gemini Dallas, was present with camera crew and audio recording gear.

Suzy spoke into a microphone and camera. "For your protection and safety, this island is annexed to the North American Central Region. You are under the authority of the Office of the Governor General. Martial law has been declared until the United States Constitution can be effectively restored. Agents of the Governor's Guard will inventory the resources of this settlement for the common welfare." Suzy was recording her raid as if it were a humanitarian enterprise.

Contrary and Pandemonium each took a unit of armed guardsmen and began an invasive inspection of crops, buildings, and woodlands. Troops removed stored food, honey, and seeds in substantial quantities. They hauled away barrels of Bruno Beer. The flowering crocuses and the heartplum trees puzzled them, but the staggering number of birds of all species mystified them even more. We'd gotten used the arrival of our many feathered friends, who seemed to instinctively understand the changed geography better than their reasoning human counterparts. I was gratified when Contrary was stung by a Tellaran bee and a swarm chased the defiling mercenaries from their apiary. I was less pleased when the guardsmen began shooting birds for sport.

"Suzy," I yelled, "The only ones we need protection from are your soldiers. They're desecrating this thriving community." I was beyond fear and confronted the camera. I was not alone in my condemnation and plea for sanity. Vincent Cretzky stepped forward from our crowd of survivors. He and Suzy assessed each other, former lovers, now working to restore civilization, each according to their own vision of the common welfare. Vincent looked fine. The fresh air, manual labor, and good company had restored his natural vigor. The promise of his youth was fulfilled; the promise Gwen had fallen in love with before Shelter's toxicity had corrupted him. Gwen stepped forward to stand at her husband's side, facing down his one-time mistress and current nemesis with dignity.

Vincent spoke with quiet authority, "We operate a fair-trade market with all our mainland neighbors. We share our resources with those in need. Suzy, you don't need to do this."

"Vincent, you never understood what I needed," hissed Suzy. She raised her gun, pointed it toward the gathered crowed, and fired six bullets straight into the heart of Gwen Cretzky, who collapsed in a bloody heap.

"Nooooo! Why? Nooo!" wailed horrified onlookers, loudest among them Vincent, who was on his knees, cupping Gwen's pale face in his hands as he watched the life seep from her opened, astonished eyes. I was at his side. So was Louie. In their natural countenance, Alice, Crystal, and Cosmo formed a protective arc around the disconsolate villagers.

Suzy shouted, "Your precious Galactic Family cannot save you!"

Bruno stood by the mourners clutching his giant Bible while quoting soothing passages from scripture. When Suzy pointed her Uzi at us again, he lofted the hefty tome above his head and declared loudly "He who lives by the sword dies by the sword." Suzy started to turn toward him, smirking at his quaint homily, only to be blindsided as Bruno brought the massive force of his Biblical biceps smack upside her head, knocking her into the mud, arms and legs crumpled in an undignified sprawl. Instantly, Suzy's mercenaries were on Bruno. Pandemonium smashed the butt of his semiautomatic on Bruno's temple. Bruno fell forward in a headlong trajectory, landing splat on top of Suzy where he proceeded to vomit explosively all over her khaki uniform. Suzy shrieked and rolled out from under the stupefied Bruno, who continued to retch while crawling away from the menacing Pandemonium.

Horrified, Suzy ripped off the Bruno-barf camouflage from shoulders to knees, revealing a gold lamé bustier and matching hot pants. Her skin was morphing from creamy flesh to greenish-gold scales. Her nose receded to two vertical slits in a small protuberance beneath a widening forehead. Her irises shriveled from round brown to vertical black slits in a red sea that matched her thinning blood-red lips. Suzy's hair shrank from its sleek blonde coif to short yellow tufts. Her breasts poured out of the top of her metallic push-up top, unveiling a scaly hide that was a travesty of feminine beauty. She ripped the Uzi from Pandemonium's hands, clutched it to her chest, threw back her head, and let fly a shriek that shook the heartplum branches until they keened. Birds all over the island went berserk, flapping, cawing, and caterwauling. Other animals added their howls to the wailing cacophony. Whatever Suzy was up to, the last traces of her humanity had been stripped away by Bruno's Biblical barf. A parody of her former self, she reveled in raw reptilian power. We were all dumbstruck. Gemini Dallas continued filming.

Suzy said, "I see I have no choice but to leave behind a garrison of guardsmen. This island is clearly functioning outside reconstruction regulations. All trade is under the Mandate of the Governor General's Office. Exchange of goods and services must be inventoried and taxed in order to reestablish regional stability."

"We told you we'd cooperate," I ground out through gritted teeth, jumping to my feet, "you vicious, murdering bitch."

Louie shouted, "Who died and made you Ruler of the World?"

"I'm the last surviving elected official in the North American Central Region. The Old Guard did the world a favor and voluntarily entered underground bunkers built to shelter them while the rest of us endured global catastrophes. Once they were inside, I had all the tunnels sealed, trapping them for millennia. The 'powers that were' are in power no more."

Louie said, "You're no improvement. You're a toxic tyrant playing god with traumatized survivors."

Ignoring Louie, Suzy narrowed her gaze and took aim at my heart. Our eyes locked. In my morning rush, I'd left my vox in the cabin. I was dead certain I was dead.

Apparently not.

Above us, a moaning spirit wind parted the mist. And there in the azure sky appeared none other than Jesus Christ, Himself, seated on a massive golden throne. His white robes and dark hair fluttered in a celestial breeze. He carried a staff in his left hand. His right hand was raised in benediction. A choir of angels in silvery regalia encircled Him. Jesus spoke, "Children of the Earth, I have returned to save the faithful. Cease fighting and set down your weapons." He waited. Suzy's guardsmen looked puzzled, glancing to Suzy for their cue. "You heard me, disarm!" Jesus demanded to all assembled. And this time, the guardsmen obeyed. Suzy held fast to her Uzi but lowered it. "That's better," said Jesus-In-The-Sky. And the angelic choir sang "Hallelujah."

"Jesus Saves!" cried Bruno, raising his massive family Bible at his Lord.

"I have returned to offer one last chance to all non-believers. Follow me to Salvation and yours will be the Kingdom of Heaven." And the angelic choir sang "Hallelujah." Guardsmen and islanders were falling to their knees in confused supplication to Jesus-In-The-Sky.

Joe ran out of the sky room and declared loud enough for all to hear, "It is happening everywhere on Earth. People can see this on every channel, the internet, even in the sky." Gemini Dallas was gesticulating behind her cameraman, who was filming Jesus-In-The Sky and his angelic hosts as the whole world gazed in wonder.

Beyond Jesus and the choir of angels, an armada of spaceships materialized, simultaneously blinking into visibility from somewhere beyond. The ships were too many to count and came in all shapes and sizes. Lens-shaped, disc-shaped, and cigar-shaped ships vied for position. Gigantic mother ships, small flitting two-man vessels, silver, white, light, and inky dark ships popped into the sky from horizon to horizon.

The largest mother ship broadcast in all languages reverberating across the world, "Don't listen to Jesus-In-The-Sky. He is a holographic hoax, the latest deception of the Illuminati and the Vatican seeking to solidify humanity's blind obedience."

"I am not a holographic hoax!" declared indignant Jesus-In-The-Sky, shaking his staff. And the angelic choir sang "Hallelujah." "I am Christ the Lord, Son of God, Son of Man, the Redeemer who died for your sins. Come to Jesus!"

"Hallelujah," sang the angels.

"Amen," cried Bruno.

"Ignore the hologram," demanded voices from the largest mother ship. "We are your Galactic Family," said speakers in every conceivable language. "We are here to offer guidance and love."

Interior views displayed the bridges of many ships. There stood dozens of various alien species. Some resembled movie aliens, conspiracy theory folklore, short necked-grays, long-necked grays, mantis-like insectoids, beautiful multi-armed androgynous blues, catlike humanoids, squat large-jawed brown creatures, beautiful, tall, androgynous Pleiadians, Vegans, Arcturans, Andromedans, and Sirians, and, of course, one mother ship full of menacing Draconians. The luminous Galactic Family spoke collectively, "We are your elder brothers and sisters. Like you, we faced evolutionary challenges that threatened our survival. We overcame them and are now here to offer our guidance to Terrans."

A giant holographic screen emerged, taking center stage in the sky. Two preening Popes in full regalia on a balcony pulpit preempted the Galactic Family's ship. "It is the role of the Mother Church to guide humanity. And we have proof. Here it is: The Third Secret of Fatima: Jesus was a light being from the Galactic Family." The short Pope frothed at the mouth as he spoke. "His return is timed to coincide with the return of Earth's Second Sun, which has recently been observed via our Vatican telescope, LUCIFER. It is ordained."

"Hallelujah, Here comes the SON," sang the angels.

"Can a hologram save the world from the radiation and pollution that is destroying the waters of the Earth?" challenged voices from Galactic Council mother ship.

"Indeed, I can," vowed Jesus-In-The-Sky. "Surrender to My will and all will be healed on Earth as it is in Heaven." And the angelic choir sang, "Hallelujah."

The onscreen televised holographic Popes-In-The-Sky cried "Come to Jesus and his Holy Mother Church!" And the Angels sang a half-hearted, "Yeah, What They Said."

To our collective amazement, an unfamiliar blue light appeared in the morning sky. No larger than a pinprick, this distinct azure star was bright enough to shine in daylight.

"Blue Star Kachina," declared Sky Dancer, "Earth's second sun. The Hopi prophesy is fulfilled."

"Wormwood," cried the Popes.

"Hallelujah! Here comes the SUN!" sang the angels.

"There's a theory about an approaching brown dwarf called Nemesis," said Javier. "But that star is definitely blue."

"Stella Blue," declared the Sirians on the Galactic Family mother ship, "Sol's binary stellar sister. It has been beyond the view of the Earth for millions of years. Now it approaches, and your ages of darkness come to an end. A golden age approaches."

"Not relevant! We still own you," declared the Draconians in their ship.

"And I'm their leader!" asserted Suzy on the ground.

"We're here to rescue you," cried holoview projections from silver spaceships bearing beautiful Arcturians. "We'll take you to another planet where you can live free."

Blue Andromedans called, "We will land for you to board. All aboard the Galactic Express!"

"Not so fast," cried out a multitude of furry brown aliens from the saucer-shaped ships, their massive jaws and teeth filling the view screen. "It's our turn. The ancient treaty is abrogated. We're here to consume Earth's creatures."

"Irrelevant! If the treaty is void, we're here to plunder Earth's planetary resources," declared the mantis-like insectoids in robotic voices they declared, "We will eviscerate the Draconians and Browns in an inter-planetary war, with enslaved humanity as the prize. The Galactic Family can do nothing but sit back and watch!" The insectoids launched a fireball at the Draconian mother ship. The Draconians shot back and the fireball sputtered across the sky like a dud firecracker.

"We have a treaty permitting us to harvest your DNA," declared the Zeta Reticuli in the lens-shaped ships. We will acquire genetic materials and hybrid fetal tissue by any means necessary."

"We're here to recruit pets," cried the cat-like species in their two-man ships. "You will be pampered all of your days."

"And we are here for a front row seat," cried voices from millions of ships in unison. "We're here to see if humanity can rise to the shift. Each of you chose to incarnate at this moment, so your fate is in your own hands."

"Come to Jesus," called Jesus-In-The-Sky and the choir of angels sang, "Hallelujah."

I sat on the grass near Gwen and hugged Vincent, who was choking on sobs. "Save her, one of you, save my Gwen," Vincent railed to the heavens. Suzy sneered and waved her gun at us. She was not done playing. But someone above must have been. Lightning struck near Suzy, scorching her combat boots and searing her Uzi. Dropping her smoldering gun, she hopped from one foot to the other, shrieking threats and demanding that the Draconians acknowledge her planetary authority.

As Suzy screamed, Jesus-In-The-Sky pixelated and did a Max Headroom triple take.

"See," said the Galactic Family in their mother ship, "That Jesus is a holographic hoax."

"Will someone just fix the vertical hold?" called the tall Pope in full regalia.

Not to be left out, military fighter jets began crisscrossing the sky, taking pot shots at the spacecraft that had threatened humanity. A jet released a bomb that formed a stratospheric mushroom cloud. The Galactic Family mother ship expanded its shield to enfold the blast, which imploded with a wet raspberry.

A voice, grander and more resonant than all the others, reverberated from horizon to horizon. It was a gloriously feminine, the voice of Mother Nature. Gaia was here. A kaleidoscope of Goddesses appeared, weaving images throughout the land, water, fauna, flora, and sky. Venus rose naked from the sea on a massive shell. Artemis materialized against the crescent moon, nocked her arrow, and drew her bow. Pele rose from the tallest peak on our island and from her loins poured forth molten lava. Green Tara emerged from a grassy mound in a basket of fruit and flowers. Oshun reclined in the whitewater beneath Bruno's bridge as a waterfall cascaded over her golden sarong. Isis spread her feathered wings. Pallas Athena arose bearing helmet, shield, and spear, with an owl perched on her shoulder. Her Etruscan counterpart, Minerva, flared at her side, armed and incandescent. Blue Kali with her multitude of arms danced upon the fallen Shiva.

Tree goddesses burst forth in leaves and branches. I recognized Kwan Yin, Ishtar, Hecate, Demeter, Buffalo Woman, Nut, Psyche, Juno, Maat, Magdalene, White Tara, Ixchel, Mawu, and Lakshmi. Thousands more Goddesses from every pantheon swirled above and below. The voice of the collective divine feminine vibrated through our cells, "God has many names, but the Goddess has many faces."

One goddess emerged, engulfed in the blazing sun. Her feet rested on the crescent moon. On her head, she wore a crown of twelve stars. She was pregnant and in labor. She spoke between contractions. "That hologram is not my son. My son will not return to any planet that so horribly abuses the feminine principle! Womankind has been violated in spirit and body for six thousand years, for as long as your Abrahamic patriarchal religions celebrated the would-be sacrifice of another Mother's son. That so-called god's demand for obedience instead of mercy was textbook psychopathy, with the entire human race as his target."

"I take exception to that characterization," declared a colossal, winged Alpha Male Draconis as he emerged from his mother ship into the open sky. This was no scaly reptilian humanoid. This was a Real Dragon.

"Are you an Anunnaki?" called Contrary to the dragon.

The dragon declared, "I am the Master of Earth and of my home planet, Nibiru, which now approaches from beyond the Oort Cloud. When Nibiru is inside the solar system, I am the Lord thy God. I made you. I own you."

"You mean Wormwood!" contradicted the short Pope self-righteously. The dragon belched fire and smoke at the Popes, who collapsed in singed coughing fits.

"Some call it Planet X," called Louie. The dragon ignored him.

Suzy called out to her guardsman, "Behold, you've never seen the true Alpha Draconis before. Our actual leader can never impersonate a human. He has not appeared on Earth for three thousand six hundred years, when the dragon became the stuff of legend."

The dragon turned toward Wah'Kon-Tah and said, "It was I who demanded human sacrifice and I to whom all obedient worship is owed."

"The time for obedience is over," exhaled Mother Mary. "The vertical organization of society has failed; no more hierarchy. Decisions will now be made in an inclusive circle on a horizontal playing field." Before she could go on, Mother Mary had another powerful labor contraction.

"I will not be gainsaid!" fumed the dragon. "I demand the sacrifice of your child. That will restore the natural order."

The dragon charged at Mother Mary as she began to bear down, pushing the child from her womb. But Draco could not reach her. Pallas Athena, Minerva, Frejya, Artemis, an army of Valkyries and Amazons tackled and barricaded him with spears, lava, and arrows. During the melee, all the goddesses in Heaven midwifed the Holy Child. As Jesus in the sky, his angels, and the Popes watched uselessly, the dragon roared with rage, beat his wings, and bellowed fire. A celestial light opened in the sky enveloping Mother Mary, her newborn, and all the goddesses. Elbowing the dragon away, the goddesses ushered the newborn into a heavenly dimension, beyond the reach of the infuriated beast, and beyond the sight of all who beheld the miracle.

Draco roared, "I claim dominion over Earth and all her creatures."

A patriotic pious pilot in one of the jet fighters who had witnessed the birth and ascension of the holy child, took fierce exception to the dragon's assertions. He fired a barrage of explosive charges at Draco, who dodged the blasts while gloating, "Your puny weapons can't harm me."

To which the pilot broadcast for all to hear, "Our puny weapons ain't what they used to be," and shot a guided missile that struck the dragon's right humerus, shredding its wing. The dragon spiraled downward to Earth, crashing wounded, at Suzy's feet, right in the Wah'Kon-Tah commons.

Gazing into Suzy's eyes, Draco declared, "So, you killed Walters and Kek, my Alphas this last three thousand six hundred-year cycle. Do you think that makes you my new Alpha, Lizzie? The hierarchy rules this planet and I rule the hierarchy." Up close, his growling hiss hurt our ears.

Unbowed, Suzy picked up her microphone and hissed in his face. Our ears and noses bled from the earsplitting decibels. "Haven't you been paying attention? It'ss woman'ss turn to rule. If you don't believe me, ask your wivess, that iss, if you make it back to them with one wing. Nibiru has a Lizzie-led order waiting to greet you."

Draco howled and prepared to unleash an inferno, but instead, he choked on a torrent of water flooding from his snout into the Mizzippi. Breakers crashed north to Canada and south into to Gulf of Mexico. Humanity wailed as more coastal communities were inundated and tsunamis raced across the Atlantic basin. Now Suzy was pissed. "This is NOT your planet anymore! It's mine!" Suzy brandished her Uzi at the Lizard King and fired point blank into his eyes. Unable to fly away, he bled from every orifice and choked on blind rage. She fired relentlessly until his entire head was a bloody pulp.

"Suzy the Dragon Slayer!" cried Contrary, and all the Governor's Guards fell to their knees, bowing before Suzy Quintana, Office Manager, Whistle Blower, Corporate Savior, Governor General, and now, Queen of the World.

Louie stumbled to my side from where he had been comforting Vincent. He grabbed my arm and we gazed at each other in disbelief. His face was tear-streaked, bloody, and dirty. "Dana, do you know what this means?" he asked, gesturing to the myriad mythic dramas unfolding before us.

"No, Louie, what does this mean?"

"You're yesterday's news." I laughed in spite of myself. Absurdly, he was right. We were in the midst of murder, unnatural disasters, Holographic Jesus in a pissing contest with the Galactic Family, and Popes arguing with Goddesses from every pantheon. As if that weren't enough, the remnants of the U.S. Military blasted into the tableau, a new blue sun appeared in the daytime sky, and apparently, a planet filled with pissed dragons was approaching Earth.

"It's a deus ex machina," I exclaimed.

"More of a catastasis," Louie countered.

Suzy turned to face the camera, "Humanity has been controlled by Draconian Overlords for thousands of years. I have vanquished those tyrants. Behold your Benevolent Leader. I assume this role due to the genetic superiority and longevity of my species. Heed the Goddess' proclamation that it is women's time to lead. I alone have the vision to shepherd humanity through the coming age. Advanced technology will usher in Paradise."

Louie called out loud enough for the sound boom to pick up, "You must not have been listening to the Goddesses. We have to live in harmony with nature if we are going to survive. A true leader doesn't use technology to subjugate the masses."

Mother Mary spoke, "Thanks to Draconian interference, the human species has utterly misunderstood the power of nature and the glory of the feminine. Ancient overlords deluded themselves that Mother Nature was theirs to conquer. Until, as a species, you revere womankind and work in resonance with nature, no one is coming to save you. You have to save yourselves."

"How dare you!" demanded the indignant short Popes in full regalia. "I have just revealed the third secret of Fatima. The real Jesus is a galactic light being and He is here to save humanity."

"Come to Jesus!" said Jesus-In-The-Sky. But, again, his face scrambled in a pixelated triple take. The angelic choir glitched, "Hallabubala".

The tall Pope said to Mother Mary, "The Holy Mother Church is the infallible voice of God on Earth. Your role in humanity's saga is over."

"Let it go Pops," said Mother Mary, gently but firmly, to the soot-covered Popes.

"Bitch!" snarled the tall Pope, waving his rosary.

"Don't you talk to my mother-in-law that way!" A youthful brunette goddess glided forth from the field of divine feminine aspects. "That would make my husband a son of a bitch."

"You're not his wife, you whore!" yelled the short Pope, recognizing Mary Magdalene.

"So says the pedophile," said Mary Magdalene.

"Deceiver!" wailed the tall Pope.

"Money launderer!" said Mary Magdalene.

"Jezebel!" said the short Pope.

"Bed wetter!" said Mary Magdalene.

"Original sinner!" snarled the tall Pope.

Mother Mary spoke, "Be still all of you." To the Popes she said, "You boys have had six thousand years to figure it out. Now go to your rooms and stay there until I tell you to come out and play. The human race is about to get a glimpse of exactly what the Reptilian Illuminati and churches have been afraid of and why the Y-chromosomally challenged patriarchy worked so hard to undermine feminine power."

The Popes scowled, crossed their arms, and refused to budge. Mother Mary addressed all Terrans: Don't trust promises of salvation. They come from self-serving entities who want nothing more than your obedience. Do consider guidance from sources who have no attachment to whether or not you heed their message. Stop being so scared of death. Consciousness never ends. It always evolves, sometimes at a snail's pace and sometimes faster than lightning. Treat every woman like your well-being depends on her well-being. Treat Mother Earth like a precious treasure. When Mother gets mad, the world shakes."

Military jets continued to crisscross the sky, shooting missiles at random alien ships. The more they shot, the more spaceships filled they sky. A voice from a mother ship announced: "These ships are here to transport any Terran who wants to escape to a better world."

"What is going on?" I cried out to no one in particular.

"It looks like all kinds of end time prophecies are happening simultaneously," answered Sky Dancer serenely. She, alone, seemed unperturbed by the insane display. "Here comes Ragnarök. The boys have come out to play."

The God of Thunder literally thundered into the sky. Thor, in all his muscle-bound Nordic arrogance, wielded his massive hammer and demolished the Draconian mother ship into smithereens, sending millions of reptiles sprawling to Earth. He pulled back to smash another ship but was forestalled by the colossal forearm of Woden. The two Nordic Gods began an epic battle of celestial fisticuffs, only to be joined by Loki, who cackled while taking pot shots at their vulnerable flanks by tossing jet fighters at them like darts.

"Freyja help me!" cried Thor.

"Not bloody likely, Thunderboy," called Freyja, emerging into the foreground. "Didn't you hear? Mother is back and she's going to have to clean up your mess. I join with my sister Goddesses. If you're smart, you'll make peace and pay attention to the Mothers." She rode off in her feline-drawn sleigh, accompanied by a slew of Valkyries along a rainbow arch. In his frustration, Thor sent a barrage of lightning bolts to Earth. Suzy screamed and leapt from foot to foot.

The short Pope wailed in exasperation, "Jesus, do something about all these females and aliens!"

Holographic Jesus whined, "I wasn't prepared for any competition for my attention. I expected the heavens to myself."

The tall Pope reproached, "Look, you're supposed to appear as a being of light from the Galactic Family. Put on a light show, for Christsakes. When we reveal the existence of ETs as the third secret of Fatima, the Vatican can maintain global monotheistic authority. If and when alien disclosure happens… which… as it turns out, is today," he finished lamely.

The short Pope wailed, "Give it up. Our ruse was revealed when our hologram glitched. That's not the third secret of Fatima and we both know it."

Mother Mary responded, "No, it certainly is not what I prophesied to Lucia.

I warned that unless the Vatican reformed, the church would face a terrible chastisement as a rain of fire and bullets, that the Vatican would be violently crushed, and its authoritarian reign ended. Consider the scope of your hypocrisy, misogyny, money laundering, secret Satanic factions, and pedophilia protection. The suppressed knowledge in the Vatican library contains scrolls from the library of Alexandria which describe Earth's cyclic civilizations and ancient technology that would have prevented the Dark Ages. It's no wonder you old goats withheld my revelation."

"It won't ever be revealed!" boasted the tall Pope.

"I just revealed it!" Mother Mary sighed, and a terrible wind stirred the land.

Seven angels blew their trumpets in a resounding blast. Angels throughout the heavens cried: "The Kingdom is at hand!"

As the world gazed at the Papal holoscreen in horror, hundreds of flaming meteorites crashed down upon the Holy City. The Popes fled the scene. Clerics in black, purple, red, and white robes fled in every direction, but to no avail. People and buildings were smashed into blazing infernos and burnt cinders. Even the unfaithful wept for the savagery of chastisement. When the reign of fire finally ceased, the two wounded Popes climbed out of a panic room buried beneath the debris. They were forced to crawl over the bodies of lifeless clerics toward a helipad adjacent to the Holy City. Seeking escape and rescue, the short Pope cried, "Someone of the faithful will surely save us." And to their relief, there, before them, an army was being airlifted onto the helipad. The Popes hurried toward the troops and cavalry who stood at the ready. Four horsemen flanked the armed soldiers. To their horror, the soldiers were ISIS terrorists, faithful warriors who had sworn to Allah to bring down the Vatican, the enemy of Islam. As the Popes rose to greet deliverance, the soldiers opened fire and the Popes were mowed down in a spray of bullets. The four horsemen rode off toward the four corners of the Old World. The Isis soldiers were then airlifted away. The Holy City lay silent and smoldering. The entire world went still, unable to fathom the end of the center of power that had dominated western civilization for two millennia. We surrendered to the Biblical moment.

Biblical was the right word. Before our very eyes, Bruno, Abby, and dozens of other Children of Abraham separated from their bodies, becoming luminescent translucent forms. They cried out in joyful unison, "Rapture, O Rapture!" Some cried out to God, others to Allah. The rest of us watched in awe as our beloved friends dissolved into the ethers. Then, wonder to behold, the ground shook as millions of resurrected souls from every continent floated upward, joining the faithful who had been raptured to Heaven.

Jesus-In-The-Sky pixelated. The Angels sang "Hallabubala."

Scarcely giving us mortals a chance to catch our breath, another mindboggling vision filled our vista. Mary and all the goddesses merged, swirling together into one immense visage that expanded to fill earth, sky, and water from horizon to horizon. Gaia basked in the glow of her twin suns, familiar Golden Sol and new Blue Kachina.

When she spoke, all our cells reverberated.

"Harken unto me. I am Gaia, the heart, spirit, and mind of this planet. Sophia is the heart, spirit, and mind of our galaxy. As I am your mother, Sophia is my mother. As I am in labor, she is in labor. Prepare for birth pangs. A blast of celestial radiation is coming our way from Sophia. You may have heard of the galactic superwave. There is infinitely more energy coming to Earth from the galactic center than from old gold Sol and new Blue. We're about to go on a whitewater ride of radiative whirlpools. Don't cling to shore. Go with the flow if you want to survive with your sanity intact. Your DNA is about to blast you where no one has gone before."

"Follow me to Salvation before the superwave hits!" called Jesus-In-The-Sky. And the Choir of Angels sang, "Hallelujah."

"The Galactic Express will convey you to a safe planet," called a multitude of alien spaceships.

"There is no safe planet in this galaxy," said Gaia patiently. "Sophia's Superwave is an equal-opportunity, multi-directional blaster."

Everyone in the sky except Gaia began arguing: Jesus, the angels, Thor, Loki, and the aliens were all shouting together. On Wah'Kon-Tah, domesticated animals chimed in with neighs, brays, moos, and loos. Above us, thousands of birds cried out in agitated calls. Then the creatures of the forest and fields released a discordance of howls and roars. The entire planet resonated with a storm of wounded rage from the animal kingdom. Creatures were calling out their wrath at humanity's treatment of our shared world. Animals in confinement pulled violently at their restraints and broke their bonds by the millions, ripping out bars and chains at the cost of limb and life, in many cases turning on their captors and giving mad chase. Above us, the sky was darkened by the deafening beating of billions of wings. Fish leapt from water. Whale and dolphin song added to the dissonance.

At the peak of the din woman and children joined in the voice of the planet, howling, screaming in a rage that terrified their beholders. Proud, arrogant men backed away in fear from the planetary pandemonium of billions of wounded women, children, fauna and flora. The voices of good men rose in collective righteous reckoning. The ocean rose in screaming waves. The wind shrieked. Gaia herself shuddered. The unspeakable howl continued, and all Wah'Kon-Tah joined in. Suzy hissed with hysterical abandon. The screaming gradually gave way to weeping as people and creatures backed away from their oppressors. The few abusers that dared restrain and pursue their tormented victims found the ground shift beneath their feet until they could not balance to stand, much less walk.

"That was me," said Gaia. "That was Mother Nature reclaiming her sovereignty." Finally, the beasts, the birds, and the sea creatures settled. Gradually, human weeping grew softer and more isolated. The end time prophets in the sky stopped quarreling. We all turned inward, contemplating wounds we had suffered and wounds we had inflicted. The world fell silent, awaiting the approaching galactic superwave, Sophia's burst.

The pensive peace was shattered by a new shrill voice. An apparition in the heavens sounded like a fast-talking game show host. His emergent face looked like Poindexter Q Nerd in Buddy Holly spectacles. "That's right kids - Gabriel Galaxy - GG here, talking atcha from the pie-in-the-sky arcade known as the Milky Midway. Incarnation on Planet Earth is all a game, dontcha know, a computer-programmed virtual reality roller coaster ride. And you're all here because when the game began, you raised your hand to come out and play. You signed up for this simulated reality in order to learn about 3D manifestation with all its pesky rules and restrictions. Your entire reality is a subset of 5D rules. Gamesters who play you against each other for fun and profit control the simulation. The stakes are all or nothing!

"But wait! That's not all! You're a 5D being too! You've just forgotten. Want to get off the ride? Want to leave the game? Well you can if you have enough points. And by points, I mean good karma. Salvation is just a wake-up call away! You too can resume your Cosmic Consciousness! How does that sound?"

Gabriel Galaxy paused for questions, but on our island, the only response he got was from Vincent Cretzky, "Can you save Gwen?"

"No can do!" exclaimed GG with exaggerated cheerfulness. "The game has to play itself out. Life and death are part of the rules. And so are prizes! Yes, prizes. In addition to Cosmic Consciousness, you get to be the God of Your Own Universe. Haven't you always wanted to play god? Well, wake up and spin the wheel of fortune!"

"Sorry to interrupt, bro," intruded a garrulous specter who looked like the love child of Soupy Sales and RuPaul. "I'm Larry Luminous, tonight's host of The Earth Factor! Humanity is not a virtual reality game; it is a cosmic reality show!! The whole galaxy has been viewing you for millions of years, placing bets, and voting entire cultures off the island. Who's on top for the next roll around Sol? Audience, it's time to vote." He paused as millions of beeps and toots sounded from the armada of UFOs. "Bombshell result! It's a narrow, but decisive victory for Suzy Quintana! In the next age, all the world's a stage!"

"All the world's a playground," argued Gabriel Galaxy.

Louie called out, "Gee willikers, Mr. Peabody. I think there is a glitch in the WABAC machine!"

"Good one, Louie!" called Larry Luminous.

"That's a thousand points for Louie!" said Gabriel Galaxy.

A third manifestation appeared. This tightly wrapped woman resembled a constipated Madam Mao. She read from a scroll. "Creatures of this Galaxy, beyond all your games, shows, and suffering; beyond your wars and treaties; you are all under the purview of The Great Experiment. Angels, both fallen and risen, designed the procedures. We gave some of you free will, some of you the illusion of free will, and others a rigorously structured hive mind. We gave you planets to thrive upon, minds to contemplate reality, and emotions to guide your actions. For billions of years, we've observed results, tweaked the conditions, and kept meticulous records. Despite Earth's precarious place on the precipice of the apocalypse, the experiment endures. If you have to rebuild from sticks and stones, no big deal. You've done so before."

Louie called out, "You must know about Tellara and the ascension of planets!"

Madam Mao scowled, "Other dimensions are not part of our experiment."

Louie retorted, "Your results will be inconclusive when planets and creatures evolve beyond your experimental design. What's the point of letting creatures suffer just to satisfy your curiosity?"

"Have you even seen The Matrix?!" snorted Madam Mao.

"This is great for ratings!" cried Larry Luminous.

"It raises the stakes in the game!" declared Gabriel Galaxy. "The jackpot is at an all-time high!"

"Hush," Gaia whispered in her omnipresent voice. To humanity's collective relief, the obnoxious announcers shut the Hell up.

"Manifestation is a collective dream that has a life of its own. You did volunteer to be in this dreamscape, and you can wake up. You involuted into 3D, the densest layer of manifestation, a subset of higher dimensions. When you began to contemplate the nature of reality, your evolutionary journey began. Your collective consciousness controls the rules and restrictions of your existence. The secret is, the more you cooperate with Nature, the easier it is to navigate those rules. Manifestation goes through vast cycles that redistribute matter and energy throughout spacetime. The laws of nature are inertial habits that change slowly and rarely, but often ungently. Sophia has reversed her polarity and burst forth the galactic superwave. As a planet, I will roll through the breakers as I have done so before. Trust Mother and roll with me."

The long day had passed. Night was falling as the Earth began to tremble everywhere. The largest remaining holo-screen in the sky broadcast a series of coronal mass ejections striking the daytime side of Earth. Solar winds enveloped the planet and blasted every surface with flashing sparks and invisible shock waves from the solar flare. The holo-screen displayed Earth undergoing its dimensional division. One Earth emerged at a higher vibrational frequency in the morphogenic field. Another Earth stabilized beneath us. At this point, the holo-screen shattered into thousands of glittering shards and the image of the planetary mitosis faded.

Externally, the solar wind shimmered in kaleidoscopic colors. Internally, all my prior incarnations swirled into my consciousness. The vision expanded to connect me with all other Terrans living and dead, all animals, plants, and minerals. Faces reflected back to me with aching familiarity: long lost friends, family, and foes. I was Water, Earth, Air, Fire, and Spirit. We were experiencing a global mind meld that spanned the ages. "You are all one. You are all the center of your own universe. Take what you love with you into the next realm," vibrated Gaia inside our heads.

Some people in my immediate vicinity were unable to cope with this shared global awareness. A woman I did not know was babbling incoherently about dragons. Gemini Dallas was curled up in a fetal position hugging Bruno's Bible. People's nervous systems were unprepared to handle the overload. Fourth-dimensional creatures who had genetically engineered us in order to dumb down humanity, were with us in this conscious web. Alice was here. So were Huckleberry and Finn. So was Suzy. Crystal and Cosmo beamed lucid knowledge of an ancient war for Earth. The Arcturans and Pleiadians had lost to the Draconians, whose agenda was enslavement of humanity. Our newly emergent species of Homo spiritualis was what the reptilians had fought for millennia to suppress.

This telepathic web should have been terrifying, but it had a sense of familiarity. Once upon a time, we had all been here together. We decided collectively to enter this third density and learn about physical manifestation, karma, sexuality, suffering, polarity, life, and death. Was this global awareness the protective web the Tellarans spoke of? Even as I had this notion, everyone on Earth, friend and foe alike, apprehended our Tellaran sojourns. Thousands of reptilians were involuntarily revealing their secrets. They were dumbfounded to realize the assistance humanity had received from 5D Tellara. They could handle the expanded collective consciousness, but they hated being immersed in liquid loving light.

Gaia reassured us, "This revelation is your birthright. During this Quickening, unused regions of your brains will open. Latent segments of your DNA will activate. No power in the galaxy can prevent what is about to happen next. Sophia is here!"

A delightfully sensual tingling began in my loins. The sensation grew and became urgent as a spectacular buildup began to move through every cell in my body. I dropped to my knees and clutched my groin, emitting an unrestrained groan of ecstatic delight. All around me, others were doing the same. A collective moan of sexual pleasure erupted from everyone on the island, everyone in the world. We were all stupefied with mindless ecstasy as wave upon wave suffused us with contractions of pleasure more intense than any orgasm I'd ever experienced. As the full body orgasm spread, a collective cry went out from all Earth's inhabitants. A global orgasm united us in simultaneous bliss. I tuned into a love so poignantly sweet that it was unbearable. Just as I thought I would go mad from the intensity of the crashing contractions, the waves subsided. I could breathe again. I sobbed and rolled back and forth, clutching my heart. I bumped into Javier and we had a moment of recognition where all I could do was whimper and all he could do was grunt.

Just as my heartbeat returned to normal, another series of sexually ecstatic waves began to build. A second global orgasmic shockwave was overtaking Earth's entire population. Again, we were powerless in its grip. We could do nothing but ride the waves to that strange and distant shore where we were overwhelmed with sexual, physical, mental, emotional, psychic, and spiritual bliss. I was in love with everyone who ever existed, and everyone was in love with me. As the second orgasmic shockwave climaxed, I felt my spine would shatter from my pulsating tail bone to my shuddering skull.

"Ooooooooh, God!" cried three billion men who gasped in an agony of ecstasy as they ejaculated simultaneously. Every woman shared that penile release. Every male felt the heat of women's cores as our erogenous zones simultaneously convulsed.

"What is this?" "What is happening?" "How can this be?" reverberated billions of masculine voices.

"It's a multiple orgasm, dear," answered billions of women who had better tolerated the second wave.

"Thank you, Goddess," cried the voices of woman who had been genitally mutilated and denied their sexual birthright. Little children sighed collectively, experiencing an innocent ecstasy that did not arouse their lower chakras, but opened their hearts and minds like flowers. Sexually wounded people felt healed in body, mind, and spirit. Rapists and sexual predators felt the full impact of their misuse of this beautiful lifeforce as their sexuality and vitality dampened to nearly zero. They too, had been sexually wounded, and felt release from the darkness that had corrupted their passion. Globally, we healed each other. Globally we were linked at all chakras.

There were orgasmic aftershocks that pulsated across the planet for hours, depriving us of the coordination to speak, or rise, or acknowledge our own names. A sweet stupefaction engulfed the transformed human species.

"Now that was a Second Coming!" A voice I recognized as Louie's penetrated my brain fog.

Even as I assimilated the bliss, others collapsed in death throes from the unbearable sweetness. Millions of souls exhaled their last breath, the relief of their final heartbeat apprehended globally. Millions of others clung to life but went mad as their most cherished paradigms were shattered. People lay about the island laughing, sighing, and bleating inarticulate groans. The human mythos had been transformed We were no longer Homo sapiens. Were we Homo spiritualis? Homo sexualis? Homo-What-The-Fuck-Was-That?

Dawn was breaking. "Wake up," whispered Gaia.

"You won't be waking up; you'll be Quaking Up!" shrilled Gabriel Galaxy.

"Quake Up!" called Jesus-In-The-Sky. And the angels sang, "Hallelujah," then pixelated and dissipated. One by one the alien spaceships blinked out of our dimension. The over-the-top presenters dissolved. The jet fighters were gone. The Goddesses were reabsorbed by Gaia. Earth stilled.

Cosmo said, "So, that was a galactic superwave, Sophia's birth pangs." Crystal and Cosmo were walking among us, passing out water and heartplums. Even as I reflected on the global mind meld, the global orgasm, and the possibility that we are inside a simulation or experiment, the sensation began to fade, like waking from a dream. People were recovering their sensibilities. In dawn's early light, the new blue sun flickered on the distant southern horizon, conjunct old golden Sol.

We thought this incomparable night was over. There was a collective gasp as we witnessed a massive asteroid slowly glide between the Earth and Sol, causing an unnatural eclipse. Ol' Sol disappeared by increments, leaving no umbra or penumbra to even peek behind this massive intruder. Conjunct New Blue was also eclipsed. The solar wind lifted dust from meteorites and volcanoes to an eerie layer that blanketed the sky, blocking all starlight. All electronic devices were fried. None of us had our voxes. Disoriented, we could not feel our way to our cabins to retrieve them. Someone lit a torch and it fizzled out. Earth was in total darkness.

"Three Days of Darkness, according to a Catholic prophecy," said Louie's familiar voice.

"Another miserable prophesy happening during our interesting times." Joe Two Feathers replied.

We all began to call each other's names and crawl to the sounds of voices, both human and animal. It got cold. We moved together, seeking warmth. As we climbed in a pile together, deer, horses, birds, sheep, dogs, cats, chickens, pigs, goats, and humans joined the huddle of our collective flesh. A more primitive a survival tactic I could not envision. Louie was near me and said, "According to the prophesy, the air will be filled with pestilence and demons."

"After everything that's happened, I would have thought Gaia could prevent this assault." Bizarre animalistic sounds spewed in the dark. We all snuggled closer in terror.

Unperturbed, Sky Dancer began to chant. After hearing several refrains, we joined together in the Osage recitation, part prayer, part song, part mantra.

"Look at us... Heart of Heaven... Heart of Earth...

Give us our descendants, our succession as long as the sun shall move...

Let it dawn... Let the day come...

May the people have peace... May they be happy...

Grandmother of the Sun... Grandmother of the light...

Let there be dawn... Let the light come."

Then, someone began to sing a familiar Christian hymn and our voices blended together. Although none of us was faithful enough to have been raptured, we all knew the words. Other voices chanted Om Mani Padme Hum and more Om Shanti Oms that I did not know, but I was soon repeating them along with everybody else. A Hebrew prayer was chanted, and again, after several refrains, we intoned along. A beautiful Muslim chant arose. We all listened reverently and then joined in, feeling religious divisions fade and the Oneness of all Terrans arise. Our collective vocalization gave us an internal cadence that allayed our panic. Time passed. The threatening voices receded.

I wondered what others around the world were doing. How were they coping? Were others huddled together or trapped in isolation? Why didn't one of those benevolent aliens blast the comet fragment out from in front of the sun? Oh, right, I remembered now. They were here for a front row seat. Humanity was facing an unprecedented challenge alone. Few species had ever been pressured to evolve so swiftly. Throughout the cyclic rise and fall of civilizations, we had given away our power to the worst sociopaths among us. They had silenced compassionate voices raised to oppose them. So now, we clung together, singing, crying, shivering, and waiting.

After an agonizing interval, there was a peak of light in the distant sky. It was the small blue sun. "Kachina," someone called. "New Blue!" called another. The blue sun offered no heat, but its light was a miracle. After what seemed like hours, our beloved Ol' Sol began to rise on the horizon. People wept but stayed huddled until Sol was high enough to warm the day. Finally, warm, I fell asleep and dreamed.

Something was gently shaking me. I knew that voice. "What huh wha?" I was drooling.

"Dana... Dana"

"Huh?" I knew that name. I had heard it before. It was familiar. Did I know Dana?

"Wake up Dana," I heard that now familiar name in a now familiar voice. Javier was speaking to me. I was lying on my back with the sun warming my face. I was flanked between my dog Rip and a good-natured sow and her squirming piglets. My eyes fluttered open and gazed into my husband's ruggedly handsome face. Javier looked spent. His eyes were bloodshot. He needed a shave, a shower, and a shampoo. He needed mouthwash. I imagined I did as well. I rolled over to my belly and pushed myself up on all fours. Around us, others were regaining consciousness, dazed and confused. Animals milled about humans in confusion. Rip snuggled at my side, placing wet doggie kisses on my cheek. I clung to him. We were all so glad to be alive.

Still on the island, Suzy advanced on us, unarmed. Contrary and Pandemonium flanked her. "Another round goes to you Dana Dimbulb. You've got the devil's own dumb luck. Why on Earth would those Tellarans choose a third-rate pencil pusher as their emissary to humanity?" Suzy was magnificently reptilian and disturbingly female.

"It's been my destiny since the fall of Atlantis. But you know that, since you were inside my mind."

We were all eating heartplums and I tossed one to Suzy, "Here, have a plum."

"Your Tellaran magic fruit," she sneered, taking a bite and savoring the nectar, while I contemplated its effects on her shriveled chakras. "You and I are not done," she threatened.

"You'll be too busy putting out fires. The whole world got a visual download of the stepping-stones you screwed, abused, or killed in your cold-blooded campaign for dominance."

"Who's left for you to exploit, Squeezy?" asked Louie, sidling up to my side.

"I cannot believe I ever found you attractive!" roared a revolted, heartbroken Vincent, standing over Gwen's body.

Suzy said to Vincent, "I had such plans for you. You loved me once. You would have been my consort."

"In Hell!" Vincent roared.

"You'll overplay your hand," said Alice, handing Suzy another heartplum.

"How can you hope to deceive humanity?" yelled Huckleberry. "Everyone's seen your naked ambition."

Suzy sneered, "Humanity will forget. They always do, with their short, insignificant lives. Come join the winning side," she urged Huckleberry and Finn. "Reptilian mind control resources are ancient, effective, and vast. And now, they're mine."

"We've been to Tellara," said Finn simply, settling all debate.

Javier challenged, "Our DNA is altered, our mental capacity expanded, our chakras aligned. You can't take that away from us. Do you imagine we'll forget the global mind meld, the global orgasm, the Revelations, or the three days of darkness? Gaia called it the Quickening."

"Yours aren't the only minds and genes that were enhanced," Suzy boasted. "Reptilians play a long game. All I have to do is wait a few generations and no one will be left alive who experienced this 'mass hallucination.'" She made air quotes. "Your version of events will fade into oral history of mythic proportions, while my official story will indoctrinate the masses for generations."

"You're a demon from Hell," burst a horrified Gemini Dallas, waving Bruno's Bible menacingly. Suzy flinched and backed away from the Good Book as if it were an armed grenade. Dozens of us roared with laughter, which incensed her.

I said, "You're no match for Gaia Sophia, Suzy Quintana. Follow the example of the Raza Clan and open your heart."

She scoffed, "I'll be satisfied with ruining everything you care about. Don't get comfortable. The next time we meet, I will destroy you, Dana Travers."

"Hopefully, that won't be for thirteen thousand years."

Suzy hissed. "Until then, I have a world to conquer!" Almost every time she had confronted me, she had been defeated or humiliated, no thanks to any ingenuity on my part. She was right about two things. I had dumb luck and she had a world to conquer. Suzy and her mercenaries withdrew across Bruno's Bridge, transporting more loads of Wah'Kon-Tah commodities, including heartplums. They blew up the bridge behind them and bombed our small harbor, sinking all boats. With Bruno's bridge collapsed and all boats sunk, we were effectively isolated.

Wah'Kon-Tah was in shambles. There was work to be done. But first, we had to see to Gwen's final resting place. Using our voxes, Javier, Louie, and I levitated Gwen and Vincent to Hal's island. As we buried her on the embankment within the cave, Vincent collapsed. Louie rocked him in his arms, both men weeping for lost love. I carved out a headstone for "Beautiful, Magical Gwen Delaney Cretzky. Revered Wife, Mother, and Storyteller." We stayed on Hal's island until late afternoon, crying, hugging, and reminiscing. Gwen and Hal had been with us during the global mind meld and orgasm.

Returning to the Commons, we soaked in the hot springs. Ol' Sol had risen in the southeast and was setting to the northwest. Its blue companion shone farther to the south; the second star to the right. As Sol set, even the stars came out in the wrong place. The Southern Cross hovered near our south western horizon.

"Pole shift," said someone.

"Pole reversal," said another

"Poleaxed," said a third.

"Axis of rotation or magnetic?" asked another.

"Maybe both?" suggested Joe.

Someone organized food. I ate sparingly. Someone told me I had to eat and pressed broth-soaked bread into my hands. It was Jesse. He and I embraced, and I asked. "Where is Ruth?"

"With Mick, Dad, and the horses."

We were joined by Vincent, Louie, and Alice.

Louie said, "Suzy has us blockaded. There is no way off or on Wah'Kon-Tah."

Javier said, "Maybe she'll leave us alone for a while."

I shook my head, "Since the mind meld, Suzy knows we can transport with voxes."

Jesse replied, "But even Suzy can't be everywhere at once. She's got Quickening crises on every continent."

"The Quickening," Vincent said. "That really happened." Louie, Javier, Alice, Vincent, and I stood shoulder-to-shoulder gazing at the unfamiliar sky.

"Look there," Javier pointed to Ol'Sol in the northwest, where it had no business being during an autumn evening.

I said "I can't tell if it's dawn or dusk. I don't even know what day it is."

Javier turned and pointed to the new blue sun in the southern sky, "It's Day One of the New Calendar."

Part 5

Magic Seasons

Tellara Rising

During the Megaportal, we witnessed Tellara's ascension. Like Earth, she had undergone a pole shift. The Ascension heartdance allowed the population to survive as Tellara's surface was transformed. Much of her landscape was marbled with muddy scars and scorched earth. Still, Antarctica was a verdant sanctuary at a temperate latitude. Ice was melting fast. Animals by the millions cohabitated. Indeed, lions lay down with lambs and well-fed animals shared feed, water, and husbandry. Hundreds of humans and thousands of grays remained as caretakers, while preserved seeds and DNA pods floated above in orbiting Arks.

Tellara was gone from my daily life, although I dreamed of her often. Phoenix, Saffron, and Bo Raza often visited my dreams and told me of their new life as ascended beings. They were floating orbs communicating with me telepathically. In their newly ascended state, Tellarans were gender fluid. Taking corporeal form was a matter of choice. Evolved humans entered and exited physical manifestation at will, joyfully and reverently. No need for sex, birth, or death, incarnation, or reincarnation. Each soul had integrated all its incarnations. If they chose corporeal bodies, they were mostly androgynous, like Crystal and Cosmo. They didn't need gender to experience union. Celestial spheres could interpenetrate with delightful bliss.

Their reality was timeless. Tellarans would have the ability to cultivate embryonic fauna and flora, to make their planet habitable for emergent species in mere eons. Tellarans were now capable of visiting many other planets throughout the galaxy at the speed of thought. No longer tethered to their home world, they were invited to join the Galactic Family. They created individual and shared realities with directed, intentional thoughts.

In one dream, Saffron said, "You see, Dana, the surface of planets sustains living conditions for only so many eons before becoming geologically or climatologically uninhabitable. Earth's Holocene epoch has passed. Earth's Anthropocene has passed. You avoided a scorched world. You avoided an ice age. Humans spent decades exacerbating man-made climate changes, all the while soiling your own den beyond reclamation."

"Still lecturing me Saffron, even now in post-apocalyptic dreams?"

"I come to praise your Wah'Kon-Tah community. I believe you said it means People of the Sky, Land, and Water."

"Wah'Kon-Tah is also an Osage prayer that means reverence to the divinity in all nature. Gaia guided us through the Quickening."

"Terrans survived the presaged end of an age."

"We have two suns now. A distant blue star far to the south is visible all day long at southern latitudes."

"Tellara also has a blue sun. It approaches from the new south pole which is now open ocean. We call the former Antarctica the Verdant Isles."

"Nibiru or Planet X is approaching with a fresh population of reptilians."

"This planet approaches Tellara as well. Their population also lives in 5D."

"Well, here on 3D Earth, the patriarchal reptilian order has been replaced by a ruthless female. Fortunately, the Reptilian Individual Movement is growing, vitalized water is flowing, Tellaran queen bees are breeding, and heartplums are flourishing."

"It will take Nibiru a hundred years to be in proximity to Earth. Terrans have time to prepare."

Phoenix entered my dream. "In Atlantis, we were ignorant and arrogant, sowing the seeds of our own destruction. We were unprepared for the end."

"I remember." I replied. "Back then we did not understand that planets, as well as species, evolve."

"Your Wah'Kon-Tah is one of many oases on Earth that are practicing resonance with nature for the mutual benefit of all life. Well done, wayshower."

"That's the highest praise you've ever given me, Phoenix."

"Well deserved, Little Janka."

"Thank you Captain Zalko."

Leel and Jeej once came to my dream to tell me that they had learned to dance. In their verdant haven, they hopped in a strangely graceful, weird, arrhythmic shuffle.

"That was wonderful, evolutionary."

"We have voxes now." Leel almost preened. "They are helping grays to develop compassion." Jeej demonstrated levitating.

"Levitation and dancing! Congratulations, Zetas, you rock!"

Leel said, "Until we activate all our chakras, we will not be able to ascend. That is why we choose to serve all surviving life on Tellara and participate in the heartdance with the remaining humans."

Jeej said, "Between the Earthborn DNA, music, and vox biofeedback our species fecundity is greatly enhanced. Four fertile Zeta-human hybrids have been born here on Verdant Isles. They are too young to breed, but the tide has turned, and our species will be saved."

In another dream, Phoenix showed me images from his higher dimensional artistic medium. Holographic interference waves generated dancing geometric fractals that conveyed stories and events. I recognized some that were based on Earth literature. But as wholistic as the images were, they moved almost too swiftly to grasp. It was more of a mental download than a movie, but multi-layered, with inner symbology and outer expression. All of Shakespeare was apprehended in one wholistic cerebral surge.

I was not the only one to dream of Tellara. All of us who had traveled to our sister world received dream visitations.

Louie dreamed of Phoenix who shared news of the Galactic Council. Louie attended a Galactic Conference in his dream body and was on a first name basis with several council members. He grew evermore remote and otherworldly.

Javier dreamed about vitalized water with Heron. "So, the Universe behaves like vitalized water?" Javier pondered, and was rewarded with a guided tour into the mysterious heart of water. From then on, Javier was our water whisperer.

Minerva dreamed of Tellaran Elders who shared legends of tribes that had migrated from Atlantis in the first wave. On Earth, she gifted Lavatlan treasures to surviving Romani, Domari, and Lomavren communities around the world. She stayed away longer each visit, using her vox to enrich her people with abundant survival necessities. The acknowledged Lavatlan Queen always returned with stories from other clans.

Joe Two Feathers spent dreamtime with Robin. They toured the Verdant Isles and orbiting bioships. Robin communicated with animals and taught Joe the fundamentals. Joe used his audio-telepathy vox skills with native, domesticated, and newly migrated species now living on Wah'Kon-Tah. He showed migratory species what they could eat. We nicknamed him Dr. Doolittle.

Ruth spent dream time with Jasmine and learned of the intelligence of plants and their healing properties. She learned of plant's soul matter and memories from when the world was young. Ruth drank plant medicine, triggering parts of her brain that enhanced her communion with flora. Her already green thumb blossomed. She was our plant whisperer.

Alice communed with Bo and Guna Raza in dreamtime. She developed psychic healing abilities that arose from manipulation of cells at the P-soup level. Our medicine woman took a page from her teacher Reva's book, and healed without her vox.

Huckleberry and Finn told us of their dreams with the Raza clan. More and more, they were off Wah'Kon-Tah, rescuing individuals who sought refuge in sustainable communities around the globe. They were leading the burgeoning Reptilian Individual Movement.

Our dreams of Tellara were vivid and lucid. But they were not to last. They grew fewer, fainter, and farther between. Saffron and Phoenix slowly drifted away.

In one last dream, Phoenix told me, "Dana, the planetary connection between Earth and Tellara will fade within several months. Our frequencies are growing ever more out of sync. The connection between Terra Nova and Terra Familiar will hold until the last soul present at the shift has died and chosen where to reincarnate. That's about seven human generations."

"The Native Americans say each decision should be made for the seventh generation in order to preserve a healthy world for posterity."

In one dream, I saw Juniper on Verdant Isles herding yaks and caribou across the grasslands. I was surprised she had not ascended and went to ask Jesse, "Why is Juniper still corporeal?" I couldn't keep track of everyone during the Megaportal.

Jesse replied, "Mom, I have something to tell you. Juniper chose not to ascend because she is pregnant with my child."

Stunned, I replied, "A child of two worlds. You will never see your child grow."

"I will in dreams. And she will know all about me from the many recordings, art, and artifacts I left with Juniper, including home movies of you and dad when we were babies."

"She? It's a girl?"

"Yes, my daughter—your granddaughter—will be born on Tellara."

"This is unprecedented. Has anything like this ever happened before? How will it affect Tellaran karmic balance?"

"We don't know."

"Talk about a long-distance relationship." I was going to be a grandmother to a child on another world. "How did this happen?"

"Mom, I was alone with *Shasta Solstice* for months. What did you think I was doing?"

"Art."

"Among other things. Juniper and I spent every day together. We fell deeply in love."

In a dream, I asked Saffron, "Has there ever been cross-breeding between worlds in Gaia's history?"

She answered, "If there has been, it was in times so ancient, to civilizations so long forgotten, that no record remains. But now, Jesse's child is part of Tellara's saga."

Leel entered the dream, "Your granddaughter's DNA will be part of our galactic posterity and your galactic legacy."

In my last Tellaran dream, I saw Juniper give birth to a girl she named Eartha. Rejoicing loved ones surrounded her, including Robin, Leel, and Jeej. Dozens of gentle animals attended the birth. Jesse dreamt with Juniper and Eartha for years.

I entreated my mentor, "Saffron, will I ever see you again?"
"We'll dance together in the Great Mother Sea."
I missed my Tellaran dreams for the rest of my life.

Terra Nova

When the violent shaking ended, Terra Nova emerged along a higher frequency trajectory. She was aligned with Terra Familiar, but one fractal octave above us. In her infancy, her population experimented with utopian ideas, holding on to the best of old Earth, while testing Tellaran concepts.

People were shifting to Terra Nova in different ways. Many enlightened masters ascended during the Quickening. Sky Dancer and Minerva were among the second wave. They phased during deep meditative states and woke up in each other's company in newly formed population hubs. As others died, they became newborns on a new world. Multiple births became the norm on Terra Nova as millions of recently deceased souls vied to enter the new world as twins and triplets.

Until the dreams began, we knew little of the whereabouts of many of Earth's most beloved teachers. For the first two years after the Quickening, dreams of Tellara commingled with dreams of Terra Nova.

Alice was the next to phase. It happened shortly after the Tellaran dreams ended. She patiently forbore threats from Suzy's boot-heeled dictatorship but ached for unity consciousness. She told us, that from all of Earth, only twenty-nine Draconians had evolved enough to phase to Terra Nova. She wanted to be there to greet them. Huckleberry and Finn committed to carry the baton for reptilian spiritual evolution and held a ceremony for Alice's death and transfiguration. The sting of losing Alice was eased when she came to us in dreams to share that each of the evolved reptiles had a unique story of repentance and redemption. She shared dreams with Draconians throughout Terra Familiar, providing inspiration to resist Suzy and seek the Individual Movement.

On Terra Nova, the reptilian enclave resided with other non-human Terrans. Pleiadians, Arcturans, Vegans, Sirrians, and Zeta hybrids who had lived among us for millennia were now 'out.' Some of those on Terra Nova had lived on Earth long enough to acquire karma and consider themselves native to Earth. Being non-human did not spare them from the foibles of attachments. All Terrans were co-mingling, co-habituating, and sharing the wisdom and wealth of Terra Nova.

About a year after Alice phased, Jesse came to tell us that he was leaving Wah'Kon-Tah. Despite Suzy's propaganda, thousands of individuals throughout the American Central Region vividly remembered the Quickening. They remembered our island and considered Wah'Kon-Tah a promised land. Many died trying to get to us. The Governor General stationed troops along the Mizzippi coasts to shoot on sight anyone attempting to launch a boat toward our island chain. Some got through by taking long detours south and navigating upstream. The newly formed Underground had no reliable connection between the mainlands and the island.

Jesse said, "What's the point of having a vox if I don't use it to help people come to sanctuary? I'm going to join Huckleberry and Finn to manage regional safe houses." With his vox, Jesse could provide refuge to hundreds, using invisibility, levitation, transportation, and remote viewing. I was not thrilled, but realized it was something he had to do. We had needed safe houses, ourselves, more than once. Crystal and Cosmo went with Jesse to our old safe house outside Chicago. We promised to remote view frequently. Louie, Vincent, Javier, and I stayed close. We were old-timers now.

Each day, individuals were sorting themselves out between two Earths. On Terra Nova, there was a collective investment in recovering the best of civilization. It took months, but running water, hydroelectric power, and communications were restored. Housing and plumbing were primitive, but universal. Science based on resonance with nature exploded. Healing was based on understanding of body, mind, and spirit. Art was celebrated. Painting, writing, pottery, and weaving flourished. Technology was renovated. Communications and transportation were reinvented via Terra-friendly discoveries. Free energy and vitalized water sources were developed.

In a dream, Sky Dancer told me, "Political lies, corruption, and scandal have been unable to gain a foothold. If we have any religion at all, it's universal reverence for both the masculine and feminine aspects of creation. We have no hierarchy and dance daily. A new concept of leadership has emerged where all voices are equal. Young and old, all Terrans participate. Our new firmament requires new ideas.

I said, "It sounds perfect."

"Not really," she answered, "There have been trials and errors aplenty. We're navigating an unprecedented learning curve. But while we're figuring things out, there has been water, food, and shelter for all. In the decades since I've been here, sustainability on Terra Nova became abundance."

"I can't wait to join you."

"We can't wait for you to transition."

Minerva came to Javier in a dream, youthful and pregnant with twins. "Within a generation, civilization on Terra Nova has developed. Voxes are being produced in foundling cottage industries. Violence against women and subjugation of humans and animals is unknown. We have schools and healing centers. Terra Nova lives by a system of Contributionism, where each gives according to their abilities and no one takes more than they need. All goods and services are available without the use of money, credits, or any system of debt or servitude. All resources are the common birthright of all of inhabitants, not just a select few."

Louie's death hit me hard. He had been hanging on to Terra Familiar by a thread since the Quickening; aching to migrate to Terra Nova and reunite with Hal. Since dreamtime with Phoenix had ended, he'd been spending his days alone in Hal's cave. Oh! Louie, my teacher, my brother, my friend, the harshest thing you ever did was create snarky nicknames for evil people.

With me at his side, Louie died in bed, his vox radiating light and heat. Vincent, Javier, and I moved his body to the mouth of the cave where Louie and I had once emerged into the waiting arms of Crystal and Cosmo. This time, we moved beyond the embankment where Gwen was buried. We moved up the subterranean river, along the excavated tunnels, precision stone walls, and deep into the small cave to Hal's grave. In preparation, Louie had carved his own stone sarcophagus alongside Hal's.

We now saw what Louie had been doing all this time. He had carved petroglyphs of his Tellaran chakra ritual into the limestone walls of the burial chamber. Intricate pictographs of his personal journey including his animal guides, his grasshopper, Sage, a salamander, and twin wolves. Chakra by chakra, lifetime by lifetime, he'd preserved a piece of his soul in the Terra Familiar firmament. He'd left it for us, and perhaps, someday, for Earth's distant descendants to find.

Javier and I resolved to do the same. In the following days, we returned to Hal's Cave to etch our soul journeys in the subterranean stone edifice. Using our vox cutting tools, we covered the entire chamber with engraved images of animal guides, human guides, and geometry. Three karmic journeys merged throughout labyrinthine megaliths. Chakra by chakra, we recreated our stories from genesis through ascension and beyond. My caterpillar was a better likeness than my phoenix or crows, but in the shadow of our vox light, the carvings took on multi-dimensional lives of their own. Javier and I became keenly aware of each other's incarnations, including our Atlantean sojourns. The carving tools became adept in our hands, as our artistry grew intricate. The project took years, covering walls, tunnels, ceilings, and floors.

Louie and Hal visited me in my dreams for months after Louie's passing. They approved the decoration of their tomb, and Louie even suggested a few irreverent additions to the art. He wanted to give the caterpillar just the hint of a penis in one of his poses in order to confound future archaeologists. A turtle, a queen bee, and a black stallion had guided Javier in his Blue Henge journey. In a dream, Louie reminded Javier that he had once joked of feeding honey to the queen bee. Javier engraved a naughty, almost cartoonish image of the queen in sated repose surrounded by her spent drones. Someday, someone would find this laser-carved mausoleum and speculate as to the meaning of these mythic stories, the tools used to carve them, and the reverence shown to the two enshrined men. But with any luck, not soon and not Suzy.

Vincent often came with us to Hal's Island. He stayed in the woodlands outside the cave and set up a remote apiary. I think it soothed him to be near Gwen's resting place. We invited friends and family to view the finished artwork, an underground temple and mausoleum dedicated to Tellara. Then Javier and I used our voxes to seal off the tunnel to the inner cave. Massive rock walls safeguarded Louie and Hal's remains on Terra Familiar while they frolicked as children on Terra Nova.

In my last dream of Louie, he told me, "Karma is a funny thing, Dana. You think it is biting you on the butt, when really it's kissing your ass."

"Or the other way around," we laughed together.

Terra Familiar

Only one television station was broadcasting. It was Suzy's *Women's World Order* propaganda machine, the WWO. Her media was meant to pacify. Instead it threatened. By contrast, the Undernet was rife with reports from all over the world. Recovering communities were sharing how they were rebuilding cooperatively. Resource-based economies and resonant technologies were being implemented. Tellara was like a new Atlantean myth and wayshowers were being quoted like folk heroes.

According to scattered reports, millions were dead, perhaps billions. In dreams, we learned that many had not died, but migrated directly to Terra Nova. Anyone who wanted to could reincarnate on Terra Nova. Those who still valued the lessons of duality could remain here on Terra Familiar rebuilding this Woman's World Order. As Bruno had said, there was a season for everything.

Gemini Dallas had been stranded on Wah'Kon-Tah when Suzy barricaded us. She ws hanging on to her sanity by a thread. She missed her old life, her celbrty, and finally escaped to the mainland, perhaps hoping for a job at the WWO. We never heard from her again.

Val's vlog was viral. Jesse filmed conversations among our community members that she posted online. Vincent recorded a heartfelt reading of Gwen's last parable, *The Paths Are Many, The Truth Is One*. Then he reminded everyone that Suzy Quintana was a reptile who had murdered his wife in cold blood. We had advantages our Atlantean ancestors did not. Heartplums, bees, vitalized water, flora, and fauna thrived on Wah'Kon-Tah and were being disseminated globally by Huckleberry and Finn. We also had a handful of voxes, our remaining Tellaran technology.

Even with voxes, rebuilding was slow. There were setbacks. The seasons were off. It took us years to figure out the new cycle. There were long transition seasons during spring and fall. Both were intermittently sunny and rainy. Summer was short and scorching. Winter was short and freezing. The altered seasons required us to guess when to sow and when to reap. But, with extralong, wet growing seasons, we got lucky and were able to harvest and store twice a year. I thanked Gaia. Javier thanked New Blue. Joe Two Feathers thanked his ancestors.

Seasons passed. Years passed. The lunar calendar was most accurate. Good Old Luna still rolled around heaven in her 28-day cycle. We renamed thirteen months. The path of Ol' Sol was changed, but not her 365-day annual cycle. New Blue's path and annual cycle were being charted. It approached from the far south and was only visible as far north as Chicago, which was now west of the Ozarks on our tilted world. New Blue was sometimes out in the daytime and sometimes out at night, depending on which side of the Earth was facing Sophia. According to Undernet sources in Tasmania, Nibiru appeared as a distant speck approaching the South Pole. We never saw it in our part of the world. It was decades, if not centuries away.

After having our crops appropriated seasonally as tribute to the Governor General, we learned to plant fruits and vegetables in patches throughout the islands. Permaculture meant sharing our harvest with the local wildlife, but it was worth the trade-off. Edible plants grew wild and plentiful. The islands gave up their secrets to those who lived in harmony with nature.

Even though our islands were blockaded, there were still exchanges of goods and news with our neighbors across the Mizzippi Sea. We became an island of smugglers. Some of our contacts were informants, some traders, and some spies. If Suzy knew that we violated the embargo, she left us alone, biding her time, consolidating her power. Smuggling went on in endlessly inventive schemes. The inland Mizzippi Sea was deep enough to allow small, pedal-operated submarines. Our chief exports were heartplums, honey, and saffron. Our biggest imports were refugees and animals migrating to our green oases in the midst of a scorched continent.

Jesse, Crystal, Cosmo, Huckleberry, and Finn had been gone for years, operating the Underground passage for refugees. Crystal and Cosmo worked throughout the Americas to identify Terrans clinging to memories of the Quickening and resisting WWO's propaganda. Suzy had been right about the forgetting. Humans could be controlled by reptilian brainwashing techniques. Those who remembered the Quickening had to gather in secret to share their recollections. Having lived through the Tellaran megaportal, those throughout the Mizzippi basin had the most vivid memories.

During the Quickening, everyone on the planet had shared an unprecedented moment as a consciously connected species. The connection faded. But for a time, all Terrans realized that Tellara was real and that a handful of wayshowers had visited her and brought keys to thriving in peace. All Terrans briefly shared the knowledge that Suzy had killed Sheldon Walters, Kek, and Gwen, and that she tried to frame me but ended up framing Frank Fretz. Suzy realized we used Tellaran technology to outwit her. So, did everyone else on the planet before The Forgetting began.

The Draconians under Suzy's command used reptilian technology, both subtle and gross, to make the Quickening seem like a staged, mass hallucination, with some threads of truth woven in to create a plausible narrative. Suzy had been right. The easiest way for humans to forget our galactic birthright was to wait for everyone who had experienced the Quickening to die. Our descendants only heard of the Quickening as stories that took on mythic qualities. The fables varied from continent to continent. To consolidate her power, long-lived Suzy only needed to wait. We are a foolhardy species, we humans, we Homo WTFs.

Over the years, the anniversary of the Quickening, rather than a celebration of humanity's galactic birthright, became a secular holiday, sort of Carnival meets Diwali. Like sacred scriptures, some believed, some didn't. Conspiracy researchers were debunked. Mainstream media discredited evidence and broadcast WWO approved stories. Suzy was governing the Americas, from Hudson Bay to Patagonia, usurping contributionism with 'benevolent' dictatorship one community at a time. People by the billions either forgot she was a murdering reptile or considered her activities righteous. Sheldon Walters was the Antichrist. Suzy the Dragon Slayer, mythic heroine, was humanity's trailblazer to the Golden Age. She was a busy little tyrant, controlling the media, putting down rebellions, conquering continents, rebuilding infrastructure, and recovering land from unprecedented natural disasters. Her science team genetically modified wheat to suppress our newly activated DNA while discounting proliferating heartplums.

Wah'Kon-Tah residents' recollection of the Quickening infuriated Suzy. For years, she left us alone, save for the biannual tribute. We survived by smuggling discreetly, assimilating new refugees quickly, and paying exorbitant tributes. I never doubted for a moment her vengeance would resurface. Every year, the surprise 'inspections' by her Governor's Guardsmen grew more savage. When they came, our residents headed for the hills, literally into our labyrinthine system of well-provisioned caves.

Jesse and I checked in regularly via our voxes. He moved from safe house to safe house while covertly reaching out to individuals and families seeking refuge. Crystal and Cosmo were his frequent companions. Every few months, they escorted small groups of evacuees to Wah'Kon-Tah. Their hippie van had been replaced by an old yellow school bus that traveled the back roads with shielded impunity. Our reunions were brief and far too infrequent. Each small cohort of refugees brought news, supplies, and praises for my undercover son.

I knew Jesse was dead before anyone told me. His vox went silent. I later learned that an infiltrator murdered him in the Chicago safe house. The news blasted across the WWO, which issued warnings to any who would follow in the refugees' footsteps. Those seeking asylum on our island were declared terrorists. Huckleberry and Finn brought his body back to the island. We mourned Jesse privately. A public memorial would have been dangerous. Drones spied on us daily. I wept with Javier. I wept with Ruth and her family. I wept with Nick and Carmela. Jesse would reincarnate on Terra Nova, one fractal octave closer to his wife and child, Juniper and Eartha. The residents who had found their way to our island due to Jesse's courage named a hydroelectric water mill after him. Beyond that, we kept our quiet counsel.

Crystal gave me Jesse's vox. It would work for no one else, and after passing it to others to try, including his father, we gave up hope that it could be maintained as a functional tool. Vincent had the notion to try to reverse engineer the vox, so he and Nick took on that years-long project. Finally, they were able to activate the cutting, heating, and lighting tools. But all the other functions remained unworkable. The technical team poo-pooed the cutting devices as the least valuable vox tool, but I recalled my long-ago days as a fugitive in a nearby cave. That simple cutting tool provided shield, sanctuary, and deliverance for Louie and me. Later, when Vincent and Nick saw the carved mausoleum enshrining the story of our chakra journeys, they were duly impressed and began engraving petroglyphs all around the island. As those of us who had been to Tellara died, one by one, our voxes were turned over to the reverse-engineering team, which now included some younger techno-geeks who had come to the island in the recent waves of refugees.

Wah'Kon-Tah emulated Tellaran customs. We had rules but no rulers, no chain of command. We danced the heartdance. It did not manifest the multidimensional web like those on Tellara, until during one particularly magical heartdance. We must have been holding simultaneous dances on Terra Nova and Terra Familiar. Joe Two Feathers, now a grown man, phased over to Terra Nova. Before our eyes, he flowed through multiphasic waves of color and music. Through the window between worlds, we saw Sky Dancer and Minerva. We recognized other departed loved ones as elders, adults (many of them pregnant women), young children, and babies. Just like that, Joe, was gone from our company and dancing with his grandmother on Terra Nova. After that, the heartdance became more real, less symbolic. It wasn't long before Ruth, Mick, and their daughters phased to Terra Nova. Seeing our loved ones depart was bittersweet. Val Andrews and her grown, married daughters phased during another simultaneous heartdance and were reunited with Jay.

One hot summer night, on the eve of his ninety-sixth birthday, Javier's heart stopped beating. My soul mate was gone. Javier and I had made a pact to wait for each other and reincarnate together on Terra Nova. Vincent and I buried him on the embankment inside Hal's cave alongside Gwen. I gave his vox to Vincent and clung to my own, the last fully operational vox on the island. After that, I spent hours alone in the sky room gazing at the *Magic Seasons* paintings. I yearned for the hills and orchards, wind and waters of Tellara, and I wept.

One by one, my loved ones died or phased to Terra Nova. I had outlived my children and grandchildren. I spent my days with Vincent. We were the last of our old tribe with pre-apocalyptic memories, the oldest remaining elders who had experienced the Quickening. There were younger people who had lived through the revelations, but now, two generations had been born for whom it was only oral tradition. I was in my nineties now, an Elder. I had never sought to take on Sky Dancer's mantle, but it had been thrust upon me by generations of islanders. Younger people came to me with perplexing questions. I usually gave examples of the way activities were conducted on Tellara or insights from my chakra journey.

Crystal and Cosmo roamed the wider world, guiding and protecting other communities. They brought fewer and fewer refuges to Wah'Kon-Tah. Huckleberry and Finn spent their time facilitating the Reptilian Individual Movement among awakening reptilians. I missed them all terribly. I missed everything from the old days. I had no fear of death but fretted over to whom I must pass the baton as wayshower for the future thirteen thousand-year shift. There was only Vincent, once foe, now friend; once a corrupt corporate tool, now a selfless Elder.

***

Suzy bided her time. On the day her army attacked to destroy Wah'Kon-Tah once and for all, we had only moments of warning. Troops had overrun the island before we heard their attack. Vincent and I were at his remote apiary on Hal's Island. I was gathering honey. Vincent was carving a scene from Gwen's last story, *The paths are many, the truth is one.* When we heard the shots, we fled toward the cave. An incessant torrent of bullets flew across the islands from an arsenal of automatic assault weapons in the hands of the Governor's Guardsmen. In the distant orchards we heard screaming, running, the crash of felled bodies, and the stampede of frightened animals. The cave opening was thickly overgrown, but we clawed our way through the underbrush.

Things stilled to slow motion as a volley of bullets whizzed past my cheek deafening me. Before we could slip down to safety, my left shoulder exploded into hundreds of bloody pieces, nearly severing my arm. In a desperate effort to save me, Vincent grabbed the remnants of my limb and shoved me down the hole into the mouth of the cavern. I landed on the embankment in a heap. The rock surface became slick with my blood. I felt rather than heard myself shriek, deafened as I was by the shots. Vincent was at my side applying pressure to my wound. He was speaking, his lips were moving, but through my haze of pain and the hollow roar in my ears, I understood nothing he said. I was mortally wounded, bleeding to death, and my closest companion was Vincent: my selfish, flawed, redeemed, heroic, complex friend, Vincent R. Cretzky, R for Raymond, a strong and wise ruler.

Vincent gestured above us and put a cautionary finger to his lips. Shadows were moving about. He signaled that he could hear the voices of our trackers. Vincent left my side, and through a red haze of pain I saw him use the cutting tool on his reverse-engineered vox to seal off the opening above us. Panting with exhaustion, Vincent piled blocks of stone in a makeshift pillar that supported the sod and closed off the light. He had bought us time. He guided my good hand to my vox and gestured for me to illuminate the cavern. It took all my strength.

I must have passed out. I awoke to insane pain and heavy, labored breathing. At first, I thought it was mine, but then I realized it was Vincent struggling to stifle his sobs as he kept up the pressure on my shoulder. Some hearing had returned. I was weak from blood loss and knew my time was short. I had much to speak of with Vincent, my inevitable successor as wayshower. "Of course it is you. It has always been you."

"Stay with me, Dana."

"Vincent, you could ascend to Terra Nova if you choose. Your karma is balanced," I rasped. "Listen to me. Time is short and I have much to say. Do you remember the story of how Phoenix chose me to be a wayshower for Earth? He nodded, and I continued. Terra Familiar needs you. You are humanity's next wayshower." I was gasping for breath and my vision was fading. "You will be the last elder of a lost civilization."

"I don't want to be the last."

"I am asking you to lead the way to Terra Nova in thirteen thousand years. Being a wayshower is like being a flawed and reluctant Bodi Sattva. You agree to remain behind to help others see the light. It's a sacrifice. When I was falsely accused of murder, I became a lightning rod for the reptilians. They still rule Terra Familiar. Suzy is their leader and she will remember, if not recognize, you through your future incarnations. If you accept, you will be a better person.

"How so?"

"Humbled and raised up at the same time. You will help millions, maybe billions, willingly, but not always easily. You'll be a beacon for the segment of humanity waking up to unity consciousness. But you won't do it alone. Like me, you will be surrounded by tribe."

I fought for my voice. Vincent and I were replaying the scene from the beach when Janka had held dying Captain Valko in her arms. Phoenix, in his Atlantean incarnation, had entreated me to take on the mantle of wayshower, to stay behind and fight the good fight in exchange for ineffable rewards.

"Dana, I accept your request. I think I accepted it when I could not enter the portal to Tellara. Then, when Suzy killed Gwen, there was no way back to my old life."

"It means waiting hundreds of lifetimes to ascend to Terra Nova, but there will always be communities like Wah'Kon-Tah."

"When will I see you again?"

"In thirteen thousand years, I will come to you as Phoenix came to me, through a portal from Terra Nova to Terra Familiar. Polarity is a harsh, but effective, teacher."

"I'll be alone," Vincent lamented.

"Huckleberry and Finn will come to your aid as Alice came to mine. They have voxes and are very long-lived. Crystal and Cosmo also remain on Terra Familiar."

"I never realized what I'd sacrificed until I came to Wah'Kon-Tah. I accept the role of wayshower, but my heart breaks with the two worlds, the one that leaves me behind, and the one that remains polarized. When shall I see Gwen again?"

"She must be waiting for you somewhere between life and death."

Vincent mused, "Between worlds. I made my commitment to be a wayshower before seeing Gwen again."

"I had to decide without consulting my mate, Solan of Atlantis. He went on to Tellara without me. I reconnected with him, an elder, named Buffalo, one of the last to ascend."

My consciousness was drifting. In the dark cavern, on the sandy embankment along the underground watercourse, I clung to the sound of Vincent's gruff voice. "Those of us remaining are going to have to take to the hills and live off the land for the rest of our lives. We can never return to the compound."

I whispered, "You have the voxes with their carving tools, perpetual light, and heat. You have the hybrid bees, vitalized water, hemp, and heartplums." My voice faded.

Vincent mused, "Not to mention humanity's enhanced DNA from Sophia. Oh, Dana, the *Magic Seasons* megaportal is the closest I ever got to Tellara. The experience is seared into my memory."

"Don't forget to dance," I whispered. My voice gave out. I traced my fingers across Vincent's face and left a trail of blood on his cheek.

"Dana, Dana…" I heard him call me from a distant tunnel. My eyes fluttered open. I was in the cave on the embankment near Javier's grave. Vincent was weeping, clinging to me as I clung to life. My vox dimly lit the cave. Once I died, the light would glow like an eternal flame.

I heard the rushing water, the underground river that had brought Louie and me to deliverance from the underworld. Then wind was rushing by my face. I was in a tunnel. A compelling white light emerged in the distance. I glided toward it and found myself in the embrace of Javier and Gwen. A cluster of spirits hovered, weightless, in a softly illuminated void with no structured boundaries.

"What of Bruno and the others who raptured?" I asked

Gwen answered, "They just flitted through, I know not where."

From our ethereal vantage point, we could see Vincent, still in the cave, still cradling my body. At length, he laid me down by Javier. He cut bricks and entombed my remains in a stone crypt. As he carved, he reminisced about our life on the island. Shots rang out for days. Vincent stayed underground until all went still.

At length, he withdrew from the cave, sealing the entrance behind him. For weeks, he reconnoitered Wah'Kon-Tah, often rafting between islands at night. Our friends were either in hiding, captured, or dead. He moved stealthily across the raw terrain, noting the location of wild edible vegetation that had been sown to protect our harvest. As weeks turned into months, no one emerged from hiding. Vincent realized he was truly alone. He never went back to the main compound that housed our worldly goods and tools.

Vincent set up camp at the mouth of our cave. He expanded the grotto and built a shack from hemp stalks and a fire pit from chiseled rock. He foraged and stored for the months and seasons ahead. Two dogs, a cow and her calf, and a small herd of horses found their way to him and became his companions. The animals found their own food and kept Vincent grounded. His companion animals grew to include feral cats, sheep, and birds of diverse species. They lived in harmony with this strange old hermit. As Vincent tended to the island, the fauna and flora revealed their secrets to him, keeping him hearty and serene. He dressed in a homespun hemp toga belted with a braided grass cord. His hair was long. His beard was full.

Meanwhile, we hovered in the space between life and death, between Terra

Nova and Terra Familiar. Vincent chatted with us, his departed friends, and we answered, although we doubted he could hear us. Gwen hovered close to Terra Familiar, keeping vigil over Vincent. Javier and I felt a pull toward Terra Nova that grew ever more insistent.

Seasons passed. Vincent had become the proverbial hermetic wild man. He lived off the land and seemed at once ageless and ancient. One day, while he was roasting onions and green peppers over his fire pit, shouting and machinery disrupted the peace. An army had arrived on Hal's Island. Again.

He waited calmly. Suzy trampled through the underbrush, tracking the smoke from his fire. Vincent saw her before she saw him. Her reptilian nature was unconcealed and her taste in fashion had reverted to hideous glitz. She wore sequined camouflage; a skin-hugging fashion disaster accessorized with her trademark high-heeled combat boots. Her shoulders were flanked with gold epaulets and her breastplate was covered with garish, jewel-encrusted medals. She was alone, separated from her patrol.

"Hello Suzy," Vincent spoke softly in his homespun simplicity.

She turned and their eyes met. "Vincent," she replied, pointing her weapon at his heart. He shrugged and smiled benignly.

Suzy mused, "I wondered if you were still alive. We never found your body or Dana's. You were the only two we could not account for."

"I am all that remains of a once thriving community."

"You're alone."

"As you see."

"I could kill you."

"As you like."

"You are remarkably calm."

"I am remarkably old."

"Shall I put you out of your misery? You've degenerated into an uncivilized animal."

"Thank you." Vincent bowed his head, gesturing to his animal companions.

Frustrated by Vincent's indifference, Suzy snarled, "You're not worth the trouble. You never were." As Vincent shrugged and sank down to sit on a log, Suzy lowered her weapon. His dogs, sensing a meal and conversation, joined them. They sniffed Suzy and rapidly retreated to Vincent's side.

"You've left the islands in good shape. We're moving in, building a base camp adjacent the old bridge site. This island is centrally located to the northern, southern, eastern, and western sectors of the continent. Your precious Wah'Kon-Tah has been renamed Quint Isles, for Quintana"

"As you like," was all he said.

"You are so full of nothing, Vincent Cretzky. I never realized you were so vacant. I once thought you were the perfect mammal."

"What would you have me contribute to your world vision, Suzy?"

"Nothing! Your time is spent. Your death would be a gift to the world."

"I am unarmed."

"You are a terrorist."

"If you say so. The old mythos has passed. We are all living our new stories."

"What's yours?" she asked.

"I am just starting to figure that out," he laughed ruefully. "Alone in the wilderness, I am just waking up. You, on the other hand, are going to be long remembered as the female Hitler, Attila, and Genghis, combined into a one-world despot. You have turned the divine feminine on its head. It is to your credit that you are open about your reptilian nature."

Suzy looked down at her ensemble. "I'm not. You're the last remaining human who can see my real nature. You damn islanders. You just couldn't let go of the Quickening."

"You will not be able to keep your true nature a secret for much longer. Over the generations, everyone will see what you are."

Suzy sneered, "By the time people recognize my reptilian nature, I'll have consolidated my global stranglehold on authority. I plan to live a long, long time, supported by millions who consider me their savior."

"You've promoted yourself, yet again, Suzy. From dictator to deity."

Suzy sneered, "You, on the other hand, are going to die alone, a jungle-dwelling lunatic."

"I am not alone." Vincent cuddled several of his animal companions.

"You are crazy."

At this, Vincent threw back his head and roared with laughter. "That makes two of us." This made Suzy laugh too and for a moment they were in rapport, former lovers who had diverged in circumstances and regard as far as any two Terrans could. "Suzy, the island takes care of her own. Treat her respectfully and she will reveal her secrets to you in her own good time."

"That's utter nonsense." Suzy stood, hoisted her Uzi, walked off a few paces, pivoted, and swung back toward Vincent. "Well, Hell, I can't leave it at that." Aiming at his heart, Suzy discharged a dozen bullets into Vincent's chest, neck, and head. He slumped to the ground and the animals ran off into the wilderness. Suzy watched Vincent bleed out while soldiers in a jeep drove up to investigate.

"Bury this terrorist," Suzy commanded, appropriating their jeep. She drove off, ripping through the undergrowth, heedless of the golden harvest.

As the grunts dug his grave, Vincent's spirit rose to join Gwen, Javier, and me in the softly lit Bardo between life and death. Vincent met his death with tranquility. He looked around for his son, Raymond, but Gwen assured him

Raymond was alive and well on Terra Familiar.

Vincent said, "I promised Dana to remain on Terra Familiar as humanity's next wayshower."

"So I understand," said Gwen. "We'll walk our path together, this time, with fewer illusions."

"Or attachments," he concurred.

Gwen said, "We'll return to Terra Familiar together."

"You mean reincarnate?" Vincent acknowledged.

I said, "Yes, but there's no hurry. You can remain here to rest, recover, prepare, and plan. You have thirteen thousand years of work ahead of you. Let the DNA, bees, heartplums, hemp, and water do their work for a few generations. And let Suzy get comfortable as the rest of humanity slowly awakens."

Javier said, "Dana and I must incarnate on Terra Nova anon."

Gwen declared, "Next time around, I am going to cross through the portal into your world, Dana."

"Count on it," I promised.

Vincent observed, "At some point in Terra Familiar's future, someone will discover the voxes and the carvings in Hal's cave. If it's Suzy, she will try to suss out their meaning and reverse engineer the technology."

"Remember," I said, "voxes only operate on love."

"Besides," Vincent said, "it will be impossible to activate vox technology without your DNA."

"She might try to use the DNA from our remains," Javier speculated. "We couldn't, but who knows what our clever lizzie can accomplish? Suzy Quintana has surpassed all expectations."

"We'll compare notes in thirteen thousand years." Vincent beamed at us. "What will be our portal, Dana? Art? Music? Poetry?"

I replied, "Maybe petroglyphs on rock walls. I'll know when the time comes, just as Phoenix knew I loved art."

Javier called urgently, "Our time on Terra Nova draws nigh. Dana, I am being pulled home." A silver cord, pulsating with light, coalesced in his solar plexus. Away he swung in a ribbon of arcs until he passed through a veil and was lost to our world.

"I must follow him. It is my time." I too felt a silver cord coalesce at my solar plexus and tug me away in undulating curls.

Receding, Terra Familiar, the planet I called home for hundreds of lifetimes, tugged at my heart, but not at my silver chord. Earth was no longer the iconic blue green marble, but a haze-covered, brown and gray waste dotted with oases of green and blue. I recognized Wah'Kon-Tah, the verdant islands in the inland sea. Gwen and Vincent faded beyond the veil and vanished from my view.

Terra Nova now appeared on my distant vista. I could see Javier far ahead of me accelerating in sweeping curves toward his new planet, his new life. To whom would he be born? When would we next meet?

Far beyond Terra Nova, a small globe of golden light shone along the spiral strand. It was Tellara settling into her next 6D octave, a beacon of higher harmonic resonance.

My ribbon wended slowly, and I hovered, untethered, in the deep vacuum of interdimensional space. After a seeming eternity, I heard a familiar, mellow voice ring out, "Still wandering, Dana Mae Travers?" I turned to face Sapphire, the brilliant caterpillar guide from my throat chakra. He was now a bioluminescent azure and indigo butterfly the size of a nebula. "We meet again," he trilled.

I replied, "Just as you predicted."

"Not predicted, Dear One, I'm an interdimensional being. I remember the future."

"I do recall your telling me that. And now, we've both ascended. I'm starting over again."

"And again and again and again."

"It's so wonderful to see you in all your glory, Sapphy."

"Call me Sapphire now. I have metamorphosed into a higher frequency, as is the destiny of all Nymphalidae Galactica." He fluttered his magnificent wings and the stars themselves formed a halo around him.

"I am so glad to find you here between worlds. What is next for you?" I asked.

"Journeys beyond reckoning. Stories beyond imagination."

"Will we meet again?"

"Count on it."

"Is that a prediction or a memory of the future?"

"Try to keep up, Dana," he chided gently.

As an urgent pull yanked my silver cord in accelerating ribbons across the celestial expanse toward Terra Nova, I called, "Farewell, Sapphire, I bid you wondrous adventures."

"Don't you remember, Dana Travers?" Sapphire crooned, "The butterfly always gets the last word."

Delighted, I exclaimed, "Tell me, Sapphire! What's the last word?"

As I receded billions of miles away from my galactic guide, his golden voice reverberated across the Universe: "Magic."

ABOUT THE AUTHOR

L.D. Leslie is a science fiction aficionado, fringe researcher, physics and metaphysics student. Mystical science fiction stories and visionary art are the tools she uses to translate her reality into relatable paradigms. L.D. Leslie is currently at work on her second novel, *Timequakes*. For the self-published author, ratings and reviews are the currency that provide visibility. Thank you for reading.

Made in the USA
Columbia, SC
29 September 2020